THE
AMERICAN
FANTASY TRADITION

THE
AMERICAN
FANTASY TRADITION

EDITED BY BRIAN M. THOMSEN

TOR®

A TOM DOHERTY ASSOCIATES BOOK
NEW YORK

THE AMERICAN FANTASY TRADITION

Copyright © 2002 by Brian M. Thomsen and Tekno Books

Introduction copyright © 2002 by Brian M. Thomsen

Edited by James Minz

Book design by Jane Adele Regina

A Tor Book
Published by Tom Doherty Associates, LLC
175 Fifth Avenue
New York, NY 10010

www.tor.com

Library of Congress Cataloging-in-Publication Data

    The American fantasy tradition / edited by Brian M. Thomsen.—1st ed.
      p.   cm.
    "A Tom Doherty Associates book."
    ISBN 0-765-30152-0 (alk. paper)
    1. Fantasy fiction, American. I. Thomsen, Brian.
  PS648.F3 A64 2002
  813'.0876608—dc21   2002068565

First Edition: September 2002

Printed in the United States of America

0 9 8 7 6 5 4 3 2 1

COPYRIGHT ACKNOWLEDGMENTS

Part of the American tradition is the Everyman Hero,
the regular guy who proves himself far beyond his expected limitations
and winds up saving the day.

For Rockaway Beach's Own
John Moran and Richard Allen,
Firefighters and Heroes of September 11th

this changed everything

I WOKE TO FIND THE SKY ON FIRE
ONE PLANE HIT LOW AND ONE HIT HIGHER
I WATCHED THE TUMBLING TOWERS HIT THE GROUND
THOUGH I DIDN'T KNOW IT THEN
I PROBABLY COULD POINT TO WHEN
HE DISAPPEARED NOT TO BE FOUND

SO LET THE FLAG FLY PROUD AND FREE
RED WHITE AND BLUE FOR ALL TO SEE
LISTEN FOR THAT BELL LET FREEDOM RING
COUNT YOUR BLESSINGS COUNT YOUR FRIENDS
RECONNECT THE BROKEN ENDS
BUT THIS CHANGED EVERYTHING

THERE'S DESPAIR INSIDE THE EYES
OF STRANGERS WHO NOW SYMPATHIZE
AND SHARE THE PAIN OF HOLDING ON WITH HOPE
THERE'S A BOND STRONG AND NEW
FROM THEM TO ME, FROM ME TO YOU
REACHING OUT TO HELP EACH OTHER COPE

THE FIGHTER PLANE IS IN THE SKY
THE BATTLESHIP JUST CAUGHT MY EYE
SIDE BY SIDE, SAFETY AND FEAR
I COULD NOT HELP BUT THINK ABOUT
WHICH WILL REMAIN WHEN THEY PULL OUT
WHEN THE COAST IS CLEAR

SO LET THE FLAG FLY PROUD AND FREE
RED WHITE AND BLUE FOR ALL TO SEE
LISTEN FOR THAT BELL LET FREEDOM RING
AND IF YOU EVER HAD A DOUBT
JUST HOW STRONG WELL YOU'LL FIND OUT
'CAUSE THIS CHANGED EVERYTHING

—GERALD BAIR

CONTENTS

PART III: LANDS OF ENCHANTMENT AND EVERYDAY LIFE

FOREWORD

The American tradition has been a useful subject of conversations at American universities (and nearby pubs and taverns) since the first courses to exclude the works of our European cousins were offered. Indeed, names such as Charles Brockden Brown (the true father of the American gothic) and James Fenimore Cooper (the true father of the Western) rose to popular literary prominence, becoming the patriarchal literary standard in a newly established subgenre of world literature that was defining itself as it tried to retroactively separate itself from its transatlantic predecessors.

Themes such as "manifest destiny" and "rugged individualism" ran rampant in comments laced with references to *deus ex machina* and democratic egalitarianism, all general themes on general topics that were of concern to the American reading public.

But just as it had become necessary to differentiate American lit from English lit, it is equally appropriate to further differentiate other genres from their British counterparts. Just as Brown became the American equivalent of Radcliffe or Maturin in the gothic, other genres must also come under scrutiny in order to try and define what "native" quality differentiates them from their transatlantic cousins.

The American Fantasy Tradition represents a single approach to the literature of the fantastic as it falls within the larger cavalcade of American fiction, particularly as a subset of English literature in general. The moniker of "the American Tradition" (a term adequately chosen by scholars and critics such as Richard Chase) and the prevalent concern that it is largely made up of the works of dead white men as chosen by other soon-to-be-dead white men is unfortunately evident in the selection of stories herewith, largely due to the narrow interpretation that I have chosen for the book's theme.

This is not to say that there aren't many substantial, indeed invaluable, female American authors of the fantastic whose work I admire. There are, but unfortunately their seminal works don't fall within the limited thematic criteria I have chosen for this volume. Indeed, a substantial amount of major American authors (such as Edgar Allan Poe and Robertson Davies) who have dabbled in the fantastic realms fall outside of the thematic canon with greater affinities to the European roots of the genre rather than that of the "homegrown" variety.

Another criteria for selection that led to numerous exclusions was the limitation that only self-contained short form works (no "excerpts from a larger work") were to be included.[1] Authors such as Robert Jordan, David Eddings, Terry Goodkind, and

---

[1] Though ironically numerous of the selections herewith (notably "Shoeless Joe Jackson Comes to Iowa," "Hatrack River," "The Coin Collector," and "The Black Ferris") all served as precursors to longer treatments and expansions of the same story.

other masters of the long form fantasy are obviously integral to the genre despite the paucity of their output in the short form.

Grateful acknowledgment is made to all of my teachers and mentors in the literary milieu, including Jerold Kappes, Frank Walsh, John Mullen, Hildreth Kritzer, Terence and Kathleen Malley, Kenneth Scott, Robert Spector, Seymour Kleinberg, Frank Brady, Irving Howe, Alfred Kazin and Baird Searles.

Grateful acknowledgment is made to the following authors/critics whose insights into the genre and/or the American tradition have always been an inspiration: Richard Chase, Leslie Fiedler, Stephen King, Michael Korda, L. Sprague de Camp, Andrew Delbanco, David Denby, Jack Cady and Jane Tompkins.

And last but not least, grateful acknowledgment is made to the following individuals whose assistance made this book possible: Tom Doherty, Jim Minz, Martin Greenberg, John Helfers, A. C. Kupfer and, of course, Donna Thomsen.

The blame for the idiosyncratic selections herewith, however, is mine alone.

THE
AMERICAN
FANTASY TRADITION

INTRODUCTION

AN APPROACH TO AN
AMERICAN FANTASY TRADITION

They [the Metaphysical Club] believed that ideas are not "out there" waiting to be discovered, but are tools—like forks and knives and microchips—that people devise to cope with the world in which they find themselves. They believed that ideas are produced not by individuals, but by groups of individuals—that ideas are social. They believed that ideas do not develop according to some inner logic of their own, but are entirely dependent, like germs, on their human carriers and the environment. And they believed that since ideas are provisional responses to particular and unreproducible circumstances, their survival depends not on their own immutability but on their adaptability.

—Louis Menand, *The Metaphysical Club*

When one looks at fantasy literature, one is immediately struck by the presence of certain predominant themes and subgenre strains. At least two of the most popular strains have their roots solidly in the British tradition, namely the Arthurian epic of *The Once and Future King*, and the Tolkien quest of *The Lord of the Rings*, both of which can trace their roots back through many centuries of Anglo-English history and lore. Other strains, such as the fairy tales of Grimm and Hoffmann, the fey of Dunsany and the Wagnerian Ring of the Nibelung are also present, and constantly available for reinterpretation, whether in modern retellings such as those by Angela Carter and Tanith Lee or psychologically metaphoric works of magic realism such as those by Borges or Marquez.

But what of the American tradition?

Literary critics such as Chase, Howe and Fiedler have all dealt with overlapping theories of what makes up the American literary tradition, dealing with such early roots as the sermons of Jonathan Edwards and Cotton Mather, through the frontier literature of Charles Brockden Brown and James Fenimore Cooper; the nineteenth-century tradition of Melville, Emerson, Twain and James; the twentieth-century realists Dos Passos, Dreiser and Sinclair; the ruralists Steinbeck and Faulkner; the moderns Hemingway and Mailer; and the post-moderns Vonnegut and Pynchon. Themes such as "religion and reform," "western expansionism," "manifest destiny," "man vs. nature," and "the metaphoric second chance" are all examined in light of the American experience as opposed to the Anglo-European tradition.

But what of the fantasy genre or, more specifically, the American tradition of fantasy?

Noted fantasy editor Lin Carter in his introduction to L. Sprague de Camp's *Literary Swordsmen and Sorcerers—The Making of Heroic Fantasy* states that "this heroic school of fantasy dates, of course, from remote antiquity and boasts an illustrious lineage," a declaration that even the most naive student of genre studies would be forced to concede. Unfortunately this esteemed fantasy historian of yesteryear takes his point a bit further by saying that "most national literatures spring from bodies of heroic and fabulous legendry—except in countries like America, too recently founded to have enjoyed a mythmaking period . . . but America . . . has to make do with such feeble follow-ups to the doughty dragon-slayers of yore as the likes of Hiawatha, Davy Crockett and Daniel Boone." Though one is hard-pressed to disagree that America's youth does indeed narrow the canvas upon which its legendary tales of yore can be told, I am nonetheless troubled by his reference to "feeble follow-ups" where he mentions real names from history as our equivalent to the great names that may never have really existed in our European ancestral history lore. When exactly did doughty dragon-slayers exist? What about magical wizards like Merlin, or perhaps the fey folk, or barbarous trolls?

Carter's prejudices spotlight a strain of literary criticism that has always cited American literature as being somehow less legitimate than its European counterparts due to the shortness of its lineage—rather than acknowledging the depth and breadth of work that has existed within its short lifespan. Noted critics such as Richard Chase, Irving Howe, Alfred Kazin and Leslie Fiedler have all addressed this issue/criticism in terms of all American literature, each stressing more or less the same general refutation that just because the American school may have derived its pre-1776 lineage from other sources, it has nonetheless developed a tradition all its own in direct contrast to its transatlantic brethren. True, a substantial amount of American writers have written pseudo-European tradition novels (such as Nathaniel Hawthorne with *The Marble Faun* or Henry James with *The Wings of the Dove*), but this has usually been done in conjunction with their writing of more traditionally American works (Hawthorne's *The Scarlet Letter* and James's *Daisy Miller*). What is more common is for members of the American school to adapt European genre motifs to the American tradition such as Mark Twain's lampoon of the Age of Chivalry in *A Connecticut Yankee in King Arthur's Court* or William Faulkner's twentieth-century interpretation of the gothic in his novel *Sanctuary*.

With the possible exception of the Western, American literature has inherited all of its literary forms and genres from its transatlantic cousins, transforming them through a process of "Americanization" into a new and very different tradition of literature. The actual changes are hard to pin down, as even Richard Chase is quick to point out in his landmark work *The American Novel and Its Tradition* citing "the originality and *Americanness*" of the works in question while conceding that "the precise nature of these qualities is often debatable." Both Kazin and Howe further this emphasis on "Americanization" by comparing it to the entire immigrant tradition of the United States, which culminated in a melting pot yielding the best and brightest of all nations of the world in the twentieth century.

It is only fair, therefore, to approach the fantasy genre with the same American-centric eye. As with the mainstream of literature, many authors have opted to write in the European tradition. Authors such as Terry Brooks, in his Shannara series, and Marion Zimmer Bradley, in her Avalon books, are obviously following the British traditions of J. R. R. Tolkien and the Arthurian school, while various works of Poe show his dedication to both French and German schools of the short story. However, to single these works out as being representative of the entire canon of American fantasy literature would be tantamount to equating King Arthur with Daniel Boone or, more absurdly, Pecos Bill with Oliver Cromwell.

It is my contention that there exists an American tradition within the fantasy genre much in the same manner as Chase discusses in his landmark study of the American novel. Like its mainstream counterpart, fantasy draws from its ancestral lineage, incorporating myth, mode, and device, while at the same time incorporating the *very* American virtue that Henry David Thoreau calls "wildness," drawing on the contradictions, alienation and disorders that were a direct result of our ancestral European forefathers coming into collision with the virginal American frontier and being forced to redefine itself in terms of a democratic society by means of a bloody revolution. The literary byproduct of this process is inherently transformed much in the way that *West Side Story* is not just a restaging of *Romeo and Juliet* but rather a wholly new work inspired by it.

The American fantasy tradition incorporates the frontier legacies of the pioneers complete with their heroism and adventure as well as with its sense of danger and primitive savagery. It incorporates the egalitarian vision of democracy, the self-made man, and the American dream with the harsh realities of both the rural and urban wildernesses, and the ups and downs of a newly born society that is prone to making up the rules as it goes along. (If there is a dominant theme in this American tradition it is one of surprise—the trick ending or the unexpected and, perhaps, unexplained turn of events.) It is filled with mythic heroes such as Rip Van Winkle (who Leslie Fiedler singles out as our first truly American literary archetype) and Pecos Bill, freely mixed with everymen like Benét's Jabez Stone in "The Devil and Daniel Webster" or Kinsella in "Shoeless Joe Jackson Comes to Iowa."

In many ways it is indeed the heroes and villains (or in many cases the singular "villain") that personify the very "American-ness" of many of these tales. The everyman is not usually a prince in hiding or a larger-than-life figure from history. Indeed, there isn't any American equivalent of Arthur Rex, king of all England, and with the exception of the occasional mythmaking of such second-rate historians as Parson Weems (credited with the invention of Washington's boyhood cherry tree incident), most writers have refrained from fantasizing the exploits of our founding fathers and other great Americans. Even the exploits of legendary frontiersman and statesman Davy Crockett, the Disney musical ballad exempted, are kept within bragging and exaggeration limits rather than distorted to extremes of magic and mysticism or superhero-dom. On the rare occasion that the historical figure does grace the pages of a fantastic tale such as the nineteenth-century statesman Daniel Webster in Stephen Vincent Benét's entertaining series of stories, they usually persevere and conquer in a very human and common way. Benét goes to great pains to stress Webster's erudition as a debater, and his powers of faith, perseverance and loyalty as befitting a son of the great state of New Hampshire, but in the end it is his day-to-day skills as a lawyer that allow him to rescue the supernaturally bound Jabez Stone from damnation ... and even the most whimsical believer in backwoods magic would have to admit that there is nothing magical or enchanting about lawyers.

For the most part, the American fantasy hero is an everyday person with everyday concerns. Sometimes he/she is gifted with a special talent or knack but usually nothing like the omnipotent powers usually afforded to their European cousins and ancestors.

Even wizards and magic men like Silver John, Mad Amos Malone and Old Nathan are a far cry from the awe-inspiring figures of Merlin and Gandalf.

More important, our homespun heroes have mundane problems, interests, concerns and passions that allow the reader to more fully identify with them. The fairy tale princess or knight is replaced by someone you can imagine running into during your normal day-to-day routine or even, in most cases, rationally recognize as an extension of one's self. When one of Stephen King's old fogies gives you a warning down at some archetypal general store, the words resonate, not because they sound clichéd and hackneyed, but because King's focal characters recognize that they *are* clichéd and hackneyed. Indeed, King's proficiency as a purveyor of the fantastic realm is only overshadowed by his abilities as a purveyor of the mundane world of brand names, whining kids and awkward adolescence.

Likewise, the seminal American fantasy antagonists are either other folk just like you and me (such as Shirley Jackson's townspeople in "The Lottery" or the spectral dopplegangers in Henry James's "The Jolly Corner" or Charlotte Perkins Gilman's "The Yellow Wallpaper"), the Devil (either literally as with Benét's Mr. Scratch, Orson Scott Card's Unmaker or Charles Beaumont's "howling man," or metaphorically as with Ray Bradbury's dark carny folk), or the awesome unknown itself. Is it any coincidence that these foes are virtually interchangeable with those faced (at least in their own minds) by the early settlers who traveled from Europe to the new land of America? As Andrew Delbanco pointed out in *The Death of Satan,* "the more stringent Protestants of New England also brought with them a tradition that claimed the New World wilderness had been reserved as 'Satan's hunting park' until their own arrival." Is it any wonder that the principal villains in our fantasies are based in original sin (sinners like ourselves), the Devil, and the unknown (or more precisely that which lies outside of the bounds of normal civilization), the exact fears and concerns of the founding fathers of our nation's founding fathers?

Beyond the heroes and villains, the "American-ness" of our fantasy tradition has flourished in a wide variety of settings and times (some as "real" as a Civil War battlefield or late-twentieth-century New York City or as imaginary as Frank Stockton's village from a medieval age that never existed or any of the numerous borderlands between heaven and hell as envisioned by Greg Bear, Gene Wolfe or Michael Bishop). In some cases the fantasy element is the main focus of the story (as when the warrior doll comes to life in Richard Matheson's "Prey" or the creeping unknown threat that lives beneath the kudzu in Karl Edward Wagner's "Where the Summer Ends"), while in others it is incidental (as with the scientifically based miracle cure for cancer which is never really explained in Ted Sturgeon's "Slow Sculpture" or the afterlife-staffed baseball diamond in the cornfield in W. P. Kinsella's "Shoeless Joe Jackson Comes to Iowa"). In some cases the outcome is survival and a return to day-to-day life forever changed (as in Harlan Ellison's "The Whimper of Whipped Dogs"), while in other cases the resolution only brings madness (H. P. Lovecraft's numerous tales as well as Avram Davidson's pastiche of them in "Twenty-Three"), death (Robert Chambers's "The Yellow Sign") or even worse, the ineffable and unimaginable (Fredric Brown's "The Geezenstacks").

FOR THE PURPOSE OF CLASSIFICATION in this anthology, I have divided the American tradition into three concurrent (and occasionally overlapping) strains to provide an organized overview of this evolving genre.

The first part, "Folk, Tall and Weird Tales" incorporates those stories which might be said to be fables or legends based in the same way that tales of the fairy folk are classified in the European tradition or the fables of Aesop and the epics of the Age of Heroes of the classical eras of Rome and Greece.

The so-called "Satan's hunting park" of the frontier (whether it be the New England woods, Appalachia or the Wild West) provided a perfect setting for folk and tall tales told around the hearth or campfire. They were filled with danger to excite the young with stories of days gone by from the country's early years or even from imaginary times, from the so-called American fairy tales to the so politically incorrect and overly idealized (and racist) plantation days' setting of the "Uncle Remus" tales where wild ingenuity (of Brer Rabbit) triumphs over the savage wild (of Brer Fox and Brer Bear).

After the savage frontier disappeared, and the nation was allegedly settled, a third form of "the tale" came into being that transposed the fear and excitement of the unknown to the thought-to-be civilized quarters (such as New York and New England in the twentieth century) by injecting threats from the unknown and ineffable into our day-to-day lives. These so-called weird tales merely innovated the campfire tales of the past with a more mysterious and unexpected dose of the contemporary with the mysterious.

THE SECOND SECTION IS CALLED "Fantastic Americana" and it gathers together fantasy stories that are directly set within the American historic landscape much as the Arthurian tradition is set within the confines of British history. Unlike its British counterpart, there is an even stronger resonance of credibility, since even a story set in our country's far past is still within the bounds of recorded history. Where the Arthurian tradition saw fit to incorporate chivalric tales from the European continent, Americana is much more clearly defined by recorded history. Crispus Attucks was killed at the Boston Massacre (as in Brad Denton's "The Hero of the Night"), the North fought the South in the Civil War (as in Ambrose Bierce's "The Other Lodgers" and Manly Wade Wellman's "The Valley Was Still") and the twentieth century saw the coming of more than one world war (as in Beaumont's "The Howling Man"). It is in fact one of the greatest virtues of this subgenre that history itself is respected despite the fantastic innovations that enable the writer to more magically tell the story, conveying a sense of credibility to a history that *might* have been.

THE THIRD AND FINAL PART OF THIS BOOK, "Lands of Enchantment and Everyday Life," evolves around what might be called the American spirit, focusing on worlds that might be different from our own but nonetheless entice us to explore them, even if they only exist in the shadow down the hall or in the space that exists between worlds that are glimpsed in the blink of an eye. More succinctly, these are the lands that exist just beyond Rod Serling's famous signpost for "The Twilight Zone." In some cases, it is an accidental discovery of things unknown that have existed "right around the corner" from us for a long time (as in the parallel universe of Jack Finney's "The Coin Collector" or the otherworldly shortcut in Stephen King's "Mrs. Todd's Shortcut"). In other cases it is a close encounter with the encroachment of darkness on our world (as in Bradbury's "The Black Ferris") or a personal revelation of the unknown as instigated by the intrepid scientist (as in Alan Brennart's "Her Pilgrim

Soul") or the "accidental bystander who becomes involved" (as in Harlan Ellison's "Paladin of the Lost Hour").

In all of these cases, the unknown is encountered and we deal with it, whether it is a man-eating griffin in the Middle Ages or a knife-wielding doll that has unexpectedly come to life.

We're Americans, and our characters deal with it whatever *it* may be (though not necessarily guaranteeing their own survival).

THOUGH EUROPEAN AND OTHER INFLUENCES are all too clear in all of these stories, they are nonetheless all solidly entrenched in the American tradition, wholly unique and as homegrown as Iowa corn or Virginia tobacco. Leslie Fiedler, in his classic work *Love and Death in the American Novel*, states: "How could one tell where the American dream ended and the Faustian nightmare began; they held in common the hope of breaking through all limits and restraints, of reaching a place of total freedom where one could with impunity deny the Fall, and live as if innocence rather than guilt were the birthright of all men."

Such a borderland of dream and nightmare could only exist within the fantasy landscape of the American tradition, its characters adapting and responding in order to cope with the world around them, fantastic or otherwise, in which they finally do indeed find themselves.

PART ONE

FOLK, TALL AND WEIRD TALES

RIP VAN WINKLE

A POSTHUMOUS WRITING
OF DIEDRICH KNICKERBOCKER

BY WASHINGTON IRVING

Born in 1783, Washington Irving grew up with tales of how America used to be back before it was its own nation. He incorporated much of this background into his fanciful *A History of New York*, written under the pseudonym of Diedrich Knickerbocker, and *The Sketch Book of Geoffrey Crayon, Gent*. It is noteworthy that both editorial and authorial personae actually appear in the notes attached to "Rip Van Winkle," strengthening the "tale-told" aspects of his story. Rip is a ne'er-do-well everyman who encounters magical minions from the past who treat him to a nap that runs right through the crucible known as the American Revolution.

The following Tale was found among the papers of the late Diedrich Knickerbocker, an old gentleman of New York, who was very curious in the Dutch history of the province, and the manners of the descendants from its primitive settlers. His historical researches, however, did not lie so much among books, as among men; for the former are lamentably scanty on his favourite topics; whereas he found the old burghers, and still more, their wives, rich in that legendary lore so invaluable to true history. Whenever, therefore, he happened upon a genuine Dutch family, snugly shut up in its low roofed farm house, under a spreading sycamore, he looked upon it as a little clasped volume of black letter, and studied it with the zeal of a bookworm.

The result of all these researches was a history of the province, during the reign of the Dutch governors, which he published some years since. There have been various opinions as to the literary character of his work and, to tell the truth, it is not a whit better than it should be. Its chief merit is its scrupulous accuracy, which indeed was a little questioned on its first appearance, but has since been completely established; and it is now admitted into all historical collections as a book of unquestionable authority.

The old gentleman died shortly after the publication of his work, and now that he is dead and gone, it cannot do much harm to his memory to say that his time might have been much better employed in weightier labours. He, however, was apt to ride his hobby his own way; and though it did now and then kick up the dust a little in the eyes of his neighbours, and grieve the spirit of some friends for whom he felt the truest deference and affection; yet his errors and follies are remembered "more in sorrow than in anger," and it begins to be suspected that he never intended to injure or offend. But however his memory may be appreciated by criticks it is still held dear by many folk whose good opinion is well worth having; particularly by certain biscuit bakers, who have gone so far as to imprint his likeness on their new year cakes, and have thus given him a chance for immortality, almost equal to being stamped on a Waterloo medal, or a Queen Anne's farthing.

> By Woden, God of Saxons,
> From whence comes Wensday, that is Wodensday,
> Truth is a thing that ever I will keep
> Unto thylke day in which I creep into
> My sepulchre—
>
> CARTWRIGHT

Whoever has made a voyage up the Hudson must remember the Kaatskill mountains. They are a dismembered branch of the great Appalachian family, and are seen away to the west of the river swelling up to noble height and lording it over the surrounding country. Every change of season, every change of weather, indeed every hour of the day, produces some change in the magical hues and shapes of these mountains, and they are regarded by all the good wives far and near as perfect barometers. When the weather is fair and settled they are clothed in blue and purple, and print their bold outlines on the clear evening sky; but sometimes, when the rest of the landscape is cloudless, they will gather a hood of grey vapours about their summits, which, in the last rays of the setting sun, will glow and light up like a crown of glory.

At the foot of these fairy mountains the voyager may have descried the light smoke curling up from a village, whose shingle roofs gleam among the trees, just where the blue tints of the upland melt away into the fresh green of the nearer landscape. It is a little village of great antiquity, having been founded by some of the Dutch colonists in the early times of the province, just about the beginning of the government of the good Peter Stuyvesant, (may he rest in peace!) and there were some of the houses of the original settlers standing within a few years; built of small yellow bricks brought from Holland, having latticed windows and gable fronts, surmounted with weathercocks.

In that same village, and in one of these very houses (which to tell the precise truth was sadly time worn and weather beaten) there lived many years since, while the country was yet a province of Great Britain, a simple good natured fellow of the name of Rip Van Winkle. He was a descendant of the Van Winkles who figured so gallantly in the chivalrous days of Peter Stuyvesant, and accompanied him to the siege of Fort Christina. He inherited, however, but little of the martial character of his ancestors. I have observed that he was a simple good natured man; he was moreover a kind neighbour, and an obedient, henpecked husband. Indeed to the latter circumstance might be owing that meekness of spirit which gained him such universal popularity; for those men are most apt to be obsequious and conciliating abroad, who are under the discipline of shrews at home. Their tempers doubtless are rendered pliant and malleable in the fiery furnace of domestic tribulation, and a curtain lecture is worth all the sermons in the world for teaching the virtues of patience and long suffering. A termagant wife may therefore in some respects be considered a tolerable blessing—and if so, Rip Van Winkle was thrice blessed.

Certain it is that he was a great favourite among all the good wives of the village, who as usual with the amiable sex, took his part in all family squabbles, and never failed, whenever they talked those matters over in their evening gossippings, to lay all the blame on Dame Van Winkle. The children of the village too would shout with joy whenever he approached. He assisted at their sports, made their play things, taught them to fly kites and shoot marbles, and told them long stories of ghosts, witches and Indians. Whenever he went dodging about the village he was surrounded by a troop of them hanging on his skirts, clambering on his back and playing a thousand tricks on him with impunity; and not a dog would bark at him throughout the neighbourhood.

The great error in Rip's composition was an insuperable aversion to all kinds of profitable labour. It could not be from the want of assiduity or perseverance; for he would sit on a wet rock, with a rod as long and heavy as a Tartar's lance, and fish all day without a murmur, even though he should not be encouraged by a single nibble. He would carry a fowling piece on his shoulder for hours together, trudging through woods, and swamps and up hill and down dale, to shoot a few squirrels or wild pigeons; he would never refuse to assist a neighbour even in the roughest toil, and was a foremost man at all country frolicks for husking Indian corn, or building stone fences; the women of the village too used to employ him to run their errands and to do such little odd jobs as their less obliging husbands would not do for them— in a word Rip was ready to attend to any body's business but his own; but as to doing family duty, and keeping his farm in order, he found it impossible.

In fact he declared it was of no use to work on his farm; it was the most pestilent little piece of ground in the whole country; every thing about it went wrong and would go wrong in spite of him. His fences were continually falling to pieces; his cow would either go astray or get among the cabbages, weeds were sure to grow quicker in his fields than any where else; the rain always made a point of setting in just as he had some outdoor work to do. So that though his patrimonial estate had dwindled away under his management, acre by acre until there was little more left than a mere patch of Indian corn and potatoes, yet it was the worst conditioned farm in the neighbourhood.

His children too were as ragged and wild as if they belonged to nobody. His son Rip, an urchin begotten in his own likeness, promised to inherit the habits with the old clothes of his father. He was generally seen trooping like a colt at his mother's heels, equipped in a pair of his father's cast off galligaskins, which he had much ado to hold up with one hand, as a fine lady does her train in bad weather.

Rip Van Winkle, however, was one of those happy mortals of foolish, well oiled dispositions, who take the world easy, eat white bread or brown, whichever can be got with least thought or trouble, and would rather starve on a penny than work for a pound. If left to himself, he would have whistled life away in perfect contentment, but his wife kept continually dinning in his ears about his idleness, his carelessness and the ruin he was bringing on his family. Morning noon and night her tongue was incessantly going, and every thing he said or did was sure to produce a torrent of household eloquence. Rip had but one way of replying to all lectures of the kind, and that by frequent use had grown into a habit. He shrugged his shoulders, shook his head, cast up his eyes, but said nothing. This, however, always provoked a fresh volley from his wife, so that he was fain to draw off his forces and take to the outside of the house—the only side which in truth belongs to a henpecked husband.

Rip's sole domestic adherent was his dog Wolf who was as much henpecked as his master, for Dame Van Winkle regarded them as companions in idleness, and even looked upon Wolf with an evil eye as the cause of his master's going so often astray. True it is, in all points of spirit befitting an honourable dog, he was as courageous an animal as ever scoured the woods—but what courage can withstand the ever during and all besetting terrors of a woman's tongue? The moment Wolf entered the house his crest fell, his tail drooped to the ground or curled between his legs, he sneaked about with a gallows air, casting many a sidelong glance at Dame Van Winkle, and at the least flourish of a broomstick or ladle he would fly to the door with yelping precipitation.

Times grew worse and worse with Rip Van Winkle as years of matrimony rolled on; a tart temper never mellows with age, and a sharp tongue is the only edged tool that grows keener with constant use. For a long while he used to console himself when driven from home, by frequenting a kind of perpetual club of the sages, philosophers and other idle personages of the village which held its sessions on a bench before a small inn, designated by a rubicund portrait of his majesty George the Third. Here they used to sit in the shade, through a long lazy summer's day, talking listlessly over village gossip, or telling endless sleepy stories about nothing. But it would have been worth any statesman's money to have heard the profound discussions that sometimes took place, when by chance an old newspaper fell into their hands from some passing traveller. How solemnly they would listen to the contents as drawled out by Derrick Van Bummel the schoolmaster, a dapper, learned little man, who was not to be daunted by the most gigantic word in the dictionary; and how sagely they would deliberate upon public events some months after they had taken place.

The opinions of this junto were completely controlled by Nicholaus Vedder, a patriarch of the village, and landlord of the inn, at the door of which he took his seat from morning till night, just moving sufficiently to avoid the sun and keep in the shade of a large tree; so that the neighbours could tell the hour by his movements as accurately as by a sun dial. It is true he was rarely heard to speak, but smoked his pipe incessantly. His adherents, however (for every great man has his adherents), perfectly understood him and knew how to gather his opinions. When any thing that was read or related displeased him, he was observed to smoke his pipe vehemently and to send forth short, frequent and angry puffs; but when pleased he would inhale the smoke slowly and tranquilly and emit it in light and placid clouds, and sometimes taking the pipe from his mouth and letting the fragrant vapour curl about his nose, would gravely nod his head in token of perfect approbation.

From even this strong hold the unlucky Rip was at length routed by his termagant wife who would suddenly break in upon the tranquility of the assemblage and call the members all to naught; nor was that august personage Nicholaus Vedder himself sacred from the daring tongue of this terrible virago, who charged him outright with encouraging her husband in habits of idleness.

Poor Rip was at last reduced almost to despair; and his only alternative to escape from the labour of the farm and the clamour of his wife, was to take gun in hand and stroll away into the woods. Here he would sometimes seat himself at the foot of a tree and share the contents of his wallet with Wolf, with whom he sympathised as a fellow sufferer in persecution. "Poor Wolf," he would say, "thy mistress leads thee a dog's life of it, but never mind my lad, whilst I live thou shalt never want a friend to stand by thee!" Wolf would wag his tail, look wistfully in his master's face, and if dogs can feel pity I verily believe he reciprocated the sentiment with all his heart.

In a long ramble of the kind on a fine autumnal day, Rip had unconsciously scrambled to one of the highest parts of the Kaatskill mountains. He was after his favourite sport of squirrel shooting and the still solitudes had echoed and re-echoed with the reports of his gun. Panting and fatigued he threw himself, late in the afternoon, on a green knoll, covered with mountain herbage, that crowned the brow of a precipice. From an opening between the trees he could overlook all the lower country for many a mile of rich woodland. He saw at a distance the lordly Hudson, far, far below him, moving on its silent but majestic course, with the reflection of a purple cloud, or the sail of a lagging bark here and there sleeping on its glassy bosom, and at last losing itself in the blue highlands.

On the other side he looked down into a deep mountain glen, wild, lonely and shagged, the bottom filled with fragments from the impending cliffs and scarcely lighted by the reflected rays of the setting sun. For some time Rip lay musing on this scene, evening was gradually advancing, the mountains began to throw their long blue shadows over the valleys, he saw that it would be dark, long before he could reach the village, and he heaved a heavy sigh when he thought of encountering the terrors of Dame Van Winkle.

As he was about to descend he heard a voice from a distance hallooing "Rip Van Winkle! Rip Van Winkle!" He looked around, but could see nothing but a crow winging its solitary flight across the mountain. He thought his fancy must have deceived him and turned again to descend, when he heard the same cry ring through the still evening air: "Rip Van Winkle! Rip Van Winkle!"—at the same time Wolf bristled up his back and giving a low growl, skulked to his master's side, looking fearfully down into the glen. Rip now felt a vague apprehension stealing over him; he looked anxiously in the same direction and perceived a strange figure slowly toiling up the rocks and bending under the weight of something he carried on his back. He was surprised to see any human being in this lonely and unfrequented place, but supposing it to be some one of the neighbourhood in need of his assistance he hastened down to yield it.

On nearer approach he was still more surprised at the singularity of the stranger's appearance. He was a short, square built old fellow, with thick bushy hair and a grizzled beard. His dress was of the antique Dutch fashion, a cloth jerkin strapped round the waist, several pair of breeches, the outer one of ample volume decorated with rows of buttons down the sides and bunches at the knees. He bore on his shoulder a stout keg that seemed full of liquor, and made signs for Rip to approach and assist him with the load. Though rather shy and distrustful of this new acquaintance Rip complied with his usual alacrity, and mutually relieving each other they clambered up a narrow gully apparently the dry bed of a mountain torrent. As they ascended Rip every now and then heard long rolling peals like distant thunder, that seemed to issue out of a deep ravine or rather cleft between lofty rocks, toward which their rugged path conducted. He paused for an instant, but supposing it to be the muttering of one of those transient thunder showers which often take place in mountain heights, he proceeded. Passing through the ravine they came to a hollow like a small amphitheatre, surrounded by perpendicular precipices, over the brinks of which impending trees shot their branches, so that you only caught glimpses of the azure sky and the bright evening cloud. During the whole time Rip and his companion had laboured on in silence, for though the former marvelled greatly what could be the object of carrying a keg of liquor up this wild mountain, yet there was something strange and incomprehensible about the unknown, that inspired awe and checked familiarity.

On entering the amphitheatre new objects of wonder presented themselves. On a level spot in the centre was a company of odd looking personages playing at ninepins. They were dressed in a quaint outlandish fashion—some wore short doublets, others jerkins with long knives in their belts and most of them had enormous breeches of similar style with that of the guide's. Their visages too were peculiar. One had a large head, broad face and small piggish eyes. The face of another seemed to consist entirely of nose, and was surmounted by a white sugarloaf hat, set off with a little red cock's tail. They all had beards of various shapes and colours. There was one who seemed to be the Commander. He was a stout old gentleman, with a weatherbeaten countenance. He wore a laced doublet, broad belt and hanger, high crowned hat and feather, red stockings and high heel'd shoes with roses in them. The whole group reminded Rip of the figures in an old Flemish painting, in the parlour of Dominie Van Schaick the village parson, and which had been brought over from Holland at the time of the settlement.

What seemed particularly odd to Rip was, that though these folks were evidently amusing themselves, yet they maintained the gravest faces, the most mysterious silence, and were, withal, the most melancholy party of pleasure he had ever witnessed. Nothing interrupted the stillness of the scene, but the noise of the balls, which, whenever they were rolled, echoed along the mountains like rumbling peals of thunder.

As Rip and his companion approached them they suddenly desisted from their play and stared at him with such fixed statue like gaze, and such strange uncouth, lack lustre countenances, that his heart turned within him, and his knees smote together. His companion now emptied the contents of the keg into large flagons and made signs to him to wait upon the company. He obeyed with fear and trembling; they quaffed the liquor in profound silence and then returned to their game.

By degrees Rip's awe and apprehension subsided. He even ventured, when no eye was fixed upon him, to taste the beverage, which he found had much of the flavour of excellent hollands. He was naturally a thirsty soul and was soon tempted to repeat the draught. One taste provoked another, and he reiterated his visits to the flagon so often that at length his senses were overpowered, his eyes swam in his head—his head gradually declined and he fell into a deep sleep.

On awaking he found himself on the green knoll from whence he had first seen the old man of the glen. He rubbed his eyes—it was a bright, sunny morning. The birds were hopping and twittering among the bushes, and the eagle was wheeling aloft and breasting the pure mountain breeze. "Surely," thought Rip, "I have not slept here all night." He recalled the occurrences before he fell asleep. The strange man with a keg of liquor—the mountain ravine—the wild retreat among the rocks—the woe begone party at ninepins—the flagon—"ah! that flagon! that wicked flagon!" thought Rip—"what excuse shall I make to Dame Van Winkle?"

He looked round for his gun, but in place of the clean well oiled fowling piece he found an old firelock lying by him, the barrel encrusted with rust; the lock falling off and the stock worm eaten. He now suspected that the grave roysters of the mountain had put a trick upon him, and having dosed him with liquor, had robbed him of his gun. Wolf too had disappeared, but he might have strayed away after a squirrel or partridge. He whistled after him and shouted his name—but all in vain; the echoes repeated his whistle and shout, but no dog was to be seen.

He determined to revisit the scene of the last evening's gambol, and if he met with any of the party, to demand his dog and gun. As he arose to walk he found himself stiff in the joints and wanting in his usual activity. "These mountain beds do not agree with me," thought Rip, "and if this frolick should lay me up with a fit of the rheumatism, I shall have a blessed time with Dame Van Winkle." With some difficulty he got down into the glen; he found the gully up which he and his companion had ascended the preceding evening, but to his astonishment a mountain stream was now foaming down it; leaping from rock to rock, and filling the glen with babbling murmurs. He, however, made shift to scramble up its sides working his toilsome way through thickets of birch, sassafras and witch hazel, and sometimes tripped up or entangled by the wild grape vines that twisted their coils and tendrils from tree to tree, and spread a kind of net work in his path.

At length he reached to where the ravine had opened through the cliffs, to the amphitheatre—but no traces of such opening remained. The rocks presented a high impenetrable wall over which the torrent came tumbling in a sheet of feathery foam, and fell into a broad deep basin black from the shadows of the surrounding forest. Here then poor Rip was brought to a stand. He again called and whistled after his dog—he was only answered by the cawing of a flock of idle crows, sporting high in air about a dry tree that overhung a sunny precipice; and who, secure in their elevation seemed to look down and scoff at the poor man's perplexities.

What was to be done? The morning was passing away and Rip felt famished for want of his breakfast. He grieved to give up his dog and gun; he dreaded to meet his wife; but it would not do to starve among the mountains. He shook his head, shouldered the rusty fire lock and with a heart full of trouble and anxiety, turned his steps homeward.

As he approached the village he met a number of people, but none whom he knew, which somewhat surprised him, for he had thought himself acquainted with every one in the country round. Their dress too was of a different fashion from that to which he was accustomed. They all stared at him with equal marks of surprise, and whenever they cast their eyes upon him, invariably stroked their chins. The constant recurrence of this gesture induced Rip involuntarily to do the same, when to his astonishment he found his beard had grown a foot long!

He had now entered the skirts of the village. A troop of strange children ran at his heels, hooting after him and pointing at his grey beard. The dogs too, not one of which he recognized for an old acquaintance, barked at him as he passed. The very village was altered—it was larger and more populous. There were rows of houses which he had never seen before, and those which had been his familiar haunts had disappeared. Strange names were over the doors—strange faces at the windows— every thing was strange. His mind now misgave him; he began to doubt whether both he and the world around him were not bewitched. Surely this was his native village which he had left but the day before. There stood the Kaatskill mountains—there ran the silver Hudson at a distance—there was every hill and dale precisely as it had always been—Rip was sorely perplexed—"That flagon last night," thought he, "has addled my poor head sadly!"

It was with some difficulty that he found the way to his own house, which he approached with silent awe, expecting every moment to hear the shrill voice of Dame Van Winkle. He found the house gone to decay—the roof fallen in, the windows shattered and the doors off the hinges. A half starved dog that looked like Wolf was skulking about it. Rip called him by name but the cur snarled, shewed his teeth and passed on. This was an unkind cut indeed—"My very dog," sighed poor Rip, "has forgotten me!"

He entered the house, which, to tell the truth, Dame Van Winkle had always kept in neat order. It was empty, forlorn and apparently abandoned. This desolateness overcame all his connubial fears—he called loudly for his wife and children—the lonely chambers rung for a moment with his voice, and then all again was silence.

He now hurried forth and hastened to his old resort, the village inn—but it too was gone. A large, ricketty wooden building stood in its place, with great gaping windows, some of them broken, and mended with old hats and petticoats, and over the door was printed "The Union Hotel, by Jonathan Doolittle." Instead of the great tree, that used to shelter the quiet little Dutch inn of yore, there now was reared a tall naked pole with something on top that looked like a red night cap, and from it was fluttering a flag on which was a singular assemblage of stars and stripes—all this was strange and incomprehensible. He recognized on the sign, however, the ruby face of King George under which he had smoked so many a peaceful pipe, but even this was singularly metamorphosed. The red coat was changed for one of blue and buff; a sword was held in the hand instead of a sceptre; the head was decorated with a cocked hat, and underneath was printed in large characters GENERAL WASHINGTON.

There was as usual a crowd of folk about the door; but none that Rip recollected. The very character of the people seemed changed. There was a busy, bustling disputatious tone about it, instead of the accustomed phlegm and drowsy tranquility. He looked in vain for the sage Nicholaus Vedder with his broad face, double chin and fair long pipe, uttering clouds of tobacco smoke instead of idle speeches. Or Van Bummel the schoolmaster doling forth the contents of an ancient newspaper. In place of these a lean bilious looking fellow with his pockets full of hand bills, was haranguing vehemently about rights of citizens—elections—members of Congress—liberty—Bunker's hill—heroes of seventy six—and other words which were a perfect babylonish jargon to the bewildered Van Winkle.

The appearance of Rip with his long grizzled beard, his rusty fowling piece his uncouth dress and an army of women and children at his heels soon attracted the attention of the tavern politicians. They crowded around him eying him from head to foot, with great curiosity. The orator bustled up to him, and drawing him partly aside, enquired "on which side he voted?"—Rip stared in vacant stupidity. Another short but busy little fellow, pulled him by the arm and rising on tiptoe, enquired in his ear "whether he was Federal or Democrat?"—Rip was equally at a loss to comprehend the question—when a knowing, self important old gentleman, in a sharp cocked hat, made his way through the crowd, putting them to the right and left with his elbows as he passed, and planting himself before Van Winkle, with one arm akimbo, the other resting on his cane, his keen eyes and sharp hat penetrating as it were into his very soul, demanded in an austere tone—"what brought him to the election with a gun on his shoulder and a mob at his heels, and whether he meant to breed a riot in the village?"—"Alas gentlemen," cried Rip, somewhat dismayed, "I am a poor quiet man, a native of the place, and a loyal subject of the King—God bless him!"

Here a general shout burst from the byestanders—"A tory! a tory! a spy! a Refugee! hustle him! away with him!"—It was with great difficulty that the self important man in the cocked hat restored order; and having assumed a ten fold austerity of brow demanded again of the unknown culprit, what he came there for and whom he was seeking. The poor man humbly assured him that he meant no harm; but merely came there in search of some of his neighbours, who used to keep about the tavern.

"—Well—who are they?—name them."

Rip bethought himself a moment and enquired, "Where's Nicholaus Vedder?"

There was a silence for a little while, when an old man replied, in a thin, piping voice, "Nicholaus Vedder? why he is dead and gone these eighteen years! There was a wooden tombstone in the church yard that used to tell all about him, but that's rotted and gone too."

"Where's Brom Dutcher?"

"Oh he went off to the army in the beginning of the war; some say he was killed at the storming of Stoney Point—others say he was drowned in a squall at the foot of Antony's Nose—I don't know—he never came back again."

"Where's Van Bummel the schoolmaster?"

"He went off to the wars too—was a great militia general, and is now in Congress."

Rip's heart died away at hearing of these sad changes in his home and friends, and finding himself thus alone in the world—every answer puzzled him too by treating of such enormous lapses of time and of matters which he could not understand—war—Congress, Stoney Point—he had no courage to ask after any more friends, but cried out in despair, "Does nobody here know Rip Van Winkle?"

"Oh. Rip Van Winkle?" exclaimed two or three—"oh to be sure!—that's Rip Van Winkle—yonder—leaning against the tree."

Rip looked and beheld a precise counterpart of himself, as he went up the mountain: apparently as lazy and certainly as ragged! The poor fellow was now completely confounded. He doubted his own identity, and whether he was himself or another man. In the midst of his bewilderment the man in the cocked hat demanded who he was,—what was his name?

"God knows," exclaimed he, at his wit's end, "I'm not myself—I'm somebody else—that's me yonder—no—that's somebody else got into my shoes—I was myself last night; but I fell asleep on the mountain—and they've changed my gun—and every thing's changed—and I'm changed—and I can't tell what's my name, or who I am!"

The byestanders began now to look at each other, nod, wink significantly and tap their fingers against their foreheads. There was a whisper also about securing the gun, and keeping the old fellow from doing mischief—at the very suggestion of which, the self important man in the cocked hat retired with some precipitation. At this critical moment a fresh likely looking woman pressed through the throng to get a peep at the greybearded man. She had a chubby child in her arms, which frightened at his looks began to cry. "Hush Rip," cried she, "hush you little fool, the old man won't hurt you." The name of the child, the air of the mother, the tone of her voice all awakened a train of recollections in his mind. "What is your name my good woman?" asked he.

"Judith Gardenier."

"And your father's name?"

"Ah, poor man, Rip Van Winkle was his name, but it's twenty years since he went away from home with his gun and never has been heard of since—his dog came home without him—but whether he shot himself, or was carried away by the Indians no body can tell. I was then but a little girl."

Rip had but one question more to ask, but he put it with a faltering voice—

"Where's your mother?"—

"Oh she too had died but a short time since—she broke a blood vessel in a fit of passion at a New England pedlar.—"

There was a drop of comfort at least in this intelligence. The honest man could contain himself no longer—he caught his daughter and her child in his arms.—"I am your father!" cried he—"Young Rip Van Winkle once—old Rip Van Winkle now!—does nobody know poor Rip Van Winkle!"

All stood amazed, until an old woman tottering out from among the crowd put her hand to her brow and peering under it in his face for a moment exclaimed—"Sure enough!—it is Rip Van Winkle—it is himself—welcome home again old neighbour—why, where have you been these twenty long years?"

Rip's story was soon told, for the whole twenty years had been to him but as one night. The neighbours stared when they heard it; some were seen to wink at each other and put their tongues in their cheeks, and the self important man in the cocked hat, who when the alarm was over had returned to the field, screwed down the corners of his mouth and shook his head—upon which there was a general shaking of the head throughout the assemblage.

It was determined, however, to take the opinion of old Peter Vanderdonk, who was seen slowly advancing up the road. He was a descendant of the historian of that name, who wrote one of the earliest accounts of the province. Peter was the most ancient inhabitant of the village and well versed in all the wonderful events and traditions of the neighbourhood. He recollected Rip at once, and corroborated his story in the most satisfactory manner. He assured the company that it was a fact handed down from his ancestor the historian, that the Kaatskill mountains had always been haunted by strange beings. That it was affirmed that the great Hendrick Hudson, the first discoverer of the river and country, kept a kind of vigil there every twenty years, with his crew of the Half Moon—being permitted in this way to revisit the scenes of his enterprize and keep a guardian eye upon the river and the great city called by his name. That his father had once seen them in their old Dutch dresses playing at nine pins in a hollow of the mountain; and that he himself had heard one summer afternoon the sound of their balls, like distant peals of thunder.

To make a long story short—the company broke up, and returned to the more important concerns of the election. Rip's daughter took him home to live with her; she had a snug well furnished house, and a stout cheery farmer for a husband whom Rip recollected for one of the urchins that used to climb upon his back. As to Rip's son and heir, who was the ditto of himself seen leaning against the tree; he was employed to work on the farm; but evinced an hereditary disposition to attend to any thing else but his business.

Rip now resumed his old walks and habits; he soon found many of his former cronies, though all rather the worse for the wear and tear of time; and preferred making friends among the rising generation, with whom he soon grew into great favour. Having nothing to do at home, and being arrived at that happy age when a man can be idle, with impunity, he took his place once more on the bench at the inn door and was reverenced as one of the patriarchs of the village and a chronicle of the old times "before the war." It was some time before he could get into the regular track of gossip, or could be made to comprehend the strange events that had taken place during his torpor. How that there had been a revolutionary war—that the country had thrown off the yoke of Old England and that instead of being a subject of his majesty George the Third, he was now a free citizen of the United States. Rip in fact was no politician; the changes of states and empires made but little impression on him; but there was one species of despotism under which he had long groaned and that was petticoat government. Happily that was at an end—he had got his neck out of the yoke of matrimony, and could go in and out whenever he pleased without dreading the tyranny of Dame Van Winkle. Whenever her name was mentioned, however, he shook his head, shrugged his shoulders and cast up his eyes; which might pass either for an expression of resignation to his fate or joy at his deliverance.

He used to tell his story to every stranger that arrived at Mr. Doolittle's Hotel. He was observed at first to vary on some points, every time he told it, which was doubtless owing to his having so recently awaked. It at last settled down precisely to the tale I have related and not a man woman or child in the neighbourhood but knew it by heart. Some always pretended to doubt the reality of it, and insisted that Rip had been out of his head, and that this was one point on which he always remained flighty. The old Dutch inhabitants, however, almost universally gave it full credit—Even to this day they never hear a thunder storm of a summer afternoon about the Kaatskill, but they say Hendrick Hudson and his crew are at their game of nine pins; and it is a common wish of all henpecked husbands in the neighbourhood, when life hangs heavy on their hands, that they might have a quieting draught out of Rip Van Winkle's flagon.

Note

The foregoing tale one would suspect had been suggested to Mr. Knickerbocker by a little German superstition about the emperor Frederick *der Rothbart* and the Kyphauser Mountain; the subjoined note, however, which he had appended to the tale, shews that it is an absolute fact, narrated with his usual fidelity.—

"The story of Rip Van Winkle may seem incredible to many, but nevertheless I give it my full belief, for I know the vicinity of our old Dutch settlements to have been very subject to marvellous events and appearances. Indeed I have heard many stranger stories than this, in the villages along the Hudson; all of which were too well authenticated to admit of a doubt. I have even talked with Rip Van Winkle myself, who when last I saw him was a very venerable old man and so perfectly rational and consistent on every other point, that I think no conscientious person could refuse to take this into the bargain—nay I have seen a certificate on the subject taken before a country justice and signed with a cross in the justice's own hand writing. The story therefore is beyond the possibility of doubt. D. K."

Postscript

The following are travelling notes from a memorandum book of Mr. Knickerbocker.

THE KAATSBERG OR CATSKILL MOUNTAINS have always been a region full of fable. The Indians considered them the abode of spirits who influenced the weather, spreading sunshine or clouds over the landscape and sending good or bad hunting seasons. They were ruled by an old squaw spirit, said to be their mother. She dwelt on the highest peak of the Catskills and had charge of the doors of day and night to open and shut them at the proper hour. She hung up the new moons in the skies and cut up the old ones into stars. In times of drought, if properly propitiated, she would spin light summer clouds out of cobwebs and morning dew, and send them off, from the crest of the mountain, flake after flake, like flakes of carded cotton to float in the air: until, dissolved by the heat of the sun, they would fall in gentle showers, causing the grass to spring, the fruits to ripen and the corn to grow an inch an hour. If displeased, however, she would brew up clouds black as ink, sitting in the midst of them like a bottle bellied spider in the midst of its web; and when these clouds broke—woe betide the valleys!

In old times say the Indian traditions, there was a kind of Manitou or Spirit, who kept about the wildest recesses of the Catskill mountains, and took a mischievous pleasure in wreaking all kinds of evils and vexations upon the red men. Sometimes he would assume the form of a bear a panther or a deer, lead the bewildered hunter a weary chace through tangled forests and among rugged rocks; and then spring off with a loud ho! ho! leaving him aghast on the brink of a beetling precipice or raging torrent.

The favorite abode of this Manitou is still shewn. It is a great rock or cliff in the loneliest part of the mountains, and, from the flowering vines which clamber about it, and the wild flowers which abound in its neighborhood, is known by the name of the Garden Rock. Near the foot of it is a small lake the haunt of the solitary bittern, with water snakes basking in the sun on the leaves of the pond lillies which lie on the surface. This place was held in great awe by the Indians, insomuch that the boldest hunter would not pursue his game within its precincts. Once upon a time, however, a hunter who had lost his way, penetrated to the garden rock where he beheld a number of gourds placed in the crotches of trees. One of these he seized and made off with it, but in the hurry of his retreat he let it fall among the rocks, when a great stream gushed forth which washed him away and swept him down precipices where he was dashed to pieces, and the stream made its way to the Hudson and continues to flow to the present day; being the identical stream known by the name of the Kaaters-kill.

FEATHERTOP: A MORALIZED LEGEND

BY NATHANIEL HAWTHORNE

NATHANIEL HAWTHORNE WAS BORN IN SALEM, MASSACHUSETTS, IN 1804 AND IS THOUGHT BY MANY TO BE ONE OF THE DARKEST OF THE EARLY AMERICAN WRITERS. (INDEED, HE EVEN HAD AN ANCESTOR WHO PRESIDED AT THE INFAMOUS SALEM WITCH TRIALS.) THOUGH FAMOUS FOR HIS NOVEL OF PURITAN CRIME AND PUNISHMENT, *THE SCARLET LETTER*, HIS STORY "FEATHERTOP" TAKES A MUCH MORE PLAYFUL TONE IN ITS TALE OF A WITCH AND HER DEMONICALLY AIDED CONSTRUCT WHO DARE TO ACT WITH MORE NOBILITY AND HUMANITY THAN THOSE WHO SURROUND THEM.

"Dickon," cried Mother Rigby, "a coal for my pipe!"

The pipe was in the old dame's mouth when she said these words. She had thrust it there after filling it with tobacco, but without stooping to light it at the hearth, where indeed there was no appearance of a fire having been kindled that morning. Forthwith, however, as soon as the order was given, there was an intense red glow out of the bowl of the pipe, and a whiff of smoke from Mother Rigby's lips. Whence the coal came, and how brought thither by an invisible hand, I have never been able to discover.

"Good!" quoth Mother Rigby, with a nod of her head. "Thank ye, Dickon! And now for making this scarecrow. Be within call, Dickon, in case I need you again."

The good woman had risen thus early (for as yet it was scarcely sunrise) in order to set about making a scarecrow, which she intended to put in the middle of her corn-patch. It was now the latter week of May, and the crows and blackbirds had already discovered the little, green, rolled-up leaf of the Indian corn just peeping out of the soil. She was determined, therefore, to contrive as lifelike a scarecrow as ever was seen, and to finish it immediately, from top to toe, so that it should begin its sentinel's duty that very morning. Now Mother Rigby (as everybody must have heard) was one of the most cunning and potent witches in New England, and might, with very little trouble, have made a scarecrow ugly enough to frighten the minister himself. But on this occasion, as she had awakened in an uncommonly pleasant humor, and was further dulcified by her pipe of tobacco, she resolved to produce something fine, beautiful, and splendid, rather than hideous and horrible.

"I don't want to set up a hobgoblin in my own corn-patch, and almost at my own doorstep," said Mother Rigby to herself, puffing out a whiff of smoke; "I could do it if I pleased, but I'm tired of doing marvellous things, and so I'll keep within the bounds of every-day business just for variety's sake. Besides, there is no use in scaring the little children for a mile roundabout, though 't is true I'm a witch."

It was settled, therefore, in her own mind, that the scarecrow should represent a fine gentleman of the period, so far as the materials at hand would allow. Perhaps it may be as well to enumerate the chief of the articles that went to the composition of this figure.

The most important item of all, probably, although it made so little show, was a certain broomstick, on which Mother Rigby had taken many an airy gallop at midnight, and which now served the scarecrow by way of a spinal column, or, as the unlearned phrase it, a backbone. One of its arms was a disabled flail which used to be wielded by Goodman Rigby, before his spouse worried him out of this troublesome world; the other, if I mistake not, was composed of the pudding stick and a broken rung of a chair, tied loosely together at the elbow. As for its legs, the right was a hoe handle, and the left an undistinguished and miscellaneous stick from the woodpile. Its lungs, stomach, and other affairs of that kind were nothing better than a meal bag stuffed with straw. Thus we have made out the skeleton and entire corporosity of the scarecrow, with the exception of its head; and this was admirably supplied by a somewhat withered and shrivelled pumpkin, in which Mother Rigby cut two holes for the eyes, and a slit for the mouth, leaving a bluish-colored knob in the middle to pass for a nose. It was really quite a respectable face.

"I've seen worse ones on human shoulders, at any rate," said Mother Rigby. "And many a fine gentleman has a pumpkin head, as well as my scarecrow."

But the clothes, in this case, were to be the making of the man. So the good old woman took down from a peg an ancient plum-colored coat of London make, and with relics of embroidery on its seams, cuffs, pocket-flaps, and button-holes, but lamentably worn and faded, patched at the elbows, tattered at the skirts, and threadbare all over. On the left breast was a round hole, whence either a star of nobility had been rent away, or else the hot heart of some former wearer had scorched it through and through. The neighbors said that this rich garment belonged to the Black Man's wardrobe, and that he kept it at Mother Rigby's cottage for the convenience of slipping it on whenever he wished to make a grand appearance at the governor's table. To match the coat there was a velvet waistcoat of very ample size, and formerly embroidered with foliage that had been as brightly golden as the maple leaves in October, but which had now quite vanished out of the substance of the velvet. Next came a pair of scarlet breeches, once worn by the French governor of Louisbourg, and the knees of which had touched the lower step of the throne of Louis le Grand. The Frenchman had given these smallclothes to an Indian powwow, who parted with them to the old witch for a gill of strong waters, at one of their dances in the forest. Furthermore, Mother Rigby produced a pair of silk stockings and put them on the figure's legs, where they showed as unsubstantial as a dream, with the wooden reality of the two sticks making itself miserably apparent through the holes. Lastly, she put her dead husband's wig on the bare scalp of the pumpkin, and surmounted the whole with a dusty three-cornered hat, in which was stuck the longest tail feather of a rooster.

Then the old dame stood the figure up in a corner of her cottage and chuckled to behold its yellow semblance of a visage, with its nobby little nose thrust into the air. It had a strangely self-satisfied aspect, and seemed to say, "Come look at me!"

"And you are well worth looking at, that's a fact!" quoth Mother Rigby, in admiration at her own handiwork. "I've made many a puppet since I've been a witch, but methinks this is the finest of them all. 'T is almost too good for a scarecrow. And, by the by, I'll just fill a fresh pipe of tobacco and then take him out to the corn-patch."

While filling her pipe the old woman continued to gaze with almost motherly affection at the figure in the corner. To say the truth, whether it were chance, or skill, or downright witchcraft, there was something wonderfully human in this ridiculous shape, bedizened with its tattered finery; and as for the countenance, it appeared to shrivel its yellow surface into a grin—a funny kind of expression betwixt scorn and merriment, as if it understood itself to be a jest at mankind. The more Mother Rigby looked the better she was pleased.

"Dickon," cried she sharply, "another coal for my pipe!"

Hardly had she spoken, than, just as before, there was a red-glowing coal on the top of the tobacco. She drew in a long whiff and puffed it forth again into the bar of morning sunshine which struggled through the one dusty pane of her cottage window. Mother Rigby always liked to flavor her pipe with a coal of fire from the particular chimney corner whence this had been brought. But where that chimney corner might be, or who brought the coal from it,—further than that the invisible messenger seemed to respond to the name of Dickon,—I cannot tell.

"That puppet yonder," thought Mother Rigby, still with her eyes fixed on the scare-crow, "is too good a piece of work to stand all summer in a corn-patch, frightening away the crows and blackbirds. He's capable of better things. Why, I've danced with a worse one, when partners happened to be scarce, at our witch meetings in the forest! What if I should let him take his chance among the other men of straw and empty fellows who go bustling about the world?"

The old witch took three or four more whiffs of her pipe and smiled.

"He'll meet plenty of his brethren at every street corner!" continued she. "Well; I didn't mean to dabble in witchcraft today, further than the lighting of my pipe, but a witch I am, and a witch I'm likely to be, and there's no use trying to shirk it. I'll make a man of my scarecrow, were it only for the joke's sake!"

While muttering these words, Mother Rigby took the pipe from her own mouth and thrust it into the crevice which represented the same feature in the pumpkin visage of the scarecrow.

"Puff, darling, puff!" said she. "Puff away, my fine fellow! your life depends on it!"

This was a strange exhortation, undoubtedly, to be addressed to a mere thing of sticks, straw, and old clothes, with nothing better than a shrivelled pumpkin for a head,—as we know to have been the scarecrow's case. Nevertheless, as we must carefully hold in remembrance, Mother Rigby was a witch of singular power and dexterity; and, keeping this fact duly before our minds, we shall see nothing beyond credibility in the remarkable incidents of our story. Indeed, the great difficulty will be at once got over, if we can only bring ourselves to believe that, as soon as the old dame bade him puff, there came a whiff of smoke from the scarecrow's mouth. It was the very feeblest of whiffs, to be sure; but it was followed by another and another, each more decided than the preceding one.

"Puff away, my pet! puff away, my pretty one!" Mother Rigby kept repeating, with her pleasantest smile. "It is the breath of life to ye; and that you may take my word for."

Beyond all question the pipe was bewitched. There must have been a spell either in the tobacco or in the fiercely glowing coal that so mysteriously burned on top of it, or in the pungently aromatic smoke which exhaled from the kindled weed. The figure, after a few doubtful attempts, at length blew forth a volley of smoke extending all the way from the obscure corner into the bar of sunshine. There it eddied and melted away among the motes of dust. It seemed a convulsive effort; for the two or three next whiffs were fainter, although the coal still glowed and threw a gleam over the scarecrow's visage. The old witch clapped her skinny hands together, and smiled encouragingly upon her handiwork. She saw that the charm worked well. The shrivelled, yellow face, which heretofore had been no face at all, had already a thin, fantastic haze, as it were of human likeness, shifting to and fro across it; sometimes vanishing entirely, but growing more perceptible than ever with the next whiff from the pipe. The whole figure, in like manner, assumed a show of life, such as we impart to ill-defined shapes among the clouds, and half deceive ourselves with the pastime of our own fancy.

If we must needs pry closely into the matter, it may be doubted whether there was any real change, after all, in the sordid, worn-out, worthless, and ill-jointed substance of the scarecrow; but merely a spectral illusion, and a cunning effect of light and shade so colored and contrived as to delude the eyes of most men. The miracles of witchcraft seem always to have had a very shallow subtlety; and, at least, if the above explanation do not hit the truth of the process, I can suggest no better.

"Well puffed, my pretty lad!" still cried old Mother Rigby. "Come, another good stout whiff, and let it be with might and main. Puff for thy life, I tell thee! Puff out of the very bottom of thy heart, if any heart thou hast, or any bottom to it! Well done, again! Thou didst suck in that mouthful as if for the pure love of it."

And then the witch beckoned to the scarecrow, throwing so much magnetic potency into her gesture that it seemed as if it must inevitably be obeyed, like the mystic call of the loadstone when it summons the iron.

"Why lurkest thou in the corner, lazy one?" said she. "Step forth! Thou hast the world before thee!"

Upon my word, if the legend were not one which I heard on my grandmother's knee, and which had established its place among things credible before my childish judgment could analyze its probability, I question whether I should have the face to tell it now.

In obedience to Mother Rigby's word, and extending its arm as if to reach her outstretched hand, the figure made a step forward—a kind of hitch and jerk, however, rather than a step—then tottered and almost lost its balance. What could the witch expect? It was nothing, after all, but a scarecrow stuck upon two sticks. But the strong-willed old beldam scowled, and beckoned, and flung the energy of her purpose so forcibly at this poor combination of rotten wood, and musty straw, and ragged garments, that it was compelled to show itself a man, in spite of the reality of things. So it stepped into the bar of sunshine. There it stood—poor devil of a contrivance that it was!—with only the thinnest vesture of human similitude about it, through which was evident the stiff, rickety, incongruous, faded, tattered, good-for-nothing patchwork of its substance, ready to sink in a heap upon the floor, as conscious of its own unworthiness to be erect. Shall I confess the truth? At its present point of vivification, the scarecrow reminds me of some of the lukewarm and abortive characters, composed of heterogeneous materials, used for the thousandth time, and never worth using, with which romance writers (and myself, no doubt, among the rest) have so over-peopled the world of fiction.

But the fierce old hag began to get angry and show a glimpse of her diabolic nature (like a snake's head, peeping with a hiss out of her bosom), at this pusillanimous behavior of the thing which she had taken the trouble to put together.

"Puff away, wretch!" cried she, wrathfully. "Puff, puff, puff, thou thing of straw and emptiness! thou rag or two! thou meal bag! thou pumpkin head! thou nothing! Where shall I find a name vile enough to call thee by? Puff, I say, and suck in thy fantastic life along with the smoke! else I snatch the pipe from thy mouth and hurl thee where that red coal came from."

Thus threatened, the unhappy scarecrow had nothing for it but to puff away for dear life. As need was, therefore, it applied itself lustily to the pipe, and sent forth such abundant volleys of tobacco smoke that the small cottage kitchen became all vaporous. The one sunbeam struggled mistily through, and could but imperfectly define the image of the cracked and dusty window pane on the opposite wall. Mother Rigby, meanwhile, with one brown arm akimbo and the other stretched towards the figure, loomed grimly amid the obscurity with such port and expression as when she was wont to heave a ponderous nightmare on her victims and stand at the bedside to enjoy their agony. In fear and trembling did this poor scarecrow puff. But its efforts, it must be acknowledged, served an excellent purpose; for, with each successive whiff, the figure lost more and more of its dizzy and perplexing tenuity and seemed to take denser substance. Its very garments, moreover, partook of the magical change, and shone with the gloss of novelty and glistened with the skilfully embroidered gold that had long ago been rent away. And, half revealed among the smoke, a yellow visage bent its lustreless eyes on Mother Rigby.

At last the old witch clinched her fist and shook it at the figure. Not that she was positively angry, but merely acting on the principle—perhaps untrue, or not the only truth, though as high a one as Mother Rigby could be expected to attain—that feeble and torpid natures, being incapable of better inspiration, must be stirred up by fear. But here was the crisis. Should she fail in what she now sought to effect, it was her ruthless purpose to scatter the miserable simulacre into its original elements.

"Thou hast a man's aspect," said she, sternly. "Have also the echo and mockery of a voice! I bid thee speak!"

The scarecrow gasped, struggled, and at length emitted a murmur, which was so incorporated with its smoky breath that you could scarcely tell whether is were indeed a voice or only a whiff of tobacco. Some narrators of this legend hold the opinion that Mother Rigby's conjurations and the fierceness of her will had compelled a familiar spirit into the figure, and that the voice was his.

"Mother," mumbled the poor stifled voice, "be not so awful with me! I would fain speak; but being without wits, what can I say?"

"Thou canst speak, darling, canst thou?" cried Mother Rigby, relaxing her grim countenance into a smile. "And what shalt thou say, quotha! Say, indeed! Art thou of the brotherhood of the empty skull, and demandest of me what thou shalt say? Thou shalt say a thousand things, and saying them a thousand times over, thou shalt still have said nothing! Be not afraid, I tell thee! When thou comest into the world (whither

I purpose sending thee forthwith) thou shalt not lack the wherewithal to talk. Talk! Why, thou shall babble like a mill-stream, if thou wilt. Thou hast brains enough for that, I trow!"

"At your service, mother," responded the figure.

"And that was well said, my pretty one," answered Mother Rigby. "Then thou speakest like thyself, and meant nothing. Thou shalt have a hundred such set phrases, and five hundred to the boot of them. And now, darling, I have taken so much pains with thee and thou art so beautiful, that, by my troth, I love thee better than any witch's puppet in the world; and I've made them of all sorts—clay, wax, straw, sticks, night fog, morning mist, sea foam, and chimney smoke. But thou art the very best. So give heed to what I say."

"Yes, kind mother," said the figure, "with all my heart!"

"With all thy heart!" cried the old witch, setting her hands to her sides and laughing loudly. "Thou hast such a pretty way of speaking. With all thy heart! And thou didst put thy hand to the left side of thy waistcoat as if thou really hadst one!"

So now, in high good humor with this fantastic contrivance of hers, Mother Rigby told the scarecrow that it must go and play its part in the great world, where not one man in a hundred, she affirmed, was gifted with more real substance than itself. And, that he might hold up his head with the best of them, she endowed him, on the spot, with an unreckonable amount of wealth. It consisted partly of a gold mine in Eldorado, and of ten thousand shares in a broken bubble, and of half a million acres of vineyard at the North Pole, and of a castle in the air, and a chateau in Spain, together with all the rents and income therefrom accruing. She further made over to him the cargo of a certain ship, laden with salt of Cadiz, which she herself, by her necromantic arts, had caused to founder, ten years before, in the deepest part of mid-ocean. If the salt were not dissolved, and could be brought to market, it would fetch a pretty penny among the fishermen. That he might not lack ready money, she gave him a copper farthing of Birmingham manufacture, being all the coin she had about her, and likewise a great deal of brass, which she applied to his forehead, thus making it yellower than ever.

"With that brass alone," quoth Mother Rigby, "thou canst pay thy way all over the earth. Kiss me, pretty darling! I have done my best for thee."

Furthermore, that the adventurer might lack no possible advantage towards a fair start in life, this excellent old dame gave him a token by which he was to introduce himself to a certain magistrate, member of the council, merchant, and elder of the church (the four capacities constituting but one man), who stood at the head of society in the neighboring metropolis. The token was neither more nor less than a single word, which Mother Rigby whispered to the scarecrow, and which the scarecrow was to whisper to the merchant.

"Gouty as the old fellow is, he'll run thy errands for thee, when once thou hast given him that word in his ear," said the old witch. "Mother Rigby knows the worshipful Justice Gookin, and the worshipful Justice knows Mother Rigby!"

Here the witch thrust her wrinkled face close to the puppet's, chuckling irrepressibly, and fidgeting all through her system, with delight at the idea which she meant to communicate.

"The worshipful Master Gookin," whispered she, "hath a comely maiden to his daughter. And hark ye, my pet! Thou hast a fair outside, and a pretty wit enough of thine own. Yea, a pretty wit enough! Thou wilt think better of it when thou hast seen more of other people's wits. Now, with thy outside and thy inside, thou art the very man to win a young girl's heart. Never doubt it! I tell thee it shall be so. Put but a bold face on the matter, sigh, smile, flourish thy hat, thrust forth thy leg like a dancing-master, put thy right hand to the left side of thy waistcoat, and pretty Polly Gookin is thine own!"

All this while the new creature had been sucking in and exhaling the vapory fragrance of his pipe, and seemed now to continue this occupation as much for the enjoyment it afforded as because it was an essential condition of his existence. It was wonderful to see how exceedingly like a human being it behaved. Its eyes (for it appeared to possess a pair) were bent on Mother Rigby, and at suitable junctures it nodded or shook its head. Neither did it lack words proper for the occasion: "Really! Indeed! Pray tell me! Is it possible! Upon my word! By no means! Oh! Ah! Hem!" and other such weighty utterances as imply attention, inquiry, acquiescence, or dissent on the part of the auditor. Even had you stood by and seen the scarecrow made, you could scarcely have resisted the conviction that it perfectly understood the cunning counsels which the old witch poured into its counterfeit of an ear. The more earnestly it applied its lips to the pipe, the more distinctly was its human likeness stamped among visible realities, the more sagacious grew its expression, the more lifelike its gestures and movements, and the more intelligibly audible its voice. Its garments, too, glistened so much the brighter with an illusory magnificence. The very pipe, in which burned the spell of all this wonderwork, ceased to appear as a smoke-blackened earthen stump, and became a meerschaum, with painted bowl and amber mouthpiece.

It might be apprehended, however, that as the life of the illusion seemed identical with the vapor of the pipe, it would terminate simultaneously with the reduction of the tobacco to ashes. But the beldam foresaw the difficulty.

"Hold thou the pipe, my precious one," said she, "while I fill it for thee again."

It was sorrowful to behold how the fine gentleman began to fade back into a scarecrow while Mother Rigby shook the ashes out of the pipe and proceeded to replenish it from her tobacco-box.

"Dickon," cried she, in her high, sharp tone, "another coal for this pipe!"

No sooner said than the intensely red speck of fire was glowing within the pipe-bowl; and the scarecrow, without waiting for the witch's bidding, applied the tube to his lips and drew in a few short, convulsive whiffs, which soon, however, became regular and equable.

"Now, mine own heart's darling," quoth Mother Rigby, "whatever may happen to thee, thou must stick to thy pipe. Thy life is in it; and that, at least, thou knowest well, if thou knowest nought besides. Stick to thy pipe, I say! Smoke, puff, blow thy cloud; and tell the people, if any question be made, that it is for thy health, and that so the physician orders thee to do. And, sweet one, when thou shalt find thy pipe getting low, go apart into some corner, and (first filling thyself with smoke) cry sharply, 'Dickon, a fresh pipe of tobacco!' and 'Dickon, another coal for my pipe!' and have it into thy pretty mouth as speedily as may be. Else, instead of a gallant gentleman in a gold-laced coat, thou wilt be but a jumble of sticks and tattered clothes, and a bag of straw, and a withered pumpkin! Now depart, my treasure, and good luck go with thee!"

"Never fear, mother!" said the figure, in a stout voice, and sending forth a courageous whiff of smoke, "I will thrive, if an honest man and a gentleman may!"

"Oh, thou wilt be the death of me!" cried the old witch, convulsed with laughter. "That was well said. If an honest man and a gentleman may! Thou playest thy part to perfection. Get along with thee for a smart fellow; and I will wager on thy head, as a man of pith and substance, with a brain and what they call a heart, and all else that a man should have, against any other thing on two legs. I hold myself a better witch than yesterday, for thy sake. Did not I make thee? And I defy any witch in New England to make such another! Here; take my staff along with thee!"

The staff, though it was but a plain oaken stick, immediately took the aspect of a gold-headed cane.

"That gold head has as much sense in it as thine own," said Mother Rigby, "and it will guide thee straight to worshipful Master Gookin's door. Get thee gone, my pretty pet, my darling, my precious one, my treasure; and if any ask thy name, it is Feathertop. For thou hast a feather in thy hat, and I have thrust a handful of feathers into the hollow of thy head, and thy wig, too, is of the fashion they call Feathertop,— so be Feathertop thy name!"

And, issuing from the cottage, Feathertop strode manfully towards town. Mother Rigby stood at the threshold, well pleased to see how the sunbeams glistened on him, as if all his magnificence were real, and how diligently and lovingly he smoked his pipe, and how handsomely he walked, in spite of a little stiffness of his legs. She watched him until out of sight, and threw a witch benediction after her darling, when a turn of the road snatched him from her view.

Betimes in the forenoon, when the principal street of the neighboring town was just at its acme of life and bustle, a stranger of very distinguished figure was seen on the sidewalk. His port as well as his garments betokened nothing short of nobility. He wore a richly embroidered plum-colored coat, a waistcoat of costly velvet, magnificently adorned with golden foliage, a pair of splendid scarlet breeches, and the finest and glossiest of white silk stockings. His head was covered with a peruke, so daintily powdered and adjusted that it would have been sacrilege to disorder it with a hat; which, therefore (and it was a gold-laced hat, set off with a snowy feather), he carried beneath his arm. On the breast of his coat glistened a star. He managed his gold-headed cane with an airy grace, peculiar to the fine gentlemen of the period; and, to give the highest possible finish to his equipment, he had lace ruffles at his wrist, of a most ethereal delicacy, sufficiently avouching how idle and aristocratic must be the hands which they half concealed.

It was a remarkable point in the accourtrement of this brilliant personage that he held in his left hand a fantastic kind of a pipe, with an exquisitely painted bowl and an amber mouthpiece. This he applied to his lips as often as every five or six paces, and inhaled a deep whiff of smoke, which, after being retained a moment in his lungs, might be seen to eddy gracefully from his mouth and nostrils.

As may well be supposed, the street was all astir to find out the stranger's name.

"It is some great nobleman, beyond question," said one of the townspeople. "Do you see the star at his breast?"

"Nay; it is too bright to be seen," said another. "Yes; he must needs be a nobleman, as you say. But by what conveyance, think you, can his lordship have voyaged or travelled hither? There has been no vessel from the old country for a month past; and if he have arrived overland from the southward, pray where are his attendants and equipage?"

"He needs no equipage to set off his rank," remarked a third.

"If he came among us in rags, nobility would shine through a hole in his elbow. I never saw such dignity of aspect. He has the old Norman blood in his veins, I warrant him."

"I rather take him to be a Dutchman, or one of your high Germans," said another citizen. "The men of those countries have always the pipe at their mouths."

"And so has a Turk," answered his companion. "But, in my judgment, this stranger hath been bred at the French court, and hath there learned politeness and grace of manner, which none understand so well as the nobility of France. That gait, now! A vulgar spectator might deem it stiff—he might call it a hitch and jerk—but, to my eye, it hath an unspeakable majesty, and must have been acquired by constant observation of the deportment of the Grand Monarque. The stranger's character and office are evident enough. He is a French ambassador, come to treat with our rulers about the cession of Canada."

"More probably a Spaniard," said another, "and hence his yellow complexion; or, most likely, he is from the Havana, or from some port on the Spanish main, and comes to make investigation about the piracies which our government is thought to connive at. Those settlers in Peru and Mexico have skins as yellow as the gold which they dig out of their mines."

"Yellow or not," cried a lady, "he is a beautiful man!—so tall, so slender! such a fine, noble face, with so well-shaped a nose, and all that delicacy of expression about the mouth! And, bless me, how bright his star is! It positively shoots out flames!"

"So do your eyes, fair lady," said the stranger, with a bow and a flourish of his pipe; for he was just passing at the instant. "Upon my honor, they have quite dazzled me."

"Was ever so original and exquisite a compliment?" murmured the lady, in an ecstasy of delight.

Amid the general admiration excited by the stranger's appearance, there were only two dissenting voices. One was that of an impertinent cur, which, after snuffing at the heels of the glistening figure, put its tail between its legs and skulked into its master's back yard, vociferating an execrable howl. The other dissentient was a young child, who squalled at the fullest stretch of his lungs, and babbled some unintelligible nonsense about a pumpkin.

Feathertop meanwhile pursued his way along the street. Except for the few complimentary words to the lady, and now and then a slight inclination of the head in requital of the profound reverences of the bystanders, he seemed wholly absorbed in his pipe. There needed no other proof of his rank and consequence than the perfect equanimity with which he comported himself, while the curiosity and admiration of the town swelled almost into clamor around him. With a crowd gathering behind his footsteps, he finally reached the mansion-house of the worshipful Justice Gookin, entered the gate, ascended the steps of the front door, and knocked. In the interim, before his summons was answered, the stranger was observed to shake the ashes out of his pipe.

"What did he say in that sharp voice?" inquired one of the spectators.

"Nay, I know not," answered his friend. "But the sun dazzles my eyes strangely. How dim and faded his lordship looks all of a sudden! Bless my wits, what is the matter with me?"

"The wonder is," said the other, "that his pipe, which was out only an instant ago, should be all alight again, and with the reddest coal I ever saw. There is something mysterious about this stranger. What a whiff of smoke was that! Dim and faded did you call him? Why, as he turns about the star on his breast is all ablaze."

"It is, indeed," said his companion; "and it will go near to dazzle pretty Polly Gookin, whom I see peeping at it out of the chamber window."

The door being now opened, Feathertop turned to the crowd, made a stately bend of his body like a great man acknowledging the reverence of the meaner sort, and vanished into the house. There was a mysterious kind of a smile, if it might not better be called a grin or grimace, upon his visage; but, of all the throng that beheld him, not an individual appears to have possessed insight enough to detect the illusive character of the stranger except a little child and a cur dog.

Our legend here loses somewhat of its continuity, and, passing over the preliminary explanation between Feathertop and the merchant, goes in quest of the pretty Polly Gookin. She was a damsel of a soft, round figure, with light hair and blue eyes, and a fair, rosy face, which seemed neither very shrewd nor very simple. This young lady had caught a glimpse of the glistening stranger while standing at the threshold, and had forthwith put on a laced cap, a string of beads, her finest kerchief, and her stiffest damask petticoat in preparation for the interview. Hurrying from her chamber to the parlor, she had ever since been viewing herself in the large looking-glass and practising pretty airs—now a smile, now a ceremonious dignity of aspect, and now a softer smile than the former, kissing her hand likewise, tossing her head, and managing her fan; while within the mirror an unsubstantial little maid repeated every gesture and did all the foolish things that Polly did, but without making her ashamed of them. In short, it was the fault of pretty Polly's ability rather than her will if she failed to be as complete an artifice as the illustrious Feathertop himself; and, when she thus tampered with her own simplicity, the witch's phantom might well hope to win her.

No sooner did Polly hear her father's gouty footsteps approaching the parlor door, accompanied with the stiff clatter of Feathertop's high-heeled shoes, than she seated herself bolt upright and innocently began warbling a song.

"Polly! daughter Polly!" cried the old merchant. "Come hither, child."

Master Gookin's aspect, as he opened the door, was doubtful and troubled.

"This gentleman," continued he, presenting the stranger, "is the Chevalier Feathertop,—nay, I beg his pardon, my Lord Feathertop,—who hath brought me a token of remembrance from an ancient friend of mine. Pay your duty to his lordship, child, and honor him as his quality deserves."

After these few words of introduction, the worshipful magistrate immediately quitted the room. But, even in that brief moment, had the fair Polly glanced aside at her father instead of devoting herself wholly to the brilliant guest, she might have taken warning of some mischief nigh at hand. The old man was nervous, fidgety, and very pale. Purposing a smile of courtesy, he had deformed his face with a sort of galvanic grin, which, when Feathertop's back was turned, he exchanged for a scowl, at the same time shaking his fist and stamping his gouty foot—an incivility which brought its retribution along with it. The truth appears to have been that Mother Rigby's word of introduction, whatever it might be, had operated far more on the rich merchant's fears than on his good will. Moreover, being a man of wonderfully acute observation, he had noticed that these painted figures on the bowl of Feathertop's pipe were in motion. Looking more closely, he became convinced that these figures were a party of little demons, each duly provided with horns and a tail, and dancing hand in hand, with gestures of diabolical merriment, round the circumference of the pipe bowl. As if to confirm his suspicions, while Master Gookin ushered his guest along a dusky passage from his private room to the parlor, the star on Feathertop's breast had scintillated actual flames, and threw a flickering gleam upon the wall, the ceiling, and the floor.

With such sinister prognostics manifesting themselves on all hands, it is not to be marvelled at that the merchant should have felt that he was committing his daughter to a very questionable acquaintance. He cursed, in his secret soul, the insinuating elegance of Feathertop's manners, as this brilliant personage bowed, smiled, put his hand on his heart, inhaled a long whiff from his pipe, and enriched the atmosphere with the smoky vapor of a fragrant and visible sigh. Gladly would poor Master Gookin have thrust his dangerous guest into the street; but there was a constraint and terror within him. This respectable old gentleman, we fear, at an earlier period of life, had given some pledge or other to the evil principle, and perhaps was now to redeem it by the sacrifice of his daughter.

It so happened that the parlor door was partly of glass, shaded by a silken curtain, the folds of which hung a little awry. So strong was the merchant's interest in witnessing what was to ensue between the fair Polly and the gallant Feathertop that, after quitting the room, he could by no means refrain from peeping through the crevice of the curtain.

But there was nothing very miraculous to be seen; nothing—except the trifles previously noticed—to confirm the idea of a supernatural peril environing the pretty Polly. The stranger it is true was evidently a thorough and practised man of the world, systematic and self-possessed, and therefore the sort of a person to whom a parent ought not to confide a simple, young girl without due watchfulness for the result. The worthy magistrate, who had been conversant with all degrees and qualities of mankind, could not but perceive every motion and gesture of the distinguished Feathertop came in its proper place; nothing had been left rude or native in him; a well-digested conventionalism had incorporated itself thoroughly with his substance and transformed him into a work of art. Perhaps it was this peculiarity that invested him with a species of ghastliness and awe. It is the effect of anything completely and consummately artificial, in human shape, that the person impresses us as an unreality and as having hardly pith enough to cast a shadow upon the floor. As regarded Feathertop, all this resulted in a wild, extravagant, and fantastical impression, as if his life and being were akin to the smoke that curled upward from his pipe.

But pretty Polly Gookin felt not thus. The pair were now promenading the room: Feathertop with his dainty stride and no less dainty grimace; the girl with a native maidenly grace, just touched, not spoiled, by a slightly affected manner, which seemed caught from the perfect artifice of her companion. The longer the interview continued, the more charmed was pretty Polly, until, within the first quarter of an hour (as the old magistrate noted by his watch), she was evidently beginning to be in love. Nor need it have been witchcraft that subdued her in such a hurry; the poor child's heart, it may be, was so very fervent that it melted her with its own warmth as reflected from the hollow semblance of a lover. No matter what Feathertop said, his words found depth and reverberation in her ear; no matter what he did, his action was heroic to her eye. And by this time it is to be supposed there was a blush on Polly's cheek, a tender smile about her mouth, and a liquid softness in her glance; while the star kept coruscating on Feathertop's breast, and the little demons careered with more frantic merriment than ever about the circumference of his pipe bowl. O pretty Polly Gookin, why should these imps rejoice so madly that a silly maiden's heart was about to be given to a shadow! Is it so unusual a misfortune, so rare a triumph?

By and by Feathertop paused, and throwing himself into an imposing attitude, seemed to summon the fair girl to survey his figure and resist him longer if she could. His star, his embroidery, his buckles glowed at that instant with unutterable splendor; the picturesque hues of his attire took a richer depth of coloring; there was a gleam and polish over his whole presence betokening the perfect witchery of well-ordered manners. The maiden raised her eyes and suffered them to linger upon her companion with a bashful and admiring gaze. Then, as if desirous of judging what value her own simple comeliness might have side by side with so much brilliancy, she cast a glance towards the full-length looking-glass in front of which they happened to be standing. It was one of the truest plates in the world and incapable of flattery. No sooner did the images therein reflected meet Polly's eye than she shrieked, shrank from the stranger's side, gazed at him for a moment in the wildest dismay, and sank insensible upon the floor. Feathertop likewise had looked towards the mirror, and there beheld, not the glittering mockery of his outside show, but a picture of the sordid patchwork of his real composition, stripped of all witchcraft.

The wretched simulacrum! We almost pity him. He threw up his arms with an expression of despair that went further than any of his previous manifestations towards vindicating his claims to be reckoned human; for, perchance the only time since this so often empty and deceptive life of mortals began its course, an illusion had seen and fully recognized itself.

Mother Rigby was seated by her kitchen hearth in the twilight of this eventful day, and had just shaken the ashes out of a new pipe, when she heard a hurried tramp along the road. Yet it did not seem so much the tramp of human footsteps as the clatter of sticks or the rattling of dry bones.

"Ha!" thought the old witch, "what step is that? Whose skeleton is out of its grave now, I wonder?"

A figure burst headlong into the cottage door. It was Feathertop! His pipe was still alight; the star still flamed upon his breast; the embroidery still glowed upon his garments; nor had he lost, in any degree or manner that could be estimated, the aspect that assimilated him with our mortal brotherhood. But yet, in some indescribable way (as is the case with all that has deluded us when once found out), the poor reality was felt beneath the cunning artifice.

"What has gone wrong?" demanded the witch. "Did yonder sniffling hypocrite thrust my darling from his door? The villain! I'll set twenty fiends to torment him till he offer thee his daughter on his bended knees!"

"No, mother," said Feathertop despondingly; "it was not that."

"Did the girl scorn my precious one?" asked Mother Rigby, her fierce eyes glowing like two coals of Tophet. "I'll cover her face with pimples! Her nose shall be as red as the coal in thy pipe! Her front teeth shall drop out! In a week hence she shall not be worth thy having!"

"Let her alone, mother," answered poor Feathertop; "the girl was half won; and methinks a kiss from her sweet lips might have made me altogether human. But," he added, after a brief pause and then a howl of self-contempt, "I've seen myself, mother! I've seen myself for the wretched, ragged, empty thing I am! I'll exist no longer!"

Snatching the pipe from his mouth, he flung it with all his might against the chimney, and at the same instant sank upon the floor, a medley of straw and tattered garments, with some sticks protruding from the heap, and a shrivelled pumpkin in the midst. The eyeholes were now lustreless; but the rudely carved gap, that just before had been a mouth, still seemed to twist itself into a despairing grin, and· was so far human.

"Poor fellow!" quoth Mother Rigby, with a rueful glance at the relics of her ill-fated contrivance. "My poor, dear, pretty Feathertop! There are thousands upon thousands of coxcombs and charlatans in the world, made up of just such a jumble of wornout, forgotten, and good-for-nothing trash as he was! Yet they live in fair repute, and never see themselves for what they are. And why should my poor puppet be the only one to know himself and perish for it?"

While thus muttering, the witch had filled a fresh pipe of tobacco, and held the stem between her fingers, as doubtful whether to thrust it into her own mouth or Feathertop's.

"Poor Feathertop!" she continued. "I could easily give him another chance and send him forth again tomorrow. But no; his feelings are too tender, his sensibilities too deep. He seems to have too much heart to bustle for his own advantage in such an empty and heartless world. Well! well! I'll make a scarecrow of him after all. 'T is an innocent and useful vocation, and will suit my darling well; and, if each of his human brethren had as fit a one, 't would be the better for mankind; and as for this pipe of tobacco, I need it more than he."

So saying, Mother Rigby put the stem between her lips. "Dickon!" cried she, in her high, sharp tone, "another coal for my pipe!"

UNCLE REMUS

BY JOEL CHANDLER HARRIS

JOEL CHANDLER HARRIS HAS, IN RECENT YEARS, FALLEN OUT OF FAVOR DUE TO HIS DECIDEDLY POLITICALLY INCORRECT CHARACTERIZATIONS. INDEED HIS UNCLE REMUS IS PROBABLY SECOND ONLY TO STOWE'S UNCLE TOM IN ITS CARICATURING OF BLACK SLAVES IN THE OLD SOUTH AS SEEN BY WHITE PEOPLE. THIS NOTWITHSTANDING, HARRIS DID INDEED GIFT AMERICAN LITERATURE WITH ITS OWN PSEUDO-AESOP, COMPLETE WITH TALKING ANIMALS AND BIBLICAL METAPHORS, ALL TOLD IN A PSEUDO RURAL DIALECT THAT FIRMLY PLACES IT WITHIN THE AMERICAN ORAL TRADITION.

Uncle Remus Initiates the Little Boy

One evening recently, the lady whom Uncle Remus calls "Miss Sally" missed her little seven-year-old boy. Making search for him through the house and through the yard, she heard the sound of voices in the old man's cabin, and, looking through the window, saw the child sitting by Uncle Remus. His head rested against the old man's arm, and he was gazing with an expression of the most intense interest into the rough, weather-beaten face, that beamed so kindly upon him. This is what "Miss Sally" heard:

"Bimeby, one day, atter Brer Fox bin doin' all dat he could fer ter ketch Brer Rabbit, en Brer Rabbit bin doin' all he could fer to keep 'im fum it, Brer Fox say to hisse'f dat he'd put up a game on Brer Rabbit, en he ain't mo'n got de wuds out'n his mouf twel Brer Rabbit come a lopin' up de big road, lookin' des ez plump, en ez fat, en ez sassy ez a Moggin hoss in a barley-patch.

" 'Hol' on dar, Brer Rabbit,' sez Brer Fox, sezee.

" 'I ain't got time, Brer Fox,' sez Brer Rabbit, sezee, sorter mendin' his licks.

" 'I wanter have some confab wid you, Brer Rabbit,' sez Brer Fox, sezee.

" 'All right, Brer Fox, but you better holler fum whar you stan'. I'm monstus full er fleas dis mawnin',' sez Brer Rabbit, sezee.

" 'I seed Brer B'ar yistiddy,' sez Brer Fox, sezee, 'en he sorter rake me over de coals kaze you en me ain't make fr'en's en live neighborly, en I tole 'im dat I'd see you.'

"Den Brer Rabbit scratch one year wid his off hinefoot sorter jubously, en den he ups en sez, sezee:

" 'All a settin', Brer Fox. Spose'n you drap roun' termorrer en take dinner wid me. We ain't got no great doin's at our house, but I speck de old 'oman en de chilluns kin sorter scramble roun' en git up sump'n fer ter stay yo' stummick.'

" 'I'm 'gree'ble, Brer Rabbit,' sez Brer Fox, sezee.

" 'Den I'll 'pen' on you,' sez Brer Rabbit, sezee.

"Nex' day, Mr. Rabbit en Miss Rabbit got up soon, 'fo' day, en raided on a gyarden like Miss Sally's out dar, en got some cabbiges en some roas'n-years, en some sparrer-grass, en dey fix up a smashin' dinner. Bimeby one er de little Rabbits, playin' out in de backyard, come runnin' in hollerin', 'Oh, ma! oh, ma! I seed Mr. Fox a comin'!' En den Brer Rabbit he tuck de chilluns by der years en make um set down, en den him and Miss Rabbit sorter dally roun' waitin' for Brer Fox. En dey keep on waitin', but no Brer Fox ain't come. Atter 'while Brer Rabbit goes to de do', easy like, en peep out, en dar, stickin' fum behime de cornder, wuz de tip-een' er Brer Fox tail. Den Brer Rabbit shot de do' en sot down, en put his paws behime his years en begin fer ter sing:

" 'De place wharbouts you spill de grease,
    Right dar you er boun' ter slide,
  An' whar you fin' a bunch er ha'r,
    You'll sholy fine de hide.'

"Nex' day, Brer Fox sont word by Mr. Mink, en skuze hisse'f kaze he wuz too sick fer ter come, en he ax Brer Rabbit fer to come en take dinner wid him, en Brer Rabbit say he wuz 'gree'ble.

"Bimeby, w'en de shadders wuz at der shortes', Brer Rabbit he sorter brush up en sa'nter down ter Brer Fox's house, en w'en he got dar, he hear somebody groanin', en he look in de do' an dar he see Brer Fox settin' up in a rockin'-cheer all wrop up wid flannil, en he look mighty weak. Brer Rabbit look all 'roun', he did, but he ain't see no dinner. De dishpan wuz settin' on de table, en close by wuz a kyarvin' knife.

" 'Look like you gwine ter have chicken fer dinner, Brer Fox,' sez Brer Rabbit, sezee.

" 'Yes, Brer Rabbit, dey er nice, en fresh, en tender,' sez Brer Fox, sezee.

"Den Brer Rabbit sorter pull his mustash, en say: 'You ain't got no calamus root, is you, Brer Fox? I done got so now dat I can't eat no chicken ceppin' she's seasoned up wid calamus root.' En wid dat Brer Rabbit lipt out er de do' and dodge 'mong de bushes, en sot dar watchin' fer Brer Fox; en he ain't watch long, nudder, kaze Brer Fox flung off de flannil en crope out er de house en got whar he could cloze in on Brer Rabbit, en bimeby Brer Rabbit holler out: 'Oh, Brer Fox! I'll des put yo' calamus root out yer on dish yer stump. Better come git it while hit's fresh,' and wid dat Brer Rabbit gallop off home. En Brer Fox ain't never cotch 'im yit, en w'at's mo', honey, he ain't gwine ter."

The Wonderful Tar-Baby Story

"Didn't the fox *never* catch the rabbit, Uncle Remus?" asked the little boy the next evening.

"He come mighty nigh it, honey, sho's you born—Brer Fox did. One day atter Brer Rabbit fool 'im wid dat calamus root, Brer Fox went ter wuk en got 'im some tar, en mix it wid some turkentime, en fix up a contrapshun w'at he call a Tar-Baby, en he tuck dish yer Tar-Baby en he sot 'er in de big road, en den he lay off in de bushes fer to see what de news wuz gwine ter be. En he didn't hatter wait long, nudder, kaze bimeby here come Brer Rabbit pacin' down de road—lippity-clippity, clippity-lippity—dez ez sassy ez a jay-bird. Brer Fox, he lay low. Brer Rabbit come prancin' 'long twel he spy de Tar-Baby, en den he fotch up on his behime legs like he wuz 'stonished. De Tar-Baby, she sot dar, she did, en Brer Fox, he lay low.

" 'Mawnin'!' sez Brer Rabbit, sezee—'nice wedder dis mawnin',' sezee.

"Tar-Baby ain't sayin' nothin', en Brer Fox, he lay low.

" 'How duz yo' sym'tums seem ter segashuate?' sez Brer Rabbit, sezee.

"Brer Fox, he wink his eye slow, en lay low, en de Tar-Baby, she ain't sayin' nothin'.

" 'How you come on, den? Is you deaf?' sez Brer Rabbit, sezee. 'Kaze if you is, I kin holler louder,' sezee.

"Tar-Baby stay still, en Brer Fox, he lay low.

" 'You er stuck up, dat's w'at you is,' says Brer Rabbit, sezee, 'en I'm gwine ter kyore you, dat's w'at I'm a gwine ter do,' sezee.

"Brer Fox, he sorter chuckle in his stummick, he did, but Tar-Baby ain't sayin' nothin'.

" 'I'm gwine ter larn you how ter talk ter 'spectubble folks ef hit's de las' ack,' sez Brer Rabbit, sezee. 'Ef you don't take off dat hat en tell me howdy, I'm gwine ter bus' you wide open,' sezee.

"Tar-Baby stay still, en Brer Fox, he lay low.

"Brer Rabbit keep on axin' 'im, en de Tar-Baby, she keep on sayin' nothin', twel present'y Brer Rabbit draw back wid his fis', he did, en blip he tuck 'er side er de head. Right dar's whar he broke his merlasses jug. His fis' stuck, en he can't pull loose. De tar hilt 'im. But Tar-Baby, she stay still, en Brer Fox, he lay low.

" 'Ef you don't lemme loose, I'll knock you agin,' sez Brer Rabbit, sezee, en wid dat he fotch 'er a wipe wid de udder han', en dat stuck. Tar-Baby, she ain't sayin' nothin', en Brer Fox, he lay low.

" 'Tu'n me loose, fo' I kick de natchul stuffin' out'n you,' sez Brer Rabbit, sezee, but de Tar-Baby, she ain't sayin' nothin'. She des hilt on, en den Brer Rabbit lose de use er his feet in de same way. Brer Fox, he lay low. Den Brer Rabbit squall out dat ef de Tar-Baby don't tu'n 'im loose he butt 'er cranksided. En den he butted, en his head got stuck. Den Brer Fox, he sa'ntered fort', lookin' des ez innercent ez one er yo' mammy's mockin'-birds.

" 'Howdy, Brer Rabbit,' sez Brer Fox, sezee. 'You look sorter stuck up dis mawnin',' sezee, en den he rolled on de groun', en laughed en laughed twel he couldn't laugh no mo'.

'I speck you'll take dinner wid me dis time, Brer Rabbit. I done laid in some calamus root, en I ain't gwine ter take no skuse,' sez Brer Fox, sezee."

Here Uncle Remus paused, and drew a two-pound yam out of the ashes.

"Did the Fox eat the Rabbit?" asked the little boy to whom the story had been told.

"Dat's all de fur de tale goes," replied the old man. "He mought, en den again he moughtent. Some say Jedge B'ar come long en loosed 'im—some say he didn't. I hear Miss Sally callin'. You better run 'long."

Why Mr. Possum Loves Peace

"One night," said Uncle Remus—taking Miss Sally's little boy on his knee, and stroking the child's hair thoughtfully and caressingly—"one night Brer Possum call by fer Brer Coon, 'cordin' ter 'greement, en atter gobblin' up a dish er fried greens en smokin' a seegyar, dey rambled fort' fer ter see how de balance er de settlement wuz gittin' 'long. Brer Coon, he wuz one er deze yer natchul pacers, en he racked 'long same ez Mars John's bay pony, en Brer Possum he went in a han'-gallup; en dey got over heap er groun', mon. Brer Possum, he got his belly full er 'simmons, en Brer Coon, he scoop up a 'bunnunce er frogs en tadpoles. Dey amble 'long, dey did, des ez sociable ez a basket er kittens, twel bimeby dey hear Mr. Dog talkin' ter hisse'f way off in de woods.

" 'Sposen he runs up on us, Brer Possum, w'at you gwine ter do?' sez Brer Coon, sezee. Brer Possum sorter laugh 'round de cornders un his mouf.

" 'Oh, ef he come, Brer Coon, I'm gwine ter stan' by you,' sez Brer Possum. 'W'at you gwine ter do?' sezee.

" 'Who? me?' sez Brer Coon. 'Ef he run up onter me, I lay I give 'im one twis',' sezee."

"Did the dog come?" asked the little boy.

"Go 'way, honey!" responded the old man, in an impressive tone. "Go way! Mr. Dog, he come en he come a zoonin'. En he ain't wait fer ter say howdy, nudder. He des sail inter de two un um. De ve'y fus pass he make Brer Possum fetch a grin fum year ter year, en keel over like he wuz dead. Den Mr. Dog, he sail inter Brer Coon, en right dar's whar he drap his money purse, kaze Brer Coon wuz cut out fer dat kinder bizness, en he fa'rly wipe up de face er de yeth wid 'im. You better b'lieve dat w'en Mr. Dog got a chance to make hisse'f skace he tuck it, en w'at der wuz lef' un him went skaddlin' thoo de woods like hit wuz shot out'n a muskit. En Brer Coon, he sorter lick his cloze inter shape en rack off, en Brer Possum, he lay dar like he wuz dead, twel bimeby he raise up sorter keerful like, en w'en he fin' de coas' cle'r he scramble up en scamper off like sumpin' was atter 'im."

Here Uncle Remus paused long enough to pick up a live coal of fire in his fingers, transfer it to the palm of his hand, and thence to his clay pipe, which he had been filling—a proceeding that was viewed by the little boy with undisguised admiration. The old man then proceeded:

"Nex' time Brer Possum met Brer Coon, Brer Coon 'fuse ter 'spon' ter his howdy, en dis make Brer Possum feel mighty bad, seein' ez how dey useter make so many, 'scurshuns tergedder.

" 'W'at make you hol' yo head so high, Brer Coon?' sez Brer Possum, sezee.

" 'I ain't runnin' wid cowerds deze days,' sez Brer Coon. 'W'en I wants you I'll sen' fer you,' sezee.

"Den Brer Possum git mighty mad.

" 'Who's enny cowerd?' sezee.

" 'You is,' sez Brer Coon, 'dat's who. I ain't soshatin' wid dem w'at lays down on de groun' en plays dead w'en dar's a free fight gwine on,' sezee.

"Den Brer Possum grin en laugh fit to kill hisse'f.

" 'Lor', Brer Coon, you don't speck I done dat kaze I wuz feard, duz you?' sezee. 'W'y I want no mo' feard dan you is dis minnit. W'at wuz dey fer ter be skeered un?' sezee. 'I know'd you'd git away wid Mr. Dog ef I didn't, en I des lay dar watchin' you shake him, waitin' fer ter put in w'en de time come,' sezee.

"Brer Coon tu'n up his nose.

" 'Dat's a mighty likely tale,' sezee, 'w'en Mr. Dog ain't mo'n tech you 'fo' you keel over, en lay dar stiff,' sezee.

" 'Dat's des w'at I wuz gwine ter tell you 'bout,' sez Brer Possum, sezee. 'I want no mo' skeer'd dan you is right now, en' I wuz fixin' ter give Mr. Dog a sample er my jaw,' sezee, 'but I'm de most ticklish chap w'at you ever laid eyes on, en no sooner did Mr. Dog put his nose down yer 'mong my ribs dan I got ter laughin', en I laughed twel I ain't had no use er my lim's,' sezee, 'en it's a mussy unto Mr. Dog dat I wuz ticklish, kaze a little mo' en I'd e't 'im up,' sezee. 'I don't min' fightin', Brer Coon, no mo' dan you duz,' sezee, 'but I declar' ter gracious ef I kin stan' ticklin'. Git me in a row whar dey ain't no ticklin' 'lowed, en I'm your man,' sezee.

"En down ter dis day"—continued Uncle Remus, watching the smoke from his pipe curl upward over the little boy's head—"down ter dis day, Brer Possum's bound ter s'render w'en you tech him in de short ribs, en he'll laugh ef he knows he's gwine ter be smashed fer it."

How Mr. Rabbit Was Too Sharp For Mr. Fox

"Uncle Remus," said the little boy one evening, when he had found the old man with little or nothing to do, "did the Fox kill and eat the Rabbit when he caught him with the Tar-Baby?"

"Law, honey, ain't I tell you 'bout dat?" replied the old darkey, chuckling slyly. "I 'clar ter gracious I ought er tole you dat, but old man Nod wuz ridin' on my eyeleds twel a leetle mo'n I'd a dis'member'd my own name, en den on to dat here come yo' mammy hollerin' atter you.

"W'at I tell you w'en I fus' begin? I tole you Brer Rabbit wuz a monstus soon creetur; leas'ways dat's w'at I laid out fer ter tell you. Well, den, honey, don't you go en make no udder calkalashuns, kaze in dem days Brer Rabbit en his fambly wuz at de head er de gang w'en enny racket wuz on han', en dar dey stayed. 'Fo' you begins fer ter wipe yo' eyes 'bout Brer Rabbit, you wait en see whar'bouts Brer Rabbit gwine ter fetch up at. But dat's needer yer ner dar.

"W'en Brer Fox fin' Brer Rabbit mixt up wid de Tar-Baby, he feel mighty good, en he roll on de groun' en laugh. Bimeby he up'n say, sezee:

" 'Well, I speck I got you dis time, Brer Rabbit, sezee; 'maybe I ain't, but I speck I is. You bin runnin' roun' here sassin' atter me a mighty long time, but I speck you done come ter de een' er de row. You bin cuttin' up yo' capers en bouncin' 'roun' in dis neighborhood ontwel you come ter b'lieve yo'se'f de boss er de whole gang. En den you er allers somers whar you got no bizness,' sez Brer Fox, sezee. 'Who ax you fer ter come en strike up a 'quaintance wid dish yer Tar-Baby? En who stuck you up dar whar you iz? Nobody in de roun' worl'. You des tuck en jam yo'se'f on dat Tar-Baby widout waitin' fer enny invite,' sez Brer Fox, sezee, 'en dar you is, en dar you'll stay twel I fixes up a bresh-pile and fiers her up, kaze I'm gwine ter bobbycue you dis day, sho,' sez Brer Fox, sezee.

"Den Brer Rabbit talk mighty 'umble.

" 'I don't keer w'at you do wid me, Brer Fox,' sezee, 'so you don't fling me in dat brier-patch. Roas' me, Brer Fox,' sezee, 'but don't fling me in dat brier-patch,' sezee.

" 'Hit's so much trouble fer ter kindle a fier,' sez Brer Fox, sezee, 'dat I speck I'll hatter hang you,' sezee.

" 'Hang me des ez high as you please, Brer Fox,' sez Brer Rabbit, sezee, 'but do fer de Lord's sake don't fling me in dat brier-patch,' sezee.

" 'I ain't got no string,' sez Brer Fox, sezee, 'en now I speck I'll hatter drown you,' sezee.

" 'Drown me des ez deep ez you please, Brer Fox,' sez Brer Rabbit, sezee, 'but don't fling me in dat brier-patch,' sezee.

" 'Dey ain't no water nigh,' sez Brer Fox, sezee, 'en now I speck I'll hatter skin you,' sezee.

" 'Skin me, Brer Fox,' sez Brer Rabbit, sezee, 'snatch out my eye-balls, t'ar out my years by de roots, en cut off my legs,' sezee, 'but do please, Brer Fox, don't fling me in dat brier-patch,' sezee.

"Co'se Brer Fox wanter hurt Brer Rabbit bad ez he kin, so he cotch 'im by de behime legs en slung 'im right in de middle er de brier-patch. Dar wuz a considerabul flutter whar Brer Rabbit struck de bushes, en Brer Fox sorter hang 'roun' fer ter see w'at wuz gwine ter happen. Bimeby he hear somebody call 'im, en way up de hill he see Brer Rabbit settin' cross-legged on a chinkapin log koamin' de pitch out'n his ha'r wid a chip. Den Brer Fox know dat he bin swop off mighty bad. Brer Rabbit wuz bleedzd fer ter fling back some er his sass, en he holler out:

" 'Bred en bawn in a brier-patch, Brer Fox—bred en bawn in a brier-patch!' en wid dat he skip out des ez lively ez a cricket in de embers."

The Story of the Deluge, and How It Came About

"One time," said Uncle Remus—adjusting his spectacles so as to be able to see how to thread a large darning-needle with which he was patching his coat—"one time, way back yander, 'fo you wuz bawn, honey, en 'fo' Mars John er Miss Sally wuz borned—way back yander 'fo' enny un us wuz borned, de animils en de creeturs sorter 'lecshuneer roun' 'mong deyselves, twel at las' dey 'greed fer ter have a 'se-mbly. In dem days," continued the old man, observing a look of incredulity on the little boy's face, "in dem days creeturs had lots mo' sense dan dey got now; let 'lone dat, dey had sense same like folks. Hit was tech en go wid um, too, mon, en w'en dey make up der min's w'at hatter be done, 'twa'n't mo'n menshun'd 'fo' hit wuz done. Well, dey 'lected dat dey hatter hol' er 'sembly fer ter sorter straighten out marters en hear de complaints, en w'en de day come dey wuz on han'. De Lion, he wuz dar, kaze he wuz de king, en he hatter be der. De Rhynossyhoss, he wuz dar, en de Elephant, he wuz dar, en de Cammils, en de Cows, en plum' down ter de Craw-fishes, dey wuz dar. Dey wuz all dar. En w'en de Lion shuck his mane, en tuck his seat in de big cheer, den de sesshun begun fer ter commence."

"What did they do, Uncle Remus?" asked the little boy.

"I can't skacely call to mine 'zackly w'at dey did do, but dey spoke speeches, en hollered, en cusst, en flung der langwidge 'roun' des like w'en yo' daddy wuz gwine ter run fer de legislater en got lef'. Howsomever, dey 'ranged der 'fairs, en splained der bizness. Bimeby, w'ile dey wuz 'sputin' 'longer one er nudder, de Elephant trompled on one er de Crawfishes. Co'se w'en dat creetur put his foot down, w'atsumever's under dar wuz boun' fer ter be squshed, en dey wa'n't nuff er dat Crawfish lef' fer ter tell dat he'd bin dar.

"Dis make de udder Crawfishes mighty mad, en dey sorter swarmed tergedder en draw'd up a kinder peramble wid some wharfo'es in it, en read her out in de 'sembly. But, bless gracious! sech a racket wuz a gwine on dat nobody ain't hear it, ceppin' maybe de Mud Turkle en de Spring Lizzud, en dere enfloons wuz pow'ful lackin'.

"Bimeby, w'iles de Nunicorn wuz 'sputin' wid de Lion, en w'ile de Hyener wuz a laughin' ter hisse'f, de Elephant squshed anudder one er de Crawfishes, en a little mo'n he'd er ruint de Mud Turkle. Den de Crawfishes, w'at dey wuz lef' un um, swarmed tergedder en draw'd up anudder peramble wid sum mo' wharfo'es; but dey mought ez well er sung Ole Dan Tucker ter a harrycane. De udder creeturs wuz too busy wid der fussin' fer ter 'spon' unto de Crawfishes. So dar dey wuz, de Crawfishes, en dey didn't know w'at minnit wuz gwine ter be de nex'; en dey kep' on gittin madder en madder en skeer'der en skeer'der, twel bimeby dey gun de wink ter de Mud Turkle en de Spring Lizzud, en den dey bo'd little holes in de groun' en went down outer sight."

"Who did, Uncle Remus?" asked the little boy.

"De Crawfishes, honey. Dey bo'd inter de groun' en kep' on bo'in' twel dey onloost de fountains er de yeth; en de waters squirt out, en riz higher en higher twel de hills wuz kivvered, en de creeturs wuz all drowned; en all bekaze dey let on 'mong deyselves dat dey wuz bigger dan de Crawfishes."

Then the old man blew the ashes from a smoking yam, and proceeded to remove the peeling.

"Where was the ark, Uncle Remus?" the little boy inquired, presently.

"W'ich ark's dat?" asked the old man, in a tone of well-feigned curiosity.

"Noah's ark," replied the child.

"Don't you pester wid ole man Noah, honey. I boun' he tuck keer er dat ark. Dat's w'at he wuz dar fer, en dat's w'at he done. Leas'ways, dat's w'at dey tells me. But don't you bodder longer dat ark, ceppin' your mammy fetches it up. Dey mought er bin two deloojes, en den agin dey moughtent. Ef dey wuz enny ark in dish yer w'at de Crawfishes brung on, I ain't heern tell un it, en w'en dey ain't no arks 'roun, I ain't got no time fer ter make um en put em in dar. Hit's gittin' yo' bedtime, honey."

THE SAGA OF PECOS BILL

BY EDWARD O'REILLY

PECOS BILL, ALONG WITH PAUL BUNYON, MIKE FINK AND JOHN HENRY ARE TRULY THE BIG MEN OF THE AMERICAN TALL TALE. THEIR "TALLNESS" DOES NOT JUST REFER TO THEIR HEIGHTS, BUT TO THEIR REPUTATIONS AND ACCOMPLISHMENTS AS WELL, AND EVEN THOUGH THEY ARE BIGGER THAN LIFE AND CAPABLE OF MOMENTOUS ACTS, THEIR HUMBLE ORIGINS AND STATIONS IN LIFE FIRMLY PLACE THEM IN THE EVERYMAN CATEGORY.

EVEN MORE THAN HIS TALL TALE CONTEMPORARIES, PECOS BILL IS ALL-AMERICAN, A HERO OF THE WEST AND FANTASTIC ARCHETYPE OF THE WESTERN HERO OF THE NOVELS OF OWEN WISTER, ZANE GREY AND MAX BRAND.

It is highly probable that Paul Bunyan, whose exploits were told in a recent number of *The Century Magazine,* and Pecos Bill, mythical cow-boy hero of the Southwest, were blood brothers. At all events, they can meet on one common ground: they were both fathered by a liar.

Pecos Bill is not a new-comer in the Southwest. His mighty deeds have been sung for generations by the men of the range. In my boyhood days in west Texas I first heard of Bill, and in later years I have often listened to chapters of his history told around the chuck-wagon by gravely mendacious cow-boys.

The stranger in cattle-land usually hears of Bill if he shows an incautious curiosity about the cow business. Some old-timer is sure to remark mournfully:

"Ranchin' ain't what it was in the days Bill staked out New Mexico."

If the visitor walks into the trap and inquires further about Bill, he is sure to receive an assortment of misinformation that every cow-hand delights in unloading on the unwary.

Although Bill has been quoted in a number of Western stories, the real history of his wondrous deeds has never been printed. I have here collected a few of the tales about him which will doubtless be familiar to cow-men, but deserve to be passed on to a larger audience.

Bill invented most of the things connected with the cow business. He was a mighty man of valor, the king killer of the bad men, and it was Bill who taught the broncho how to buck. It is a matter of record that he dug the Rio Grande one dry year when he grew tired of packin' water from the Gulf of Mexico.

According to the most veracious historians, Bill was born about the time Sam Houston discovered Texas. His mother was a sturdy pioneer woman who once killed forty-five Indians with a broom-handle, and weaned him on moonshine liquor when he was three days old. He cut his teeth on a bowie-knife, and his earliest playfellows were the bears and catamounts of east Texas.

When Bill was about a year old, another family moved into the country, and located about fifty miles down the river. His father decided the place was gettin' too crowded, and packed his family in a wagon and headed west.

One day after they crossed the Pecos River, Bill fell out of the wagon. As there were sixteen or seventeen other children in the family, his parents didn't miss him for four or five weeks, and then it was too late to try to find him.

That's how Bill came to grow up with the coyotes along the Pecos. He soon learned the coyote language, and used to hunt with them and sit on the hills and howl at night. Being so young when he got lost, he always thought he was a coyote. That's where he learned to kill deer by runnin' them to death.

One day when he was about ten years old a cow-boy came along just when Bill had matched a fight with two grizzly bears. Bill hugged the bears to death, tore off a hind leg, and was just settin' down to breakfast when this cow-boy loped up and asked him what he meant by runnin' around naked that way among the varmints.

"Why, because I am a varmint," Bill told him. "I'm a coyote."

The cow-boy argued with him that he was a human, but Bill wouldn't believe him.

"Ain't I got fleas?" he insisted. "And don't I howl around all night, like a respectable coyote should do?"

"That don't prove nothin'," the cow-boy answered. "All Texans have fleas, and most of them howl. Did you ever see a coyote that didn't have a tail? Well, you ain't got no tail; so that proves you ain't a varmint."

Bill looked, and, sure enough, he didn't have a tail.

"You sure got me out on a limb," says Bill. "I never noticed that before. It shows what higher education will do for a man. I believe you're right. Lead me to them humans, and I'll throw in with them."

Bill went to town with this cow-hand, and in due time he got to enjoyin' all the pleasant vices of mankind, and decided that he certainly was a human. He got to runnin' with the wild bunch, and sunk lower and lower, until finally he became a cow-boy.

It wasn't long until he was famous as a bad man. He invented the six-shooter and train-robbin' and most of the crimes popular in the old days of the West. He didn't invent cow-stealin'. That was discovered by King David in the Bible, but Bill improved on it.

There is no way of tellin' just how many men Bill did kill. Deep down he had a tender heart, however, and never killed women or children, or tourists out of season. He never scalped his victims; he was too civilized for that. He used to skin them gently and tan their hides.

It wasn't long before Bill had killed all the bad man in west Texas, massacred all the Indians, and eat all the buffalo. So he decided to migrate to a new country where hard men still thrived and a man could pass the time away.

He saddled up his horse and hit for the West. One day he met an old trapper and told him what he was lookin' for.

"I want the hardest cow outfit in the world," he says. "Not one of these ordinary cow-stealin', Mexican-shootin' bunches of amateurs, but a real hard herd of hand-picked hellions that make murder a fine art and take some proper pride in their slaughter."

"Stranger, you're headed in the right direction," answers the trapper. "Keep right on down this draw for a couple of hundred miles, and you'll find that very outfit. They're so hard they can kick fire out of a flint rock with their bare toes."

Bill single-footed down that draw for about a hundred miles that afternoon; then he met with an accident. His horse stubbed his toe on a mountain and broke his leg, leavin' Bill afoot.

He slung his saddle over his shoulder and set off hikin' down that draw, cussin' and a-swearin'. Profanity was a gift with Bill.

All at once a big ten-foot rattlesnake quiled up in his path, set his tail to singin', and allowed he'd like to match a fight. Bill laid down his saddle, and just to be fair about it, he gave the snake the first three bites. Then he waded into that reptile and everlastingly frailed the pizen out of him.

By and by that old rattler yelled for mercy, and admitted that when it came to fightin', Bill started where he let off. So Bill picked up his saddle and started on, carryin' the snake in his hand and spinnin' it in short loops at the Gila monsters.

About fifty miles further on, a big old mountain-lion jumped off a cliff and lit all spraddled out on Bill's neck. This was no ordinary lion. It weighed more than three steers and a yearlin', and was the very same lion the State of Nuevo León was named after down in old Mexico.

Kind of chucklin' to himself, Bill laid down his saddle and his snake and went into action. In a minute the fur was flyin' down the cañon until it darkened the sun. The way Bill knocked the animosity out of that lion was a shame. In about three minutes that lion hollered:

"I'll give up, Bill. Can't you take a joke?"

Bill let him up, and then he cinched the saddle on him and went down that cañon whoopin' and yellin', ridin' that lion a hundred feet at a jump, and quirtin' him down the flank with the rattlesnake.

It wasn't long before he saw a chuck-wagon with a bunch of cow-boys squattin' around it. He rode up to that wagon, splittin' the air with his war-whoops, with that old lion a-screechin', and that snake singin' his rattles.

When he came to the fire he grabbed the old cougar by the ear, jerked him back on his haunches, stepped off him, hung his snake around his neck, and looked the outfit over. Them cow-boys sat there sayin' less than nothin'.

Bill was hungry, and seein' a boilerful of beans cookin' on the fire, he scooped up a few handfuls and swallowed them, washin' them down with a few gallons of boilin' coffee out of the pot. Wipin' his mouth on a handful of prickly-pear cactus, Bill turned to the cow-boys and asked:

"Who the hell is boss around here?"

A big fellow about eight feet tall, with seven pistols and nine bowie-knives in his belt, rose up and, takin' off his hat, said:

"Stranger, I was; but you be."

Bill had many adventures with this outfit. It was about this time he staked out New Mexico, and used Arizona for a calf-pasture. It was here that he found his noted horse Widow-Maker. He raised him from a colt on nitroglycerin and dynamite, and Bill was the only man that could throw a leg over him.

There wasn't anythin' that Bill couldn't ride, although I have heard of one occasion when he was thrown. He made a bet that he could ride an Oklahoma cyclone slick-heeled, without a saddle.

He met the cyclone, the worst that was ever known, up on the Kansas line. Bill eared that tornado down and climbed on its back. That cyclone did some pitchin' that is unbelievable, if it were not vouched for by many reliable witnesses.

Down across Texas it went sunfishin', back-flippin', side-windin', knockin' down mountains, blowin' the holes out of the ground, and tyin' rivers into knots. The Staked Plains used to be heavily timbered until that big wind swiped the trees off and left it a bare prairie.

Bill just sat up there, thumbin' that cyclone in the withers, floppin it across the ears with his hat, and rollin' a cigarette with one hand. He rode it through three States, but over in Arizona it got him.

When it saw it couldn't throw him, it rained out from under him. This is proved by the fact that it washed out the Grand Cañon. Bill came down over in California. The spot where he lit is now known as Death Valley, a hole in the ground more than one hundred feet below sea-level, and the print of his hip-pockets can still be seen in the granite.

I have heard this story disputed in some of its details. Some historians claim that Bill wasn't thrown; that he slid down on a streak of lightnin' without knockin' the ashes off his cigarette. It is also claimed that the Grand Cañon was dug by Bill one week when he went prospectin'; but the best authorities insist on the first version. They argue that that streak of lightnin' story comes from the habit he always had of usin' one to light his cigarette.

Bill was a great roper. In fact, he invented ropin'. Old-timers who admit they knew him say that his rope was as long as the equator, although the more conservative say that it was at least two feet shorter on one end. He used to rope a herd of cattle at one throw.

This skill once saved the life of a friend. The friend had tried to ride Widow-Maker one day, and was thrown so high he came down on top of Pike's Peak. He was in the middle of a bad fix, because he couldn't get down, and seemed doomed to a lingerin' death on high.

Bill came to the rescue, and usin' only a short calf-loop, he roped his friend around the neck and jerked him down to safety in the valley, twenty thousand feet below. This man was always grateful, and became Bill's horse-wrangler at the time he staked out New Mexico.

In his idle moments in New Mexico Bill amused himself puttin' thorns on the trees and horns on the toads. It was on this ranch he dug the Rio Grande and invented the centipede and the tarantula as a joke on his friends.

When the cow business was dull, Pecos Bill occasionally embarked in other ventures; for instance, at one time he took a contract to supply the S. P. Railroad with wood. He hired a few hundred Mexicans to chop and haul the wood to the railroad line. As pay for the job, Bill gave each Mexican one fourth of the wood he hauled.

These Mexicans are funny people. After they received their share of the wood they didn't know what to do with it; so Bill took it off their hands and never charged them a cent.

On another occasion Bill took the job of buildin' the line fence that forms the boundary from El Paso across to the Pacific. He rounded up a herd of prairie-dogs and set them to dig holes, which by nature a prairie-dog likes to do.

Whenever one of them finished a nice hole and settled down to live in it, Bill evicted him and stuck a fence-post in the hole. Everybody admired his foresight except the prairie-dogs, and who cares what a prairie-dog thinks?

Old Bill was always a very truthful man. To prove this, the cow-boys repeat one of his stories, which Bill claimed happened to him. Nobody ever disputed him; that is, no one who is alive now.

He threw in with a bunch of Kiowa Indians one time on a little huntin'-trip. It was about the time the buffalo were getting scarce, and Bill was huntin' with his famous squatter-hound named Norther.

Norther would run down a buffalo and hold him by the ear until Bill came up and skinned him alive. Then he would turn it loose to grow a new hide. The scheme worked all right in the summer, but in the winter most of them caught colds and died.

The stories of Bill's love-affairs are especially numerous. One of them may be told. It is the sad tale of the fate of his bride, a winsome little maiden called Slue-Foot Sue. She was a famous rider herself, and Bill lost his heart when he saw her riding a catfish down the Rio Grande with only a surcingle. You must remember that the catfish in the Rio Grande are bigger than whales and twice as active.

Sue made a sad mistake, however, when she insisted on ridin' Widow-Maker on her weddin'-day. The old horse threw her so high she had to duck her head to let the moon go by. Unfortunately, she was wearin' her weddin'-gown, and in those days the women wore those big steel-spring bustles.

Well, when Sue lit, she naturally bounced, and every time she came down she bounced again. It was an awful sad sight to see Bill implorin' her to quit her bouncin' and not be so nervous; but Sue kept right on, up and down, weepin', and throwin' kisses to her distracted lover, and carryin' on as a bride naturally would do under those circumstances.

She bounced for three days and four nights, and Bill finally had to shoot her to keep her from starvin' to death. It was mighty tragic. Bill never got over it. Of course he married lots of women after that. In fact, it was one of his weaknesses; but none of them filled the place in his heart once held by Slue-Foot Sue, his bouncin' bride.

There is a great difference of opinion as to the manner of Bill's demise. Many claim that it was his drinkin' habits that killed him. You see, Bill got so that liquor didn't have any kick for him, and he fell into the habit of drinkin' strychnine and other forms of wolf pizen.

Even the wolf bait lost its effect, and he got to puttin' fish-hooks and barbed wire in his toddy. It was the barbed wire that finally killed him. It rusted his interior and gave him indigestion. He wasted away to a mere skeleton, weighin' not more than two tons; then up and died, and went to his infernal reward.

Many of the border bards who knew Pecos Bill at his best have a different account of his death.

They say that he met a man from Boston one day, wearing a mail-order cow-boy outfit, and askin' fool questions about the West; and poor old Bill laid down and laughed himself to death.

ROSY'S JOURNEY

BY LOUISA MAY ALCOTT

ALONG WITH FRANK STOCKTON, LOUISA MAY ALCOTT, THE RENOWNED AU-
THOR OF SUCH CLASSIC WORKS OF "GIRL'S FICTION" AS *LITTLE WOMEN* AND
LITTLE MEN, WAS AN ACCOMPLISHED MASTER (MISTRESS) AT ADAPTING THE
CONVENTIONAL EUROPEAN FAIRY TALE TO THE AMERICAN MODE. IN ADDITION
TO ITS THEMES OF RUGGED INDIVIDUALISM AND SELF-RELIANCE, "ROSY'S JOUR-
NEY" ALSO INCLUDES REFERENCES TO SUCH NINETEENTH-CENTURY BITS OF
AMERICANA AS THE LEGENDARY GOLD RUSH.

Rosy was a nice little girl who lived with her mother in a small house in the
woods. They were very poor, for the father had gone away to dig gold, and did
not come back; so they had to work hard to get food to eat and clothes to wear. The
mother spun yarn when she was able, for she was often sick, and Rosy did all she
could to help. She milked the red cow and fed the hens; dug the garden, and went to
town to sell the yarn and the eggs.

She was very good and sweet, and everyone loved her; but the neighbors were all
poor, and could do little to help the child. So, when at last the mother died, the cow
and hens and house had to be sold to pay the doctor and the debts. Then Rosy was
left all alone, with no mother, no home, and no money to buy clothes and dinners
with.

"What will you do?" said the people, who were very sorry for her.

"I will go and find my father," answered Rosy, bravely.

"But he is far away, and you don't know just where he is, up among the mountains.
Stay with us and spin on your little wheel, and we will buy the yarn, and take care
of you, dear little girl," said the kind people.

"No, I must go; for mother told me to, and my father will be glad to have me. I'm
not afraid, for everyone is good to me," said Rosy, gratefully.

Then the people gave her a warm red cloak, and a basket with a little loaf and
bottle of milk in it, and some pennies to buy more to eat when the bread was gone.
They all kissed her, and wished her good luck; and she trotted away through the wood
to find her father.

For some days she got on very well; for the wood-cutters were kind, and let her
sleep in their huts, and gave her things to eat. But by and by she came to lonely
places where there were no houses; and then she was afraid, and used to climb up in
the trees to sleep, and had to eat berries and leaves, like the Children in the Wood.

She made a fire at night, so wild beasts would not come near her; and if she met
other travelers, she was so young and innocent no one had the heart to hurt her. She

was kind to everything she met; so all little creatures were friends to her, as we shall see.

One day, as she was resting by a river, she saw a tiny fish on the bank, nearly dead for want of water.

"Poor thing! Go and be happy again," she said, softly taking him up, and dropping him into the nice cool river.

"Thank you, dear child; I'll not forget, but will help you some day," said the fish, when he had taken a good drink, and felt better.

"Why, how can a tiny fish help such a great girl as I am?" laughed Rosy.

"Wait and see," answered the fish, as he swam away with a flap of his little tail.

Rosy went on her way, and forgot all about it. But she never forgot to be kind; and soon after, as she was looking in the grass for strawberries, she found a field-mouse with a broken leg.

"Help me to my nest, or my babies will starve," cried the poor thing.

"Yes, I will, and bring these berries so that you can keep still till your leg is better, and have something to eat."

Rosy took the mouse carefully in her little hand, and tied up the broken leg with a leaf of spearmint and a blade of grass. Then she carried her to the nest under the roots of an old tree, where four baby mice were squeaking sadly for their mother. She made a bed of thistledown for the sick mouse, and put close within reach all the berries and seeds she could find, and brought an acorn-cup of water from the spring, so they could be comfortable.

"Good little Rosy, I shall pay you for all this kindness some day," said the mouse, when she was done.

"I'm afraid you are not big enough to do much," answered Rosy, as she ran off to go on her journey.

"Wait and see," called the mouse; and all the little ones squeaked as if they said the same.

Some time after, as Rosy lay up in a tree, waiting for the sun to rise, she heard a great buzzing close by, and saw a fly caught in a cobweb that went from one twig to another. The big spider was trying to spin him all up, and the poor fly was struggling to get away before his legs and wings were helpless.

Rosy put up her finger and pulled down the web, and the spider ran away at once to hide under the leaves. But the happy fly sat on Rosy's hand, cleaning his wings, and buzzing so loud for joy that it sounded like a little trumpet.

"You've saved my life, and I'll save yours, if I can," said the fly, twinkling his bright eye at Rosy.

"You silly thing, you can't help me," answered Rosy, climbing down, while the fly buzzed away, saying, like the mouse and the fish, "Wait and see; wait and see."

Rosy trudged on and on, till at last she came to the sea. The mountains were on the other side; but how should she get over the wide water? No ships were there, and she had no money to hire one if there had been any; so she sat on the shore, very tired and sad, and cried a few big tears as salty as the sea.

"Hullo!" called a bubbly sort of voice close by; and the fish popped up his head.

Rosy ran to see what he wanted.

"I've come to help you over the water," said the fish.

"How can you, when I want a ship, and someone to show me the way?" answered Rosy.

"I shall just call my friend the whale, and he will take you over better than a ship, because he won't get wrecked. Don't mind if he spouts and flounces about a good deal, he is only playing; so you needn't be frightened."

Down dived the little fish, and Rosy waited to see what would happen; for she didn't believe such a tiny thing could really bring a whale to help her.

Presently what looked like a small island came floating through the sea; and turning round, so that its tail touched the shore, the whale said, in a roaring voice that made her jump, "Come aboard, little girl, and hold on tight, I'll carry you wherever you like."

It was rather a slippery bridge, and Rosy was rather scared at this big, strange boat; but she got safely over, and held on fast; then, with a roll and a plunge, off went the whale, spouting two fountains, while his tail steered him like the rudder of a ship.

Rosy liked it, and looked down into the deep sea, where all sorts of queer and lovely things were to be seen. Great fishes came and looked at her; dolphins played near to amuse her; the pretty nautilus sailed by in its transparent boat; and porpoises made her laugh with their rough play. Mermaids brought her pearls and red coral to wear, sea-apples to eat, and at night sung her to sleep with their sweet lullabies.

So she had a very pleasant voyage, and ran on shore with many thanks to the good whale, who gave a splendid spout, and swam away.

Then Rosy traveled along till she came to a desert. Hundreds of miles of hot sand, with no trees or brooks or houses.

"I never can go that way," she said; "I should starve, and soon be worn out walking in that hot sand. What *shall* I do?"

"Quee, quee!
Wait and see:
You were good to me;
So here I come,
From my little home,
To help you willingly,"

said a friendly voice; and there was the mouse, looking at her with its bright eyes full of gratitude.

"Why, you dear little thing, I'm very glad to see you; but I'm sure you can't help me across this desert," said Rosy, stroking its soft back.

"That's easy enough," answered the mouse, rubbing its paws briskly. "I'll just call my friend the lion; he lives here, and he'll take you across with pleasure."

"Oh, I'm afraid he'd rather eat me. How dare you call that fierce beast?" cried Rosy, much surprised.

"I gnawed him out of a net once, and he promised to help me. He is a noble animal, and he will keep his word."

Then the mouse sang, in its shrill little voice,

"O lion, grand,
Come over the sand,

And help me now, I pray!
Here's a little lass,
Who wants to pass;
Please carry her on her way."

In a moment a loud roar was heard, and a splendid yellow lion, with fiery eyes and a long mane, came bounding over the sand to meet them.

"What can I do for you, tiny friend?" he said, looking at the mouse, who was not a bit frightened, though Rosy hid behind a rock, expecting every moment to be eaten.

Mousie told him, and the good lion said pleasantly,—"I'll take the child along. Come on, my dear; sit on my back and hold fast to my mane, for I'm a swift horse, and you might fall off."

Then he crouched down like a great cat, and Rosy climbed up, for he was so kind she could not fear him; and away they went, racing over the sand till her hair whistled in the wind. As soon as she got her breath, she thought it great fun to go flying along, while other lions and tigers rolled their fierce eyes at her, but dared not touch her; for this lion was king of all, and she was quite safe. They met a train of camels with loads on their backs; and the people traveling with them wondered what queer thing was riding that fine lion. It looked like a very large monkey in a red cloak, but went so fast they never saw that it was a little girl.

"How glad I am that I was kind to the mouse; for if the good little creature had not helped me, I never could have crossed this desert," said Rosy, as the lion walked awhile to rest himself.

"And if the mouse had not gnawed me out of the net I never should have come at her call. You see, little people can conquer big ones, and make them gentle and friendly by kindness," answered the lion.

Then away they went again, faster than ever, till they came to the green country. Rosy thanked the good beast, and he ran back; for if anyone saw him, they would try to catch him.

"Now I have only to climb up these mountains and find father," thought Rosy, as she saw the great hills before her, with many steep roads winding up to the top; and far, far away rose the smoke from the huts where the men lived and dug for gold. She started off bravely, but took the wrong road, and after climbing a long while found the path ended in rocks over which she could not go. She was very tired and hungry; for her food was gone, and there were no houses in this wild place. Night was coming on, and it was so cold she was afraid she would freeze before morning, but dared not go on lest she should fall down some steep hole and be killed. Much discouraged, she lay down on the moss and cried a little; then she tried to sleep, but something kept buzzing in her ear, and looking carefully she saw a fly prancing about on the moss, as if anxious to make her listen to his song,

"Rosy, my dear,
Don't cry—I'm here
To help you all I can.
I'm only a fly,
But you'll see that I
Will keep my word like a man."

Rosy couldn't help laughing to hear the brisk little fellow talk as if he could do great things; but she was very glad to see him and hear his cheerful song, so she held out her finger, and while he sat there told him all her troubles.

"Bless your heart! my friend the eagle will carry you right up the mountains and leave you at your father's door," cried the fly; and he was off with a flirt of his gauzy wings, for he meant what he said.

Rosy was ready for her new horse, and not at all afraid after the whale and the lion; so when a great eagle swooped down and alighted near her, she just looked at his sharp claws, big eyes, and crooked beak as coolly as if he had been a cock-robin.

He liked her courage, and said kindly in his rough voice, "Hop up, little girl, and sit among my feathers. Hold me fast round the neck, or you may grow dizzy and get a fall."

Rosy nestled down among the thick gray feathers, and put both arms round his neck; and whiz they went, up, up, up, higher and higher, till the trees looked like grass, they were so far below. At first it was very cold, and Rosy cuddled deeper into her feather bed; then, as they came nearer to the sun, it grew warm, and she peeped out to see the huts standing in a green spot on the top of the mountain.

"Here we are. You'll find all the men are down in the mine at this time. They won't come up till morning; so you will have to wait for your father. Goodbye; good luck, my dear." And the eagle soared away, higher still, to his nest among the clouds.

It was night now, but fires were burning in all the houses; so Rosy went from hut to hut trying to find her father's, that she might rest while she waited; at last in one the picture of a pretty little girl hung on the wall, and under it was written, "My Rosy." Then she knew that this was the right place; and she ate some supper, put on more wood, and went to bed, for she wanted to be fresh when her father came in the morning.

While she slept a storm came on—thunder rolled and lightning flashed, the wind blew a gale, and rain poured—but Rosy never waked till dawn, when she heard men shouting outside, "Run, run! The river is rising! We shall all be drowned!"

Rosy ran out to see what was the matter, though the wind nearly blew her away; she found that so much rain had made the river overflow till it began to wash the banks away.

"What shall I do? What shall I do?" cried Rosy, watching the men rush about like ants, getting their bags of gold ready to carry off before the water swept them away, if it became a flood.

As if in answer to her cry, Rosy heard a voice say close by,

"Splash, dash!
Rumble and crash!
Here come the beavers gay;
See what they do,
Rosy, for you
Because you helped *me* one day."

And there in the water was the little fish swimming about, while an army of beavers began to pile up earth and stones in a high bank to keep the river back. How they worked, digging and heaping with teeth and claws, and beating the earth hard with their queer tails like shovels!

Rosy and the men watched them work, glad to be safe, while the storm cleared up; and by the time the dam was made, all danger was over. Rosy looked into the faces of the rough men, hoping her father was there, and was just going to ask about him, when a great shouting rose again, and all began to run to the pit hole, saying, "The sand has fallen in! The poor fellows will be smothered! How can we get them out? how can we get them out?"

Rosy ran too, feeling as if her heart would break; for her father was down in the mine, and would die soon if air did not come to him. The men dug as hard as they could; but it was a long job, and they feared they would not be in time.

Suddenly hundreds of moles came scampering along, and began to burrow down through the earth, making many holes for air to go in; for they know how to build galleries through the ground better than men can. Everyone was so surprised they stopped to look on; for the dirt flew like rain as the busy little fellows scratched and bored as if making an underground railway.

"What does it mean?" said the men. "They work faster than we can, and better; but who sent them? Is this strange little girl a fairy?"

Before Rosy could speak, all heard a shrill, small voice singing,

"They come at my call;
And though they are small,
They'll dig the passage clear;
I never forget;
We'll save them yet,
For love of Rosy dear."

Then all saw a little gray mouse sitting on a stone, waving her tail about, and pointing with her tiny paw to show the moles where to dig.

The men laughed; and Rosy was telling them who she was, when a cry came from the pit, and they saw that the way was clear so they could pull the buried men up. In a minute they got ropes, and soon had ten poor fellows safe on the ground; pale and dirty, but all alive, and all shouting as if they were crazy, "Tom's got it! Tom's got it! Hooray for Tom!"

"What is it?" cried the others; and then they saw Tom come up with the biggest lump of gold ever found in the mountains.

Everyone was glad of Tom's luck; for he was a good man, and had worked a long time, and been sick, and couldn't go back to his wife and child. When he saw Rosy, he dropped the lump, and caught her up, saying, "My little girl! She's better than a million pounds of gold."

Then Rosy was very happy, and went back to the hut, and had a lovely time telling her father all about her troubles and her travels. He cried when he heard that the poor mother was dead before she could have any of the good things the gold would buy them.

"We will go away and be happy together in the pleasantest home I can find, and never part any more, my darling," said the father, kissing Rosy as she sat on his knee with her arms round his neck.

She was just going to say something very sweet to comfort him, when a fly lit on her arm and buzzed very loud,

"Don't drive me away,
But hear what I say:
Bad men want the gold;
They will steal it tonight,
And you must take flight;
So be quiet and busy and bold."

"I was afraid someone would take my lump away. I'll pack up at once, and we will creep off while the men are busy at work; though I'm afraid we can't go fast enough to be safe, if they miss us and come after," said Tom, bundling his gold into a bag and looking very sober; for some of the miners were wild fellows, and might kill him for the sake of that great lump.

But the fly sang again,

"Slip away with me,
And you will see
What a wise little thing am I;
For the road I show
No man can know,
Since it's up in the pathless sky."

Then they followed Buzz to a quiet nook in the wood; and there were the eagle and his mate waiting to fly away with them so fast and so far that no one could follow. Rosy and the bag of gold were put on the mother eagle; Tom sat astride the king bird; and away they flew to a great city, where the little girl and her father lived happily together all their lives.

THE YELLOW SIGN

BY ROBERT W. CHAMBERS

ROBERT W. CHAMBERS IS PRIMARILY KNOWN TODAY FOR HIS COLLECTION OF SHORT STORIES ENTITLED *THE KING IN YELLOW*, WHICH INCLUDED "THE YELLOW SIGN." IN MANY WAYS HE FUNCTIONED AS A PRECURSOR TO THE WEIRD TALES OF OTHER LUMINARIES (SUCH AS LOVECRAFT) IN HIS INVENTED MYTHOS OF UNSPEAKABLE OLD GODS AND DEMON-INSPIRED BOOKS. HE FURTHER ENTRENCHED HIS MYTHOS BY SETTING HIS STORIES IN THE SAME DOWNTOWN NEW YORK AREAS THAT HAD ALREADY BEEN BROUGHT TO PUBLIC PROMINENCE IN HENRY JAMES'S MORE LITERARY NOVELS, LIKE *WASHINGTON SQUARE*.

> *Let the red dawn surmise*
> *What we shall do,*
> *When this blue starlight dies*
> *And all is through.*

I

There are so many things which are impossible to explain! Why should certain chords in music make me think of the brown and golden tints of autumn foliage? Why should the Mass of Sainte Cécile send my thoughts wandering among caverns whose walls blaze with ragged masses of virgin silver? What was it in the roar and turmoil of Broadway at six o'clock that flashed before my eyes the picture of a still Breton forest where sunlight filtered through spring foliage and Sylvia bent, half curiously, half tenderly, over a small green lizard, murmuring: "To think that this also is a little ward of God!"

When I first saw the watchman his back was toward me. I looked at him indifferently until he went into the church. I paid no more attention to him than I had to any other man who lounged through Washington Square that morning, and when I shut my window and turned back into my studio I had forgotten him. Late in the afternoon, the day being warm, I raised the window again and leaned out to get a sniff of air. A man was standing in the courtyard of the church, and I noticed him again with as little interest as I had that morning. I looked across the square to where the fountain was playing and then, with my mind filled with vague impressions of trees, asphalt drives, and the moving groups of nursemaids and holiday-makers, I started to walk back to my easel. As I turned, my listless glance included the man below in the churchyard. His face was toward me now, and with a perfectly involuntary movement

I bent to see it. At the same moment he raised his head and looked at me. Instantly I thought of a coffin-worm. Whatever it was about the man that repelled me I did not know, but the impression of a plump white grave-worm was so intense and nauseating that I must have shown it in my expression, for he turned his puffy face away with a movement which made me think of a disturbed grub in a chestnut.

I went back to my easel and motioned the model to resume her pose. After working awhile I was satisfied that I was spoiling what I had done as rapidly as possible, and I took up a palette knife and scraped the color out again. The flesh tones were sallow and unhealthy, and I did not understand how I could have painted such sickly color into a study which before that had glowed with healthy tones.

I looked at Tessie. She had not changed, and the clear flush of health dyed her neck and cheeks as I frowned.

"Is it something I've done?" she said.

"No—I've made a mess of this arm, and for the life of me I can't see how I came to paint such mud as that into the canvas," I replied.

"Don't I pose well?" she insisted.

"Of course, perfectly."

"Then it's not my fault?"

"No, it's my own."

"I'm very sorry," she said.

I told her she could rest while I applied rag and turpentine to the plague spot on my canvas, and she went off to smoke a cigarette and look over the illustrations in the *Courier Français*.

I did not know whether it was something in the turpentine or a defect in the canvas, but the more I scrubbed the more that gangrene seemed to spread. I worked like a beaver to get it out, and yet the disease appeared to creep from limb to limb of the study before me. Alarmed I strove to arrest it, but now the color on the breast changed and the whole figure seemed to absorb the infection as a sponge soaks up water. Vigorously I plied palette knife, turpentine, and scraper, thinking all the time what a séance I should hold with Duval who had sold me the canvas; but soon I noticed it was not the canvas which was defective, nor yet the colors of Edward. "It must be the turpentine," I thought angrily, "or else my eyes have become so blurred and confused by the afternoon light that I can't see straight." I called Tessie, the model. She came and leaned over my chair blowing rings of smoke into the air.

"What *have* you been doing to it?" she exclaimed.

"Nothing," I growled, "it must be this turpentine!"

"What a horrible color it is now," she continued. "Do you think my flesh resembles green cheese?"

"No, I don't," I said angrily. "Did you ever know me to paint like that before?"

"No, indeed!"

"Well, then!"

"It must be the turpentine, or something," she admitted.

She slipped on a Japanese robe and walked to the window. I scraped and rubbed until I was tired and finally picked up my brushes and hurled them through the canvas with a forcible expression, the tone alone of which reached Tessie's ears.

Nevertheless she promptly began: "That's it! Swear and act silly and ruin your brushes. You've been three weeks on that study, and now look! What's the good of ripping the canvas? What creatures artists are!"

I felt about as much ashamed as I usually did after such an outbreak, and I turned the ruined canvas to the wall. Tessie helped me clean my brushes, and then danced away to dress. From the screen she regaled me with bits of advice concerning whole or partial loss of temper, until, thinking, perhaps, I had been tormented sufficiently, she came out to implore me to button her waist where she could not reach it on the shoulder.

"Everything went wrong from the time you came back from the window and talked about that horrid-looking man you saw in the churchyard," she announced.

"Yes, he probably bewitched the picture," I said yawning. I looked at my watch.

"It's after six, I know," said Tessie, adjusting her hat before the mirror.

"Yes," I replied, "I didn't mean to keep you so long." I leaned out of the window but recoiled with disgust, for the young man with the pasty face stood below in the churchyard. Tessie saw my gesture of disapproval and leaned from the window.

"Is that the man you don't like?" she whispered.

I nodded.

"I can't see his face, but he does look fat and soft. Someway or other," she continued, turning to look at me, "he reminds me of a dream,—an awful dream I once had. Or," she mused, looking down at her shapely shoes, "was it a dream after all?"

"How should I know?" I smiled.

Tessie smiled in reply.

"You were in it," she said, "so perhaps you might know something about it."

"Tessie! Tessie!" I protested, "don't you dare flatter by saying that you dream about me!"

"But I did," she insisted; "shall I tell you about it?"

Tessie leaned back on the open window-sill and began very seriously.

"One night last winter I was lying in bed thinking about nothing at all in particular. I had been posing for you and I was tired out, yet it seemed impossible for me to sleep. I heard the bells in the city ring, ten, eleven, and midnight. I must have fallen asleep about midnight because I don't remember hearing the bells after that. It seemed to me that I had scarcely closed my eyes when I dreamed that something impelled me to go to the window. I rose, and raising the sash leaned out. Twenty-fifth Street was deserted as far as I could see. I began to be afraid; everything outside seemed so— so black and uncomfortable. Then the sound of wheels in the distance came to my ears, and it seemed to me as though that was what I must wait for. Very slowly the wheels approached, and, finally, I could make out a vehicle moving along the street. It came nearer and nearer, and when it passed beneath my window I saw it was a hearse. Then, as I trembled with fear, the driver turned and looked straight at me. When I awoke I was standing by the open window shivering with cold, but the black-plumed hearse and the driver were gone. I dreamed this dream again in March last, and again awoke beside the open window. Last night the dream came again. You remember how it was raining; when I awoke, standing at the open window, my night-dress was soaked."

"But where did I come into the dream?" I asked.

"You—you were in the coffin; but you were not dead."

"In the coffin?"

"Yes."

"How did you know? Could you see me?"

"No; I only knew you were there."

"Had you been eating Welsh rarebits, or lobster salad?" I began laughing, but the girl interrupted me with a frightened cry.

"Hello! What's up?" I said, as she shrank into the embrasure by the window.

"The—the man below in the churchyard;—he drove the hearse."

"Nonsense," I said, but Tessie's eyes were wide with terror. I went to the window and looked out. The man was gone. "Come, Tessie," I urged, "don't be foolish. You have posed too long; you are nervous."

"Do you think I could forget that face?" she murmured. "Three times I saw the hearse pass below my window, and every time the driver turned and looked up at me. Oh, his face was so white and—and soft? It looked dead—it looked as if it had been dead a long time."

I induced the girl to sit down and swallow a glass of Marsala. Then I sat down beside her, and tried to give her some advice.

"Look here, Tessie," I said, "you go to the country for a week or two, and you'll have no more dreams about hearses. You pose all day, and when night comes your nerves are upset. You can't keep this up. Then again, instead of going to bed when your day's work is done, you run off to picnics at Sulzer's Park, or go to the Eldorado or Coney Island, and when you come down here next morning you are fagged out. There was no real hearse. That was a soft-shell crab dream."

She smiled faintly.

"What about the man in the churchyard?"

"Oh, he's only an ordinary unhealthy, everyday creature."

"As true as my name is Tessie Reardon, I swear to you, Mr. Scott, that the face of the man below in the churchyard is the face of the man who drove the hearse!"

"What of it?" I said. "It's an honest trade."

"Then you think I *did* see the hearse?"

"Oh," I said diplomatically, "if you really did, it might not be unlikely that the man below drove it. There is nothing in that."

Tessie rose, unrolled her scented handkerchief and taking a bit of gum from a knot in the hem, placed it in her mouth. Then drawing on her gloves she offered me her hand, with a frank, "Good-night, Mr. Scott," and walked out.

II

The next morning, Thomas, the bellboy, brought me the *Herald* and a bit of news. The church next door had been sold. I thanked Heaven for it, not that it being a Catholic I had any repugnance for the congregation next door, but because my nerves were shattered by a blatant exhorter, whose every word echoed through the aisle of the church as if it had been my own rooms, and who insisted on his r's with a nasal persistence which revolted my every instinct. Then, too, there was a fiend in human shape, an organist, who reeled off some of the grand old hymns with an interpretation of his own, and I longed for the blood of a creature who could play the doxology with an amendment of minor chords which one hears only in a quartet of very young undergraduates. I believe the minister was a good man, but when he bellowed: "And the Lorrrd said unto Moses, the Lorrrd is a man of war; the Lorrrd is his name. My wrath shall wax hot and I will kill you with the sworrrd!" I wondered how many centuries of purgatory it would take to atone for such a sin.

"Who bought the property?" I asked Thomas.

"Nobody that I knows, sir. They do say the gent wot owns this 'ere 'Amilton flats was lookin' at it. 'E might be a bildin' more studios."

I walked to the window. The young man with the unhealthy face stood by the churchyard gate, and at the mere sight of him the same overwhelming repugnance took possesion of me.

"By the way, Thomas," I said, "who is that fellow down there?"

Thomas sniffed. "That there worm, sir? 'E's night-watchman of the church, sir. 'E maikes me tired a-sittin' out all night on them steps and lookin' at you insultin' like. I'd a punched 'is 'ed, sir—beg pardon, sir—"

"Go on, Thomas."

"One night a comin' 'ome with 'Arry, the other English boy, I sees 'im a-sittin' there on them steps. We 'ad Molly and Jen with us, sir, the two girls on the tray service, an' 'e looks so insultin' at us that I up and sez: 'Wat you looking hat, you fat slug?'—beg pardon, sir, but that's 'ow I sez, sir. Then 'e don't say nothin' and I sez: 'Come out and I'll punch that puddin' 'ed.' Then I hopens the gate and goes in, but 'e don't say nothin', only looks insultin' like. Then I 'its 'im one, but ugh! 'is 'ed was that cold and mushy it ud sicken you to touch 'im."

"What did he do then?" I asked, curiously.

"Im? Nawthin'."

"And you, Thomas?"

The young fellow flushed with embarrassment and smiled uneasily.

"Mr. Scott, sir, I ain't no coward an' I can't make it out at all why I run. I was in the 5th Lawncers, sir, bugler at Tel-el-Kebir, an' was shot by the wells."

"You don't mean to say you ran away?"

"Yes, sir; I run."

"Why?"

"That's just what I want to know, sir. I grabbed Molly an' run, an' the rest was as frightened as I."

"But what were they frightened at?"

Thomas refused to answer for a while, but now my curiosity was aroused about the repulsive young man below and I pressed him. Three years' sojourn in America had not only modified Thomas' cockney dialect but had given him the American's fear of ridicule.

"You won't believe me, Mr. Scott, sir?"

"Yes, I will."

"You will lawf at me, sir?"

"Nonsense!"

He hesitated. "Well, sir, it's Gawd's truth that when I 'it 'im 'e grabbed me wrists, sir, and when I twisted 'is soft, mushy fist one of 'is fingers come off in me 'and."

The utter loathing and horror of Thomas' face must have been reflected in my own for he added:

"It's orful, an' now when I see 'im I just go away. 'E maikes me hill."

When Thomas had gone I went to the window. The man stood beside the church-railing with both hands on the gate, but I hastily retreated to my easel again, sickened and horrified, for I saw that the middle finger of his right hand was missing.

At nine o'clock Tessie appeared and vanished behind the screen with a merry "Good morning, Mr. Scott." When she had reappeared and taken her pose upon the model-stand I started a new canvas much to her delight. She remained silent as long as I was on the drawing, but as soon as the scrape of the charcoal ceased and I took up my fixative she began to chatter.

"Oh, I had such a lovely time last night. We went to Tony Pastor's."

"Who are 'we'?" I demanded.

"Oh, Maggie, you know, Mr. Whyte's model, and Pinkie McCormack—we call her Pinkie because she's got that beautiful red hair you artists like so much—and Lizzie Burke."

I sent a shower of spray from the fixative over the canvas, and said: "Well, go on."

"We saw Kelly and Baby Barnes the skirt-dancer and—and all the rest. I made a mash."

"Then you have gone back on me, Tessie?"

She laughed and shook her head.

"He's Lizzie Burke's brother, Ed. He's a perfect gen'l'man."

I felt constrained to give her some parental advice concerning mashing, which she took with a bright smile.

"Oh, I can take care of a strange mash," she said, examining her chewing gum, "but Ed is different. Lizzie is my best friend."

Then she related how Ed had come back from the stocking mill in Lowell, Massachusetts, to find her and Lizzie grown up, and what an accomplished young man he was, and how he thought nothing of squandering half a dollar for ice-cream and oysters to celebrate his entry as a clerk into the woollen department of Macy's. Before she finished I began to paint, and she resumed the pose, smiling and chattering like a sparrow. By noon I had the study fairly well rubbed in and Tessie came to look at it.

"That's better," she said.

I thought so too, and ate my lunch with a satisfied feeling that all was going well. Tessie spread her lunch on a drawing table opposite me and we drank our claret from the same bottle and lighted our cigarettes from the same match. I was very much attached to Tessie. I had watched her shoot up into a slender but exquisitely formed woman from a frail, awkward child. She had posed for me during the last three years, and among all my models she was my favorite. It would have troubled me very much indeed had she become "tough" or "fly," as the phrase goes, but I never noticed any deterioration of her manner, and felt at heart that she was all right. She and I never discussed morals at all, and I had no intention of doing so, partly because I had none myself, and partly because I knew she would do what she liked in spite of me. Still I did hope she would steer clear of complications, because I wished her well, and then also I had a selfish desire to retain the best model I had. I knew that mashing, as she termed it, had no significance with girls like Tessie, and that such things in America did not resemble in the least the same things in Paris. Yet having lived with my eyes open, I also knew that somebody would take Tessie away some day, in one manner or another, and though I professed to myself that marriage was nonsense, I sincerely hoped that, in this case, there would be a priest at the end of the vista. I am a Catholic. When I listen to high mass, when I sign myself, I feel that everything, including myself, is more cheerful, and when I confess, it does me good. A man who lives as much alone as I do, must confess to somebody. Then, again, Sylvia was Catholic, and it was reason enough for me. But I was speaking of Tessie, which is very different. Tessie also was Catholic and much more devout than I, so, taking it all in all, I had little fear for my pretty model until she should fall in love. But *then* I knew that fate alone would decide her future for her, and I prayed inwardly that fate would keep her away from men like me and throw into her path nothing but Ed Burkes and Jimmy McCormacks, bless her sweet face!

Tessie sat blowing rings of smoke up to the ceiling and tinkling the ice in her tumbler.

"Do you know that I also had a dream last night?" I observed.

"Not about that man," she laughed.

"Exactly. A dream similar to yours, only much worse."

It was foolish and thoughtless of me to say this, but you know how little tact the average painter has.

"I must have fallen asleep about 10 o'clock," I continued, "and after awhile I dreamt that I awoke. So plainly did I hear the midnight bells, the wind in the tree branches, and the whistle of steamers from the bay, that even now I can scarcely believe I was not awake. I seemed to be lying in a box which had a glass cover. Dimly I saw the street lamps as I passed, for I must tell you, Tessie, the box in which I reclined appeared to lie in a cushioned wagon which jolted me over a stony pavement. After a while I became impatient and tried to move but the box was too narrow. My hands were crossed on my breast so I could not raise them to help myself. I listened and then tried to call. My voice was gone. I could hear the trample of the horses attached to the wagon and even the breathing of the driver. Then another sound broke upon my ears like the raising of a window sash. I managed to turn my head a little, and found I could look, not only through the glass cover of my box, but also through the glass panes in the side of the covered vehicle. I saw houses, empty and silent, with neither light nor life about any of them excepting one. In that house a window was open on the first floor and a figure all in white stood looking down into the street. It was you."

Tessie had turned her face away from me and leaned on the table with her elbow.

"I could see your face," I resumed, "and it seemed to me to be very sorrowful. Then we passed on and turned into a narrow black lane. Presently the horses stopped. I waited and waited, closing my eyes with fear and impatience, but all was as silent as the grave. After what seemed to me hours, I began to feel uncomfortable. A sense that somebody was close to me made me unclose my eyes. Then I saw the white face of the hearse-driver looking at me through the coffin-lid—"

A sob from Tessie interrupted me. She was trembling like a leaf. I saw I had made an ass of myself and attempted to repair the damage.

"Why, Tess," I said, "I only told you this to show you what influence your story might have on another person's dreams. You don't suppose I really lay in a coffin, do you? What are you trembling for? Don't you see that your dream and my unreasonable dislike for that inoffensive watchman of the church simply set my brain working as soon as I fell asleep?"

She laid her head between her arms and sobbed as if her heart would break. What a precious triple donkey I had made of myself? But I was about to break my record. I went over and put my arm about her.

"Tessie, dear, forgive me," I said; "I had no business to frighten you with such nonsense. You are too sensible a girl, too good a Catholic to believe in dreams."

Her hand tightened on mine and her head fell back upon my shoulder, but she still trembled and I petted and comforted her.

"Come, Tess, open your eyes and smile."

Her eyes opened with a slow languid movement and met mine, but their expression was so queer that I hastened to reassure her again.

"It's all humbug, Tessie, you surely are not afraid that any harm will come to you because of that."

"No," she said, but her scarlet lips quivered.

"Then what's the matter? Are you afraid?"

"Yes. Not for myself."

"For me, then?" I demanded gayly.

"For you," she murmured in a voice almost inaudible, "I—I care for you."

At first I started to laugh, but when I understood her, a shock passed through me and I sat like one turned to stone. This was the crowning bit of idiocy I had committed. During the moment which elapsed between her reply and my answer I thought of a thousand responses to that innocent confession. I could pass it by with a laugh, I could misunderstand her and reassure her as to my health, I could simply point out that it was impossible she could love me. But my reply was quicker than my thoughts, and I might think and think now when it was too late, for I had kissed her on the mouth.

That evening I took my usual walk in Washington Park, pondering over the occurrences of the day. I was thoroughly committed. There was no back out now, and I stared the future straight in the face. I was not good, not even scrupulous, but I had no idea of deceiving either myself or Tessie. The one passion of my life lay buried in the sunlit forests of Brittany. Was it buried there forever? Hope cried "No!" For three years I had been listening to the voice of Hope, and for three years I had waited for a footstep on my threshold. Had Sylvia forgotten? "No!" cried Hope.

I said that I was not good. That is true, but still I was not exactly a comic opera villain. I had led an easy-going reckless life, taking what invited me of pleasure, deploring and sometimes bitterly regretting consequences. In one thing alone, except my painting, was I serious, and that was something which lay hidden if not lost in the Breton forests.

It was too late now for me to regret what had occurred during the day. Whatever it had been, pity, a sudden tenderness for sorrow, or the more brutal instinct of gratified vanity, it was all the same now, and unless I wished to bruise an innocent heart my path lay marked before me. The fire and strength, the depth of passion of a love which I had never even suspected, with all my imagined experience in the world, left me no alternative but to respond or send her away. Whether because I am so cowardly about giving pain to others, or whether it was that I have little of the gloomy Puritan in me, I do not know, but I shrank from disclaiming responsibility for that thoughtless kiss, and in fact had no time to do so before the gates of her heart opened and the flood poured forth. Others who habitually do their duty and find a sullen satisfaction in making themselves and everybody else unhappy, might have withstood it. I did not. I dared not. After the storm had abated I did tell her that she might better have loved Ed Burke and worn a plain gold ring, but she would not hear of it, and I thought perhaps that as long as she had decided to love somebody she could not marry, it had better be me. I, at least, could treat her with an intelligent affection, and whenever she became tired of her infatuation she could go none the worse for it. For I was decided on that point although I knew how hard it would be. I remember the usual termination of Platonic liaisons and thought how disgusted I had been whenever I heard of one. I knew I was undertaking a great deal for unscrupulous a man as I was, and I dreaded the future, but never for one moment did I doubt that she was safe with me. Had it been anybody but Tessie I should not have bothered my head about scruples. For it did not occur to me to sacrifice Tessie as I would have sacrificed a woman of the world. I looked the future squarely in the face and saw the several probable endings to the affair. She would either tire of the whole thing, or become so unhappy that I should have either to marry her or go away. If I married her we would be unhappy. I with a wife unsuited to me, and she with a husband unsuitable for any woman. For my past life could scarcely entitle me to marry. If I went away she might either fall ill, recover, and marry some Eddie Burke, or she might recklessly or deliberately go and do something foolish. On the other hand if she tired of me, then her whole life would be before her with beautiful vistas of Eddie Burkes and marriage rings and twins and Harlem flats and Heaven knows what. As I strolled along through the trees by the Washington Arch, I decided that she should find a substantial friend in me anyway and the future could take care of itself. Then I went into the house and put on my evening dress for the little faintly perfumed note on my dresser said, "Have a cab at the stage door at eleven," and the note was signed "Edith Carmichel, Metropolitan Theater."

I took supper that night, or rather we took supper, Miss Carmichel and I, at Solari's and the dawn was just beginning to gild the cross on the Memorial Church as I entered Washington Square after leaving Edith at the Brunswick. There was not a soul in the park as I passed among the trees and took the walk which leads from the Garibaldi statue to the Hamilton Apartment House, but as I passed the churchyard I saw a figure sitting on the stone steps. In spite of myself a chill crept over me at the sight of the white puffy face, and I hastened to pass. Then he said something which might have been addressed to me or might merely have been a mutter to himself, but a sudden furious anger flamed up within me that such a creature should address me. For an instant I felt like wheeling about and smashing my stick over his head, but I walked on, and entering the Hamilton went to my apartment. For some time I tossed about the bed trying to get the sound of his voice out of my ears, but could not. It filled my head, that muttering sound, like thick oily smoke from a fat-rendering vat or an odor of noisome decay. And as I lay and tossed about, the voice in my ears seemed more distinct, and I began to understand the words he had muttered. They came to me slowly as if I had forgotten them, and at last I could make some sense out of the sounds. It was this:

"Have you found the Yellow Sign?"

"Have you found the Yellow Sign?"

"Have you found the Yellow Sign?"

I was furious. What did he mean by that? Then with a curse upon him and his I rolled over and went to sleep, but when I awoke later I looked pale and haggard, for I had dreamed the dream of the night before and it troubled me more than I cared to think.

I dressed and went down into my studio. Tessie sat by the window, but as I came in she rose and put both arms around my neck for an innocent kiss. She looked so sweet and dainty that I kissed her again and then sat down before the easel.

"Hello! Where's the study I began yesterday?" I asked.

Tessie looked conscious, but did not answer. I began to hunt among the piles of canvases, saying, "Hurry up, Tess, and get ready; we must take advantage of the morning light."

When at last I gave up the search among the other canvases and turned to look around the room for the missing study I noticed Tessie standing by the screen with her clothes still on.

"What's the matter," I asked, "don't you feel well?"

"Yes."

"Then hurry."

"Do you want me to pose as—as I have always posed?"

Then I understood. Here was a new complication. I had lost, of course, the best nude model I had ever seen. I looked at Tessie. Her face was scarlet. Alas! Alas! We had eaten of the tree of knowledge, and Eden and native innocence were dreams of the past—I mean for her.

I suppose she noticed the disappointment on my face, for she said: "I will pose if you wish. The study is behind the screen here where I put it."

"No," I said, "we will begin something new;" and I went into my wardrobe and picked out a Moorish costume which fairly blazed with tinsel. It was a genuine costume, and Tessie retired to the screen with it enchanted. When she came forth again I was astonished. Her long black hair was bound above her forehead with a circlet of turquoises, and the ends curled about her glittering girdle. Her feet were encased in the embroidered pointed slippers and the skirt of her costume, curiously wrought with arabesques in silver, fell to her ankles. The deep metallic blue vest embroidered with silver and the short Mauresque jacket spangled and sewn with turquoises became her wonderfully. She came up to me and held up her face smiling. I slipped my hand into my pocket and drawing out a gold chain with a cross attached, dropped it over her head.

"It's yours, Tessie."

"Mine?" she faltered.

"Yours. Now go and pose." Then with a radiant smile she ran behind the screen and presently reappeared with a little box on which was written my name.

"I had intended to give it to you when I went home to-night," she said, "but I can't wait now."

I opened the box. On the pink cotton inside lay a clasp of black onyx, on which was inlaid a curious symbol or letter in gold. It was neither Arabic nor Chinese, nor as I found afterwards did it belong to any human script.

"It's all I had to give you for a keepsake," she said, timidly.

I was annoyed, but I told her how much I should prize it, and promised to wear it always. She fastened it on my coat beneath the lapel.

"How foolish, Tess, to go and buy me such a beautiful thing as this," I said.

"I did not buy it," she laughed.

Then she told me how she had found it one day while coming from the Aquarium in the Battery, how she had advertised it and watched the papers, but at last gave up all hopes of finding the owner.

"That was last winter," she said, "the very day I had the first horrid dream about the hearse."

I remembered my dream of the previous night but said nothing, and presently my charcoal was flying over a new canvas, and Tessie stood motionless on the model stand.

III

The day following was a disastrous one for me. While moving a framed canvas from one easel to another my foot slipped on the polished floor and I fell heavily on both wrists. There were so badly sprained that it was useless to attempt to hold a brush, and I was obliged to wander about the studio, glaring at unfinished drawings and sketches until despair seized me and I sat down to smoke and twiddle my thumbs with rage. The rain blew against the windows and rattled on the roof of the church, driving me into a nervous fit with its interminable patter. Tessie sat sewing by the window, and every now and then raised her head and looked at me with such innocent compassion that I began to feel ashamed of my irritation and looked about for something to occupy me. I had read all the papers and all the books in the library, but for the sake of something to do I went to the bookcases and shoved them open with my elbow. I knew every volume by its color and examined them all, passing slowly around the library and whistling to keep up my spirits. I was turning to go into the dining-room when my eye fell upon a book bound in serpent skin, standing in a corner of the top shelf of the last bookcase. I did not remember it and from the floor could not decipher the pale lettering on the back, so I went to the smoking-room and called Tessie. She came in from the studio and climbed up to reach the book.

"What is it?" I asked.

" 'The King in Yellow.' "

I was dumfounded. Who had placed it there? How came it in my rooms? I had long ago decided that I should never open that book, and nothing on earth could have persuaded me to to buy it. Fearful lest curiosity might tempt me to open it, I had never even looked at it in book-stores. If I ever had had any curiosity to read it, the awful tragedy of young Castaigne, whom I knew, prevented me from exploring its wicked pages. I had always refused to listen to any description of it, and indeed, nobody ever ventured to discuss the second part aloud, so I had absolutely no knowledge of what those leaves might reveal. I stared at the poisonous mottled binding as I would at a snake.

"Don't touch it, Tessie," I said; "come down."

Of course my admonition was enough to arouse her curiosity, and before I could prevent it she took the book and, laughing, danced off into the studio with it. I called to her but she slipped away with a tormenting smile at my helpless hands, and I followed her with some impatience.

"Tessie!" I cried, entering the library, "listen, I am serious. Put that book away. I do not wish you to open it!" The library was empty. I went into both drawing-rooms, then into the bedrooms, laundry, kitchen, and finally returned to the library and began a systematic search. She had hidden herself so well that it was half an hour later when I discovered her crouching white and silent by the latticed window in the store-room above. At first glance I saw she had been punished for her foolishness. "The King in Yellow" lay at her feet, but the book was open at the second part. I looked at Tessie and saw it was too late. She had opened "The King in Yellow." Then I took her by the hand and led her into the studio. She seemed dazed, and when I told her to lie down on the sofa she obeyed me without a word. After a while she closed her eyes and her breathing became regular and deep, but I could not determine whether or not she slept. For a long while I sat silently beside her, but she neither stirred nor spoke, and at last I rose and entering the unused store-room took the book in my least injured hand. It seemed heavy as lead, but I carried it into the studio again; and sitting down on the rug beside the sofa, opened it and read it through from beginning to end.

When, faint with the excess of my emotions, I dropped the volume and leaned wearily back against the sofa, Tessie opened her eyes and looked at me.

WE HAD BEEN SPEAKING for some time in a dull monotonous strain before I realized that we were discussing "The King in Yellow." Oh the sin of writing such words,— words which are clear as crystal, limpid and musical as bubbling springs, words which sparkle and glow like the poisoned diamonds of the Medicis! Oh the wickedness, the hopeless damnation of a soul who could fascinate and paralyze human creatures with such words,—words understood by the ignorant and wise alike, words which are more precious than jewels, more soothing than music, more awful than death!

We talked on, unmindful of the gathering shadows, and she was begging me to throw away the clasp of black onyx quaintly inlaid with what we now knew to be the Yellow Sign. I never shall know why I refused, though even at this hour, here in my bedroom as I write this confession, I should be glad to know *what* it was that prevented me from tearing the Yellow Sign from my breast and casting it into the fire. I am sure I wished to do so, and yet Tessie pleaded with me in vain. Night fell and the hours dragged on, but still we murmured to each other of the King and the Pallid Mask, and midnight sounded from the misty spires in the fog-wrapped city. We spoke of Hastur and of Cassilda, while outside the fog rolled against the blank window-panes as the cloud waves roll and break on the shores of Hali.

The house was very silent now and not a sound came up from the misty streets. Tessie lay among the cushions, her face a gray blot in the gloom, but her hands were clasped in mine and I knew that she knew and read my thoughts as I read hers, for we had understood the mystery of the Hyades and the Phantom of Truth was laid. Then as we answered each other, swiftly, silently, thought on thought, the shadows stirred in the gloom about us, and far in the distant streets we heard a sound. Nearer and nearer it came, the dull crunching wheels, nearer and yet nearer, and now, outside before the door it ceased, and I dragged myself to the window and saw a black-plumed hearse. The gate below opened and shut, and I crept shaking to my door and bolted it, but I knew no bolts, no locks, could keep that creature out who was coming for the Yellow Sign. And now I heard him moving very softly along the hall. Now he was at the door, and the bolts rotted at his touch. Now he had entered. With eyes starting from my head I peered into the darkness, but when he came into the room I did not see him. It was only when I felt him envelop me in his cold soft grasp that I cried out and struggled with deadly fury, but my hands were useless and he tore the onyx clasp from my coat and struck me full in the face. Then, as I fell, I heard Tessie's soft cry and her spirit fled: and even while falling I longed to follow her, for I knew that the King in Yellow had opened his tattered mantle and there was only God to cry to now.

I would tell more, but I cannot see what help it will be to the world. As for me I am past human help or hope. As I lie here, writing, careless even whether or not I die before I finish, I can see the doctor gathering up his powders and phials with a vague gesture to the good priest beside me, which I understand.

They will be very curious to know the tragedy—they of the outside world who write books and print millions of newspapers, but I shall write no more, and the father confessor will seal my last words with the seal of sanctity when his holy office is done. They of the outside world may send their creatures into wrecked homes and death-smitten firesides, and their newspapers will batten on blood and tears, but with me their spies must halt before the confessional. They know that Tessie is dead and that I am dying. They know how the people in the house, aroused by an infernal scream, rushed into my room and found one living and two dead, but they do not know what I shall tell them now; they do not know that the doctor said as he pointed to a horrible decomposed heap on the floor—the livid corpse of the watchman from the church: "I have no theory, no explanation. That man must have been dead for months!"

I THINK I AM DYING. I wish the priest would—

THE SHADOW OVER INNSMOUTH

BY H. P. LOVECRAFT

PROBABLY NO NAME IS MORE SYNONYMOUS WITH THE WEIRD TALE THAN H. P. LOVECRAFT, WHOSE TALES OF THE CTHULHU MYTHOS AND THE DREADED *NECRONOMICON* CONTINUE TO INSPIRE DEVOTEES TODAY. "THE SHADOW OVER INNSMOUTH" IS LITERALLY SET IN HIS OWN BACKYARD, AN ISOLATED NEW ENGLAND SEACOAST TOWN WITH A HAUNTED PAST AND STRANGE TOWNSFOLK WHO LIKE TO KEEP TO THEMSELVES. I PARTICULARLY LIKE THE SENSE OF DREAD, FEAR AND LOATHING APPARENT IN THE NARRATION AS WELL AS THE PLAUSIBLE EXCUSE, RENDERED BEFORE THE TALE IS EVEN TOLD TO DISCOURAGE NONBELIEVERS FROM TRYING TO DISPROVE WHETHER THE EVENTS REALLY OCCURRED (AT LEAST ACCORDING TO THE TYPICAL LOVECRAFTIAN NARRATOR OF DUBIOUS SANITY AND VERACITY).

I

During the winter of 1927–28 officials of the Federal government made a strange and secret investigation of certain conditions in the ancient Massachusetts seaport of Innsmouth. The public first learned of it in February, when a vast series of raids and arrests occurred, followed by the deliberate burning and dynamiting—under suitable precautions—of an enormous number of crumbling, worm-eaten, and supposedly empty houses along the abandoned waterfront. Uninquiring souls let this occurrence pass as one of the major clashes in a spasmodic war on liquor.

Keener news-followers, however, wondered at the prodigious number of arrests, the abnormally large force of men used in making them, and the secrecy surrounding the disposal of the prisoners. No trials, or even definite charges, were reported; nor were any of the captives seen thereafter in the regular gaols of the nation. There were vague statements about disease and concentration camps, and later about dispersal in various naval and military prisons, but nothing positive ever developed. Innsmouth itself was left almost depopulated, and it is even now only beginning to show signs of a sluggishly revived existence.

Complaints from many liberal organisations were met with long confidential discussions, and representatives were taken on trips to certain camps and prisons. As a result, these societies became surprisingly passive and reticent. Newspaper men were harder to manage, but seemed largely to cooperate with the government in the end. Only one paper—a tabloid always discounted because of its wild policy—mentioned the deep-diving submarine that discharged torpedoes downward in the marine abyss just beyond Devil Reef. That item, gathered by chance in a haunt of sailors, seemed indeed rather far-fetched; since the low, black reef lies a full mile and a half out from Innsmouth Harbour.

People around the country and in the nearby towns muttered a great deal among themselves, but said very little to the outer world. They had talked about dying and half-deserted Innsmouth for nearly a century, and nothing new could be wilder or more hideous than what they had whispered and hinted years before. Many things had taught them secretiveness, and there was no need to exert pressure on them. Besides, they really knew little; for wide salt marshes, desolate and unpeopled, kept neighbours off from Innsmouth on the landward side.

But at last I am going to defy the ban on speech about this thing. Results, I am certain, are so thorough that no public harm save a shock of repulsion could ever accrue from a hinting of what was found by those horrified raiders at Innsmouth. Besides, what was found might possibly have more than one explanation. I do not know just how much of the whole tale has been told even to me, and I have many reasons for not wishing to probe deeper. For my contact with this affair has been closer than that of any other layman, and I have carried away impressions which are yet to drive me to drastic measures.

It was I who fled frantically out of Innsmouth in the early morning hours of July 16, 1927, and whose frightened appeals for government inquiry and action brought on the whole reported episode. I was willing enough to stay mute while the affair was fresh and uncertain; but now that it is an old story, with public interest and curiosity gone, I have an odd craving to whisper about those few frightful hours in that ill-rumoured and evilly-shadowed seaport of death and blasphemous abnormality. The mere telling helps me to restore confidence in my own faculties; to reassure myself that I was not simply the first to succumb to a contagious nightmare halluci-nation. It helps me, too, in making up my mind regarding a certain terrible step which lies ahead of me.

I never heard of Innsmouth till the day before I saw it for the first and—so far—last time. I was celebrating my coming of age by a tour of New England—sightseeing, antiquarian, and genealogical—and had planned to go directly from ancient Newbury-port to Arkham, whence my mother's family was derived. I had no car, but was travelling by train, trolley and motor-coach, always seeking the cheapest possible route. In Newburyport they told me that the steam train was the thing to take to Arkham; and it was only at the station ticket-office, when I demurred at the high fare, that I learned about Innsmouth. The stout, shrewd-faced agent, whose speech shewed him to be no local man, seemed sympathetic toward my efforts at economy, and made a suggestion that none of my other informants had offered.

"You could take that old bus, I suppose," he said with a certain hesitation, "but it ain't thought much of hereabouts. It goes through Innsmouth—you may have heard about that—and so the people don't like it. Run by an Innsmouth fellow—Joe Sargent—but never gets any custom from here, or Arkham either, I guess. Wonder it keeps running at all. I s'pose it's cheap enough, but I never see mor'n two or three people in it—nobody but those Innsmouth folks. Leaves the Square—front of Ham-mond's Drug Store—at 10 a.m. and 7 p.m. unless they've changed lately. Looks like a terrible rattletrap—I've never been on it."

That was the first I ever heard of shadowed Innsmouth. Any reference to a town not shown on common maps or listed in recent guidebooks would have interested me, and the agent's odd manner of allusion roused something like real curiosity. A town able to inspire such dislike in its neighbours, I thought, must be at least rather unusual, and worthy of a tourist's attention. If it came before Arkham I would stop off there—and so I asked the agent to tell me something about it. He was very deliberate, and spoke with an air of feeling slightly superior to what he said.

"Innsmouth? Well, it's a queer kind of a town down at the mouth of the Manuxet. Used to be almost a city—quite a port before the War of 1812—but all gone to pieces in the last hundred years or so. No railroad now—B. and M. never went through, and the branch line from Rowley was given up years ago.

"More empty houses than there are people, I guess, and no business to speak of except fishing and lobstering. Everybody trades mostly either here or in Arkham or Ipswich. Once they had quite a few mills, but nothing's left now except one gold refinery running on the leanest kind of part time.

"That refinery, though, used to be a big thing, and old man Marsh, who owns it, must be richer'n Croesus. Queer old duck, though, and sticks mighty close in his home. He's supposed to have developed some skin disease or deformity late in life that makes him keep out of sight. Grandson of Captain Obed Marsh, who founded the business. His mother seems to've been some kind of foreigner—they say a South Sea islander—so everybody raised Cain when he married an Ipswich girl fifty years ago. They always do that about Innsmouth people, and folks here and hereabouts always try to cover up any Innsmouth blood they have in 'em. But Marsh's children and grandchildren look just like anyone else so far's I can see. I've had 'em pointed out to me here—though, come to think of it, the elder children don't seem to be around lately. Never saw the old man.

"And why is everybody so down on Innsmouth? Well, young fellow, you mustn't take too much stock in what people here say. They're hard to get started, but once they do get started they never let up. They've been telling things about Innsmouth—whispering 'em, mostly—for the last hundred years, I guess, and I gather they're more scared than anything else. Some of the stories would make you laugh—about old Captain Marsh driving bargains with the devil and bringing imps out of hell to live in Innsmouth, or about some kind of devil-worship and awful sacrifices in some place near the wharves that people stumbled on around 1845 or thereabouts—but I come from Panton, Vermont, and that kind of story don't go down with me.

"You ought to hear, though, what some of the old-timers tell about the black reef off the coast—Devil Reef, they call it. It's well above water a good part of the time, and never much below it, but at that you could hardly call it an island. The story is that there's a whole legion of devils seen sometimes on that reef—sprawled about, or darting in and out of some kind of caves near the top. It's a rugged, uneven thing, a good bit over a mile out, and toward the end of shipping days sailors used to make big detours just to avoid it.

"That is, sailors that didn't hail from Innsmouth. One of the things they had against old Captain Marsh was that he was supposed to land on it sometimes at night when the tide was right. Maybe he did, for I dare say the rock formation was interesting, and it's just barely possible he was looking for pirate loot and maybe finding it; but there was talk of his dealing with demons there. Fact is, I guess on the whole it was really the Captain that gave the bad reputation to the reef.

"That was before the big epidemic of 1846, when over half the folks in Innsmouth was carried off. They never did quite figure out what the trouble was, but it was probably some foreign kind of disease brought from China or somewhere by the shipping. It surely was bad enough—there was riots over it, and all sorts of ghastly doings that I don't believe ever got outside of town—and it left the place in awful shape. Never came back—there can't be more'n 300 or 400 people living there now.

"But the real thing behind the way folks feel is simply race prejudice—and I don't say I'm blaming those that hold it. I hate those Innsmouth folks myself, and I wouldn't care to go to their town. I s'pose you know—though I can see you're a Westerner by your talk—what a lot our New England ships used to have to do with queer ports in Africa, Asia, the South Seas, and everywhere else, and what queer kinds of people they sometimes brought back with 'em. You've probably heard about the Salem man that came home with a Chinese wife, and maybe you know there's still a bunch of Fiji Islanders somewhere around Cape Cod.

"Well, there must be something like that back of the Innsmouth people. The place always was badly cut off from the rest of the country by marshes and creeks, and we can't be sure about the ins and outs of the matter; but it's pretty clear that old Captain Marsh must have brought home some odd specimens when he had all three of his ships in commission back in the twenties and thirties. There certainly is a strange kind of streak in the Innsmouth folks today—I don't know how to explain it, but it sort of makes you crawl. You'll notice a little in Sargent if you take his bus. Some of 'em have queer narrow heads with flat noses and bulgy, stary eyes that never seem to shut, and their skin ain't quite right. Rough and scabby, and the sides of the necks are all shrivelled or creased up. Get bald, too, very young. The older fellows look the worst—fact is, I don't believe I've ever seen a very old chap of that kind. Guess they must die of looking in the glass! Animals hate 'em—they used to have lots of horse trouble before autos came in.

"Nobody around here or in Arkham or Ipswich will have anything to do with 'em, and they act kind of offish themselves when they come to town or when anyone tries to fish on their grounds. Queer how fish are always thick off Innsmouth Harbour when there ain't any anywhere else around—but just try to fish there yourself and see how the folks chase you off! Those people used to come here on the railroad—walking and taking the train at Rowley after the branch was dropped—but now they use that bus.

"Yes, there's a hotel in Innsmouth—called the Gilman House—but I don't believe it can amount to much. I wouldn't advise you to try it. Better stay over here and take the ten o'clock bus tomorrow morning; then you can get an evening bus there for Arkham at eight o'clock. There was a factory inspector who stopped at the Gilman a couple of years ago and he had a lot of unpleasant hints about the place. Seems they get a queer crowd there, for this fellow heard voices in other rooms—though most of 'em was empty—that gave him the shivers. It was foreign talk, he thought, but he said the bad thing about it was the kind of voice that sometimes spoke. It sounded so unnatural—sloppinglike, he said—that he didn't dare undress and go to sleep. Just waited up and lit out the first thing in the morning. The talk went on most all night.

"This fellow—Casey, his name was—had a lot to say about how the Innsmouth folks watched him and seemed kind of on guard. He found the Marsh refinery a queer place—it's in an old mill on the lower falls of the Manuxet. What he said tallied up with what I'd heard. Books in bad shape, and no clear account of any kind of dealings.

You know it's always been a kind of mystery where the Marshes get the gold they refine. They've never seemed to do much buying in that line, but years ago they shipped out an enormous lot of ingots.

"Used to be talk of a queer foreign kind of jewellery that the sailors and refinery men sometimes sold on the sly, or that was seen once or twice on some of the Marsh women-folks. People allowed maybe old Captain Obed traded for it in some heathen port, especially since he always ordered stacks of glass beads and trinkets such as seafaring men used to get for native trade. Others thought and still think he'd found an old pirate cache out on Devil Reef. But here's a funny thing. The old Captain's ben dead these sixty years, and there's ain't ben a good-sized ship out of the place since the Civil War; but just the same the Marshes still keep on buying a few of those native trade things—mostly glass and rubber gewgaws, they tell me. Maybe the Innsmouth folks like 'em to look at themselves—Gawd knows they've gotten to be about as bad as South Sea cannibals and Guinea savages.

"That plague of '46 must have taken off the best blood in the place. Anyway, they're a doubtful lot now, and the Marshes and other rich folks are as bad as any. As I told you, there probably ain't more'n 400 people in the whole town in spite of all the streets they say there are. I guess they're what they call 'white trash' down South—lawless and sly, and full of secret things. They get a lot of fish and lobsters and do exporting by truck. Queer how the fish swarm right there and nowhere else.

"Nobody can ever keep track of these people, and state school officials and census men have a devil of a time. You can bet that prying strangers ain't welcome around Innsmouth. I've heard personally of more'n one business or government man that's disappeared there, and there's loose talk of one who went crazy and is out at Danvers now. They must have fixed up some awful scare for that fellow.

"That's why I wouldn't go at night if I was you. I've never ben there and have no wish to go, but I guess a daytime trip couldn't hurt you—even though the people hereabouts will advise you not to make it. If you're just sightseeing, and looking for old-time stuff, Innsmouth ought to be quite a place for you."

And so I spent part of that evening at the Newburyport Public Library looking up data about Innsmouth. When I had tried to question the natives is the shops, the lunchroom, the garages, and the fire station, I had found them even harder to get started than the ticket agent had predicted; and realised that I could not spare the time to overcome their first instinctive reticences. They had a kind of obscure suspiciousness, as if there were something amiss with anyone too much interested in Innsmouth. At the Y.M.C.A., where I was stopping, the clerk merely discouraged my going to such a dismal, decadent place; and the people at the library shewed much the same attitude. Clearly, in the eyes of the educated, Innsmouth was merely an exaggerated case of civic degeneration.

The Essex County histories on the library shelves had very little to say, except that the town was founded in 1643, noted for shipbuilding before the Revolution, a seat of great marine prosperity in the early 19th century, and later a minor factory centre using the Manuxet as power. The epidemic and riots of 1846 were very sparsely treated, as if they formed a discredit to the county.

References to decline were few, though the significance of the later record was unmistakable. After the Civil War all industrial life was confined to the Marsh Refining Company, and the marketing of gold ingots formed the only remaining bit of major commerce aside from the eternal fishing. That fishing paid less and less as the price of the commodity fell and large-scale corporations offered competition, but there was never a dearth of fish around Innsmouth Harbour. Foreigners seldom settled there, and there was some discreetly veiled evidence that a number of Poles and Portuguese who had tried it had been scattered in a peculiarly drastic fashion.

Most interesting of all was a glancing reference to the strange jewellery vaguely associated with Innsmouth. It had evidently impressed the whole countryside more than a little, for mention was made of specimens in the museum of Miskatonic University at Arkham, and in the display room of the Newburyport Historical Society. The fragmentary descriptions of these things were bald and prosaic, but they hinted to me an undercurrent of persistent strangeness. Something about them seemed so odd and provocative that I could not put them out of my mind, and despite the relative lateness of the hour I resolved to see the local sample—said to be a large, queerly-proportioned thing evidently meant for a tiara—if it could possibly be arranged.

The librarian gave me a note of introduction to the curator of the Society, a Miss Anna Tilton, who lived nearby, and after a brief explanation that ancient gentlewoman was kind enough to pilot me into the closed building, since the hour was not outrageously late. The collection was a notable one indeed, but in my present mood I had eyes for nothing but the bizarre object which glistened in a corner cupboard under the electric lights.

It took no excessive sensitiveness to beauty to make me literally gasp at the strange, unearthly splendour of the alien, opulent phantasy that rested there on a purple velvet cushion. Even now I can hardly describe what I saw, though it was clearly enough a sort of tiara, as the description had said. It was tall in front, and with a very large and curiously irregular periphery, as if designed for a head of almost freakishly elliptical outline. The material seemed to be predominantly gold, though a weird lighter lustrousness hinted at some strange alloy with an equally beautiful and scarcely identifiable metal. Its condition was almost perfect, and one could have spent hours in studying the striking and puzzlingly untraditional designs—some simply geometrical, and some plainly marine—chased or moulded in high relief on its surface with a craftsmanship of incredible skill and grace.

The longer I looked, the more the thing fascinated me; and in this fascination there was a curiously disturbing element hardly to be classified or accounted for. At first I decided that it was the queer other-worldly quality of the art which made me uneasy. All other art objects I had ever seen either belonged to some known racial or national stream, or else were consciously modernistic defiances of every recognised stream. This tiara was neither. It clearly belonged to some settled technique of infinite maturity and perfection, yet that technique was utterly remote from any—Eastern or Western, ancient or modern—which I had ever heard of or seen exemplified. It was as if the workmanship were that of another planet.

However, I soon saw that my uneasiness had a second and perhaps equally potent source residing in the pictorial and mathematical suggestion of the strange designs. The patterns all hinted of remote secrets and unimaginable abysses in time and space, and the monotonously aquatic nature of the reliefs became almost sinister. Among these reliefs were fabulous monsters of abhorrent grotesqueness and malignity—half ichthyic and half batrachian in suggestion—which one could not dissociate from a certain haunting and uncomfortable sense of pseudo-memory, as if they called up some image from deep cells and tissues whose retentive functions are wholly primal and awesomely ancestral. At times I fancied that every contour of these blasphemous fish-frogs was overflowing with the ultimate quintessence of unknown and inhuman evil.

In odd contrast to the tiara's aspect was its brief and prosy history as related by Miss Tilton. It had been pawned for a ridiculous sum at a stop in State Street in 1873, by a drunken Innsmouth man shortly afterward killed in a brawl. The Society had acquired it directly from the pawnbroker, at once giving it a display worthy of its quality. It was labelled as of probable East-Indian or Indo-Chinese provenance, though the attribution was frankly tentative.

Miss Tilton, comparing all possible hypotheses regarding its origin and its presence in New England, was inclined to believe that it formed part of some exotic pirate hoard discovered by old Captain Obed Marsh. This view was surely not weakened by the insistent offers of purchase at a high price which the Marshes began to make as soon as they knew of its presence, and which they repeated to this day despite the Society's unvarying determination not to sell.

As the good lady shewed me out of the building she made it clear that the pirate theory of the Marsh fortune was a popular one among the intelligent people of the region. Her own attitude toward shadowed Innsmouth—which she had never seen— was one of disgust at a community slipping far down the cultural scale, and she assured me that the rumours of devil-worship were partly justified by a peculiar secret cult which had gained force there and engulfed all the orthodox churches.

It was called, she said, "The Esoteric Order of Dagon", and was undoubtedly a debased, quasi-pagan thing imported from the East a century before, at a time when the Innsmouth fisheries seemed to be going barren. Its persistence among a simple people was quite natural in view of the sudden and permanent return of abundantly fine fishing, and it soon came to be the greatest influence in the town, replacing Freemasonry altogether and taking up headquarters in the old Masonic Hall on New Church Green.

All this, to the pious Miss Tilton, formed an excellent reason for shunning the ancient town of decay and desolation; but to me it was merely a fresh incentive. To my architectural and historical anticipations was now added an acute anthropological zeal, and I could scarcely sleep in my small room at the "Y" as the night wore away.

II

Shortly before ten the next morning I stood with one small valise in front of Hammond's Drug Store in old Market Square waiting for the Innsmouth bus. As the hour for its arrival drew near I noticed a general drift of the loungers to other places up the street, or to the Ideal Lunch across the square. Evidently the ticket-agent had not exaggerated the dislike which local people bore toward Innsmouth and its denizens. In a few moments a small motor-coach of extreme decrepitude and dirty grey colour rattled down State Street, made a turn, and drew up at the curb beside me. I felt immediately that it was the right one; a guess which the half-legible sign on the windshield—*Arkham-Innsmouth-Newb'port*—soon verified.

There were only three passengers—dark, unkempt men of sullen visage and somewhat youthful cast—and when the vehicle stopped they clumsily shambled out and began walking up State Street in a silent, almost furtive fashion. The driver also alighted, and I watched him as he went into the drug store to make some purchase. This, I reflected, must be the Joe Sargent mentioned by the ticket-agent; and even before I noticed any details there spread over me a wave of spontaneous aversion which could be neither checked nor explained. It suddenly struck me as very natural that the local people should not wish to ride on a bus owned and driven by this man, or to visit any oftener than possible the habitat of such a man and his kinsfolk.

When the driver came out of the store I looked at him more carefully and tried to determine the source of my evil impression. He was a thin, stoop-shouldered man not much under six feet tall, dressed in shabby blue civilian clothes and wearing a frayed golf cap. His age was perhaps thirty-five, but the odd, deep creases in the sides of his neck made him seem older when one did not study his dull, expressionless face. He had a narrow head, bulging, watery-blue eyes that seemed never to wink, a flat nose, a receding forehead and chin, and singularly undeveloped ears. His long thick lip and coarse-pored, greyish cheeks seemed almost beardless except for some sparse yellow hairs that straggled and curled in irregular patches; and in places the surface seemed queerly irregular, as if peeling from some cutaneous disease. His hands were large and heavily veined, and had a very unusual greyish-blue tinge. The fingers were strikingly short in proportion to the rest of the structure, and seemed to have a tendency to curl closely into the huge palm. As he walked toward the bus I observed his peculiarly shambling gait and saw that his feet were inordinately immense. The more I studied them the more I wondered how he could buy any shoes to fit them.

A certain greasiness about the fellow increased my dislike. He was evidently given to working or lounging around the fish docks, and carried with him much of their characteristic smell. Just what foreign blood was in him I could not even guess. His oddities certainly did not look Asiatic, Polynesian, Levantine or negroid, yet I could see why the people found him alien. I myself would have thought of biological degeneration rather than alienage.

I was sorry when I saw there would be no other passengers on the bus. Somehow I did not like the idea of riding alone with this driver. But as leaving time obviously approached I conquered my qualms and followed the man aboard, extending him a dollar bill and murmuring the single word "Innsmouth." He looked curiously at me for a second as he returned forty cents change without speaking. I took a seat far behind him, but on the same side of the bus, since I wished to watch the shore during the journey.

At length the decrepit vehicle started with a jerk, and rattled noisily past the old brick buildings of State Street amidst a cloud of vapour from the exhaust. Glancing at the people on the sidewalks, I thought I detected in them a curious wish to avoid looking at the bus—or at least a wish to avoid seeming to look at it. Then we turned to the left into High Street, where the going was smoother; flying by stately old mansions of the early republic and still older colonial farmhouses, passing the Lower Green and Parker River, and finally emerging into a long, monotonous stretch of open shore country.

The day was warm and sunny, but the landscape of sand, sedge-grass, and stunted shrubbery became more and more desolate as we proceeded. Out the window I could see the blue water and the sandy line of Plum Island, and we presently drew very near the beach as our narrow road veered off from the main highway to Rowley and Ipswich. There were no visible houses, and I could tell by the state of the road that traffic was very light hereabouts. The small, weather-worn telephone poles carried only two wires. Now and then we crossed crude wooden bridges over tidal creeks that wound far inland and promoted the general isolation of the region.

Once in a while I noticed dead stumps and crumbling foundation-walls above the drifting sand, and recalled the old tradition quoted in one of the histories I had read, that this was once a fertile and thickly-settled countryside. The change, it was said, came simultaneously with the Innsmouth epidemic of 1846, and was thought by simple folk to have a dark connexion with hidden forces of evil. Actually, it was caused by the unwise cutting of woodlands near the shore, which robbed the soil of its best protection and opened the way for waves of wind-blown sand.

At last we lost sight of Plum Island and saw the vast expanse of the open Atlantic on our left. Our narrow course began to climb steeply, and I felt a singular sense of disquiet in looking at the lonely crest ahead where the rutted roadway met the sky. It was as if the bus were about to keep on in its ascent, leaving the sane earth altogether and merging with the unknown arcana of upper air and cryptical sky. The smell of the sea took on ominous implications, and the silent driver's bent, rigid back and narrow head became more and more hateful. As I looked at him I saw that the back of his head was almost as hairless as his face, having only a few straggling yellow strands upon a grey scabrous surface.

Then we reached the crest and beheld the outspread valley beyond, where the Manuxet joins the sea just north of the long line of cliffs that culminate in Kingsport Head and veer off toward Cape Ann. On the far misty horizon I could just make out the dizzy profile of the Head, topped by the queer ancient house of which so many legends are told; but for the moment all my attention was captured by the nearer panorama just below me. I had, I realised, come face to face with rumour-shadowed Innsmouth.

It was a town of wide extent and dense construction, yet one with a portentous dearth of visible life. From the tangle of chimney-pots scarcely a wisp of smoke came, and the three tall steeples loomed stark and unpainted against the seaward horizon. One of them was crumbling down at the top, and in that and another there were only black gaping holes where clock-dials should have been. The vast huddle of sagging gambrel roofs and peaked gables conveyed with offensive clearness the idea of wormy decay, and as we approached along the now descending road I could see that many roofs had wholly caved in. There were some large square Georgian houses, too, with hipped roofs, cupolas, and railed "widow's walks." These were mostly well back from the water, and one or two seemed to be in moderately sound condition. Stretching inland from among them I saw the rusted, grass-grown line of the abandoned railway, with leaning telegraph-poles now devoid of wires, and the half-obscured lines of the old carriage roads to Rowley and Ipswich.

The decay was worst close to the waterfront, though in its very midst I could spy the white belfry of a fairly well-preserved brick structure which looked like a small factory. The harbour, long clogged with sand, was enclosed by an ancient stone breakwater; on which I could begin to discern the minute forms of a few seated fishermen, and at whose end were what looked like the foundations of a bygone lighthouse. A sandy tongue had formed inside this barrier, and upon it I saw a few decrepit cabins, moored dories, and scattered lobster-pots. The only deep water seemed to be where the river poured out past the belfried structure and turned southward to join the ocean at the breakwater's end.

Here and there the ruins of wharves jutted out from the shore to end in indeterminate rottenness, those farthest south seeming the most decayed. And far out at sea, despite a high tide, I glimpsed a long, black line scarcely rising above the water yet carrying a suggestion of odd latent malignancy. This, I knew, must be Devil Reef. As I looked, a subtle, curious sense of beckoning seemed superadded to the grim repulsion; and oddly enough, I found this overtone more disturbing than the primary impression.

We met no one on the road, but presently began to pass deserted farms in varying stages of ruin. Then I noticed a few inhabited houses with rags stuffed in the broken windows and shells and dead fish lying about the littered yards. Once or twice I saw listless-looking people working in barren gardens or digging clams on the fishy-smelling beach below, and groups of dirty, simian-visaged children playing around weed-grown doorsteps. Somehow these people seemed more disquieting than the dismal buildings, for almost every one had certain peculiarities of face and motions which I instinctively disliked without being able to define or comprehend them. For a second I thought this typical physique suggested some picture I had seen, perhaps in a book, under circumstances of particular horror or melancholy; but this pseudo-recollection passed very quickly.

As the bus reached a lower level I began to catch the steady note of a waterfall through the unnatural stillness. The leaning, unpainted houses grew thicker, lined both sides of the road, and displayed more urban tendencies than did those we were leaving behind. The panorama ahead had contracted to a street scene, and in spots I could see where a cobblestone pavement and stretches of brick sidewalk had formerly existed. All the houses were apparently deserted, and there were occasional gaps where tumbledown chimneys and cellar walls told of buildings that had collapsed. Pervading everything was the most nauseous fishy odour imaginable.

Soon cross streets and junctions began to appear; those on the left leading to shoreward realms of unpaved squalor and decay, while those on the right shewed vistas of departed grandeur. So far I had seen no people in the town, but there now came signs of a sparse habitation—curtained windows here and there, and an occasional battered motorcar at the curb. Pavement and sidewalks were increasingly well-defined, and though most of the houses were quite old—wood and brick structures of the early 19th century—they were obviously kept fit for habitation. As an amateur antiquarian I almost lost my olfactory disgust and my feeling of menace and repulsion amidst this rich, unaltered survival from the past.

But I was not to reach my destination without one very strong impression of poignantly disagreeably quality. The bus had come to a sort of open concourse or radial point with churches on two sides and the bedraggled remains of a circular green in the centre, and I was looking at a large pillared hall on the right-hand junction ahead. The structure's once white paint was now grey and peeling, and the black and gold sign on the pediment was so faded that I could only with difficulty make out the words "Esoteric Order of Dagon". This, then was the former Masonic Hall now given over to a degraded cult. As I strained to decipher this inscription my notice was distracted by the raucous tones of a cracked bell across the street, and I quickly turned to look out the window on my side of the coach.

The sound came from a squat-towered stone church of manifestly later date than most of the houses, built in a clumsy Gothic fashion and having a disproportionately high basement with shuttered windows. Though the hands of its clock were missing on the side I glimpsed, I knew that those hoarse strokes were tolling the hour of eleven. Then suddenly all thoughts of time were blotted out by an onrushing image of sharp intensity and unaccountable horror which had seized me before I knew what it really was. The door of the church basement was open, revealing a rectangle of blackness inside. And as I looked, a certain object crossed or seemed to cross that dark rectangle; burning into my brain a momentary conception of nightmare which was all the more maddening because analysis could not shew a single nightmarish quality in it.

It was a living object—the first except the driver that I had seen since entering the compact part of the town—and had I been in a steadier mood I would have found nothing whatever of terror in it. Clearly, as I realised a moment later, it was the pastor; clad in some peculiar vestments doubtless introduced since the Order of Dagon had modified the ritual of the local churches. The thing which had probably caught my first subconscious glance and supplied the touch of bizarre horror was the tall tiara he wore; an almost exact duplicate of the one Miss Tilton had shown me the previous evening. This, acting on my imagination, had supplied namelessly sinister qualities to the indeterminate face and robed, shambling form beneath it. There was not, I soon decided, any reason why I should have felt that shuddering touch of evil pseudo-memory. Was it not natural that a local mystery cult should adopt among its regimentals an unique type of head-dress made familiar to the community in some strange way—perhaps as treasure-trove?

A very thin sprinkling of repellent-looking youngish people now became visible on the sidewalks—lone individuals, and silent knots of two or three. The lower floors of the crumbling houses sometimes harboured small shops with dingy signs, and I noticed a parked truck or two as we rattled along. The sound of waterfalls became more and more distinct, and presently I saw a fairly deep river-gorge ahead, spanned by a wide, iron-railed highway bridge beyond which a large square opened out. As we clanked over the bridge I looked out on both sides and observed some factory buildings on the edge of the grassy bluff or part way down. The water far below was very abundant, and I could see two vigorous sets of falls upstream on my right and at least one downstream on my left. From this point the noise was quite deafening. Then we rolled into the large semicircular square across the river and drew up on the right-hand side in front of a tall, cupola-crowned building with remnants of yellow paint and with a half-effaced sign proclaiming it to be the Gilman House.

I was glad to get out of that bus, and at once proceeded to check my valise in the shabby hotel lobby. There was only one person in sight—an elderly man without what I had come to call the "Innsmouth look"—and I decided not to ask him any of the questions which bothered me; remembering that odd things had been noticed in this hotel. Instead, I strolled out on the square, from which the bus had already gone, and studied the scene minutely and appraisingly.

One side of the cobblestoned open space was the straight line of the river; the

other was a semicircle of slant-roofed brick buildings of about the 1800 peri<del></del> which several streets radiated away to the southeast, south, and southwest. were depressingly few and small—all low-powered incandescents—and I was glad that my plans called for departure before dark, even though I knew the moon would be bright. The buildings were all in fair condition, and included perhaps a dozen shops in current operation; of which one was a grocery of the First National chain, others a dismal restaurant, a drug store, and a wholesale fish-dealer's office, and still another, at the eastward extremity of the square near the river an office of the town's only industry—the Marsh Refining Company. There were perhaps ten people visible, and four or five automobiles and motor trucks stood scattered about. I did not need to be told that this was the civic centre of Innsmouth. Eastward I could catch blue glimpses of the harbour, against which rose the decaying remains of three once beautiful Georgian steeples. And toward the shore on the opposite bank of the river I saw the white belfry surmounting what I took to be the Marsh refinery.

For some reason or other I chose to make my first inquiries at the chain grocery, whose personnel was not likely to be native to Innsmouth. I found a solitary boy of about seventeen in charge, and was pleased to note the brightness and affability which promised cheerful information. He seemed exceptionally eager to talk, and I soon gathered that he did not like the place, its fishy smell, or its furtive people. A word with any outsider was a relief to him. He hailed from Arkham, boarded with a family who came from Ipswich, and went back whenever he got a moment off. His family did not like him to work in Innsmouth, but the chain had transferred him there and he did not wish to give up his job.

There was, he said, no public library or chamber of commerce in Innsmouth, but I could probably find my way about. The street I had come down was Federal. West of that were the fine old residence streets—Broad, Washington, Lafayette, and Adams—and east of it were the shoreward slums. It was in these slums—along Main Street—that I would find the old Georgian churches, but they were all along abandoned. It would be well not to make oneself too conspicuous in such neighbourhoods—especially north of the river—since the people were sullen and hostile. Some strangers had even disappeared.

Certain spots were almost forbidden territory, as he had learned at considerable cost. One must not, for example, linger much around the Marsh refinery, or around any of the still used churches, or around the pillared Order of Dagon Hall at New Church Green. Those churches were very odd—all violently disavowed by their respective denominations elsewhere, and apparently using the queerest kind of ceremonials and clerical vestments. Their creeds were heterodox and mysterious, involving hints of certain marvellous transformations leading to bodily immortality—of a sort—on this earth. The youth's own pastor—Dr. Wallace of Asbury M. E. Church in Arkham—had gravely urged him not to join any church in Innsmouth.

As for the Innsmouth people—the youth hardly knew what to make of them. They were as furtive and seldom seen as animals that live in burrows, and one could hardly imagine how they passed the time apart from their desultory fishing. Perhaps—judging from the quantities of bootleg liquor they consumed—they lay for most of the daylight hours in an alcoholic stupor. They seemed sullenly banded together in some sort of fellowship and understanding—despising the world as if they had access to other and preferable spheres of entity. Their appearance—especially those staring, unwinking eyes which one never saw shut—was certainly shocking enough; and their voices were disgusting. It was awful to hear them chanting in their churches at night, and especially during their main festivals or revivals, which fell twice a year on April 30th and October 31st.

They were very fond of the water, and swam a great deal in both river and harbour. Swimming races out to Devil Reef were very common, and everyone in sight seemed well able to share in this arduous sport. When one came to think of it, it was generally only rather young people who were seen about in public, and of these the oldest were apt to be the most tainted-looking. When exceptions did occur, they were mostly persons with no trace of aberrancy, like the old clerk at the hotel. One wondered what became of the bulk of the older folk, and whether the "Innsmouth look" were not a strange and insidious disease-phenomenon which increased its hold as years advanced.

Only a very rare affliction, of course, could bring about such vast and radical anatomical changes in a single individual after maturity—changes involving osseous factors as basic as the shape of the skull—but then, even this aspect was no more baffling and unheard-of than the visible features of the malady as a whole. It would be hard, the youth implied, to form any real conclusions regarding such a matter; since one never came to know the natives personally no matter how long one might live in Innsmouth.

The youth was certain that many specimens even worse than the worst visible ones were kept locked indoors in some places. People sometimes heard the queerest kind of sounds. The tottering waterfront hovels north of the river were reputedly connected by hidden tunnels, being thus a veritable warren of unseen abnormalities. What kind of foreign blood—if any—these beings had, it was impossible to tell. They sometimes kept certain especially repulsive characters out of sight when government agents and others from the outside world came to town.

It would be of no use, my informant said, to ask the natives anything about the place. The only one who would talk was a very aged but normal-looking man who lived at the poorhouse on the north rim of the town and spent his time walking about or lounging around the fire station. This hoary character, Zadok Allen, was 96 years old and somewhat touched in the head, besides being the town drunkard. He was a strange, furtive creature who constantly looked over his shoulder as if afraid of something, and when sober could not be persuaded to talk at all with strangers. He was, however, unable to resist any offer of his favourite poison; and once drunk would furnish the most astonishing fragments of whispered reminiscence.

After all, though, little useful data could be gained from him; since his stories were all insane, incomplete hints of impossible marvels and horrors which could have no source save in his own disordered fancy. Nobody ever believed him, but the natives did not like him to drink and talk with strangers; and it was not always safe to be seen questioning him. It was probably from him that some of the wildest popular whispers and delusions were derived.

Several non-native residents had reported monstrous glimpses from time to time, but between old Zadok's tales and the malformed inhabitants it was no wonder such illusions were current. None of the non-natives ever stayed out late at night, there being a widespread impression that it was not wise to do so. Besides, the streets were loathsomely dark.

As for business—the abundance of fish, was certainly almost uncanny, but the natives were taking less and less advantage of it. Moreover, prices were falling and competition was growing. Of course the town's real business was the refinery, whose commercial office was on the square only a few doors east of where we stood. Old Man Marsh was never seen, but sometimes went to the works in a closed, curtained car.

There were all sorts of rumours about how Marsh had come to look. He had once been a great dandy, and people said he still wore the frock-coated finery of the Edwardian age curiously adapted to certain deformities. His sons had formerly conducted the office in the square, but latterly they had been keeping out of sight a good deal and leaving the brunt of affairs to the younger generation. The sons and their sisters had come to look very queer, especially the elder ones; and it was said that their health was failing.

One of the Marsh daughters was a repellent, reptilian-looking woman who wore an excess of weird jewellery clearly of the same exotic tradition as that to which the strange tiara belonged. My informant had noticed it many times, and had heard it spoken of as coming from some secret hoard, either of pirates or of demons. The clergymen—or priests, or whatever they were called nowadays—also wore this kind of ornament as a head-dress; but one seldom caught glimpses of them. Other specimens the youth had not seen, though many were rumoured to exist around Innsmouth.

The Marshes, together with the other three gently bred families of the town—the Waites, the Gilmans, and the Eliots—were all very retiring. They lived in immense houses along Washington Street, and several were reputed to harbour in concealment certain living kinsfolk whose personal aspect forbade public view, and whose deaths had been reported and recorded.

Warning me that many of the street signs were down, the youth drew for my benefit a rough but ample and painstaking sketch map of the town's salient features. After a moment's study I felt sure that it would be of great help, and pocketed it with profuse thanks. Disliking the dinginess of the single restaurant I had seen, I bought a fair supply of cheese crackers and ginger wafers to serve as a lunch later on. My programme, I decided, would be to thread the principal streets, talk with any non-natives I might encounter, and catch the eight o'clock coach for Arkham. The town, I could see, formed a significant and exaggerated example of communal decay; but being no sociologist I would limit my serious observations to the field of architecture.

Thus I began my systematic though half-bewildered tour of Innsmouth's narrow, shadow-blighted ways. Crossing the bridge and turning toward the roar of the lower falls, I passed close to the Marsh refinery, which seemed to be oddly free from the noise of industry. This building stood on the steep river bluff near a bridge and an open confluence of streets which I took to be the earliest civic centre, displaced after the Revolution by the present Town Square.

Re-crossing the gorge on the Main Street bridge, I struck a region of utter desertion which somehow made me shudder. Collapsing huddles of gambrel roofs formed a jagged and fantastic skyline, above which rose the ghoulish, decapitated steeple of an ancient church. Some houses along Main Street were tenanted, but most were tightly boarded up. Down unpaved side streets I saw the black, gaping windows of deserted hovels, many of which leaned at perilous and incredible angles through the sinking of part of the foundations. Those windows stared so spectrally that it took courage to turn eastward toward the waterfront. Certainly, the terror of a deserted house swells in geometrical rather than arithmetical progression as houses multiply to form a city of stark desolation. The sight of such endless avenues of fishy-eyed vacancy and death, and the thought of such linked infinities of black, brooding compartments given over to cobwebs and memories and the conqueror worm, start up vestigial fears and aversions that not even the stoutest philosophy can disperse.

Fish Street was as deserted as Main, though it differed in having many brick and stone warehouses still in excellent shape. Water Street was almost its duplicate, save that there were great seaward gaps where wharves had been. Not a living thing did I see except for the scattered fishermen on the distant break-water, and not a sound did I hear save the lapping of the harbour tides and the roar of the falls in the Manuxet. The town was getting more and more on my nerves, and I looked behind me furtively as I picked my way back over the tottering Water Street bridge. The Fish Street bridge, according to the sketch, was in ruins.

North of the river there were traces of squalid life—active fish-packing houses in Water Street, smoking chimneys and patched roofs here and there, occasional sounds from indeterminate sources, and infrequent shambling forms in the dismal streets and unpaved lanes—but I seemed to find this even more oppressive than the southerly desertion. For one thing, the people were more hideous and abnormal than those near the centre of the town; so that I was several times evilly reminded of something utterly fantastic which I could not quite place. Undoubtedly the alien strain in the Innsmouth folk was stronger here than farther inland—unless, indeed, the "Innsmouth look" were a disease rather than a blood stain, in which case this district might be held to harbour the more advanced cases.

One detail that annoyed me was the distribution of the few faint sounds I heard. They ought naturally to have come wholly from the visibly inhabited houses, yet in reality were often strongest inside the most rigidly boarded-up facades. There were creakings, scurryings, and hoarse doubtful noises; and I thought uncomfortably about the hidden tunnels suggested by the grocery boy. Suddenly I found myself wondering what the voices of those denizens would be like. I had heard no speech so far in this quarter, and was unaccountably anxious not to do so.

Pausing only long enough to look at two fine but ruinous old churches at Main and Church Streets, I hastened out of that vile waterfront slum. My next logical goal was New Church Green, but somehow or other I could not bear to repass the church in whose basement I had glimpsed the inexplicably frightening form of that strangely diademmed priest or pastor. Besides, the grocery youth had told me that churches, as well as the Order of Dagon Hall, were not advisable neighbourhoods for strangers.

Accordingly I kept north along Main to Martin, then turning inland, crossing Federal Street safely north of the Green, and entering the decayed patrician neighbourhood of northern Broad, Washington, Lafayette, and Adams Streets. Though these stately old avenues were ill-surfaced and unkempt, their elm-shaded dignity had not entirely departed. Mansion after mansion claimed my gaze, most of them decrepit and boarded up amidst neglected grounds, but one or two in each street shewing signs of occupancy. In Washington Street there was a row of four or five in excellent repair and with finely-tended lawns and gardens. The most sumptuous of these—with wide terraced parterres extending back the whole way to Lafayette Street—I took to be the home of Old Man Marsh, the afflicted refinery owner.

In all these streets no living thing was visible, and I wondered at the complete absence of cats and dogs from Innsmouth. Another thing which puzzled and disturbed me, even in some of the best-preserved mansions, was the tightly shuttered condition of many third-storey and attic windows. Furtiveness and secretiveness seemed universal in this hushed city of alienage and death, and I could not escape the sensation of being watched from ambush on every hand by sly, staring eyes that never shut.

I shivered as the cracked stroke of three sounded from a belfry on my left. Too well did I recall the squat church from which those notes came. Following Washington Street toward the river, I now faced a new zone of former industry and commerce; noting the ruins of a factory ahead, and seeing others, with the traces of an old railway station and covered railway bridge beyond, up the gorge on my right.

The uncertain bridge now before me was posted with a warning sign, but I took the risk and crossed again to the south bank where traces of life reappeared. Furtive, shambling creatures stared cryptically in my direction, and more normal faces eyed me coldly and curiously. Innsmouth was rapidly becoming intolerable, and I turned down Paine Street toward the Square in the hope of getting some vehicle to take me to Arkham before the still-distant starting-time of that sinister bus.

It was then that I saw the tumbledown fire station on my left, and noticed the red-faced, bushy-bearded, watery-eyed old man in nondescript rags who sat on a bench in front of it talking with a pair of unkempt but not abnormal-looking firemen. This, of course, must be Zodak Allen, the half-crazed liquorish nonagenarian whose tales of old Innsmouth and its shadow were so hideous and incredible.

III

It must have been some imp of the perverse—or some sardonic pull from dark, hidden sources—which made me change my plans as I did. I had long before resolved to limit my observations to architecture alone, and I was even then hurrying toward the Square in an effort to get quick transportation out of this festering city of death and decay; but the sight of old Zadok Allen set up new currents in my mind and made me slacken my pace uncertainly.

I had been assured that the old man could do nothing but hint at wild, disjointed, and incredible legends, and I had been warned that the natives made it unsafe to be seen talking with him; yet the thought of this aged witness to the town's decay, with memories going back to the early days of ships and factories, was a lure that no amount of reason could make me resist. After all, the strangest and maddest of myths are often merely symbols or allegories based upon truth—and old Zadok must have seen everything which went on around Innsmouth for the last ninety years. Curiosity flared up beyond sense and caution, and in my youthful egotism I fancied I might be able to sift a nucleus of real history from the confused, extravagant outpouring I would probably extract with the aid of raw whiskey.

I knew that I could not accost him then and there, for the firemen would surely notice and object. Instead, I reflected, I would prepare by getting some bootleg liquor at a place where the grocery boy had told me it was plentiful. Then I would loaf near the fire station in apparent casualness, and fall in with old Zadok after he had started on one of his frequent rambles. The youth had said that he was very restless, seldom sitting around the station for more than an hour or two at a time.

A quart bottle of whiskey was easily, though not cheaply, obtained in the rear of a dingy variety-store just off the Square in Eliot Street. The dirty-looking fellow who waited on me had a touch of the staring "Innsmouth look", but was quite civil in his way; being perhaps used to the custom of such convivial strangers—truckmen, gold-buyers, and the like—as were occasionally in town.

Reentering the Square I saw that luck was with me; for—shuffling out of Paine Street around the corner of the Gilman House—I glimpsed nothing less than the tall, lean, tattered form of old Zadok Allen himself. In accordance with my plan, I attracted his attention by brandishing my newly-purchased bottle: and soon realised that he had begun to shuffle wistfully after me as I turned into Waite Street on my way to the most deserted region I could think of.

I was steering my course by the map the grocery boy had prepared, and was aiming for the wholly abandoned stretch of southern waterfront which I had previously visited. The only people in sight there had been the fishermen on the distant breakwater; and by going a few squares south I could get beyond the range of these, finding a pair of seats on some abandoned wharf and being free to question old Zadok unobserved for an indefinite time. Before I reached Main Street I could hear a faint and wheezy "Hey, Mister!" behind me, and I presently allowed the old man to catch up and take copious pulls from the quart bottle.

I began putting out feelers as we walked amidst the ominipresent desolation and crazily tilted ruins, but found that the aged tongue did not loosen as quickly as I had expected. At length I saw a grass-grown opening toward the sea between crumbling brick walls, with the weedy length of an earth-and-masonry wharf projecting beyond. Piles of moss-covered stones near the water promised tolerable seats, and the scene was sheltered from all possible view by a ruined warehouse on the north. Here, I thought, was the ideal place for a long secret colloquy; so I guided my companion down the lane and picked out spots to sit in among the mossy stones. The air of death and desertion was ghoulish, and the smell of fish almost insufferable; but I was resolved to let nothing deter me.

About four hours remained for conversation if I were to catch the eight o'clock coach for Arkham, and I began to dole out more liquor to the ancient tippler; meanwhile eating my own frugal lunch. In my donations I was careful not to overshoot the mark, for I did not wish Zadok's vinous garrulousness to pass into a stupor. After an hour his furtive taciturnity shewed signs of disappearing, but much to my disappointment he still sidetracked my questions about Innsmouth and its shadow-haunted past. He would babble of current topics, revealing a wide acquaintance with newspapers and a great tendency to philosophise in a sententious village fashion.

Toward the end of the second hour I feared my quart of whiskey would not be enough to produce results, and was wondering whether I had better leave old Zadok and go back for more. Just then, however, chance made the opening which my questions had been unable to make; and the wheezing ancient's rambling took a turn that caused me to lean forward and listen alertly. My back was toward the fishy-smelling sea, but he was facing it, and something or other had caused his wandering gaze to light on the low, distant line of Devil Reef, then shewing plainly and almost fascinatingly above the waves. The sight seemed to displease him, for he began a series of weak curses which ended in a confidential whisper and a knowing leer. He bent toward me, took hold of my coat lapel, and hissed out some hints that could not be mistaken.

"Thar's whar it all begun—that cursed place of all wickedness whar the deep water starts. Gate o' hell—sheer drop daown to a bottom no saoundin'-line kin tech. Ol' Cap'n Obed done it—him that faound aout more'n was good fer him in the Saouth Sea islands.

"Everybody was in a bad way them days. Trade fallin' off, mills losin' business—even the new ones—an' the best of our menfolks kilt a-privateerin' in the War of 1812 or lost with the *Elizy* brig an' the *Ranger* scow—both on 'em Gilman venters. Obed Marsh he had three ships afloat—brigantine *Columby*, brig *Hetty*, an' barque *Sumatry Queen*. He was the only one as kep' on with the East-Injy an' Pacific trade, though Esdras Martin's barkentine *Malay Bride* made a venter as late as twenty-eight.

"Never was nobody like Cap'n Obed—old limb o' Satan! Heh, heh! I kin mind him a-tellin' abaout furren parts, an' callin' all the folks stupid fer goin' to Christian meetin' an' bearin' their burdens meek an' lowly. Says they'd orter git better gods like some o' the folks in the Injies—gods as ud bring 'em good fishin' in return for their sacrifices, an' ud reely answer folks's prayers.

"Matt Eliot, his fust mate, talked a lot too, only he was again' folks's doin' any heathen things. Told abaout an island east of Othaheite whar they was a lot o' stone ruins older'n anybody knew anything abaout, kind o' like them on Ponape, in the Carolines, but with carvin's of faces that looked like the big statues on Easter Island. Thar was a little volcanic island near thar, too, whar they was other ruins with diff'rent carvin's—ruins all wore away like they'd ben under the sea onct, an' with picters of awful monsters all over 'em.

"Wal, Sir, Matt he says the natives araound thar had all the fish they cud ketch, an' sported bracelets an' armlets an' head rigs made aout o' a queer kind o' gold an' covered with picters o' monsters jest like the ones carved over the ruins on the little island—sorter fishlike frogs or froglike fishes that was drawed in all kinds o' positions like they was human bein's. Nobody cud get aout o' them whar they got all the stuff, an' all the other natives wondered haow they managed to find fish in plenty even when the very next islands had lean pickin's. Matt he got to wonderin' too an' so did Cap'n Obed. Obed he notices, besides, that lots of the han'some young folks ud drop aout o' sight fer good from year to year, an' that they wan't many old folks araound. Also, he thinks some of the folks looked durned queer even for Kanakys.

"It took Obed to git the truth aout o' them heathen. I dun't know haow he done it, but he begun by tradin' fer the gold-like things they wore. Ast 'em whar they come from, an' ef they cud git more, an' finally wormed the story aout o' the old chief—Walakea, they called him. Nobody but Obed ud ever a believed the old yeller devil, but the Cap'n cud read folks like they was books. Heh, heh! Nobody never believes me naow when I tell 'em, an' I dun't s'pose you will, young feller—though come to look at ye, ye hev kind o' got them sharp-readin' eyes like Obed had."

The old man's whisper grew fainter, and I found myself shuddering at the terrible and sincere portentousness of his intonation, even though I knew his tale could be nothing but drunken phantasy.

"Wal, Sir, Obed he larnt that they's things on this arth as most folks never heerd about—an' wouldn't believe ef they did hear. It seems these Kanakys was sacrificin' heaps o' their young men an' maidens to some kind o' god-things that lived under the sea, an' gittin' all kinds o' favour in return. They met the things on the little islet with the queer ruins, an' it seems them awful picters o' frog-fish monsters was supposed to be picters o' these things. Mebbe they was the kind o' critters as got all the mermaid stories an' sech started. They had all kinds o' cities on the sea-bottom, an' this island was heaved up from thar. Seems they was some of the things alive in the stone buildin's when the island come up sudden to the surface. That's haow the Kanakys got wind they was daown thar. Made sign-talk as soon as they got over bein' skeert, an' pieced up a bargain afore long.

"Them things liked human sacrifices. Had had 'em ages afore, but lost track o' the upper world arter a time. What they done to the victims it ain't fer me to say, an' I guess Obed wa'n't none too sharp about askin'. But it was all right with the heathens, because they'd ben havin' a hard time an' was desp'rate abaout everything. They give a sarten number o' young folks to the sea-things twice every year—May-Eve an' Hallowe'en—reg'lar as cud be. Also give some o' the carved kick-knacks they made. What the things agreed to give in return was plenty o' fish—they druv 'em in from all over the sea—an' a few gold-like things naow an' then.

"Wal, as I says, the natives met the things on the little volcanic islet—goin' thar in canoes with the sacrifices et cet'ry, and bringin' back any of the gold-like jools as was comin' to 'em. At fust the things didn't never go onto the main island, but arter a time they come to want to. Seems they hankered arter mixin' with the folks, an' havin' j'int ceremonies on the big days—May-Eve an' Hallowe'en. Ye see, they was able to live both in an' aout o' water—what they call amphibians, I guess. The Kanakys told 'em as haow folks from the other islands might wanta wipe 'em aout ef they got wind o' their bein' thar, but they says they dun't keer much, because they cud wipe aout the hull brood o' humans ef they was willin' to bother—that is, any as didn't hev sarten signs sech as was used onct by the lost Old Ones, whoever they was. But not wantin' to bother, they'd lay low when anybody visited the island.

"When it come to matin' with them toad-lookin' fishes, the Kanakys kind o' balked, but finally they larnt something as put a new face on the matter. Seems that human folks has got a kind o' relation to sech water-beasts—that everything alive come aout o' the water onct, an' only needs a little change to go back agin. Them things told the Kanakys that ef they mixed bloods there'd be children as ud look human at fust, but later turn more'n more like the things, till finally they'd take to the water an' jine the main lot o' things daown har. An' this is the important part, young feller—them as turned into fish things an' went into the water wouldn't never die. Them, things never died excep' they was kilt violent.

"Wal, Sir, it seems by the time Obed knowed them islanders they was all full o' fish blood from them deep water things. When they got old an' begun to shew it, they was kep' hid until they felt like takin' to the water an' quittin' the place. Some was more teched than others, an' some never did change quite enough to take to the water; but mostly they turned out jest the way them things said. Them as was born more like the things changed arly, but them as was nearly human sometimes stayed on the island till they was past seventy, though they'd usually go daown under for trial trips afore that. Folks as had took to the water gen'rally come back a good deal to visit, so's a man ud often be a'talkin' to his own five-times-great-grandfather who'd left the dry land a couple o' hundred years or so afore.

"Everybody got aout o' the idee o' dyin'—excep' in canoe wars with the other islanders, or as sacrifices to the sea-gods daown below, or from snake-bite or plague or sharp gallopin' ailments or somethin' afore they cud take to the water—but simply looked forrad to a kind o' change that wa'n't a bit horrible arter a while. They thought what they'd got was well wuth all they'd had to give up—an' I guess Obed kind o' come to think the same hisself when he'd chewed over old Walakea's story a bit. Walakea, though, was one of the few as hadn't got none of the fish blood—bein' of a royal line that intermarried with royal lines on other islands.

"Walakea he shewed Obed a lot o' rites an' incantations as had to do with the sea things, an' let him see some o' the folks in the village as had changed a lot from human shape. Somehaow or other, though, he never would let him see one of the reg'lar things from right aout o' the water. In the end he give him a funny kind o' thingumajig made aout o' lead or something, that he said ud bring up the fish things from any place in the water whar they might be a nest o' 'em. The idee was to drop it daown with the right kind o' prayers an' sech. Walakea allaowed as the things was scattered all over the world, so's anybody that looked abaout cud find a nest an' bring 'em up ef they was wanted.

"Matt he didn't like this business at all, an' wanted Obed shud keep away from the island; but the Cap'n was sharp fer gain, an' faound he cud get them gold-like things so cheap it ud pay him to make a specialty of 'em. Things went on that way for years, an' Obed got enough o' that gold-like stuff to make him start the refinery in Waite's old run-daown fullin' mill. He didn't dass sell the pieces like they was, for folks ud be all the time askin' questions. All the same his crews ud get a piece an' dispose of it naow and then, even though they was swore to keep quiet; an' he let his women-folks wear some o' the pieces as was more human-like than most.

"Wall, come abaout 'thutty-eight—when I was seven year' old—Obed he faound the island people all wiped aout between v'yages. Seems the other islanders had got wind o' what was goin' on, and had took matters into their own hands. S'pose they must a had, after all, them old magic signs as the sea things says was the only things they was afeard of. No tellin' what any o' them Kanakys will chance to git a holt of when the sea-bottom throws up some island with ruins older'n the deluge. Pious cusses, these was—they didn't leave nothin' standin' on either the main island or the little volcanic islet excep' what parts of the ruins was too big to knock daown. In some places they was little stones strewed abaout—like charms—with somethin' on 'em like what ye call a swastika naowadays. Prob'ly them was the Old Ones' signs. Folks all wiped aout, no trace o' no gold-like things, an' none o' the nearby Kanakys ud breathe a word abaout the matter. Wouldn't even admit they'd ever ben any people on that island.

"That naturally hit Obed pretty hard, seein' as his normal trade was doin' very poor. It hit the whole of Innsmouth, too, because in seafarin' days what profited the master of a ship gen'lly profited the master of a ship gen'lly profited the crew pro- portionate. Most of the folks araound the taown took the hard times kind o' sheeplike an' resigned, but they was in bad shape because the fishin' was peterin' aout an' the mills wan't doin' none too well.

"Then's the time Obed he begun a-cursin' at the folks fer bein' dull sheep an' prayin' to a Christian heaven as didn't help 'em none. He told 'em he'd knowed o' folks as prayed to gods that give somethin' ye reely need, an' says ef a good bunch o' men ud stand by him, he cud mebbe get a holt o' sarten paowers as ud bring plenty o' fish an' quite a bit o' gold. O' course them as sarved on the *Sumatry Queen*, an' seed the island knowed what he meant, an' wa'n't none too anxious to get clost to sea-things like they'd heerd tell on, but them as didn't know what 'twas all abaout got kind o' swayed by what Obed had to say, and begun to ast him what he cud do to set 'em on the way to the faith as ud bring 'em results."

Here the old man faltered, mumbled, and lapsed into a moody and apprehensive silence; glancing nervously over his shoulder and then turning back to stare fascinatedly at the distant black reef. When I spoke to him he did not answer, so I knew I would have to let him finish the bottle. The insane yarn I was hearing interested me profoundly, for I fancied there was contained within it a sort of crude allegory based upon the strangeness of Innsmouth and elaborated by an imagination at once creative and full of scraps of exotic legend. Not for a moment did I believe that the tale had any really substantial foundation; but none the less the account held a hint of genuine terror if only because it brought in references to strange jewels clearly akin to the malign tiara I had seen at Newburyport. Perhaps the ornaments had, after all, come from some strange island; and possibly the wild stories were lies of the bygone Obed himself rather than of this antique toper.

I handed Zadok the bottle, and he drained it to the last drop. It was curious how he could stand so much whiskey, for not even a trace of thickness had come into his high, wheezy voice. He licked the nose of the bottle and slipped it into his pocket, then beginning to nod and whisper softly to himself. I bent close to catch any articulate words he might utter, and thought I saw a sardonic smile behind the stained bushy whiskers. Yes—he was really forming words, and I could grasp a fair proportion of them.

"Poor Matt—Matt he allus was agin it—tried to line up the folks on his side, an' had long talks with the preachers—no use—they run the Congregational parson aout o' taown, an' the Methodist feller quit—never did see Resolved Babcock, the Baptist parson, agin—Wrath o' Jehovy—I was a mightly little critter, but I heerd what I heerd an' seen what I seen—Dagon an' Ashtoreth—Belial an' Beelzebub—Golden Caff an' the idols o' Canaan an' the Philistines—Babylonish abominations—*Mene, mene, tekel, upharsin*—."

He stopped again, and from the look in his watery blue eyes I feared he was close to a stupor after all. But when I gently shook his shoulder he turned on me with astonishing alertness and snapped out some more obscure phrases.

"Dun't believe me, hey? Heh, heh, heh—-then jest tell me, young feller, why Cap'n Obed an' twenty odd other folks used to row aout to Devil Reef in the dead o' night an' chant things so laoud ye cud hear 'em all over taown when the wind was right? Tell me that, hey? An' tell me why Obed was allus droppin' heavy things daown into the deep water t'other side o' the reef whar the bottom shoots daown like a cliff lower'n ye kin saound? Tell me what he done with that funny-shaped lead thingamajig as Walakea give him? Hey, boy? An' what did they all haowl on May-Eve, an' agin the next Hallowe'en? An' why'd the new church parsons—fellers as used to be sailors—wear them queer robes an' cover theirselves with them gold-like things Obed brung? Hey?"

The watery blue eyes were almost savage and maniacal now, and the dirty white beard bristled electrically. Old Zadok probably saw me shrink back, for he began to cackle evilly.

"Heh, heh, heh, heh! Beginnin' to see hey? Mebbe ye'd like to a ben me in them days, when I seed things at night aout to sea from the cupalo top o' my haouse. Oh,

I kin tell ye' little pitchers hev big ears, an' I wa'n't missin' nothin' o' what was gossiped abaout Cap'n Obed an' the folks aout to the reef! Heh, heh, heh! Haow abaout the night I took my pa's ship's glass up to the cupalo an' seed the reef a-bristlin' thick with shapes that dove off quick soon's the moon riz? Obed an' the folks was in a dory, but them shapes dove off the far side into the deep water an' never come up . . . Haow'd ye like to be a little shaver alone up in a cupola a-watchin' *shapes as wa'n't human shapes? . . . Hey? . . . Heh, heh, heh. . . .*"

The old man was getting hysterical, and I began to shiver with a nameless alarm. He laid a gnarled claw on my shoulder, and it seemed to me that its shaking was not altogether that of mirth.

"S'pose one night ye seed somethin' heavy heaved offen Obed's dory beyond the reef, and then learned nex' day a young feller was missin' from home. Hey! Did anybody ever see hide or hair o' Hiram Gilman agin. Did they? An' Nick Pierce, an' Luelly Waite, an' Andoniram Saouthwick, an' Henry Garrison. Hey? Heh, heh, heh, heh . . . Shapes talkin' sign language with their hands . . . them as had reel hands. . . .

"Wal, Sir, that was the time Obed begun to git on his feet agin. Folks see his three darters a-wearin' gold-like things as nobody'd never see on 'em afore, an' smoke started comin' aout o' the refin'ry chimbly. Other folks was prosp'rin', too—fish begun to swarm into the harbour fit to kill, an' heaven knows what sized cargoes we begun to ship aout to Newb'ryport, Arkham, an' Boston. 'Twas then Obed got the ol' branch railrud put through. Some Kingsport fishermen heerd abaout the ketch an' come up in sloops, but they was all lost. Nobody never see 'em agin. An' jest then our folks organised the Esoteric Order o' Dagon, an' bought Masonic Hall offen Calvary Commandery for it . . . heh, heh, heh! Matt Eliot was a Mason an' agin the sellin', but he dropped aout o' sight jest then.

"Remember, I ain't sayin' Obed was set on hevin' things jest like they was on that Kanaky isle. I dun't think he aimed at fust to do no mixin', nor raise no younguns to take to the water an' turn into fishes with eternal life. He wanted them gold things, an' wan willin' to pay heavy, an' I guess the others was satisfied fer a while. . . .

"Come in 'forty-six the taown done some lookin' an' thinkin' fer itself. Too many folks missin'—too much wild preachin' at meetin' of a Sunday—too much talk abaout that reef. I guess I done a bit by tellin' Selectman Mowry what I see from the cupalo. They was a party one night as follered Obed's craowd aout to the reef, an' I heerd shots betwixt the dories. Nex' day Obed and thutty-two others was in gaol, with everybody a-wonderin' jest what was afoot and jest what charge agin 'em cud be got to holt. God, ef anybody'd look'd ahead . . . a couple o' weeks later, when nothin' had ben throwed into the sea fer thet long . . .

Zadok was shewing signs of fright and exhaustion, and I let him keep silence for a while, though glancing apprehensively at my watch. The tide had turned and was coming in now, and the sound of the waves seemed to arouse him. I was glad of that tide, for at high water the fishy smell might not be so bad. Again I strained to catch his whispers.

"That awful night . . . I seed 'em. I was up in the cupalo . . . hordes of 'em . . . swarms of 'em . . . all over the reef an' swimmin' up the harbour into the Manuxet . . . God, what happened in the streets of Innsmouth that night . . . they rattled our door, but pa wouldn't open . . . then he clumb aout the kitchen winder with his musket to find Selecman Mowry an' see what he cud; do . . . Maounds o' the dead an' the dyin' . . . shots and screams . . . shaoutin' in Ol' Squar an' Taown Squar an' New Church Green—gaol throwed open . . . —proclamation . . . treason . . . called it the plague when folks come in an' faound haff our people missin' . . . nobody left but them as ud jine in with Obed an' them things or else keep quiet . . . never heerd o' my pa no more . . ."

The old man was panting, and perspiring profusely. His grip on my shoulder tightened.

"Everything cleaned up in the mornin'—but they was *traces* . . . Obed he kinder takes charge an' says things is goin' to be changed . . . *others'll* worship with us at meetin'-time, an' sarten haouses hez got to entertain *guests* . . . they wanted to mix like they done with the Kanakys, an' he fer one didn't feel baound to stop 'em. Far gone, was Obed . . . jest like a crazy man on the subjeck. He says they brung us fish an' treasure, an' shud hev what they hankered after . . .

"Nothin' was to be diff'runt on the aoutside, only we was to keep shy o' strangers ef we knowed what was good fer us. We all hed to take the Oath o' Dagon, an' later on they was secon' an' third Oaths that some on us took. Them as ud help special, ud git special rewards—gold an' sech—No use balkin', fer they was millions of 'em daown thar. They'd ruther not start risin' an' wipin' aout human-kind, but ef they was gave away an' forced to, they cud do a lot toward jest that. We didn't hev them old charms to cut 'em off like folks in the Saouth Sea did, an' them Kanakys wudn't never give away their secrets.

"Yield up enough sacrifices an' savage knick-knacks an' harbourage in the taown when they wanted it, an' they'd let well enough alone. Wudn't bother no strangers as might bear tales aoutside—that is, withaout they got pryin'. All in the band of the faithful—Order o' Dagon—an' the children shud never die, but go back to the Mother Hydra an' Father Dagon what we all come from onct . . . *Iä! Iä! Cthulhu fhtagn! Ph'nglui mglw'nafh Cthulhu R'lyeh wgah-nagl fhtaga—*"

Old Zadok was fast lapsing into stark raving, and I held my breath. Poor old soul—to what pitiful depths of hallucination had his liquor, plus his hatred of the decay, alienage, and disease around him, brought that fertile, imaginative brain! He began to moan now, and tears were coursing down his channelled cheeks into the depths of his beard.

"God, what I seen senct I was fifteen year' old—*Mene, mene, tekel, upharsin!*—the folks as was missin', and them as kilt theirselves—them as told things in Arkham or Ipswich or sech places was all called crazy, like you're callin' me right naow—but God, what I seen—They'd a kilt me long ago fer what I know, only I'd took the fust an' secon' Oaths o' Dagon offen Obed, so was pertected unlessen a jury of 'em proved I told things knowin' an' delib'rit . . . but I wudn't take the third Oath—I'd a died ruther'n take that—

"It got wuss araound Civil War time, *when children born senct 'forty-six begun to grow up*—some of 'em, that is. I was afeared—never did no pryin' arter that awful night, an' never see one o'—*them*—clost to in all my life. That is, never no full-blooded one. I went to the war, an' ef I'd a had any guts or sense I'd a never come back, but settled away from here. But folks wrote me things wa'n't so bad. That, I s'pose, was because gov'munt draft men was in taown arter 'sixty-three. Arter the war it was jest as bad agin. People begun to fall off—mills an' shops shet daown—shippin' stopped an' the harbour choked up—railrud give up—but *they* . . . they never stopped swimmin' in an' aout o' the river from that cursed reef o' Satan—an' more an' more attic winders got a-boarded up, an' more an' more noises was heerd in haouses as wa'n't s'posed to hev nobody in 'em . . .

"Folks aoutside hev their stories abaout us—s'pose you've heerd a plenty on 'em, seein' what questions ye ast—stories abaout things they've seed naow an' then, an' abaout that queer joolry as still comes in from somewhars an' ain't quite all melted up—but nothin' never gits def'nite. Nobody'll believe nothin'. They call them gold-like things pirate loot, an' allaow the Innsmouth folks hez furren blood or is distempered or somethin'. Besides, them that lives here shoo off as many strangers as they kin, an' encourage the rest not to git very cur'ous, specially raound night time. Beasts balk at the critters—bosses wuss'n mules—but when they got autos that was all right.

"In forty-six Cap'n Obed took a second wife *that nobody in the taown never see*— some says he didn't want to, but was made to by them as he'd called in—had three children by her—two as disappeared young, but one gal as looked like anybody else an' was eddicated in Europe. Obed finally got her married off by a trick to an Arkham feller as didn't suspect nothin'. But nobody aoutside'll hev nothin' to do with Innsmouth folks naow. Barnabas Marsh that runs the refin'ry naow is Obed's grandson by his fust wife—son of Onesiphorus, his eldest son, *but his mother was another o' them as wa'n't never seed aoutdoors.*

"Right naow Barnabas is abaout changed. Can't shet his eyes no more, an' is all aout o' shape. They say he still wears clothes, but he'll take to the water soon. Mebbe he's tried it already—they do sometimes go daown fer, little spells afore they go daown for good. Ain't ben seed abaout in public fer night on ten year'. Dun't know haow his poor wife kin feel—she come from Ipswich, an' they nigh lynched Barnabas when he courted her fifty odd year' ago. Obed he died in 'seventy-eight, an' all the next gen'ration is gone naow—the *fust* wife's children dead, an' the rest . . . God knows . . ."

The sound of the incoming tide was now very insistent, and little by little it seemed to change the old man's mood from maudlin tearfulness to watchful fear. He would pause now and then to renew those nervous glances over his shoulder or out toward the reef, and despite the wild absurdity of his tale, I could not help beginning to share his vague apprehensiveness. Zadok now grew shriller, and seemed to be trying to whip up his courage with louder speech.

"Hey, yew, why dun't ye say somethin'? Haow'd ye like to be livin' in a taown like this, with everything a-rottin' an' dyin', an' boarded-up monsters crawlin' an' bleatin' an' barkin' an' hoppin' araoun' black cellars an' attics every way ye turn? Hey? Haow'd ye like to hear the haowlin' night arter night from the churches an' Order o' Dagon Hall, *an' know what's doin' part o' the haowlin'?* Haow'd ye like to hear what comes from that awful reef every May-Eve an' Hallowmass? Hey? Think the old man's crazy, eh? Wal, Sir, *let me tell ye that ain't the wust!*"

Zadok was really screaming now, and the mad frenzy of his voice disturbed me more than I care to own.

"Curse ye, dun't set thar a'starin' at me with them eyes—I tell Obed Marsh he's in hell, an' hez got to stay thar! Heh, heh . . . in hell, I says! Can't git me—I hain't done nothin' nor told nobody nothin'—

"Oh, you, young feller? Wal, even ef I hain't told nobody nothin' yet, I'm a'goin' to naow! Yew jest set still an' listen to me, boy—this is what I ain't never told nobody . . . I says I didn't get to do no pryin' arter that night—*but I faound things aout jest the same!*

"Yew want to know what the reel horror is, hey? Wal, it's this—it ain't what them fish devils *hez done, but what they're a-goin' to do!* They're a-bringin' things up aout o' whar they come from into the taown—ben doin' it fer years, an' slackenin' up lately. Them haouses north o' the river betwixt Water an' Main Streets is full of 'em— them devils *an' what they brung*—an' when they git ready . . . I say, *when they git ready* . . . ever hear tell of a *shoggoth?*

"Hey, d'ye hear me? I tell ye *I know what them things be—I seen 'em one night when . . . eh-ahhh-ah! e'yahhh . . .*"

The hideous suddenness and inhuman frightfulness of the old man's shriek almost made me faint. His eyes, looking past me toward the malodorous sea, were positively starting from his head; while his face was a mask of fear worthy of Greek tragedy. His bony claw dug monstrously into my shoulder, and he made no motion as I turned my head to look at whatever he had glimpsed.

There was nothing that I could see. Only the incoming tide, with perhaps one set of ripples more local than the long-flung line of breakers. But now Zadok was shaking me, and I turned back to watch the melting of that fear-frozen face into a chaos of twitching eyelids and mumbling gums. Presently his voice came back—albeit as a trembling whisper.

"*Git aout o' here!* Get aout o' here! *They seen us*—git aout fer your life! Dun't wait fer nothin'—*they know naow*—Run fer it—quick—*aout o' this taown*—"

Another heavy wave dashed against the loosening masonry of the bygone wharf, and changed the mad ancient's whisper to another inhuman and blood-curdling scream. "*E-yaahhhh! . . . yhaaaaaaa! . . .*"

Before I could recover my scattered wits he had relaxed his clutch on my shoulder and dashed wildly inland toward the street, reeling northward around the ruined ware-house wall.

I glanced back at the sea, but there was nothing there. And when I reached Water Street and looked along it toward the north there was no remaining trace of Zadok Allen.

IV

I can hardly describe the mood in which I was left by this harrowing episode—an episode at once mad and pitiful, grotesque and terrifying. The grocery boy had pre-pared me for it, yet the reality left me none the less bewildered and disturbed. Puerile though the story was, old Zadok's insane earnestness and horror had communicated to me a mounting unrest which joined with my earlier sense of loathing for the town and its blight of intangible shadow.

Later I might sift the tale and extract some nucleus of historic allegory; just now I wished to put it out of my head. The hour had grown perilously late—my watch said 7:15, and the Arkham bus left Town Square at eight—so I tried to give my thoughts as neutral and practical a cast as possible, meanwhile walking rapidly through the deserted streets of gaping roofs and leaning houses toward the hotel where I had checked my valise and would find my bus.

Though the golden light of late afternoon gave the ancient roofs and decrepit chimneys an air of mystic loveliness and peace, I could not help glancing over my shoulder now and then. I would surely be very glad to get out of malodorous and fear-shadowed Innsmouth, and wished there were some other vehicle than the bus driven by that sinister-looking fellow Sargent. Yet I did not hurry too precipitately, for there were architectural details worth viewing at every silent corner; and I could easily, I calculated, cover the necessary distance in a half-hour.

Studying the grocery youth's map and seeking a route I had not traversed before, I chose Marsh Street instead of State for my approach to Town Square. Near the corner of Fall Street I began to see scattered groups of furtive whisperers, and when I finally reached the Square I saw that almost all the loiterers were congregated around the door of the Gilman House. It seemed as if many bulging, watery, unwinking eyes looked oddly at me as I claimed my valise in the lobby, and I hoped that none of these unpleasant creatures would be my fellow-passengers on the coach.

The bus, rather early, rattled in with three passengers somewhat before eight, and an evil-looking fellow on the sidewalk muttered a few indistinguishable words to the driver. Sargent threw out a mail-bag and a roll of newspapers, and entered the hotel; while the passengers—the same men whom I had seen arriving in Newburyport that morning—shambled to the sidewalk and exchanged some faint guttural words with a loafer in a language I could have sworn was not English. I boarded the empty coach and took the same seat I had taken before, but was hardly settled before Sargent reappeared and began mumbling in a throaty voice of peculiar repulsiveness.

I was, it appeared, in very bad luck. There had been something wrong with the engine, despite the excellent time made from Newburyport, and the bus could not complete the journey to Arkham. No, it could not possibly be repaired that night, nor was there any other way of getting transportation out of Innsmouth either to Arkham or elsewhere. Sargent was sorry, but I would have to stop over at the Gilman. Probably the clerk would make the price easy for me, but there was nothing else to do. Almost dazed by this sudden obstacle, and violently dreading the fall of night in this decaying and half-unlighted town, I left the bus and re-entered the hotel lobby; where the sullen queer-looking night clerk told me I could have Room 428 on next the top floor— large, but without running water—for a dollar.

Despite what I had heard of this hotel in Newburyport, I signed the register, paid my dollar, let the clerk take my valise, and followed that sour, solitary attendant up three creaking flights of stairs past dusty corridors which seemed wholly devoid of life. My room, a dismal rear one with two windows and bare, cheap furnishings, overlooked a dingy court-yard otherwise hemmed in by low, deserted brick blocks, and commanded a view of decrepit westward-stretching roofs with a marshy country-side beyond. At the end of the corridor was a bathroom—a discouraging relique with ancient marble bowl, tin tub, faint electric light, and musty wooden panelling around all the plumbing fixtures.

It being still daylight, I descended to the Square and looked around for a dinner of some sort; noticing as I did so the strange glances I received from the unwholesome loafers. Since the grocery was closed, I was forced to patronise the restaurant I had shunned before; a stooped, narrow-headed man with staring, unwinking eyes, and a flat-nosed wench with unbelievably thick, clumsy hands being in attendance. The service was all of the counter type, and it relieved me to find that much was evidently served from cans and packages. A bowl of vegetable soup with crackers was enough for me, and I soon headed back for my cheerless room at the Gilman; getting an evening paper and a fly-specked magazine from the evil-visaged clerk at the rickety stand beside his desk.

As twilight deepened I turned on the one feeble electric bulb over the cheap, iron-framed bed, and tried as best I could to continue the reading I had begun. I felt it advisable to keep my mind wholesomely occupied, for it would not do to brood over the abnormalities of this ancient, blight-shadowed town while I was still within its borders. The insane yarn I had heard from the aged drunkard did not promise very pleasant dreams, and I felt I must keep the image of his wild, watery eyes as far as possible from my imagination.

Also, I must not dwell on what that factory inspector had told the Newburyport ticket-agent about the Gilman House and the voices of its nocturnal tenants—not on that, nor on the face beneath the tiara in the black church doorway; the face for whose horror my conscious mind could not account. It would perhaps have been easier to keep my thoughts from disturbing topics had the room not been so gruesomely musty. As it was, the lethal mustiness blended hideously with the town's general fishy odour, and persistently focussed one's fancy on death and decay.

Another thing that disturbed me was the absence of a bolt on the door of my room. One had been there, as marks clearly shewed, but there were signs of recent removal. No doubt it had become out of order, like so many other things in this decrepit edifice. In my nervousness I looked around and discovered a bolt on the clothespress which seemed to be of the same size, judging from the marks, as the one formerly on the door. To gain a partial relief from the general tension I busied myself by transferring this hardware to the vacant place with the aid of a handy three-in-one device including a screw-driver which I kept on my key-ring. The bolt fitted perfectly, and I was somewhat relieved when I knew that I could shoot it firmly upon retiring. Not that I had any real apprehension of its need, but that any symbol of security was welcome in an environment of this kind. There were adequate bolts on the two lateral doors to connecting rooms, and these I proceeded to fasten.

I did not undress, but decided to read till I was sleepy and then lie down with only my coat, collar, and shoes off. Taking a pocket flash light from my valise, I placed it in my trousers, so that I could read my watch if I woke up later in the dark. Drowsiness, however, did not come; and when I stopped to analyse my thoughts I found to my disquiet that I was really unconsciously listening for something—listening for something which I dreaded but could not name. That inspector's story must have worked on my imagination more deeply than I had suspected. Again I tried to read, but found that I made no progress.

After a time I seemed to hear the stairs and corridors creak at intervals as if with footsteps, and wondered if the other rooms were beginning to fill up. There were no voices, however, and it struck me that there was something subtly furtive about the creaking. I did not like it, and debated whether I had better try to sleep at all. This town had some queer people, and there had undoubtedly been several disappearances. Was this one of those inns where travelers were slain for their money? Surely I had no look of excessive prosperity. Or were the townsfolk really so resentful about curious visitors? Had my obvious sightseeing, with its frequent map-consultations, aroused unfavourable notice? It occurred to me that I must be in a highly nervous state to let a few random creakings set me off speculating in this fashion—but I regretted none the less that I was unarmed.

At length, feeling a fatigue which had nothing of drowsiness in it, I bolted the newly outfitted hall door, turned off the light, and threw myself down on the hard, uneven bed—coat, collar, shoes, and all. In the darkness every faint noise of the night seemed magnified, and a flood of doubly unpleasant thoughts swept over me. I was sorry I had put out the light, yet was too tired to rise and turn it on again. Then, after a long, dreary interval, and prefaced by a fresh creaking of stairs and corridor, there came that soft, damnably unmistakable sound which seemed like a malign fulfilment of all my apprehensions. Without the least shadow of a doubt, the lock of my door was being tried—cautiously, furtively, tentatively—with a key.

My sensations upon recognising this sign of actual peril were perhaps less rather than more tumultuous because of my previous vague fears. I had been, albeit without definite reason, instinctively on my guard—and that was to my advantage in the new and real crisis, whatever it might turn out to be. Nevertheless the change in the menace from vague premonition to immediate reality was a profound shock, and fell upon me with the force of a genuine blow. It never once occurred to me that the fumbling might be a mere mistake. Malign purpose was all I could think of, and I kept deathly quiet, awaiting the would-be intruder's next move.

After a time the cautious rattling ceased, and I heard the room to the north entered with a pass key. Then the lock of the connecting door to my room was softly tried. The bolt held, of course, and I heard the floor creak as the prowler left the room. After a moment there came another soft rattling, and I knew that the room to the south of me was being entered. Again a furtive trying of a bolted connecting door, and again a receding creaking. This time the creaking went along the hall and down the stairs, so I knew that the prowler had realised the bolted condition of my doors and was giving up his attempt for a greater or lesser time, as the future would shew.

The readiness with which I fell into a plan of action proves that I must have been subconsciously fearing some menace and considering possible avenues of escape for hours. From the first I felt that the unseen fumbler meant a danger not to be met or dealt with, but only to be fled from as precipitately as possible. The one thing to do was to get out of that hotel alive as quickly as I could, and through some channel other than the front stairs and lobby.

Rising softly and throwing my flashlight on the switch, I sought to light the bulb over my bed in order to choose and pocket some belongings for a swift, valiseless flight. Nothing, however, happened; and I saw that the power had been cut off. Clearly, some cryptic, evil movement was afoot on a large scale—just what, I could not say. As I stood pondering with my hand on the now useless switch I heard a muffled creaking on the floor below, and thought I could barely distinguish voices in conversation. A moment later I felt less sure that the deeper sounds were voices, since the apparent hoarse barkings and loose-syllabled croakings bore so little resemblance to recognized human speech. Then I thought with renewed force of what the factory inspector had heard in the night in this mouldering and pestilential building.

Having filled my pockets with the flashlight's aid, I put on my hat and tiptoed to the windows to consider chances of descent. Despite the state's safety regulations there was no fire escape on this side of the hotel, and I saw that my windows commanded only a sheer three-storey drop to the cobbled courtyard. On the right and left, however, some ancient brick business blocks abutted on the hotel; their slant roofs coming up to a reasonable jumping distance from my fourth-storey level. To reach either of these lines of buildings I would have to be in a room two doors from my own—in one case on the north and in the other case on the south—and my mind instantly set to work calculating what chances I had of making the transfer.

I could not, I decided, risk an emergence into the corridor; where my footsteps would surely be heard, and where the difficulties of entering the desired room would be insuperable. My progress, if it was to be made at all, would have to be through the less solidly-built connecting doors of the rooms; the locks and bolts of which I would have to force violently, using my shoulder as a battering-ram whenever they were set against me. This, I thought, would be possible owing to the rickety nature of the house and its fixtures; but I realised I could not do it noiselessly. I would have to count on sheer speed, and the chance of getting to a window before any hostile forces became coordinated enough to open the right door toward me with a pass-key. My own outer door I reinforced by pushing the bureau against it—little by little, in order to make a minimum of sound.

I perceived that my chances were very slender, and was fully prepared for any calamity. Even getting to another roof would not solve the problem, for there would then remain the task of reaching the ground and escaping from the town. One thing in my favour was the deserted and ruinous state of the abutting buildings, and the number of skylights gaping blackly open in each row.

Gathering from the grocery boy's map that the best route out of town was southward, I glanced first at the connecting door on the south side of the room. It was designed to open in my direction, hence I saw—after drawing the bolt and finding other fastenings in place—it was not a favorable one for forcing. Accordingly abandoning it as a route, I cautiously moved the bedstead against it to hamper any attack which might be made on it later from the next room. The door on the north was hung to open away from me, and this—though a test proved it to be locked or bolted from the other side—I knew must be my route. If I could gain the roofs of the buildings in Paine Street and descend successfully to the ground level, I might perhaps dart through the courtyard and the adjacent or opposite buildings to Washington or Bates— or else emerge in Paine and edge around southward into Washington. In any case, I would aim to strike Washington somehow and get quickly out of the Town Square region. My preference would be to avoid Paine, since the fire station there might be open all night.

As I thought of these things I looked out over the squalid sea of decaying roofs below me, now brightened by the beams of a moon not much past full. On the right the black gash of the river-gorge clove the panorama; abandoned factories and railway station clinging barnacle-like to its sides. Beyond it the rusted railway and the Rowley road led off through a flat, marshy terrain dotted with islets of higher and dryer scrubgrown land. On the left the creek-threaded countryside was nearer, the narrow road to Ipswich gleaming white in the moonlight. I could not see from my side of the hotel the southward route toward Arkham which I had determined to take.

I was irresolutely speculating on when I had better attack the northward door, and on how I could least audibly manage it, when I noticed that the vague noises underfoot had given place to a fresh and heavier creaking of the stairs. A wavering flicker of light shewed through my transom, and the boards of the corridor began to groan with a ponderous load. Muffled sounds of possible vocal origin approached, and at length a firm knock came at my outer door.

For a moment I simply held my breath and waited. Eternities seemed to elapse, and the nauseous fishy odour of my environment seemed to mount suddenly and spectacularly. Then the knocking was repeated—continuously, and with growing insistence. I knew that the time for action had come, and forthwith drew the bolt of the northward connecting door, bracing myself for the task of battering it open. The knocking waxed louder, and I hoped that its volume would cover the sound of my efforts. At last beginning my attempt, I lunged again and again at the thin panelling with my left shoulder, heedless of shock or pain. The door resisted even more than I had expected, but I did not give in. And all the while the clamour at the outer door increased.

Finally the connecting door gave, but with such a crash that I knew those outside must have heard. Instantly the outside knocking became a violent battering, while keys sounded ominously in the hall doors of the rooms on both sides of me. Rushing through the newly opened connexion, I succeeded in bolting the northerly hall door before the lock could be turned; but even as I did so I heard the hall door of the third room—the one from whose window I had hoped to reach the roof below—being tried with a pass key.

For an instant I felt absolute despair, since my trapping in a chamber with no window egress seemed complete. A wave of almost abnormal horror swept over me, and invested with a terrible but unexplainable singularity the flashlight-glimpsed dust prints made by the intruder who had lately tried my door from this room. Then, with a dazed automatism which persisted despite hopelessness, I made for the next connecting door and performed the blind motion of pushing at it in an effort to get through and—granting that fastenings might be as providentially intact as in this second room—bolt the hall door beyond before the lock could be turned from outside.

Sheer fortunate chance gave me my reprieve—for the connecting door before me was not only unlocked but actually ajar. In a second I was through, and had my right knee and shoulder against a hall door which was visibly opening inward. My pressure took the opener off guard, for the thing shut as I pushed, so that I could slip the well-conditioned bolt as I had done with the other door. As I gained this respite I heard the battering at the two other doors abate, while a confused clatter came from the connecting door I had shielded with the bedstead. Evidently the bulk of my assailants had entered the southerly room and were massing in a lateral attack. But at the same moment a pass key sounded in the next door to the north, and I knew that a nearer peril was at hand.

The northward connecting door was wide open, but there was no time to think about checking the already turning lock in the hall. All I could do was to shut and bolt the open connecting door, as well as its mate on the opposite side—pushing a bedstead against the one and a bureau against the other, and moving a washstand in front of the hall door. I must, I saw, trust to such makeshift barriers to shield me till I could get out the window and on the roof of the Paine Street block. But even in this acute moment my chief horror was something apart from the immediate weakness of my defences. I was shuddering because not one of my pursuers, despite some hideous pantings, gruntings, and subdued barkings at odd intervals, was uttering an unmuffled or intelligible vocal sound.

As I moved the furniture and rushed toward the windows I heard a frightful scurrying along the corridor toward the room north of me, and perceived that the southward battering had ceased. Plainly, most of my opponents were about to concentrate against the feeble connecting door which they knew must open directly on me. Outside, the moon played on the ridgepole of the block below, and I saw that the jump would be desperately hazardous because of the steep surface on which I must land.

Surveying the conditions, I chose the more southerly of the two windows as my avenue of escape; planning to land on the inner slope of the roof and make for the nearest skylight. Once inside one of the decrepit brick structures I would have to reckon with pursuit; but I hoped to descend and dodge in and out of yawning doorways along the shadowed courtyard, eventually getting to Washington Street and slipping out of town toward the south.

The clatter at the northerly connecting door was now terrific, and I saw that the weak panelling was beginning to splinter. Obviously, the besiegers had brought some ponderous object into play as a battering-ram. The bedstead, however, still held firm; so that I had at least a faint chance of making good my escape. As I opened the window I noticed that it was flanked by heavy velour draperies suspended from a pole by brass rings, and also that there was a large projecting catch for the shutters on the exterior. Seeing a possible means of avoiding the dangerous jump, I yanked at the hangings and brought them down, pole and all; then quickly hooking two of the rings in the shutter catch and flinging the drapery outside. The heavy folds reached fully to the abutting roof, and I saw that the rings and catch would be likely to bear my weight. So, climbing out of the window and down the improvised rope ladder, I left behind me for ever the morbid and horror-infested fabric of the Gilman House.

I landed safely on the loose slates of the steep roof, and succeeded in gaining the gaping black skylight without a slip. Glancing up at the window I had left, I observed it was still dark, though far across the crumbling chimneys to the north I could see lights ominously blazing in the Order of Dagon Hall, the Baptist church, and the Congregational church which I recalled so shiveringly. There had seemed to be no one in the courtyard below, and I hoped there would be a chance to get away before the spreading of a general alarm. Flashing my pocket lamp into the skylight, I saw that there were no steps down. The distance was slight, however, so I clambered over the brink and dropped; striking a dusty floor littered with crumbling boxes and barrels.

The place was ghoulish-looking, but I was past minding such impressions and made at once for the staircase revealed by my flashlight—after a hasty glance at my watch, which shewed the hour to be 2 a.m. The steps creaked, but seemed tolerably sound; and I raced down past a barnlike second storey to the ground floor. The desolation was complete, and only echoes answered my footfalls. At length I reached the lower hall at one end of which I saw a faint luminous rectangle marking the ruined Paine Street doorway. Heading the other way, I found the back door also open; and darted out and down five stone steps to the grass-grown cobblestones of the courtyard.

The moonbeams did not reach down here, but I could just see my way about without using the flashlight. Some of the windows on the Gilman House side were faintly glowing, and I thought I heard confused sounds within. Walking softly over to the Washington Street side I perceived several open doorways, and chose the nearest as my route out. The hallway inside was black, and when I reached the opposite end I saw that the street door was wedged immovably shut. Resolved to try another building, I groped my way back toward the courtyard, but stopped short when close to the doorway.

For out of an opened door in the Gilman House a large crowd of doubtful shapes was pouring—lanterns bobbing in the darkness, and horrible croaking voices exchanging low cries in what was certainly not English. The figures moved uncertainly, and I realised to my relief that they did not know where I had gone; but for all that they sent a shiver of horror through my frame. Their features were indistinguishable, but their crouching, shambling gait was abominably repellent. And worst of all, I perceived that one figure was strangely robed, and unmistakably surmounted by a tall tiara of a design altogether too familiar. As the figures spread throughout the courtyard, I felt my fears increase. Suppose I could find no egress from this building on the street side? The fishy odour was detestable, and I wondered I could stand it without fainting. Again groping toward the street, I opened a door off the hall and came upon an empty room with closely shuttered but sashless windows. Fumbling in the rays of my flashlight, I found I could open the shutters; and in another moment had climbed outside and was carefully closing the aperture in its original manner.

I was now in Washington Street, and for the moment saw no living thing nor any light save that of the moon. From several directions in the distance, however, I could hear the sound of hoarse voices, of footsteps, and of a curious kind of pattering which did not sound quite like footsteps. Plainly I had no time to lose. The points of the compass were clear to me, and I was glad that all the street lights were turned off, as is often the custom on strongly moonlit nights in unprosperous rural regions. Some of the sounds came from the south, yet I retained my design of escaping in that direction. There would, I knew, be plenty of deserted doorways to shelter me in case I met any person or group who looked like pursuers.

I walked rapidly, softly, and close to the ruined houses. While hatless and dishevelled after my arduous climb, I did not look especially noticeable; and stood a good chance of passing unheeded if forced to encounter any casual wayfarer. At Bates Street I drew into a yawning vestibule while two shambling figures crossed in front of me, but was soon on my way again and approaching the open space where Eliot Street obliquely crosses Washington at the intersection of South. Though I had never seen this space, it had looked dangerous to me on the grocery youth's map; since the moonlight would have free play there. There was no use trying to evade it, for any alternative course would involve detours of possibly disastrous visibility and delaying effect. The only thing to do was to cross it boldly and openly; imitating the typical shamble of the Innsmouth folk as best I could, and trusting that no one—or at least no pursuer of mine—would be there.

Just how fully the pursuit was organised—and indeed, just what its purpose might be—I could form no idea. There seemed to be unusual activity in the town, but I judged that the news of my escape from the Gilman had not yet spread. I would, of course, soon have to shift from Washington to some other southward street; for that party from the hotel would doubtless be after me. I must have left dust prints in that last old building, revealing how I had gained the street.

The open space was, as I had expected, strongly moonlit; and I saw the remains of a parklike, iron-railed green in its centre. Fortunately no one was about, though a curious sort of buzz or roar seemed to be increasing in the direction of Town Square. South Street was very wide, leading directly down a slight declivity to the waterfront and commanding a long view out at sea; and I hoped that no one would be glancing up it from afar as I crossed in the bright moonlight.

My progress was unimpeded, and no fresh sound arose to hint that I had been spied. Glancing about me, I involuntarily let my pace slacken for a second to take in the sight of the sea, gorgeous in the burning moonlight at the street's end. Far out beyond the breakwater was the dim, dark line of Devil Reef, and as I glimpsed it I could not help thinking of all the hideous legends I had heard in the last thirty-four hours—legends which portrayed this ragged rock as a veritable gateway to realms of unfathomed horror and inconceivable abnormality.

Then, without warning, I saw the intermittent flashes of light on the distant reef. They were definite and unmistakable, and awaked in my mind a blind horror beyond all rational proportion. My muscles tightened for panic flight, held in only by a certain unconscious caution and half-hypnotic fascination. And to make matters worse, there now flashed forth from the lofty cupola of the Gilman House, which loomed up to the northeast behind me, a series of analogous though differently spaced gleams which could be nothing less than an answering signal.

Controlling my muscles, and realising afresh how plainly visible I was, I resumed my brisker and feignedly shambling pace; though keeping my eyes on that hellish and ominous reef as long as the opening of South Street gave me a seaward view. What the whole proceeding meant, I could not imagine; unless it involved some strange rite connected with Devil Reef, or unless some party had landed from a ship on that sinister rock. I now bent to the left around the ruinous green; still gazing toward the ocean as it blazed in the spectral summer moonlight, and watching the cryptical flashing of those nameless, unexplainable beacons.

It was then that the most horrible impression of all was borne in upon me—the impression which destroyed my last vestige of self-control and sent me running frantically southward past the yawning black doorways and fishily staring windows of that deserted nightmare street. For at a closer glance I saw that the moonlit waters between the reef and the shore were far from empty. They were alive with a teeming horde of shapes swimming inward toward the town; and even at my vast distance and in my single moment of perception I could tell that the bobbing heads and flailing arms were alien and aberrant in a way scarcely to be expressed or consciously formulated.

My frantic running ceased before I had covered a block, for at my left I began to hear something like the hue and cry of organised pursuit. There were footsteps and gutteral sounds, and a rattling motor wheezed south along Federal Street. In a second all my plans were utterly changed—for if the southward highway were blocked ahead of me, I must clearly find another egress from Innsmouth. I paused and drew into a gaping doorway, reflecting how lucky I was to have left the moonlit open space before these pursuers came down the parallel street.

A second reflection was less comforting. Since the pursuit was down another street, it was plain that the party was not following me directly. It had not seen me, but was simply obeying a general plan of cutting off my escape. This, however, implied that all roads leading out of Innsmouth were similarly patrolled; for the people could not have known what route I intended to take. If this were so, I would have to make my retreat across country away from any road; but how could I do that in view of the marshy and creek-riddled nature of all the surrounding region? For a moment my brain reeled—both from sheer hopelessness and from a rapid increase in the omni-present fishy odour.

Then I thought of the abandoned railway to Rowley, whose solid line of ballasted, weed-grown earth still stretched off to the northwest from the crumbling station on the edge of the river-gorge. There was just a chance that the townsfolk would not think of that; since its briar-choked desertion made it half-impassable, and the un-likeliest of all avenues for a fugitive to choose. I had seen it clearly from my hotel window, and knew about how it lay. Most of its earlier length was uncomfortably visible from the Rowley road, and from high places in the town itself; but one could perhaps crawl inconspicuously through the undergrowth. At any rate, it would form my only chance of deliverance, and there was nothing to do but try it.

Drawing inside the hall of my deserted shelter, I once more consulted the grocery boy's map with the aid of the flashlight. The immediate problem was how to reach the ancient railway; and I now saw that the safest course was ahead to Babson Street, then west to Lafayette—there edging around but not crossing an open space homol-ogous to the one I had traversed—and subsequently back northward and westward in a zigzagging line through Lafayette, Bates, Adams, and Bank Streets—the latter skirt-ing the river gorge—to the abandoned and dilapidated station I had seen from my window. My reason for going ahead to Babson was that I wished neither to re-cross the earlier open space nor to begin my westward course along a cross street as broad as South.

Starting once more, I crossed the street to the right-hand side in order to edge around into Babson as inconspicuously as possible. Noises still continued in Federal Street, and as I glanced behind me I thought I saw a gleam of light near the building through which I had escaped. Anxious to leave Washington Street, I broke into a quiet dog-trot, trusting to luck not to encounter any observing eye. Next the corner of Babson Street I saw to my alarm that one of the houses was still inhabited, as attested by curtains at the window; but there were no lights within, and I passed it without disaster.

In Babson Street, which crossed Federal and might thus reveal me to the searchers, I clung as closely as possible to the sagging, uneven buildings; twice pausing in a doorway as the noises behind me momentarily increased. The open space ahead shone wide and desolate under the moon, but my route would not force me to cross it. During my second pause I began to detect a fresh distribution of vague sounds; and upon looking cautiously out from cover beheld a motor car darting across the open space, bound outward along Eliot Street, which there intersects both Babson and Lafayette.

As I watched—choked by a sudden rise in the fishy odour after a short abatement—I saw a band of uncouth, crouching shapes loping and shambling in the same direction; and knew that this must be the party guarding the Ipswich road, since that highway forms an extension of Eliot Street. Two of the figures I glimpsed were in voluminous robes, and one wore a peaked diadem which glistened whitely in the moonlight. The gait of this figure was so odd that it sent a chill through me—for it seemed to me the creature was almost hopping.

When the last of the band was out of sight I resumed my progress; darting around the corner into Lafayette Street, and crossing Eliot very hurriedly lest stragglers of the party be still advancing along that thoroughfare. I did hear some croaking and clattering sounds far off toward Town Square, but accomplished the passage without disaster. My greatest dread was in re-crossing broad and moonlit South Street—with its seaward view—and I had to nerve myself for the ordeal. Someone might easily be looking, and possible Eliot Street stragglers could not fail to glimpse me from either of two points. At the last moment I decided I had better slacken my trot and make the crossing as before in the shambling gait of an average Innsmouth native.

When the view of the water again opened out—this time on my right—I was half-determined not to look at it at all. I could not, however, resist; but cast a sidelong glance as I carefully and imitatively shambled toward the protecting shadows ahead. There was no ship visible, as I had half-expected there would be. Instead, the first thing which caught my eye was a small rowboat pulling in toward the abandoned wharves and laden with some bulky, tarpaulin-covered object. Its rowers, though distantly and indistinctly seen, were of an especially repellent aspect. Several swimmers were still discernible; while on the far black reef I could see a faint, steady glow unlike the winking beacon visible before, and of a curious colour which I could not precisely identify. Above the slant roofs ahead and to the right there loomed the tall cupola of the Gilman House, but it was completely dark. The fishy odour, dispelled for a moment by some merciful breeze, now closed in again with maddening intensity.

I had not quite crossed the street when I heard a muttering band advancing along Washington from the north. As they reached the broad open space where I had had my first disquieting glimpse of the moonlit water I could see them plainly only a block away—and was horrified by the bestial abnormality of their faces and the doglike sub-humanness of their crouching gait. One man moved in a positively simian way, with long arms frequently touching the ground; while another figure—robed and tiaraed—seemed to progress in an almost hopping fashion. I judged this party to be the one I had seen in the Gilman's courtyard—the one, therefore, most closely on my trail. As some of the figures turned to look in my direction. I was transfixed with fright, yet managed to preserve the casual, shambling gait I had assumed. To this day I do not know whether they saw me or not. If they did, my stratagem must have deceived them, for they passed on across the moonlit space without varying their course—meanwhile croaking and jabbering in some hateful gutteral patois I could not identify.

Once more in shadow, I resumed my former dog-trot past the leaning and decrepit houses that stared blankly into the night. Having crossed to the western sidewalk I rounded the nearest corner into Bates Street, where I kept close to the buildings on the southern side. I passed two houses shewing signs of habitation, one of which had faint lights in upper rooms, yet met with no obstacle. As I turned into Adams Street I felt measurably safer, but received a shock when a man reeled out of a black doorway directly in front of me. He proved, however, too hopelessly drunk to be a menace; so that I reached the dismal ruins of the Bank Street warehouses in safety.

No one was stirring in that dead street beside the river-gorge, and the roar of the waterfalls quite drowned my footsteps. It was a long dog-trot to the ruined station, and the great brick warehouse walls around me seemed somehow more terrifying than the fronts of private houses. At last I saw the ancient arcaded station—or what was left of it—and made directly for the tracks that started from its farther end.

The rails were rusty but mainly intact, and not more than half the ties had rotted away. Walking or running on such a surface was very difficult; but I did my best, and on the whole made very fair time. For some distance the line kept on along the gorge's brink, but at length I reached the long covered bridge where it crossed the chasm at a dizzy height. The condition of this bridge would determine my next step. If humanly possible, I would use it; if not, I would have to risk more street wandering and take the nearest intact highway bridge.

The vast, barnlike length of the old bridge gleamed spectrally in the moonlight, and I saw that the ties were safe for at least a few feet within. Entering, I began to use my flashlight, and was almost knocked down by the cloud of bats that flapped past me. About half-way across there was a perilous gap in the ties which I feared for a moment would halt me; but in the end I risked a desperate jump which fortunately succeeded.

I was glad to see the moonlight again when I emerged from that macabre tunnel. The old tracks crossed River Street at grade, and at once veered off into a region increasingly rural and with less and less of Innsmouth's abhorrent fishy odour. Here the dense growth of weeds and briers hindered me and cruelly tore my clothes, but I was none the less glad that they were there to give me concealment in case of peril. I knew that much of my route must be visible from the Rowley road.

The marshy region began very shortly, with the single track on a low, grassy embankment where the weedy growth was somewhat thinner. Then came a sort of island of higher ground, where the line passed through a shallow open cut choked with bushes and brambles. I was very glad of this partial shelter, since at this point the Rowley road was uncomfortably near according to my window view. At the end of the cut it would cross the track and swerve off to a safer distance; but meanwhile I must be exceedingly careful. I was by this time thankfully certain that the railway itself was not patrolled.

Just before entering the cut I glanced behind me, but saw no pursuer. The ancient spires and roofs of decaying Innsmouth gleamed lovely and ethereal in the magic yellow moonlight, and I thought of how they must have looked in the old days before the shadow fell. Then, as my gaze circled inland from the town, something less tranquil arrested my notice and held me immobile for a second.

What I saw—or fancied I saw—was a disturbing suggestion of undulant motion far to the south; a suggestion which made me conclude that a very large horde must be pouring out of the city along the level Ipswich road. The distance was great, and I could distinguish nothing in detail; but I did not at all like the look of that moving column. It undulated too much, and glistened too brightly in the rays of the now westering moon. There was a suggestion of sound, too, though the wind was blowing the other way—a suggestion of bestial scraping and bellowing even worse than the muttering of the parties I had lately overheard.

All sorts of unpleasant conjectures crossed my mind. I thought of those very extreme Innsmouth types said to be hidden in crumbling, centuried warrens near the waterfront. I thought, too, of those nameless swimmers I had seen. Counting the parties so far glimpsed, as well as those presumably covering other roads, the number of my pursuers must be strangely large for a town as depopulated as Innsmouth.

Whence could come the dense personnel of such a column as I now beheld? Did those ancient, unplumbed warrens teem with a twisted, uncatalogued, and unsuspected life? Or had some unseen ship indeed landed a legion of unknown outsiders on that hellish reef? Who were they? Why were they here? And if such a column of them was scouring the Ipswich road, would the patrols on the other roads be likewise augmented?

I had entered the brush-grown cut and was struggling along at a very slow pace when that damnable fishy odour again waxed dominant. Had the wind suddenly changed eastward so that it blew in from the sea and over the town? It must have, I concluded, since I now began to hear shocking guttural murmurs from that hitherto silent direction. There was another sound, too—a kind of wholesale, colossal flopping or pattering which somehow called up images of the most detestable sort. It made me think illogically of that unpleasantly undulating column on the far-off Ipswich road.

And then both stench and sounds grew stronger, so that I paused shivering and grateful for the cut's protection. It was here, I recalled, that the Rowley road drew so close to the old railway before crossing westward and diverging. Something was coming along that road, and I must lie low till its passage and vanishment in the distance. Thank heaven these creatures employed no dogs for tracking—though perhaps that would have been impossible amidst the omnipresent regional odour. Crouched in the bushes of that sandy cleft I felt reasonably safe, even though I knew the searchers would have to cross the track in front of me not much more than a hundred yards away. I would be able to see them, but they could not, except by a malign miracle, see me.

All at once I began dreading to look at them as they passed. I saw the close moonlit space where they would surge by, and had curious thoughts about the irredeemable pollution of that space. They would perhaps be the worst of all Innsmouth types— something one would not care to remember.

The stench waxed overpowering, and the noises swelled to a bestial babel of croaking, baying and barking without the least suggestion of human speech. Were these indeed the voices of my pursuers? Did they have dogs after all? So far I had seen none of the lower animals in Innsmouth. That flopping or pattering was monstrous—I could not look upon the degenerate creatures responsible for it. I would keep my eyes shut till the sound receded toward the west. The horde was very close now—the air foul with their hoarse snarlings, and the ground almost shaking with their alien-rhythmed footfalls. My breath nearly ceased to come, and I put every ounce of will-power into the task of holding my eyelids down.

I am not even yet willing to say whether what followed was a hideous actuality or only a nightmare hallucination. The later action of the government, after my frantic appeals, would tend to confirm it as a monstrous truth; but could not an hallucination have been repeated under the quasi-hypnotic spell of that ancient, haunted, and shadowed town? Such places have strange properties, and the legacy of insane legend might well have acted on more than one human imagination amidst those dead, stench-cursed streets and huddles of rotting roofs and crumbling steeples. Is it not possible that the germ of an actual contagious madness lurks in the depths of that shadow over Innsmouth? Who can be sure of reality after hearing things like the tale of old Zadok Allen? The government men never found poor Zadok, and have no conjectures to make as to what became of him. Where does madness leave off and reality begin? Is it possible that even my latest fear is sheer delusion?

But I must try to tell what I thought I saw that night under the mocking yellow moon—saw surging and hopping down the Rowley road in plain sight in front of me as I crouched among the wild brambles of that desolate railway cut. Of course my resolution to keep my eyes shut had failed. It was foredoomed to failure—for who could crouch blindly while a legion of croaking, baying entities of unknown source flopped noisomely past, scarcely more than a hundred yards away?

I thought I was prepared for the worst, and I really ought to have been prepared considering what I had seen before. My other pursuers had been accursedly abnormal—so should I not have been ready to face a strengthening of the abnormal element; to look upon forms in which there was no mixture of the normal at all? I did not open my eyes until the raucous clamour came loudly from a point obviously straight ahead. Then I knew that a long section of them must be plainly in sight where the sides of the cut flattened out and the road crossed the track—and I could no longer keep myself from sampling whatever horror that leering yellow moon might have to shew.

It was the end, for whatever remains to me of life on the surface of this earth, of every vestige of mental peace and confidence in the integrity of nature and of the human mind. Nothing that I could have imagined—nothing, even, that I could have gathered had I credited old Zadok's crazy tale in the most literal way—would be in any way comparable to the demoniac, blasphemous reality that I saw—or believe I saw. I have tried to hint what it was in order to postpone the horror of writing it down baldly. Can it be possible that this planet has actually spawned such things; that human eyes have truly seen, as objective flesh, what man has hitherto known only in febrile phantasy and tenuous legend?

And yet I saw them in a limitless stream—flopping, hopping, croaking, bleating—surging inhumanly through the spectral moonlight in a grotesque, malignant saraband of fantastic nightmare. And some of them had tall tiaras of that nameless whitish-gold metal . . . and some were strangely robed . . . and one, who led the way, was clad in a ghoulishly humped black coat and striped trousers, and had a man's felt hat perched on the shapeless thing that answered for a head.

I think their predominant colour was a greyish-green, though they had white bellies. They were mostly shiny and slippery, but the ridges of their backs were scaly. Their forms vaguely suggested the anthropoid, while their heads were the heads of fish, with prodigious bulging eyes that never closed. At the sides of their necks were palpitating gills, and their long paws were webbed. They hopped irregularly, some-times on two legs and sometimes on four. I was somehow glad that they had no more than four limbs. Their croaking, baying voices, clearly used for articulate speech, held all the dark shades of expression which their staring faces lacked.

But for all of their monstrousness they were not unfamiliar to me. I knew too well what they must be—for was not the memory of the evil tiara at Newburyport still fresh? They were the blasphemous fish-frogs of the nameless design—living and hor-rible—and as I saw them I knew also of what that humped, tiaraed priest in the black church basement had fearsomely reminded me. Their number was past guessing. It seemed to me that there were limitless swarms of them—and certainly my momentary glimpse could have shewn only the least fraction. In another instant everything was blotted out by a merciful fit of fainting; the first I had ever had.

V

It was a gentle daylight rain that awaked me from my stupor in the brush-grown railway cut, and when I staggered out to the roadway ahead I saw no trace of any prints in the fresh mud. The fishy odour, too, was gone, Innsmouth's ruined roofs and toppling steeples loomed up greyly toward the southeast, but not a living creature did I spy in all the desolate salt marshes around. My watch was still going, and told me that the hour was past noon.

The reality of what I had been through was highly uncertain in my mind, but I felt that something hideous lay in the background. I must get away from evil-shadowed Innsmouth—and accordingly I began to test my cramped, wearied powers of loco-motion. Despite weakness, hunger, horror, and bewilderment I found myself after a time able to walk; so started slowly along the muddy road to Rowley. Before evening I was in the village, getting a meal and providing myself with presentable clothes. I caught the night train to Arkham, and the next day talked long and earnestly with government officials there; a process I later repeated in Boston. With the main result of these colloquies the public is now familiar—and I wish, for normality's sake, there were nothing more to tell. Perhaps it is madness that is overtaking me—yet perhaps a greater horror—or a greater marvel—is reaching out.

As may well be imagined, I gave up most of the fore-planned features of the rest of my tour—the scenic, architectural, and antiquarian diversions on which I had counted so heavily. Nor did I dare look for that piece of strange jewellery said to be in the Miskatonic University Museum. I did, however, improve my stay in Arkham by collecting some genealogical notes I had long wished to possess; very rough and hasty data, it is true, but capable of good use later on when I might have time to collate and codify them. The curator of the historical society there—Mr. E. Lapham Peabody—was very courteous about assisting me, and expressed unusual interest when I told him I was a grandson of Eliza Orne of Arkham, who was born in 1867 and had married James Williamson of Ohio at the age of seventeen.

It seemed that a material uncle of mine had been there many years before on a quest much like my own; and that my grandmother's family was a topic of some local curiosity. There had, Mr. Peabody said, been considerable discussion about the mar-riage of her father, Benjamin Orne, just after the Civil War; since the ancestry of the bride was peculiarly puzzling. That bride was understood to have been an orphaned Marsh of New Hampshire—a cousin of the Essex County Marshes—but her education had been in France and she knew very little of her family. A guardian had deposited funds in a Boston bank to maintain her and her French governess; but that guardian's name was unfamiliar to Arkham people, and in time he dropped out of sight, so that the governess assumed his role by court appointment. The Frenchwoman—now long dead—was very taciturn, and there were those who said she could have told more than she did.

But the most baffling thing was the inability of anyone to place the recorded parents of the young woman—Enoch and Lydia (Meserve) Marsh—among the known fam-ilies of New Hampshire. Possibly, many suggested, she was the natural daughter of some Marsh of prominence—she certainly had the true Marsh eyes. Most of the puzzling was done after her early death, which took place at the birth of my grandmother—her only child. Having formed some disagreeable impressions connected with the name of Marsh, I did not welcome the news that it belonged on my own ancestral tree; nor was I pleased by Mr. Peabody's suggestion that I had the true Marsh eyes myself. However, I was grateful for data which I knew would prove valuable; and took copious notes and lists of book references regarding the well-documented Orne family.

I went directly home to Toledo from Boston, and later spent a month at Maumee recuperating from my ordeal. In September I entered Oberlin for my final year, and from then till the next June was busy with studies and other wholesome activities—reminded of the bygone terror only by occasional official visits from government men in connexion with the campaign which my pleas and evidence had started. Around the middle of July—just a year after the Innsmouth experience—I spent a week with my late mother's family in Cleveland; checking some of my new genealogical data with the various notes, traditions, and bits of heirloom material in existence there, and seeing what kind of a connected chart I could construct.

I did not exactly relish this task, for the atmosphere of the Williamson home had always depressed me. There was a strain of morbidity there, and my mother had never encouraged my visiting her parents as a child, although she always welcomed her father when he came to Toledo. My Arkham-born grandmother had seemed strange and almost terrifying to me, and I do not think I grieved when she disappeared. I was eight years old then, and it was said that she had wandered off in grief after the suicide of my uncle Douglas, her eldest son. He had shot himself after a trip to New England—the same trip, no doubt, which had caused him to be recalled at the Arkham Historical Society.

This uncle had resembled her, and I had never liked him either. Something about the staring, unwinking expression of both of them had given me a vague, unaccountable uneasiness. My mother and uncle Walter had not looked like that. They were like their father, though poor little cousin Lawrence—Walter's son—had been an almost perfect duplicate of his grandmother before his condition took him to the permanent seclusion of a sanitarium at Canton. I had not seen him in four years, but my uncle once implied that his state, both mental and physical, was very bad. This worry had probably been a major cause of his mother's death two years before.

My grandfather and his widowed son Walter now comprised the Cleveland household, but the memory of older times hung thickly over it. I still disliked the place, and tried to get my researches done as quickly as possible. Williamson records and traditions were supplied in abundance by my grandfather; though for Orne material I had to depend on my uncle Walter, who put at my disposal the contents of all his files, including notes, letters, cuttings, heirlooms, photographs, and miniatures.

It was in going over the letters and pictures on the Orne side that I began to acquire a kind of terror of my own ancestry. As I have said, my grandmother and uncle Douglas had always disturbed me. Now, years after their passing, I gazed at their pictured faces with a measurably heightened feeling of repulsion and alienation. I could not at first understand the change, but gradually a horrible sort of comparison began to obtrude itself on my unconscious mind despite the steady refusal of my consciousness to admit even the least suspicion of it. It was clear that the typical expression of these faces now suggested something it had not suggested before—something which would bring stark panic if too openly thought of.

But the worst shock came when my uncle shewed me the Orne jewellery in a downtown safe-deposit vault. Some of the items were delicate and inspiring enough, but there was one box of strange old pieces descended from my mysterious great-grandmother which my uncle was almost reluctant to produce. They were, he said, of very grotesque and almost repulsive design, and had never to his knowledge been publicly worn; though my grandmother used to enjoy looking at them. Vague legends of bad luck clustered around them, and my great-grandmother's French governess had said they ought not to be worn in New England, though it would be quite safe to wear them in Europe.

As my uncle began slowly and grudgingly to unwrap the things he urged me not to be shocked by the strangeness and frequent hideousness of the designs. Artists and archaeologists who had seen them pronounced their workmanship superlatively and exotically exquisite, though no one seemed able to define their exact material or assign them to any specific art tradition. There were two armlets, a tiara, and a kind of pectoral; the latter having in high relief certain figures of almost unbearable extravagance.

During this description I had kept a tight rein on my emotions, but my face must have betrayed my mounting fears. My uncle looked concerned, and paused in his unwrapping to study my countenance. I motioned to him to continue, which he did with renewed signs of reluctance. He seemed to expect some demonstration when the first piece—the tiara—became visible, but I doubt if he expected quite what actually happened. I did not expect it, either, for I thought I was thoroughly forewarned regarding what the jewellery would turn out to be. What I did was to faint silently away, just as I had done in that brier choked railway cut a year before.

From that day on my life has been a nightmare of brooding and apprehension, nor do I know how much is hideous truth and how much madness. My great-grandmother had been a Marsh of unknown source whose husband lived in Arkham—and did not old Zadok say that the daughter of Obed Marsh by a monstrous mother was married to an Arkham man through a trick? What was it the ancient toper had muttered about the likeness of my eyes to Captain Obed's? In Arkham, too, the curator had told me I had the true Marsh eyes. Was Obed Marsh my own great-great-grandfather? Who— or what—then, was my great-great-grandmother? But perhaps this was all madness. Those whitish-gold ornaments might easily have been bought from some Innsmouth sailor by the father of my great-grandmother, whoever he was. And that look in the staring-eyed faces of my grandmother and self-slain uncle might be sheer fancy on my part—sheer fancy, bolstered up by the Innsmouth shadow which had so darkly coloured my imagination. But why had my uncle killed himself after an ancestral quest in New England?

For more than two years I fought off these reflections with partial success. My father secured me a place in an insurance office, and I buried myself in routine as deeply as possible. In the winter of 1930–31, however, the dreams began. They were very sparse and insidious at first, but increased in frequency and vividness as the weeks went by. Great watery spaces opened out before me, and I seemed to wander through titanic sunken porticos and labyrinths of weedy cyclopean walls with grotesque fishes as my companions. Then the other shapes began to appear, filling me with nameless horror the moment I awoke. But during the dreams they did not horrify me at all—I was one with them; wearing their unhuman trappings, treading their aqueous ways, and praying monstrously at their evil sea-bottom temples.

There was much more than I could remember, but even what I did remember each morning would be enough to stamp me as a madman or a genius if ever I dared write it down. Some frightful influence, I felt, was seeking gradually to drag me out of the sane world of wholesome life into unnamable abysses of blackness and alienage; and the process told heavily on me. My health and appearance grew steadily worse, till finally I was forced to give up my position and adopt the static, secluded life of an invalid. Some odd nervous affliction had me in its grip, and I found myself at times almost unable to shut my eyes.

It was then that I began to study the mirror with mounting alarm. The slow ravages of disease are not pleasant to watch, but in my case there was something subtler and more puzzling in the background. My father seemed to notice it, too, for he began looking at me curiously and almost affrightedly. What was taking place in me? Could it be that I was coming to resemble my grandmother and uncle Douglas?

One night I had a frightful dream in which I met my grandmother under the sea. She lived in a phosphorescent palace of many terraces, with gardens of strange leprous corals and grotesque brachiate efflorescences, and welcomed me with a warmth that may have been sardonic. She had changed—as those who take to the water change— and told me she had never died. Instead, she had gone to a spot her dead son had learned about, and had leaped to a realm whose wonders—destined for him as well— he had spurned with a smoking pistol. This was to be my realm, too—I could not escape it. I would never die, but would live with those who had lived since before man ever walked the earth.

I met also that which had been her grandmother. For eighty thousand years Pth'thya- l'yi had lived in Y'ha-nthlei, and thither she had gone back after Obed Marsh was dead. Y'ha-nthlei was not destroyed when the upper-earth men shot death into the sea. It was hurt, but not destroyed. The Deep Ones could never be destroyed, even though the palaeogean magic of the forgotten Old Ones might sometimes check them. For the present they would rest; but some day, if they remembered, they would rise again for the tribute Great Cthulhu craved. It would be a city greater than Innsmouth next time. They had planned to spread, and had brought up that which would help them, but now they must wait once more. For bringing the upper-earth men's death I must do a penance, but that would not be heavy. This was the dream in which I saw a *shoggoth* for the first time, and the sight set me awake in a frenzy of screaming. That morning the mirror definitely told me I had acquired *the Innsmouth look*.

So far I have not shot myself as my uncle Douglas did. I bought an automatic and almost took the step, but certain dreams deterred me. The tense extremes of horror are lessening, and I feel queerly drawn toward the unknown sea-deeps instead of fearing them. I hear and do strange things in sleep, and awake with a kind of exaltation instead of terror. I do not believe I need to wait for the full change as most have waited. If I did, my father would probably shut me up in a sanitarium as my poor little cousin is shut up. Stupendous and unheard-of splendours await me below, and I shall seek them soon. *Iä-R'lyeh! Cthulhu fhtagn! Iä Iä!* No, I shall not shoot myself—I cannot be made to shoot myself!

I shall plan my cousin's escape from that Canton madhouse, and together we shall go to marvel-shadowed Innsmouth. We shall swim out to that brooding reef in the sea and dive down through black abysses to Cyclopean and many-columned Y'ha-nthlei, and in that lair of the Deep Ones we shall dwell amidst wonder and glory for ever.

O UGLY BIRD!

BY MANLY WADE WELLMAN

Manly Wade Wellman was a master at bringing the "old ways" and superstitions to life in stories that took place in the darker, less-civilized sections of rural Appalachia. Wellman's stories take place where the devils who ran away from the god-fearing Puritans (or perhaps some of Rip Van Winkle's Henry Hudson companions) might have gone to hide.

Perhaps his most famous creation of all is Silver John (sometimes called John the Balladeer), the wizard-wizened minstrel who's always ready to rescue the weak or innocent from the clutches of demonic evil.

I swear I'm licked before I start, trying to tell you all what Mr. Onselm looked like. Words give out sometimes. The way you're purely frozen to death for fit words to tell the favor of the girl you love. And Mr. Onselm and I pure poison hated each other from the start. That's a way that love and hate are alike.

He's what folks in the country call a low man, meaning he's short and small. But a low man is low other ways than in inches, sometimes. Mr. Onselm's shoulders didn't wide out as far as his big ears, and they sank and sagged. His thin legs bowed in at the knee and out at the shank, like two sickles put point to point. His neck was as thin as a carrot, and on it his head looked like a swollen-up pale gourd. Thin hair, gray as tree moss. Loose mouth, a little bit open to show long, straight teeth. Not much chin. The right eye squinted, mean and dark, while the hike of his brow stretched the left one wide open. His good clothes fitted his mean body as if they were cut to its measure. Those good clothes of his were almost as much out of match to the rest of him as his long, soft, pink hands, the hands of a man who'd never had to work a tap's worth.

You see now what I mean? I can't say just how he looked, only that he looked hateful.

I first met him when I was coming down from that high mountain's comb, along an animal trail—maybe a deer made it. I was making to go on across the valley and through a pass, on to Hark Mountain where I'd heard tell was the Bottomless Pool. No special reason, just I had the notion to go there. The valley had trees in it, and through and among the trees I saw, here and there down the slope, patchy places and cabins and yards.

I hoped to myself I might could get fed at one of the cabins, for I'd run clear out of eating some spell back. I didn't have any money, nary coin of it; just only my hickory shirt and blue jeans pants and torn old army shoes, and my guitar on its sling cord. But I knew the mountain folks. If they've got anything to eat, a decent-spoken stranger can get the half part of it. Town folks ain't always the same way about that.

Down the slope I picked my way, favoring the guitar just in case I slipped and fell down, and in an hour I'd made it to the first patch. The cabin was two rooms, dog-trotted and open through the middle. Beyond it was a shed and a pigpen. In the yard was the man of the house, talking to who I found out later was Mr. Onselm.

"You don't have any meat at all?" Mr. Onselm inquired him, and Mr. Onselm's voice was the last you'd expect his sort of man to have, it was full of broad low music, like an organ in a big town church. But I decided not to ask him to sing when I'd taken another closer glimpse of him—sickle-legged and gourd-headed, and pale and puny in his fine-fitting clothes. For, small as he was, he looked mad and danger-ous; and the man of the place, though he was a big, strong-seeming old gentleman with a square jaw, looked scared.

"I been right short this year, Mr. Onselm," he said, and it was a half-begging way he said it. "The last bit of meat I done fished out of the brine on Tuesday. And I'd sure enough rather not to kill the pig till December."

Mr. Onselm tramped over to the pen and looked in. The pig was a friendly-acting one; it reared up with its front feet against the boards and grunted up, the way you'd know he hoped for something nice to eat. Mr. Onselm spit into the pen.

"All right," he said, granting a favor. "But I want some meal."

He sickle-legged back toward the cabin. A brown barrel stood out in the dog trot. Mr. Onselm flung off the cover and pinched up some meal between the tips of his pink fingers. "Get me a sack," he told the man.

The man went quick indoors, and quick out he came, with the sack. Mr. Onselm held it open while the man scooped out enough meal to fill it up. Then Mr. Onselm twisted the neck tight shut and the man lashed the neck with twine. Finally Mr. Onselm looked up and saw me standing there with my guitar under my arm.

"Who are you?" he asked, sort of crooning.

"My name's John," I said.

"John what?" Then he never waited for me to tell him John what. "Where did you steal that guitar?"

"This was given to me," I replied him. "I strung it with the silver wires myself."

"Silver," said Mr. Onselm, and he opened his squint eye by a trifle bit.

"Yes, sir." With my left hand I clamped a chord. With my right thumb I picked the silver strings to a whisper. I began to make up a song:

"Mister Onselm,
They do what you tell 'em—"

"That will do," said Mr. Onselm, not so singingly, and I stopped with the half-made-up song. He relaxed and let his eye go back to a squint again.

"They do what I tell 'em," he said, halfway to himself. "Not bad."

We studied each other, he and I, for a few ticks of time. Then he turned away and went tramping out of the yard and off among the trees. When he was gone from sight, the man of the house asked me, right friendly enough, what he could do for me.

"I'm just a-walking through," I said. I didn't want to ask him right off for some dinner.

"I heard you name yourself John," he said. "Just so happens my name's John, too. John Bristow."

"Nice place you got here, Mr. Bristow," I said, looking around. "You cropping or you renting?"

"I own the house and the land," he told me, and I was surprised; for Mr. Onselm had treated him the way a mean-minded boss treats a cropper.

"Oh," I said, "then that Mr. Onselm was just a visitor."

"Visitor?" Mr. Bristow snorted out the word. "He visits ary living soul here around. Lets them know what thing he wants, and they pass it to him. I kindly thought you knew him, you sang about him so ready."

"Oh, I just got that up." I touched the silver strings again. "Many a new song comes to me, and I just sing it. That's my nature."

"I love the old songs better," said Mr. Bristow, and smiled; so I sang one:

"I had been in Georgia
Not a many more weeks than three
When I fell in love with a pretty fair girl
And she fell in love with me.

"Her lips were red as red could be,
Her eyes were brown as brown,
Her hair was like a thundercloud
Before the rain comes down."

Gentlemen, you'd ought to been there, to see Mr. Bristow's face shine. He said: "By God, John, you sure enough can sing it and play it. It's a pure pleasure to hark at you."

"I do my possible best," I said. "But Mr. Onselm doesn't like it." I thought for a moment, then I inquired him: "What's the way he can get ary thing he wants in this valley?"

"Shoo, can't tell you what way. Just done it for years, he has."

"Doesn't anybody refuse him?"

"Well, it's happened. Once, they say, Old Jim Desbro refused him a chicken. And Mr. Onselm pointed his finger at Old Jim's mules, they was a-plowing at the time. Them mules couldn't move nary hoof, not till Mr. Onselm had the chicken from Old Jim. Another time there was, Miss Tilly Parmer hid a cake she'd just baked when she seen Mr. Onselm a-coming. He pointed a finger and he dumbed her. She never spoke one mumbling word from that day on to the day she laid down and died. Could hear and know what was said to her, but when she tried to talk she could only just gibble."

"Then he's a hoodoo man," I said. "And that means, the law can't do a thing to him."

"No sir, not even if the law worried itself up about anything going on this far from the country seat." He looked at the meal sack, still standing in the dog-trot. "Near about time for the Ugly Bird to come fetch Mr. Onselm's meal."

"What's the Ugly Bird?" I asked, but Mr. Bristow didn't have to tell me that.

It must have been a-hanging up there over us, high and quiet, and now it dropped down into the yard, like a fish hawk into a pond.

First out I could see it was dark, heavy-winged, bigger by right much than a buzzard. Then I made out the shiny gray-black of the body, like wet slate, and how the body looked to be naked, how it seemed there were feathers only on the wide wings. Then I saw the long thin snaky neck and the bulgy head and the long crane beak. And I saw the two eyes set in the front of the head—set man-fashion in the front, not bird-fashion one on each side.

The feet grabbed for the sack and taloned onto it, and they showed pink and smooth, with five grabby toes on each one. Then the wings snapped, like a tablecloth in a high wind, and it went churning up again, and away over the tops of the trees, taking the sack of meal with it.

"That's the Ugly Bird," said Mr. Bristow to me, so low I could just about hear him. "Mr. Onselm's been companioning with it ever since I could recollect."

"Such a sort of bird I never before saw," I said. "Must be a right scared-out one. Do you know what struck me while I was a-watching it?"

"Most likely I do know, John. It's got feet look like Mr. Onselm's hands."

"Could it maybe be," I asked, "that a hoodoo man like Mr. Onselm knows what way to shape himself into a bird thing?"

But Mr. Bristow shook his gray head. "It's known that when he's at one place, the Ugly Bird's been sighted at another." He tried to change the subject. "Silver strings on your guitar; I never heard tell of aught but steel strings."

"In the olden days," I told him, "silver was used a many times for strings. It gives a more singy sound."

In my mind I had it made sure that the subject wasn't going to be changed. I tried a chord on my guitar, and began to sing:

"You all have heard of the Ugly Bird
So curious and so queer,
It flies its flight by day and night
And fills folks' hearts with fear."

"John—" Mr. Bristow began to butt in. But I sang on:

"I never came here to hide from fear,
And I give you my promised word
That I soon expect to twist the neck
Of the God damn Ugly Bird."

Mr. Bristow looked sick at me. His hand trembled as it felt in his pocket.

"I wish I could bid you stop and eat with me," he said, "but—here, maybe you better buy you something."

What he gave me was a quarter and a dime. I near about gave them back, but I saw he wanted me to have them. So I thanked him kindly and walked off down the same trail through the trees Mr. Onselm had gone. Mr. Bristow watched me go, looking shrunk up.

Why had my song scared him? I kept singing it:

"O Ugly Bird! O Ugly Bird!
You spy and sneak and thieve!
This place can't be for you and me,
And one of us got to leave."

Singing, I tried to recollect all I'd heard or read or guessed that might could help toward studying out what the Ugly Bird was.

Didn't witch folks have partner animals? I'd read, and I'd heard tell, about the animals called familiars. Mostly they were cats or black dogs or such matter as that, but sometimes they were birds.

That might could be the secret, or a right much of it. For the Ugly Bird wasn't Mr. Onselm, changed by witching so he could fly. Mr. Bristow had said the two of them were seen different places at one and the same time. So Mr. Onselm could no way turn himself into the Ugly Bird. They were close partners, no more. Brothers. With the Ugly Bird's feet looking like Mr. Onselm's pink hands.

I was ware of something up in the sky, the big black V of something that flew. It quartered over me, half as high as the highest scrap of woolly white cloud. Once or twice it made a turn, seemingly like wanting to stoop for me like a hawk for a rabbit; but it didn't do any such. Looking up at it and letting my feet find the trail on their own way, I rounded a bunch of mountain laurel and there, on a rotten log in the middle of a clearing, sat Mr. Onselm.

His gourd head was sunk down on his thin neck. His elbows set on his crooked knees, and the soft, pink, long hands hid his face, as if he felt miserable. The look of him made me feel disgusted. I came walking close to him.

"You don't feel so brash, do you?" I asked him.

"Go away," he sort of gulped, soft and tired and sick.

"What for?" I wanted to know. "I like it here." Sitting on the log next to him, I pulled my guitar across me. "I feel like singing, Mr. Onselm."

I made it up again, word by word as I sang it:

"His father got hung for hog stealing,
His mother got burnt for a witch,
And his only friend is the Ugly Bird,
The dirty son—"

Something hit me like a shooting star, a-slamming down from overhead.

It hit my back and shoulder, and it knocked me floundering forward on one hand and one knee. It was only the mercy of God I didn't fall on my guitar and smash it. I crawled forward a few quick scrambles and made to get up again, shaky and dizzy, to see what had happened.

I saw. The Ugly Bird had flown down and dropped the sack of meal on me. Now it skimmed across the clearing, at the height of the low branches. Its eyes glinted at me, and its mouth came open like a pair of scissors. I saw teeth, sharp and mean, like the teeth of agar fish. Then the Ugly Bird swooped for me, and the wind of its wings was colder than a winter tempest storm.

Without thinking or stopping to think, I flung up my both hands to box it off from me, and it gave back, it flew back from me like the biggest, devilishest humming bird you'd ever see in a nightmare. I was too dizzy and scared to wonder why it pulled off like that; I had barely the wit to be glad it did.

"Get out of here," moaned Mr. Onselm, not stirring from where he sat.

I take shame to say, I got. I kept my hands up and backed across the clearing and to the trail on the far side. Then I halfway thought I knew where my luck had come from. My hands had lifted my guitar up as the Ugly Bird flung itself at me, and some way it hadn't liked the guitar.

Reaching the trail again, I looked back. The Ugly Bird was perching on the log where I'd been sitting. It slaunched along close to Mr. Onselm, sort of nuzzling up to him. Horrible to see, I'll be sworn. They were sure enough close together. I turned and stumbled off away, along the trail down the valley and off toward the pass beyond the valley.

I found a stream, with stones making steps across it. I followed it down to where it made a wide pool. There I got on my knee and washed my face—it looked pale as clabber in the water image—and sat down with my back to a tree and hugged my guitar and had a rest.

I was shaking all over. I must have felt near about as bad for a while as Mr. Onselm had looked to feel, sitting on that rotten log to wait for his Ugly Bird and—what else?

Had he been hungry near to death? Sick? Or maybe had his own evil set back on him? I couldn't rightly say which.

But after a while I felt some better. I got up and walked back to the trail and along it again, till I came to what must have been the only store thereabouts.

It faced one way on a rough gravelly road that could carry wagon traffic, car traffic too if you didn't mind your car getting a good shakeup, and the trail joined on there, right across from the doorway. The building wasn't big but it was good, made of sawed planks, and there was paint on it, well painted on. Its bottom rested on big rocks instead of posts, and it had a roofed open front like a porch, with a bench in there where folks could sit.

Opening the door, I went in. You'll find many such stores in back country places through the land, where folks haven't built their towns up too close. Two-three counters. Shelves of cans and packages. Smoked meat hung up in one corner, a glass-fronted icebox for fresh meat in another. Barrels here and there, for beans or meal or potatoes. At the end of one counter, a sign says U.S. POST OFFICE, and there's a set of maybe half a dozen pigeonholes to put letters in, and a couple of cigar boxes for stamps and money order blanks. That's the kind of place it was.

The proprietor wasn't in just then. Only a girl, scared and shaky back of the counter, and Mr. Onselm, there ahead of me, a-telling her what it was he wanted.

He wanted her.

"I don't care a shuck if Sam Heaver did leave you in charge here," he said with the music in his voice. "He won't stop my taking you with me."

Then he heard me come in, and he swung round and fixed his squint eye and his wide-open eye on me, like two mis-matched gun muzzles. "You again," he said.

He looked right hale and hearty again. I strayed my hands over the guitar's silver strings, just enough to hear, and he twisted up his face as if it colicked him.

"Winnie," he told the girl, "wait on this stranger and get him out of here."

Her round eyes were scared in her scared face. I thought inside myself that seldom I'd seen as sweet a face as hers, or as scared a one. Her hair was dark and thick. It was like the thundercloud before the rain comes down. It made her paleness look paler. She was small and slim, and she cowered there, for fear of Mr. Onselm and what he'd been saying to her.

"Yes, sir?" she said to me, hushed and shaky.

"A box of crackers, please, ma'am," I decided, pointing to where they were on the shelf behind her. "And a can of those little sardine fish."

She put them on the counter for me. I dug out the quarter Mr. Bristow had given me up the trail, and slapped it down on the counter top between the scared girl and Mr. Onselm.

"Get away!" he squeaked, shrill and sharp and mean as a bat. When I looked at him, he'd jumped back, almost halfway across the floor from the counter. And for just once, his both eyes were big and wide.

"Why, Mr. Onselm, what's the matter?" I wondered him, and I purely was wondering. "This is a good quarter."

I picked it up and held it out for him to take and study.

But he flung himself around, and he ran out of that store like a rabbit. A rabbit with dogs running it down.

The girl he'd called Winnie just leaned against the wall as if she was bone tired. I asked her: "Why did he light out like that?"

I gave her the quarter, and she took it. "That money isn't a scary thing, is it?" I asked.

"It doesn't much scare me," she said, and rang it up on the old cash register. "All that scares me is—Mr. Onselm."

I picked up the box of crackers and sardines. "Is he courting you?"

She shivered, although it was warm in the store. "I'd sooner be in a hole with a snake than be courted by Mr. Onselm."

"Then why not just tell him to leave you be?"

"He wouldn't hark at that," she said. "He always just does what pleasures him. Nobody dares to stop him."

"So I've heard tell," I nodded. "About the mules he stopped where they stood, and the poor old lady he struck dumb." I returned to the other thing we'd been talking. "But what made him squinch away from that money piece? I'd reckon he loved money."

She shook her head, and the thundercloud hair stirred. "Mr. Onselm never needs any money. He takes what he wants, without paying for it."

"Including you?" I asked.

"Not including me yet." She shuddered again. "He reckons to do that later on."

I put down my dime I had left from what Mr. Bristow had gifted me. "Let's have a coke drink together, you and me."

She rang up the dime, too. There was a sort of dried-out chuckle at the door, like a stone flung rattling down a deep dark well. I looked quick, and I saw two long, dark wings flop away outside. The Ugly Bird had come to spy what we were doing.

But the girl Winnie hadn't seen, and she smiled over her coke drink. I asked her permission to open my fish and crackers on the bench outside. She said I could. Out there, I worried open the can with that little key that comes with it, and had my meal. When I'd finished I put the empty can and cracker box in a garbage barrel and tuned my guitar.

Hearing that, Winnie came out. She told me how to make my way to the pass and on beyond to Hark Mountain. Of the Bottomless Pool she'd heard some talk, though she'd never been to it. Then she harked while I picked the music and sang the song about the girl whose hair was like the thundercloud before the rain comes down. Harking, Winnie blushed till she was pale no more.

Then we talked about Mr. Onselm and the Ugly Bird, and how they had been seen in two different places at once. "But," said Winnie, "nobody's ever seen the two of them together."

"I have," I told her. "And not an hour back."

And I related about how Mr. Onselm had sat, all sick and miserable, on that rotten log, and how the Ugly Bird had lighted beside him and crowded up to him.

She was quiet to hear all about it, with her eyes staring off, the way she might be looking for something far away. When I was done, she said: "John, you tell me it crowded right up to him."

"It did that thing," I said again. "You'd think it was studying how to crawl right inside him."

"Inside him!"

"That's the true fact."

She kept staring off, and thinking.

"Makes me recollect something I heard somebody say once about hoodoo folks," she said after a time. "How there's hoodoo folks can sometimes put a sort of stuff out, mostly in a dark room. And the stuff is part of them, but it can take the shape and mind of some other person—and once in a while, the shape and mind of an animal."

"Shoo," I said, "now you mention it, I've heard some talk of the same thing. And somebody reckoned it might could explain those Louisiana stories about the were-wolves."

"The shape and mind of an animal," she repeated herself. "Maybe the shape and mind of a bird. And that stuff, they call it echo—no, ecto—ecto—"

"Ectoplasm." I remembered the word. "That's it. I've even seen a book with pictures in it, they say were taken of such stuff. And it seems to be alive. It'll yell if you grab it or hit it or stab at it or like that."

"Couldn't maybe—" Winnie began, but a musical voice interrupted.

"I say he's been around here long enough," Mr. Onselm was telling somebody.

Back he came. Behind him were three men, Mr. Bristow was one, and there was likewise a tall, gawky man with wide shoulders and a black-stubbly chin, and behind him a soft, smooth-grizzled old man with an old fancy vest over his white shirt.

Mr. Onselm was like the leader of a posse. "Sam Heaver," he crooned at the soft grizzled one, "do you favor having tramps come and loaf around your store?"

The soft old storekeeper looked at me, dead and gloomy. "You better get going, son," he said, as if he'd memorized it.

I laid my guitar on the bench beside me, very careful of it. "You men ail my stomach," I said, looking at them, from one to the next to the next. "You come at the whistle of this half-born, half-bred witch-man. You let him sic you on me like dogs, when I'm hurting nobody and nothing."

"Better go," said the old storekeeper again.

I stood up and faced Mr. Onselm, ready to fight him. He just laughed at me, like a sweetly played horn.

"You," he said, "without a dime in your pocket! What are you a-feathering up about? You can't do anything to anybody."

Without a dime . . .

But I had a dime. I'd spent it for the coke drinks for Winnie and me. And the Ugly Bird had spied in to see me spend it, my silver money, the silver money that scared and ailed Mr. Onselm . . .

"Take his guitar, Hobe." Mr. Onselm said an order, and the gawky man moved, clumsy but quick and grabbed my guitar off the bench and backed away to the inner door.

"There," said Mr. Onselm, sort of purring, "that takes care of him."

He fairly jumped, too, and grabbed Winnie by her wrist. He pulled her along out of the porch toward the trail, and I heard her whimper.

"Stop him!" I yelled out, but the three of them stood and looked, scared to move or say a word. Mr. Onselm, still holding Winnie with one hand, faced me. He lifted his other hand and stuck out the pink forefinger at me, like the barrel of a pistol.

Just the look his two eyes, squint and wide, gave me made me weary and dizzy to my bones. He was gong to witch me, as he'd done the mules, as he'd done the woman who'd tried to hide her cake from him. I turned away from his gaze, sick and—sure, I was afraid. And I heard him giggle, thinking he'd won already. I took a step, and I was next to that gawky fellow named Hobe, who held my guitar.

I made a quick long jump and started to wrestle it away from him.

"Hang onto that thing; Hobe!" I heard Mr. Onselm sort of choke out, and, from Mr. Bristow:

"Take care, there's the Ugly Bird!"

Its big dark wings flapped like a storm in the air just behind me. But I'd shoved my elbow into Hobe's belly-pit and I'd torn my guitar from his hands, and I turned on my heel to face what was being brought upon me.

A little way off in the open, Mr. Onselm stood stiff and straight as a stone figure in front of an old court house. He still held Winnie by the wrist. Right betwixt them came a-swooping the Ugly Bird at me, the ugliest ugly of all, its long sharp beak pointing for me like a sticky knife.

I dug my toes and smashed my guitar at it. I swung the way a player swings a ball bat at a pitched ball. Full-slam I struck its bulgy head, right above that sharp beak and across its two eyes, and I heard the loud noise as the polished wood of my music-maker crashed to splinters.

Oh, gentlemen, and down went that Ugly Bird!

Down it went, falling just short of the porch.

Quiet it lay.

Its great big feathered wings stretched out either side, without any flutter to them. Its beak was driven into the ground like a nail. It didn't kick or flop or stir once.

But Mr. Onselm, where he stood holding Winnie, screamed out the way he might scream if something had clawed out all his insides with one single tearing dig and grab.

He didn't move. I don't even know if his mouth came rightly open to make that scream. Winnie gave a pull with all the strength she had, and tottered back, loose from him. Then, as if only his hold on her had kept him standing, Mr. Onselm slapped right over and dropped down on his face, his arms flung out like the Ugly Bird's wings, his face in the dirt like the Ugly Bird's face.

Still holding onto my broken guitar by the neck, like a club, I walked quick over to him and stooped. "Get up," I bade him, and took hold of what hair he had and lifted up his face to look at it.

One look was a plenty. From the war, I know a dead man when I see one. I let go Mr. Onselm's hair, and his face went back into the dirt the way you'd know it belonged there.

The other men moved at last, slow and tottery like old men. And they didn't act like my enemies now, for Mr. Onselm who'd made them act thataway was down and dead.

Then Hobe gave a sort of shaky scared shout, and we looked where he was looking.

The Ugly Bird looked all of a sudden rotten and mushy, and while we saw that, it was soaking into the ground. To me, anyhow, its body had seemed to turn shadowy and misty, and I could see through it, to pebbles on the ground beneath. I moved close, though I didn't relish moving. The Ugly Bird was melting away, like dirty snow on top of a hot stove; only no wetness left behind.

It was gone, while we watched and wondered and felt bad all over, and at the same time glad to see it go. Nothing left but the hole punched in the dirt by its beak. I stepped closer yet, and with my shoe I stamped the hole shut.

Then Mr. Bristow kneeled on his knee and turned Mr. Onselm over. On the dead face ran lines across, thin and purple, as though he'd been struck down by a blow from a toaster or a gridiron.

"Why," said Mr. Bristow. "Why, John, them's the marks of your guitar strings." He looked up at me. "Your silver guitar strings."

"Silver?" said the storekeeper. "Is them strings silver? Why, friends, silver finishes a hoodoo man."

That was it. All of us remembered that at once.

"Sure enough," put in Hobe. "Ain't it a silver bullet that it takes to kill a witch, or hanging or burning? And a silver knife to kill a witch's cat?"

"And a silver key locks out ghosts, doesn't it?" said Mr. Bristow, getting up to stand among us again.

I looked at my broken guitar and the dangling strings of silver.

"What was the word you said?" Winnie whispered to me.

"Ectoplasm," I replied her. "Like his soul coming out of him—and getting itself struck dead outside his body."

Then there was talk, more important, about what to do now. The men did the deciding. They allowed to report to the county seat that Mr. Onselm's heart had stopped on him, which was what it had done, after all. They went over the tale three-four times, to make sure they'd all tell it the same. They cheered up while they talked it. You couldn't ever call for a bunch of gladder folks to get shed of a neighbor.

Then they tried to say their thanks to me.

"John," said Mr. Bristow, "we'd all of us sure enough be proud and happy if you'd stay here. You took his curse off us, and we can't never thank you enough."

"Don't thank me," I said. "I was fighting for my life."

Hobe said he wanted me to come live on his farm and help him work it on half shares. Sam Heaver offered me all the money he had in his old cash register. I thanked them. To each I said, no, sir, thank you kindly, I'd better not. If they wanted their tale to sound true to the sheriff and the coroner, they'd better help it along by forgetting that I'd ever been around when Mr. Onselm's heart stopped. Anyhow, I meant to go look at that Bottomless Pool. All I was truly sorry about was my guitar had got broken.

But while I was saying all that, Mr. Bristow had gone running off. Now he came back, with a guitar he'd had at his place, and he said he'd be honored if I'd take it instead of mine. It was a good guitar, had a fine tone. So I put my silver strings on it and tightened and tuned them, and tried a chord or two.

Winnie swore by all that was pure and holy she'd pray for me by name each night of her life, and I told her that that would sure enough see me safe from any assault of the devil.

"Assault of the devil, John!" she said, almost shrill in the voice, she meant it so truly. "It's been you who drove the devil from out this valley."

And the others all said they agreed her on that.

"It was foretold about you in the Bible," said Winnie, her voice soft again. "There was a man sent from God, whose name was John—"

But that was far too much for her to say, and she dropped her sweet dark head down, and I saw her mouth tremble and two tears sneak down her cheeks. And I was that abashed, I said goodbye all around in a hurry.

Off I walked toward where the pass would be, strumming my new guitar as I walked. Back into my mind I got an old, old song. I've heard tell that the song's written down in an old-timey book called *Percy's Frolics,* or *Relics,* or some such name:

"Lady, I never loved witchcraft,
Never dealt in privy wile,
But evermore held the high way
Of love and honor, free from guile. . . ."

And though I couldn't bring myself to look back yonder to the place I was leaving forever, I knew that Winnie was a-watching me, and that she listened, listened, till she had to strain her ears to catch the last, faintest end of my song.

THE FOOL

BY DAVID DRAKE

THOUGH PRIMARILY KNOWN AS AN AUTHOR OF MILITARY SCIENCE FICTION, DAVID DRAKE HAS ALSO WRITTEN NUMEROUS SUBSTANTIAL FANTASIES, INCLUDING *DRAGONLORD*, A SORT OF MARTIAL ARTHURIAN, AND THE MASTERFUL EPIC SERIES *LORD OF THE ISLES*.

HIS "OLD NATHAN" STORIES (OF WHICH "THE FOOL" IS ONE) ARE ALMOST DIRECT DESCENDANTS OF WELLMAN'S "SILVER JOHN" THOUGH DRAKE'S MOUNTAIN-HERMIT WIZARD-SHAMAN IS A BIT MORE RURALLY REALISTIC AND SCARY THAN THE MUSICAL BALLADEER.

"Now jest ignore him," said the buck to the doe as Old Nathan turned in the furrow he was hoeing twenty yards ahead of them.

"But he's *looking* at us," whispered the doe from the side of her mouth. She stood frozen, but a rapidly pulsing artery made shadows quiver across her throat in the evening sun.

"G'wan away!" called Old Nathan, but his voice sounded halfhearted even in his own ears. He lifted the hoe and shook it. A hot afternoon cultivating was the best medicine the cunning man knew for his aches . . . but the work did not become less tiring because it did him good. "Git, deer!"

"See, it's all right," said the buck as he lowered his head for another mouthful of turnip greens.

Old Nathan stooped for a clod to hurl at them. As he straightened with it the deer turned in unison and fled in great floating bounds, their heads thrust forward.

"Consarn it," muttered the cunning man, crumbling the clod between his long, knobby fingers as he watched the animals disappear into the woods beyond his plowland.

"Hi there," called a voice from behind him, beside his cabin back across the creek.

Old Nathan turned, brushing his hand against his pants leg of coarse homespun. His distance sight was as good as it ever had been, so even at the length of a decent rifleshot he had no trouble in identifying his visitor as Eldon Bowsmith. Simp Bowsmith, they called the boy down to the settlement . . . and they had reason, though the boy was more an innocent than a natural in the usual sense.

"Hi!" Bowsmith repeated, waving with one hand while the other shaded his eyes from the low sun. "There wuz two *deer* in the field jist now!"

They had reason, that was sure as the sunrise.

"Hold there," Old Nathan called as the boy started down the path to the creek and the field beyond. "I'm headed back myself." Shouldering his hoe, he suited his action to his words.

Bowsmith nodded and plucked a long grass stem. He began to chew on the soft white base of it while he leaned on the fence of the pasture which had once held a bull and two milk cows . . . and now held the cows alone. The animals, startled at first into watchfulness, returned to chewing their cud when they realized that the stranger's personality was at least as placid as their own.

Old Nathan crossed the creek on the puncheon that served as a bridge—a log of red oak, adzed flat on the top side. A fancier structure would have been pointless, because spring freshets were sure to carry *any* practicable bridge downstream once or twice a year. The simplest form of crossing was both easily replaced and adequate to the cunning man's needs.

As he climbed the sloping path to his cabin with long, slow strides, Old Nathan studied his visitor. Bowsmith was tall, as tall as the cunning man himself, and perhaps as gangling. Age had shrunk Old Nathan's flesh over its framework of bone and sinew to accentuate angles, but there was little real difference in build between the two men save for the visitor's greater juiciness.

Bowsmith's most distinguishing characteristic—the factor that permitted Old Nathan to recognize him from two hundred yards away—was his hair. It was a nondescript brown in color, but the way it stood out in patches of varying length was unmistakable. It looked as if the boy had cut it himself, using a knife.

The cunning man realized he must have been staring when Bowsmith said with an apologetic grin, "There hain't a mirror et my place, ye see. I do what I kin with a bucket uv water."

"Makes no matter with me," Old Nathan muttered. Nor should it have, and he was embarrassed that his thoughts were so transparent. He'd been late to the line hisself when they give out good looks. "Come in 'n set, and you kin tell me what brought ye here."

Bowsmith tossed to the ground his grass stem—chewed all the way to the harsh green blades—and hesitated as if to pluck another before entering the cabin. " 'Bliged t'ye," he said and, in the event, followed Old Nathan without anything to occupy his hands.

The doors, front and back, of the foursquare cabin were open when the visitor arrived, but he had walked around instead of through the structure on his way to find the cunning man. Now he stared at the interior, his look of anticipation giving way to disappointment at the lack of exotic trappings.

There were two chairs, a stool, and a table, all solidly fitted but shaped by a broadaxe and spokeshave rather than a lathe. The bed was of similar workmanship, with a rope frame and corn-shuck mattress. The quilted coverlet was decorated with a Tree-of-Life appliqué of exceptional quality, but there were women in the county who could at least brag that they could stitch its equal.

A shelf set into the wall above the bed held six books, and two chests flanked the fireplace. The chests, covered in age-blackened leather and iron-bound, could bear dark imaginings—but they surely did not require such. Five china cups and a plate stood on the fireboard where every cabin but the poorest displayed similar knick-knacks; and the rifle pegged to the wall above them would have been unusual only by its absence.

"Well . . . ," Bowsmith murmured, turning his head slowly in his survey. He had expected to feel awe, and lacking that, he did not, his tongue did not know quite how to proceed. Then, on the wall facing the fireplace, he finally found something worthy of amazed comment. "Well . . . ," he said, pointing to the strop of black bullhide. The bull's tail touched the floor, while the nose lifted far past the rafters to brush the roof peak. "What en tarnation's *thet?*"

"Bull I onct hed," Old Nathan said gruffly, answering the boy as he might not have done with anyone who was less obviously an open-eyed innocent.

"Well," the boy repeated, this time in a tone of agreement. But his brow furrowed again and he asked, "But how come ye *keep* hit?"

Old Nathan grimaced and, seating himself in the rocker, pointed Bowsmith to the upright chair. "Set," he ordered.

But there was no harm in the lad, so the older man explained, "I could bring him back, I could. Don't choose to, is all, cuz hit'd cost too much. There's a price for ever'thing, and I reckon that 'un's more thin the gain."

"Well," said the boy, beaming now that he was sure Old Nathan wasn't angry with him after all.

He sat down on the chair as directed and ran a hand through his hair while he paused to collect his thoughts. Bowsmith must be twenty-five or near it, but the cunning man was sure that he would halve his visitor's age if he had nothing to go by except voice and diction.

"Ma used t' barber me 'fore she passed on last year," the boy said in embarrassment renewed by the touch of his ragged scalp. "Mar' Beth Neill, she tried the onct, but hit wuz worser'n what I done."

He smiled wanly at the memory, tracing his fingers down the center of his scalp. "Cut me bare, right along here," he said. "*Land* but people laughed. She hed t' laugh herself."

"Yer land lies hard by the Neill clan's, I b'lieve?" the cunning man said with his eyes narrowing.

"Thet's so," agreed Bowsmith, bobbing his head happily. "We're great friends, thim en me, since Ma passed on." He looked down at the floor, grinning fiercely, and combed the fingers of both hands through his hair as if to shield the memories that were dancing through his skull. "Specially Mar' Beth, I reckon."

"First I heard," said Old Nathan, "thet any uv Baron Neill's clan wuz a friend to ary soul but kin by blood er by marriage . . . and I'd heard they kept marriage pretty much in the clan besides."

Bowsmith looked up expectantly, though he said nothing. Perhaps he hadn't understood the cunning man's words, though they'd been blunt enough in all truth.

Old Nathan sighed and leaned back in his rocker. "No matter, boy, no matter," he said. "Tell me what it is ez brings ye here."

The younger man grimaced and blinked as he considered the request, which he apparently expected to be confusing. His brow cleared again in beaming delight and he said, "Why, I'm missin' my plowhorse, and I heard ye could find sich things. Horses what strayed."

Lives next to the Neill clan and thinks his horse strayed, the cunning man thought. Strayed right through the wall of a locked barn, no doubt. He frowned like thunder as he considered the ramifications, for the boy and for himself, if he provided the help requested.

"The Bar'n tried t' hep me find Jen," volunteered Bowsmith. "Thet's my horse. He knows about findin' and sichlike, too, from old books. . . ." He turned, uncomfortably, to glance at the volumes on the shelf here.

"I'd heard thet about the Baron," said Old Nathan grimly.

"But it wuzn't no good," the boy continued. "He says, the Bar'n does, must hev been a painter et Jen." He shrugged and scrunched his face up under pressure of an emotion the cunning man could not identify from the expression alone. "So I reckon thet's so . . . but she wuz a good ol' horse, Jen wuz, and it don't seem right somehows t' leave her bones out in the woods thet way. I thought maybe . . . ?"

Well, by God if there was one, and by Satan who was as surely loose in the world as the Neill clan—and the Neills' good evidence for the Devil—Old Nathan wasn't going to pass this by. Though *finding* the horse would be dangerous, and there was no need for that. . . .

"All right, boy," said the cunning man as he stood up. The motion of his muscles helped him find the right words, sometimes, so he walked toward the fireplace alcove. "Don't ye be buryin' yer Jen till she's dead, now. I reckon I kin bring her home fer ye."

A pot of vegetables had been stewing all afternoon on the banked fire. Old Nathan pivoted to the side the prong holding the pot and set a knot of pitchy lightwood on the coals. "Now," he continued, stepping away from the fire so that when the pine knot flared up its sparks would not spatter him, "you fetch me hair from Jen, her mane and her tail partikalarly. Ye kin find thet, cain't ye, clingin' in yer barn and yer fences?"

Bowsmith leaped up happily, "Why, sure I kin," he said. "Thet's all ye need?" Then his face darkened. "There's one thing, though," he said, then swallowed to prime his voice for what he had to admit next. "I've a right strong back, and I reckon there hain't much ye kin put me to around yer fields here ez I cain't do fer ye. But I hain't got money t' pay ye, and since Ma passed on"—he swallowed again—"seems like ever' durn thing we owned, I cain't find whur I put it. So effen my labor's not enough fer ye, I don't know what I could give."

The boy met Old Nathan's eyes squarely and there weren't many folk who would do that, for fear that the cunning man would draw out the very secrets of their hearts. Well, Simp Bowsmith didn't seem to have any secrets; and perhaps there were worse ways to be.

"Don't trouble yerself with thet," said Old Nathan aloud, "until we fetch yer horse back."

The cunning man watched the boy tramping cheerfully back up the trail, unconcerned by the darkness and without even a stick against the threat of bears and cougars which would keep his neighbors from traveling at night. Hard to believe, sometimes, that the same world held that boy and the Neill clan besides.

A thought struck him. "Hoy!" he called, striding to the edge of his porch to shout up the trail. "Eldon Bowsmith!"

"Sir?" wound the boy's reply from the dark. He must already be to the top of the knob, among the old beeches that were its crown.

"Ye bring me a nail from a shoe Jen's cast besides," Old Nathan called back. "D'ye hear me?"

"Yessir."

"Still, we'll make a fetch from the hair first, and thet hed ought t'do the job," the cunning man muttered; but his brow was furrowing as he considered consequences, things that would happen despite him and things that he—needs must—would initiate.

"I BRUNG YE WHAT YE CALLED FER," said Bowsmith, sweating and cheerful from his midday hike. His whistling had announced him as soon as he topped the knob, the happiest rendition of "Bonny Barbry Allen" Old Nathan had heard in all his born days.

The boy held out a gob of gray-white horsehair in one hand and a tapered horseshoe nail in the other. Then his eyes lighted on movement in a corner of the room, the cat slinking under the bedstead.

"Oh!" said Bowsmith, kneeling and setting the nail on the floor to be able to extend his right hand toward the animal. "Ye've a cat. Here, pretty boy. Here, handsome." He clucked his tongue.

"Hain't much fer strangers, that 'un," said Old Nathan, and the cat promptly made a liar of him by flowing back from cover and flopping down in front of Bowsmith to have his belly rubbed.

"Oh," said the cat, "he's all right, ain't he," as he gripped the boy's wrist with his forepaws and tugged it down to his jaws.

"Watch—" the cunning man said in irritation to one or the other, he wasn't sure which. The pair of them ignored him, the cat purring in delight and closing his jaws so that the four long canines dimpled the boy's skin but did not threaten to puncture it.

Bowsmith looked up in sudden horror.

"Don't stop, damn ye!" growled the cat and kicked a knuckle with a hind paw.

"Is he . . . ?" the boy asked. "I mean, I thought he wuz a cat, but . . . ?"

"He's a cat, sure ez I'm a man"—Old Nathan snapped. He had started to add—"and you're a durn fool," but that was too close to the truth, and there was no reason to throw it in Bowsmith's face because he made up to Old Nathan's cat better than the cunning man himself generally did.

"Spilesport," grumbled the cat as he rolled to his feet and stalked out the door.

"Oh well," said the boy, rising and then remembering to pick up the horseshoe nail. "I wouldn't want, you know, t' trifle with yer familiars, coo."

"Don't hold with sich," the cunning man retorted. Then a thought occurred to him and he added, "Who is it been tellin' ye about familiar spirits and sechlike things?"

"Well," admitted the boy, and "admit" was the right word for there was embarrassment in his voice, "I reckon the Bar'n might could hev said somethin'. He knows about thet sort uv thing."

"Well, ye brung the horsehair," said Old Nathan softly, his green eyes slitted over the thoughts behind them. He took the material from the boy's hand and carried it with him to the table.

The first task was to sort the horsehair—long white strands from the tail; shorter but equally coarse bits of mane; and combings from the hide itself, matted together and gray-hued. The wad was more of a blur to his eyes than it was even in kinky reality. Sighing, the old man started up to get his spectacles from one of the chests.

Then, pausing, he had a better idea. He turned and gestured Bowsmith to the straight chair at the table. "Set there and sort the pieces fer length," he said gruffly.

The cunning man was harsh because he was angry at the signs that he was aging; angry that the boy was too great a fool to see how he was being preyed upon; and angry that he, Old Nathan the Devil's Master, should care about the fate of one fool more in a world that already had a right plenty of such.

"Yessir," said the boy, jumping to obey with such clumsy alacrity that his thigh bumped the table and slid the solid piece several inches along the floor. "And thin what do we do?"

Bowsmith's fingers were deft enough, thought Old Nathan as he stepped back a pace to watch. "No *we* about it, boy," said the cunning man. "You spin it to a bridle whilst I mebbe say some words t' help."

Long hairs from the tail to form the reins; wispy headbands and throat latch bent from the mane, and the whole felted together at each junction by tufts of gray hair from the hide.

"And I want ye t' think uv yer Jen as ye do thet, boy," Old Nathan said aloud while visions of the coming operation drifted through his mind. "Jest ez t'night ye'll think uv her as ye set in her stall, down on four legs like a beast yerself, and ye wear this bridle you're makin'. And ye'll call her home, so ye will, and thet'll end the matter, I reckon."

" 'Bliged t' ye, sir," said Eldon Bowsmith, glancing up as he neared the end of the sorting. There was no more doubt in his eyes than a more sophisticated visitor would have expressed at the promise the sun would rise.

Old Nathan wished he were as confident. He especially wished that he were confident the Neill clan would let matters rest when their neighbor had his horse back.

OLD NATHAN WAS TOSSING the dirt with which he had just scoured his cookware off the side of the porch the next evening when he saw Bowsmith trudging back down the trail. The boy was not whistling, and his head was bent despondently.

His right hand was clenched. Old Nathan knew, as surely as if he could see it, that Bowsmith was bringing back the fetch bridle.

"Come and set," the cunning man called, rising and flexing the muscles of his back as if in preparation to shoulder a burden.

"Well," the boy said, glumly but without the reproach Old Nathan had expected, "I reckon I'm in a right pickle now," as he mounted the pair of steps to the porch.

The two men entered the cabin; Old Nathan laid another stick of lightwood on the fire. It was late afternoon in the flatlands, but here in the forested hills the sun had set and the glow of the sky was dim even outdoors.

"I *tried* t' do what ye said," Bowsmith said, fingering his scalp with his free hand, "but someways I must hev gone wrong like usual."

The cat, alerted by voices, dropped from the rafters to the floor with a loud thump. "Good t' see ye agin," the animal said as he curled, tail high, around the boots of the younger man. Even though Bowsmith could not understand the words as such, he knelt and began kneading the cat's fur while much of the frustrated distress left his face.

"Jen didn't fetch t' yer summons, thin?" the cunning man prodded. Durn fool, durn cat, durn *nonsense*. He set down the pot he carried with a clank, not bothering at present to rinse it with a gourdful of water.

"Worsen thet," the boy explained. "I brung the ol' mule from Neills', and wuzn't they mad ez *hops*." He looked up at the cunning man. "The Bar'n wuz right ready t' hev the sheriff on me fer horse stealin', even thoughs he's a great good friend t' me."

The boy's brow clouded with misery, then cleared into the same beatific, full-face smile Old Nathan had seen cross it before. "Mar' Beth, though, she quietened him. She told him I hadn't meant t' take their mule, and thet I'd clear off the track uv newground they been meanin' t' plant down on Cane Creek."

"You figger t' do thet?" the cunning man asked sharply. "Clear cane-brake fer the Neill clan, whin there's ten uv thim and none willin' t' break his back with sich a chore?"

"Why I reckon hit's the least I could do," Bowsmith answered in surprise. "Why, I took their mule, didn't I?"

Old Nathan swallowed his retort, but the taste of the words soured his mouth. "Let's see the fetch bridle," he said instead, reaching out his hand.

The cunning man knelt close by the spluttering fire to examine the bridle while his visitor continued to play with the cat in mutual delight. The bridle was well made, as good a job as Old Nathan himself could have done with his spectacles on.

It was a far more polished piece than the bridle Eldon Bowsmith had carried off the day before, and the hairs from which it was hand-spun were brown and black.

"Where'd ye stop yestiddy, on yer way t' home?" Old Nathan demanded.

Bowsmith popped upright, startling the cat out the door with an angry curse. "Now, how did *you* know thet?" he said—in amazement, and in delight at being amazed.

"Boy, boy," the cunning man said, shaking his head. He was too astounded at such innocence even to snarl in frustration. "Where'd ye stop?"

"Well, I reckon I might uv met Mary Beth Neill," Bowsmith said, tousling his hair like a dog scratching his head with a forepaw. "They're right friendly folk, the Neills, so's they hed me stay t' supper."

"Where you told thim all about the fetch bridle, didn't ye?" Old Nathan snapped, angry at last.

"Did I?" said the boy in open-eyed wonder. "Why, not so's I kin recolleck, sir . . . but I reckon ef you say I did, thin—"

Old Nathan waved the younger man to silence. Bowsmith might have blurted the plan to the Neills and not remember doing so. Equally, a mind less subtle than Baron Neill's might have drawn the whole story from a mere glimpse of the bridle woven of Jen's hair. That the Neill patriarch had been able to counter in the way he had done suggested he was deeper into the lore than Old Nathan would otherwise have believed.

"Well, what's done is done," said the cunning man as he stepped to the fireboard. "Means we need go a way I'd not hev gone fer choice."

He took the horseshoe nail from where he had lodged it, beside the last in line of his five china cups. He wouldn't have asked the boy to bring the nail if he hadn't expected—or at least feared—such a pass. If Baron Neill chose to raise the stakes, then that's what the stakes would be.

Old Nathan set the nail back, for the nonce. There was a proper bed of coals banked against the wall of the fireplace now during the day. The cunning man chose two splits of hickory and set them sharp-edge down on the ashes and bark-sides close together. When the clinging wood fibers ignited, the flames and the blazing gases they drove out would be channeled up between the flats to lick the air above the log in blue lambency. For present purposes, that would be sufficient.

"Well, come on, thin, boy," the cunning man said to his visitor. "We'll git a rock fer en anvil from the crik and some other truck, and thin we'll forge ye a pinter t' pint out yer horse. Wheriver she be."

OLD NATHAN HAD CHOSEN for the anvil an egg of sandstone almost the size of a man's chest. It was at a good location for easy lifting, standing clear of the streambed on a pedestal of limestone blocks from which all the sand and lesser gravel had been sluiced away since the water was speeded by constriction.

For all that the rock's placement was a good one, Old Nathan had thought that its weight might be too much for Bowsmith to carry up to the cabin. The boy had not hesitated, however, to wade into the stream running to mid-thigh and raise the egg with the strength of his arms and shoulders alone.

Bowsmith walked back out of the stream, feeling cautiously for his footing but with no other sign of the considerable weight he balanced over his head. He paused a moment on the low bank, where mud squelched from between his bare toes. Then he resumed his steady stride, pacing up the path.

Old Nathan had watched to make sure the boy could handle the task set him. As a result, he had to rush to complete his own part of the business in time to reach the cabin when Bowsmith did.

A flattened pebble, fist-sized and handfilling, would do nicely for the hammer. It was a smaller bit of the same dense sandstone that the cunning man had chosen for the anvil. He tossed it down beside a clump of alders and paused with his eyes closed. His fingers crooked, groping for the knife he kept in a place he could "see" only within his skull.

It was there where it should be, a jackknife with two blades of steel good enough to accept a razor edge—which was how Old Nathan kept the shorter one. His fingers closed on the yellow bone handle and drew the knife out into the world that he and others watched with their eyes.

The cunning man had never been sure where it was that he put his knife. Nor, for that matter, would he have bet more than he could afford to lose that the little tool would be there the next time he sought it. Thus far, it always had been. That was all he knew.

He opened the longer blade, the one sharpened to a 30° angle, and held the edge against a smooth-barked alder stem that was of about the same diameter as his thumb. Old Nathan's free hand gripped the alder above the intended cut, and a single firm stroke of the knife severed the stem at a slant across the tough fibers.

Whistling himself—"The Twa Corbies," in contrast to Bowsmith's rendition of "Bonny Barbry Allen" on the path ahead—Old Nathan strode back to the cabin. The split hickory should be burning to just the right extent by now.

"And I'll set down on his white neck bone," the cunning man sang aloud as he trimmed the alder's branches away, "T' pluck his eyes out one and one."

The Neill clan had made their bed. Now they could sleep in it with the sheriff.

"GITTIN' RIGHT HOT," said Bowsmith as he squatted and squinted at the nail he had placed on the splits according to the cunning man's direction. "Reckon the little teensie end's so hot hit's nigh yaller t' look et."

Old Nathan gripped the trimmed stem with both hands and twisted as he folded it, so that the alder doubled at the notch he had cut in the middle. What had been a yard-long wand was now a pair of tongs with which the cunning man bent to grip the heated nail by its square head.

"Ready now," he directed. "Remember thet you're drawin' out the iron druther thin bangin' hit flat."

"Wisht we hed a proper sledge," the boy said. He slammed the smaller stone accurately onto the glowing nail the instant Old Nathan's tongs laid it on the anvil stone.

Sparks hissed from the nail in red anger, though the sound of the blow was a *clock!* rather than a ringing crash. A dimple near the tip of the nail brightened to orange. Before it had faded, the boy struck again. Old Nathan turned the workpiece 90° on its axis, and the hand-stone hit it a third time.

While the makeshift hammer was striking, the iron did not appear to change. When the cunning man's tongs laid it back in the blue sheet of hickory flame, however, the workpiece was noticeably longer than the smith had forged it originally.

Old Nathan had been muttering under his breath as the boy hammered. They were forging the scale on the face of the nail into the fabric of the pointer, amalgamating the proteins of Jen's hoof with the hot iron. Old Nathan murmured, "As least is to great," each time the hammer struck. Now, as the nail heated again, the gases seemed to flow by it in the pattern of a horse's mane.

"Cain't use an iron sledge, boy," the cunning man said aloud. "Not fer this, not though the nail be iron hisself."

He lifted out the workpiece again. "Strike on," he said. "And the tip this time, so's hit's pinted like an awl."

The stone clopped like a horse's hoof and clicked like horses' teeth, while beside them in the chimney corner the fire settled itself with a burbling whicker.

"As least is to great. . . ."

ELDON BOWSMITH'S FACE was sooty from the fire and flushed where runnels of sweat had washed the soot away, but there was a triumphant gleam in his eyes as he prepared to leave Old Nathan's cabin that evening. He held the iron pointer upright in one hand and his opposite index finger raised in balance. The tip of his left ring finger was bandaged with a bit of tow and spiderweb to cover a puncture. The cunning man had drawn three drops of the boy's blood to color the water in which they quenched the iron after its last heating.

"I cain't say how much I figger I'm 'bliged t' ye fer this," said Bowsmith, gazing at the pointer with a fondness inexplicable to anyone who did not know what had gone into creating the instrument.

The bit of iron had been hammered out to the length of a man's third finger. It looked like a scrap of bent wire, curved and recurved by blows from stone onto stone, each surface having a rounded face. The final point had been rolled onto it between the stones, with the boy showing a remarkable delicacy and ability to coordinate his motions with those of the cunning man who held the tongs.

"Don't thank me till ye've got yer Jen back in her stall," said Old Nathan. His mind added, "And not thin, effen the Neills burn ye out and string ye to en oak limb." Aloud he said, "Anyways, ye did the heavy part yerself."

That was true only when limited to the physical portion of what had gone on that afternoon. Were the hammering of primary importance, then every blacksmith would have been a wizard. Old Nathan, too, was panting and worn from exertion; but like Bowsmith, the success he felt at what had been accomplished made the effort worthwhile. He had seen the plowhorse pacing in her narrow stall when steam rose as the iron was quenched.

The boy cocked his head aside and started to comb his fingers through his hair in what Old Nathan had learned was a gesture of embarrassment. He looked from the pointer to his bandaged finger, then began to rub his scalp with the heel of his right hand. "Well . . . ," he said. "I want ye t' know thet I . . ."

Bowsmith grimaced and looked up to meet the eyes of the cunning man squarely. "Lot uv folk," he said, "they wouldn't hev let me hep. They call me Simp, right t' my face they do thet. . . . En, en I reckon there's no harm t' thet, but . . . sir, ye treated me like Ma used to. You air ez good a friend ez I've got in the world, 'ceptin' the Neills."

"So good a friend ez thet?" said the cunning man drily. He had an uncomfortable urge to turn his own face away and comb fingers through his hair.

"Well," he said instead and cleared his throat in order to go on. "Well. Ye remember what I told ye. Ye don't speak uv this t' ary soul. En by the grace uv *yer* Ma in heaven whur she watches ye—"

Old Nathan gripped the boy by both shoulders, and the importance of what he had to get across made emotionally believable words that were not part of the world's truth as the cunning man knew it "—*don't* call t' Jen and foller the pinter to her without ye've the sheriff et yer side. Aye, en ef he wants t' bring half the settlement along t' boot, thin I reckon thet might be a wise notion."

"Ain't goin' t' fail ye this time, sir," promised the boy brightly. "Hit'll all be jist like you say."

He was whistling again as he strode up the hill into the dusk. Old Nathan imagined a cabin burning and a lanky form dangling from a tree beside it.

He spat to avoid the omen.

OLD NATHAN SAT MOROSELY in the chimney corner, reading with his back to the fire, when his cat came in the next night.

"Caught a rabbit nigh on up t' the road," the cat volunteered cheerfully. "Land *sakes* didn't it squeal and thrash."

He threw himself down on the puncheon floor, using Old Nathan's booted foot as a brace while he licked his belly and genitals. "Let it go more times thin I kin count," the cat went on. "When it wouldn't run no more, thin I killed it en et it down t' the head en hide."

"I reckon ye did," said the cunning man. To say otherwise to the cat would be as empty as railing against the sky for what it struck with its thunderbolts. He carefully folded his reading glasses and set them in the crease of his book so that he could stroke the animal's fur.

"Hev ye seen thet young feller what wuz here t'other day?" the cat asked, pawing his master's hand but not—for a wonder—hooking in his claws.

"I hev not," Old Nathan replied flatly. He had ways by which he could have followed Bowsmith's situation or even anticipated it. Such sources of information came with a price, however, and they graved an otherwise fluid future on the stone of reality. He would enter that world of knowledge for others whose perceived need was great enough, but he would not enter it for himself. Old Nathan had experienced no greater horror in his seventy years of life than the certain knowledge of a disaster which he could not change.

"Well," said the cat, "reckon ye'll hev a chanct to purty quick, now. Turned down yer trail, he did, 'bout time I licked off them rabbit guts en come home myself."

"Halloo the house!" called Eldon Bowsmith from beyond the front door, and the cat bit Old Nathan's forearm solidly as the cunning man tried to rise from the rocking chair.

"Bless en *save* ye, cat!" roared the old man, gripping the animal before the hind legs, feeling the warm distended belly squishing with rabbit meat. "Come in, boy," he cried, "come in en set," and he surged upright with the open book in one hand and the cat cursing in the other.

Bowsmith wore a look of such dejection that he scarcely brightened with surprise at the cunning man's incongruous appearance. A black iron pointer dangled from the boy's right hand, and the scrap of bandage had fallen from his left ring finger without being replaced.

"Ev'nin' t' ye, sir," he said to Old Nathan. "Wisht I could say I'd done ez ye told me, but I don't reckon I kin."

When the cat released Old Nathan's forearm, the cunning man let him jump to the floor. The animal promptly began to insinuate himself between Bowsmith's feet and rub the boy's knees with his tailtip, muttering, "Good t' see ye, good thet ye've come."

"Well, you're alive," said Old Nathan, "en you're here, which ain't a bad start fer fixin' sich ez needs t' be fixed. Set yerself en we'll talk about it."

Bowsmith obeyed his host's gesture and seated himself in the rocker, still warm and clicking with the motion of the cunning man rising from it. He held out the pointer but did not look at his host as he explained, "I wint to the settlemint, and I told the sheriff what ye said. He gathered up mebbe half a dozen uv the men thereabouts, all totin' their guns like they wuz en army. En I named Jen, like you said, and this nail, hit like t' pull outen my *hand* it wuz so fierce t' find her."

Old Nathan examined by firelight the pointer he had taken from the boy. He was frowning, and when he measured the iron against his finger the frown became a thundercloud in which the cunning man's eyes were flashes of green lightning. The pointer was a quarter inch longer than the one that had left his cabin the morning before.

"En would ye b'lieve it, but hit took us straight ez straight t' the Neill place?" continued the boy with genuine wonderment in his voice. He shook his head. "I told the sheriff I reckoned there wuz a mistake, but mebbe the Bar'n had found Jen en he wuz keepin' her t' give me whin I next come by."

Bowsmith shook his head again. He laced his fingers together on his lap and stared glumly at them as he concluded, "But I be hanged ef thet same ol' spavined mule warn't tied t' the door uv the barn, and the pinter wouldn't leave afore it touched hit's hoof." He sucked in his lips in frustration.

"Here, I'd admire ef you sleeked my fur," purred the cat, and he leaped into the boy's lap. Bowsmith's hands obeyed as aptly as if he could have understood the words of the request.

"What is it happened thin, boy?" Old Nathan asked in a voice as soft as the whisper of powder being poured down the barrel of a musket.

"Well, I'm feared to guess what might hev happened," explained Bowsmith, "effen the Baron hisself hedn't come out the cabin and say hit made no matter."

He began to nod in agreement with the words in his memory, saying, "The Bar'n, he told the sheriff I wuzn't right in the head sometimes, en he give thim all a swig outen his jug uv wildcat so's they wouldn't hammer me fer runnin' thim off through the woods like a durned fool. They wuz laughin' like fiends whin they left, the sheriff and the folk from the settlement."

Bowsmith's hands paused. The cat waited a moment, then rose and battered his chin against the boy's chest until the stroking resumed.

"Reckon I am a durn fool," the boy said morosely. "Thet en worse."

"How long did ye stop over t' the Neills after ye left here yestiddy?" Old Nathan asked in the same soft voice.

"Coo," said Bowsmith, meeting the cunning man's eyes as wonder drove the gloom from his face. "Well, I *niver*. . . . Wuzn't goin' t' tell ye thet, seein's ez ye'd said I oughtn't t' stop. But Mar' Beth, she seed me on the road en hollered me up t' the cabin t' set fer a spell. Don't guess I was there too long, though. The Baron asked me whin I was going t' clear his newground. And then whin he went out, me en the boys, we passed the jug a time er two."

He frowned. "Reckon hit might uv been longer thin I'd recollected."

"Hit wuz dark by the time ye passed the Neills', warn't it?" Old Nathan said. "How'd Mary Beth see down t' the road?"

"Why, I be," replied the boy. "Why—" His face brightened. "D'ye reckon she wuz waiting on me t' come back by? She's powerful sweet on me, ye know, though I say thet who oughtn't."

"Reckon hit might be she wuz waitin'," said the cunning man, his voice leaden and implacable. He lifted his eyes from Bowsmith to the end wall opposite the fireplace. The strop that was all the material remains of Spanish King shivered in a breeze that neither man could feel.

"Pinter must hev lost all hit's virtue whin I went back on what ye told me," the boy said miserably. "You bin so good t' me, en I step on my dick ever' time I turn around. Reckon I'll git back t' my place afore I cause more trouble."

"Set, boy," said Old Nathan. "Ye'll go whin I say go . . . and ye'll do this time what I say ye'll do."

"Yessir," replied Bowsmith, taken aback. When he tried instinctively to straighten his shoulders, the chair rocked beneath him. He lurched to his feet in response. Instead of spilling the cat, he used the animal as a balancer and then clutched him back to his chest.

"Yessir," he repeated, standing upright and looking confused but not frightened. And not, somehow, ridiculous, for all his ragged spray of hair and the grumbling tomcat in his arms.

Old Nathan set the book he held down on the table, his spectacles still marking his place against the stiff binding which struggled to close the volume. With both hands free, he gripped the table itself and walked over to the fireplace alcove.

Bowsmith poured the cat back onto the floor as soon as he understood what his host was about, but he paused on realizing that his help was not needed. The table top was forty inches to a side, sawn from thick planks and set on an equally solid framework—all of oak. The cunning man shifted the table without concern for its weight and awkwardness. He had never been a giant for strength, but even now he was no one to trifle with either.

"Ye kin fetch the straight chair to it," he said over his shoulder while he fumbled with the lock of one of the chests flanking the fireplace. "I'll need the light t' copy out the words ye'll need."

"Sir, I cain't read," the boy said in a voice of pale, peeping despair.

"Hit don't signify," replied the cunning man. The lid of the chest creaked open. "Fetch the chair."

Old Nathan set a bundle of turkey quills onto the table, then a pot of ink stoppered with a cork. The ink moved sluggishly and could have used a dram of water to thin it, but it was fluid enough for writing as is.

Still kneeling before the chest, the cunning man raised a document case and untied the ribbon which closed it. Bowsmith placed the straight chair by the table, moving the rocker aside to make room. Then he watched over the cunning man's shoulder, finding in the written word a magic as real as anything Old Nathan had woven or forged on previous visits.

"Not this one," the older man said, laying aside the first of the letters he took from the case. It was in a woman's hand, the paper fine but age-spotted. He could not read the words without his glasses, but he did not need to reread what he had not been able to forget even at this distance in time. "Nor this."

"Coo . . . ," Bowsmith murmured as the first document was covered by the second, this one written on parchment with a wax seal and ribbons which the case had kept a red as bright as that of the day they were impressed onto the document.

Old Nathan smiled despite his mood. "A commendation from General Sevier," he said in quiet pride as he took another letter from the case.

"You fit the Redcoats et New Or-leens like they say, thin?" the younger man asked.

Old Nathan looked back at him with an expression suddenly as blank as a board. "No, boy," he said, "hit was et Kings Mountain, en they didn't wear red coats, the most uv thim."

He paused and then added in a kindlier tone, "En I reckon thet when I was yer age en ol' fools wuz jawin' about Quebec and Cartagena and all thet like, hit didn't matter a bean betwixt them t' me neither. And mebbe there wuz more truth t' thet thin I've thought since."

"I don't rightly foller," said Bowsmith.

"Don't reckon ye need to," the older man replied. "Throw a stick uv lightwood on the fire."

Holding the sheet he had just removed from the case, Old Nathan stood upright and squinted to be sure of what he had. It seemed to be one of his brother's last letters to him, a decade old but no more important for that. It was written on both sides of the sheet, but the cuttlefish ink had faded to its permanent state of rich brown. The paper would serve as well for the cunning man's present need as a clean sheet which could not have been found closer than Hewitt's store in the settlement—and that dearly.

He sat down on the chair and donned his spectacles, using the letter as a placeholder in the book in their stead. The turkey quills were held together by a wisp of twine which, with his glasses on, he could see to untie.

After choosing a likely quill, Old Nathan scowled and said, "Turn yer head, boy." When he felt the movement of Bowsmith behind him, obedient if uncertain, the cunning man reached out with his eyes closed and brought his hand back holding the jackknife.

Some of Old Nathan's magic was done in public to impress visitors and those to whom they might babble in awe. Some things that he might have hidden from others he did before Bowsmith, because he knew that the boy would never attempt to duplicate the acts on his own. But this one trick was the cunning man's secret of secrets.

The knife is the most useful of Mankind's tools, dating from ages before he was even human. But a knife is also a weapon, and the sole reason for storing it—somewhere else—rather than in a pants pocket was that on some future date an enemy might remove a weapon from your pants. Better to plan for a need which never eventuated than to be caught by unexpected disaster.

"Ye kin turn and help me now, Eldon Bowsmith," the cunning man said as he trimmed his pen with the wire edge of the smaller blade. "Ye kin hold open the book fer me."

"Yessir," said the boy and obeyed with the clumsy nervousness of a bachelor asked to hold an infant for the first time. He gripped the volume with an effort which an axehelve would have better justified. The shaking of his limbs would make the print even harder to read.

Old Nathan sighed. "Gently, boy," he said. "Hit won't bite ye."

Though there was reason to fear this book. It named itself *Testamentum Athanasii* on a title page which gave no other information regarding its provenance. The volume was old, but it had been printed with movable type and bound or rebound recently enough that the leather hinges showed no sign of cracking.

The receipt to which the book now opened was one Old Nathan had read frequently in the months since Spanish King had won his last battle and, winning, had died. Not till now had he really considered employing the formula. Not really.

"Boy," lied the cunning man, "we cain't git yer horse back, so I'll give ye the strength uv a bull thet ye kin plow."

Bowsmith's face found a neutral pattern and held it while his mind worked on the sentence he had just been offered. Usually conversations took standard patterns. "G'day t' ye, Simp." "G'day t' ye, Mister/Miz . . ." "Ev'nin', Eldon. Come en set." "Ev'nin', Mar' Beth. Don' mind effen I do." Patterns like that made a conversation easier, without the confusing precipices which talking to Old Nathan entailed.

"Druther hev Jen back, sir," said the boy at last. "Effen *you* don't mind."

The cunning man raised his left hand. The gesture was not quite a physical threat because the hand held his spectacles, and their lenses refracted spitting orange firelight across the book and the face of the younger man. "Mind, boy?" said Old Nathan. "Mind? You mind *me*, thet's the long and the short uv it now, d'ye hear?"

"Yessir."

The cunning man dipped his pen in the ink and wiped it on the bottle's rim, cursing the fluid's consistency. "Give ye the strength uv a bull," he lied again, "en a strong bull et thet." He began to write, his present strokes crossing those of his brother in the original letter. He held the spectacles a few inches in front of his eyes, squinting and adjusting them as he copied from the page of the book.

"Ever ketch rabbits, feller?" asked the cat as he leaped to the tabletop and landed without a stir because all four paws touched down together.

"Good feller," muttered Bowsmith, holding the book with the thumb and spread fingers of one hand so that the other could stroke the cat. The trembling which had disturbed the pages until then ceased, though the cat occasionally bumped a corner of the volume. "Good feller. . . ."

The click of clawtips against oak, the scritch of the pen nib leaving crisp black lines across the sepia complaints beneath, and the sputtering pine knot that lighted the cabin wove themselves into a sinister unity that was darker than the nighted forest outside.

Yet not so dark as the cunning man's intent.

When he finished, the boy and the cat were both staring at him, and it was the cat who rumbled, "Bad ez all thet?" smelling the emotions in the old man's sweat.

"What'll be," Old Nathan rasped through a throat drier than he had realized till he spoke, "will be." He looked down at the document he had just indited, folded his spectacles one-handed, and then turned to hurl the quill pen into the fire with a violence that only hinted his fury at what he was about to do.

"Sir?" said Bowsmith.

"Shut the book, boy," said Old Nathan wearily. His fingers made a tentative pass toward the paper, to send it the way the quill had gone. A casuist would have said that he was not acting and therefore bore no guilt . . . but a man who sets a snare for a rabbit cannot claim the throttled rabbit caused its own death by stepping into the noose.

The cunning man stood and handed the receipt to his visitor, folding it along the creases of the original letter. "Put it in yer pocket fer now, lad," he said. He took the book, closed now as he had directed, and scooped up the cat gently with a hand beneath the rib cage and the beast's haunches in the crook of his elbow.

"Now, carry the table across t' the other side," the cunning man continued, motioning Bowsmith with a thrust of his beard because he did not care to point with the leather-covered book. "Fetch me down the strop uv bullhide there. Hit's got a peg drove through each earhole t' hold it."

"That ol' bull," said the cat, turning his head to watch Bowsmith walk across the room balancing the heavy table on one hand. "Ye know, I git t' missin' him sometimes?"

"As do I," Old Nathan agreed grimly. "But I don't choose t' live in a world where I don't see the prices till the final day."

"Sir?" queried the boy, looking down from the table which he had mounted in a flat-footed jump that crashed its legs down on the puncheons.

"Don't let it trouble ye, boy," the cunning man replied. "I talk t' my cat, sometimes. Fetch me down Spanish King, en I'll deal with yer problem the way I've set myself t' do."

The cat sprang free of the encircling arm, startled by what he heard in his master's voice.

IT WAS AN HOUR PAST SUNSET, and Baron Ncill held court on the porch over an entourage of two of his three sons and four of the six grandsons. Inside the cabin, built English-fashion of sawn timber but double-sized, the women of the clan cleared off the truck from supper and talked in low voices among themselves. The false crow calls from the lookout tree raucously penetrated the background of cicadas and tree frogs.

" 'Bout time," said the youngest son, taking a swig from the jug. He was in his early forties, balding and feral.

"Mar' Beth," called Baron Neill without turning his head or taking from his mouth the long stem of his meerschaum pipe.

There was silence from within the cabin but no immediate response.

The Baron dropped his feet from the porch rail with a crash and stood up. The Neill patriarch looked more like a rat than anything on two legs had a right to do. His nose was prominent, and the remainder of his body seemed to spread outward from it down to the fleshy buttocks supported by a pair of spindly shanks. "Mar' Beth!" he shouted, hunched forward as he faced the cabin door.

"Well, I'm comin', ain't I?" said a woman who was by convention the Baron's youngest daughter and was in any case close kin to him. She stepped out of the lamplit cabin, hitching the checked apron a little straighter on her homespun dress. The oil light behind her colored her hair more of a yellow than the sun would have brought out, emphasizing the translucent gradations of her single tortoiseshell comb.

"Simp's comin' back," said the Baron, relaxing enough to clamp the pipe again between his teeth. "Tyse jist called. Git down t' the trail en bring him back."

The woman stood hipshot, the desire to scowl tempered by the knowledge that the patriarch would strike her if the expression were not hidden by the angle of the light. "I'm *poorly*," she said.

One of the boys snickered, and Baron Neill roared, "Don't I *know* thet? You do ez I tell ye, girl."

Mary Beth stepped off the porch with an exaggerated sway to her hips. The pair of hogs sprawled beneath the boards awakened but snorted and flopped back down after questing with their long flexible snouts.

"Could be I don't mind," the woman threw back over her shoulder from a safe distance. "Could be Simp looks right good stacked up agin some I've seed."

One of her brothers sent after her a curse and the block of poplar he was whittling, neither with serious intent.

"Jeth," said the Baron, "go fetch Dave and Sim from the still. Never know when two more guns might be the difference betwixt somethin' er somethin' else. En bring another jug back with ye."

"Lotta durn work for a durned old plowhorse," grumbled one of the younger Neills.

The Baron sat down again on his chair and lifted his boots to the porch rail. "Ain't about a horse," he said, holding out his hand and having it filled by the stoneware whiskey jug without him needing to ask. "Hain't been about a horse since he brung Old Nathan into hit. Fancies himself, that 'un does."

The rat-faced old man took a deep draw on his pipe and mingled in his mouth the harsh flavors of burley tobacco and raw whiskey. "Well, I fancy myself, too. We'll jist see who's got the rights uv it."

ELDON BOWSMITH TRIED TO STEP apart from the woman when the path curved back in sight of the cabin. Mary Beth giggled throatily and pulled herself close again, causing the youth to sway like a sapling in the wind. He stretched out the heavy bundle in his opposite hand in order to recover his balance.

"What in *tarnation* is that ye got, boy?" demanded Baron Neill from the porch. The air above his pipe bowl glowed orange as he drew on the mouthpiece.

"Got a strop uv bullhide, Bar'n," Bowsmith called back. "Got the horns, tail, and the strip offen the backbone besides."

He swayed again, then said in a voice that carried better than he would have intended, "Mar' *Beth*, ye mustn't touch me like thet here." But the words were not a serious reproach, and his laughter joined the woman's renewed giggle.

There was snorting laughter from the porch as well. One of the men there might have spoken had not Baron Neill snarled his offspring to silence.

The couple separated when they reached the steps, Mary Beth leading the visitor with her hips swaying in even greater emphasis than when she had left the cabin.

"Tarnation," the Baron repeated as he stood and took the rolled strip of hide from Bowsmith. The boy's hand started to resist, but he quickly released the bundle when he remembered where he was.

"Set a spell, boy," said the patriarch. "Zeph, hand him the jug."

"I reckon I need yer help, Bar'n," Bowsmith said, rubbing his right sole against his left calf. The stoneware jug—a full one just brought from the still by the Baron's other two grandsons—was pressed into his hands and he took a brief sip.

"Now, don't ye insult my squeezin's, boy," said one of the younger men. "Drink hit down like a man er ye'll answer t' me." In this, as in most things, the clan worked as a unit to achieve its ends. Simp Bowsmith was little enough of a problem sober; but with a few swallows of wildcat in him, the boy ran like butter.

"Why, you know we'd do the world for ye, lad," said the rat-faced elder as he shifted to bring the bundle into the lamplight spilling from the open door. It was just what the boy had claimed, a strop of heavy leather, tanned with the hair still on, and including the stiff-boned tail as well as the long, translucent horns.

Bowsmith handed the jug to one of the men around him, then spluttered and coughed as he swallowed the last of the mouthful he had taken. "Ye see, sir," he said quickly in an attempt to cover the tears which the liquor had brought to his eyes, "I've a spell t' say, but I need some'un t' speak the words over whilst I git thim right. He writ thim down fer me, Mister Nathan did. But I cain't read, so's he told me go down t' the settlemint en hev Mister Hewitt er the sheriff say thim with me."

He carefully unbuttoned the pocket of his shirt, out at the elbows now that his mother was not alive to patch it. With the reverence for writing that other men might have reserved for gold, he handed the rewritten document to Baron Neill.

The patriarch thrust the rolled bullhide to the nearest of his offspring and took the receipt. Turning, he saw Mary Beth and said, "You—girl. Fetch the lamp out here, and thin you git back whar ye belong. Ye know better thin t' nose around whin thar's men talkin'."

"But I mustn't speak the spell out whole till ever'thing's perpared," Bowsmith went on, gouging his calf again with the nail of his big toe. "Thet's cuz hit'll work only the onct, Mister Nathan sez. En effen I'm not wearin' the strop over me when I says it, thin I'll gain some strength but not the whole strength uv the bull."

There was a sharp altercation within the cabin, one female voice shrieking, "En what're *we* s'posed t' do with no more light thin inside the Devil's butthole? You put that lamp down, Mar' Beth Neill!"

"Zeph," said the Baron in a low voice, but two of his sons were already moving toward the doorway, shifting their rifles to free their right hands.

"Anyhows, I thought ye might read the spell out with me, sir," Bowsmith said. "Thim folk down t' the settlemint, I reckon they don't hev much use fer me."

"I wuz jist—" a woman cried on a rising inflection that ended with the thud of knuckles instead of a slap. The light through the doorway shifted, then brightened. The men came out, one of them carrying a copper lamp with a glass chimney.

The circle of lamplight lay like the finger of God on the group of men. That the Neills were all one family was obvious; that they were a species removed from humanity was possible. They were short men; in their midst, Eldon Bowsmith looked like a scrawny chicken surrounded by rats standing upright. The hair on their scalps was black and straight, thinning even on the youngest, and their foreheads sloped sharply.

Several of the clan were chewing tobacco, but the Baron alone smoked a pipe. The stem of that yellow-bowled meerschaum served him as an officer's swagger stick or a conductor's baton.

"Hold the durn lamp," the patriarch snapped to the son who tried to hand him the instrument. While Bowsmith clasped his hands and watched the Baron in nervous hopefulness, the remainder of the Neill clan eyed the boy sidelong and whispered at the edge of the lighted circle.

Baron Neill unfolded the document carefully and held it high so that the lamp illuminated the writing from behind his shoulder. Smoke dribbled from his nostrils in short puffs as his teeth clenched on the stem of his pipe.

When the Baron lowered the receipt, he removed the pipe from his mouth. His eyes were glaring blank fury, but his tongue said only, "I wonder, boy, effen yer Mister Nathan warn't funnin' ye along. This paper he give ye, hit don't hev word one on it. Hit's jist Babel."

One of the younger Neills took the document which the Baron held spurned at his side. Three of the others crowded closer and began to argue in whispers, one of them tracing with his finger the words written in sepia ink beneath the receipt.

"Well, they hain't words, Bar'n," said the boy, surprised that he knew something which the other man—any other man, he might have said—did not. "I mean, not like we'd speak. Mister Nathan, he said what he writ out wuz the sounds, so's I didn't hev occasion t' be consarned they wuz furrin words."

Baron Neill blinked, as shocked to hear a reasoned exposition from Simp Bowsmith as the boy was to have offered it. After momentary consideration, he decided to treat the information as something he had known all the time. "*Leave* thet be!" he roared, whirling on the cluster of his offspring poring over the receipt.

Two of the men were gripping the document at the same time. Both of them released it and jumped back, bumping their fellows and joggling the lantern dangerously. They collided again as they tried unsuccessfully to catch the paper before it fluttered to the board floor.

The Baron cuffed the nearer and swatted at the other as well, missing when the younger man dodged back behind the shelter of his kin. Deliberately, his agitation suggested only by the vehemence of the pull he took on his pipe, the old man bent and retrieved the document. He peered at it again, then fixed his eyes on Bowsmith. "You say you're t' speak the words on this. Would thet be et some particular time?"

"No sir," said the boy, bobbing his head as if in an effort to roll ideas to the surface of his mind. "Not thet Mister Nathan told me."

As Baron Neill squinted at the receipt again, silently mouthing the syllables which formed no language of which he was cognizant, Bowsmith added, "Jist t' set down with the bullhide over my back, en t' speak out the words. En I'm ez strong ez a bull."

"Give him another pull on the jug," the Baron ordered abruptly.

"I don't—" Bowsmith began as three Neills closed on him, one offering the jug with a gesture as imperious as that of a highwayman presenting his pistol.

"Boy," the Baron continued, "I'm goin' t' help ye, jist like you said. But hit's a hard task, en ye'll hev t' bear with me till I'm ready. Ain't like reg'lar readin', this parsin' out things ez ain't words."

He fixed the boy with a fierce glare which was robbed of much of its effect because the lamp behind him threw his head into bald silhouette. "Understand?"

"Yessir."

"Drink my liquor, boy," suggested the man with the jug. "Hit'll straighten yer quill for sure."

"Yessir."

"Now," Baron Neill went on, refolding the receipt and sliding it into the pocket of his own blue frock coat, "you set up with the young folks, hev a good time, en we'll make ye up a bed with us fer the night. Meanwhiles, I'm goin' down t' the barn t' study this over so's I kin help ye in the mornin'."

"Oh," said Bowsmith in relief, then coughed as fumes of the whiskey he had just drunk shocked the back of his nostrils. "Lordy," he muttered, wheezing to get his breath. "Lordy!"

One of the Neills thumped him hard on the back and said, "Chase thet down with another, so's they fight each other en leave you alone."

"Thet bullhide," said the Baron, calculation underlying the appearance of mild curiosity, "hit's somethin' special, now, ain't it?"

"Reckon it might be," the boy agreed, glad to talk because it delayed by that much the next swig of the liquor that already spun his head and his stomach. "Hit was pegged up t' Mister Nathan's wall like hit hed been thar a right long time."

"Figgered thet," Baron Neill said in satisfaction. "Hed t' be somethin' more thin ye'd said."

Bowsmith sighed and took another drink. For a moment there was no sound but the hiss of the lamp and a whippoorwill calling from the middle distance.

"Reckon I'll take the hide with me t' the barn," said the Baron, reaching for the rolled strop, "so's hit won't git trod upon."

The grandson holding the strip of hide turned so that his body blocked the Baron's intent. "Reckon we kin keep it here en save ye the burden, ol' man," he said in a sullen tone raised an octave by fear of the consequences.

"What's *this*, now?" the patriarch said, backing a half step and placing his hands on his hips.

"Like Len sez," interjected the man with the lamp, stepping between his father and his son,"we'll keep the hide safe back here."

"Tar*nation*," Baron Neill said, throwing up his hands and feigning good-natured exasperation. "Ye didn't think yer own pa 'ud shut ye out wholesale, did ye?"

"Bar'n," said Eldon Bowsmith, emboldened by the liquor, "I don't foller ye."

"Shet yer mouth whin others er talkin' family matters, boy," snapped one of the clan from the fringes. None of the women could be seen through the open door of the cabin, but their hush was like the breathing of a restive cow.

"You youngins hev fun," said the Baron, turning abruptly. "I've got some candles down t' the barn. I'll jist study this"—he tapped with the pipestem on the pocket in which paper rustled—"en we'll talk agin, mebbe 'long about moonrise."

Midnight.

"Y'all hev fun," repeated the old man as he began to walk down the slippery path to the barn.

The Neill women, led by Mary Beth with her comb readjusted to let her hair fall to her shoulders, softly joined the men on the porch.

IN SUCH NUMBERS, even the bare feet of his offspring were ample warning to Baron Neill before Zephaniah opened the barn door. The candle of molded tallow guttered and threatened to go out.

"Simp?" the old man asked. He sat on the bar of an empty stall with the candle set in the slot cut higher in the endpost for another bar.

It had been years since the clan kept cows. The only animal now sharing the barn with the patriarch and the smell of sour hay was Bowsmith's horse, her jaws knotted closed with a rag to keep her from neighing. Her stall was curtained with blankets against the vague possibility that the boy would glance into the building.

"Like we'd knocked him on the head," said the third man in the procession entering the barn. The horse wheezed through her nostrils and pawed the bars of her stall.

"Why ain't we done jist thet?" demanded Mary Beth. "Nobody round here's got a scrap uv use fer him, 'ceptin' mebbe thet ol' bastard cunning man. En *he's* not right in the head neither."

The whole clan was padding into the barn, but the building's volume was a good match for their number. There were several infants, one of them continuing to squall against its mother's breast until a male took it from her. The mother cringed, but she relaxed when the man only pinched the baby's lips shut with a thumb and forefinger. He increased the pressure every time the infant swelled itself for another squawl.

"Did I raise ye up t' be a fool, girl?" Baron Neill demanded angrily, jabbing with his pipestem. "Sure, they've a use fer him—t' laugh et. Effen we slit his throat en weight his belly with stones, the county'll be here with rope and torches fer the whole lot uv us."

He took a breath and calmed as the last of the clan trooped in. "Besides, hain't needful. Never do what hain't needful."

One of the men swung the door to and rotated a peg to hold it closed. The candleflame thrashed in the breeze, then steadied to a dull, smoky light as before.

"Now . . . ," said the Baron slowly, "I'll tell ye what we're goin' t' do."

Alone of the Neill clan, he was seated. Some of those spread into the farther corners could see nothing of the patriarch save his legs crossed as he sat on the stall bar. There were over twenty people in the barn, including the infants, and the faint illumination accentuated the similiarity of their features.

Len, the grandson who held the bullhide, crossed his arms to squeeze the bundle closer to his chest. He spread his legs slightly, and two of his bearded, rat-faced kin stepped closer as if to defend him from the Baron's glare.

The patriarch smiled. "We're all goin' t' be stronger thin strong," he said in a sinuous, enticing whisper. "Ye heard Simp—he'd gain strength whether er no the strop wuz over his back. So . . . I'll deacon the spell off, en you all speak the lines out after me, standin' about in the middle."

He paused in order to stand up and search the faces from one side of the room to the other. "Hev I ever played my kinfolk false?" he demanded. The receipt in his left hand rustled, and the stem of his pipe rotated with his gaze. Each of his offspring lowered his or her eyes as the pointer swept the clan.

Even Len scowled at the rolled strop instead of meeting the Baron's eyes, but the young man said harshly, "Who's t' hold the hide, thin? You?"

"The hide'll lay over my back," Baron Neill agreed easily, "en the lot uv you'll stand about close ez ye kin git and nobody closer thin the next. I reckon we all gain, en I gain the most."

The sound of breathing made the barn itself seem a living thing, but no one spoke and even the sputter of the candle was audible. At last Mary Beth, standing hipshot and only three-quarters facing the patriarch, broke the silence with, "You're not ez young ez ye onct were, Pa. Seems ez if the one t' git the most hed ought t' be one t' be around t' use hit most."

Instead of retorting angrily, Baron Neill smiled and said, "Which one, girl? Who do *you* pick in my place?"

The woman glanced about her. Disconcerted, she squirmed backward, out of the focus into which she had thrown herself.

"He's treated us right," murmured another woman, half-hidden in the shadow of the post which held the candle. "Hit's best we git on with the business."

"All right, ol' man," said Len, stepping forward to hold out the strop. "What er ye waitin' on?"

"Mebbe fer my kin t' come t' their senses," retorted the patriarch with a smile of triumph.

Instead of snatching the bullhide at once, Baron Neill slid his cold pipe into the breast pocket of his coat, then folded the receipt he had taken from Bowsmith and set it carefully on the endpost of the stall.

Len pursed his lips in anger, demoted from central figure in the clan's resistance to the Baron back to the boy who had been ordered to hold the bullhide. The horns, hanging from the section of the bull's coarse poll which had been lifted, rattled together as the young man's hands began to tremble with emotion.

Baron Neill took off his frock coat and hung it from the other post supporting the bar on which he had waited. Working deliberately, the Baron shrugged the straps of his galluses off his shoulders and lowered his trousers until he could step out of them. His boots already stood toes-out beside the stall partition. None of the others of the clan were wearing footgear.

"Should we . . . ?" asked one of the men, pinching a pleat of his shirt to finish the question.

"No need," the Baron said, unbuttoning the front of his own store-bought shirt. "Mebbe not fer me, even. But best t' be sure."

One of the children started to whine a question. His mother hushed him almost instantly by clasping one hand over his mouth and the other behind the child's head to hold him firmly.

The shirt was the last of Baron Neill's clothing. When he had draped it over his trousers and coat, he looked even more like the white-furred rodent he resembled clothed. His body was pasty, its surface colored more by grime and the yellow candlelight than by blood vessels beneath it. The epaulettes on the Baron's coat had camouflaged the extreme narrowness of his shoulders and chest, and the only place his skin was taut was where the potbelly sagged against it.

His eyes had a terrible power, and they seemed to glint even before he took the candle to set it before him on the floor compacted of earth, dung, and ancient straw.

The Baron removed the receipt from the post on which it waited, opened it and smoothed the folds, and placed it beside the candle. Only then did he say to Len, "*Now* I'll take the strop, boy."

His grandson nodded sharply and passed the bundle over. The mood of the room was taut, like that of a stormy sky in the moments before the release of lightning. The anger and embarrassment which had twisted Len's face into a grimace earlier was now replaced by blank fear. Baron Neill smiled at him grimly.

The bull's tail was stiff with the bones still in it, so the length of hide had been wound around the base of that tail like thread on a spindle. Baron Neill held the strop by the head end, one hand on the hairless muzzle and the other on the poll between the horns, each the length of a man's arm along the curve. He shook out the roll with a quick jerk that left the brush of the tail scratching on the boards at the head of the stall.

The Baron cautiously held the strop against his back with the clattering horns dangling down to his knees. The old man gave a little shudder as the leather touched his bare skin, but he knelt and leaned forward, tugging the strop upward until the muzzle flopped loosely in front of his face.

The Baron muttered something that started as a curse and blurred into nondescript syllables when he recalled the task he was about. He rested the palm of one hand on the floor, holding the receipt flat and in the light of the candle. With his free hand, he folded the muzzle and forehead of the bull back over the poll so that he could see.

"Make a circle around me," ordered the patriarch in a voice husky with its preparations for declaiming the spell.

He should have been ridiculous, a naked old man on all fours like a dog, his head and back crossed by a strip of bullhide several times longer than the human torso. The tension in the barn kept even the children of the clan from seeing humor in the situation, and the muzzled plowhorse froze to silence in her curtained stall.

The Neills shuffled into motion, none of them speaking. The man who held the infant's lips pinched shut handed the child back to its mother. It whimpered only minutely and showed no interest in the breast which she quickly offered it to suck.

Two of the grandsons joined hands. The notion caught like gunpowder burning, hands leaping into hands. In the physical union, the psychic pressure that weighted the barn seemed more bearable though also more intense.

"Remember," said the Baron as he felt his offspring merge behind him, two of them linking hands over the trailing strop, "Ye'll not hev another chance. En ye'll git no pity from me effen ye cain't foller my deaconin' en you're no better off thin ye are now."

"Go *on*, ol' man," Mary Beth demanded in a savage whisper as she looked down on Baron Neill and the candle on the floor between her and the patriarch.

Baron Neill cocked his head up to look at the woman. She met his eyes with a glare as fierce as his own. Turning back to the paper on the ground, the old man read, "Ek neckroo say mettapempomie."

The candle guttered at his words. The whole clan responded together, "Ek neckroo say mettapempomie," their merged voices hesitant but gaining strength and unity toward the last of the Greek syllables like the wind in advance of a rainstorm.

"Soy sowma moo didomie," read the Baron. His normal voice was high-pitched and unsteady, always on the verge of cracking. Now it had dropped an octave and had power enough to drive straw into motion on the floor a yard away.

"Soy sowma moo didomie," thundered the Neill clan. Sparrows, nested on the roof trusses, fluttered and peeped as they tried furiously to escape from the barn. In the darkness, they could not see the vents under the roof peaks by which they flew in and out during daylight.

Baron Neill read the remainder of the formula, line by line. The process was becoming easier, because the smoky candle had begun to burn with a flame as white as the noonday sun. The syllables which had been written on age-yellowed paper and a background of earlier words now stood out and shaped themselves to the patriarch's tongue.

At another time, the Baron would have recognized the power which his tongue released but could not control. This night the situation had already been driven over a precipice. Caution was lost in exhilaration at the approaching climax, and the last impulse to stop was stilled by the fear that stopping might already be impossible.

The shingles above shuddered as the clan repeated the lines, and the candleflame climbed with the icy purpose of a stalagmite reaching for completion with a cave roof. Jen kicked at her stall in blind panic, cracking through the old crossbar, but none of the humans heard the sound.

"Hellon moy," shouted Baron Neill in triumph. "Hellon moy! Hellon moy!"

Mary Beth suddenly broke the circle and twisted. "Hit's *hot!*" she cried as she tore the front of her dress from neckline to waist in a single hysterical effort.

The woman's breasts swung free, their nipples erect and longer than they would have seemed a moment before. She tried to scream, but the sound fluted off into silence as her body ran like wax in obedience to the formula she and her kin had intoned.

The circle of the Neill clan flowed toward its center, flesh and bone alike taking on the consistency of magma. Clothing dropped and quivered as the bodies it had covered runneled out of sleeves and through the weave of the fabrics.

The bullhide strop sagged also as Baron Neill's body melted beneath it. As the pink, roiling plasm surged toward the center of the circle, the horns lifted and bristles that had lain over the bull's spine in life sprang erect.

The human voices were stilled, but the sparrows piped a mad chorus and Jen's hooves crashed again onto the splintering crossbar.

There was a slurping, gurgling sound. The bull's tail stood upright, its brush waving like a flag, and from the seething mass that had been the Neill clan rose the mighty, massive form of a black bull.

Eldon Bowsmith lurched awake on the porch of the Neill house. He had dreamed of a bull's bellow so loud that it shook the world.

Fuddled but with eyes adapted to the light of the crescent moon, he looked around him. The house was still and dark.

Then, as he tried to stand with the help of the porch rail, the barn door flew apart with a shower of splinters. Spanish King, bellowing again with the fury of which only a bull is capable, burst from the enclosure and galloped off into the night.

Behind him whinnied a horse which, in the brief glance vouchsafed by motion and the light, looked a lot like Jen.

WHEN ELDON BOWSMITH REACHED the cabin, Old Nathan was currying his bull by the light of a burning pine knot thrust into the ground beside the porch. A horse was tethered to the rail with a makeshift neck halter of twine.

"Sir, is thet you?" the boy asked cautiously.

"Who en *blazes* d'ye think hit 'ud be?" the cunning man snapped.

"Don't know thet 'un," snorted Spanish King. His big head swung toward the visitor, and one horn dipped menacingly.

"Ye'd not *be* here, blast ye," said Old Nathan, slapping the bull along the jaw, " 'ceptin' fer him."

"Yessir," said Bowsmith. "I'm right sorry. Only, a lot uv what I seed t'night, I figgered must be thet I wuz drinkin'."

"Took long enough t' fetch me," rumbled the bull as he snuffled the night air. He made no comment about the blow, but the way he studiously ignored Bowsmith suggested that the reproof had sunk home. "Summer's nigh over."

He paused and turned his head again so that one brown eye focused squarely on the cunning man. "Where *wuz* I, anyhow? D'ye know?"

"Not yet," said Old Nathan, stroking the bull's sweat-matted shoulders fiercely with the curry comb.

"Pardon, sir?" said the boy, who had walked into the circle of torchlight, showing a well-justified care to keep Old Nathan between him and Spanish King. Then he blinked and rose up on his bare toes to peer over the bull's shoulder at the horse. "Why," he blurted, "thet's the spit en image uv my horse Jen, only thet this mare's too bony!"

"Thet's yer Jen, all right," said the cunning man. "There's sacked barley in the lean-to out back, effen ye want t' feed her some afore ye take her t' home. Been runnin' the woods, I reckon."

"We're goin' back home?" asked the horse, speaking for almost the first time since she had followed Spanish King rather than be alone in the night.

"Oh, my God, Jen!" said the boy, striding past Spanish King with never a thought for the horns. "I'm so *glad* t' see ye!" He threw his arms around the horse's neck while she whickered, nuzzling the boy in hopes of finding some of the barley Old Nathan had mentioned.

"Durn fool," muttered Spanish King; but then he stretched himself deliberately, extending one leg at a time until his deep chest was rubbing the sod. "Good t' be back, though," he said. "Won't say it ain't."

Eldon Bowsmith straightened abruptly and stepped away from his mare, though he kept his hand on her mane. "Sir," he said, "ye found my Jen, en ye brung her back. What do I owe ye?"

Old Nathan ran the fingers of his free hand along the bristly spine of his bull. "Other folk hev took care uv thet," the cunning man said as Spanish King rumbled in pleasure at his touch. "Cleared yer account, so t' speak."

The pine torch was burning fitfully, close to the ground, so that Bowsmith's grimace of puzzlement turned shadows into a devil's mask. "Somebody paid for me?" he asked. "Well, I niver. Friends, hit must hev been?"

Spanish King lifted himself and began to walk regally around the cabin to his pasture and the two cows who were his property.

"Reckon ye could say thet," replied Old Nathan. "They wuz ez nigh t' bein' yer friends ez anybody's but their own."

The cunning man paused and grinned like very Satan. "In the end," he said, "they warn't sich good friends t' themselves."

A gust of wind rattled the shingles, as if the night sky were remembering what it had heard at the Neill place. Then it was silent again.

NARROW VALLEY

BY R. A. LAFFERTY

R. A. LAFFERTY WAS A MASTER OF THE DEADPAN TALL TALE, THE TYPE OF STORY THAT DARES YOU TO DISBELIEVE IT DESPITE THE GENIUS OF ITS STYLE AND CONSTRUCTION AS WEIGHED AGAINST THE OVERALL ABSURDITY OF ITS PREMISE AND PLOT. HE CONTINUES THE TRADITION OF AMERICAN MAGIC MEN FURTHER WESTWARD TO HIS OWN LOCALES OF INDIAN COUNTRY IN HIS NATIVE OKLAHOMA, THOUGH ITS PRACTITIONER MIGHT NOT SEEM AS ADEPT AS SOME OF HIS PRECURSORS.

In the year 1893, land allotments in severalty were made to the remaining eight hundred and twenty-one Pawnee Indians. Each would receive one hundred and sixty acres of land and no more, and thereafter the Pawnees would be expected to pay taxes on their land, the same as the White-Eyes did.

"Kitkehahke!" Clarence Big-Saddle cussed. "You can't kick a dog around proper on a hundred and sixty acres. And I sure am not hear before about this pay taxes on land."

Clarence Big-Saddle selected a nice green vally for his allotment. It was one of the half dozen plots he had always regarded as his own. He sodded around the summer lodge that he had there and made it an all-season home. But he sure didn't intend to pay taxes on it.

So he burned leaves and bark and made a speech:

"That my valley be always wide and flourish and green and such stuff as that!" he orated in Pawnee chant style. "But that it be narrow if an intruder come."

He didn't have any balsam bark to burn. He threw on a little cedar bark instead. He didn't have any elder leaves. He used a handful of jack-oak leaves. And he forgot the word. How you going to work it if you forget the word?

"Petahauerat!" he howled out with the confidence he hoped would fool the fates.

"That's the same long of a word," he said in a low aside to himself. But he was doubtful. "What am I, a White Man, a burr-tailed jack, a new kind of nut to think it will work?" he asked. "I have to laugh at me. Oh well, we see."

He threw the rest of the bark and the leaves on the fire, and he hollered the wrong word out again.

And he was answered by a dazzling sheet of summer lightning.

"Skidi!" Clarence Big-Saddle swore. "It worked. I didn't think it would."

Clarence Big-Saddle lived on his land for many years, and he paid no taxes. Intruders were unable to come down to his place. The land was sold for taxes three times, but nobody ever came down to claim it. Finally, it was carried as open land on the books. Homesteaders filed on it several times, but none of them fulfilled the qualification of living on the land.

Half a century went by. Clarence Big-Saddle called his son.

"I've had it, boy," he said. "I think I'll just go in the house and die."

"Okay, Dad," the son Clarence Little-Saddle said. "I'm going in to town to shoot a few games of pool with the boys. I'll bury you when I get back this evening."

So the son Clarence Little-Saddle inherited. He also lived on the land for many years without paying taxes.

There was a disturbance in the courthouse one day. The place seemed to be invaded in force, but actually there were but one man, one woman, and five children. "I'm Robert Rampart," said the man, "and we want the Land Office."

"I'm Robert Rampart Junior," said a nine-year-old gangler, "and we want it pretty blamed quick."

"I don't think we have anything like that," the girl at the desk said. "Isn't that something they had a long time ago?"

"Ignorance is no excuse for inefficiency, my dear," said Mary Mabel Rampart, an eight-year-old who could easily pass for eight and a half. "After I make my report, I wonder who will be sitting at your desk tomorrow."

"You people are either in the wrong state or the wrong century," the girl said.

"The Homestead Act still obtains," Robert Rampart insisted. "There is one tract of land carried as open in this county. I want to file on it."

Cecilia Rampart answered the knowing wink of a beefy man at the distant desk. "Hi," she breathed as she slinked over. "I'm Cecilia Rampart, but my stage name is Cecilia San Juan. Do you think that seven is too young to play ingenue roles?"

"Not for you," the man said. "Tell your folks to come over here."

"Do you know where the Land Office is?" Cecilia asked.

"Sure. It's the fourth left-hand drawer of my desk. The smallest office we got in the whole courthouse. We don't use it much any more."

The Ramparts gathered around. The beefy man started to make out the papers.

"This is the land description," Robert Rampart began. "Why, you've got it down already. How did you know?"

"I've been around here a long time," the man answered.

They did the paper work, and Robert Rampart filed on the land.

"You won't be able to come onto the land itself, though," the man said.

"Why won't I?" Rampart demanded. "Isn't the land description accurate?"

"Oh, I suppose so. But nobody's ever been able to get to the land. It's become a sort of joke."

"Well, I intend to get to the bottom of that joke," Rampart insisted. "I will occupy the land or I will find out why not."

"I'm not sure about that," the beefy man said. "The last man to file on the land, about a dozen years ago, wasn't able to occupy the land. And he wasn't able to say why he couldn't. It's kind of interesting, the look on their faces after they try it for a day or two, and then give it up."

The Ramparts left the courthouse, loaded into their camper, and drove out to find their land. They stopped at the house of a cattle and wheat farmer named Charley Dublin. Dublin met them with a grin which indicated he'd been tipped off.

"Come along if you want to, folks," Dublin said. "The easiest way is on foot across my short pasture here. Your land's directly west of mine."

They walked the short distance to the border.

"My name is Tom Rampart, Mr. Dublin." Six-year-old Tom made conversation as they walked. "But my name is really Ramires, and not Tom. I am the issue of an indiscretion of my mother in Mexico several years ago."

"The boy is a kidder, Mr. Dublin," said the mother, Nina Rampart, defending herself. "I have never been in Mexico, but sometimes I have the urge to disappear there forever."

"Ay yes, Mrs. Rampart. And what is the name of the youngest boy here?" Charley Dublin asked.

"Fatty," said Fatty Rampart.

"But surely that is not your given name?"

"Audifax," said five-year-old Fatty.

"Ah well, Audifax, Fatty, are you a kidder too?"

"He's getting better at it, Mr. Dublin," Mary Mabel said. "He was a twin till last week. His twin was named Skinny. Mama left Skinny unguarded while she was out tippling, and there were wild dogs in the neighborhood. When Mama got back, do you know what was left of Skinny? Two neck bones and an ankle bone. That was all."

"Poor Skinny," Dublin said. "Well, Rampart, this is the fence and the end of my land. Yours is just beyond."

"Is that ditch on my land?" Rampart asked.

"That ditch *is* your land."

"I'll have it filled in. It's a dangerous deep cut even if it is narrow. And the other fence looks like a good one, and I sure have a pretty plot of land beyond it."

"No, Rampart, the land beyond the second fence belongs to Holister Hyde," Charley Dublin said. "That second fence is the *end* of your land."

"Now, just wait a minute, Dublin! There's something wrong here. My land is one hundred and sixty acres, which would be a half mile on a side. Where's my half-mile width?"

"Between the two fences."

"That's not eight feet."

"Doesn't look like it, does it, Rampart? Tell you what—there's plenty of throwing-sized rocks around. Try to throw one across it."

"I'm not interested in any such boys' games," Rampart exploded. "I want my land."

But the Rampart children *were* interested in such games. They got with it with those throwing rocks. They winged them out over the little gully. The stones acted funny. They hung in the air, as it were, and diminished in size. And they were small as pebbles when they dropped down, down into the gully. None of them could throw a stone across that ditch, and they were throwing kids.

"You and your neighbor have conspired to fence open land for your own use," Rampart charged.

"No such thing, Rampart," Dublin said cheerfully. "My land checks perfectly. So does Hyde's. So does yours, if we knew how to check it. It's like one of those trick topological drawings. It really is half a mile from here to there, but the eye gets lost somewhere. It's your land. Crawl through the fence and figure it out."

Rampart crawled through the fence, and drew himself up to jump the gully. Then he hesitated. He got a glimpse of just how deep that gully was. Still, it wasn't five feet across.

There was a heavy fence post on the ground, designed for use as a corner post. Rampart up-ended it with some effort. Then he shoved it to fall and bridge the gully. But it fell short, and it shouldn't have. An eight-foot post should bridge a five-foot gully.

The post fell into the gully, and rolled and rolled and rolled. It spun as though it were rolling outward, but it made no progress except vertically. The post came to rest on a ledge of the gully, so close that Rampart could almost reach out and touch it, but it now appeared no bigger than a match stick.

"There is something wrong with that fence post, or with the world, or with my eyes," Robert Rampart said. "I wish I felt dizzy so I could blame it on that."

"There's a little game that I sometimes play with my neighbor Hyde when we're both out," Dublin said. "I've a heavy rifle and I train it on the middle of his forehead as he stands on the other side of the ditch apparently eight feet away. I fire it off then (I'm a good shot), and I hear it whine across. It'd kill him dead if things were as they seem. But Hyde's in no danger. The shot always bangs into that little scuff of rocks and boulders about thirty feet below him. I can see it kick up the rock dust there, and the sound of it rattling into those little boulders comes back to me in about two and a half seconds."

A bull-bat (poor people call it the night-hawk) raveled around in the air and zoomed out over the narrow ditch, but it did not reach the other side. The bird dropped below ground level and could be seen against the background of the other side of the ditch. It grew smaller and hazier as though at a distance of three or four hundred yards. The white bars on its wings could no longer be discerned; then the bird itself could hardly be discerned; but it was far short of the other side of the five-foot ditch.

A man identified by Charley Dublin as the neighbor Hollister Hyde had appeared on the other side of the little ditch. Hyde grinned and waved. He shouted something, but could not be heard.

"Hyde and I both read mouths," Dublin said, "so we can talk across the ditch easy enough. Which kid wants to play chicken? Hyde will barrel a good-sized rock right at your head, and if you duck or flinch you're chicken."

"Me! Me!" Audifax Rampart challenged. And Hyde, a big man with big hands, did barrel a fearsome jagged rock right at the head of the boy. It would have killed him if things had been as they appeared. But the rock diminished to nothing and disappeared into the ditch. Here was a phenomenon: things seemed real-sized on either side of the ditch, but they diminished coming out over the ditch either way.

"Everybody game for it?" Robert Rampart Junior asked.

"We won't get down there by standing here," Mary Mabel said.

"Nothing wenchered, nothing gained," said Cecilia. "I got that from an ad for a sex comedy."

Then the five Rampart kids ran down into the gully. Ran *down* is right. It was almost as if they ran down the vertical face of a cliff. They couldn't do that. The gully was no wider than the stride of the biggest kids. But the gully diminished those children, it ate them alive. They were doll-sized. They were acorn-sized. They were running for minute after minute across a ditch that was only five feet across. They were going, deeper in it, and getting smaller. Robert Rampart was roaring his alarm, and his wife Nina was screaming. Then she stopped. "What am I carrying on so loud about?" she asked herself. "It looks like fun. I'll do it too."

She plunged into the gully, diminished in size as the children had done, and ran at a pace to carry her a hundred yards away across a gully only five feet wide.

That Robert Rampart stirred things up for a while then. He got the sheriff there, and the highway patrolmen. A ditch had stolen his wife and five children, he said, and maybe killed them. And if anybody laughs, there may be another killing. He got the colonel of the State National Guard there, and a command post set up. He got a couple of airplane pilots. Robert Rampart had one quality: when he hollered, people came.

He got the newsmen out from T-Town, and the eminent scientists, Dr. Velikof Vonk, Arpad Arkabaranan, and Willy McGilly. That bunch turns up every time you get on a good one. They just happen to be in that part of the country where something interesting is going on.

They attacked the thing from all four sides and the top, and by inner and outer theory. If a thing measures half a mile on each side, and the sides are straight, there just has to be something in the middle of it. They took pictures from the air, and they turned out perfect. They proved that Robert Rampart had the prettiest hundred and sixty acres in the country, the larger part of it being a lush green valley, and all of it being half a mile on a side, and situated just where it should be. They took ground-level photos then, and it showed a beautiful half-mile stretch of land between the boundaries of Charley Dublin and Hollister Hyde. But a man isn't a camera. None of them could see that beautiful spread with the eyes in their heads. Where was it?

Down in the valley itself everything was normal. It really was half a mile wide and no more than eighty feet deep with a very gentle slope. It was warm and sweet, and beautiful with grass and grain.

Nina and the kids loved it, and they rushed to see what squatter had built that little house on their land. A house, or a shack. It had never known paint, but paint would have spoiled it. It was built of split timbers dressed near smooth with ax and draw knife, chinked with white clay, and sodded up to about half its height. And there was an interloper standing by the little lodge.

"Here, here what are you doing on our land?" Robert Rampart Junior demanded of the man. "Now you just shamble off again wherever you came from. I'll bet you're a thief too, and those cattle are stolen."

"Only the black-and-white calf," Clarence Little-Saddle said. "I couldn't resist him, but the rest are mine. I guess I'll just stay around and see that you folks get settled all right."

"Is there any wild Indians around here?" Fatty Rampart asked.

"No, not really. I go on a bender about every three months and get a little bit wild, and there's a couple Osage boys from Gray Horse that get noisy sometimes, but that's about all," Clarence Little-Saddle said.

"You certainly don't intend to palm yourself off on us as an Indian," Mary Mabel challenged. "You'll find us a little too knowledgeable for that."

"Little girl, you might as well tell this cow there's no room for her to be a cow since you're so knowledgeable. She thinks she's a short-horn cow named Sweet Virginia. I think I'm a Pawnee Indian named Clarence. Break it to us real gentle if we're not."

"If you're an Indian where's your war bonnet? There's not a feather on you anywhere."

"How you be sure? There's a story that we got feathers instead of hair on—Aw, I can't tell a joke like that to a little girl! How come you're not wearing the Iron Crown of Lombardy if you're a white girl? How you expect me to believe you're a little white girl and your folks came from Europe a couple hundred years ago if you don't wear it? There are six hundred tribes, and only one of them, the Oglala Sioux, had the war bonnet, and only the big leaders, never more than two or three alive at one time, wore it."

"Your analogy is a little strained," Mary Mabel said. "Those Indians we saw in Florida and the ones at Atlantic City had war bonnets, and they couldn't very well have been the kind of Sioux you said. And just last night on the TV in the motel, those Massachusetts Indians put a war bonnet on the President and called him the Great White Father. You mean to tell me that they were all phonies? Hey, who's laughing at who here?"

"If you're an Indian where's your bow and arrow?" Tom Rampart interrupted. "I bet you can't even shoot one."

"You're sure right there," Clarence admitted. "I never shot one of those things but once in my life. They used to have an archery range in Boulder Park over in T-Town, and you could rent the things and shoot at targets tied to hay bales. Hey, I barked my whole forearm and nearly broke my thumb when the bow-string thwacked home. I couldn't shoot that thing at all. I don't see how anybody ever could shoot one of them."

"Okay, kids," Nina Rampart called to her brood. "Let's start pitching this junk out of the shack so we can move in. Is there any way we can drive our camper down here, Clarence?"

"Sure, there's a pretty good dirt road, and it's a lot wider than it looks from the top. I got a bunch of green bills in an old night charley in the shack. Let me get them, and I'll clear out for a while. The shack hasn't been cleaned out for seven years, since the last time this happened. I'll show you the road to the top, and you can bring your car down it."

"Hey, you old Indian, you lied!" Cecilia Rampart shrilled from the doorway of the shack. "You *do* have a war bonnet. Can I have it?"

"I didn't mean to lie, I forgot about that thing," Clarence Little-Saddle said. "My son Clarence Bareback sent that to me from Japan for a joke a long time ago. Sure, you can have it."

All the children were assigned tasks carrying the junk out of the shack and setting fire to it. Nina Rampart and Clarence Little-Saddle ambled up to the rim of the valley by the vehicle road that was wider than it looked from the top.

"Nina, you're back! I thought you were gone forever," Robert Rampart jittered at seeing her again. "What—where are the children?"

"Why, I left them down in the valley, Robert. That is, ah, down in that little ditch right there. Now you've got me worried again. I'm going to drive the camper down there and unload it. You'd better go on down and lend a hand too, Robert, and quit talking to all these funny-looking men here."

And Nina went back to Dublin's place for the camper.

"It would be easier for a camel to go through the eye of a needle than for that intrepid woman to drive a car down into that narrow ditch," the eminent scientist Dr. Velikof Vonk said.

"You know how that camel does it?" Clarence Little-Saddle offered, appearing all of a sudden from nowhere. "He just closes one of his own eyes and flops back his ears and plunges right through. A camel is mighty narrow when he closes one eye and flops back his ears. Besides, they use a big-eyed needle in the act."

"Where'd this crazy man come from?" Robert Rampart demanded, jumping three feet in the air. "Things are coming out of the ground now. I want my land! I want my children! I want my wife! Whoops, here she comes driving it. Nina, you can't drive a loaded camper into a ditch like that! You'll be killed or collapsed!"

Nina Rampart drove the loaded camper into the little ditch at a pretty good rate of speed. The best of belief is that she just closed one eye and plunged right through. The car diminished and dropped, and it was smaller than a toy car. But it raised a pretty good cloud of dust as it bumped for several hundred yards across a ditch that was only five feet wide.

"Rampart, it's akin to the phenomenon known as looming, only in reverse," the eminent scientist Arpad Arkabaranan explained as he attempted to throw a rock across the narrow ditch. The rock rose very high in the air, seemed to hang at its apex while it diminished to the size of a grain of sand, and then fell into the ditch not six inches of the way across. There isn't anybody going to throw across a half-mile valley even if it looks five feet. "Look at a rising moon sometimes, Rampart. It appears very large, as though covering a great sector of the horizon, but it only covers one-half of a degree. It is hard to believe that you could set seven hundred and twenty of such large moons side by side around the horizon, or that it would take one hundred and eighty of the big things to reach from the horizon to a point overhead. It is also hard to believe that your valley is five hundred times as wide as it appears, but it has been surveyed, and it is."

"I want my land. I want my children. I want my wife," Robert chanted dully. "Damn, I let her get away again."

"I'll tell you, Rampy," Clarence Little-Saddle squared on him, "a man that lets his wife get away twice doesn't deserve to keep her. I give you till nightfall; then you forfeit. I've taken a liking to the brood. One of us is going to be down there tonight."

After a while a bunch of them were off in that little tavern on the road between Cleveland and Osage. It was only a half a mile away. If the valley had run in the other direction, it would have been only six feet away.

"It is a psychic nexus in the form of an elongated dome," said the eminent scientist Velikof Vonk. "It is maintained subconsciously by the concatenation of at least two minds, the stronger of them belonging to a man dead for many years. It has apparently existed for a little less than a hundred years, and in another hundred years it will be considerably weakened. We know from our checking out folk tales of Europe as well as Cambodia that these ensorceled areas seldom survive for more than two hundred and fifty years. The person who first set such a thing in being will usually lose interest in it, and in all worldly things, within a hundred years of his own death. This is a simple thanato-psychic limitation. As a short-term device, the thing has been used several times as a military tactic.

"This psychic nexus, as long as it maintains itself, causes group illusion, but it is really a simple thing. It doesn't fool birds or rabbits or cattle or cameras, only humans. There is nothing meteorological about it. It is strictly psychological. I'm glad I was able to give a scientific explanation to it or it would have worried me."

"It is continental fault coinciding with a noospheric fault," said the eminent scientist Arpad Arkabaranan. "The valley really is half a mile wide, and at the same time it really is only five feet wide. If we measured correctly, we would get these dual measurements. Of course it is meteorological! Everything including dreams is meteorological. It is the animals and cameras which are fooled, as lacking a true dimension; it is only humans who see the true duality. The phenomenon should be common along the whole continental fault where the earth gains or loses half a mile that has to go somewhere. Likely it extends through the whole sweep of the Cross Timbers. Many of those trees appear twice, and many do not appear at all. A man in the proper state of mind could farm that land or raise cattle on it, but it doesn't really exist. There is a clear parallel in the Luftspiegelungthal sector in the Black Forest of Germany which exists, or does not exist, according to the circumstances and to the attitude of the beholder. Then we have the case of Mad Mountain in Morgan County, Tennessee, which isn't there all the time, and also the Little Lobo Mirage south of Presidio, Texas, from which twenty thousand barrels of water were pumped in one two-and-a-half-year period before the mirage reverted to a mirage status. I'm glad I was able to give a scientific explanation to this or it would have worried me."

"I just don't understand how he worked it," said the eminent scientist Willy McGilly. "Cedar bark, jack-oak leaves, and the word 'Petahauerat.' The thing's impossible! When I was a boy and we wanted to make a hideout, we used bark from the skunk-spruce tree, the leaves of a box-elder, and the word was 'Boadicea.' All three elements are wrong here. I cannot find a scientific explanation for it, and it does worry me."

They went back to Narrow Valley. Robert Rampart was still chanting dully: "I want my land. I want my children. I want my wife."

Nina Rampart came chugging up out of the narrow ditch in the camper and emerged through that little gate a few yards down the fence row.

"Supper's ready and we're tired of waiting for you, Robert," she said. "A fine homesteader you are! Afraid to come onto your own land! Come along now; I'm tired of waiting for you."

"I want my land! I want my children! I want my wife!" Robert Rampart still chanted. "Oh, there you are, Nina. You stay here this time. I want my land! I want my children! I want an answer to this terrible thing!"

"It is time we decided who wears the pants in this family," Nina said stoutly. She picked up her husband, slung him over her shoulder, carried him to the camper and dumped him in, slammed (as it seemed) a dozen doors at once, and drove furiously into the Narrow Valley, which already seemed wider.

Why, the place was getting normaler and normaler by the minute! Pretty soon it looked almost as wide as it was supposed to be. The psychic nexus in the form of an elongated dome had collapsed. The continental fault that coincided with the noospheric fault had faced facts and decided to conform. The Ramparts were in effective possession of their homestead, and Narrow Valley was as normal as any place anywhere.

"I have lost my land," Clarence Little-Saddle moaned. "It was the land of my father Clarence Big-Saddle, and I meant it to be the land of my son Clarence Bareback. It looked so narrow that people did not notice how wide it was, and people did not try to enter it. Now I have lost it."

Clarence Little-Saddle and the eminent scientist Willy McGilly were standing on the edge of Narrow Valley, which now appeared its true half-mile extent. The moon was just rising, so big that it filled a third of the sky. Who would have imagined that it would take a hundred and eight of such monstrous things to reach from the horizon to a point overhead, and yet you could sight it with sighters and figure it so.

"I had a little bear-cat by the tail and I let go," Clarence groaned. "I had a fine valley for free, and I have lost it. I am like that hard-luck guy in the funny-paper or Job in the Bible. Destitution is my lot."

Willy McGilly looked around furtively. They were alone on the edge of the half-mile-wide valley.

"Let's give it a booster shot," Willy McGilly said.

Hey, those two got with it! They started a snapping fire and began to throw the stuff onto it. Bark from the dog-elm tree—how do you know it won't work?

It *was* working! Already the other side of the valley seemed a hundred yards closer, and there were alarmed noises coming up from the people in the valley.

Leaves from a black locust tree—and the valley narrowed still more! There was, moreover, terrified screaming of both children and big people from the depths of Narrow Valley, and the happy voice of Mary Mabel Rampart chanting "Earthquake! Earthquake!"

"That my valley be always wide and flourish and such stuff, and green with money and grass!" Clarence Little-Saddle orated in Pawnee chant style, "but that it be narrow if intruders come, smash them like bugs!"

People, that valley wasn't over a hundred feet wide, now, and the screaming of the people in the bottom of the valley had been joined by the hysterical coughing of the camper car starting up.

Willy and Clarence threw everything that was left on the fire. But the word? The word? Who remembers the word?

"Corsicanatexas!" Clarence Little-Saddle howled out with confidence he hoped would fool the fates.

He was answered not only by a dazzling sheet of summer lightning, but also by thunder and raindrops.

"Chahiksi!" Clarence Little-Saddle swore. "It worked. I didn't think it would. It will be all right now. I can use the rain.

The valley was again a ditch only five feet wide.

The camper car struggled out of Narrow Valley through the little gate. It was smashed flat as a sheet of paper, and the screaming kids and people in it had only one dimension.

"It's closing in! It's closing in!" Robert Rampart roared, and he was no thicker than if he had been made out of cardboard.

"We're smashed like bugs," the Rampart boys intoned. "We're thin like paper."

"Mort, ruine, ecrasement!" spoke-acted Cecilia Rampart like the great tragedienne she was.

"Help! Help!" Nina Rampart croaked, but she winked at Willy and Clarence as they rolled by. "This homesteading jag always did leave me a little flat."

"Don't throw those paper dolls away. They might be the Ramparts," Mary Mabel called.

The camper car coughed again and bumped along on level ground. This couldn't last forever. The car was widening out as it bumped along.

"Did we overdo it, Clarence?" Willy McGilly asked. "What did one flatlander say to the other?"

"Dimension of us never got around," Clarence said. "No, I don't think we overdid it, Willy. That car must be eighteen inches wide already, and they all ought to be normal by the time they reach the main road. The next time I do it, I think I'll throw wood-grain plastic on the fire to see who's kidding who."

JACKALOPE

BY ALAN DEAN FOSTER

ALAN DEAN FOSTER HAS WRITTEN EXTENSIVELY WITHIN THE GENRES OF SCI-
ENCE FICTION AND FANTASY, WITH SUBJECTS RANGING FROM ALIEN FIRST-
CONTACT STORIES TO EPIC FANTASIES OF TALKING ANIMALS TO BESTSELLING
MOVIE TIE-INS SUCH AS *STAR WARS*, *ALIEN*, AND *STAR TREK*. FOSTER IS A
RESIDENT OF THE SOUTHWEST, AND HIS AMOS MALONE STORIES OF A MAGICAL
MOUNTAINMAN WHO COULD HAVE WALKED OUT OF THE PAGES OF AN A. B.
GUTHRIE OR LARRY MCMURTRY NOVEL (IF IT WASN'T FOR THE FACT THAT HE
WAS RIDING A UNICORN WITH A SAWED-OFF HORN), ARE NEAR AND DEAR TO
HIS HEART. "JACKALOPE" IS A MIXTURE OF WESTERN TALL TALE WITH THE
FANTASTIC, AS TOLD BY SOME OLD-TIMERS SITTING AROUND A CAMPFIRE.

I'm, sorry, Gentlemen, but there is nothing left to tempt me. I've killed everything
there is to be killed.

Lord Guy Ruxton extracted an imported Havana cigar from a jacket pocket, utilized
an engraved Italian cutter to snip the end, and turned slightly to his left so Manners
could light it for him. As he puffed it to life, there was a subtle but unmistakable
shifting of bodies in the saloon as cardplayers and drinkers leaned in his direction in
a vain but hopeful attempt to partake, however infinitesimally, of that expensive aromatic smoke which would forever lie beyond their modest means.

Though they shared the best table in the house with him, Ruxton's audience of
Butte's leading citizens was equally appreciative, if not nearly so obvious. Being
connoisseurs of silver, they admired the cigar cutter as much as the smoke. The town
of Butte would not exist save for silver.

Ruxton was a rara avis in Montana Territory: a wide-ranging world traveler and
hunter of big game. A fine orator, he held his after-dinner companions spellbound
with his tales of tracking exotic animals to the far corners of the earth. Miners and
bankers alike were enthralled by stories of stalking tiger in British India, oryx in
Arabia, and all manner of dangerous game in Darkest Africa. Ruxton was only mildly
condescending to the colonials, and they responded in kind. Still, it was clear he was
bored. He took a sip of the best scotch Butte had to offer.

"I think the time has come for me to pack it all in, gentlemen, and retire to my
estate in Hampshire. You see, there is nothing left for me to hunt. The walls of my
trophy room will see no further additions because there is nothing further to add. I
lament the end of excitement!"

Silas Hooten had founded the town's first bank and watched it grow along with
the production of silver. Now he smiled and put down his drink.

"If it's excitement you crave, why not have a go at hunting buffalo in Sioux Territory?"

Ruxton regarded his cigar rather than the banker. "Because there is nothing to hunt in the eastern portion of your benighted territory *except* buffalo, and I have found that animal a singularly uninspiring quarry, though I have hunted it with bow and arrow in the fashion of the savages as well as with rifle. The presence of Red Hostiles in the vicinity does not alter the object of the hunt." He sighed tiredly.

"No, gentlemen. I have sampled the best of your cuisine, your scenery, and your women. Now I fear it is time I return permanently to England. I do not fault your bucolic hospitality. America was the only land remaining to be hunted. That I have done. Would that there were more truth and less wind to some of the tales I have heard of this country."

"Jackalope."

Ruxton frowned, peered past Hooten. "I beg your pardon, sir?" His drinking companions turned to stare with him.

"Jackalope, I said. Got ears, ain'tcha?"

The mouth that had given birth to the word was hidden by a massive buckskin-clad back. The individual seated at the bar looked like a chunk of dark granite blasted from the depths of one of the town's mines, hauled in by mine trolley and set up on a stool like some Druidic monolith. A hat fashioned of an unidentifiable golden fur crowned the huge head. Black curly hair lightly flecked with white tumbled in an undisciplined waterfall from beneath the headgear.

As miners and bankers and visiting nobility looked on, the man turned like an Egyptian statue come to life. Deep-sunk black eyes regarded them from beneath Assyrian brows. The hair at the back was matched in front by a dense beard that might have been forged of wrought-iron wire. Two thick, gnarled fingers supported a beer mug full of whiskey.

"I was sayin', sir, bein' unable to avoid overhearin' part of your conversation, that it might be you've never hunted for jackalope."

"Yes. Well." Ruxton noted that his companions were now smiling and chuckling softly among themselves. He lowered his voice. "Who is this extremely large chap, and what is he nattering on about?"

"Malone." Orin Waxman ran the biggest general store in town. "Amos Malone."

"*Mad* Amos Malone." Hooten pointed a finger at the side of his head. "The man's crazier than a bedbug, but it's a rare soul who'll say so to his face."

"Looking upon him, I can understand that. You say he's mad?" Several of the men nodded. "What's this 'jackalope' thing he's on about?"

Waxman shook his head, grinning. "There is no such animal. Somebody somewhere faked one up, and it's turned into a long-standing gag for foolin' easterners. No offense, Your Lordship. Someone will shoot a jackrabbit and a small deer or antelope. They'll take both to a good taxidermist with a sense of humor, and he'll stick the deer antlers on the rabbit's head. And there's your jackalope."

"I see. It is quite imaginary? You're positive of that?"

The men eyed one another uncertainly, left it to Hooten to reply. "Of course it is, sir. The mountain man's just having a little joke at your expense."

"A good joke, is it? At my expense?" Ruxton's eyes glittered as he turned back to the bar. "Here now, my good fellow. I am intrigued by your comment. Do come and join us."

Mutters of disbelief and distress came from Ruxton's companions, but none dared object when Malone lurched over to assume the lone empty chair at the table. Such men were not famed for their hygiene. Waxman and the others were relieved to discover that Malone, at least, seemed to have bathed some time in the not too distant past.

Obviously enjoying himself hugely, Ruxton swept a hand toward his hosts. "These gentlemen insist vehemently that there is no such creature as the one you speak of. I interpret that to mean they are calling you a liar, sir."

Waxman choked on his liquor, while Hooten's eyes widened in horror. Malone simply eyed them intently for a long moment, then sipped at his tenth of whiskey. The resultant sighs of relief were inaudible.

"None of 'em knows enough to call me a liar. I ain't insulted by the denials of the ignorant."

His response delighted Ruxton. "Sir, you are a man of surprises! For the moment I intend to leave aside the matter of your sanity. As you overheard, I am something of a sportsman."

"Your claim, not mine."

Ruxton bristled slightly at that, but restrained himself. "True enough. You claim I have not hunted this creature you call a jackalope. These good citizens dispute the assertion that it exists. I would put you and them to the test, sir." He made sure he met Malone's gaze evenly. "If you are game."

"I ain't, but the jackalope is."

Ruxton hesitated a moment, then burst out laughing when he was sure. "Upon my word! A rustic with wit. I like you, sir. 'Pon my word I do!" He stubbed out his half-finished cigar and tossed it over his shoulder, ignoring the near riot that followed its descending trajectory as a dozen men scrambled for possession of the butt.

"I would engage you, Mr. Malone, to direct me to the place where I might find such an animal and add it to my collection. I will pay you well, in gold, to serve as my guide in such a venture. Our bargain will be that should we find nothing except fast talk, all expenses will be borne by you."

Malone considered, seeing the doubt in the others' faces. Then he gently set down his mug. "Done. It'll be you and me alone, though. I don't like travelin' with a crowd." He glanced at Ruxton's valet. "Especially slaves."

The valet stiffened. Ruxton only smiled. "Manners is a valued member of my household staff, not a slave. However, it shall be as you wish. I will accompany you alone. Where are we going, sir, or is it to remain a mysterious secret?" He was clearly amused.

Malone turned and nodded westward. "Up thataway. Into the Bitterroots."

"The Bitterroots!" Hooten half-rose out of his seat. "Lord Ruxton, I implore you to reconsider this foolishness. The veracity of this—gentleman—is to be doubted. His reputation is eccentric in the extreme. There's nothing up in those mountains except Nez Percé and Blackfeet. You'll find only trouble and danger in that range, not non-existent game!"

"Come now, gentlemen. Are you again openly disputing the good Mr. Malone's word?" Waxman's lower lip trembled, but, like the others, he said no more. "Then it is agreed. When do we depart, Mr. Malone?"

"Morning'd be fine with me. We'll be gone a few weeks. Take what you need, but it's best to travel light."

"As you say, sir. I understand the weather is good this time of year. I am looking forward to our excursion."

THEY HEADED NORTHWEST out of town despite the last-minute pleas of Hooten and his friends. The death of so distinguished a visitor to their territory would not be the best of publicity for a growing community, and they feared it; yes, they did. Ruxton's valet tried to reassure them.

"Lord Ruxton, gentlemen, is used to the life of the camp and the trail. He had been in difficult circumstances many times and has always emerged unscathed. He is a crack shot and an athlete, a man who relishes danger and its challenges. Your concern does him an injustice. No harm will befall him. If you must worry about someone, concern yourselves with this crude Malone person."

"Mad Amos is no genius, but he ain't dumb, neither," said one of the men who'd gathered on the porch of the hotel to bid the hunters farewell. "Ain't nobody never been able to figure him out noways."

"I assure you," Manners continued, "Lord Ruxton is more than a match for any situation this lout can place him in."

"Oh, I wasn't worried about how your boss is going to get on with Malone," said the man who'd spoken. "I was wondering how he was going to cope with the Rockies."

ONCE THEY LEFT town, they commenced a steady climb into mountains as serene and lovely as any in the world. They reminded Ruxton of the Alps, without the spas and fine hotels and other amenities of that ancient region. By way of compensation, there was a freshness in the air, a newness not to be found at the watering holes of the wealthy that dotted the continent. Ruxton's packhorse trailed behind Malone's.

"That is an unusual animal you ride, sir." He nodded at Malone's mount.

The mountain man spoke without looking at his guest. "Useless has been called plenty of names, Lord. Most of 'em less complimentary than that."

The animal Malone called Useless was black except for patches of white at tail and fetlocks. A single white ring encircled one eye, giving the horse the aspect of a permanent squint. He was a cross among half a dozen breeds. For reasons Malone chose not to elaborate on, a heavy leather patch was affixed permanently to the animal's forehead.

Have to attend to that again soon, he mused. He didn't worry about it out in the backcountry, but it was just the sort of thing to provoke consternation among simple city folk.

The horse snorted, just to let the two riders know he was listening.

"Magnificent country, your West. Do you think we might encounter some Red Indians, as Mr. Hooten seemed to fear?"

"Only if they're in the mood for company. Nobody sees the Blackfeet unless they want to be seen, and sometimes the Nez Percé don't even see each other. I don't anticipate any trouble, if that's what you mean. I've an understandin' with the folks hereabouts. If we do meet up with any, you keep your mouth shut and let me do the talkin'. I ain't sure how they'd take you."

"As you wish, Mr. Malone. How long before," he bent to hide a smile, "we stand to encounter one of your jackalopes?"

"Hard to say. They're shy critters, and there seem to be fewer of 'em each year. Seems to be as folks start movin' into this part of the world, certain critters start movin' out."

"Indeed? How inconvenient. Well, I am in no hurry. I am enjoying our excursion immensely. I took the liberty of stocking up on the finest victuals your community could provide. I shall enjoy dining au camp at your expense, Mr. Malone."

"Ain't my expense unless we don't git you a jackalope, Lord."

"Of course. I am remiss."

"Don't know about that, but you're sure as hell premature."

Many days went by without them encountering evidence of any other humans of any color. Malone seemed content to lead ever deeper into the mountains. Snow-clad peaks soared ten thousand feet overhead as they picked their way across a rocky slope above a wide, white-flecked river. Ruxton marveled at Malone's ability to find a path where none was visible. The man was a fine tracker, like many of the primitives Ruxton had engaged in other lands.

He was watching his guide carefully now. Perhaps robbery had been his motive all along in agreeing to this trek. Ruxton had considered the possibility back in the saloon, but, instead of deterring him, it only added spice to an expedition such as this. He lived for such excitement. If thuggery was indeed in the mountain man's plans, he was in for a surprise. Ruxton had dealt with drunken cossacks and silent-footed dacoits. Despite Malone's size, Ruxton knew that in the event of a fight, it would be an Englishman who returned to tell the tale.

He was careful to sleep on the opposite side of their campfire, Colt pistol at his side, the intricately carved pepperbox snug in its special holster inside his boot. Malone would not surprise him in the middle of the night.

So he was more than mildly shocked when he found himself being shaken awake the following morning. His hand lunged for the Colt, paused when he saw that Malone was looking not at him but past him.

"Whisper," Malone instructed him, "and then speak softer than that."

"What is it?" Ruxton was up quickly, pulling on his jacket. "Savages?"

Malone shook his head.

"What then?" Chilled fingers buttoned the coat. Even in late spring, dawn was cold in these mountains.

"What you come fer, Lord."

Ruxton's hands stopped. "Pardon, Mr. Malone?"

"Jackalopes, you damn idjit! You want that trophy or not?"

Ruxton gaped at him, then hurriedly resumed his dressing.

Malone led him away from camp. They crossed two small ridges before surmounting one slightly higher. The roar of the river masked their climb.

Clutching his .30=30, Ruxton peered over the crest of the ridge. There was no need for Malone to remind him to keep his voice down, because he had no words for what he was seeing.

Not one, not two, but a whole herd of the utterly impossible creatures were feeding and frolicking in a small grassy meadow. They were bigger than he would have imagined, bigger than the largest jackrabbits he'd shot in New Mexico. They nibbled contentedly at the grass or preened themselves or lay on their sides soaking up the early-morning sun. Several pairs of young males were play-fighting. They would eye each other intently, then drop their heads and leap like rutting rams. Heads made contact six feet above the ground. Antlers locked and clacked loudly before the combatants separated, tumbled back to earth, and gathered themselves for another charge.

"I don't believe it," he mumbled under his breath.

Malone was impatient. "I don't care whether you believe it or not, Lord, but I never did cotton to havin' my word doubted. I reckon we won't be hearin' no more of such nonsense. You think you can shoot one, or you want me to do it fer you?"

"What? Oh yes."

Ruxton checked his weapon. He'd come to Montana in search of trophies, had gone along with Malone for the excitement of the wager, and now found himself in the position of obtaining far more than he'd sought. This expedition would yield much more. There would be articles in *The Times,* scientific honors, perhaps a special room in the British Museum.

Oh, he would take care to acknowledge Malone as his guide to this wonder. That would be proper. But recognition as discoverer would mean nothing to such a simple soul. The honor would be wasted on him. Ruxton therefore would graciously relieve him of the burdens it would entail.

Though nervous, he knew he could not miss. Not at this range. His valet had not exaggerated his master's skill with a rifle. Ruxton settled on the biggest buck in the herd, a magnificent ten-pointer. It was squatting off to one side, grazing contentedly. *Sorry, old fellow*, he thought as he squeezed the trigger.

The gun's report echoed noisily up the canyon. The buck screamed once as it jumped convulsively. By the time it hit the ground, it was dead, shot cleanly through the heart. Like fleas exploding from an old mattress, the rest of the herd vanished in seconds.

But the dead buck jackalope did not vanish like a character from *Through the Looking-Glass.* It was real. Malone followed behind as the excited Ruxton scrambled over the rocks toward it.

He lifted it triumphantly by the antlers. It was heavy, at least twenty pounds. This was not some clever fake conceived at great expense to deceive him.

"Mr. Malone," he told the mountain man when he finally arrived, "I am sorry for doubting your word. Oh, I confess to being as skeptical as your fellow citizens. I thought I would be the one to have the good laugh. I apologize profusely."

"No need to apologize, Lord. Leastwise you had the guts to back up your words. And there's worse things to go a-huntin' fer than a good laugh. Come on now and let's be gettin' away from here."

"Why the rush? I thought I might have a shot at another one."

"I promised you one trophy. You bagged it, and a big one at that." He was scanning the canyon walls as he spoke. "Now it's time you and I were makin' tracks."

Ruxton frowned, joined Malone in studying river and enclosing canyon. "Why? Surely we're in no danger here. Or do you fear Indians may have heard my shot?"

"Nope. Ain't worried about Indians. Ain't none in this place. They won't come down this canyon."

"Well, then, what troubles you? Pumas, perhaps, or a bear?"

"Not them, neither."

Ruxton sighed, not wishing to spoil this historic moment with an argument. "I warn you, sir, I have little patience for linguistic obfuscation."

"Tell me somethin', Lord. What kind of critter do you think would be fast enough and strong enough to catch somethin' like a jackalope?"

"Why, I don't know. I should imagine that the usual predators manage to   " But Malone had turned and was already taking long strides back toward camp. Ruxton followed, too elated by his kill to remain angry with his irritating guide.

Having put the incident completely out of his mind, he was furious when Malone woke him in the middle of the night. He could see the mountain man outlined by the glow of the dying campfire.

"Sir, I have no idea what your absurd intention may be in disturbing me thus, but I am accustomed to enjoying a full night's rest, and I—"

"Shut up."

"Now listen to me, my good fellow, if you—"

He went silent as the muzzle of an enormous rifle tilted toward him. "I told you to shut up, Lord. If you do, maybe I can keep you alive."

Ruxton had plenty more to say, but forced himself to keep quiet so that Malone could explain. That was when he noticed that his guide was staring anxiously at the sky.

A diadem of stars flattered a half-moon that turned the granite slopes around them the color of used steel. Far below, the unnamed river ran nervously toward the distant Missouri. Ruxton was about to mention the possibility of marauding Indians once again, when something man-sized filled his field of vision. Its eyes were like saucers of molten lead. He let out a scream and fell backward even as the gun in Malone's hands thundered. Something like a Malay dirk cut his shoulder, slicing through his shirt. Then all was still.

He lay panting as Malone rushed to reload the buffalo gun. Putting a hand to his shoulder, Ruxton found not one but three parallel cuts through shirt and skin. They were shallow but bloody, and beginning to sting as his body reacted to the injury.

Wordlessly, he started to stand, only to drop to hands and knees on Malone's terse command. He crawled over to the thing the mountain man had shot out of the sky.

It was not intact. Malone's Sharps blasted a three-inch-long cartridge through an octagonal barrel. The nocturnal attacker had been blown apart. But enough remained to show Ruxton it was no creature known to modern science.

"What the blazes is it, Malone?"

The mountain man continued to survey the sky, his eyes seeming to flick from star to star as though he knew each intimately. The horses pawed nervously at the ground, rolling their eyes and tugging at their reins. Of the four, only Malone's mount Useless stood calmly, occasionally shaking his head and turning it sideways to gaze sourly at the two men.

"Wolful," Malone replied curtly. He set the rifle aside and drew his peculiar LeMat pistol.

The body was certainly that of a very large wolf. What lifted Ruxton's hackles were not so much the powerful, now-broken wings that sprouted from just above and behind the enlarged shoulders, nor the grasping talons on all four feet, one of which had slashed his shoulder and just missed his throat. It was the face that was really disturbing. The familiar long wolf muzzle was curved slightly, like some furry beak. The ears were too wide and long for any member of the *Canis* genus. And the now-dark eyes that had shone like the lamps of Hell were so swollen in size they nearly met above the bridge of the muzzle. It was a creature worthy of the imagination of a Dante.

He crawled back to camp and began pulling on his boots. Malone grunted satisfaction.

"Good. Reckon I don't have to tell you everythin'. We got to get under some cover." He nodded upslope from their trail. "Thought I might've seen a cave on our way in. Don't much care for dark places, but it might be big enough to hide us and the horses both." He rose and holstered the rifle, began assembling their equipment with one hand. Ruxton noted that he did not at any time let go of the LeMat.

They lost one of the horses despite their caution. Neither man rode, and the unflappable Useless led, but Ruxton's pack mare still broke her tether and bolted for the nearest stand of tall trees. As she charged across the slope, she shed cooking pots and utensils and food and tools, the equipment making a terrible racket as it banged and bounced off the rocks. Malone and Ruxton watched her go.

"She'll be all right," Ruxton declared hopefully. "We'll track her down come morning."

Malone's expression was grim in the moonlight. "Why do you think I didn't head for the woods?"

As the mare approached the first trees, the entire forest canopy appeared to rise from the topmost branches. Ruxton's mouth went dry, and he shivered. But what more natural than for nocturnal flying creatures to roost in flocks? The fleeing mare had disturbed them.

There were at least thirty of the huge wolfuls. They swooped down on the terrified animal, circling low and snapping with wolf jaws at her withers and neck. She kicked out frantically and sent one of her tormentors spinning. It yelped unnaturally.

There were too many to prevent the inevitable. A pair landed on her back, using their talons to cling to flesh and pack straps. They tore at her face and flanks. Others cut her legs out from under her, striking at the tendons until they had her hamstrung. Unable to run or kick, the mare was buried beneath an avalanche of snarling, tearing bodies. She whinnied wildly to the last.

Malone and Ruxton didn't linger for the end. Even as the mare went down, a couple of the flock were making exploratory passes at the remaining horses and men. Ruxton felt heavy feathers brush his head as he ducked. He was not ashamed to admit that he screamed. Malone's LeMat boomed several times. Once there was a deeper, sharper explosion as he fired the .410 shotgun barrel that was mounted beneath the revolver barrel. Ruxton found himself surrounded by blood and feathers. He had a brief glimpse of feral yellow eyes. Then the sky disappeared as they stumbled into the cave.

It tunneled far back into the mountain. As Malone had hoped, there was more than enough room for all of them, including the horses. They tied them to boulders near the back wall of the cave.

Bored with the carcass of the already dismembered mare, the flock began to gather outside the entrance, padding back and forth and flapping their wings excitedly. The cave was actually larger than Malone would have liked. There was flying room inside. A lower ceiling would have been much more comforting.

Ruxton was breathing hard, his eyes nearly as wild as those of his mount. While it had stopped bleeding, his injured shoulder was throbbing mercilessly. But he could still hold a rifle.

"I regret the loss of my large-bore," he told Malone as he checked the .30=30. "It was packed with my other supplies on the mare."

The mountain man grunted. There followed an uncomfortable silence.

"Look here, Malone," said Ruxton finally, "I'm sorry I doubted you, old chap. I've been a bit of an ass all along, and I apologize." He stuck out his hand.

Malone eyed it, then enveloped it in his own huge paw and squeezed briefly. "I like a man who can own up to his own mistakes. I just hope you'll live to regret it." He turned back to the cave entrance. "There'll still be some meat left on your mare. When they've cracked all the marrow out of the bones, they'll work themselves up for a go at us. We have to stop 'em before they get inside, or we're done."

Ruxton nodded, resting his rifle atop a boulder that had fallen from the ceiling. "I've never even heard rumors of such a creature."

"Any folks whut sees one never gets away to tell of it. The Nez Percé know about 'em. They call 'em Sha-hoo-ne-wha-teh. Spirit wolves of the air. But the Nez Percé are unusual folk. They see things the Blackfeet and even the Cheyenne miss. 'Course, white folks don't find their way into this particular part of the Bitterroots.

"Way I figger it, no ordinary predator's fast enough or strong enough to take down a jackalope, especially when they stand and fight together. So these here wolfuls evolved to prey on 'em. Unfortunately, they ain't real particular about their supper. You and me, we're a dam sight slower than a sick jackalope. As for the horses, well, they're regular walkin' general stores far as these critters are concerned."

"Listen, Malone. Most of my shells were packed on that poor mare along with my big guns. If things start to look bad, I'd appreciate it if you'd save a round in that LeMat for me. I don't mean for my rifle."

"I know what you mean. We ain't somebody's supper yet, Lord. They got to get in here first. Meanwhile, why not have a go at askin' your name-sake for help?"

"My namesake?" Malone's eyes rose as he jerked a finger upward. "Oh," Ruxton nodded somberly.

The wolfuls continued to gather outside, their massed wingbeats a vast rushing that soon drowned out the livelier, healthier babble of the river below.

"First they'll sing for courage," Malone explained. "Then they'll start circlin' as they decide which one of 'em will get the honor of goin' for our throats first. After that they'll come for us. Try and pick your shots. One way or the other, it'll all be over quick."

Ruxton nodded, his teeth tightly clenched as he stared at the moonlit oval that marked the entrance of their sanctuary.

When the flock began their howling, it was as if all the graves at Battersea had opened to release the long dead. The sounds were higher in pitch than normal wolf calls, a sort of moan mixed with the kind of screech an enormous vulture might make. The horses panicked at it, kicking up dust and gravel, pawing at the unyielding stone.

Foam spilled from their lips. Only Useless stood placidly, one eye half-opened, swaying on his legs as if asleep. It made Ruxton wonder. Perhaps the animal was partly
deaf and blind.

The flock leader was silver across his muzzle. He came in low and then rose
abruptly toward the ceiling, awful talons spread wide to grasp and rend, vast yellow
eyes staring hypnotically. They froze the startled Ruxton for an instant, but not Malone. The Sharps blew the wolful in half, the huge shell tearing through flesh and
bone. Ruxton had no time to appreciate the difficult shot, because the rest of the flock
followed close on the heels of their dead leader.

The terrified whinnying of the horses, the howls and roars of the wolfuls, and the
rapid firing of both men's guns were deafening in the enclosed space. Ruxton saw
Malone put down the empty LeMat and race to reload, his thick fingers moving as
precisely as those of a concert pianist. He'd drawn his big bowie knife and used it to
fend off his attackers as he worked.

Then Ruxton saw him go down, the golden-furred hat flying as a diving wolful
struck him across the forehead. The claws missed his eyes, but the impact was severe.

"Malone!" Ignoring the pain shooting through his shoulder, Ruxton rushed to the
other man's side. His rifle cracked, and another wolful dropped, snapping mindlessly
at its own damaged wing.

The mountain man blinked dazedly up at him, bleeding from the gash in his head.
It was a shallow wound. He was only stunned.

That was when the flapping and howling and gnashing of teeth ceased. So concerned was he with the guide that Ruxton didn't notice it at first. Only when he helped
the much larger man to his feet did he see that the last of the wolfuls had turned tail
and was fleeing the cave.

"They're leaving. We beat them, old man! Gave them a sound hiding!"

"I think not, Lord." Malone fought to penetrate the oil that seemed to be floating
on his retinas. "The Sharps—gotta get the Sharps." He stumbled, blinking dizzily.

"Hang on. I'll get it. But we don't need it anymore. They've gone, you see, and—"

He stopped in mid-sentence, holding his breath even as he left Malone to pick up
the heavy buffalo rifle. The last howling of the wolfuls had faded into the distance,
but it was not silent outside. A dull booming, as of some heavy tread, was clearly
audible and growing steadily louder as he listened. He forced himself to keep his
hands steady as he loaded the Sharps.

The massive breathing was right outside the cave. Evidently they were not the first
creatures to make use of its shelter. The horses were too terrified to whinny. They
huddled together against the back wall, trembling.

The moon went out as something immense blocked the entrance. Ruxton raised
the Sharps and tried to hold it steady. Though he was a strong man, it sent shivers
along the muscles of his arms.

Whatever stood there had to bend to fit beneath the twenty-foot-high ceiling. Its
eyes were red instead of yellow like those of the wolful. An overpowering musk
assailed Ruxton's nostrils as the hairy leviathan paused to sniff loudly.

It growled, and Ruxton felt his knees go weak. Imagine a whale, growling. The
growl became a snarl that revealed teeth the size of railroad ties in the blunt, dark
muzzle. It was coming for them.

Ruxton pulled the trigger, and the Sharps erupted. He thought he'd prepared himself for the recoil, but he was wrong. It knocked him on his back. The echo of the gun's report was drowned by an incredible bellow of pain and anger as the monster stumbled backward.

The rifle was pulled from his numb fingers. Malone reloaded as Ruxton staggered erect. The owner of the cave was already recovering from the shock and preparing to charge again. This time it would not hesitate curiously. A second slug from the Sharps wouldn't stop it. Not this time. As well to try shooting a runaway locomotive.

Something went flying past him like black lightning. Ruxton had a glimpse of white fetlocks and flying mane. Useless slammed headfirst into the belly of the monster like a Derby winner pounding for the finish line. The gargantua went backward, falling head over heels down the slope.

"Dumb, stupid son of a spasmed mare!" Malone growled as he gripped Ruxton by the shoulder. "Let's git out of this damn possum trap!"

They stumbled outside. There was no need to lead the remaining horses. Freed from their tethers, they sprinted madly past the two men. Malone and Ruxton ran downslope toward the forest, now devoid of roosting wolfuls.

Ruxton risked a look backward. A less brave man might have fainted dead away right then and there, or swallowed his tongue at the sight.

Useless had become a darting, spinning black dervish on four legs, nipping at the ankles of the immensity that now stood on its hind feet. It swiped at the much smaller but nimbler horse with paws the size of carriages. Each time a blow capable of demolishing a house descended, Useless would skip just out of its reach.

Only when the two men were safely in among trees too old and thick even for the leviathan to tear down did Useless abandon his efforts. With a roar, the monster chased the horse a few yards. Then it bellowed a final defiance before dropping to all fours. Like a piece of the mountain come to life, it turned and lumbered back to reclaim its cave.

Running easily, Useless galloped past both winded men. He turned the fleeing horses, circling them until they slowed, nuzzling Malone's own pack mare until she stood quietly, spittle dribbling from her jaws. Then he snorted once, shook his head, and bent to crop the tops of some wild onions that were growing nearby.

"Mr. Malone, that is quite a remarkable animal you have there." Ruxton fought for breath as he rested his hands on his knees. "How did you ever train him to do something like that? 'Pon my word, but that was the most gallant action I have seen a horse take on behalf of its master."

"Train 'im? Gallant? The idjit bastard like to got hisself killed! I had a clean shot. Coulda stopped it."

"Stopped that behemoth?" Ruxton nodded in the direction of the cave that had initially been their refuge and had nearly ended as their grave. "Not even with that cannon you call a rifle, old chap. Your animal saved us for sure."

"Well—mebbee. But it was still a damnfool thing to do."

Malone repeated the assertion to his mount's face, shoving his beard against that squinty-eyed visage while holding it by the neck.

"You hear me, you moronic offspring of a mule? Don't you never try nothin' like that again!"

Useless bit him on the nose.

———

WHAT WAS IT, anyway?" Now that they were well away from the nameless river and the canyon it had carved, Ruxton found he was able to relax a little. The sun was rising over his unsatisfied curiosity.

Malone had spent much of the morning muttering curses at his mount while occasionally feeling gingerly of the bandage Ruxton had applied to his nose. It was an incongruous slash of white above the black beard. Personally, Ruxton had felt the animal justified in its response.

"Somethin' big enough to snatch a wolful right out of the sky. Nez Percé, they call it—wal, never mind what the Nez Percé call it. You wouldn't be able to pronounce it anyway. Me, I call it a grizzephant. Only the second one I've ever seen. If the good Lord wills it, I'll never see another. Reckon you could call it *Ursus loxodonta*."

"Why, Mr. Malone, sir. Latin? I do believe you are at pains to conceal a real education."

"Nope. Just don't use it much 'cause nobody around here cares one way or t'other. They don't believe half of what I try to tell 'em anyways, so I just keep my mouth shut." He leaned over to give his mount a reluctant pat on the neck. "Old Useless here, I reckon he deserves a genus of his own. I just ain't come up with the right one yet, though I kinda lean toward *Equus idioticus*. With the emphasis on the 'cuss.' "

Ruxton leaned forward for a better look. As he did so, he noticed that the leather patch that normally covered the animal's forehead was hanging loose, having been dislodged in the fight.

"Mr. Malone, would I be remiss if I were to suggest that your horse has a horn growing from the center of his forehead?"

Malone leaned out for a look, straightened. "Drat. Got to fix that before we git to Randle's Farm. Folks in these parts don't rightly understand such things as unicorns."

Ruxton couldn't keep from staring. The horn was six inches long and looked sharp. Undoubtedly it had helped keep the grizzephant's attention last night. He could just make out the marks where Malone had kept it filed down.

"I know an elderly Chinese gentleman who will give you a million pounds sterling and six of the most attentive and beautiful women you ever set eyes upon for that horn, sir."

"No, thanks, Lord. Be happy you got your jackalope."

"Yes, my jacka—" Ruxton's eyes got very wide. "The jackalope! It was tied to the packhorse the wolfuls killed!"

Malone eyed him evenly. "Want to go back and try again?"

Ruxton turned around in his saddle. His shoulder still throbbed, but the injury was almost completely healed thanks to some strange-smelling herb powder Malone had rubbed on it while mumbling some nonsense about Tibet and Samarkand. He straightened resolutely, bringing his gaze back to the trail ahead.

"I will mount the memory in my mind," he said firmly, "and make do with that."

For the first time since they'd met, Amos Malone smiled. "I reckon mebbe you ain't as dumb as you look, then, Lord. Even if you do ride funny. Ain't that right, sweetie-dumplin'?" He caressed his mount's neck.

Useless looked back out of his half-closed squint eye. A kind of thunder rolled across the Bitterroots one more time as the unicorn farted.

THE LOTTERY

BY SHIRLEY JACKSON

SHIRLEY JACKSON'S CLASSIC NOVELS IN THE CONTEMPORARY GOTHIC STYLE (SUCH AS *THE HAUNTING OF HILL HOUSE* AND *WE HAVE ALWAYS LIVED IN THE CASTLE*) ARE A BRILLIANT COUNTERPOINT TO HER DOWN-HOME HUMOROUS TALES OF FAMILY LIFE IN *LIFE AMONG THE SAVAGES*. THE CREEPIEST THING ABOUT HER CLASSIC STORY "THE LOTTERY" IS THAT IT MERGES AN EVERYTOWN USA SETTING WITH THE UNSPEAKABLE SECRET TRADITION THAT WE SEE UNFOLDING RIGHT BEFORE OUR EYES IN REAL TIME. THOUGH NOTHING FANTASTIC OR MAGICAL OCCURS, THE UNREALITY OF THE ACTION AND ITS THOROUGHLY MODERN SETTING ARE LIKELY PRODUCTS OF FANTASY.

The morning of June 27th was clear and sunny, with the fresh warmth of a full-summer day; the flowers were blossoming profusely and the grass was richly green. The people of the village began to gather in the square, between the post office and the bank, around ten o'clock; in some towns there were so many people that the lottery took two days and had to be started on June 26th, but in this village, where there were only about three hundred people, the whole lottery took less than two hours, so it could begin at ten o'clock in the morning and still be through in time to allow the villagers to get home for noon dinner.

The children assembled first, of course. School was recently over for the summer, and the feeling of liberty sat uneasily on most of them; they tended to gather together quietly for a while before they broke into boisterous play, and their talk was still of the classroom and the teacher, of books and reprimands. Bobby Martin had already stuffed his pockets full of stones, and the other boys soon followed his example, selecting the smoothest and roundest stones; Bobby and Harry Jones and Dickie Delacroix—the villagers pronounced this name "Dellacroy"—eventually made a great pile of stones in one corner of the square and guarded it against the raids of the other boys. The girls stood aside, talking among themselves, looking over their shoulders at the boys, and the very small children rolled in the dust or clung to the hands of their older brothers or sisters.

Soon the men began to gather, surveying their own children, speaking of planting and rain, tractors and taxes. They stood together, away from the pile of stones in the corner, and their jokes were quiet and they smiled rather than laughed. The women, wearing faded house dresses and sweaters, came shortly after their menfolk. They greeted one another and exchanged bits of gossip as they went to join their husbands. Soon the women, standing by their husbands, began to call to their children, and the children came reluctantly, having to be called four or five times. Bobby Martin ducked under his mother's grasping hand and ran, laughing, back to the pile of stones. His father spoke up sharply, and Bobby came quickly and took his place between his father and his oldest brother.

The lottery was conducted—as were the square dances, the teenage club, the Halloween program—by Mr. Summers, who had time and energy to devote to civic activities. He was a round-faced, jovial man and he ran the coal business, and people were sorry for him, because he had no children and his wife was a scold. When he arrived in the square, carrying the black wooden box, there was a murmur of conversation among the villagers, and he waved and called, "Little late today, folks." The postmaster, Mr. Graves, followed him, carrying a three-legged stool, and the stool was put in the center of the square and Mr. Summers set the black box down on it. The villagers kept their distance, leaving a space between themselves and the stool, and when Mr. Summers said, "Some of you fellows want to give me a hand?" there was a hesitation before two men, Mr. Martin and his oldest son, Baxter, came forward to hold the box steady on the stool while Mr. Summers stirred up the papers inside it.

The original paraphernalia for the lottery had been lost long ago, and the black box now resting on the stool had been put into use even before Old Man Warner, the oldest man in town, was born. Mr. Summers spoke frequently to the villagers about making a new box, but no one liked to upset even as much tradition as was represented by the black box. There was a story that the present box had been made with some pieces of the box that had preceded it, the one that had been constructed when the first people settled down to make a village here. Every year, after the lottery, Mr. Summers began talking again about a new box, but every year the subject was allowed to fade off without anything's being done. The black box grew shabbier each year; by now it was no longer completely black but splintered badly along one side to show the original wood color, and in some places faded or stained.

Mr. Martin and his oldest son, Baxter, held the black box securely on the stool until Mr. Summers had stirred the papers thoroughly with his hand. Because so much of the ritual had been forgotten or discarded, Mr. Summers had been successful in having slips of paper substituted for the chips of wood that had been used for generations. Chips of wood, Mr. Summers had argued, had been all very well when the village was tiny, but now that the population was more than three hundred and likely to keep on growing, it was necessary to use something that would fit more easily into the black box. The night before the lottery, Mr. Summers and Mr. Graves made up the slips of paper and put them in the box, and it was then taken to the safe of Mr. Summers's coal company and locked up until Mr. Summers was ready to take it to the square next morning. The rest of the year, the box was put away, sometimes one place, sometimes another; it had spent one year in Mr. Graves's barn and another year underfoot in the post office, and sometimes it was set on a shelf in the Martin grocery and left there.

There was a great deal of fussing to be done before Mr. Summers declared the lottery open. There were the lists to make up—of heads of families, heads of households in each family, members of each household in each family. There was the proper swearing-in of Mr. Summers by the postmaster, as the official of the lottery; at one time, some people remembered, there had been a recital of some sort, performed by the official of the lottery, a perfunctory, tuneless chant that had been rattled off duly each year; some people believed that the official of the lottery used to stand just so when he said or sang it, others believed that he was supposed to walk among the people, but years and years ago this part of the ritual had been allowed to lapse. There had been, also, a ritual salute, which the official of the lottery had had to use in addressing each person who came up to draw from the box, but this also had changed with time, until now it was felt necessary only for the official to speak to each person approaching. Mr. Summers was very good at all this; in his clean white shirt and blue jeans, with one hand resting carelessly on the black box, he seemed very proper and important as he talked interminably to Mr. Graves and the Martins.

Just as Mr. Summers finally left off talking and turned to the assembled villagers, Mrs. Hutchinson came hurriedly along the path to the square, her sweater thrown over her shoulders, and slid into place in the back of the crowd. "Clean forgot what day it was," she said to Mrs. Delacroix, who stood next to her, and they both laughed softly. "Thought my old man was out back stacking wood," Mrs. Hutchinson went on, "and then I looked out the window and the kids was gone, and then I remembered it was the twenty-seventh and came a-running." She dried her hands on her apron, and Mrs. Delacroix said, "You're in time, though. They're still talking away up there."

Mrs. Hutchinson craned her neck to see through the crowd and found her husband and children standing near the front. She tapped Mrs. Delacroix on the arm as a farewell and began to make her way through the crowd. The people separated good-humoredly to let her through; two or three people said, in voices just loud enough to be heard across the crowd, "Here comes your Missus, Hutchinson," and "Bill, she made it after all." Mrs. Hutchinson reached her husband, and Mr. Summers, who had been waiting, said cheerfully, "Thought we were going to have to get on without you, Tessie." Mrs. Hutchinson said, grinning, "Wouldn't have me leave m'dishes in the sink, now, would you, Joe?" and soft laughter ran through the crowd as the people stirred back into position after Mrs. Hutchinson's arrival.

"Well, now," Mr. Summers said soberly, "guess we better get started, get this over with, so's we can go back to work. Anybody ain't here?"

"Dunbar," several people said. "Dunbar, Dunbar."

Mr. Summers consulted his list. "Clyde Dunbar," he said. "That's right. He's broke his leg, hasn't he? Who's drawing for him?"

"Me, I guess," a woman said, and Mr. Summers turned to look at her. "Wife draws for her husband," Mr. Summers said. "Don't you have a grown boy to do it for you, Janey?" Although Mr. Summers and everyone else in the village knew the answer perfectly well, it was the business of the official of the lottery to ask such questions formally. Mr. Summers waited with an expression of polite interest while Mrs. Dunbar answered.

"Horace's not but sixteen yet," Mrs. Dunbar said regretfully. "Guess I gotta fill in for the old man this year."

"Right," Mr. Summers said. He made a note on the list he was holding. Then he asked, "Watson boy drawing this year?"

A tall boy in the crowd raised his hand. "Here," he said. "I'm drawing for m'mother and me." He blinked his eyes nervously and ducked his head as several voices in the crowd said things like "Good fellow, Jack," and "Glad to see your mother's got a man to do it."

"Well," Mr. Summers said, "guess that's everyone. Old Man Warner make it?"

"Here," a voice said, and Mr. Summers nodded.

A SUDDEN HUSH FELL on the crowd as Mr. Summers cleared his throat and looked at the list. "All ready?" he called. "Now, I'll read the names—heads of families first—and the men come up and take a paper out of the box. Keep the paper folded in your hand without looking at it until everyone has had a turn. Everything clear?"

The people had done it so many times that they only half listened to the directions; most of them were quiet, wetting their lips, not looking around. Then Mr. Summers raised one hand high and said, "Adams." A man disengaged himself from the crowd and came forward. "Hi, Steve," Mr. Summers said, and Mr. Adams said, "Hi, Joe." They grinned at one another humorlessly and nervously. Then Mr. Adams reached into the black box and took out a folded paper. He held it firmly by one corner as he turned and went hastily back to his place in the crowd, where he stood a little apart from his family, not looking down at his hand.

"Allen," Mr. Summers said. "Anderson . . . Bentham."

"Seems like there's no time at all between lotteries any more," Mrs. Delacroix said to Mrs. Graves in the back row. "Seems like we got through with the last one only last week."

"Time sure goes fast," Mrs. Graves said.

"Clark . . . Delacroix."

"There goes my old man," Mrs. Delacroix said. She held her breath while her husband went forward.

"Dunbar," Mr. Summers said, and Mrs. Dunbar went steadily to the box while one of the women said, "Go on, Janey," and another said, "There she goes."

"We're next," Mrs. Graves said. She watched while Mr. Graves came around from the side of the box, greeted Mr. Summers gravely, and selected a slip of paper from the box. By now, all through the crowd there were men holding the small folded papers in their large hands, turning them over and over nervously. Mrs. Dunbar and her two sons stood together, Mrs. Dunbar holding the slip of paper.

"Harburt . . . Hutchinson."

"Get up there, Bill," Mrs. Hutchinson said, and the people near her laughed.

"Jones."

"They do say," Mr. Adams said to Old Man Warner, who stood next to him, "that over in the north village they're talking of giving up the lottery."

Old Man Warner snorted. "Pack of crazy fools," he said. "Listening to the young folks, nothing's good enough for *them*. Next thing you know, they'll be wanting to go back to living in caves, nobody work any more, live *that* way for a while. Used to be a saying about 'Lottery in June, corn be heavy soon.' First thing you know, we'd all be eating stewed chickweed and acorns. There's *always* been a lottery," he added petulantly. "Bad enough to see young Joe Summers up there joking with everybody."

"Some places have already quit lotteries," Mrs. Adams said.

"Nothing but trouble in *that*," Old Man Warner said stoutly. "Pack of young fools."

"Martin." And Bobby Martin watched his father go forward. "Overdyke . . . Percy."

"I wish they'd hurry," Mrs. Dunbar said to her older son. "I wish they'd hurry."

"They're almost through," her son said.

"You get ready to run tell Dad," Mrs. Dunbar said.

Mr. Summers called his own name and then stepped forward precisely and selected a slip from the box. Then he called, "Warner."

"Seventy-seventh year I been in the lottery," Old Man Warner said as he went through the crowd. "Seventy-seventh time."

"Watson." The tall boy came awkwardly through the crowd. Someone said, "Don't be nervous, Jack," and Mr. Summers said, "Take your time, son."

"Zanini."

AFTER THAT, there was a long pause, a breathless pause, until Mr. Summers, holding his slip of paper in the air, said, "All right, fellows." For a minute, no one moved, and then all the slips of paper were opened. Suddenly, all the women began to speak at once, saying, "Who is it?," "Who's got it?," "Is it the Dunbars?," "Is it the Watsons?" Then the voices began to say, "It's Hutchinson. It's Bill," "Bill Hutchinson's got it."

"Go tell your father," Mrs. Dunbar said to her older son.

People began to look around to see the Hutchinsons. Bill Hutchinson was standing quiet, staring down at the paper in his hand. Suddenly, Tessie Hutchinson shouted to Mr. Summers, "You didn't give him time enough to take any paper he wanted. I saw you. It wasn't fair!"

"Be a good sport, Tessie," Mrs. Delacroix called, and Mrs. Graves said, "All of us took the same chance."

"Shut up, Tessie," Bill Hutchinson said.

"Well, everyone," Mr. Summers said, "that was done pretty fast, and now we've got to be hurrying a little more to get done in time." He consulted his next list. "Bill," he said, "you draw for the Hutchinson family. You got any other households in the Hutchinsons?"

"There's Don and Eva," Mrs. Hutchinson yelled. "Make *them* take their chance!"

"Daughters draw with their husbands' families, Tessie," Mr. Summers said gently. "You know that as well as anyone else."

"It wasn't *fair*," Tessie said.

"I guess not, Joe," Bill Hutchinson said regretfully. "My daughter draws with her husband's family, that's only fair. And I've got no other family except the kids."

"Then, as far as drawing for families is concerned, it's you," Mr. Summers said in explanation, "and as far as drawing for households is concerned, that's you, too. Right?"

"Right," Bill Hutchinson said.

"How many kids, Bill?" Mr. Summers asked formally.

"Three," Bill Hutchinson said. "There's Bill, Jr., and Nancy, and little Dave. And Tessie and me."

"All right, then," Mr. Summers said. "Harry, you got their tickets back?"

Mr. Graves nodded and held up the slips of paper. "Put them in the box, then," Mr. Summers directed. "Take Bill's and put it in."

"I think we ought to start over," Mrs. Hutchinson said, as quietly as she could. "I tell you it wasn't *fair*. You didn't give him time enough to choose. *Every*body saw that."

Mr. Graves had selected the five slips and put them in the box, and he dropped all the papers but those onto the ground, where the breeze caught them and lifted them off.

"Listen, everybody," Mrs. Hutchinson was saying to the people around her.

"Ready, Bill?" Mr. Summers asked, and Bill Hutchinson, with one quick glance around at his wife and children, nodded.

"Remember," Mr. Summers said, "take the slips and keep them folded until each person has taken one. Harry, you help little Dave." Mr. Graves took the hand of the little boy, who came willingly with him up to the box. "Take a paper out of the box, Davy," Mr. Summers said. Davy put his hand into the box and laughed. "Take just *one* paper," Mr. Summers said. "Harry, you hold it for him." Mr. Graves took the child's hand and removed the folded paper from the tight fist and held it while little Dave stood next to him and looked up at him wonderingly.

"Nancy next," Mr. Summers said. Nancy was twelve, and her school friends breathed heavily as she went forward, switching her skirt, and took a slip daintily from the box. "Bill, Jr.," Mr. Summers said, and Billy, his face red and his feet overlarge, nearly knocked the box over as he got a paper out. "Tessie," Mr. Summers said. She hesitated for a minute, looking around defiantly, and then set her lips and went up to the box. She snatched a paper out and held it behind her.

"Bill," Mr. Summers said, and Bill Hutchinson reached into the box and felt around, bringing his hand out at last with the slip of paper in it.

The crowd was quiet. A girl whispered, "I hope it's not Nancy," and the sound of the whisper reached the edges of the crowd.

"It's not the way it used to be," Old Man Warner said clearly. "People ain't the way they used to be."

"All right," Mr. Summers said. "Open the papers. Harry, you open little Dave's."

Mr. Graves opened the slip of paper and there was a general sigh through the crowd as he held it up and everyone could see that it was blank. Nancy and Bill, Jr., opened theirs at the same time, and both beamed and laughed, turning around to the crowd and holding their slips of paper above their heads.

"Tessie," Mr. Summers said. There was a pause, and then Mr. Summers looked at Bill Hutchinson, and Bill unfolded his paper and showed it. It was blank.

"It's Tessie," Mr. Summers said, and his voice was hushed. "Show us her paper, Bill."

Bill Hutchinson went over to his wife and forced the slip of paper out of her hand. It had a black spot on it, the black spot Mr. Summers had made the night before with the heavy pencil in the coal-company office. Bill Hutchinson held it up, and there was a stir in the crowd.

"All right, folks," Mr. Summers said. "Let's finish quickly."

Although the villagers had forgotten the ritual and lost the original black box, they still remembered to use stones. The pile of stones the boys had made earlier was ready; there were stones on the ground with the blowing scraps of paper that had come out of the box. Mrs. Delacroix selected a stone so large she had to pick it up with both hands and turned to Mrs. Dunbar. "Come on," she said. "Hurry up."

Mrs. Dunbar had small stones in both hands, and she said, gasping for breath, "I can't run at all. You'll have to go ahead and I'll catch up with you."

The children had stones already, and someone gave little Davy Hutchinson a few pebbles.

Tessie Hutchinson was in the center of a cleared space by now, and she held her hands out desperately as the villagers moved in on her. "It isn't fair," she said. A stone hit her on the side of the head.

Old Man Warner was saying, "Come on, come on, everyone." Steve Adams was in the front of the crowd of villagers, with Mrs. Graves beside him.

"It isn't fair, it isn't right," Mrs. Hutchinson screamed, and then they were upon her.

CHILDREN OF THE CORN

BY STEPHEN KING

More than any other author, Stephen King has singlehandedly brought contemporary horror back in vogue with stories that even the most jaded rationalist can enjoy. Indeed it is the voiced disbelief and skepticism of his own characters at the existence of supernatural threats before meeting it head-on that help to lull the reader into page-turning rapture. One of his favorite setups concerns a couple of travelers who invariably take a wrong turn somewhere and wind up encountering the unknown that lurks right around the next bend, or as in "Children of the Corn" (a literary descendant of "The Lottery"), an overtly supernatural presence who goes by the moniker of "he who walks among the rows."

B urt turned the radio on too loud and didn't turn it down because they were on the verge of another argument and he didn't want it to happen. He was desperate for it not to happen.

Vicky said something.

"What?" he shouted.

"Turn it down! Do you want to break my eardrums?"

He bit down hard on what might have come through his mouth and turned it down.

Vicky was fanning herself with her scarf even though the T-Bird was air-conditioned. "Where are we, anyway?"

"Nebraska."

She gave him a cold, neutral look. "Yes, Burt. I know we're in Nebraska, Burt. But where the hell *are* we?"

"You've got the road atlas. Look it up. Or can't you read?"

"Such wit. This is why we got off the turnpike. So we could look at three hundred miles of corn. And enjoy the wit and wisdom of Burt Robeson."

He was gripping the steering wheel so hard his knuckles were white. He decided he was holding it that tightly because if he loosened up, why, one of those hands might just fly off and hit the ex-Prom Queen beside him right in the chops. We're saving our marriage, he told himself. Yes. We're doing it the same way us grunts went about saving villages in the war.

"Vicky," he said carefully. "I have driven fifteen hundred miles on turnpikes since we left Boston. I did that driving myself because you refused to drive. Then—"

"I did not refuse!" Vicky said hotly. "Just because I get migraines when I drive for a long time—"

"Then when I asked you if you'd navigate for me on some of the secondary roads, you said sure, Burt. Those were your exact words. Sure, Burt. Then—"

"Sometimes I wonder how I ever wound up married to you."

"By saying two little words."

She stared at him for a moment, white-lipped, and then picked up the road atlas. She turned the pages savagely.

It *had* been a mistake leaving the turnpike. Burt thought morosely. It was a shame, too, because up until then they had been doing pretty well, treating each other almost like human beings. It had sometimes seemed that this trip to the coast, ostensibly to see Vicky's brother and his wife but actually a last-ditch attempt to patch up their own marriage, was going to work.

But since they left the pike, it had been bad again. How bad? Well, terrible, actually.

"We left the turnpike at Hamburg, right?"

"Right."

"There's nothing more until Gatlin," she said. "Twenty miles. Wide place in the road. Do you suppose we could stop there and get something to eat. Or does your almighty schedule say we have to go until two o'clock like we did yesterday?"

He took his eyes off the road to look at her. "I've about had it, Vicky. As far as I'm concerned, we can turn around right here and go home and see that lawyer you wanted to talk to. Because this isn't working at—"

She had faced forward again, her expression stonily set. It suddenly turned to surprise and fear. *"Burt look out you're going to—"*

He turned his attention back to the road just in time to see something vanish under the T-Bird's bumper. A moment later, while he was only beginning to switch from gas to brake, he felt something thump sickeningly under the front and then the back wheels. They were thrown forward as the car braked along the centerline, decelerating from fifty to zero along black skidmarks.

"A dog," he said. "Tell me it was a dog, Vicky."

Her face was a pallid, cottage-cheese color. "A boy. A little boy. He just ran out of the corn and . . . congratulations, tiger."

She fumbled the car door open, leaned out, threw up.

Burt sat straight behind the T-Bird's wheel, hands still gripping it loosely. He was aware of nothing for a long time but the rich, dark smell of fertilizer.

Then he saw that Vicky was gone and when he looked in the outside mirror he saw her stumbling clumsily back toward a heaped bundle that looked like a pile of rags. She was ordinarily a graceful woman but now her grace was gone, robbed.

It's manslaughter. That's what they call it. I took my eyes off the road.

He turned the ignition off and got out. The wind rustled softly through the growing man-high corn, making a weird sound like respiration. Vicky was standing over the bundle of rags now, and he could hear her sobbing.

He was halfway between the car and where she stood and something caught his eye on the left, a gaudy splash of red amid all the green, as bright as barn paint.

He stopped, looking directly into the corn. He found himself thinking (anything to untrack from those rags that were not rags) that it must have been a fantastically growing season for corn. It grew close together, almost ready to bear. You could plunge into those neat, shaded rows and spend a day trying to find your way out again. But the neatness was broken here. Several tall cornstalks had been broken and leaned askew. And what was that farther back in the shadows?

"Burt!" Vicky screamed at him. "Don't you want to come see? So you can tell all your poker buddies what you bagged in Nebraska? Don't you—" But the rest was lost in fresh sobs. Her shadow was puddled starkly around her feet. It was almost noon.

Shade closed over him as he entered the corn. The red barn paint was blood. There was a low, somnolent buzz as flies lit, tasted, and buzzed off again . . . maybe to tell others. There was more blood on the leaves farther in. Surely it couldn't have splattered this far? And then he was standing over the object he had seen from the road. He picked it up.

The neatness of the rows was disturbed here. Several stalks were canted drunkenly, two of them had been broken clean off. The earth had been gouged. There was blood. The corn rustled. With a little shiver, he walked back to the road.

Vicky was having hysterics, screaming unintelligible words at him, crying, laughing. Who would have thought it could end in such a melodramatic way? He looked at her and saw he wasn't having an identity crisis or a difficult life transition or any of those trendy things. He hated her. He gave her a hard slap across the face.

She stopped short and put a hand against the reddening impression of his fingers. "You'll go to jail, Burt," she said solemnly.

"I don't think so," he said, and put the suitcase he had found in the corn at her feet.

"What—?"

"I don't know. I guess it belonged to him." He pointed to the sprawled, face-down body that lay in the road. No more than thirteen, from the look of him.

The suitcase was old. The brown leather was battered and scuffed. Two hanks of clotheslines had been wrapped around it and tied in large, clownish grannies. Vicky bent to undo one of them, saw the blood greased into the knot, and withdrew.

Burt knelt and turned the body over gently.

"I don't want to look," Vicky said, staring down helplessly anyway. And when the staring, sightless face flopped up to regard them, she screamed again. The boy's face was dirty, his expression a grimace of terror. His throat had been cut.

Burt got up and put his arms around Vicky as she began to sway. "Don't faint," he said very quietly. "Do you hear me, Vicky? Don't faint."

He repeated it over and over and at last she began to recover and held him tight. They might have been dancing, there on the noon-struck road with the boy's corpse at their feet.

"Vicky?"

"What?" Muffled against his shirt.

"Go back to the car and put the keys in your pocket. Get the blanket out of the back seat, and my rifle. Bring them here."

"The rifle?"

"Someone cut his throat. Maybe whoever is watching us."

Her head jerked up and her wide eyes considered the corn. It marched away as far as the eye could see, undulating up and down small dips and rises of land.

"I imagine he's gone, But why take chances? Go on. Do it."

She walked stiltedly back to the car, her shadow following, a dark mascot who stuck close at this hour of the day. When she leaned into the back seat, Burt squatted beside the boy. White male, no distinguishing marks. Run over, yes, but the T-Bird hadn't cut the kid's throat. It had been cut raggedly and inefficiently—no army sergeant had shown the killer the finer points of hand-to-hand assassination—but the final effect had been deadly. He had either run or been pushed through the last thirty feet of corn, dead or mortally wounded. And Burt Robeson had run him down. If the boy had still been alive when the car hit him, his life had been cut short by thirty seconds at most.

Vicky tapped him on the shoulder and he jumped.

She was standing with the brown army blanket over her left arm, the cased pump shotgun in her right hand, her face averted. He took the blanket and spread it on the road. He rolled the body onto it. Vicky uttered a desperate little moan.

"You okay?" He looked up at her. "Vicky?"

"Okay," she said in a strangled voice.

He flipped the sides of the blanket over the body and scooped it up, hating the thick, dead weight of it. It tried to make a U in his arms and slither through his grasp. He clutched it tighter and they walked back to the T-Bird.

"Open the trunk," he grunted.

The trunk was full of travel stuff, suitcases and souvenirs. Vicky shifted most of it into the back seat and Burt slipped the body into the made space and slammed the trunklid down. A sigh of relief escaped him.

Vicky was standing by the driver's side door, still holding the cased rifle.

"Just put it in the back and get in."

He looked at his watch and saw only fifteen minutes had passed. It seemed like hours.

"What about the suitcase?" she asked.

He trotted back down the road to where it stood on the white line, like the focal point in an Impressionist painting. He picked it up by its tattered handle and paused for a moment. He had a strong sensation of being watched. It was a feeling he had read about in books, mostly cheap fiction, and he had always doubted its reality. Now he didn't. It was as if there were people in the corn, maybe a lot of them, coldly estimating whether the woman could get the gun out of the case and use it before they could grab him, drag him into the shady rows, cut his throat—

Heart beating thickly, he ran back to the car, pulled the keys out of the trunk lock, and got in.

Vicky was crying again. Burt got them moving, and before a minute had passed, he could no longer pick out the spot where it had happened in the rearview mirror.

"What did you say the next town was?" he asked.

"Oh." She bent over the road atlas again. "Gatlin. We should be there in ten minutes."

"Does it look big enough to have a police station?"

"No. It's just a dot."

"Maybe there's a constable."

They drove in silence for a while. They passed a silo on the left. Nothing else but corn. Nothing passed them going the other way, not even a farm truck.

"Have we passed anything since we got off the turnpike, Vicky?"

She thought about it. "A car and a tractor. At that intersection."

"No, since we got on this road. Route 17."

"No. I don't think we have." Earlier this might have been the preface to some cutting remark. Now she only stared out of her half of the windshield at the unrolling road and the endless dotted line.

"Vicky? Could you open the suitcase?"

"Do you think it might matter?"

"Don't know. It might."

While she picked at the knots (her face was set in a peculiar way—expressionless but tight-mouthed—that Burt remembered his mother wearing when she pulled the innards out of the Sunday chicken), Burt turned on the radio again.

The pop station they had been listening to was almost obliterated in static and Burt switched, running the red marker slowly down the dial. Farm reports. Buck Owens. Tammy Wynette. All distant, nearly distorted into babble. Then, near the end of the dial, one single word blared out of the speaker, so loud and clear that the lips which uttered it might have been directly beneath the grill of the dashboard speaker.

"ATONEMENT!" this voice bellowed.

Burt made a surprised grunting sound. Vicky jumped.

"ONLY BY THE BLOOD OF THE LAMB ARE WE SAVED!" the voice roared, and Burt hurriedly turned the sound down. This station was close, all right. So close that . . . yes, there it was. Poking out of the corn at the horizon, a spidery red tripod against the blue. The radio tower.

"Atonement is the word, brothers 'n' sisters," the voice told them, dropping to a more conversational pitch. In the background, offmike, voices murmured amen. "There's some that thinks it's okay to get out in the world, as if you could work and walk in the world without being smirched by the world. Now is that what the word of God teaches us?"

Offmike but still loud: "No!"

"HOLY JESUS!" the evangelist shouted, and now the words came in a powerful, pumping cadence, almost as compelling as a driving rock-and-roll beat: "When they gonna know that way is death? When they gonna know that the wages of the world are paid on the other side? Huh? Huh? The Lord has said there's many mansions in His house. But there's no room for the fornicator. No room for the covetor. No room for the defiler of the corn. No room for the hommasexshul. No room—"

Vicky snapped it off. "That drivel makes me sick."

"What did he say?" Burt asked her. "What did he say about corn?"

"I didn't hear it." She was picking at the second clothesline knot.

"He said something about corn. I know he did."

"I got it!" Vicky said, and the suitcase fell open in her lap. They were passing a sign that said: GATLIN 5 MI. DRIVE CAREFULLY PROTECT OUR CHILDREN. The sign had been put up by the Elks. There were .22 bullet holes in it.

"Socks," Vicky said. "Two pairs of pants . . . a shirt . . . a belt . . . a string tie with a—" She held it up, showing him the peeling gilt neck clasp. "Who's that?"

Burt glanced at it. "Hopalong Cassidy, I think."

"Oh." She put it back. She was crying again.

After a moment, Burt said: "Did anything strike you funny about that radio sermon?"

"No. I heard enough of that stuff as a kid to last me forever. I told you about it."

"Didn't you think he sounded kind of young? That preacher?"

She uttered a mirthless laugh. "A teen-ager, maybe, so what? That's what's so monstrous about that whole trip. They like to get hold of them when their minds are still rubber. They know how to put all the emotional checks and balances in. You should have been at some of the tent meetings my mother and father dragged me to . . . some of the ones I was 'saved' at.

"Let's see. There was Baby Hortense, the Singing Marvel. She was eight. She'd come on and sing 'Leaning on the Everlasting Arms' while her daddy passed the plate, telling everybody to 'dig deep, now, let's not let this little child of God down.' Then there was Norman Staunton. He used to preach hellfire and brimstone in this little Lord Fauntleroy suit with short pants. He was only seven."

She nodded at his look of unbelief.

"They weren't the only two, either. There were plenty of them on the circuit. They were good *draws*." She spat the word. "Ruby Stampnell. She was a ten-year-old faith healer. The Grace Sisters. They used to come out with little tin-foil haloes over their heads and— *oh!*"

"What is it?" He jerked around to look at her, and what she was holding in her hands. Vicky was staring at it raptly. Her slowly seining hands had snagged it on the bottom of the suitcase and had brought it up as she talked. Burt pulled over to take a better look. She gave it to him wordlessly.

It was crucifix that had been made from twists of corn husk, once green, now dry. Attached to this by woven cornsilk was a dwarf corncob. Most of the kernels had been carefully removed, probably dug out one at a time with a pocketknife. Those kernels remaining formed a crude cruciform figure in yellowish bas-relief. Corn-kernel eyes, each slit longways to suggest pupils. Outstretched kernel arms, the legs together, terminating in a rough indication of bare feet. Above, four letters also raised from the bone-white cob: I N R I.

"That's a fantastic piece of workmanship," he said.

"It's hideous," she said in a flat, strained voice. "Throw it out."

"Vicky, the police might want to see it."

"Why?"

"Well, I don't know why. Maybe—"

"Throw it out. Will you please do that for me? I don't want it in the car."

"I'll put it in back. And as soon as we see the cops, we'll get rid of it one way or the other. I promise. Okay?"

"Oh, do whatever you want with it!" she shouted at him. "You will anyway!"

Troubled, he threw the thing in back, where it landed on a pile of clothes. Its corn-kernel eyes stared raptly at the T-Bird's dome light. He pulled out again, gravel splurting from beneath the tires.

"We'll give the body and everything that was in the suitcase to the cops," he promised. "Then we'll be shut of it."

Vicky didn't answer. She was looking at her hands.

A mile farther on, the endless cornfields drew away from the road, showing farmhouses and outbuildings. In one yard they saw dirty chickens pecking listlessly at the soil. There were faded cola and chewing-tobacco ads on the roofs of barns. They passed a tall billboard that said: ONLY JESUS SAVES. They passed a café with a Conoco gas island, but Burt decided to go on into the center of town, if there was one. If not, they could come back to the café. It only occurred to him after they had passed it that the parking lot had been empty except for a dirty old pickup that had looked like it was sitting on two flat tires.

Vicky suddenly began to laugh, a high, giggling sound that struck Burt as being dangerously close to hysteria.

"What's so funny?"

"The signs," she said, gasping and hiccuping. "Haven't you been reading them? When they called this the Bible Belt, they sure weren't kidding. Oh, Lordy, there's another bunch." Another burst of hysterical laughter escaped her, and she clapped both hands over her mouth.

Each sign had only one word. They were leaning on whitewashed sticks that had been implanted in the sandy shoulder, long ago by the looks; the whitewash was flaked and faded. They were coming up at eighty-foot intervals and Burt read:

A . . . CLOUD . . . BY . . . DAY . . . A . . . PILLAR . . . OF . . . FIRE . . . BY . . . NIGHT

"They only forgot one thing," Vicky said, still giggling helplessly.

"What?" Burt asked, frowning.

"Burma Shave." She held a knuckled fist against her open mouth to keep in the laughter, but her semi-hysterical giggles flowed around it like effervescent ginger-ale bubbles.

"Vicky, are you all right?"

"I will be. Just as soon as we're a thousand miles away from here, in sunny sinful California with the Rockies between us and Nebraska."

Another group of signs came up and they read them silently.

TAKE . . . THIS . . . AND . . . EAT . . . SAITH . . . THE . . . LORD . . . GOD . . .

Now why, Burt thought, should I immediately associate that indefinite pronoun with corn? Isn't that what they say when they give you communion? It had been so long since he had been to church that he really couldn't remember. He wouldn't be surprised if they used cornbread for holy wafer around these parts. He opened his mouth to tell Vicky that, and then thought better of it.

They breasted a gentle rise and there was Gatlin below them, all three blocks of it, looking like a set from a movie about the Depression.

"There'll be a constable," Burt said, and wondered why the sight of that hick one-timetable town dozing in the sun should have brought a lump of dread into his throat.

They passed a speed sign proclaiming that no more than thirty was now in order, and another sign, rust-flecked, which said: YOU ARE NOW ENTERING GATLIN, NICEST LITTLE TOWN IN NEBRASKA — OR ANYWHERE ELSE! POP. 5431.

Dusty elms stood on both sides of the road, most of them diseased. They passed the Gatlin Lumberyard and a '76 gas station, where the price signs swung slowly in a hot noon breeze: REG 35.9 HI-TEST 38.9, and another which said: HI TRUCKERS DIESEL FUEL AROUND BACK.

They crossed Elm Street, then Birch Street, and came up on the town square. The houses lining the streets were plain wood with screened porches. Angular and functional. The lawns were yellow and dispirited. Up ahead a mongrel dog walked slowly out into the middle of Maple Street, stood looking at them for a moment, then lay down in the road with its nose on its paws.

"Stop," Vicky said. "Stop right here."

Burt pulled obediently to the curb.

"Turn around. Let's take the body to Grand Island. That's not too far, is it? Let's do that."

"Vicky, what's wrong?"

"What do you mean, what's wrong?" she asked, her voice rising thinly. "This town is empty, Burt. There's nobody here but us. Can't you feel that?"

He had felt something, and still felt it. But—

"It just seems that way," he said. "But it sure is a one-hydrant town. Probably all up in the square, having a bake sale or a bingo game."

"There's no one here." She said the words with a queer, strained emphasis. "Didn't you see that '76 station back there?"

"Sure, by the lumberyard, so what?" His mind was elsewhere, listening to the dull buzz of a cicada burrowing into one of the nearby elms. He could smell corn, dusty roses, and fertilizer—of course. For the first time they were off the turnpike and in a town. A town in a state he had never been in before (although he had flown over it from time to time in United Airlines 747s) and somehow it felt all wrong but all right. Somewhere up ahead there would be a drugstore with a soda fountain, a movie house named the Bijou, a school named after JFK.

"Burt, the prices said thirty-five-nine for regular and thirty-eight-nine for high octane. Now how long has it been since anyone in this country paid those prices?"

"At least four years," he admitted. "But, Vicky—"

"We're right in town, Burt, and there's not a car! *Not one car!*"

"Grand Island is seventy miles away. It would look funny if we took him there."

"I don't care."

"Look, let's just drive up to the courthouse and—"

"No!"

There, damn it, there. Why our marriage is falling apart, in a nutshell. No I won't. No sir. And furthermore, I'll hold my breath till I turn blue if you don't let me have my way.

"Vicky," he said.

"I want to get out of here, Burt."

"Vicky, listen to me."

"Turn around. Let's go."

"Vicky, will you stop a minute?"

"I'll stop when we're driving the other way. Now let's go."

"We have a dead child in the trunk of our car!" he roared at her, and took a distinct pleasure at the way she flinched, the way her face crumbled. In a slightly lower voice he went on: "His throat was cut and he was shoved out into the road and I ran him over. Now I'm going to drive up to the courthouse or whatever they have here, and I'm going to report it. If you want to start walking back toward the pike, go to it. I'll pick you up. But don't you tell me to turn around and drive seventy miles to Grand Island like we had nothing in the trunk but a bag of garbage. He happens to be some mother's son, and I'm going to report it before whoever killed him gets over the hills and far away."

"You bastard," she said, crying. "What am I doing with you?"

"I don't know," he said. "I don't know anymore. But the situation can be remedied, Vicky."

He pulled away from the curb. The dog lifted its head at the brief squeal of tires and then lowered it to its paws again.

They drove the remaining block to the square. At the corner of Main and Pleasant, Main Street split in two. There actually was a town square, a grassy park with a bandstand in the middle. On the other end, where Main Street became one again, there were two official-looking buildings. Burt could make out the lettering on one: GATLIN MUNICIPAL CENTER.

"That's it," he said. Vicky said nothing.

Halfway up the square, Burt pulled over again. They were beside a lunch room, the Gatlin Bar and Grill.

"Where are you going?" Vicky asked with alarm as he opened his door.

"To find out where everyone is. Sign in the window there says 'open.' "

"You're not going to leave me here alone."

"So come. Who's stopping you?"

She unlocked her door and stepped out as he crossed in front of the car. He saw how pale her face was and felt an instant of pity. Hopeless pity.

"Do you hear it?" she asked as he joined her.

"Hear what?"

"The nothing. No cars. No people. No tractors. Nothing."

And then, from a block over, they heard the high and joyous laughter of children.

"I hear kids," he said, "Don't you?"

She looked at him, troubled.

He opened the lunchroom door and stepped into dry, antiseptic heat. The floor was dusty. The sheen on the chrome was dull. The wooden blades of the ceiling fans stood still. Empty tables. Empty counter stools. But the mirror behind the counter had been shattered and there was something else . . . in a moment he had it. All the beer taps had been broken off. They lay along the counter like bizarre party favors.

Vicky's voice was gay and near to breaking. "Sure, ask anybody. Pardon me, sir, but could you tell me—"

"Oh, shut up." But his voice was dull and without force: They were standing in a bar of dusty sunlight that fell through the lunchroom's big plate-glass window and again he had that feeling of being watched and he thought of the boy they had in their trunk and of the high laughter of children. A phrase came to him for no reason, a legal-sounding phrase, and it began to repeat mystically in his mind: *Sight unseen. Sight unseen. Sight unseen.*

His eyes traveled over the age-yellowed cards thumbtacked up behind the counter: CHEESBURG 35¢ WORLD'S BEST JOE 10¢ STRAWBERRY RHUBARB PIE 25¢ TODAY'S SPECIAL HAM & RED EYE GRAVY W/MASHED POT 80¢.

How long since he had seen lunchroom prices like that?

Vicky had the answer. "Look at this," she said shrilly. She was pointing at the calendar on the wall. "They've been at that bean supper for twelve years, I guess." She uttered a grinding laugh.

He walked over. The picture showed two boys swimming in a pond while a cute little dog carried off their clothes. Below the picture was the legend: COMPLIMENTS OF GATLIN LUMBER & HARDWARE *You Breakum, We Fixum*. The month on view was August 1964.

"I don't understand," he faltered, "but I'm sure—"

"You're sure!" she cried hysterically. "Sure, you're sure! That's part of your trouble, Burt, you've spent your whole life being *sure!*"

He turned back to the door and she came after him.

"Where are you going?"

"To the Municipal Center."

"Burt, why do you have to be so stubborn? You know something's wrong here. Can't you just admit it?"

"I'm not being stubborn. I just want to get shut of what's in that trunk."

They stepped out onto the sidewalk, and Burt was struck afresh with the town's silence, and with the smell of fertilizer. Somehow you never thought of that smell when you buttered an ear and salted it and bit in. Compliments of sun, rain, all sorts of manmade phosphates, and a good healthy dose of cow shit. But somehow this smell was different from the one he had grown up with in rural upstate New York. You could say whatever you wanted to about organic fertilizer, but there was something almost fragrant about it when the spreader was laying it down in the fields. Not one of your great perfumes, God no, but when the late-afternoon spring breeze would pick up and waft it over the freshly turned fields, it *was* a smell with good associations. It meant winter was over for good. It meant that school doors were going to bang closed in six weeks or so and spill everyone out into summer. It was a smell tied irrevocably in his mind with other aromas that *were* perfume: timothy grass, clover, fresh earth, hollyhocks, dogwood.

But they must do something different out here, he thought. The smell was close but not the same. There was a sickish-sweet undertone. Almost a death smell. As a medical orderly in Vietnam, he had become well versed in that smell.

Vicky was sitting quietly in the car, holding the corn crucifix in her lap and staring at it in a rapt way Burt didn't like.

"Put that thing down," he said.

"No," she said without looking up. "You play your games and I'll play mine."

He put the car in gear and drove up to the corner. A dead stoplight hung overhead, swinging in a faint breeze. To the left was a neat white church. The grass was cut. Neatly kept flowers grew beside the flagged path up to the door. Burt pulled over.

"What are you doing?"

"I'm going to go in and take a look," Burt said. "It's the only place in town that looks as if there isn't ten years' dust on it. And look at the sermon board."

She looked. Neatly pegged white letters under glass read: THE POWER AND GRACE OF HE WHO WALKS BEHIND THE ROWS. The date was July 24, 1976—the Sunday before.

"He Who Walks Behind the Rows," Burt said, turning off the ignition. "One of nine thousand names of God only used in Nebraska, I guess. Coming?"

She didn't smile. "I'm not going in with you."

"Fine. Whatever you want."

"I haven't been in a church since I left home and I don't want to be in *this* church and I don't want to be in *this* town, Burt. I'm scared out of my mind, can't we just *go?*"

"I'll only be a minute."

"I've got my keys, Burt. If you're not back in five minutes, I'll just drive away and leave you here."

"Now just wait a minute, lady."

"That's what I'm going to do. Unless you want to assault me like a common mugger and take my keys. I suppose you could do that."

"But you don't think I will."

"No."

Her purse was on the seat between them, he snatched it up. She screamed and grabbed for the shoulder strap. He pulled it out of her reach. Not bothering to dig, he simply turned the bag upside down and let everything fall out. Her keyring glittered amid tissues, cosmetics, change, old shopping lists. She lunged for it but he beat her again and put the keys in his own pocket.

"You didn't have to do that," she said, crying. "Give them to me."

"No," he said, and gave her a hard, meaningless grin. "No way."

"Please, Burt! I'm scared!" She held her hand out, pleading now.

"You'd wait two minutes and decide that was long enough."

"I wouldn't—"

"And then you'd drive off laughing and saying to yourself, 'That'll teach Burt to cross me when I want something.' Hasn't that pretty much been your motto during our married life? That'll teach Burt to cross me?"

He got out of the car.

"Please, Burt!" she screamed, sliding across the seat. "Listen . . . I know . . . we'll drive out of town and call from a phone booth, okay? I've got all kinds of change. I just . . . we can . . . *don't leave me alone, Burt, don't leave me out here alone!*"

He slammed the door on her cry and then leaned against the side of the T-Bird for a moment, thumbs against his closed eyes. She was pounding on the driver's side window and calling his name. She was going to make a wonderful impression when he finally found someone in authority to take charge of the kid's body. Oh yes.

He turned and walked up the flagstone path to the church doors. Two or three minutes, just a look-around, and he would be back out. Probably the door wasn't even unlocked.

But it pushed in easily on silent, well-oiled hinges (reverently oiled, he thought, and that seemed funny for no really good reason) and he stepped into a vestibule so cool it was almost chilly. It took his eyes a moment to adjust to the dimness.

The first thing he noticed was a pile of wooden letters in the far corner, dusty and jumbled indifferently together. He went to them, curious. They looked as old and forgotten as the calendar in the bar and grill, unlike the rest of the vestibule, which was dustfree and tidy. The letters were about two feet high, obviously part of a set. He spread them out on the carpet—there were eighteen of them—-and shifted them around like anagrams. HURT BITE CRAG CHAP CS. Nope. CRAP TARGET CHIBS HUG. That wasn't much good either. Except for the CH in CHIBS. He quickly assembled the word CHURCH and was left looking at RAPTAGET CIBS. Foolish. He was squatting here playing idiot games with a bunch of letters while Vicky was going nuts out in the car. He started to get up, and then saw it. He formed BAPTIST, leaving RAG EC—and by changing two letters he had GRACE. GRACE BAPTIST CHURCH. The letters must have been out front. They had taken them down and had thrown them indifferently in the corner, and the church had been painted since then so that you couldn't even see where the letters had been.

Why?

It wasn't the Grace Baptist Church anymore, that was why. So what kind of church was it? For some reason that question caused a trickle of fear and he stood up quickly, dusting his fingers. So they had taken down a bunch of letters, so what? Maybe they had changed the place into Flip Wilson's Church of What's Happening Now.

But what had happened then?

He shook it off impatiently and went through the inner doors. Now he was standing at the back of the church itself, and as he looked toward the nave, he felt fear close around his heart and squeeze tightly. His breath drew in, loud in the pregnant silence of this place.

The space behind the pulpit was dominated by a gigantic portrait of Christ, and Burt thought: If nothing else in this town gave Vicky the screaming meemies, this would.

The Christ was grinning, vulpine. His eyes were wide and staring, reminding Burt uneasily of Lon Chaney in *The Phantom of the Opera*. In each of the wide black pupils someone (a sinner, presumably) was drowning in a lake of fire. But the oddest thing was that this Christ had green hair . . . hair which on closer examination revealed itself to be a twining mass of early-summer corn. The picture was crudely done but effective. It looked like a comic-strip mural done by a gifted child—an Old Testament Christ, or a pagan Christ that might slaughter his sheep for sacrifice instead of leading them.

At the foot of the left-hand rank of pews was a pipe organ, and Burt could not at first tell what was wrong with it. He walked down the left-hand aisle and saw with slowly dawning horror that the keys had been ripped up, the stops had been pulled out . . . and the pipes themselves filled with dry cornhusks. Over the organ was a carefully lettered plaque which read: MAKE NO MUSIC EXCEPT WITH HUMAN TONGUE SAITH THE LORD GOD.

Vicky was right. Something was terribly wrong here. He debated going back to Vicky without exploring any further, just getting into the car and leaving town as quickly as possible, never mind the Municipal Building. But it grated on him. Tell the truth, he thought. You want to give her Ban 5000 a workout before going back and admitting she was right to start with.

He would go back out in a minute or so.

He walked toward the pulpit, thinking: People must go through Gatlin all the time. There must be people in the neighboring towns who have friends and relatives here. The Nebraska SP must cruise through from time to time. And what about the power company? The stoplight had been dead. Surely they'd know if the power had been off for twelve long years. Conclusion: What seemed to have happened in Gatlin was impossible.

Still, he had the creeps.

He climbed the four carpeted steps to the pulpit and looked out over the deserted pews, glimmering in the half-shadows. He seemed to feel the weight of those eldritch and decidedly unchristian eyes boring into his back.

There was a large Bible on the lectern, opened to the thirty-eighth chapter of Job. Burt glanced down at it and read: "Then the Lord answered Job out of the whirlwind, and said, 'Who is this that darkeneth counsel by words without knowledge? . . . Where

wast thou when I laid the foundations of the earth? Declare, if thou hast understanding.' The Lord. He Who Walks Behind the Rows. Declare if thou hast understanding.
And please pass the corn."

He fluttered the pages of the Bible, and they made a dry whispering sound in the
quiet—the sound that ghosts might make if there really were such things. And in a
place like this you could almost believe it. Sections of the Bible had been chopped
out. Mostly from the New Testament, he saw. Someone had decided to take on the
job of amending Good King James with a pair of scissors.

But the Old Testament was intact.

He was about to leave the pulpit when he saw another book on a lower shelf and
took it out, thinking it might be a church record of weddings and confirmations and
burials.

He grimaced at the words stamped on the cover, done inexpertly in gold leaf: THUS
LET THE INIQUITOUS BE CUT DOWN SO THAT THE GROUND MAY BE FERTILE AGAIN
SAITH THE LORD GOD OF HOSTS.

There seemed to be one train of thought around here, and Burt didn't care much
for the track it seemed to ride on.

He opened the book to the first wide, lined sheet. A child had done the lettering,
he saw immediately. In places an ink eraser had been carefully used, and while there
were no misspellings, the letters were large and childishly made, drawn rather than
written. The first column read:

Amos Deigan (Richard), b. Sept. 4, 1945	Sept. 4, 1964
Isaac Renfrew (William), b. Sept. 19, 1945	Sept. 19, 1964
Zepeniah Kirk (George), b. Oct. 14, 1945	Oct. 14, 1964
Mary Wells (Roberta), b. Nov. 12, 1945	Nov. 12, 1964
Yemen Hollis (Edward), b. Jan 5, 1946	Jan. 5, 1965

Frowning, Burt continued to turn through the pages. Three-quarters of the way
through, the double columns ended abruptly:

Rachel Stigman (Donna), b. June 21, 1957	June 21, 1976
Moses Richardson (Henry), b. July 29, 1957	
Malachi Boardman (Craig), b. August 15, 1957	

The last entry in the book was for Ruth Clawson (Sandra), b. April 30, 1961. Burt
looked at the shelf where he had found this book and came up with two more. The
first had the same INIQUITOUS BE CUT DOWN logo, and it continued the same record,
the single column tracing birth dates and names. In early September of 1964 he found
Job Gilman (Clayton), b. September 6, and the next entry was Eve Tobin, b. June 16,
1965. No second name in parentheses.

The third book was blank.

Standing behind the pulpit, Burt thought about it.

Something had happened in 1964. Something to do with religion, and corn . . . and
children.

Dear God we beg thy blessing on the crop. For Jesus' sake, amen.

And the knife raised high to sacrifice the lamb—but had it been a lamb? Perhaps a religious mania had swept them. Alone, all alone, cut off from the outside world by hundreds of square miles of the rustling secret corn. Alone under seventy million acres of blue sky. Alone under the watchful eye of God, now a strange green God, a God of corn, grown old and strange and hungry. He Who Walks Behind the Rows.

Burt felt a chill creep into his flesh.

Vicky, let me tell you a story. It's about Amos Deigan, who was born Richard Deigan on September 4, 1945. He took the name Amos in 1964, fine Old Testament name, Amos, one of the minor prophets. Well, Vicky, what happened—don't laugh—is that Dick Deigan and his friends—Billy Renfrew, George Kirk, Roberta Wells, and Eddie Hollis among others—they got religion and they killed off their parents. All of them. Isn't that a scream? Shot them in their beds, knifed them in their bathtubs, poisoned their suppers, hung them, or disemboweled them, for all I know.

Why? The corn. Maybe it was dying. Maybe they got the idea somehow that it was dying because there was too much sinning. Not enough sacrifice. They would have done it in the corn, in the rows.

And somehow, Vicky, I'm quite sure of this, somehow they decided that nineteen was as old as any of them could live. Richard "Amos" Deigan, the hero of our little story, had his nineteenth birthday on September 4, 1964—the date in the book. I think maybe they killed him. Sacrificed him in the corn. Isn't that a silly story?

But let's look at Rachel Stigman, who was Donna Stigman until 1964. She turned nineteen on June 21, just about a month ago. Moses Richardson was born on July 29—just three days from today he'll be nineteen. Any idea what's going to happen to ole Mose on the twenty-ninth?

I can guess.

Burt licked his lips, which felt dry.

One other thing, Vicky. Look at this. We have Job Gilman (Clayton) born on September 6, 1964. No other births until June 16, 1965. A gap of ten months. Know what I think? They killed all the parents, even the pregnant ones, that's what I think. And one of *them* got pregnant in October of 1964 and gave birth to Eve. Some sixteen- or seventeen-year-old girl. *Eve. The first woman.*

He thumbed back through the book feverishly and found the Eve Tobin entry. Below it: "Adam Greenlaw, b. July 11, 1965."

They'd be just eleven now, he thought, and his flesh began to crawl. And maybe they're out there. Someplace.

But how could such a thing be kept secret? How could it go on?

How unless the God in question approved?

"Oh Jesus," Burt said into the silence, and that was when the T-Bird's horn began to blare into the afternoon, one long continuous blast.

Burt jumped from the pulpit and ran down the center aisle. He threw open the outer vestibule door, letting in hot sunshine, dazzling. Vicky was bolt upright behind the steering wheel, both hands plastered on the horn ring, her head swiveling wildly. From all around the children were coming. Some of them were laughing gaily. They held knives, hatchets, pipes, rocks, hammers. One girl, maybe eight, with beautiful long blond hair, held a jackhandle. Rural weapons. Not a gun among them. Burt felt a wild urge to scream out: *Which of you is Adam and Eve? Who are the mothers? Who are the daughters? Fathers? Sons?*

Declare if thou hast understanding.

They came from the side streets, from the town green, through the gate in the chain-link fence around the school playground a block farther west. Some of them glanced indifferently at Burt, standing frozen on the church steps, and some nudged each other and pointed and smiled . . . the sweet smiles of children.

The girls were dressed in long brown wool and faded sunbonnets. The boys, like Quaker parsons, were all in black and wore round-crowned flat-brimmed hats. They streamed across the town square toward the car, across the lawns, a few came across the front yard of what had been the Grace Baptist Church until 1964. One or two of them almost close enough to touch.

"The shotgun!" Burt yelled. "Vicky, get the shotgun!"

But she was frozen in her panic, he could see that from the steps. He doubted if she could even hear him through the closed windows.

They converged on the Thunderbird. The axes and hatchets and chunks of pipe began to rise and fall. My God, am I seeing this? he thought frozenly. An arrow of chrome fell off the side of the car. The hood ornament went flying, Knives scrawled spirals through the sidewalls of the tires and the car settled. The horn blared on and on. The windshield and side windows went opaque and cracked under the on-slaught . . . and then the safety glass sprayed inward and he could see again. Vicky was crouched back, only one hand on the horn ring now, the other thrown up to protect her face. Eager young hands reached in, fumbling for the lock/unlock button. She beat them away wildly. The horn became intermittent and then stopped altogether.

The beaten and dented driver's side door was hauled open. They were trying to drag her out but her hands were wrapped around the steering wheel. Then one of them leaned in, knife in hand and—

His paralysis broke and he plunged down the steps, almost falling, and ran down the flagstone walk, toward them. One of them, a boy of about sixteen with long red hair spilling out from beneath his hat, turned toward him, almost casually, and some-thing flicked through the air. Burt's left arm jerked backward, and for a moment he had the absurd thought that he had been punched at long distance. Then the pain came, so sharp and sudden that the world went gray.

He examined his arm with a stupid sort of wonder. A buck-and-a-half Pensy jack-knife was growing out of it like a strange tumor. The sleeve of his J. C. Penney sport shirt was turning red. He looked at it for what seemed like forever, trying to under-stand how he could have grown a jackknife . . . was it possible?

When he looked up, the boy with the red hair was almost on top of him. He was grinning, confident.

"Hey, you bastard," Burt said. His voice was creaking, shocked.

"Remand your soul to God, for you will stand before His throne momentarily," the boy with the red hair said, and clawed for Burt's eyes.

Burt stepped back, pulled the Pensy out of his arm, and stuck it into the red-haired boy's throat. The gush of blood was immediate, gigantic. Burt was splashed with it. The red-haired boy began to gobble and walk in a large circle. He clawed at the knife, trying to pull it free, and was unable. Burt watched him, jaw hanging agape. None of this was happening. It was a dream. The red-haired boy gobbled and walked. Now his sound was the only one in the hot early afternoon. The others watched, stunned.

This part of it wasn't in the script, Burt thought numbly. Vicky and I, we were in the script. And the boy in the corn, who was trying to run away. But not one of their own. He stared at them savagely, wanting to scream, *How do you like it?*

The red-haired boy gave one last weak gobble, and sank to his knees. He stared up at Burt for a moment, and then his hands dropped away from the haft of the knife, and he fell forward.

A soft sighing sound from the children gathered around the Thunderbird. They stared at Burt. Burt stared back at them, fascinated . . . and that was when he noticed that Vicky was gone.

"Where is she?" he asked. "Where did you take her?"

One of the boys raised a blood-streaked hunting knife toward his throat and made a sawing motion there. He grinned. That was the only answer.

From somewhere in back, an older boy's voice, soft: "Get him."

The boys began to walk toward him. Burt backed up. They began to walk faster. Burt backed up faster. The shotgun, the goddamned shotgun! Out of reach. The sun cut their shadows darkly on the green church lawn . . . and then he was on the sidewalk. He turned and ran.

"Kill him!" someone roared, and they came after him.

He ran, but not quite blindly. He skirted the Municipal Building—no help there, they would corner him like a rat—and ran on up Main Street, which opened out and became the highway again two blocks farther up. He and Vicky would have been on that road now and away, if he had only listened.

His loafers slapped against the sidewalk. Ahead of him he could see a few more business buildings, including the Gatlin Ice Cream Shoppe and—sure enough—the Bijou Theater. The dust-clotted marquee letters read NOW HOWING L MITED EN AGE- MEN ELI A TH TAYLOR CLEOPA RA. Beyond the next cross street was a gas station that marked the edge of town. And beyond that the corn, closing back in to the sides of the road. A green tide of corn.

Burt ran. He was already out of breath and the knife wound in his upper arm was beginning to hurt. And he was leaving a trail of blood. As he ran he yanked his handkerchief from his back pocket and stuck it inside his shirt.

He ran. His loafers pounded the cracked cement of the sidewalk, his breath rasped in his throat with more and more heat. His arm began to throb in earnest. Some mordant part of his brain tried to ask if he thought he could run all the way to the next town, if he could run twenty miles of two-lane blacktop.

He ran. Behind him he could hear them, fifteen years younger and faster than he was, gaining. Their feet slapped on the pavement. They whooped and shouted back and forth to each other. They're having more fun than a five-alarm fire, Burt thought disjointedly. They'll talk about it for years.

Burt ran.

He ran past the gas station marking the edge of town. His breath gasped and roared in his chest. The sidewalk ran out under his feet. And now there was only one thing to do, only one chance to beat them and escape with his life. The houses were gone, the town was gone. The corn had surged in a soft green wave back to the edges of the road. The green, swordlike leaves rustled softly. It would be deep in there, deep and cool, shady in the rows of man-high corn.

He ran past a sign that said: YOU ARE NOW LEAVING GATLIN, NICEST LITTLE TOWN IN NEBRASKA—OR ANYWHERE ELSE? DROP IN ANYTIME!

I'll be sure to do that, Burt thought dimly.

He ran past the sign like a sprinter closing on the tape and then swerved left, crossing the road, and kicked his loafers away. Then he was in the corn and it closed behind him and over him like the waves of a green sea, taking him in. Hiding him. He felt a sudden and wholly unexpected relief sweep him, and at the same moment ge hot his second wind. His lungs, which had been shallowing up, seemed to unlock and give him more breath.

He ran straight down the first row he had entered, head ducked, his broad shoulders swiping the leaves and making them tremble. Twenty yards in he turned right, parallel to the road again, and ran on, keeping low so they wouldn't see his dark head of hair bobbing amid the yellow corn tassels. He doubled back toward the road for a few moments, crossed more rows, and then put his back to the road and hopped randomly from row to row, always delving deeper and deeper into the corn.

At last, he collapsed onto his knees and put his forehead against the ground. He could only hear his own taxed breathing, and the thought that played over and over in his mind was: *Thank God I gave up smoking, thank God I gave up smoking, thank God—*

Then he could hear them, yelling back and forth to each other, in some cases bumping into each other ("Hey, this is my row!"), and the sound heartened him. They were well away to his left and they sounded very poorly organized.

He took his handkerchief out of his shirt, folded it, and stuck it back in after looking at the wound. The bleeding seemed to have stopped in spite of the workout he had given it.

He rested a moment longer, and was suddenly aware that he felt *good*, physically better than he had in years . . . excepting the throb of his arm. He felt well exercised, and suddenly grappling with a clearcut (no matter how insane) problem after two years of trying to cope with the incubotic gremlins that were sucking his marriage dry.

It wasn't right that he should feel this way, he told himself. He was in deadly peril of his life, and his wife had been carried off. She might be dead now. He tried to summon up Vicky's face and dispel some of the odd good feeling by doing so, but her face wouldn't come. What came was the red-haired boy with the knife in his throat.

He became aware of the corn fragrance in his nose now, all around him. The wind through the tops of the plants made a sound like voices. Soothing. Whatever had been done in the name of this corn, it was now his protector.

But they were getting closer.

Running hunched over, he hurried up the row he was in, crossed over, doubled back, and crossed over more rows. He tried to keep the voices always on his left, but as the afternoon progressed, that became harder and harder to do. The voices had grown faint, and often the rustling sound of the corn obscured them altogether. He would run, listen, run again. The earth was hard-packed, and his stockinged feet left little or no trace.

When he stopped much later the sun was hanging over the fields to his right, red and inflamed, and when he looked at his watch he saw that it was quarter past seven. The sun had stained the corntops a reddish gold, but here the shadows were dark and deep. He cocked his head, listening. With the coming of sunset the wind had died entirely and the corn stood still, exhaling its aroma of growth into the warm air. If they were still in the corn they were either far away or just hunkered down and listening. But Burt didn't think a bunch of kids, even crazy ones, could be quiet for that long. He suspected they had done the most kidlike thing, regardless of the consequences for them: they had given up and gone home.

He turned toward the setting sun, which had sunk between the raftered clouds on the horizon, and began to walk. If he cut on a diagonal through the rows, always keeping the setting sun ahead of him, he would be bound to strike Route 17 sooner or later.

The ache in his arm had settled into a dull throb that was nearly pleasant. And the good feeling was still with him. He decided that as long as he was here, he would let the good feeling exist in him without guilt. The guilt would return when he had to face the authorities and account for what had happened in Gatlin. But that could wait.

He pressed through the corn, thinking he had never felt so keenly aware. Fifteen minutes later the sun was only a hemisphere poking over the horizon and he stopped again, his new awareness clicking into a pattern he didn't like. It was vaguely . . . well, vaguely frightening.

He cocked his head. The corn was rustling.

Burt had been aware of that for some time, but he had just put it together with something else. The wind was still. How could that be?

He looked around warily, half expecting to see the smiling boys in their Quaker coats creeping out of the corn, their knives clutched in their hands. Nothing of the sort. There was still that rustling noise. Off to the left.

He began to walk in that direction, not having to bull through the corn anymore. The row was taking him in the direction he wanted to go, naturally. The row ended up ahead. Ended? No, emptied out into some sort of clearing. The rustling was there.

He stopped, suddenly afraid.

The scent of the corn was strong enough to be cloying. The rows held onto the sun's heat and he became aware that he was plastered with sweat and chaff and thin spider strands of cornsilk. The bugs ought to be crawling all over him . . . but they weren't.

He stood still, staring toward that place where the corn opened out onto what looked like a large circle of bare earth.

There were no midges or mosquitoes in here, no blackflies or chiggers—what he and Vicky had called "drive-in-bugs" when they had been courting, he thought with sudden and unexpectedly sad nostalgia. And he hadn't seen a single crow. How was that for weird, a cornpatch with no crows?

In the last of the daylight he swept his eyes closely over the row of corn to his left. And saw that every leaf and stalk was perfect, which was just not possible. No yellow blight. No tattered leaves, no caterpillar eggs, no burrows, no—

His eyes widened.

My God, there aren't any weeds!

Not a single one. Every foot and a half the corn plants rose from the earth. There was no witchgrass, jimson, pikeweed, whore's hair, or poke salad. Nothing.

Burt stared up, eyes wide. The light in the west was fading. The raftered clouds had drawn back together. Below them the golden light had faded to pink and ocher. It would be dark soon enough.

It was time to go down to the clearing in the corn and see what was there—hadn't that been the plan all along? All the time he had thought he was cutting back to the highway, hadn't he been being led to this place?

Dread in his belly, he went on down to the row and stood at the edge of the clearing. There was enough light left for him to see what was here. He couldn't scream. There didn't seem to be enough air left in his lungs. He tottered in on legs like slats of splintery wood. His eyes bulged from his sweaty face.

"Vicky," he whispered. "Oh, Vicky, my God—"

She had been mounted on a crossbar like a hideous trophy, her arms held at the wrists and her legs at the ankles with twists of common barbed wire, seventy cents a yard at any hardware store in Nebraska. Her eyes had been ripped out. The sockets were filled with the moonflax of cornsilk. Her jaws were wrenched open in a silent scream, her mouth filled with cornhusks.

On her left was a skeleton in a moldering surplice. The nude jawbone grinned. The eye sockets seemed to stare at Burt jocularly, as if the onetime minister of the Grace Baptist Church was saying: *It's not so bad, being sacrificed by pagan devil-children in the corn is not so bad, having your eyes ripped out of your skull according to the Laws of Moses is not so bad—*

To the left of the skeleton in the surplice was a second skeleton, this one dressed in a rotting blue uniform. A hat hung over the skull, shading the eyes, and on the peak of the cap was a greenish-tinged badge reading POLICE CHIEF.

That was when Burt heard it coming: not the children but something much larger, moving through the corn and toward the clearing. Not the children, no. The children wouldn't venture into the corn at night. This was the holy place, the place of He Who Walks Behind the Rows.

Jerkily Burt turned to flee. The row he had entered the clearing by was gone. Closed up. All the rows had closed up. It was coming closer now and he could hear it, pushing through the corn. He could hear it breathing. An ecstasy of superstitious terror seized him. It was coming. The corn on the far side of the clearing had suddenly darkened, as if a gigantic shadow had blotted it out.

Coming.

He Who Walks Behind the Rows.

It began to come into the clearing. Burt saw something huge, bulking up to the sky . . . something green with terrible red eyes the size of footballs.

Something that smelled like dried cornhusks years in some dark barn.

He began to scream. But he did not scream long.

Some time later, a bloated orange harvest moon came up.

THE CHILDREN OF THE CORN stood in the clearing at midday, looking at the two crucified skeletons and the two bodies . . . the bodies were not skeletons yet, but they would be. In time. And here, in the heartland of Nebraska, in the corn, there was nothing but time.

"Behold, a dream came to me in the night, and the Lord did shew all this to me."

They all turned to look at Isaac with dread and wonder, even Malachi. Isaac was only nine, but he had been the Seer since the corn had taken David a year ago. David had been nineteen and he had walked into the corn on his birthday, just as dusk had come drifting down the summer rows.

Now, small face grave under his round-crowned hat, Isaac continued:

"And in my dream, the Lord was a shadow that walked behind the rows, and he spoke to me in the words he used to our older brothers years ago. He is much displeased with this sacrifice."

They made a sighing, sobbing noise and looked at the surrounding walls of green.

"And the Lord did say: Have I not given you a place of killing, that you might make sacrifice there? And have I not shewn you favor? But this man has made a blasphemy within me, and I have completed this sacrifice myself. Like the Blue Man and the false minister who escaped many years ago."

"The Blue Man . . . the false minister," they whispered, and looked at each other uneasily.

"So now is the Age of Favor lowered from nineteen plantings and harvestings to eighteen," Isaac went on relentlessly. "Yet be fruitful and multiply as the corn multiplies, that my favor may be shewn you, and be upon you."

Isaac ceased.

The eyes turned to Malachi and Joseph, the only two among this party who were eighteen. There were others back in town, perhaps twenty in all.

They waited to hear what Malachi would say, Malachi who had led the hunt for Japheth, who evermore would be known as Ahaz, cursed of God. Malachi had cut the throat of Ahaz and had thrown his body out of the corn so the foul body would not pollute it or blight it.

"I obey the word of God," Malachi whispered.

The corn seemed to sigh its approval.

In the weeks to come the girls would make many corncob crucifixes to ward off further evil.

And that night all of those now above the Age of Favor walked silently into the corn and went to the clearing, to gain the continued favor of He Who Walks Behind the Rows.

"Goodbye, Malachi," Ruth called. She waved disconsolately. Her belly was big with Malachi's child and tears coursed silently down her cheeks. Malachi did not turn. His back was straight. The corn swallowed him.

Ruth turned away, still crying. She had conceived a secret hatred for the corn and sometimes dreamed of walking into it with a torch in each hand when dry September came and the stalks were dead and explosively combustile. But she also feared it. Out there, in the night, something walked, and it saw everything . . . even the secrets kept in human hearts.

Dusk deepened into night. Around Gatlin the corn rustled and whispered secretly. It was well pleased.

BUFFALO GALS,
WON'T YOU COME OUT TONIGHT

BY URSULA K. LE GUIN

URSULA K. LE GUIN IS EQUALLY ADEPT AT SCIENCE FICTION, FANTASY, ALLE-GORY AND FAIRY TALE, AND A MASTER OF PORTRAYING THE MARVELOUS OVER-LAPS BETWEEN THE FANTASTIC AND REALITY. "BUFFALO GALS, WON'T YOU COME OUT TONIGHT" READS LIKE A CAMPFIRE TALE OF THE OLD WEST, BUT AS WITH MOST OF LE GUIN'S WORK, IS IN REALITY MUCH MORE.

i

"You fell out of the sky," the coyote said.

Still curled up tight, lying on her side, her back pressed against the over-hanging rock, the child watched the coyote with one eye. Over the other eye she kept her hand cupped, its back on the dirt.

"There was a burned place in the sky, up there alongside the rimrock, and then you fell out of it," the coyote repeated, patiently, as if the news was getting a bit stale. "Are you hurt?"

She was all right. She was in the plane with Mr. Michaels, and the motor was so loud she couldn't understand what he said even when he shouted, and the way the wind rocked the wings was making her feel sick, but it was all right. They were flying to Canyonville. In the plane.

She looked. The coyote was still sitting there. It yawned. It was a big one, in good condition, its coat silvery and thick. The dark tear-line from its long yellow eye was as clearly marked as a tabby cat's.

She sat up, slowly, still holding her right hand pressed to her right eye.

"Did you lose an eye?" the coyote asked, interested.

"I don't know," the child said. She caught her breath and shivered. "I'm cold."

"I'll help you look for it," the coyote said. "Come on! If you move around you won't have to shiver. The sun's up."

Cold lonely brightness lay across the falling land, a hundred miles of sagebrush. The coyote was trotting busily around, nosing under clumps of rabbit-brush and cheat-grass, pawing at a rock. "Aren't you going to look?" it said, suddenly sitting down on its haunches and abandoning the search. "I knew a trick once where I could throw my eyes way up into a tree and see everything from up there, and then whistle, and they'd come back into my head. But that goddam bluejay stole them, and when I whistled nothing came. I had to stick lumps of pine pitch into my head so I could see anything. You could try that. But you've got one eye that's OK, what do you need two for? Are you coming, or are you dying there?"

The child crouched, shivering.

"Well, come if you want to," said the coyote, yawned again, snapped at a flea, stood up, turned, and trotted away among the sparse clumps of rabbit-brush and sage, along the long slope that stretched on down and down into the plain streaked across by long shadows of sagebrush. The slender, grey-yellow animal was hard to keep in sight, vanishing as the child watched.

She struggled to her feet, and without a word, though she kept saying in her mind, "Wait, please wait," she hobbled after the coyote. She could not see it. She kept her hand pressed over the right eyesocket. Seeing with one eye there was no depth; it was like a huge, flat picture. The coyote suddenly sat in the middle of the picture, looking back at her, its mouth open, its eyes narrowed, grinning. Her legs began to steady and her head did not pound so hard, though the deep, black ache was always there. She had nearly caught up to the coyote when it trotted off again. This time she spoke. "Please wait!" she said.

"OK," said the coyote, but it trotted right on. She followed, walking downhill into the flat picture that at each step was deep.

Each step was different underfoot; each sage bush was different, and all the same. Following the coyote she came out from the shadow of the rimrock cliffs, and the sun at eyelevel dazzled her left eye. Its bright warmth soaked into her muscles and bones at once. The air, that all night had been so hard to breathe, came sweet and easy.

The sage bushes were pulling in their shadows and the sun was hot on the child's back when she followed the coyote along the rim of a gully. After a while the coyote slanted down the undercut slope and the child scrambled after, through scrub willows to the thin creek in its wide sandbed. Both drank.

The coyote crossed the creek, not with a careless charge and splashing like a dog, but singlefoot and quiet like a cat; always it carried its tail low. The child hesitated, knowing that wet shoes make blistered feet, and then waded across in as few steps as possible. Her right arm ached with the effort of holding her hand up over her eye. "I need a bandage," she said to the coyote. It cocked its head and said nothing. It stretched out its forelegs and lay watching the water, resting but alert. The child sat down nearby on the hot sand and tried to move her right hand. It was glued to the skin around her eye by dried blood. At the little tearing-away pain, she whimpered; though it was a small pain it frightened her. The coyote came over close and poked its long snout into her face. Its strong, sharp smell was in her nostrils. It began to lick the awful, aching blindness, cleaning and cleaning with its curled, precise, strong, wet tongue, until the child was able to cry a little with relief, being comforted. Her head was bent close to the grey-yellow ribs, and she saw the hard nipples, the whitish belly-fur. She put her arm around the she-coyote, stroking the harsh coat over back and ribs.

"OK," the coyote said, "let's go!" And set off without a backward glance. The child scrambled to her feet and followed. "Where are we going?" she said, and the coyote, trotting on down along the creek, answered, "On down along the creek . . ."

THERE MUST HAVE BEEN a while she was asleep while she walked, because she felt like she was waking up, but she was walking along, only in a different place. She didn't know how she knew it was different. They were still following the creek, though the gully was flattened out to nothing much, and there was still sagebrush range as far as the eye could see. The eye—the good one—felt rested. The other one still ached, but not so sharply, and there was no use thinking about it. But where was the coyote?

She stopped. The pit of cold into which the plane had fallen re-opened and she fell. She stood falling, a thin whimper making itself in her throat.

"Over here!"

The child turned. She saw a coyote gnawing at the half-dried-up carcass of a crow, black feathers sticking to the black lips and narrow jaw.

She saw a tawny-skinned woman kneeling by a campfire, sprinkling something into a conical pot. She heard the water boiling in the pot, though it was propped between rocks, off the fire. The woman's hair was yellow and grey, bound back with a string. Her feet were bare. The upturned soles looked as dark and hard as shoe soles, but the arch of the foot was high, and the toes made two neat curving rows. She wore bluejeans and an old white shirt. She looked over at the girl. "Come on, eat crow!" she said. The child slowly came toward the woman and the fire, and squatted down. She had stopped falling and felt very light and empty; and her tongue was like a piece of wood stuck in her mouth.

Coyote was now blowing into the pot or basket or whatever it was. She reached into it with two fingers, and pulled her hand away shaking it and shouting, "Ow! Shit! Why don't I ever have any spoons?" She broke off a dead twig of sagebrush, dipped it into the pot, and licked it. "Oh, boy," she said. "Come on!"

The child moved a little closer, broke off a twig, dipped. Lumpy pinkish mush clung to the twig. She licked. The taste was rich and delicate.

"What is it?" she asked after a long time of dipping and licking.

"Food. Dried salmon mush," Coyote said. "It's cooling down." She stuck two fingers into the mush again, this time getting a good load, which she ate very neatly. The child, when she tried, got mush all over her chin. It was like chopsticks, it took practice. She practiced. They ate turn and turn until nothing was left in the pot but three rocks. The child did not ask why there were rocks in the mush-pot. They licked the rocks clean. Coyote licked out the inside of the pot-basket, rinsed it once in the creek, and put it onto her head. It fit nicely, making a conical hat. She pulled off her bluejeans. "Piss on the fire!" she cried, and did so, standing straddling it. "Ah, steam between the legs!" she said. The child, embarrassed, thought she was supposed to do the same thing, but did not want to, and did not. Bareassed, Coyote danced around the dampened fire, kicking her long thin legs out and singing,

> *"Buffalo gals, won't you come out tonight,*
> *Come out tonight, come out tonight,*
> *Buffalo gals, won't you come out tonight,*
> *And dance by the light of the moon?*

She pulled her jeans back on. The child was burying the remains of the fire in creek-sand, heaping it over, seriously, wanting to do right. Coyote watched her.

"Is that you?" she said. "A Buffalo Gal? What happened to the rest of you?"

"The rest of me?" The child looked at herself, alarmed.

"All your people."

"Oh. Well, Mom took Bobbie, he's my little brother, away with Uncle Norm. He isn't really my uncle, or anything. So Mr. Michaels was going there anyway so he was going to fly me over to my real father, in Canyonville. Linda, my stepmother, you know, she said it was OK for the summer anyhow if I was there, and then we could see. But the plane."

In the silence the girl's face became dark red, then greyish white. Coyote watched, fascinated. "Oh," the girl said, "Oh—Oh—Mr. Michaels—he must be—Did the—"

"Come on!" said Coyote, and set off walking.

The child cried, "I ought to go back—"

"What for?" said Coyote. She stopped to look round at the child, then went on faster. "Come on, Gal!" She said it as a name; maybe it was the child's name, Myra, as spoken by Coyote. The child, confused and despairing, protested again, but followed her. "Where are we going? Where *are* we?"

"This is my country," Coyote answered, with dignity, making a long, slow gesture all round the vast horizon. "I made it. Every goddam sage bush."

And they went on. Coyote's gait was easy, even a little shambling, but she covered the ground; the child struggled not to drop behind. Shadows were beginning to pull themselves out again from under the rocks and shrubs. Leaving the creek, they went up a long, low, uneven slope that ended away off against the sky in rimrock. Dark trees stood one here, another way over there; what people called a juniper forest, a desert forest, one with a lot more between the trees than trees. Each juniper they passed smelled sharply, cat-pee smell the kids at school called it, but the child liked it; it seemed to go into her mind and wake her up. She picked off a juniper berry and held it in her mouth, but after a while spat it out. The aching was coming back in huge black waves, and she kept stumbling. She found that she was sitting down on the ground. When she tried to get up her legs shook and would not go under her. She felt foolish and frightened, and began to cry.

"We're home!" Coyote called from way on up the hill.

The child looked with her one weeping eye, and saw sagebrush, juniper, cheatgrass, rimrock. She heard a coyote yip far off in the dry twilight.

She saw a little town up under the rimrock, board houses, shacks, all unpainted. She heard Coyote call again, "Come on, pup! Come on, Gal, we're home!" She could not get up, so she tried to go on all fours, the long way up the slope to the houses under the rimrock. Long before she got there, several people came to meet her. They were all children, she thought at first, and then began to understand that most of them were grown people, but all were very short; they were broad-bodied, fat, with fine, delicate hands and feet. Their eyes were bright. Some of the women helped her stand up and walk, coaxing her, "It isn't much farther, you're doing fine." In the late dusk lights shone yellow-bright through doorways and through unchinked cracks between boards. Woodsmoke hung sweet in the quiet air. The short people talked and laughed all the time, softly. "Where's she going to stay?"—"Put her in with Robin, they're all asleep already!"—"Oh, she can stay with us."

The child asked hoarsely. "Where's Coyote?"

"Out hunting," the short people said.

A deeper voice spoke: "Somebody new has come into town?"

"Yes, a new person," one of the short men answered.

Among these people the deep-voiced man bulked impressive; he was broad and tall, with powerful hands, a big head, a short neck. They made way for him respectfully. He moved very quietly, respectful of them also. His eyes when he stared down at the child were amazing. When he blinked, it was like the passing of a hand before a candle-flame.

"It's only an owlet," he said. "What have you let happen to your eye, new person?"

"I was—We were flying—"

"You're too young to fly," the big man said in his deep, soft voice. "Who brought you here?"

"Coyote."

And one of the short people confirmed: "She came here with Coyote, Young Owl."

"Then maybe she should stay in Coyote's house tonight," the big man said.

"It's all bones and lonely in there," said a short woman with fat cheeks and a striped shirt. "She can come with us."

That seemed to decide it. The fat-cheeked woman patted the child's arm and took her past several shacks and shanties to a low, windowless house. The doorway was so low even the child had to duck down to enter. There were a lot of people inside, some already there and some crowding in after the fat-cheeked woman. Several babies were fast asleep in cradle-boxes in corners. There was a good fire, and a good smell, like toasted sesame seeds. The child was given food, and ate a little, but her head swam and the blackness in her right eye kept coming across her left eye so she could not see at all for a while. Nobody asked her name or told her what to call them. She heard the children call the fat-cheeked woman Chipmunk. She got up courage finally to say, "Is there somewhere I can go to sleep, Mrs. Chipmunk?"

"Sure, come on," one of the daughters said, "in here," and took the child into a back room, not completely partitioned off from the crowded front room, but dark and uncrowded. Big shelves with mattresses and blankets lined the walls. "Crawl in!" said Chipmunk's daughter, patting the child's arm in the comforting way they had. The child climbed onto a shelf, under a blanket. She laid down her head. She thought, "I didn't brush my teeth."

ii

She woke; she slept again. In Chipmunk's sleeping room it was always stuffy, warm, and half-dark, day and night. People came in and slept and got up and left, night and day. She dozed and slept, got down to drink from the bucket and dipper in the front room, and went back to sleep and doze.

She was sitting up on the shelf, her feet dangling, not feeling bad any more, but dreamy, weak. She felt in her jeans pockets. In the left front one was a pocket comb and a bubblegum wrapper, in the right front, two dollar bills and a quarter and a dime.

Chipmunk and another woman, a very pretty dark-eyed plump one, came in. "So you woke up for your dance!" Chipmunk greeted her, laughing, and sat down by her with an arm around her.

"Jay's giving you a dance," the dark woman said. "He's going to make you all right. Let's get you all ready!"

There was a spring up under the rimrock, that flattened out into a pool with slimy, reedy shores. A flock of noisy children splashing in it ran off and left the child and the two women to bathe. The water was warm on the surface, cold down on the feet and legs. All naked, the two soft-voiced laughing women, their round bellies and breasts, broad hips and buttocks gleaming warm in the late afternoon light, sluiced the child down, washed and stroked her limbs and hands and hair, cleaned around the cheekbone and eyebrow of her right eye with infinite softness, admired her, sudsed her, rinsed her, splashed her out of the water, dried her off, dried each other off, got dressed, dressed her, braided her hair, braided each other's hair, tied feathers on the braid-ends, admired her and each other again, and brought her back down into the little straggling town and to a kind of playing field or dirt parking lot in among the houses. There were no streets, just paths and dirt, no lawns and gardens, just sagebrush and dirt. Quite a few people were gathering or wandering around the open place, looking dressed up, wearing colorful shirts, print dresses, strings of beads, earrings. "Hey there, Chipmunk, Whitefoot!" they greeted the women.

A man in new jeans, with a bright blue velveteen vest over a clean, faded blue workshirt, came forward to meet them, very handsome, tense, and important. "All right, Gal!" he said in a harsh, loud voice, which startled among all these soft-speaking people. "We're going to get that eye fixed right up tonight! You just sit down here and don't worry about a thing." He took her wrist, gently despite his bossy, brassy manner, and led her to a woven mat that lay on the dirt near the middle of the open place. There, feeling very foolish, she had to sit down, and was told to stay still. She soon got over feeling that everybody was looking at her, since nobody paid her more attention than a checking glance or, from Chipmunk or Whitefoot and their families, a reassuring wink. Every now and then Jay rushed over to her and said something like, "Going to be as good as new!" and went off again to organize people, waving his long blue arms and shouting.

Coming up the hill to the open place, a lean, loose, tawny figure—and the child started to jump up, remembered she was to sit still, and sat still, calling out softly, "Coyote! Coyote!"

Coyote came lounging by. She grinned. She stood looking down at the child. "Don't let that Bluejay fuck you up, Gal," she said, and lounged on.

The child's gaze followed her, yearning.

People were sitting down now over on one side of the open place, making an uneven half-circle that kept getting added to at the ends until there was nearly a circle of people sitting on the dirt around the child, ten or fifteen paces from her. All the people wore the kind of clothes the child was used to, jeans and jeans-jackets, shirts, vests, cotton dresses, but they were all barefoot, and she thought they were more beautiful than the people she knew, each in a different way, as if each one had invented beauty. Yet some of them were also very strange: thin black shining people with whispery voices, a long-legged woman with eyes like jewels. The big man called Young Owl was there, sleepy-looking and dignified, like Judge McCown who owned a sixty-thousand acre ranch; and beside him was a woman the child thought might be his sister, for like him she had a hook nose and big, strong hands; but she was lean and dark, and there was a crazy look in her fierce eyes. Yellow eyes, but round, not long and slanted like Coyote's. There was Coyote sitting yawning, scratching her armpit, bored. Now somebody was entering the circle: a man, wearing only a kind of kilt and a cloak painted or beaded with diamond shapes, dancing to the rhythm of the rattle he carried and shook with a buzzing fast beat. His limbs and body were thick yet supple, his movements smooth and pouring. The child kept her gaze on him as he danced past her, around her, past again. The rattle in his hand shook almost too fast to see, in the other hand was something thin and sharp. People were singing around the circle now, a few notes repeated in time to the rattle, soft and tuneless. It was exciting and boring, strange and familiar. The Rattler wove his dancing closer and closer to her, darting at her. The first time she flinched away, frightened by the lunging movement and by his flat, cold face with narrow eyes, but after that she sat still, knowing her part. The dancing went on, the singing went on, till they carried her past boredom into a floating that could go on forever.

Jay had come strutting into the circle, and was standing beside her. He couldn't sing, but he called out, "Hey! Hey! Hey! Hey!" in his big, harsh voice, and everybody answered from all round, and the echo came down from the rimrock on the second beat. Jay was holding up a stick with a ball on it in one hand, and something like a marble in the other. The stick was a pipe: he got smoke into his mouth from it and blew it in four directions and up and down and then over the marble, a puff each time. Then the rattle stopped suddenly, and everything was silent for several breaths. Jay squatted down and looked intently into the child's face, his head cocked to one side. He reached forward, muttering something in time to the rattle and the singing that had started up again louder than before; he touched the child's right eye in the black center of the pain. She flinched and endured. His touch was not gentle. She saw the marble, a dull yellow ball like beeswax, in his hand; then she shut her seeing eye and set her teeth.

"There!" Jay shouted. "Open up. Come on! Let's see!"

Her jaw clenched like a vise, she opened both eyes. The lid of the right one stuck and dragged with such a searing white pain that she nearly threw up as she sat there in the middle of everybody watching.

"Hey, can you see? How's it work? It looks great!" Jay was shaking her arm, railing at her. "How's it feel? Is it working?"

What she saw was confused, hazy, yellowish. She began to discover, as everybody came crowding around peering at her, smiling, stroking and patting her arms and shoulders, that if she shut the hurting eye and looked with the other, everything was clear and flat; if she used them both, things were blurry and yellowish, but deep.

There, right close, was Coyote's long nose and narrow eyes and grin. "What is it, Jay?" she was asking peering at the new eye. "One of mine you stole that time?"

"It's pine pitch," Jay shouted furiously. "You think I'd use some stupid secondhand coyote eye? I'm a doctor!"

"Ooooh, ooooh, a doctor," Coyote said. "Boy, that is one ugly eye. Why didn't you ask Rabbit for a rabbit-dropping? That eye looks like shit." She put her lean face yet closer, till the child thought she was going to kiss her; instead, the thin, firm tongue once more licked accurate across the pain, cooling, clearing. When the child opened both eyes again the world looked pretty good.

"It works fine," she said.

"Hey!" Jay yelled. "She says it works fine! It works fine, she says so! I told you! What'd I tell you?" He went off waving his arms and yelling. Coyote had disappeared. Everybody was wandering off.

The child stood up, stiff from long sitting. It was nearly dark; only the long west held a great depth of pale radiance. Eastward the plains ran down into night.

Lights were on in some of the shanties. Off at the edge of town somebody was playing a creaky fiddle, a lonesome chirping tune.

A person came beside her and spoke quietly: "Where will you stay?"

"I don't know," the child said. She was feeling extremely hungry. "Can I stay with Coyote?"

"She isn't home much," the soft-voiced woman said. "You were staying with Chipmunk, weren't you? Or there's Rabbit or Jackrabbit, they have families . . ."

"Do you have a family?" the girl asked, looking at the delicate, soft-eyed woman.

"Two fawns," the woman answered, smiling. "But I just came into town for the dance."

"I'd really like to stay with Coyote," the child said after a little pause, timid, but obstinate.

"OK, that's fine. Her house is over here." Doe walked along beside the child to a ramshackle cabin on the high edge of town. No light shone from inside. A lot of junk was scattered around the front. There was no step up to the half-open door. Over the door a battered pine board, nailed up crooked, said BIDE-A-WEE.

"Hey, Coyote? Visitors," Doe said. Nothing happened.

Doe pushed the door farther open and peered in. "She's out hunting, I guess. I better be getting back to the fawns. You going to be OK? Anybody else here will give you something to eat—you know . . . OK?"

"Yeah. I'm fine. Thank you," the child said.

She watched Doe walk away through the clear twilight, a severely elegant walk, small steps, like a woman in high heels, quick, precise, very light.

Inside Bide-A-Wee it was too dark to see anything and so cluttered that she fell over something at every step. She could not figure out where or how to light a fire. There was something that felt like a bed, but when she lay down on it, it felt more like a dirty-clothes pile, and smelt like one. Things bit her legs, arms, neck, and back. She was terribly hungry. By smell she found her way to what had to be a dead fish hanging from the ceiling in one corner. By feel she broke off a greasy flake and tasted it. It was smoked dried salmon. She ate one succulent piece after another until she was satisfied, and licked her fingers clean. Near the open door starlight shone on water in a pot of some kind; the child smelled it cautiously, tasted it cautiously, and drank just enough to quench her thirst, for it tasted of mud and was warm and stale. Then she went back to the bed of dirty clothes and fleas, and lay down. She could have gone to Chipmunk's house, or other friendly households; she thought of that as she lay forlorn in Coyote's dirty bed. But she did not go. She slapped at fleas until she fell asleep.

Along in the deep night somebody said, "Move over, pup," and was warm beside her.

BREAKFAST, EATEN SITTING in the sun in the doorway, was dried-salmon-powder mush. Coyote hunted, mornings and evenings, but what they ate was not fresh game but salmon, and dried stuff, and any berries in season. The child did not ask about this. It made sense to her. She was going to ask Coyote why she slept at night and waked in the day like humans, instead of the other way round like coyotes, but when she framed the question in her mind she saw at once that night is when you sleep and day when you're awake; that made sense too. But one question she did ask, one hot day when they were lying around slapping fleas.

"I don't understand why you all look like people," she said.

"We are people."

"I mean, people like me, humans."

"Resemblance is in the eye," Coyote said. "How is that lousy eye, by the way?"

"It's fine. But—like you wear clothes—and live in houses—with fires and stuff—"

"That's what you think . . . If that loudmouth Jay hadn't horned in, I could have done a really good job."

The child was quite used to Coyote's disinclination to stick to any one subject, and to her boasting. Coyote was like a lot of kids she knew, in some respects. Not in others.

"You mean what I'm seeing isn't true? Isn't real—like on TV, or something?"

"No," Coyote said. "Hey, that's a tick on your collar." She reached over, flicked the tick off, picked it up on one finger, bit it, and spat out the bits.

"Yecch!" the child said. "So?"

"So, to me you're basically greyish yellow and run on four legs. To that lot—" she waved disdainfully at the warren of little houses next down the hill—"you hop around twitching your nose all the time. To Hawk, you're an egg, or maybe getting pinfeathers. See? It just depends on how you look at things. There are only two kinds of people."

"Humans and animals?"

"No. The kind of people who say. 'There are two kinds of people' and the kind of people who don't." Coyote cracked up, pounding her thigh and yelling with delight at her joke. The child didn't get it, and waited.

"OK," Coyote said. "There's the first people, and then the others. That's the two kinds."

"The first people are—?"

"Us, the animals . . . and things. All the old ones. You know. And you pups, kids, fledglings. All first people."

"And the—others?"

"Them," Coyote said. "You know. The others. The new people. The ones who came." Her fine, hard face had gone serious, rather formidable. She glanced directly, as she seldom did, at the child, a brief gold sharpness. "We were here," she said. "We were always here. We are always here. Where we are is here. But it's their country now. They're running it . . . Shit, even I did better!"

The child pondered and offered a word she had used to hear a good deal: "They're illegal immigrants."

"Illegal!" Coyote said, mocking, sneering. "Illegal is a sick bird. What the fuck's illegal mean? You want a code of justice from a coyote? Grow up, kid!"

"I don't want to."

"You don't want to grow up?"

"I'll be the other kind if I do."

"Yeah. So," Coyote said, and shrugged. "That's life." She got up and went around the house, and the child heard her pissing in the back yard.

A lot of things were hard to take about Coyote as a mother. When her boyfriends came to visit, the child learned to go stay with Chipmunk or the Rabbits for the night, because Coyote and her friend wouldn't even wait to get on the bed but would start doing that right on the floor or even out in the yard. A couple of times Coyote came back late from hunting with a friend, and the child had to lie up against the wall in the same bed and hear and feel them doing that right next to her. It was something like fighting and something like dancing, with a beat to it, and she didn't mind too much except that it made it hard to stay asleep.

Once she woke up and one of Coyote's friends was stroking her stomach in a creepy way: She didn't know what to do, but Coyote woke up and realized what he was doing, bit him hard, and kicked him out of bed. He spent the night on the floor, and apologized next morning—"Aw, hell, Ki, I forgot the kid was there, I thought it was you—"

Coyote, unappeased, yelled, "You think I don't got any standards? You think I'd let some coyote rape a kid in my bed?" She kicked him out of the house, and grumbled about him all day. But a while later he spent the night again, and he and Coyote did that three or four times.

Another thing that was embarrassing was the way Coyote peed anywhere, taking her pants down in public. But most people here didn't seem to care. The thing that worried the child most, maybe, was when Coyote did number two anywhere and then turned around and talked to it. That seemed so awful. As if Coyote was—the way she often seemed, but really wasn't—crazy.

The child gathered up all the old dry turds from around the house one day while Coyote was having a nap, and buried them in a sandy place near where she and Bobcat and some of the other people generally went and did and buried their number twos.

Coyote woke up, came lounging out of Bide-A-Wee, rubbing her hands through her thick, fair, greyish hair and yawning, looked all around once with those narrow eyes, and said, "Hey! Where are they?" Then she shouted, "Where are you? Where are you?"

And a faint, muffled chorus came from over in the sandy draw, "Mommy! Mommy! We're here!"

Coyote trotted over, squatted down, raked out every turd, and talked with them for a long time. When she came back she said nothing, but the child, redfaced and heart pounding, said, "I'm sorry I did that."

"It's just easier when they're all around close by," Coyote said, washing her hands (despite the filth of her house, she kept herself quite clean, in her own fashion).

"I kept stepping on them," the child said, trying to justify her deed.

"Poor little shits," said Coyote, practicing dance-steps.

"Coyote," the child said timidly. "Did you ever have any children? I mean real pups?"

"Did I? Did I have children? Litters! That one that tried feeling you up, you know? that was my son. Pick of the litter . . . Listen, Gal. Have daughters. When you have anything, have daughters. At least they clear out."

iii

The child thought of herself as Gal, but also sometimes as Myra. So far as she knew, she was the only person in town who had two names. She had to think about that, and about what Coyote had said about the two kinds of people; she had to think about where she belonged. Some persons in town made it clear that as far as they were concerned she didn't and never would belong there. Hawk's furious stare burned through her; the Skunk children made audible remarks about what she smelled like. And though Whitefoot and Chipmunk and their families were kind, it was the generosity of big families, where one more or less simply doesn't count. If one of them, or Cottontail, or Jackrabbit, had come upon her in the desert lying lost and half-blind, would they have stayed with her, like Coyote? That was Coyote's craziness, what they called her craziness. She wasn't afraid. She went between the two kinds of people, she crossed over. Buck and Doe and their beautiful children weren't really afraid, because they lived so constantly in danger. The Rattler wasn't afraid, because he was so dangerous. And yet maybe he was afraid of her, for he never spoke, and never came close to her. None of them treated her the way Coyote did. Even among the children, her only constant playmate was one younger than herself, a preposterous and fearless little boy called Horned Toad Child. They dug and built together, out among the sagebrush, and played at hunting and gathering and keeping house and holding dances, all the great games. A pale, squatty child with fringed eyebrows, he was a self-contained but loyal friend; and he knew a good deal for his age.

"There isn't anybody else like me here," she said, as they sat by the pool in the morning sunlight.

"There isn't anybody much like me anywhere," said Horned Toad Child.

"Well, you know what I mean."

"Yeah . . . There used to be people like you around, I guess."

"What were they called?"

"Oh—people. Like everybody . . ."

"But where do my people live? They have towns. I used to live in one. I don't know where they are, is all. I ought to find out. I don't know where my mother is now, but my daddy's in Canyonville. I was going there when."

"Ask Horse," said Horned Toad Child, sagaciously. He had moved away from the water, which he did not like and never drank, and was plaiting rushes.

"I don't know Horse."

"He hangs around the butte down there a lot of the time. He's waiting till his uncle gets old and he can kick him out and be the big honcho. The old man and the women don't want him around till then. Horses are weird. Anyway, he's the one to ask. He gets around a lot. And his people came here with the new people, that's what they say, anyhow."

Illegal immigrants, the girl thought. She took Horned Toad's advice, and one long day when Coyote was gone on one of her unannounced and unexplained trips, she took a pouchful of dried salmon and salmonberries and went off alone to the flat-topped butte miles away in the southwest.

There was a beautiful spring at the foot of the butte, and a trail to it with a lot of footprints on it. She waited there under willows by the clear pool, and after a while

Horse came running, splendid, with copper-red skin and long, strong legs, deep chest, dark eyes, his black hair whipping his back as he ran. He stopped, not at all winded, and gave a snort as he looked at her. "Who are you?"

Nobody in town asked that—ever. She saw it was true: Horse had come here with her people, people who had to ask each other who they were.

"I live with Coyote," she said, cautiously.

"Oh, sure, I heard about you," Horse said. He knelt to drink from the pool, long deep drafts, his hands plunged in the cool water. When he had drunk he wiped his mouth, sat back on his heels, and announced, "I'm going to be king."

"King of the Horses?"

"Right! Pretty soon now. I could lick the old man already, but I can wait. Let him have his day," said Horse, vainglorious, magnanimous. The child gazed at him, in love already, forever.

"I can comb your hair, if you like," she said.

"Great!" said Horse, and sat still while she stood behind him, tugging her pocket comb through his coarse, black, shining, yard-long hair. It took a long time to get it smooth. She tied it in a massive ponytail with willowbark when she was done. Horse bent over the pool to admire himself. "That's great," he said. "That's really beautiful!"

"Do you ever go . . . where the other people are?" she asked in a low voice.

He did not reply for long enough that she thought he wasn't going to; then he said, "You mean the metal places, the glass places? The holes? I go around them. There are all the walls now. There didn't used to be so many. Grandmother said there didn't used to be any walls. Do you know Grandmother?" he asked naively, looking at her with his great dark eyes.

"Your grandmother?"

"Well, yes—Grandmother—You know. Who makes the web. Well, anyhow. I know there's some of my people, horses, there. I've seen them across the walls. They act really crazy. You know, we brought the new people here. They couldn't have got here without us, they only have two legs, and they have those metal shells. I can tell you that whole story. The King has to know the stories."

"I like stories a lot."

"It takes three nights to tell it. What do you want to know about them?"

"I was thinking that maybe I ought to go there. Where they are."

"It's dangerous. Really dangerous. You can't go through—they'd catch you."

"I'd just like to know the way."

"I know the way," Horse said, sounding for the first time entirely adult and reliable; she knew he did know the way. "It's a long run for a colt." He looked at her again. "I've got a cousin with different-color eyes," he said, looking from her right to her left eye. "One brown and one blue. But she's an Appaloosa."

"Bluejay made the yellow one," the child explained. "I lost my own one. In the . . . when . . . You don't think I could get to those places?"

"Why do you want to?"

"I sort of feel like I have to."

Horse nodded. He got up. She stood still.

"I could take you, I guess," he said.

"Would you? When?"

"Oh, now, I guess. Once I'm King I won't be able to leave, you know. Have to protect the women. And I sure wouldn't let my people get anywhere near those places!" A shudder ran right down his magnificent body, yet he said, with a toss of his head, "They couldn't catch me, of course, but the others can't run like I do . . ."

"How long would it take us?"

Horse thought a while. "Well, the nearest place like that is over by the red rocks. If we left now we'd be back here around tomorrow noon. It's just a little hole."

She did not know what he meant by "a hole," but did not ask.

"You want to go?" Horse said, flipping back his ponytail.

"OK," the girl said, feeling the ground go out from under her.

"Can you run?"

She shook her head. "I walked here, though."

Horse laughed, a large, cheerful laugh. "Come on," he said, and knelt and held his hands backturned like stirrups for her to mount to his shoulders. "What do they call you?" he teased, rising easily, setting right off at a jogtrot. "Gnat? Fly? Flea?"

"Tick, because I stick!" the child cried, gripping the willowbark tie of the black mane, laughing with delight at being suddenly eight feet tall and traveling across the desert without even trying, like the tumbleweed, as fast as the wind.

MOON, A NIGHT PAST full, rose to light the plains for them. Horse jogged easily on and on. Somewhere deep in the night they stopped at a Pygmy Owl camp, ate a little, and rested. Most of the owls were out hunting, but an old lady entertained them at her campfire, telling them tales about the ghost of a cricket, about the great invisible people, tales that the child heard interwoven with her own dreams as she dozed and half-woke and dozed again. Then Horse put her up on his shoulders and on they went at a tireless slow lope. Moon went down behind them, and before them the sky paled into rose and gold. The soft nightwind was gone; the air was sharp, cold, still. On it, in it, there was a faint, sour smell of burning. The child felt Horse's gait change, grow tighter, uneasy.

"Hey, Prince!"

A small, slightly scolding voice: the child knew it, and placed it as soon as she saw the person sitting by a juniper tree, neatly dressed, wearing an old black cap.

"Hey, Chickadee!" Horse said, coming round and stopping. The child had observed, back in Coyote's town, that everybody treated Chickadee with respect. She didn't see why. Chickadee seemed an ordinary person, busy and talkative like most of the small birds, nothing like so endearing as Quail or so impressive as Hawk or Great Owl.

"You're going on that way?" Chickadee asked Horse.

"The little one wants to see if her people are living there," Horse said, surprising the child. Was that what she wanted?

Chickadee looked disapproving, as she often did. She whistled a few notes thoughtfully, another of her habits, and then got up. "I'll come along."

"That's great," Horse said, thankfully.

"I'll scout," Chickadee said, and off she went, surprisingly fast, ahead of them, while Horse took up his steady long lope.

The sour smell was stronger in the air.

Chickadee halted, way ahead of them on a slight rise, and stood still. Horse dropped to a walk, and then stopped. "There," he said in a low voice.

The child stared. In the strange light and slight mist before sunrise she could not see clearly, and when she strained and peered she felt as if her left eye were not seeing at all. "What is it?" she whispered.

"One of the holes. Across the wall—see?"

It did seem there was a line, a straight, jerky line drawn across the sagebrush plain, and on the far side of it—nothing? Was it mist? Something moved there—"It's cattle!" she said. Horse stood silent, uneasy. Chickadee was coming back towards them.

"It's a ranch," the child said. "That's a fence. There's a lot of Herefords." The words tasted like iron, like salt in her mouth. The things she named wavered in her sight and faded, leaving nothing—a hole in the world, a burned place like a cigarette burn. "Go closer!" she urged Horse. "I want to see."

And as if he owed her obedience, he went forward, tense but unquestioning.

Chickadee came up to them. "Nobody around," she said in her small, dry voice, "but there's one of those fast turtle things coming."

Horse nodded, but kept going forward.

Gripping his broad shoulders, the child stared into the blank, and as if Chickadee's words had focused her eyes, she saw again: the scattered whitefaces, a few of them looking up with bluish, rolling eyes—the fences—over the rise a chimneyed house-roof and a high barn—and then in the distance something moving fast, too fast, burning across the ground straight at them at terrible speed. "Run!" she yelled to Horse, "run away! Run!" As if released from bonds he wheeled and ran, flat out, in great reaching strides, away from sunrise, the fiery burning chariot, the smell of acid, iron, death. And Chickadee flew before them like a cinder on the air of dawn.

iv

"Horse?" Coyote said. "That prick? Catfood!"

Coyote had been there when the child got home to Bide-A-Wee, but she clearly hadn't been worrying about where Gal was, and maybe hadn't even noticed she was gone. She was in a vile mood, and took it all wrong when the child tried to tell her where she had been.

"If you're going to do damn fool things, next time do 'em with me, at least I'm an expert," she said, morose, and slouched out the door. The child saw her squatting down, poking an old, white turd with a stick, trying to get it to answer some question she kept asking it. The turd lay obstinately silent. Later in the day the child saw two coyote men, a young one and a mangy-looking older one, loitering around near the spring, looking over at Bide-A-Wee. She decided it would be a good night to spend somewhere else.

The thought of the crowded rooms of Chipmunk's house was not attractive. It was going to be a warm night again tonight, and moonlit. Maybe she would sleep outside. If she could feel sure some people wouldn't come around, like the Rattler . . . She was standing indecisive halfway through town when a dry voice said, "Hey, Gal."

"Hey, Chickadee."

The trim, black-capped woman was standing on her doorstep shaking out a rug. She kept her house neat, trim like herself. Having come back across the desert with her the child now knew, though she still could not have said, why Chickadee was a respected person.

"I thought maybe I'd sleep out tonight," the child said, tentative.

"Unhealthy," said Chickadee. "What are nests for?"

"Mom's kind of busy," the child said.

"Tsk!" went Chickadee, and snapped the rug with disapproving vigor. "What about your little friend? At least they're decent people."

"Horny-toad? His parents are so shy . . ."

"Well. Come in and have something to eat, anyhow," said Chickadee.

The child helped her cook dinner. She knew now why there were rocks in the mush-pot.

"Chickadee," she said, "I still don't understand, can I ask you? Mom said it depends who's seeing it, but still, I mean if I see you wearing clothes and everything like humans, then how come you cook this way, in baskets, you know, and there aren't any—any of the things like they have—there where we were with Horse this morning?"

"I don't know," Chickadee said. Her voice indoors was quite soft and pleasant. "I guess we do things the way they always were done. When your people and my people lived together, you know. And together with everything else here. The rocks, you know. The plants and everything." She looked at the basket of willowbark, fernroot and pitch, at the blackened rocks that were heating in the fire. "You see how it all goes together . . . ?"

"But you have fire—That's different—"

"Ah!" said Chickadee, impatient, "you people! Do you think you invented the sun?"

She took up the wooden tongs, plopped the heated rocks into the water-filled basket with a terrific hiss and steam and loud bubblings. The child sprinkled in the pounded seeds, and stirred.

Chickadee brought out a basket of fine blackberries. They sat on the newly-shaken-out rug, and ate. The child's two-finger scoop technique with mush was now highly refined.

"Maybe I didn't cause the world," Chickadee said, "but I'm a better cook than Coyote."

The child nodded, stuffing.

"I don't know why I made Horse go there," she said, after she had stuffed. "I got just as scared as him when I saw it. But now I feel again like I have to go back there. But I want to stay here. With my, with Coyote. I don't understand."

"When we lived together it was all one place," Chickadee said in her slow, soft home-voice. "But now the others, the new people, they live apart. And their places are so heavy. They weigh down on our place, they press on it, draw it, suck it, eat it, eat holes in it, crowd it out . . . Maybe after a while longer there'll only be one place again, their place. And none of us here. I knew Bison, out over the mountains. I knew Antelope right here. I knew Grizzly and Greywolf, up west there. Gone. All gone. And the salmon you eat at Coyote's house, those are the dream salmon, those are the true food; but in the rivers, how many salmon now? The rivers that were red with them in spring? Who dances, now, when the First Salmon offers himself? Who dances by the river? Oh, you should ask Coyote about all this. She knows more than I do! But she forgets . . . She's hopeless, worse than Raven, she has to piss on every post, she's a terrible housekeeper . . ." Chickadee's voice had sharpened. She whistled a note or two, and said no more.

After a while the child asked very softly, "Who is Grandmother?"

"Grandmother," Chickadee said. She looked at the child, and ate several blackberries thoughtfully. She stroked the rug they sat on.

"If I built the fire on the rug, it would burn a hole in it," she said. "Right? So we build the fire on sand, on dirt . . . Things are woven together. So we call the weaver the Grandmother." She whistled four notes, looking up the smokehole. "After all," she added, "maybe all this place, the other places too, maybe they're all only one side of the weaving, I don't know. I can only look with one eye at a time, how can I tell how deep it goes?"

LYING THAT NIGHT rolled up in a blanket in Chickadee's back yard, the child heard the wind soughing and storming in the cottonwoods down in the draw, and then slept deeply, weary from the long night before. Just at sunrise she woke. The eastern mountains were a cloudy dark red as if the level light shone through them as through a hand held before the fire. In the tobacco patch—the only farming anybody in this town did was to raise a little wild tobacco—Lizard and Beetle were singing some kind of growing song or blessing song, soft and desultory, huh-huh-huh-huh, huh-huh-huh-huh, and as she lay warm-curled on the ground the song made her feel rooted in the ground, cradled on it and in it, so where her fingers ended and the dirt began she did not know, as if she were dead, but she was wholly alive, she was the earth's life. She got up dancing, left the blanket folded neatly on Chickadee's neat and already empty bed, and danced up the hill to Bide-A-Wee. At the half-open door she sang,

> "Danced with a gal with a hole in her stocking
> And her knees kept a knocking and her toes kept
>   a rocking,
> Danced with a gal with a hole in her stocking,
> Danced by the light of the moon!"

Coyote emerged, tousled and lurching, and eyed her narrowly. "Sheeeoot," she said. She sucked her teeth and then went to splash water all over her head from the gourd by the door. She shook her head and the waterdrops flew. "Let's get out of here," she said. "I have had it. I don't know what got into me. If I'm pregnant again, at my age, oh, shit. Let's get out of town. I need a change of air."

In the foggy dark of the house, the child could see at least two coyote men sprawled snoring away on the bed and floor. Coyote walked over to the old white turd and kicked it. "Why didn't you stop me?" she shouted.

"I *told* you," the turd muttered sulkily.

"Dumb shit," Coyote said. "Come on, Gal. Let's go. Where to?" She didn't wait for an answer. "I know. Come on!"

And she set off through town at that lazy-looking rangy walk that was so hard to keep up with. But the child was full of pep, and came dancing, so that Coyote began dancing too, skipping and pirouetting and fooling around all the way down the long slope to the level plains. There she slanted their way off north-eastward. Horse Butte was at their backs, getting smaller in the distance.

Along near noon the child said, "I didn't bring anything to eat."

"Something will turn up," Coyote said, "sure to." And pretty soon she turned aside, going straight to a tiny grey shack hidden by a couple of half-dead junipers and a

stand of rabbit-brush. The place smelled terrible. A sign on the door said: FOX. PRI-
VATE. NO TRESPASSING!—but Coyote pushed it open, and trotted right back out with
half a small smoked salmon. "Nobody home but us chickens," she said, grinning
sweetly.

"Isn't that stealing?" the child asked, worried.

"Yes," Coyote answered, trotting on.

They ate the fox-scented salmon by a dried-up creek, slept a while, and went on.

Before long the child smelled the sour burning smell, and stopped. It was as if a
huge, heavy hand had begun pushing her chest, pushing her away, and yet at the same
time as if she had stepped into a strong current that drew her forward, helpless.

"Hey, getting close!" Coyote said, and stopped to piss by a juniper stump.

"Close to what?"

"Their town. See?" She pointed to a pair of sage-spotted hills. Between them was
an area of greyish blank.

"I don't want to go there."

"We won't go all the way in. No way! We'll just get a little closer and look. It's
fun," Coyote said, putting her head on one side, coaxing. "They do all these weird
things in the air."

The child hung back.

Coyote became business-like, responsible. "We're going to be very careful," she
announced. "And look out for big dogs, OK? Little dogs I can handle. Make a good
lunch. Big dogs, it goes the other way. Right? Let's go, then."

Seemingly as casual and lounging as ever, but with a tense alertness in the carriage
of her head and the yellow glance of her eyes, Coyote led off again, not looking back;
and the child followed.

All around them the pressures increased. It was if the air itself was pressing on
them, as if time was going too fast, too hard, not flowing but pounding, pounding,
pounding, faster and harder till it buzzed like Rattler's rattle. Hurry, you have to hurry!
everything said, there isn't time! everything said. Things rushed past screaming and
shuddering. Things turned, flashed, roared, stank, vanished. There was a boy—he
came into focus all at once, but not on the ground: he was going along a couple of
inches above the ground, moving very fast, bending his legs from side to side in a
kind of frenzied swaying dance, and was gone. Twenty children sat in rows in the air
all singing shrilly and then the walls closed over them. A basket no a pot no a can,
a garbage can, full of salmon smelling wonderful no full of stinking deerhides and
rotten cabbage stalks, keep out of it, Coyote! Where was she?

"Mom!" the child called. "Mother!"—standing a moment at the end of an ordinary
small-town street near the gas station, and the next moment in a terror of blanknesses,
invisible walls, terrible smells and pressures and the overwhelming rush of Time
straight forward rolling her helpless as a twig in the race above a waterfall. She clung,
held on trying not to fall—"Mother!"

Coyote was over by the big basket of salmon, approaching it, wary, but out in the
open, in the full sunlight, in the full current. And a boy and a man borne by the same
current were coming down the long, sage-spotted hill behind the gas station, each
with a gun, red hats, hunters, it was killing season. "Hell, will you look at that damn
coyote in broad daylight big as my wife's ass," the man said, and cocked aimed shot

all as Myra screamed and ran against the enormous drowning torrent. Coyote fled past her yelling, "Get out of here!" She turned and was borne away.

Far out of sight of that place, in a little draw among low hills, they sat and breathed air in searing gasps until after a long time it came easy again.

"Mom, that was *stupid*," the child said furiously.

"Sure was," Coyote said. "But did you see all that food!"

"I'm not hungry," the child said sullenly. "Not till we get all the way away from here."

"But they're your folks," Coyote said. "All yours. Your kith and kin and cousins and kind. Bang! Pow! There's Coyote! Bang! There's my wife's ass! Pow! There's anything—BOOOOM! Blow it away, man! BOOOOOOM!"

"I want to go home," the child said.

"Not yet," said Coyote. "I got to take a shit." She did so, then turned to the fresh turd, leaning over it. "It says I have to stay," she reported, smiling.

"It didn't say anything! I was listening!"

"You know how to understand? You hear everything, Miss Big Ears? Hears all— Sees all with her crummy gummy eye—"

"You have pine-pitch eyes too! You told me so!"

"That's a story," Coyote snarled. "You don't even know a story when you hear one! Look, do what you like, it's a free country. I'm hanging around here tonight. I like the action." She sat down and began patting her hands on the dirt in a soft four-four rhythm and singing under her breath, one of the endless tuneless songs that kept time from running too fast, that wove the roots of trees and bushes and ferns and grass in the web that held the stream in the streambed and the rock in the rock's place and the earth together. And the child lay listening.

"I love you," she said.

Coyote went on singing.

Sun went down the last slope of the west and left a pale green clarity over the desert hills.

Coyote had stopped singing, She sniffed. "Hey," she said. "Dinner." She got up and moseyed along the little draw. "Yeah," she called back softly. "Come on!"

Stiffly, for the fear-crystals had not yet melted out of her joints, the child got up and went to Coyote. Off to one side along the hill was one of the lines, a fence. She didn't look at it. It was OK. They were outside it.

"Look at that!"

A smoked salmon, a whole chinook, lay on a little cedarbark mat. "An offering! Well, I'll be darned!" Coyote was so impressed she didn't even swear. "I haven't seen one of these for years! I thought they'd forgotten!"

"Offering to who?"

"Me! Who else? Boy, *look* at that!"

The child looked dubiously at the salmon.

"It smells funny."

"How funny?"

"Like burned."

"It's smoked, stupid! Come on."

"I'm not hungry."

"OK. It's not your salmon anyhow. It's mine. My offering, for me. Hey, you people! You people over there! Coyote thanks you! Keep it up like this and maybe I'll do some things for you too!"

"Don't, don't yell, Mom! They're not that far away—"

"They're all my people," said Coyote with a great gesture, and then sat down cross-legged, broke off a big piece of salmon, and ate.

Evening Star burned like a deep, bright pool of water in the clear sky. Down over the twin hills was a dim suffusion of light, like a fog. The child looked away from it, back at the star.

"Oh," Coyote said. "Oh, shit."

"What's wrong?"

"That wasn't so smart, eating that," Coyote said, and then held herself and began to shiver, to scream, to choke—her eyes rolled up, her long arms and legs flew out jerking and dancing, foam spurted out between her clenched teeth. Her body arched tremendously backwards, and the child, trying to hold her, was thrown violently off by the spasms of her limbs. The child scrambled back and held the body as it spasmed again, twitched, quivered, went still.

By moonrise Coyote was cold. Till then there had been so much warmth under the tawny coat that the child kept thinking maybe she was alive, maybe if she just kept holding her, keeping her warm, she would recover, she would be all right. She held her close, not looking at the black lips drawn back from the teeth, the white balls of the eyes. But when the cold came through the fur as the presence of death, the child let the slight, stiff corpse lie down on the dirt.

She went nearby and dug a hole in the stony sand of the draw, a shallow pit. Coyote's people did not bury their dead, she knew that. But her people did. She carried the small corpse to the pit, laid it down, and covered it with her blue and white bandanna. It was not large enough; the four stiff paws stuck out. The child heaped the body over with sand and rocks and a scurf of sagebrush and tumbleweed held down with more rocks. She also went to where the salmon had lain on the cedar mat, and finding the carcass of a lamb heaped dirt and rocks over the poisoned thing. Then she stood up and walked away without looking back.

At the top of the hill she stood and looked across the draw toward the misty glow of the lights of the town lying in the pass between the twin hills.

"I hope you all die in pain," she said aloud. She turned away and walked down into the desert.

v

It was Chickadee who met her, on the second evening, north of Horse Butte.

"I didn't cry," the child said.

"None of us do," said Chickadee. "Come with me this way now. Come into Grandmother's house."

It was underground, but very large, dark and large, and the Grandmother was there at the center, at her loom. She was making a rug or blanket of the hills and the black rain and the white rain, weaving in the lightning. As they spoke she wove.

"Hello, Chickadee. Hello, New Person."

"Grandmother," Chickadee greeted her.

The child said, "I'm not one of them."

Grandmother's eyes were small and dim. She smiled and wove. The shuttle thrummed through the warp.

"Old Person, then," said Grandmother. "You'd better go back there now, Grand-daughter. That's where you live."

"I lived with Coyote. She's dead. They killed her."

"Oh, don't worry about Coyote!" Grandmother said, with a little huff of laughter. "She gets killed all the time."

The child stood still. She saw the endless weaving.

"Then I—Could I go back home—to her house?"

"I don't think it would work," Grandmother said. "Do you, Chickadee?"

Chickadee shook her head once, silent.

"It would be dark there now, and empty, and fleas . . . You got outside your people's time, into our place; but I think that Coyote was taking you back, see. Her way. If you go back now, you can still live with them. Isn't your father there?"

The child nodded.

"They've been looking for you."

"They have?"

"Oh, yes, ever since you fell out of the sky. The man was dead, but you weren't there—they kept looking."

"Serves him right. Serves them all right," the child said. She put her hands up over her face and began to cry terribly, without tears.

"Go on, little one, Granddaughter," Spider said. "Don't be afraid. You can live well there. I'll be there too, you know. In your dreams, in your ideas, in dark corners in the basement. Don't kill me, or I'll make it rain . . ."

"I'll come around," Chickadee said. "Make gardens for me."

The child held her breath and clenched her hands until her sobs stopped and let her speak.

"Will I ever see Coyote?"

"I don't know," the Grandmother replied.

The child accepted this. She said, after another silence, "Can I keep my eye?"

"Yes. You can keep your eye."

"Thank you, Grandmother," the child said. She turned away then and started up the night slope towards the next day. Ahead of her in the air of dawn for a long way a little bird flew, black-capped, light-winged.

PART TWO

FANTASTIC AMERICANA

THE JOLLY CORNER

BY HENRY JAMES

HENRY JAMES HAS ALWAYS BEEN A DARLING OF LITERARY ACADEMIA WITH HIS MARVELOUS NOVELS OF AMERICANS ABROAD AND THE CONFLICTS OF THE SOCIALLY CONSCIOUS UPPER-CRUST, AND LIKEWISE HIS SHORT NOVEL *THE TURN OF THE SCREW* IS CONSIDERED TO BE ONE OF THE TRULY GREAT GHOST STORIES OF ALL TIME. IT IS IN "THE JOLLY CORNER," HOWEVER, THAT HE IS AT HIS MOST AMERICAN. HIS TALE OF AN EXPATRIATE RETURNING TO HIS ANCESTRAL HOME ONLY TO CONFRONT THE GRIM GHOST OF THE PERSON HE MIGHT HAVE BECOME HAD HE STAYED IN AMERICA IS A PERFECT METAPHOR FOR THE LOST GENTILITY OF GILDED AGE NEW YORK, AND INDEED THE LOST INNOCENCE OF THE UNITED STATES AFTER THE TRAUMA OF HER CIVIL WAR.

I

"Everyone asks me what I 'think' of everything," said Spencer Brydon; "and I make answer as I can—begging or dodging the question, putting them off with any nonsense. It wouldn't matter to any of them really," he went on, "for, even were it possible to meet in that stand-and-deliver way so silly a demand on so big a subject, my 'thoughts' would still be almost altogether about something that concerns only myself." He was talking to Miss Staverton, with whom for a couple of months now he had availed himself of every possible occasion to talk; this disposition and this resource, this comfort and support, as the situation in fact presented itself, having promptly enough taken the first place in the considerable array of rather unattenuated surprises attending his so strangely belated return to America. Everything was somehow a surprise; and that might be natural when one had so long and so consistently neglected everything, taken pains to give surprises so much margin for play. He had given them more than thirty years—thirty-three, to be exact; and they now seemed to him to have organized their performance quite on the scale of that license. He had been twenty-three on leaving New York—he was fifty-six today: unless indeed he were to reckon as he had sometimes, since his repatriation, found himself feeling; in which case he would have lived longer than is often allotted to man. It would have taken a century, he repeatedly said to himself, and said also to Alice Staverton, it would have taken a longer absence and a more averted mind than those even of which he had been guilty, to pile up the differences, the newnesses, the queernesses, above all the bignesses, for the better or the worse, that at present assaulted his vision wherever he looked.

The great fact all the while however had been the incalculability; since he *had* supposed himself, from decade to decade, to be allowing, and in the most liberal and intelligent manner, for brilliancy of change. He actually saw that he had allowed for nothing; he missed what he would have been sure of finding, he found what he would never have imagined. Proportions and values were upside-down; the ugly things he had expected, the ugly things of his faraway youth, when he had too promptly waked up to a sense of the ugly—these uncanny phenomena placed him rather, as it happened, under the charm; whereas the "swagger" things, the modern, the monstrous, the famous things, those he had more particularly, like thousands of ingenuous inquirers every year, come over to see, were exactly his sources of dismay. They were as so many set traps for displeasure, above all for reaction, of which his restless tread was constantly pressing the spring. It was interesting, doubtless, the whole show, but it would have been too disconcerting hadn't a certain finer truth saved the situation. He had distinctly not, in this steadier light, come over *all* for the monstrosities; he had come, not only in the last analysis but quite on the face of the act, under an impulse with which they had nothing to do. He had come—putting the thing pompously—to look at his "property," which he had thus for a third of a century not been within four thousand miles of; or, expressing it less sordidly, he had yielded to the humor of seeing again his house on the jolly corner, as he usually, and quite fondly, described it—the one in which he had first seen the light, in which various members of his family had lived and had died, in which the holidays of his overschooled boyhood had been passed and the few social flowers of his chilled adolescence gathered, and which, alienated then for so long a period, had, through the successive deaths of his two brothers and the termination of old arrangements, come wholly into his hands. He was the owner of another, not quite so "good"—the jolly corner having been, far from back, superlatively extending and consecrated; and the value of the pair represented his main capital, with an income consisting, in these later years, of their respective rents which (thanks precisely to their original excellent type) had never been depressingly low. He could live in "Europe," as he had been in the habit of living, on the product of these flourishing New York leases, and all the better since, that of the second structure, the mere number in its long row, having within a twelve-month fallen in, renovation at a high advance had proved beautifully possible.

These were items of property indeed, but he had found himself since his arrival distinguishing more than ever between them. The house within the street, two bristling blocks westward, was already in course of reconstruction as a tall mass of flats; he had acceded, some time before, to overtures for this conversion—in which, now that it was going forward, it had been not the least of his astonishments to find himself able, on the spot, and though without a previous ounce of such experience, to participate with a certain intelligence, almost with a certain authority. He had lived his life with his back so turned to such concerns and his face addressed to those of so different an order that he scarce knew what to make of this lively stir, in a compartment of his mind never yet penetrated, of a capacity for business and a sense for construction. These virtues, so common all round him now, had been dormant in his own organism—where it might be said of them perhaps that they had slept the sleep of the just. At present, in the splendid autumn weather—the autumn as least was a pure boon in the terrible place—he loafed about his "work" undeterred, secretly agitated; not in the least "minding" that the whole proposition, as they said, was vulgar and sordid, and ready to climb ladders, to walk the plank, to handle materials and look wise about them, to ask questions, in fine, and challenge explanations and really "go into" figures.

It amused, it verily quite charmed him; and, by the same stroke, it amused, and even more, Alice Staverton, though perhaps charming her perceptibly less. She wasn't however going to be better off for it, as *he* was—and so astonishingly much: nothing was now likely, he knew, even to make her better off than she found herself, in the afternoon of life, as the delicately frugal possessor and tenant of the small house in Irving Place to which she had subtly managed to cling through her almost unbroken New York career. If he knew the way to it now better than to any other address among the dreadful multiplied numberings which seemed to him to reduce the whole place to some vast ledger page, overgrown, fantastic, of ruled and crisscrossed lines and figures—if he had formed, for his consolation, that habit, it was really not a little because of the charm of his having encountered and recognized, in the vast wilderness of the wholesale, breaking through the mere gross generalization of wealth and force and success, a small still scene where items and shades, all delicate things, kept the sharpness of the notes of a high voice perfectly trained, and where economy hung about like the scent of a garden. His old friend lived with one maid and herself dusted her relics and trimmed her lamps and polished her silver; she stood off, in the awful modern crush, when she could, but she sallied forth and did battle when the challenge was really to "spirit," the spirit she after all confessed to, proudly and a little shyly, as to that of the better time, that of *their* common, their quite far away and antediluvian social period and order. She made use of the street cars when need be, the terrible things that people scrambled for as the panic-stricken at sea scramble for the boats; she affronted, inscrutably, under stress, all the public concussions and ordeals; and yet, with that slim mystifying grace of her appearance, which defied you to say if she were a fair young woman who looked older through trouble, or fine smooth older one who looked young through successful indifference; with her precious reference, above all, to memories and histories into which he could enter, she was as exquisite for him as some pale pressed flower (a rarity to begin with), and, failing other sweetnesses, she was a sufficient reward of his effort. They had communities of knowledge, "their" knowledge (this discriminating possessive was always on her lips) of presences of the other age, presences all overlaid, in his case, by the experience of a man and the freedom of a wanderer, overlaid by pleasure, by infidelity, by passages of life that were strange and dim to her, just by "Europe" in short, but still unobscured, still exposed and cherished, under that pious visitation of the spirit from which she had never been diverted.

She had come with him one day to see how his "apartment house" was rising; he had helped her over gaps and explained to her plans, and while they were there had happened to have, before her, a brief but lively discussion with the man in charge, the representative of the building firm that had undertaken his work. He had found himself quite "standing-up" to this personage over a failure on the latter's part to observe some detail of one of their noted conditions, and had so lucidly argued his case that, besides ever so prettily flushing, at the time, for sympathy in his triumph, she had afterwards said to him (though to a slightly greater effect of irony) that he had clearly for too many years neglected a real gift. If he had but stayed at home he would have anticipated the inventor of the skyscraper. If he had but stayed at home he would have discovered his genius in time really to start some new variety of awful architectual hare and run it till it burrowed in the gold mine. He was to remember these words, while the weeks elapsed, for the small silver ring they had sounded over the queerest and deepest of his own lately most disguised and most muffled vibrations.

It had begun to be present to him after the first fortnight, it had broken out with the oddest abruptness, this particular wanton wonderment: it met him there—and this was the image under which he himself judged the matter, or at least, not a little, thrilled and flushed with it—very much as he might have been met by some strange figure, some unexpected occupant, at a turn of one of the dim passages of an empty house. The quaint analogy quite hauntingly remained with him, when he didn't indeed rather improve it by a still intenser form: that of his opening a door behind which he would have made sure of finding nothing, a door into a room shuttered and void, and yet so coming, with a great suppressed start, on some quite erect confronting presence, sometimes planted in the middle of the place and facing him through the dusk. After that visit to the house in construction he walked with his companion to see the other and always so much the better one, which in the eastward direction formed one of the corners, the "jolly" one precisely, of the street now so generally dishonored and disfigured in its westward reaches, and of the comparatively conservative avenue. The avenue still had pretensions, as Miss Staverton said, to decency; the old people had mostly gone, the old names were unknown, and here and there an old association seemed to stray, all vaguely, like some very aged person, out too late, whom you might meet and feel the impulse to watch or follow, in kindness, for safe restoration to shelter.

They went in together, our friends; he admitted himself with his key, as he kept no one there, he explained, preferring, for his reasons, to leave the place empty, under a simple arrangement with a good woman living in the neighborhood and who came for a daily hour to open windows and dust and sweep. Spencer Brydon had his reasons and was growingly aware of them; they seemed to him better each time he was there, though he didn't name them all to his companion, any more than he told her as yet how often, how quite absurdly often, he himself came. He only let her see for the present, while they walked through the great blank rooms, that absolute vacancy reigned and that, from top to bottom, there was nothing but Mrs. Muldoon's broom-stick, in the corner, to tempt the burglar. Mrs. Muldoon was then on the premises, and she loquaciously attended the visitors, preceding them from room to room and pushing back shutters and throwing up sashes—all to show them, as she remarked, how little there was to see. There was little indeed to see in the great gaunt shell where the main dispositions and the general apportionment of space, the style of an age of ampler allowances, had nevertheless for its master their honest pleading message, affecting him as some good old servant's, some lifelong retainer's appeal for a character, or even for a retiring pension; yet it was also a remark of Mrs. Muldoon's that, glad as she was to oblige him by her noonday round, there was a request she greatly hoped he would never make of her. If he should wish her for any reason to come in after dark she would just tell him, if he "plased," that he must ask it of somebody else.

The fact that there was nothing to see didn't militate for the worthy woman against what one *might* see, and she put it frankly to Miss Staverton that no lady could be expected to like, could she? "scraping up to thim top storys in the ayvil hours." The gas and electric light were off the house, and she fairly evoked a gruesome vision of her march through the great gray rooms—so many of them as there were too!—with her glimmering taper. Miss Staverton met her honest glare with a smile and the profession that she herself certainly would recoil from such an adventure. Spencer Brydon meanwhile held his peace—for the moment; the question of the "evil" hours in his old home had already become too grave for him. He had begun some time since to "crape," and he knew just why a packet of candles addressed to that pursuit had been stowed by his own hand, three weeks before, at the back of a drawer of the fine old sideboard that occupied, as a "fixture," the deep recess in the dining room. Just now he laughed at his companions—quickly however changing the subject; for the reason that, in the first place, his laugh struck him even at that moment as starting the odd echo, the conscious human resonance (he scarce knew how to qualify it) that sounds made while he was there alone sent back to his ear or his fancy; and that, in the second, he imagined Alice Staverton for the instant on the point of asking him, with a divination, if he ever so prowled. There were divinations he was unprepared for, and he had at all events averted inquiry by the time Mrs. Muldoon had left them, passing on to other parts.

There was happily enough to say, on so consecrated a spot, that could be said freely and fairly; so that a whole train of declarations was precipitated by his friend's having herself broken out, after a yearning look round: "But I hope you don't mean they want you to pull *this* to pieces!" His answer came, promptly, with his reawakened wrath: it was of course exactly what they wanted, and what they were "at" him for, daily, with the iteration of people who couldn't for their life understand a man's liability to decent feelings. He had found the place, just as it stood and beyond that he could express, an interest and a joy. There were values other than the beastly rent values, and in short, in short—! But it was thus Miss Staverton took him up. "In short you're to make so good a thing of your skyscraper that, living in luxury on *those* ill-gotten gains, you can afford for a while to be sentimental here!" Her smile had for him, with the words, the particular mild irony with which he found half her talk suffused; an irony without bitterness and that came, exactly, from her having so much imagination—not, like the cheap sarcasms with which one heard most people, about the world of "society," bid for the reputation of cleverness, from nobody's really having any. It was agreeable to him at this very moment to be sure that when he had answered, after a brief demur, "Well yes: so, precisely, you may put it!" her imagination would still do him justice. He explained that even if never a dollar were to come to him from the other house he would nevertheless cherish this one; and he dwelt, further, while they lingered and wandered, on the fact of the stupefaction he was already exciting, the positive mystification he felt himself create.

He spoke of the value of all he read into it, into the mere sight of the walls, mere shapes of the rooms, mere sound of the floors, mere feel, in his hand, of the old silverplated knobs of the several mahogany doors, which suggested the pressure of the palms of the dead; the seventy years of the past in fine that these things represented, the annals of nearly three generations, counting his grandfather's, the one that had ended there, and the impalpable ashes of his long-extinct youth, afloat in the very air like microscopic motes. She listened to everything; she was a woman who answered intimately but who utterly didn't chatter. She scattered abroad therefore no cloud of words; she could assent, she could agree, above all she could encourage, without doing that. Only at the last she went a little further than he had done himself. "And then how do you know? You may still, after all, want to live here." It rather indeed pulled him up, for it wasn't what he had been thinking, at least in her sense of the words. "You mean I may decide to stay on for the sake of it?"

"Well, *with* such a home—!" But, quite beautifully, she had too much tact to dot so monstrous an *i*, and it was precisely an illustration of the way she didn't rattle. How could any one—of any wit—insist on anyone else's "wanting" to live in New York?

"Oh," he said, "I *might* have lived here (since I had my opportunity early in life); I might have put in here all these years. Then everything would have been different enough—and, I dare say, 'funny' enough. But that's another matter. And then the beauty of it—I mean of my perversity, of my refusal to agree to a 'deal'—is just in the total absence of a reason. Don't you see that if I had a reason about the matter at all it would *have* to be the other way, and would then be inevitably a reason of dollars? There are no reasons here *but* of dollars. Let us therefore have none whatever—not the ghost of one."

They were back in the hall then for departure, but from where they stood the vista was large, through an open door, into the great square main saloon, with its almost antique felicity of brave spaces between windows. Her eyes came back from that reach and met his own a moment. "Are you very sure the 'ghost' of one doesn't, much rather, serve—?"

He had a positive sense of turning pale. But it was as near as they were then to come. For he made answer, he believed, between a glare and a grin: "Oh ghosts—of course the place must swarm with them! I should be ashamed of it if it didn't. Poor Mrs. Muldoon's right, and it's why I haven't asked her to do more than look in."

Miss Staverton's gaze again lost itself, and things she didn't utter, it was clear, came and went in her mind. She might even for the minute, off there in the fine room, have imagined some element dimly gathering. Simplified like the death mask of a handsome face, it perhaps produced for her just then an effect akin to the stir of an expression in the "set" commemorative plaster. Yet whatever her impression may have been she produced instead a vague platitude. "Well, if it were only furnished and lived in—!"

She appeared to imply that in case of its being still furnished he might have been a little less opposed to the idea of a return. But she passed straight into the vestibule, as if to leave her words behind her, and the next moment he had opened the house door and was standing with her on the steps. He closed the door and, while he re-pocketed his key, looking up and down, they took in the comparatively harsh actuality of the avenue, which reminded him of the assault of the outer light of the desert on the traveler emerging from an Egyptian tomb. But he risked before they stepped into the street his gathered answer to her speech. "For me it *is* lived in. For me it *is* furnished." At which it was easy for her to sigh "Ah yes—!" all vaguely and discreetly; since his parents and his favorite sister, to say nothing of other kin, in numbers, had run their course and met their end there. That represented, within the walls, ineffaceable life.

It was a few days after this that, during an hour passed with her again, he had expressed his impatience of the too flattering curiosity—among the people he met—about his appreciation of New York. He had arrived at none at all that was socially producible, and as for that matter of his "thinking" (thinking the better or the worse of anything there) he was wholly taken up with one subject of thought. It was mere vain egoism, and it was moreover, if she liked, a morbid obsession. He found all things come back to the question of what he personally might have been, how he might have led his life and "turned out," if he had not so, at the outset, given it up. And confessing for the first time to the intensity within him of this absurd speculation—which but proved also, no doubt, the habit of too selfishly thinking—he affirmed the impotence there of any other source of interest, any other native appeal. "What would it have made of me, what would it have made of me? I keep forever wondering, all idiotically; as if I could possibly know! I see what it has made of dozens of others, those I meet, and it positively aches within me, to the point of exasperation, that it would have made something of me as well. Only I can't make out *what*, and the worry of it, the small rage of curiosity never to be satisfied, brings back what I remember to have felt, once or twice, after judging best, for reasons, to burn some important letter unopened. I've been sorry, I've hated it—I've never known what was in the letter. You may of course say it's a trifle—!"

"I don't say it's a trifle," Miss Staverton gravely interrupted.

She was seated by her fire, and before her, on his feet and restless, he turned to and fro between this intensity of his idea and a fitful and unseeing inspection, through his single eyeglass, of the dear little old objects on her chimney-piece. Her interruption made him for an instant look at her harder. "I shouldn't care if you did!" he laughed, however; "and it's only a figure, at any rate, for the way I now feel. *Not* to have followed my perverse young course—and almost in the teeth of my father's curse, as I may say; not to have kept it up, so, 'over there,' from that day to this, without a doubt or a pang; not, above all, to have liked it, to have loved it, so much, loved it, no doubt, with such an abysmal conceit of my own preference: some variation from *that*, I say, must have produced some different effect for my life and for my 'form.' I should have stuck here—if it had been possible; and I was too young, at twenty-three, to judge, *pour deux sous*, whether it *were* possible. If I had waited I might have seen it was, and then I might have been, by staying here, something nearer to one of these types who have been hammered so hard and made so keen by their conditions. It isn't that I admire them so much—the question of any charm in them, or of any charm, beyond that of the rank money passion, exerted by their conditions *for* them, has nothing to do with the matter: it's only a question of what fantastic, yet perfectly possible, development of my own nature I mayn't have missed. It comes over me that I had then a strange *alter ego* deep down somewhere within me, as the full-blown flower is in the small tight bud, and that I just took the course, I just transferred him to the climate, that blighted him for once and forever."

"And you wonder about the flower," Miss Staverton said. "So do I, if you want to know; and so I've been wondering these several weeks. I believe in the flower," she continued, "I felt it would have been quite splendid, quite huge and monstrous."

"Monstrous above all!" her visitor echoed; "and I imagine, by the same stroke, quite hideous and offensive."

"You don't believe that," she returned; "if you did you wouldn't wonder. You'd know, and that would be enough for you. What you feel—and what I feel *for* you—is that you'd have had power."

"You'd have liked me that way?" he asked.

She barely hung fire. "How should I not have liked you?"

"I see. You'd have liked me, have preferred me, a billionaire!"

"How should I not have liked you?" she simply again asked.

He stood before her still—her question kept him motionless. He took it in, so much there was of it; and indeed his not otherwise meeting it testified to that. "I know at least what I am," he simply went on; "the other side of the medal's clear enough. I've not been edifying—I believe I'm thought in a hundred quarters to have been barely decent. I've followed strange paths and worshipped strange gods; it must have come to you again and again—in fact you've admitted to me as much—that I was leading, at any time these thirty years, a selfish frivolous scandalous life. And you see what it has made of me."

She just waited, smiling at him. "You see what it has made of *me*."

"Oh you're a person whom nothing can have altered. You were born to be what you are, anywhere, anyway: you've the perfection nothing else could have blighted. And don't you see how, without my exile, I shouldn't have been waiting till now—?" But he pulled up for the strange pang.

"The great thing to see," she presently said, "seems to me to be that it has spoiled nothing. It hasn't spoiled your being here at last. It hasn't spoiled this. It hasn't spoiled your speaking—" She also however faltered.

He wondered at everything her controlled emotion might mean. "Do you believe then—too dreadfully!—that I *am* as good as I might ever have been?"

"Oh no! Far from it!" With which she got up from her chair and was nearer to him. "But I don't care," she smiled.

"You mean I'm good enough?"

She considered a little. "Will you believe it if I say so? I mean will you let that settle your question for you?" And then as if making out in his face that he drew back from this, that he had some idea which, however absurd, he couldn't yet bargain away: "Oh you don't care either—but very differently: you don't care for anything but yourself."

Spencer Brydon recognized it—it was in fact what he had absolutely professed. Yet he importantly qualified. "*He* isn't myself. He's the just so totally other person. But I do want to see him," he added. "And I can. And I shall."

Their eyes met for a minute while he guessed from something in hers that she divined his strange sense. But neither of them otherwise expressed it, and her apparent understanding, with no protesting shock, no easy derision, touched him more deeply than anything yet, constituting for his stifled perversity, on the spot, an element that was like breathable air. What she said however was unexpected. "Well, *I*'ve seen him."

"You—?"

"I've see him in a dream."

"Oh a 'dream'—!" It let him down.

"But twice over," she continued. "I saw him as I see you now."

"You've dreamed the same dream—?"

"Twice over," she repeated. "The very same."

This did somehow a little speak to him, as it also gratified him. "You dream about me at that rate?"

"Ah about *him*!" she smiled.

His eyes again sounded her. "Then you know all about him."

And as she said nothing more: "What's the wretch like?"

She hesitated, and it was as if he were pressing her so hard that, resisting for reasons of her own, she had to turn away. "I'll tell you some other time!"

II

It was after this that there was most of a virtue for him, most of a cultivated charm, most of a preposterous secret thrill, in the particular form of surrender to his obsession and of address to what he more and more believed to be his privilege. It was what in these weeks he was living for—since he really felt life to begin but after Mrs. Muldoon had retired from the scene and, visiting the ample house from attic to cellar, making sure he was alone, he knew himself in safe possession and, as he tacitly expressed it, let himself go. He sometimes came twice in the twenty-four hours; the moments he liked best were those of gathering dusk, of the short autumn twilight; this was the time of which, again and again, he found himself hoping most. Then he could, as seemed to him, most intimately wander and wait, linger and listen, feel his fine attention, never in his life before so fine, on the pulse of the great vague place: he preferred the lampless hour and only wished he might have prolonged each day the deep crepuscular spell. Later—rarely much before midnight, but then for a considerable vigil—he watched with his glimmering light; moving slowly, holding it high, playing it far, rejoicing above all, as much as he might, in open vistas, reaches of communication between rooms and by passages; the long straight chance or show, as he would have called it, for the revelation he pretended to invite. It was a practice he found he could perfectly "work" without exciting remark; no one was in the least the wiser for it; even Alice Staverton, who was moreover a well of discretion, didn't quite fully imagine.

He let himself in and let himself out with the assurance of calm proprietorship; and accident so far favored him that, if a fat avenue "officer" had happened on occasion to see him entering at eleven-thirty, he had never yet, to the best of his belief, been noticed as emerging at two. He walked there on the crisp November nights, arrived regularly at the evening's end; it was as easy to do this after dining out as to take his way to a club or to his hotel. When he left his club, if he hadn't been dining out, it was ostensibly to go to his hotel; and when he left his hotel, if he had spent a part of the evening there, it was ostensibly to go to his club. Everything was easy in fine; everything conspired and promoted: there was truly even in the strain of his experience something that glossed over, something that salved and simplified, all the rest of consciousness. He circulated, talked, renewed, loosely and pleasantly, old relations—met indeed, so far as he could, new expectations and seemed to make out on the whole that in spite of the career, of such different contacts, which he had spoken of to Miss Staverton as ministering so little, for those who might have watched it, to edification, he was positively rather liked than not. He was a dim secondary social success—and all with people who had truly not an idea of him. It was all mere surface sound, this murmur of their welcome, this popping of their corks—just as his gestures of response were the extravagant shadows, emphatic in proportion as they meant little, of some game of *ombres chinoises*. He projected himself all day, in thought, straight over the bristling line of hard unconscious heads and into the other, the real, the waiting life; the life that, as soon as he had heard behind him the click of his great house door, began for him, on the jolly corner, as beguilingly as the slow opening bars of some rich music follows the tap of the conductor's wand.

He always caught the first effect of the steel point of his stick on the old marble of the hall pavement, large black-and-white squares that he remembered as the admiration of his childhood and that had then made in him, as he now saw, for the growth of an early conception of style. This effect was the dim reverberating tinkle as of some far-off bell hung who should say where?—in the depths of the house, of the past, of that mystical other world that might have flourished for him had he not, for weal or woe, abandoned it. On this impression he did ever the same thing; he put his stick noiselessly away in a corner—feeling the place once more in the likeness of some great glass bowl, all precious concave crystal, set delicately humming by the play of a moist finger round its edge. The concave crystal held, as it were, this mystical other world, and the indescribably fine murmur of its rim was the sigh there, the scarce audible pathetic wail to his strained ear, of all the old baffled forsworn possibilities. What he did therefore by this appeal of his hushed presence was to wake them into such measure of ghostly life as they might still enjoy. They were shy, all but unappeasably shy, but they weren't really sinister; at least they weren't as he had hitherto felt them—before they had taken the Form he so yearned to make them take, the Form he at moments saw himself in the light of fairly hunting on tiptoe, the points of his evening shoes, from room to room and from story to story.

That was the essence of his vision—which was all rank folly, if one would, while he was out of the house and otherwise occupied, but which took on the last verisimilitude as soon as he was placed and posted. He knew what he meant and what he wanted; it was as clear as the figure on a check presented in demand for cash. His *alter ego* "walked"—that was the note of his image of him, while his image of his motive for his own odd pastime was the desire to waylay him and meet him. He roamed, slowly, warily, but all restlessly, he himself did—Mrs. Muldoon had been right, absolutely, with her figure of their "craping;" and the presence he watched for would roam restlessly too. But it would be as cautious and as shifty; the conviction of its probable, in fact its already quite sensible, quite audible evasion of pursuit grew for him from night to night, laying on him finally a rigor to which nothing in his life had been comparable. It had been the theory of many superficially judging persons, he knew, that he was wasting that life in a surrender to sensations, but he had tasted of no pleasure so fine as his actual tension, had been introduced to no sport that demanded at once the patience and the nerve of this stalking of a creature more subtle, yet at bay perhaps more formidable, than any beast of the forest. The terms, the comparisons, the very practices of the chase positively came again into play; there were even moments when passages of his occasional experience as a sportsman, stirred memories, from his younger time, of moor and mountain and desert, revived for him—and to the increase of his keenness—by the tremendous force of analogy. He found himself at moments—once he had placed his single light on some mantel shelf or in some recess—stepping back into shelter or shade, effacing himself behind a door or in an embrasure, as he had sought of old the vantage of rock and tree; he found himself holding his breath and living in the joy of the instant, the supreme suspense created by big game alone.

He wasn't afraid (though putting himself the question as he believed gentlemen on

Bengal tiger shoots or in close quarters with the great bear of the Rockies had been known to confess to having put it); and this indeed—since here at least he might be frank!—because of the impression, so intimate and so strange, that he himself produced as yet a dread, produced certainly a strain, beyond the liveliest he was likely to feel. They fell for him into categories, they fairly became familiar, the signs, for his own perception, of the alarm his presence and his vigilance created; though leaving him always to remark, portentously, on his probably having formed a relation, his probably enjoying a consciousness, unique in the experience of man. People enough, first and last, had been in terror apparitions, but who had ever before so turned the tables and become himself, in the apparitional world, an incalculable terror? He might have found this sublime had he quite dared to think of it; but he didn't too much insist, truly, on that side of his privilege. With habit and repetition he gained to an extraordinary degree the power to penetrate the dusk of distances and the darkness of corners, to resolve back into their innocence the treacheries of uncertain light, the evil-looking forms taken in the gloom by mere shadows, by accidents of the air, by shifting effects of perspective; putting down his dim luminary he could still wander on without it, pass into other rooms and, only knowing it was there behind him in case of need, see his way about, visually project for his purpose a comparative clearness. It made him feel, this acquired faculty, like some monstrous stealthy cat; he wondered if he would have glared at these moments with large shining yellow eyes, and what it mightn't verily be, for the poor hard-pressed *alter ego*, to be confronted with such a type.

He liked however the open shutters; he opened everywhere those Mrs. Muldoon had closed, closing them as carefully afterwards, so that she shouldn't notice: he liked—oh this he did like, and above all in the upper rooms!—the sense of the hard silver of the autumn stars through the window panes, and scarcely less the flare of the street lamps below, the white electric luster which it would have taken curtains to keep out. This was human actual social; this was of the world he had lived in, and he was more at his ease certainly for the countenance, coldly general and impersonal, that all the while and in spite of his detachment it seemed to give him. He had support of course mostly in the rooms at the wide front and the prolonged side; it failed him considerably in the central shades and the parts at the back. But if he sometimes, on his rounds, was glad of his optical reach, so none the less often the rear of the house affected him as the very jungle of his prey. The place was there more subdivided; a large "extension" in particular, where small rooms for servants had been multiplied, abounded in nooks and corners, in closets and passages, in the ramifications especially of an ample back staircase over which he leaned, many a time, to look far down—not deterred from his gravity even while aware that he might, for a spectator, have figured some solemn simpleton playing at hide-and-seek. Outside in fact he might himself make that ironic *rapprochement*; but within the walls, and in spite of the clear windows, his consistency was proof against the cynical light of New York.

It had belonged to the idea of the exasperated consciousness of his victim to become a real test for him; since he had quite put it to himself from the first that, oh distinctly! he could "cultivate" his whole perception. He had felt it as above all open to cultivation—which indeed was but another name for his manner of spending his time. He was bringing it on, bringing it to perfection, by practice; in consequence of which it had grown so fine that he was now aware of impressions, attestations of his general postulate, that couldn't have broken upon him at once. This was the case more specifically with a phenomenon at last quite frequent for him in the upper rooms, the recognition—absolutely unmistakable, and by a turn dating from a particular hour, his resumption of his campaign after a diplomatic drop, a calculated absence of three nights—of his being definitely followed, tracked at a distance carefully taken and to the express end that he should the less confidently, less arrogantly, appear to himself merely to pursue. It worried, it finally quite broke him up, for it proved, of all the conceivable impressions, the one least suited to his book. He was kept in sight while remaining himself—as regards the essence of his position—sightless, and his only recourse then was in abrupt turns, rapid recoveries of ground. He wheeled about, retracing his steps, as if he might so catch in his face at least the stirred air of some other quick revolution. It was indeed true that his fully dislocalized thought of these maneuvers recalled to him Pantaloon, at the Christmas farce, buffeted and tricked from behind by ubiquitous Harlequin; but it left intact the influence of the conditions themselves each time he was reexposed to them, so that in fact this association, had he suffered it to become constant, would on a certain side have but ministered to his intenser gravity. He had made, as I have said, to create on the premises the baseless sense of a reprieve, his three absences; and the result of the third was to confirm the aftereffect of the second.

On his return, that night—the night succeeding his last intermission—he stood in the hall and looked up the staircase with a certainty more intimate than any he had yet known. "He's *there*, at the top, and waiting—not, as in general, falling back for disappearance. He's holding his ground, and it's the first time—which is a proof, isn't it? that something has happened for him." So Brydon argued with his hand on the banister and his foot on the lowest stair; in which position he felt as never before the air chilled by his logic. He himself turned cold in it, for he seemed of a sudden to know what now was involved. "Harder pressed?—yes, he takes it in, with its thus making clear to him that I've come, as they say, 'to stay.' He finally doesn't like and can't bear it, in the sense, I mean, that his wrath, his menaced interest, now balances with his dread. I've hunted him till he has 'turned': that, up there, is what has happened—he's the fanged or the antlered animal brought at last to bay." There came to him, as I say—but determined by an influence beyond my notation!—the acuteness of this certainty; under which however the next moment he had broken into a sweat that he would as little have consented to attribute to fear as he would have dared immediately to act upon it for enterprise. It marked nonetheless a prodigious thrill, a thrill that represented sudden dismay, no doubt, but also represented, and with the self-same throb, the strangest, the most joyous, possibly the next minute almost the proudest, duplication of consciousness.

"He has been dodging, retreating, hiding, but now, worked up to anger, he'll fight"—this intense impression made a single mouthful, as it were, of terror and applause. But what was wondrous was that the applause, for the felt fact, was so eager, since, if it was his other self he was running to earth, this ineffable identity was thus in the last resort not unworthy of him. It bristled there—somewhere near at hand, however unseen still—as the hunted thing, even as the trodden worm of the adage *must* at last bristle; and Brydon at this instant tasted probably of a sensation more complex than had ever before found itself consistent with sanity. It was as if it would have shamed him that a character so associated with his own should triumphantly succeed in just skulking, should to the end not risk the open, so that the drop of this danger was, on the spot, a great lift of the whole situation. Yet with another rare shift of the same subtlety he was already trying to measure by how much more he himself might now be in peril of fear; so rejoicing that he could, in another form, actively inspire that fear, and simultaneously quaking for the form in which he might passively know it.

The apprehension of knowing it must after a little have grown in him, and the strangest moment of his adventure perhaps, the most memorable or really most interesting, afterwards, of his crisis, was the lapse of certain instants of concentrated conscious *combat*, the sense of a need to hold on to something, even after the manner of a man slipping and slipping on some awful incline; the vivid impulse, above all, to move, to act, to charge, somehow and upon something—to show himself, in a word, that he wasn't afraid. The state of "holding on" was thus the state to which he was momentarily reduced; if there had been anything, in the great vacancy, to seize, he would presently have been aware of having clutched it as he might under a shock at home have clutched the nearest chair back. He had been surprised at any rate—of this he *was* aware—into something unprecedented since his original appropriation of the place; he had closed his eyes, held them tight, for a long minute, as with that instinct of dismay and that terror of vision. When he opened them the room, the other contiguous rooms, extraordinarily, seemed lighter—so light, almost, that at first he took the change for day. He stood firm, however that might be, just where he had paused; his resistance had helped him—it was as if there were something he had tided over. He knew after a little what this was—it had been in the imminent danger of flight. He had stiffened his will against going; without this he would have made for the stairs, and it seemed to him that, still with his eyes closed, he would have descended them, would have known how, straight and swiftly, to the bottom.

Well, as he had held out, here he was—still at the top, among the more intricate upper rooms and with the gauntlet of the others, of all the rest of the house, still to run when it should be his time to go. He would go at his time—only at his time: didn't he go every night very much at the same hour? He took out his watch—there was light for that: it was scarcely a quarter past one, and he had never withdrawn so soon. He reached his lodgings for the most part at two—with his walk of a quarter of an hour. He would wait for the last quarter—he wouldn't stir till then; and he kept his watch there with his eyes on it, reflecting while he held it that this deliberate wait, a wait with an effort, which he recognized, would serve perfectly for the attestation he desired to make. It would prove his courage—unless indeed the latter might most be proved by his budging at last from his place. What he mainly felt now was that, since he hadn't scuttled, he had his dignities—which had never in his life seemed so many—all to preserve and to carry aloft. This was before him in truth as a physical image, an image almost worthy of an age of greater romance. That remark indeed glimmered for him only to glow the next instant with a finer light; since what age of romance, after all, could have matched either the state of his mind or, "objectively," as they said, the wonder of his situation? The only difference would have been that, brandishing his dignities over his head as in a parchment scroll, he might then—that is in the heroic time—have proceeded downstairs with a drawn sword in his other grasp.

At present, really, the light he had set down on the mantel of the next room would have to figure his sword; which utensil, in the course of a minute, he had taken the requisite number of steps to possess himself of. The door between the rooms was open, and from the second another door opened to a third. These rooms, as he remembered, gave all three upon a common corridor as well, but there was a fourth, beyond them, without issue save through the preceding. To have moved, to have heard his step again, was appreciably a help; though even in recognizing this he lingered once more a little by the chimney-piece on which his light had rested. When he next moved, just hesitating where to turn, he found himself considering a circumstance that, after his first and comparatively vague apprehension of it, produced in him the start that often attends some pang of recollection, the violent shock of having ceased happily to forget. He had come into sight of the door in which the brief chain of communication ended and which he now surveyed from the nearer threshold, the one not directly facing it. Placed at some distance to the left of this point, it would have admitted him to the last room of the four, the room without other approach or egress, had it not, to his intimate conviction, been closed since his former visitation, the matter probably of a quarter of an hour before. He stared with all his eyes at the wonder of the fact, arrested again where he stood and again holding his breath while he sounded its sense. Surely it had been *subsequently* closed—that is it had been on his previous passage indubitably open!

He took it full in the face that something had happened between—that he couldn't not have noticed before (by which he meant on his original tour of all the rooms that evening) that such a barrier had exceptionally presented itself. He had indeed since that moment undergone an agitation so extraordinary that it might have muddled for him any earlier view; and he tried to convince himself that he might perhaps then have gone into the room and, inadvertently, automatically, on coming out, have drawn the door after him. The difficulty was that this exactly was what he never did; it was against his whole policy, as he might have said, the essence of which was to keep vistas clear. He had them from the first, as he was well aware, quite on the brain: the strange apparition, at the far end of one of them, of his baffled "prey" (which had become by so sharp an irony so little the term now to apply!) was the form of success his imagination had most cherished, projecting into it always a refinement of beauty. He had known fifty times the start of perception that had afterwards dropped; had fifty times gasped to himself "There!" under some fond brief hallucination. The house, as the case stood, admirably lent itself; he might wonder at the taste, the native architecture of the particular time, which could rejoice so in the multiplication of doors—the opposite extreme to the modern, the actual almost complete proscription of them; but it had fairly contributed to provoke this obsession of the presence encountered telescopically, as he might say, focused and studied in diminishing perspective and as by a rest for the elbow.

It was with these considerations that his present attention was charged—they perfectly availed to make what he saw portentous. He *couldn't,* by any lapse, have blocked that aperture; and if he hadn't, if it was unthinkable, why what else was clear but that there had been another agent? Another agent?—he had been catching, as he felt, a moment back, the very breath of him; but when had he been so close as in this simple, this logical, this completely personal act? It was so logical, that is, that one might have *taken* it for personal; yet for what did Brydon take it, he asked himself, while, softly panting, he felt his eyes almost leave their sockets. Ah this time at last they *were*, the two, the opposed projections of him, in presence; and this time, as much as one would, the question of danger loomed. With it rose, as not before, the question of courage—for what he knew the blank face of the door to say to him was "Show us how much you have!" It stared, it glared back at him with that challenge; it put to him the two alternatives: should he just push it open or not? Oh to have this consciousness was to *think*—and to think, Brydon knew, as he stood there, was, with the lapsing moments, not to have acted! Not to have acted—that was the misery and the pang—was even still not to act; was in fact *all* to feel the thing in another, in a new and terrible way. How long did he pause and how long did he debate? There was presently nothing to measure it; for his vibration had already changed—as just by the effect of its intensity. Shut up there, at bay, defiant, and with the prodigy of the thing palpably provably *done*, thus giving notice like some stark signboard—under that accession of accent the situation itself had turned; and Brydon at last remarkably made up his mind on what it had turned to.

It had turned altogether to a different admonition; to a supreme hint, for him, of the value of discretion! This slowly dawned, no doubt—for it could take its time; so perfectly, on his threshold, had he been stayed, so little as yet had he either advanced or retreated. It was the strangest of all things that now when, by his taking ten steps and applying his hand to the latch, or even his shoulder and his knee, if necessary, to a panel, all the hunger of his prime need might have been met, his high curiosity crowned, his unrest assuaged—it was amazing, but it was also exquisite and rare, that insistence should have, at a touch, quite dropped from him. Discretion—he jumped at that; and yet not, verily, at such a pitch, because it saved his nerves or his skin, but because, much more valuably, it saved the situation. When I say he "jumped" at it I feel the consonance of this term with the fact that—at the end indeed of I know not how long—he did move again, he crossed straight to the door. He wouldn't touch it—it seemed now that he might *if* he would: he would only just wait there a little, to show, to prove, that he wouldn't. He had thus another station, close to the thin partition by which revelation was denied him; but with his eyes bent and his hands held off in a mere intensity of stillness. He listened as if there had been something to hear, but this attitude, while it lasted, was his own communication. "If you won't then—good: I spare you and I give up. You affect me as by the appeal positively for pity: you convince me that for reasons rigid and sublime—what do I know?—we both of us should have suffered. I respect them then, and, though moved and privileged as, I believe, it has never been given to man, I retire, I renounce—never, on my honor, to try again. So rest forever—and let *me*!"

That, for Brydon was the deep sense of this last demonstration—solemn, measured, directed, as he felt it to be. He brought it to a close, he turned away; and now verily he knew how deeply he had been stirred. He retraced his steps, taking up his candle, burnt, he observed, well-nigh to the socket, and marking again, lighten it as he would, the distinctness of his footfall; after which, in a moment, he knew himself at the other side of the house. He did here what he had not yet done at these hours—he opened half a casement, one of those in the front, and let in the air of the night; a thing he would have taken at any time previous for a sharp rupture of his spell. His spell was broken now, and it didn't matter—broken by his concession and his surrender, which made it idle henceforth that he should ever come back. The empty street—its other life so marked even by the great lamplit vacancy—was within call, within touch; he stayed there as to be in it again, high above it though he was still perched; he watched as for some comforting common fact, some vulgar human note, the passage of a scavenger or a thief, some nightbird however base. He would have blessed that sign of life; he would have welcomed positively the slow approach of his friend the policeman, whom he had hitherto only sought to avoid, and was not sure that if the patrol had come into sight he mightn't have felt the impulse to get into relation with it, to hail it, on some pretext, from his fourth floor.

The pretext that wouldn't have been too silly or too compromising, the explanation that would have saved his dignity and kept his name, in such a case, out of the papers, was not definite to him: he was so occupied with the thought of recording his discretion—as an effect of the vow he had just uttered to his intimate adversary—that the importance of this loomed large and something had overtaken all ironically his sense of proportion. If there had been a ladder applied to the front of the house, even one of the vertiginous perpendiculars employed by painters and roofers and sometimes left standing overnight, he would have managed somehow, astride of the windowsill, to compass by outstretched leg and arm that mode of descent. If there had been some such uncanny thing as he had found in his room at hotels, a workable fire-escape in the form of notched cable or a canvas shoot, he would have availed himself of it as a proof—well, of his present delicacy. He nursed that sentiment, as the question stood, a little in vain, and even—at the end of he scarcely knew, once more, how long—found it, as by the action on his mind of the failure of response of the outer world, sinking back to vague anguish. It seemed to him he had waited an age for some stir of the great grim hush; the life of the town was itself under a spell—so unnaturally, up and down the whole prospect of known and rather ugly objects, the blankness and the silence lasted. Had they ever, he asked himself, the hard-faced houses, which had begun to look livid in the dim dawn, had they ever spoken so little to any need of his spirit? Great builded voids, great crowded stillnesses put on, often, in the heart of cities, for the small hours, a sort of sinister mask, and it was of this large collective negation that Brydon presently became conscious—all the more that the break of day was, almost incredibly, now at hand, proving to him what a night he had made of it.

He looked again at his watch, saw what had become of his time values (he had taken hours for minutes—not, as in other tense situations, minutes for hours) and the strange air of the streets was but the weak, the sullen flush of a dawn in which everything was still locked up. His choked appeal from his own open window had been the sole note of life, and he could but break off at last as for a worse despair. Yet while so deeply demoralized he was capable again of an impulse denoting—at least by his present measure—extraordinary resolution; of retracing his steps to the spot where he had turned cold with the extinction of his last pulse of doubt as to there being in the place another presence than his own. This required an effort strong enough to sicken him; but he had his reason, which overmastered for the moment everything else. There was the whole of the rest of the house to traverse, and how should he screw himself to that if the door he had seen closed were at present open? He could hold to the idea that the closing had practically been for him an act of mercy, a chance offered him to descend, depart, get off the ground and never again profane it. This conception held together, it worked; but what it meant for him depended now clearly on the amount of forbearance his recent action, or rather his recent inaction, had engendered. The image of the "presence," whatever it was, waiting there for him to go—this image had not yet been so concrete for his nerves as when he stopped short of the point at which certainty would have come to him. For, with all his resolution, or more exactly with all his dread, he did stop short—he hung back from really seeing. The risk was too great and his fear too definite: it took at this moment an awful specific form.

He knew—yes, as he had never known anything—that, *should* he see the door open, it would all too abjectly be the end of him. It would mean that the agent of his shame—for his shame was the deep abjection—was once more at large and in general possession; and what glared him thus in the face was the act that this would determine for him. It would send him straight about to the window he had left open, and by that window, be long ladder and dangling rope as absent as they would, he saw himself uncontrollably insanely fatally take his way to the street. The hideous chance of this he at least could avert; but he could only avert it by recoiling in time from assurance. He had the whole house to deal with, this fact was still there; only he now knew that uncertainty alone could start him. He stole back from where he had checked himself— merely to do so was suddenly like safety—and, making blindly for the greater stair-case, left gaping rooms and sounding passages behind. Here was the top of the stairs, with a fine large dim descent and three spacious landings to mark off. His instinct was all for mildness, but his feet were harsh on the floors, and strangely, when he had in a couple of minutes become aware of this, it counted somehow for help. He couldn't have spoken, the tone of his voice would have scared him, and the common conceit or resource of "whistling in the dark" (whether literally or figuratively) have appeared basely vulgar; yet he liked nonetheless to hear himself go, and when he had reached his first landing—taking it all with no rush, but quite steadily—that stage of success drew from him a gasp of relief.

The house, withal, seemed immense, the scale of space again inordinate; the open rooms, to no one of which his eyes deflected, gloomed in their shuttered state like mouths of caverns; only the high skylight that formed the crown in the deep well created for him a medium in which he could advance, but which might have been, for queerness of color, some watery underworld. He tried to think of something noble, as that his property was really grand, a splendid possession; but this nobleness took the form too of the clear delight with which he was finally to sacrifice it. They might come in now, the builders, the destroyers—they might come as soon as they would. At the end of two flights he had dropped to another zone, and from the middle of the third, with only one more left, he recognized the influence of the lower windows, of half-drawn blinds, of the occasional gleam of street lamps, of the glazed spaces of the vestibule. This was the bottom of the sea, which showed an illumination of its own and which he even saw paved—when at a given moment he drew up to sink a long look over the banisters—with the marble squares of his childhood. By that time in-dubitably he felt, as he might have said in a commoner cause, better; it had allowed him to stop and draw breath, and the ease increased with the sight of the old black-and-white slabs. But what he most felt was that now surely, with the element of impunity pulling him as by hard firm hands, the case was settled for what he might have seen above had he dared that last look. The closed door, blessedly remote now, was still closed—and he had only in short to reach that of the house.

He came down further, he crossed the passage forming the access to the last flight; and if here again he stopped an instant it was almost for the sharpness of the thrill of assured escape. It made him shut his eyes—which opened again to the straight slope of the remainder of the stairs. Here was impunity still, but impunity almost excessive; inasmuch as the side lights and the high fan tracery of the entrance were glimmering straight into the hall; an appearance produced, he the next instant saw, by the fact that the vestibule gaped wide, that the hinged halves of the inner door had been thrown far back. Out of that again the *question* sprang at him, making his eyes, as he felt, half-start from his head, as they had done, at the top of the house, before the sign of the other door. If he had left that one open, hadn't he left this one closed, and wasn't he now in *most* immediate presence of some inconceivable occult activity? It was as sharp, the question, as a knife in his side, but the answer hung fire still and seemed to lose itself in the vague darkness to which the thin admitted dawn, glimmering archwise over the whole outer door, made a semicircular margin, a cold silvery nimbus that seemed to play a little as he looked—to shift and expand and contract.

It was as if there had been something within it, protected by indistinctness and corresponding in extent with the opaque surface behind, the painted panels of the last barrier to his escape, of which the key was in his pocket. The indistinctness mocked him even while he stared, affected him as somehow shrouding or challenging certitude, so that after faltering an instant on his step he let himself go with the sense that here *was* at last something to meet, to touch, to take, to know—something all unnatural and dreadful, but to advance upon which was the condition for him either of liberation or of supreme defeat. The penumbra, dense and dark, was the virtual screen of a figure which stood in it as still as some image erect in a niche or as some black-vizored sentinel guarding a treasure. Brydon was to know afterwards, was to recall and make out, the particular thing he had believed during the rest of his descent. He saw, in its great gray glimmering margin, the central vagueness diminish, and he felt it to be taking the very form toward which, for so many days, the passion of his curiosity had yearned. It gloomed, it loomed, it was something, it was somebody, the prodigy of a personal presence.

Rigid and conscious, spectral yet human, a man of his own substance and stature waited there to measure himself with his power to dismay. This only could it be—this only till he recognized, with his advance, that what made the face dim was the pair of raised hands that covered it and in which, so far from being offered in defiance, it was buried as for dark deprecation. So Brydon, before him, took him in; with every fact of him now, in the higher light, hard and acute—his planted stillness, his vivid truth, his grizzled bent head and white masking hands, his queer actuality of evening dress, of dangling double eyeglass, of gleaming silk lappet and white linen, of pearl button and gold watch guard and polished shoe. No portrait by a great modern master could have presented him with more intensity, thrust him out of his frame with more art, as if there had been "treatment," of the consummate sort, in his every shade and salience. The revulsion, for our friend, had become, before he knew it, immense—this drop, in the act of apprehension, to the sense of his adversary's inscrutable maneuver. That meaning at least, while he gaped, it offered him; for he could but gape at his other self in this other anguish, gape as a proof that *he*, standing there for the achieved, the enjoyed, the triumphant life, couldn't be faced in his triumph. Wasn't the proof in the splendid covering hands, strong and completely spread?—so spread and so intentional that, in spite of a special verity that surpassed every other, the fact that one of these hands had lost two fingers, which were reduced to stumps, as if accidentally shot away, the face was effectually guarded and saved.

"Saved," though, *would* it be?—Brydon breathed his wonder till the very impunity of his attitude and the very insistence of his eyes produced, as he felt, a sudden stir which showed the next instant as a deeper portent, which the head raised itself, the betrayal of a braver purpose. The hands, as he looked, began to move, to open; then, as if deciding in a flash, dropped from the face and left it uncovered and presented. Horror, with the sight, had leaped into Brydon's throat, gasping there in a sound he couldn't utter; for the bared identity was too hideous as *his*, and his glare was the passion of his protest. The face, *that* face, Spencer Brydon's?—he searched it still, but looking away from it in dismay and denial, falling straight from his height of sublimity. It was unknown, inconceivable, awful, disconnected from any possibility—! He had been "sold," he inwardly moaned, stalking such game as this: the presence before him was a presence, the horror within him a horror, but the waste of his nights had been only grotesque and the success of his adventure an irony. Such an identity fitted his at *no* point, made its alternative monstrous. A thousand times yes, as it came upon him nearer now—the face was the face of a stranger. It came upon him nearer now, quite as one of those expanding fantastic images projected by the magic lantern of childhood; for the stranger, whoever he might be, evil, odious, blatant, vulgar, had advanced as for aggression, and he knew himself give ground. Then harder pressed still, sick with the force of his shock, and falling back as under the hot breath and the roused passion of a life larger than his own, a rage of personality before which his own collapsed, he felt the whole vision turn to darkness and his very feet give way. His head went round; he was going; he had gone.

III

What had next brought him back, clearly—though after how long?—was Mrs. Muldoon's voice, coming to him from quite near, from so near that he seemed presently to see her as kneeling on the ground before him while he lay looking up at her; himself not wholly on the ground, but half-raised and upheld—conscious, yes, of tenderness of support and, more particularly, of a head pillowed in extraordinary softness and faintly refreshing fragrance. He considered, he wondered, his wit but half at his service; then another face intervened, bending more directly over him, and he finally knew that Alice Staverton had made her lap an ample and perfect cushion to him, and that she had to this end seated herself on the lowest degree of the staircase, the rest of his long person remaining stretched on his old black-and-white slabs. They were cold, these marble squares of his youth; but *he* somehow was not, in this rich return of consciousness—the most wonderful hour, little by little, that he had ever known, leaving him, as it did, so gratefully, so abysmally passive, and yet as with a treasure of intelligence waiting all round him for quiet appropriation; dissolved, he might call it, in the air of the place and producing the golden glow of a late autumn afternoon. He had come back, yes—come back from further away than any man but himself had ever traveled; but it was strange how with this sense what he had come back to seemed really the great thing, and as if his prodigious journey had been all for the sake of it. Slowly but surely his consciousness grew, his vision of his state thus completing itself: he had been miraculously *carried* back—lifted and carefully borne as from where he had been picked up, the uttermost end of an interminable gray passage. Even with this he was suffered to rest, and what had now brought him to knowledge was the break in the long mild motion.

It had brought him to knowledge, to knowledge—yes, this was the beauty of his state; which came to resemble more and more that of a man who has gone to sleep on some news of a great inheritance, and then, after dreaming it away, after profaning it with matters strange to it, has waked up again to serenity of certitude and has only to lie and watch it grow. This was the drift of his patience—that he had only to let it shine on him. He must moreover, with intermissions, still have been lifted and borne; since why and how else should he have known himself, later on, with the afternoon glow intenser, no longer at the foot of his stairs—situated as these now seemed at that dark other end of his tunnel—but on a deep windowbench of his high saloon, over which had been spread, couch fashion, a mantle of soft stuff lined with gray fur that was familiar to his eyes and that one of his hands kept fondly feeling as for its pledge of truth. Mrs. Muldoon's face had gone, but the other, the second he had recognized, hung over him in a way that showed how he was still propped and pillowed. He took it all in, and the more he took it the more it seemed to suffice: he was as much at peace as if he had had food and drink. It was the two women who had found him, on Mrs. Muldoon's having plied, at her usual hour, her latchkey—and on her having above all arrived while Miss Staverton still lingered near the house. She had been turning away, all anxiety, from worrying the vain bell-handle—her calculation having been of the hour of the good woman's visit; but the latter, blessedly, had come up while she was still there, and they had entered together. He had then lain, beyond the vestibule, very much as he was lying now—quite, that is, as he appeared to have fallen, but all so wondrously without bruise or gash; only in a depth of stupor. What he most took in, however, at present, with the steadier clearance, was that Alice Staverton had for a long unspeakable moment not doubted he was dead.

"It must have been that I *was*." He made it out as she held him. "Yes—I can only have died. You brought me literally to life. Only," he wondered, his eyes rising to her, "only, in the name of all the benedictions, how?"

It took her but an instant to bend her face and kiss him, and something in the manner of it, and in the way her hands clasped and locked his head while he felt the cool charity and virtue of her lips, something in all this beatitude somehow answered everything. "And now I keep you," she said.

"Oh keep me, keep me!" he pleaded while her face still hung over him: in response to which it dropped again and stayed close, clingingly close. It was the seal of their situation—of which he tasted the impress for a long blissful moment in silence. But he came back. "Yet how did you know—?"

"I was uneasy. You were to have come, you remember—and you had sent no word."

"Yes, I remember—I was to have gone to you at one today." It caught on to their "old" life and relation—which were so near and so far. "I was still out there in my strange darkness—where was it, what was it? I must have stayed there so long." He could but wonder at the depth and the duration of his swoon.

"Since last night?" she asked with a shade of fear for her possible indiscretion.

"Since this morning—it must have been; the cold dim dawn of today. Where have I been," he vaguley wailed, "where have I been?" He felt her hold him close, and it was if this helped him now to make in all security his mild moan. "What a long dark day!"

All in her tenderness she had waited a moment. "In the cold dim dawn?" she quavered.

But he had already gone on piecing together the parts of the whole prodigy. "As I didn't turn up you came straight—?"

She barely cast about. "I went first to your hotel—where they told me of your absence. You had dined out last evening and hadn't been back since. But they appeared to know you had been at your club."

"So you had the idea of *this*—?"

"Of what?" she asked in a moment.

"Well—of what has happened."

"I believed at least you'd have been here. I've known, all along," she said, "that you've been coming."

" 'Known' it—?"

"Well, I've believed it. I said nothing to you after that talk we had a month ago— but I felt sure. I knew you *would*," she declared.

"That I'd persist, you mean?"

"That you'd see him."

"Ah but I didn't!" cried Brydon with his long wail. "There's somebody—an awful beast; whom I brought, too horribly, to bay. But it's not me."

At this she bent over him again, and her eyes were in his eyes. "No—it's not you." And it was as if, while her face hovered, he might have made out in it, hadn't it been so near, some particular meaning blurred by a smile. "No, thank heaven," she re- peated—"it's not you! Of course it wasn't to have been."

"Ah but it *was*," he gently insisted. And he stared before him now as he had been staring for so many weeks. "I was to have known myself."

"You couldn't!" she returned consolingly. And then reverting, and as if to account further for what she had herself done, "But it wasn't only *that*, that you hadn't been at home," she went on. "I waited till the hour at which we had found Mrs. Muldoon that day of my going with you; and she arrived, as I've told you, while, failing to bring anyone to the door, I lingered in my despair on the steps. After a little, if she hadn't come, by such a mercy, I should have found means to hunt her up. But it wasn't," said Alice Staverton, as if once more with her fine intention—"it wasn't only that."

His eyes, as he lay, turned back to her. "What more then?"

She met it, the wonder she had stirred. "In the cold dim dawn, you say? Well, in the cold dim dawn of this morning I too saw you."

"Saw *me*—?"

"Saw *him*," said Alice Staverton. "It must have been at the same moment."

He lay an instant taking it in—as if he wished to be quite reasonable. "At the same moment?"

"Yes—in my dream again, the same one I've named to you. He came back to me. Then I knew it for a sign. He had come to you."

At this Brydon raised himself; he had to see her better. She helped him when she understood his movement, and he sat up, steadying himself beside her there on the windowbench and with his right hand grasping her left. "*He* didn't come to me."

"You came to yourself," she beautifully smiled.

"Ah I've come to myself now—thanks to you, dearest. But this brute, with his awful face—this brute's a black stranger. He's none of *me*, even as I *might* have been," Brydon sturdily declared.

But she kept the clearness that was like the breath of infallibility. "Isn't the whole point that you'd have been different?"

He almost scowled for it. "As different as *that*—?"

Her look again was more beautiful to him than the things of this world. "Haven't you exactly wanted to know *how* different? So this morning," she said, "you appeared to me."

"Like *him*?"

"A black stranger!"

"Then how did you know it was I?"

"Because, as I told you weeks ago, my mind, my imagination, had worked so over what you might, what you mightn't have been—to show you, you see, how I've thought of you. In the midst of that you came to me—that my wonder might be answered. So I knew," she went on; "and believed that, since the question held you too so fast, as you told me that day, you too would see for yourself. And when this morning I again saw I knew it would be because you had—and also then, from the first moment, because you somehow wanted me. *He* seemed to tell me of that. So why," she strangely smiled, "shouldn't I like him?"

It brought Spencer Brydon to his feet. "You 'like' that horror—?"

"I *could* have liked him. And to me," she said, "he was no horror. I had accepted him."

" 'Accepted'—?" Brydon oddly sounded.

"Before, for the interest of his difference—yes. And as *I* didn't disown him, as *I* knew him—which you at last, confronted with him in his difference, so cruelly didn't, my dear—well, he must have been, you see, less dreadful to me. And it may have pleased him that I pitied him."

She was beside him on her feet, but still holding his hand—still with her arm supporting him. But though it all brought for him thus a dim light, "You 'pitied' him?" he grudgingly, resentfully asked.

"He has been unhappy; he has been ravaged," she said.

"And haven't I been unhappy? Am not I—you've only to look at me!—ravaged?"

"Ah I don't say I like him *better*," she granted after a thought. "But he's grim, he's worn—and things have happened to him. He doesn't make shift, for sight, with your charming monocle."

"No"—it struck Brydon: "I couldn't have sported mine 'downtown.' They'd have guyed me there."

"His great convex pince-nez—I saw it, I recognized the kind—is for his poor ruined sight. And his poor right hand—!"

"Ah!" Brydon winced—whether for his proved identity or for his lost fingers. Then, "He has a million a year," he lucidly added. "But he hasn't you."

"And he isn't—no, he isn't—*you*!" she murmured as he drew her to his breast.

A GHOST STORY

BY MARK TWAIN

THERE IS PROBABLY NO MORE RECOGNIZABLE AMERICAN WRITER THAN SAMUEL CLEMENS, OR AS HE IS UNDOUBTEDLY BETTER KNOWN, "MARK TWAIN." TWAIN WAS A TALE-SPINNER OF THE HIGHEST REPUTE, UNAFRAID OF "DETRACTORS, DISBELIEVERS, AND OTHER IGNORANT FOLK." IN "A GHOST STORY" HE HAS A LITTLE FUN WITH THE CONVENTIONAL GHOST STORY GENRE WITH ITS INHERENT "BELIEVE IT OR NOT" CHALLENGE. THE SUBJECT OF ITS HAUNTING IS THE LEGENDARY CARDIFF GIANT, WHICH HAD ALREADY BEEN REVEALED AS A HOAX AT THE TIME OF THE STORY'S PUBLICATION.

I took a large room, far up Broadway, in a huge old building whose upper stories had been wholly unoccupied for years until I came. The place had long been given up to dust and cobwebs, to solitude and silence. I seemed groping among the tombs and invading the privacy of the dead, that first night I climbed up to my quarters. For the first time in my life a superstitious dread came over me; and as I turned a dark angle of the stairway and an invisible cobweb swung its slazy woof in my face and clung there, I shuddered as one who had encountered a phantom.

I was glad enough when I reached my room and locked out the mold and the darkness. A cheery fire was burning in the grate, and I sat down before it with a comforting sense of relief. For two hours I sat there, thinking of bygone times; recalling old scenes, and summoning half-forgotten faces out of the mists of the past; listening, in fancy, to voices that long ago grew silent for all time, and to once familiar songs that nobody sings now. And as my reverie softened down to a sadder and sadder pathos, the shrieking of the winds outside softened to a wail, the angry beating of the rain against the panes diminished to a tranquil patter, and one by one the noises in the street subsided, until the hurrying footsteps of the last belated straggler died away in the distance and left no sound behind.

The fire had burned low. A sense of loneliness crept over me. I arose and undressed, moving on tiptoe about the room, doing stealthily what I had to do, as if I were environed by sleeping enemies whose slumbers it would be fatal to break. I covered up in bed, and lay listening to the rain and wind and the faint creaking of distant shutters, till they lulled me to sleep.

I slept profoundly, but how long I do not know. All at once I found myself awake, and filled with a shuddering expectancy. All was still. All but my own heart—I could hear it beat. Presently the bedclothes began to slip away slowly toward the foot of the bed, as if some one were pulling them! I could not stir; I could not speak. Still the blankets slipped deliberately away, till my breast was uncovered. Then with a great effort I seized them and drew them over my head. I waited, listened, waited. Once more that steady pull began, and once more I lay torpid a century of dragging seconds till my breast was naked again. At last I roused my energies and snatched the covers back to their place and held them with a strong grip. I waited. By and by I felt a faint tug, and took a fresh grip. The tug strengthened to a steady strain—it grew stronger and stronger. My hold parted, and for the third time the blankets slid away. I groaned. An answering groan came from the foot of the bed! Beaded drops of sweat stood upon my forehead. I was more dead than alive. Presently I heard a heavy footstep in my room—the step of an elephant, it seemed to me—it was not like anything human. But it was moving *from* me—there was relief in that. I heard it approach the door—pass out without moving bolt or lock—and wander away among the dismal corridors, straining the floors and joists till they creaked again as it passed—and then silence reigned once more.

When my excitement had calmed, I said to myself, "This is a dream—simply a hideous dream." And so I lay thinking it over until I convinced myself that it *was* a dream, and then a comforting laugh relaxed my lips and I was happy again. I got up and struck a light; and when I found that the locks and bolts were just as I had left them, another soothing laugh welled in my heart and rippled from my lips. I took my pipe and lit it, and was just sitting down before the fire, when—down went the pipe out of my nerveless fingers, the blood forsook my cheeks, and my placid breathing was cut short with a gasp! In the ashes on the hearth, side by side with my own bare footprint, was another, so vast that in comparison mine was but an infant's! Then I had *had* a visitor, and the elephant tread was explained.

I put out the light and returned to bed, palsied with fear. I lay a long time, peering into the darkness, and listening. Then I heard a grating noise overhead, like the dragging of a heavy body across the floor; then the throwing down of the body, and the shaking of my windows in response to the concussion. In distant parts of the building I heard the muffled slamming of doors. I heard, at intervals, stealthy footsteps creeping in and out among the corridors, and up and down the stairs. Sometimes these noises approached my door, hesitated, and went away again. I heard the clanking of chains faintly, in remote passages, and listened while the clanking grew nearer—while it wearily climbed the stairways, marking each move by the loose surplus of chain that fell with an accented rattle upon each succeeding step as the goblin that bore it advanced. I heard muttered sentences; half-uttered screams that seemed smothered violently; and the swish of invisible garments, the rush of invisible wings. Then I became conscious that my chamber was invaded—that I was not alone. I heard sighs and breathings about my bed, and mysterious whisperings. Three little spheres of soft phosphorescent light appeared on the ceiling directly over my head, clung and glowed there a moment, and then dropped—two of them upon my face and one upon the pillow. They spattered, liquidly, and felt warm. Intuition told me they had turned to gouts of blood as they fell—I needed no light to satisfy myself of that. Then I saw pallid faces, dimly luminous, and white uplifted hands, floating bodiless in the air—floating a moment and then disappearing. The whispering ceased, and the voices and the sounds, and a solemn stillness followed. I waited and listened. I felt that I must have light or die. I was weak with fear. I slowly raised myself toward a sitting posture, and my face came in contact with a clammy hand! All strength went from me apparently, and I fell back like a stricken invalid. Then I heard the rustle of a garment—it seemed to pass to the door and go out.

When everything was still once more, I crept out of bed, sick and feeble, and lit the gas with a hand that trembled as if it were aged with a hundred years. The light brought some little cheer to my spirits. I sat down and fell into a dreamy contemplation of that great footprint in the ashes. By and by its outlines began to waver and grow dim. I glanced up and the broad gas-flame was slowly wilting away. In the same moment I heard that elephantine tread again. I noted its approach, nearer and nearer, along the musty halls, and dimmer and dimmer the light waned. The tread reached my very door and paused—the light had dwindled to a sickly blue, and all things about me lay in a spectral twilight. The door did not open, and yet I felt a faint gust of air fan my cheek, and presently was conscious of a huge, cloudy presence before me. I watched it with fascinated eyes. A pale glow stole over the Thing; gradually its cloudy folds took shape—an arm appeared, then legs, then a body, and last a great sad face looked out of the vapor. Stripped of its filmy housings, naked, muscular and comely, the majestic Cardiff Giant loomed above me!

All my misery vanished—for a child might know that no harm could come with that benignant countenance. My cheerful spirits returned at once, and in sympathy with them the gas flamed up brightly again. Never a lonely outcast was so glad to welcome company as I was to greet the friendly giant. I said:

"Why, is it nobody but you? Do you know, I have been scared to death for the last two or three hours? I am most honestly glad to see you. I wish I had a chair— Here, here, don't try to sit down in that thing!"

But it was too late. He was in it before I could stop him, and down he went—I never saw a chair shivered so in my life.

"Stop, stop, you'll ruin ev—"

Too late again. There was another crash, and another chair was resolved into its original elements.

"Confound it, haven't you got any judgment at all? Do you want to ruin all the furniture on the place? Here, here, you petrified fool—"

But it was no use. Before I could arrest him he had sat down on the bed, and it was a melancholy ruin.

"Now what sort of a way is that to do? First you come lumbering about the place bringing a legion of vagabond goblins along with you to worry me to death, and then when I overlook an indelicacy of costume which would not be tolerated anywhere by cultivated people except in a respectable theater, and not even there if the nudity were of *your* sex, you repay me by wrecking all the furniture you can find to sit down on. And why will you? You damage yourself as much as you do me. You have broken off the end of your spinal column, and littered up the floor with chips of your hams till the place looks like a marble yard. You ought to be ashamed of yourself—you are big enough to know better."

"Well, I will not break any more furniture. But what am I to do? I have not had a chance to sit down for a century." And the tears came into his eyes.

"Poor devil," I said, "I should not have been so harsh with you. And you are an orphan, too, no doubt. But sit down on the floor here—nothing else can stand your weight—and besides, we cannot be sociable with you away up there above me; I want you down where I can perch on this high counting-house stool and gossip with you face to face."

So he sat down on the floor, and lit a pipe which I gave him, threw one of my red blankets over his shoulders, inverted my sitzbath on his head, helmet fashion, and made himself picturesque and comfortable. Then he crossed his ankles, while I renewed the fire, and exposed the flat, honeycombed bottoms of his prodigious feet to the grateful warmth.

"What is the matter with the bottom of your feet and the back of your legs, that they are gouged up so?"

"Infernal chilblains—I caught them clear up to the back of my head, roosting out there under Newell's farm. But I love the place; I love it as one loves his old home. There is no peace for me like the peace I feel when I am there."

We talked along for half an hour, and then I noticed that he looked tired, and spoke of it.

"Tired?" he said. "Well, I should think so. And now I will tell you all about it, since you have treated me so well. I am the spirit of the petrified Man that lies across the street there in the museum. I am the ghost of the Cardiff Giant. I can have no rest, no peace, till they have given that poor body burial again. Now what was the most natural thing for me to do, to make men satisfy this wish? Terrify them into it!—haunt the place where the body lay! So I haunted the museum night after night. I even got other spirits to help me. But it did no good, for nobody ever came to the museum at midnight. Then it occurred to me to come over the way and haunt this place a little. I felt that if I ever got a hearing I must succeed, for I had the most efficient company that perdition could furnish. Night after night we have shivered around through these mildewed halls, dragging chains, groaning, whispering, tramping up and down stairs, till, to tell you the truth, I am almost worn out. But when I saw a light in your room to-night I roused my energies again and went at it with a deal of the old freshness. But I am tired out—entirely fagged out. Give me, I beseech you, give me some hope!"

I lit off my perch in a burst of excitement, and exclaimed:

"This transcends everything! everything that ever did occur! Why you poor blundering old fossil, you have had all your trouble for nothing—you have been haunting a *plaster cast* of yourself—the real Cardiff Giant is in Albany![1] Confound it, don't you know your own remains?"

I never saw such an eloquent look of shame, of pitiable humiliation, overspread a countenance before.

The Petrified Man rose slowly to his feet, and said:

"Honestly, is that true?"

"As true as I am sitting here."

He took the pipe from his mouth and laid it on the mantel, then stood irresolute a moment (unconsciously, from old habit, thrusting his hands where his pantaloons pockets should have been, and meditatively dropping his chin on his breast), and finally said:

[1]A fact. The original fraud was ingeniously and fraudfully duplicated, and exhibited in New York as the "only genuine" Cardiff Giant (to the unspeakable disgust of the owners of the real colossus) at the very same time that the latter was drawing crowds at a museum in Albany.

"Well—I *never* felt so absurd before. The Petrified Man has sold everybody else, and now the mean fraud has ended by selling its own ghost! My son, if there is any charity left in your heart for a poor friendless phantom like me, don't let this get out. Think how *you* would feel if you had made such an ass of yourself."

I heard his stately tramp die away, step by step down the stairs and out into the deserted street, and felt sorry that he was gone, poor fellow—and sorrier still that he had carried off my red blanket and my bathtub.

THE OTHER LODGERS

BY AMBROSE BIERCE

AMBROSE BIERCE WAS THE ONLY MAJOR AMERICAN WRITER TO ACTUALLY SERVE IN COMBAT FOR THE DURATION OF THE CIVIL WAR. AS A RESULT HIS TALES OF THE BATTLEFIELD SUCH AS "CHICKAMAUGA" AND "A HORSEMAN IN THE SKY" ARE FILLED WITH THE GRIM REALITY OF MEN FIGHTING A WAR THAT IN MANY CASES PITTED BROTHERS AGAINST BROTHERS. THOUGH "AN OCCURRENCE AT OWL CREEK BRIDGE" IS PROBABLY HIS BETTER-KNOWN TALE OF THE CIVIL WAR FANTASTIC, THE SHORT SHORT ENTITLED "THE OTHER LODGERS" IS A MUCH MORE TRADITIONAL TALE OF A HAUNTING AND THE HORRORS OF WAR.

"In order to take that train," said Colonel Levering, sitting in the Waldorf-Astoria hotel, "you will have to remain nearly all night in Atlanta. That is a fine city, but I advise you not to put up at the Breathitt House, one of the principal hotels. It is an old wooden building in urgent need of repairs. There are breaches in the walls that you could throw a cat through. The bedrooms have no locks on the doors, no furniture but a single chair in each, and a bedstead without bedding—just a mattress. Even these meager accommodations you cannot be sure that you will have in monopoly; you must take your chance of being stowed in with a lot of others. Sir, it is a most abominable hotel.

"The night that I passed in it was an uncomfortable night. I got in late and was shown to my room on the ground floor by an apologetic night-clerk with a tallow candle, which he considerately left with me. I was worn out by two days and a night of hard railway travel and had not entirely recovered from a gunshot wound in the head, received in an altercation. Rather than look for better quarters I lay down on the mattress without removing my clothing and fell asleep.

"Along toward morning I awoke. The moon had risen and was shining in at the uncurtained window, illuminating the room with a soft, bluish light which seemed, somehow, a bit spooky, though I dare say it had no uncommon quality; all moonlight is that way if you will observe it. Imagine my surprise and indignation when I saw the floor occupied by at least a dozen other lodgers! I sat up, earnestly damning the management of that unthinkable hotel, and was about to spring from the bed to go and make trouble for the night-clerk—him of the apologetic manner and the tallow candle—when something in the situation affected me with a strange indisposition to move. I suppose I was what a story-writer might call 'frozen with terror.' For those men were obviously all dead!

"They lay on their backs, disposed orderly along three sides of the room, their feet to the walls—against the other wall, farthest from the door, stood my bed and the chair. All the faces were covered, but under their white cloths the features of the two bodies that lay in the square patch of moonlight near the window showed in sharp profile as to nose and chin.

"I thought this is a bad dream and tried to cry out, as one does in a nightmare, but could make no sound. At last, with a desperate effort I threw my feet to the floor and passing between the two rows of clouted faces and the two bodies that lay nearest the door, I escaped from the infernal place and ran to the office. The night-clerk was there, behind the desk, sitting in the dim light of another tallow candle—just sitting and staring. He did not rise: my abrupt entrance produced no effect upon him, though I must have looked a veritable corpse myself. It occurred to me then that I had not before really observed the fellow. He was a little chap, with a colorless face and the whitest, blankest eyes I ever saw. He had no more expression than the back of my hand. His clothing was a dirty gray.

" 'Damn you!' I said; 'what do you mean?'

"Just the same, I was shaking like a leaf in the wind and did not recognize my own voice.

"The night-clerk rose, bowed (apologetically) and—well, he was no longer there, and at that moment I felt a hand laid upon my shoulder from behind. Just fancy that if you can! Unspeakably frightened, I turned and saw a portly, kind-faced gentleman, who asked:

" 'What is the matter, my friend?'

"I was not long in telling him, but before I made an end of it he went pale himself. 'See here,' he said, 'are you telling the truth?'

"I had now got myself in hand and terror had given place to indignation. 'If you dare to doubt it,' I said, 'I'll hammer the life out of you!'

" 'No,' he replied, 'don't do that; just sit down till I tell you. This is not a hotel. It used to be; afterward it was a hospital. Now it is unoccupied, awaiting a tenant. The room that you mention was the dead-room—there were always plenty of dead. The fellow that you call the night-clerk used to be that, but later he booked the patients as they were brought in. I don't understand his being here. He has been dead a few weeks.'

" 'And who are you?' I blurted out.

" 'Oh, I look after the premises. I happened to be passing just now, and seeing a light in here came in to investigate. Let us have a look into that room,' he added, lifting the sputtering candle from the desk.

" 'I'll see you at the devil first!' said I, bolting out of the door into the street.

"Sir, that Breathitt House, in Atlanta, is a beastly place! Don't you stop there."

"God forbid! Your account of it certainly does not suggest comfort. By the way, Colonel, when did all that occur?"

"In September, 1864—shortly after the siege."

MA'AME PELAGIE

BY KATE CHOPIN

THOUGH PRIMARILY REMEMBERED FOR HER CLASSIC PROTOFEMINIST NOVELLA "THE AWAKENING," KATE CHOPIN WAS ALSO KNOWN TO DABBLE ALONG THE EDGE OF FANTASY AS IN HER COLLECTION *BAYOU FOLK*. IN "MA'AME PELAGIE" WE ARE NOT JUST TREATED TO SOME OF THE MYSTERY OF THE CULTURE OF THE BAYOU FOLK, WE ALSO SEE FIRSTHAND THE SCARS OF THE THEN-RECENT PAST AS MANIFESTED IN VISIONS OF THE CIVIL WAR.

I.

When the war began, there stood on Côte Joyeuse an imposing mansion of redbrick, shaped like the Pantheon. A grove of majestic live-oaks surrounded it.

Thirty years later, only the thick walls were standing, with the dull redbrick showing here and there through a matted growth of clinging vines. The huge round pillars were intact; so to some extent was the stone flagging of hall and portico. There had been no home so stately along the whole stretch of Côte Joyeuse. Everyone knew that, as they knew it had cost Philippe Valmêt sixty thousand dollars to build, away back in 1840. No one was in danger of forgetting that fact, so long as his daughter Pélagie survived. She was a queenly, white-haired woman of fifty. "Ma'ame Pélagie," they called her, though she was unmarried, as was her sister Pauline, a child in Ma'ame Pélagie's eyes; a child of thirty-five.

The two lived alone in a three-roomed cabin, almost within the shadow of the ruin. They lived for a dream, for Ma'ame Pélagie's dream, which was to rebuild the old home.

It would be pitiful to tell how their days were spent to accomplish this end; how the dollars had been saved for thirty years and the picayunes hoarded; and yet, not half enough gathered! But Ma'ame Pélagie felt sure of twenty years of life before her, and counted upon as many more for her sister. And what could not come to pass in twenty—in forty—years?

Often, of pleasant afternoons, the two would drink their black coffee, seated upon the stone-flagged portico whose canopy was the blue sky of Louisiana. They loved to sit there in the silence, with only each other and the sheeny, prying lizards for company, talking of the old times and planning for the new; while light breezes stirred the tattered vines high up among the columns, where owls nested.

"We can never hope to have all just as it was, Pauline," Ma'ame Pélagie would say; "perhaps the marble pillars of the salon will have to be replaced by wooden ones, and the crystal candelabra left out. Should you be willing, Pauline?"

"Oh, yes Sesoeur, I shall be willing." It was always, "Yes, Sesoeur," or "No, Se-soeur," "Just as you please, Sesoeur," with poor little Mam'selle Pauline. For what did she remember of that old life and that old spendor? Only a faint gleam here and there; the half-consciousness of a young, uneventful existence; and then a great crash. That meant the nearness of war; the revolt of slaves; confusion ending in fire and flame through which she was borne safely in the strong arms of Pélagie, and carried to the log cabin which was still their home. Their brother, Léandre, had known more of it all than Pauline, and not so much as Pélagie. He had left the management of the big plantation with all its memories and traditions to his older sister, and had gone away to dwell in cities. That was many years ago. Now, Léandre's business called him frequently and upon long journeys from home, and his motherless daughter was coming to stay with her aunts at Côte Joyeuse.

They talked about it, sipping their coffee on the ruined portico. Mam'selle Pauline was terribly excited; the flush that throbbed into her pale, nervous face showed it; and she locked her thin fingers in and out incessantly.

"But what shall we do with La Petite, Sesoeur? Where shall we put her? How shall we amuse her? Ah, Seigneur!"

"She will sleep upon a cot in the room next to ours," responded Ma'ame Pélagie, "and live as we do. She knows how we live, and why we live; her father has told her. She knows we have money and could squander it if we chose. Do not fret, Pauline; let us hope La Petite is a true Valmêt."

Then Ma'ame Pélagie rose with stately deliberation and went to saddle her horse, for she had yet to make her last daily round through the fields; and Mam'selle Pauline threaded her way slowly among the tangled grasses toward the cabin.

The coming of La Petite, bringing with her as she did the pungent atmosphere of an outside and dimly known world, was a shock to these two, living their dream-life. The girl was quite as tall as her aunt Pélagie, with dark eyes that reflected joy as a still pool reflects the light of stars; and her rounded cheek was tinged like the pink crèpe myrtle. Mam'selle Pauline kissed her and trembled. Ma'ame Pélagie looked into her eyes with a searching gaze, which seemed to seek a likeness of the past in the living present.

And they made room between them for this young life.

II.

La Petite had determined upon trying to fit herself to the strange, narrow existence which she knew awaited her at Côte Joyeuse. It went well enough at first. Sometimes she followed Ma'ame Pélagie into the fields to note how the cotton was opening, ripe and white; or to count the ears of corn upon the hardy stalks. But oftener she was with her aunt Pauline, assisting in household offices, chattering of her brief past, or walking with the older woman arm-in-arm under the trailing moss of the giant oaks.

Mam'selle Pauline's steps grew very buoyant that summer, and her eyes were sometimes as bright as a bird's, unless La Petite were away from her side, when they would lose all other light but one of uneasy expectancy. The girl seemed to love her well in return, and called her endearingly Tan'tante. But as the time went by, La Petite became very quiet—not listless, but thoughtful, and slow in her movements. Then her cheeks began to pale, till they were tinged like the creamy plumes of the white crêpe myrtle that grew in the ruin.

One day when she sat within its shadow, between her aunts, holding a hand of each, she said: "Tante Pélagie, I must tell you something, you and Tan'tante." She spoke low, but clearly and firmly. "I love you both—please remember that I love you both. But I must go away from you. I can't live any longer here at Côte Joyeuse."

A spasm passed through Mam'selle Pauline's delicate frame. La Petite could feel the twitch of it in the wiry fingers that were intertwined with her own. Ma'ame Pélagie remained unchanged and motionless. No human eye could penetrate so deep as to see the satisfaction which her soul felt. She said: "What do you mean, Petite? Your father has sent you to us, and I am sure it is his wish that you remain."

"My father loves me, Tante Pélagie, and such will not be his wish when he knows. Oh!" she continued with a restless movement, "it is as though a weight were pressing me backward here. I must live another life; the life I lived before. I want to know things that are happening from day to day over the world, and hear them talked about. I want my music, my books, my companions. If I had known no other life but this one of privation, I suppose it would be different. If I had to live this life, I should make the best of it. But I do not have to; and you know, Tante Pélagie, you do not need to. It seems to me," she added in a whisper, "that it is a sin against myself. Ah, Tan'tante!—what is the matter with Tan'tante?"

It was nothing; only a slight feeling of faintness, that would soon pass. She entreated them to take no notice; but they brought her some water and fanned her with a palmetto leaf.

But that night, in the stillness of the room, Mam'selle Pauline sobbed and would not be comforted. Ma'ame Pélagie took her in her arms.

"Pauline, my little sister Pauline," she entreated, "I never have seen you like this before. Do you no longer love me? Have we not been happy together, you and I?"

"Oh, yes, Sesoeur."

"Is it because La Petite is going away?"

"Yes, Sesoeur."

"Then she is dearer to you than I!" spoke Ma'ame Pélagie with sharp resentment. "Than I, who held you and warmed you in my arms the day you were born; than I, your mother, father, sister, everything that could cherish you. Pauline, don't tell me that."

Mam'selle Pauline tried to talk through her sobs.

"I can't explain it to you, Sesoeur. I don't understand it myself. I love you as I have always loved you; next to God. But if La Petite goes away I shall die. I can't understand—help me, Sesoeur. She seems—she seems like a savior; like one who had come and taken me by the hand and was leading me somewhere—somewhere I want to go."

Ma'ame Pélagie had been sitting beside the bed in her peignoir and slippers. She held the hand of her sister who lay there, and smoothed down the woman's soft brown hair. She said not a word, and the silence was broken only by Mam'selle Pauline's continued sobs. Once Ma'ame Pélagie arose to mix a drink of orange-flower water, which she gave to her sister, as she would have offered it to a nervous, fretful child. Almost an hour passed before Ma'ame Pélagie spoke again. Then she said:

"Pauline, you must cease that sobbing, now, and sleep. You will make yourself ill.

La Petite will not go away. Do you hear me? Do you understand? She will stay, I promise you."

Mam'selle Pauline could not clearly comprehend, but she had great faith in the word of her sister, and soothed by the promise and the touch of Ma'ame Pélagie's strong, gentle hand, she fell asleep.

III.

Ma'ame Pélagie, when she saw that her sister slept, arose noiselessly and stepped outside upon the low-roofed narrow gallery. She did not linger there, but with a step that was hurried and agitated, she crossed the distance that divided her cabin from the ruin.

The night was not a dark one, for the sky was clear and the moon resplendent. But light or dark would have made no difference to Ma'ame Pélagie. It was not the first time she had stolen away to the ruin at nighttime, when the whole plantation slept; but she never before had been there with a heart so nearly broken. She was going there for the last time to dream her dreams; to see the visions that hitherto had crowded her days and nights, and to bid them farewell.

There was the first of them, awaiting her upon the very portal; a robust old white-haired man, chiding her for returning home so late. There are guests to be entertained. Does she not know it? Guests from the city and from the near plantations. Yes, she knows it is late. She had been abroad with Félix, and they did not notice how the time was speeding. Félix is there; he will explain it all. He is there beside her, but she does not want to hear what he will tell her father.

Ma'ame Pélagie had sunk upon the bench where she and her sister so often came to sit. Turning, she gazed in through the gaping chasm of the window at her side. The interior of the ruin is ablaze. Not with the moonlight, for that is faint beside the other one—the sparkle from the crystal candelabra, which negroes, moving noiselessly and respectfully about, are lighting, one after the other. How the gleam of them reflects and glances from the polished marble pillars!

The room holds a number of guests. There is old Monsieur Lucien Santien, leaning against one of the pillars, and laughing at something which Monsieur Lafirme is telling him, till his fat shoulders shake. His son Jules is with him—Jules, who wants to marry her. She laughs. She wonders if Félix has told her father yet. There is young Jerome Lafirme playing at checkers upon the sofa with Léandre. Little Pauline stands annoying them and disturbing the game. Léandre reproves her. She begins to cry, and old black Clémentine, her nurse, who is not far off, limps across the room to pick her up and carry her away. How sensitive the little one is! But she trots about and takes care of herself better than she did a year or two ago, when she fell upon the stone hall floor and raised a great "bo-bo" on her forehead. Pélagie was hurt and angry enough about it; and she ordered rugs and buffalo robes to be brought and laid thick upon the tiles, till the little one's steps were surer.

"Il ne faut pas faire mal à Pauline."

She was saying it aloud—"faire mal à Pauline."

But she gazes beyond the salon, back into the big dining hall, where the white crêpe myrtle grows. Ha! How low that bat has circled. It has struck Ma'ame Pélagie full on the breast. She does not know it. She is beyond there in the dining hall, where her father sits with a group of friends over their wine. As usual they are talking politics. How tiresome! She has heard them say "la guerre" oftener than once. La guerre. Bah! She and Félix have something pleasanter to talk about, out under the oaks, or back in the shadow of the oleanders.

But they were right! The sound of a cannon, shot at Sumter, has rolled across the Southern States, and its echo is heard along the whole stretch of Côte Joyeuse.

Yet Pélagie does not believe it. Not till La Ricaneuse stands before her with bare, black arms akimbo, uttering a volley of vile abuse and of brazen impudence. Pélagie wants to kill her. But yet she will not believe. Not till Félix comes to her in the chamber above the dining hall—there where that trumpet vine hangs—comes to say good-bye to her. The hurt which the big brass buttons of his new gray uniform pressed into the tender flesh of her bosom has never left it. She sits upon the sofa, and he beside her, both speechless with pain. That room would not have been altered. Even the sofa would have been there in the same spot, and Ma'ame Pélagie had meant all along, for thirty years, all along, to lie there upon it some day when the time came to die.

But there is no time to weep, with the enemy at the door. The door has been no barrier. They are clattering through the halls now, drinking the wines, shattering the crystal and glass, slashing the portraits.

One of them stands before her and tells her to leave the house. She slaps his face. How the stigma stands out red as blood upon his blanched cheek!

Now there is a roar of fire and the flames are bearing down upon her motionless figure. She wants to show them how a daughter of Louisiana can perish before her conquerors. But little Pauline clings to her knees in an agony of terror. Little Pauline must be saved.

"Il ne faut pas faire mal à Pauline."

Again she is saying it aloud—"faire mal à Pauline."

THE NIGHT WAS NEARLY SPENT; Ma'ame Pélagie had glided from the bench upon which she had rested, and for hours lay prone upon the stone flagging, motionless. When she dragged herself to her feet it was to walk like one in a dream. About the great, solemn pillars, one after the other, she reached her arms, and pressed her cheek and her lips upon the senseless brick.

"Adieu, adieu!" whispered Ma'ame Pélagie.

There was no longer the moon to guide her steps across the familiar pathway to the cabin. The brightest light in the sky was Venus, that swung low in the east. The bats had ceased to beat their wings about the ruin. Even the mockingbird that had warbled for hours in the old mulberry tree had sung himself asleep. That darkest hour before the day was mantling the earth. Ma'ame Pélagie hurried through the wet, clinging grass, beating aside the heavy moss that swept across her face, walking on toward the cabin—toward Pauline. Not once did she look back upon the ruin that brooded like a huge monster—a black spot in the darkness that enveloped it.

IV.

Little more than a year later the transformation which the old Valmêt place had undergone was the talk and wonder of Côte Joyeuse. One would have looked in vain for the ruin; it was no longer there; neither was the log cabin. But out in the open, where the sun shone upon it, and the breezes blew about it, was a shapely structure fashioned from woods that the forests of the State had furnished. It rested upon a solid foundation of brick.

Upon a corner of the pleasant gallery sat Léandre smoking his afternoon cigar, and chatting with neighbors who had called. This was to be his *pied à terre* now; the home where his sisters and his daughter dwelt. The laughter of young people was heard out under the trees, and within the house where La Petite was playing upon the piano. With the enthusiasm of a young artist she drew from the keys strains that seemed marvelously beautiful to Mam'selle Pauline, who stood enraptured near her. Mam'selle Pauline had been touched by the re-creation of Valmêt. Her cheek was as full and almost as flushed as La Petite's. The years were falling away from her.

Ma'ame Pélagie had been conversing with her brother and his friends. Then she turned and walked away; stopping to listen awhile to the music which La Petite was making. But it was only for a moment. She went on around the curve of the veranda, where she found herself alone. She stayed there, erect, holding to the banister rail and looking out calmly in the distance across the fields.

She was dressed in black, with the white kerchief she always wore folded across her bosom. Her thick, glossy hair rose like a silver diadem from her brow. In her deep, dark eyes smouldered the light of fires that would never flame. She had grown very old. Years instead of months seemed to have passed over her since the night she bade farewell to her visions.

Poor Ma'ame Pélagie! How could it be different! While the outward pressure of a young and joyous existence had forced her footsteps into the light, her soul had stayed in the shadow of the ruin.

THE DEVIL AND DANIEL WEBSTER

BY STEPHEN VINCENT BENÉT

WHEN YOU THINK OF AMERICAN DEPICTIONS OF THE DEVIL, NONE FEEL MORE HOMEGROWN THAN GOOD OLD MR. SCRATCH WHO COMES A-KNOCKING WITH AN OFFER OF 'ALL THAT MONEY CAN BUY' IN EXCHANGE FOR YOUR SOUL. STEPHEN VINCENT BENÉT'S CLASSIC TALE "THE DEVIL AND DANIEL WEBSTER" SET THE STANDARD FOR ALL FUTURE AMERICAN "DEAL WITH THE DEVIL" STORIES WITH ITS EVERYMAN VICTIM, JABEZ STONE, AND REAL AMERICAN HERO, NEW HAMPSHIRE'S OWN DANIEL WEBSTER, ARCHITECT OF THE LEGENDARY COMPROMISE OF 1850 AND A PRETTY GOOD LAWYER TO BOOT.

It's a story they tell in the border country, where Massachusetts joins Vermont and New Hampshire.

Yes, Dan'l Webster's dead—or, at least, they buried him. But every time there's a thunderstorm around Marshfield, they say you can hear his rolling voice in the hollows of the sky. And they say that if you go to his grave and speak loud and clear, "Dan'l Webster—Dan'l Webster!" the ground'll begin to shiver and the trees begin to shake. And after a while you'll hear a deep voice saying, "Neighbor, how stands the Union?" Then you better answer the Union stands as she stood, rock-bottomed and copper-sheathed, one and indivisible, or he's liable to rear right out of the ground. At least, that's what I was told when I was a youngster.

You see, for a while, he was the biggest man in the country. He never got to be President, but he was the biggest man. There were thousands that trusted in him right next to God Almighty, and they told stories about him that were like the stories of patriarchs and such. They said, when he stood up to speak, stars and stripes came right out in the sky, and once he spoke against a river and made it sink into the ground. They said, when he walked the woods with his fishing rod, Killall, the trout would jump out of the streams right into his pockets, for they knew it was no use putting up a fight against him; and, when he argued a case, he could turn on the harps of the blessed and the shaking of the earth underground. That was the kind of man he was, and his big farm up at Marshfield was suitable to him. The chickens he raised were all white meat down through the drumsticks, the cows were tended like children, and the big ram he called Goliath had horns with a curl like a morning-glory vine and could butt through an iron door. But Dan'l wasn't one of your gentlemen famers; he knew all the ways of the land, and he'd be up by candlelight to see that the chores got done. A man with a mouth like a mastiff, a brow like a mountain and eyes like burning anthracite—that was Dan'l Webster in his prime. And the biggest case he argued never got written down in the books, for he argued it against the devil, nip and tuck and no holds barred. And this is the way I used to hear it told.

There was a man named Jabez Stone, lived at Cross Corners, New Hampshire. He wasn't a bad man to start with, but he was an unlucky man. If he planted corn, he got borers; if he planted potatoes, he got blight. He had good-enough land, but it didn't prosper him; he had a decent wife and children, but the more children he had, the less there was to feed them. If stones cropped up in his neighbor's field, boulders boiled up in his; if he had a horse with the spavins, he'd trade it for one with the staggers and give something extra. There's some folks bound to be like that, apparently. But one day Jabez Stone got sick of the whole business.

He'd been plowing that morning and he'd just broke the plowshare on a rock that he could have sworn hadn't been there yesterday. And, as he stood looking at the plowshare, the off horse began to cough—that ropy kind of cough that means sickness and horse doctors. There were two children down with the measles, his wife was ailing, and he had a whitlow on his thumb. It was about the last straw for Jabez Stone. "I vow," he said, and he looked around him kind of desperate—"I vow it's enough to make a man want to sell his soul to the devil! And I would, too, for two cents!"

Then he felt a kind of queerness come over him at having said what he'd said; though, naturally, being a New Hampshireman, he wouldn't take it back. But, all the same, when it got to be evening and, as far as he could see, no notice had been taken, he felt relieved in his mind, for he was a religious man. But notice is always taken, sooner or later, just like the Good Book says. And, sure enough, next day, about suppertime, a soft-spoken, dark-dressed stranger drove up in a handsome buggy and asked for Jabez Stone.

Well, Jabez told his family it was a lawyer, come to see him about a legacy. But he knew who it was. He didn't like the looks of the stranger, nor the way he smiled with his teeth. They were white teeth, and plentiful—some say they were filed to a point, but I wouldn't vouch for that. And he didn't like it when the dog took one look at the stranger and ran away howling, with his tail between his legs. But having passed his word, more or less, he stuck to it, and they went out behind the barn and made their bargain. Jabez Stone had to prick his finger to sign, and the stranger lent him a silver pin. The wound healed clean, but it left a little white scar.

After that, all of a sudden, things began to pick up and prosper for Jabez Stone. His cows got fat and his horses sleek, his crops were the envy of the neighborhood, and lightning might strike all over the valley, but it wouldn't strike his barn. Pretty soon, he was one of the prosperous people of the county; they asked him to stand for selectman, and he stood for it; there began to be talk of running him for state senate. All in all, you might say the Stone family was as happy and contented as cats in a dairy. And so they were, except for Jabez Stone.

He'd been contented enough, the first few years. It's a great thing when bad luck turns; it drives most other things out of your head. True, every now and then, especially in rainy weather, the little white scar on his finger would give him a twinge. And once a year, punctual as clockwork, the stranger with the handsome buggy would come driving by. But the sixth year, the stranger lighted, and, after that, his peace was over for Jabez Stone.

The stranger came up through the lower field, switching his boots with a cane—they were handsome black boots, but Jabez Stone never liked the look of them, particularly the toes. And, after he'd passed the time of day, he said, "Well, Mr. Stone, you're a hummer! It's a very pretty property you've got here, Mr. Stone."

"Well, some might favor it and others might not," said Jabez Stone, for he was a New Hampshireman.

"Oh, no need to decry your industry!" said the stranger, very easy, showing his teeth in a smile. "After all, we know what's been done, and it's been according to contract and specifications. So when—ahem—the mortgage falls due next year, you shouldn't have any regrets."

"Speaking of that mortgage, mister," said Jabez Stone, and he looked around for help to the earth and the sky, "I'm beginning to have one or two doubts about it."

"Doubts?" said the stranger, not quite so pleasantly.

"Why, yes," said Jabez Stone. "This being the U.S.A. and me always having been a religious man." He cleared his throat and got bolder. "Yes, sir," he said, "I'm beginning to have considerable doubts as to that mortgage holding in court."

"There's courts and courts," said the stranger, clicking his teeth. "Still, we might as well have a look at the original document." And he hauled out a big black pocketbook, full of papers. "Sherwin, Slater, Stevens, Stone," he muttered. "I, Jabez Stone, for a term of seven years—Oh, it's quite in order, I think."

But Jabez Stone wasn't listening, for he saw something else flutter out of the black pocketbook. It was something that looked like a moth, but it wasn't a moth. And as Jabez Stone stared at it, it seemed to speak to him in a small sort of piping voice, terrible small and thin, but terrible human. "Neighbor Stone!" it squeaked. "Neighbor Stone! Help me! For God's sake, help me!"

But before Jabez Stone could stir hand or foot, the stranger whipped out a big bandanna handkerchief, caught the creature in it, just like a butterfly, and started tying up the ends of the bandanna.

"Sorry for the interruption," he said. "As I was saying—"

But Jabez Stone was shaking all over like a scared horse.

"That's Miser Stevens' voice!" he said, in a croak. "And you've got him in your handkerchief!"

The stranger looked a little embarrassed.

"Yes, I really should have transferred him to the collecting box," he said with a simper, "but there were some rather unusual specimens there and I didn't want them crowded. Well, well, these little contretemps will occur."

"I don't know what you mean by contertan," said Jabez Stone, "but that was Miser Stevens' voice! And he ain't dead! You can't tell me he is! He was just as spry and mean as a woodchuck, Tuesday!"

"In the midst of life—" said the stranger, kind of pious. "Listen!" Then a bell began to toll in the valley and Jabez Stone listened, with the sweat running down his face. For he knew it was tolled for Miser Stevens and that he was dead.

"These long-standing accounts," said the stranger with a sigh; "one really hates to close them. But business is business."

He still had the bandanna in his hand, and Jabez Stone felt sick as he saw the cloth struggle and flutter.

"Are they all as small as that?" he asked hoarsely.

"Small?" said the stranger. "Oh, I see what you mean. Why, they vary." He measured Jabez Stone with his eyes, and his teeth showed. "Don't worry, Mr. Stone," he said. "You'll go with a very good grade. I wouldn't trust you outside the collecting box. Now, a man like Dan'l Webster, of course—well, we'd have to build a special box for him, and even at that, I imagine the wing spread would astonish you. But, in your case, as I was saying—"

"Put that handkerchief away!" said Jabez Stone, and he began to beg and to pray. But the best he could get at the end was a three years' extension, with conditions.

But till you make a bargain like that, you've got no idea of how fast four years can run. By the last months of those years, Jabez Stone's known all over the state and there's talk of running him for governor—and it's dust and ashes in his mouth. For every day when he gets up, he thinks, "There's one more night gone," and every night when he lies down, he thinks of the black pocketbook and the soul of Miser Stevens, and it makes him sick at heart. Till, finally, he can't bear it any longer, and, in the last days of the last year, he hitches up his horse and drives off to seek Dan'l Webster. For Dan'l was born in New Hampshire, only a few miles from Cross Corners, and it's well known that he has a particular soft spot for old neighbors.

It was early in the morning when he got to Marshfield, but Dan'l was up already, talking Latin to the farm hands and wrestling with the ram, Goliath, and trying out a new trotter and working up speeches to make against John C. Calhoun. But when he heard a New Hampshireman had come to see him, he dropped everything else he was doing, for that was Dan'l's way. He gave Jabez Stone a breakfast that five men couldn't eat, went into the living history of every man and woman in Cross Corners, and finally asked him how he could serve him.

Jabez Stone allowed that it was a kind of mortgage case.

"Well, I haven't pleaded a mortgage case in a long time, and I don't generally plead now, except before the Supreme Court," said Dan'l, "but if I can, I'll help you."

"Then I've got hope for the first time in ten years," said Jabez Stone, and told him the details.

Dan'l walked up and down as he listened, hands behind his back, now and then asking a question, now and then plunging his eyes at the floor, as if they'd bore through it like gimlets. When Jabez Stone had finished, Dan'l puffed out his cheeks and blew. Then he turned to Jabez Stone and a smile broke over his face like the sunrise over Monadnock.

"You've certainly given yourself the devil's own row to hoe, Neighbor Stone," he said, "but I'll take your case."

"You'll take it?" said Jabez Stone, hardly daring to believe.

"Yes," said Dan'l Webster. "I've got about seventy-five other things to do and the Missouri Compromise to straighten out, but I'll take your case. For if two New Hampshiremen aren't a match for the devil, we might as well give the country back to the Indians."

Then he shook Jabez Stone by the hand and said, "Did you come down here in a hurry?"

"Well, I admit I made time," said Jabez Stone.

"You'll go back faster," said Dan'l Webster, and he told 'em to hitch up Constitution and Constellation to the carriage. They were matched grays with one white forefoot, and they stepped like greased lightning.

Well, I won't describe how excited and pleased the whole Stone family was to have the great Dan'l Webster for a guest, when they finally got there. Jabez Stone had lost his hat on the way, blown off when they overtook a wind, but he didn't take much account of that. But after supper he sent the family off to bed, for he had most particular business with Mr. Webster. Mrs. Stone wanted them to sit in the front parlor, but Dan'l Webster knew front parlors and said he preferred the kitchen. So it was there they sat, waiting for the stranger, with a jug on the table between them and a bright fire on the hearth—the stranger being scheduled to show up on the stroke of midnight, according to specifications.

Well, most men wouldn't have asked for better company than Dan'l Webster and a jug. But with every tick of the clock Jabez Stone got sadder and sadder. His eyes roved round, and though he sampled the jug you could see he couldn't taste it. Finally, on the stroke of 11:30 he reached over and grabbed Dan'l Webster by the arm.

"Mr. Webster, Mr. Webster!" he said, and his voice was shaking with fear and a desperate courage. "For God's sake, Mr. Webster, harness your horses and get away from this place while you can!"

"You've brought me a long way, neighbor, to tell me you don't like my company," said Dan'l Webster, quite peaceable, pulling at the jug.

"Miserable wretch that I am!" groaned Jabez Stone. "I've brought you a devilish way, and now I see my folly. Let him take me if he wills. I don't hanker after it, I must say, but I can stand it. But you're the Union's stay and New Hampshire's pride! He mustn't get you, Mr. Webster! He mustn't get you!"

Dan'l Webster looked at the distracted man, all gray and shaking in the firelight, and laid a hand on his shoulder.

"I'm obliged to you, Neighbor Stone," he said gently. "It's kindly thought of. But there's a jug on the table and a case in hand. And I never left a jug or a case half finished in my life."

And just at that moment there was a sharp rap on the door.

"Ah," said Dan'l Webster, very coolly, "I thought your clock was a trifle slow, Neighbor Stone." He stepped to the door and opened it. "Come in!" he said.

The stranger came in—very dark and tall he looked in the firelight. He was carrying a box under his arm—a black, japanned box with little air holes in the lid. At the sight of the box, Jabez Stone gave a low cry and shrank into a corner of the room.

"Mr. Webster, I presume," said the stranger, very polite, but with his eyes glowing like a fox's deep in the woods.

"Attorney of record for Jabez Stone," said Dan'l Webster, but his eyes were glowing too. "Might I ask your name?"

"I've gone by a good many," said the stranger carelessly. "Perhaps Scratch will do for the evening. I'm often called that in these regions."

Then he sat down at the table and poured himself a drink from the jug. The liquor was cold in the jug, but it came steaming into the glass.

"And now," said the stranger, smiling and showing his teeth, "I shall call upon you, as a law-abiding citizen, to assist me in taking possession of my property."

Well, with that the argument began—and it went hot and heavy. At first, Jabez Stone had a flicker of hope, but when he saw Dan'l Webster being forced back at point after point, he just scrunched in his corner, with his eyes on that japanned box. For there wasn't any doubt as to the deed or the signature—that was the worst of it. Dan'l Webster twisted and turned and thumped his fist on the table, but he couldn't get away from that. He offered to compromise the case; the stranger wouldn't hear of it. He pointed out the property had increased in value, and state senators ought to be worth more; the stranger stuck to the letter of the law. He was a great lawyer, Dan'l Webster, but we know who's the King of Lawyers, as the Good Book tells us, and it seemed as if, for the first time, Dan'l Webster had met his match.

Finally, the stranger yawned a little. "Your spirited efforts on behalf of your client do you credit, Mr. Webster," he said, "but if you have no more arguments to adduce, I'm rather pressed for time"—and Jabez Stone shuddered.

Dan'l Webster's brow looked dark as a thundercloud.

"Pressed or not, you shall not have this man!" he thundered. "Mr. Stone is an American citizen, and no American citizen may be forced into the service of a foreign prince. We fought England for that in '12 and we'll fight all hell for it again!"

"Foreign?" said the stranger. "And who calls me a foreigner?"

"Well, I never yet heard of the dev—of your claiming American citizenship," said Dan'l Webster with surprise.

"And who with better right?" said the stranger, with one of his terrible smiles. "When the first wrong was done to the first Indian, I was there. When the first slaver put out for the Congo, I stood on her deck. Am I not in your books and stories and beliefs, from the first settlements on? Am I not spoken of, still, in every church in New England? 'Tis true the North claims me for a Southerner and the South for a Northerner, but I am neither. I am merely an honest American like yourself—and of the best descent—for, to tell the truth, Mr. Webster, though I don't like to boast of it, my name is older in this country than yours."

"Aha!" said Dan'l Webster, with the veins standing out in his forehead. "Then I stand on the Constitution! I demand a trial for my client!"

"The case is hardly one for an ordinary court," said the stranger, his eyes flickering. "And, indeed, the lateness of the hour—"

"Let it be any court you choose, so it is an American judge and an American jury!" said Dan'l Webster in his pride. "Let it be the quick or the dead; I'll abide the issue!"

"You have said it," said the stranger, and pointed his finger at the door. And with that, and all of a sudden, there was a rushing of wind outside and a noise of footsteps. They came, clear and distinct, through the night And yet, they were not like the footsteps of living men.

"In God's name, who comes by so late?" cried Jabez Stone, in an ague of fear.

"The jury Mr. Webster demands," said the stranger, sipping at his boiling glass. "You must pardon the rough appearance of one or two; they will have come a long way."

And with that the fire burned blue and the door blew open and twelve men entered, one by one.

If Jabez Stone had been sick with terror before, he was blind with terror now. For there was Walter Butler, the loyalist, who spread fire and horror through the Mohawk Valley in the times of the Revolution; and there was Simon Girty, the renegade, who saw white men burned at the stake and whooped with the Indians to see them burn. His eyes were green, like a catamount's, and the stains on his hunting shirt did not come from the blood of the deer. King Philip was there, wild and proud as he had been in life, with the great gash in his head that gave him his death wound, and cruel Governor Dale, who broke men on the wheel. There was Morton of Merry Mount, who so vexed the Plymouth Colony, with his flushed, loose, handsome face and his hate of the godly. There was Teach, the bloody pirate, with his black beard curling on his breast. The Reverend John Smeet, with his strangler's hands and his Geneva gown, walked as daintily as he had to the gallows. The red print of the rope was still around his neck, but he carried a perfumed handkerchief in one hand. One and all, they came into the room with the fires of hell still upon them, and the stranger named their names and their deeds as they came, till the tale of twelve was told. Yet the stranger had told the truth—they had all played a part in America.

"Are you satisfied with the jury, Mr. Webster?" said the stranger mockingly, when they had taken their places.

The sweat stood upon Dan'l Webster's brow, but his voice was clear.

"Quite satisfied," he said. "Though I miss General Arnold from the company."

"Benedict Arnold is engaged upon other business," said the stranger, with glower. "Ah, you asked for a justice, I believe."

He pointed his finger once more, and a tall man, soberly clad in Puritan garb, with the burning gaze of the fanatic, stalked into the room and took his judge's place.

"Justice Hathorne is a jurist of experience," said the stranger. "He presided at certain witch trials once held in Salem. There were others who repented of the business later, but not he."

"Repent of such notable wonders and undertakings?" said the stern old justice. "Nay, hang them—hang them all!" And he muttered to himself in a way that struck ice into the soul of Jabez Stone.

Then the trial began, and, as you might expect, it didn't look anyways good for the defense. And Jabez Stone didn't make much of a witness in his own behalf. He took one look at Simon Girty and screeched, and they had to put him back in his corner in a kind of swoon.

It didn't halt the trial, though; the trial went on, as trials do. Dan'l Webster had faced some hard juries and hanging judges in his time, but this was the hardest he'd ever faced, and he knew it. They sat there with a kind of glitter in their eyes, and the stranger's smooth voice went on and on. Every time he'd raise an objection, it'd be "Objection sustained," but whenever Dan'l objected, it'd be "Objection denied." Well, you couldn't expect fair play from a fellow like this Mr. Scratch.

It got to Dan'l in the end, and he began to heat, like iron in the forge. When he got up to speak he was going to flay that stranger with every trick known to the law, and the judge and jury too. He didn't care if it was contempt of court or what would happen to him for it. He didn't care any more what happened to Jabez Stone. He just got madder and madder, thinking of what he'd say. And yet, curiously enough, the more he thought about it, the less he was able to arrange his speech in his mind.

Till, finally, it was time for him to get up on his feet, and he did so, all ready to bust out with lightnings and denunciations. But before he started he looked over the judge and jury for a moment, such being his custom. And he noticed the glitter in their eyes was twice as strong as before, and they all leaned forward. Like hounds just before they get the fox, they looked, and the blue mist of evil in the room thickened as he watched them. Then he saw what he'd been about to do, and he wiped his forehead, as a man might who's just escaped falling into a pit in the dark.

For it was him they'd come for, not only Jabez Stone. He read it in the glitter of their eyes and in the way the stranger hid his mouth with one hand. And if he fought them with their own weapons, he'd fall into their power; he knew that, though he couldn't have told you how. It was his own anger and horror that burned in their eyes; and he'd have to wipe that out or the case was lost. He stood there for a moment, his black eyes burning like anthracite. And then he began to speak.

He started off in a low voice, though you could hear every word. They say he could call on the harps of the blessed when he chose. And this was just as simple and easy as a man could talk. But he didn't start out by condemning or reviling. He was talking about the things that make a country a country, and a man a man.

And he began with the simple things that everybody's known and felt—the freshness of a fine morning when you're young, and the taste of food when you're hungry, and the new day that's every day when you're a child. He took them up and he turned them in his hands. They were good things for any man. But without freedom, they sickened. And when he talked of those enslaved, and the sorrows of slavery, his voice got like a big bell. He talked of the early days of America and the men who had made those days. It wasn't a spread-eagle speech, but he made you see it. He admitted all the wrong that had ever been done. But he showed how, out of the wrong and the right, the suffering and the starvations, something new had come. And everybody had played a part in it, even the traitors.

Then he turned to Jabez Stone and showed him as he was—an ordinary man who'd had hard luck and wanted to change it. And, because he'd wanted to change it, now he was going to be punished for all eternity. And yet there was good in Jabez Stone, and he showed that good. He was hard and mean, in some ways, but he was a man. There was sadness in being a man, but it was a proud thing too. And he showed what the pride of it was till you couldn't help feeling it. Yes, even in hell, if a man was a man, you'd know it. And he wasn't pleading for any one person any more, though his voice rang like an organ. He was telling the story and the failures and the endless journey of mankind. They got tricked and trapped and bamboozled, but it was a great journey. And no demon that was ever foaled could know the inwardness of it—it took a man to do that.

The fire began to die on the hearth and the wind before morning to blow. The light was getting gray in the room when Dan'l Webster finished. And his words came back at the end to New Hampshire ground, and the one spot of land that each man loves and clings to. He painted a picture of that, and to each one of that jury he spoke of things long forgotten. For his voice could search the heart, and that was his gift and his strength. And to one, his voice was like the forest and its secrecy, and to another like the sea and the storms of the sea; and one heard the cry of his lost nation in it, and another saw a little harmless scene he hadn't remembered for years. But each saw something. And when Dan'l Webster finished he didn't know whether or not he'd saved Jabez Stone. But he knew he'd done a miracle. For the glitter was gone from the eyes of judge and jury, and, for the moment, they were men again, and knew they were men.

"The defense rests," said Dan'l Webster, and stood there like a mountain. His ears were still ringing with his speech, and he didn't hear anything else till he heard Judge Hathorne say, "The jury will retire to consider its verdict."

Walter Butler rose in his place and his face had a dark, gay pride on it.

"The jury has considered its verdict," he said, and looked the stranger full in the eye. "We find for the defendant, Jabez Stone."

With that, the smile left the stranger's face, but Walter Butler did not flinch.

"Perhaps 'tis not strictly in accordance with the evidence," he said, "but even the damned may salute the eloquence of Mr. Webster."

With that, the long crow of a rooster split the gray morning sky, and judge and jury were gone from the room like a puff of smoke and as if they had never been there. The stranger turned to Dan'l Webster, smiling wryly.

"Major Butler was always a bold man," he said. "I had not thought him quite so bold. Nevertheless, my congratulations, as between two gentlemen."

"I'll have that paper first, if you please," said Dan'l Webster, and he took it and tore it into four pieces. It was queerly warm to the touch. "And now," he said, "I'll have you!" and his hand came down like a bear trap on the stranger's arm. For he knew that once you bested anybody like Mr. Scratch in fair fight, his power on you was gone. And he could see that Mr. Scratch knew it too.

The stranger twisted and wriggled, but he couldn't get out of that grip. "Come, come, Mr. Webster," he said, smiling palely. "This sort of thing is ridic—ouch!—is ridiculous. If you're worried about the costs of the case, naturally, I'd be glad to pay—"

"And so you shall!" said Dan'l Webster, shaking him till his teeth rattled. "For you'll sit right down at that table and draw up a document, promising never to bother Jabez Stone nor his heirs or assigns nor any other New Hampshireman till doomsday! For any hades we want to raise in this state, we can raise ourselves, without assistance from strangers."

"Ouch!" said the stranger. "Ouch! Well, they never did run very big to the barrel, but—ouch!—I agree!"

So he sat down and drew up the document. But Dan'l Webster kept his hand on his coat collar all the time.

"And, now, may I go?" said the stranger, quiet humble, when Dan'l'd seen the document was in proper and legal form.

"Go?" said Dan'l, giving him another shake. "I'm still trying to figure out what I'll do with you. For you've settled the costs of the case, but you haven't settled with me. I think I'll take you back to Marshfield," he said, kind of reflective. "I've got a ram there named Goliath that can butt through an iron door. I'd kind of like to turn you loose in his field and see what he'd do."

Well, with that the stranger began to beg and to plead. And he begged and he pled so humble that finally Dan'l, who was naturally kindhearted, agreed to let him go. The stranger seemed terrible grateful for that and said, just to show they were friends, he'd tell Dan'l's fortune before leaving. So Dan'l agreed to that, though he didn't take much stock in fortune-tellers ordinarily. But, naturally, the stranger was a little different.

Well, he pried and he peered at the lines in Dan'l's hands. And he told him one thing and another that was quite remarkable. But they were all in the past.

"Yes, all that's true, and it happened," said Dan'l Webster. "But what's to come in the future?"

The stranger grinned, kind of happily, and shook his head.

"The future's not as you think it," he said. "It's dark. You have a great ambition, Mr. Webster."

"I have," said Dan'l firmly, for everybody knew he wanted to be President.

"It seems almost within your grasp," said the stranger, "but you will not attain it. Lesser men will be made president and you will be passed over."

"And, if I am, I'll still be Daniel Webster," said Dan'l. "Say on."

"And have two strong sons," said the stranger, shaking his head. "You look to found a line. But each will die in war and neither reach greatness."

"Live or die, they are still my sons," said Dan'l Webster. "Say on."

"You have made great speeches," said the stranger. "You will make more."

"Ah," said Dan'l Webster.

"But the last great speech you make will turn many of your own against you," said the stranger. "They will call you Ichabod; they will call you by other names. Even in New England, some will say you have turned your coat and sold your country, and their voices will be loud against you till you die."

"So it is an honest speech, it does not matter what men say," said Dan'l Webster. Then he looked at the stranger and their glances locked.

"One question," he said. "I have fought for the Union all my life. Will I see that fight won against those who would tear it apart?"

"Not while you live," said the stranger, grimly, "but it will be won. And after you are dead, there are thousands who will fight for your cause, because of words that you spoke."

"Why, then, you long-barreled, slab-sided, lantern-jawed, fortune-telling note shaver!" said Dan'l Webster, with a great roar of laughter, "be off with you to your own place before I put my mark on you! For, by the thirteen original colonies, I'd go to the Pit itself to save the Union!"

And with that he drew back his foot for a kick that would have stunned a horse. It was only the tip of his shoe that caught the stranger, but he went flying out the door with his collecting box under his arm.

"And now," said Dan'l Webster, seeing Jabez Stone beginning to rouse from his swoon, "let's see what's left in the jug, for it's dry work talking all night. I hope there's pie for breakfast, Neighbor Stone."

But they say that whenever the devil comes near Marshfield, even now, he gives it a wide berth. And he hasn't been seen in the state of New Hampshire from that day to this. I'm not talking about Massachusetts or Vermont.

THE VALLEY WAS STILL

BY MANLY WADE WELLMAN

IN ADDITION TO HIS "SILVER JOHN" STORIES, MANLY WADE WELLMAN WAS ALSO A PULITZER PRIZE–WINNING CIVIL WAR SCHOLAR. "THE VALLEY WAS STILL" IS PROBABLY HIS MOST FAMOUS CIVIL WAR TALE OF THE FANTASTIC AND IT SUCCEEDS IN GIVING A CERTAIN IRONIC TWIST TO THE CONCEPT OF "DAMN YANKEES." (IT WAS ALSO SUCCESSFULLY ADAPTED BY ROD SERLING FOR HIS *TWILIGHT ZONE* TV SERIES.)

Wind touched the pines on the ridge, and stirred the thicker forest on the hills opposite; but the grassy valley between, with its red and white houses at the bottom, was as still as a painted backdrop in a theater. Not even a grasshopper sang in it.

Two cavalrymen sat their mounts at the edge of the pines. The one in the torn butternut blouse hawked and spat, and the sound was strangely loud at the brink of that silence.

"I'd reckoned the Yanks was down in that there little town," he said. "Channow, it's called. Joe, you look like a Yank yourself in them clothes."

His mate, who wore half-weathered blue, did not appear complimented. The garments had been stripped from an outraged sergeant of Pennsylvania Lancers, taken prisoner at the Seven Days. They fitted their new wearer's lean body nicely, except across the shoulders. His boots were likewise trophies of war—from the Second Manassas, where the Union Army had learned that lightning can strike twice in the same place; and his saddle-cloth, with its U. S. stamp, had also been unwillingly furnished by the Federal army. But the gray horse had come from his father's Virginia farm, and had lived through a year of fierce fighting and fiercer toil. The rider's name was Joseph Paradine, and he had recently declined, with thanks, the offer of General J.E.B. Stuart to recommend him for a commission.

He preferred to serve as a common trooper. He was a chivalric idealist, and a peerless scout.

"You'd better steal some Yankee blues yourself, Dauger," he advised. "Those home-spun pants would drop off of you if you stood up in your stirrups. . . . Yes, the enemy's expected to take up a position in Channow Valley. But if he had done so, we'd have run into his videttes by now, and that town would be as noisy as a county fair."

He rode from among the pines and into the open on the lower slope.

"You're plumb exposin' yourself, Joe," warned Dauger anxiously.

"And I'm going to expose myself more," returned Paradine, his eyes on the valley. "We've been told to find the Yankees, establish their whereabouts. Then our people will tackle them." He spoke with the confidence of triumph that in the summer of 1862 possessed Confederates who had driven the Union's bravest and best all through Virginia. "I'm going all the way down."

"There'll be Yanks hidin'," suggested Dauger pessimistically. "They'll plug you plumb full of lead."

"If they do," called Paradine, "ride back and tell the boys, because then you'll know the Yankees actually are in Channow." He put his horse to the slope, feeling actually happy at the thought that he might suffer for the sake of his cause. It is worthy of repetition that he was a chivalric idealist.

Dauger, quite as brave but more practical, bode where he was. Paradine, riding downhill, passed out of reach of any more warnings.

Paradine's eyes were kept on the village as he descended deep into silence as into water. He had never known such silence, not even at the frequent prayings of his very devout regiment. It made him nervous, a different nervousness from the tingling elation brought by battle thunders, and it fairly daunted his seasoned and intelligent horse. The beast tossed its head, sniffed, danced precariously, and had to be urged to the slope's foot and the trail that ran there.

From the bottom of the slope, the village was a scant two miles away. Its chimneys did not smoke, nor did its trees stir in the windless air. Nor was there sign or motion upon its streets and among its houses of red brick and white wood—no enemy soldiers, or anything else.

Was this a trap? But Paradine smiled at the thought of a whole Yankee brigade or more, lying low to capture one lone Southerner.

More likely they thought him a friend, wearing blue as he did; but why silence in that case, either?

He determined to make noise. If there were hostile forces in and among the houses of Channow, he would draw their attention, perhaps their musket fire. Spurring the gray so that it whickered and plunged, he forced it to canter at an angle toward the nearest houses. At the same time he drew his saber, whetted to a razor-edge contrary to regulations, and waved it over his head. He gave the rebel yell, high and fierce.

"Yee-hee!"

Paradine's voice was a strong one, and it could ring from end to end of a brigade in line; but, even as he yelled, that yell perished—dropped from his lips, as though cut away.

He could not have been heard ten yards. Had his throat dried up? Then, suddenly, he knew. There was no echo here, for all the ridge lay behind, and the hills in front to the north. Even the galloping hoofs of the gray sounded muffled, as if in cotton. Strange . . . there was no response to his defiance.

That was more surprising still. If there were no enemy troops, what about the people of the town? Paradine felt his brown neck-hair, which needed cutting badly, rise and stiffen. Something sinister lay yonder, and warned him away. But he had ridden into this valley to gather intelligence for his officers. He could not turn back, and respect himself thereafter, as a gentleman and a soldier. Has it been noted that Paradine was a chivalric idealist?

But his horse, whatever its blood and character, lacked such selfless devotion to the cause of States' Rights. It faltered in its gallop, tried first to turn back, and then to throw Paradine. He cursed it feelingly, fought it with bit, knee and spur, and finally pulled up and dismounted. He drew the reins forward over the tossing gray head, thrust his left arm through the loop, and with his left hand drew the big cap-and-ball revolver from his holster. Thus ready, with shot or saber, he proceeded on foot, and the gray followed him protestingly.

"Come on," he scolded, very loudly—he was sick of the silence. "I don't know what I'm getting into here. If I have to retreat, it won't be on foot."

Half a mile more, at a brisk walk. A quarter-mile beyond that, more slowly; for still there was no sound or movement from the village. Then the trail joined a wagon track, and Paradine came to the foot of the single street of Channow.

He looked along it, and came to an abrupt halt.

The street, with its shaded yards on either side, was littered with slack blue lumps, each the size of a human body.

The Yankee army, or its advance guard, was there—but fallen and stony still.

"Dead!" muttered Paradine, under his breath.

But who could have killed them? Not his comrades, who had not known where the enemy was. Plague, then? But the most withering plague takes hours, at least, and these had plainly fallen all in the same instant.

Paradine studied the scene. Here had been a proper entry of a strange settlement— first a patrol, watchful and suspicious; then a larger advance party, in two single files, each file hugging one side of the street with eyes and weapons commanding the other side; and, finally, the main body—men, horses and guns, with a baggage train—all as it should be; but now prone and still, like tin soldiers strewn on a floor after a game.

The house at the foot of the street had a hitching-post, cast from iron to represent a Negro boy with a ring in one lifted hand. To that ring Paradine tethered the now almost unmanageable gray. He heard a throbbing roll, as of drums, which he identified as the blood beating in his ears. The saber-hilt was slippery with the sweat of his palm.

He knew that he was afraid, and did not relish the knowledge. Stubbornly he turned his boot-toes forward, and approached the fallen ranks of the enemy. The drums in his ears beat a cadence for his lone march.

He reached and stood over the nearest of the bodies. A blue-bloused infantryman this, melted over on his face, his hands slack upon the musket lying crosswise beneath him. The peaked forage cap had fallen from rumpled, bright hair. The cheek, what Paradine could see of it, was as downy as a peach. Only a kid, young to die; but was he dead?

There was no sign of a wound. Too, a certain waxy finality was lacking in that slumped posture. Paradine extended the point of his saber and gingerly prodded a sun-reddened wrist.

No response. Paradine increased the pressure. A red drop appeared under the point, and grew. Paradine scowled. The boy could bleed. He must be alive, after all.

"Wake up, Yankee," said Joseph Paradine, and stirred the blue flank with his foot. The flesh yielded, but did not stir otherwise. He turned the body over. A vacant pink face stared up out of eyes that were fixed, but bright. Not death—and not sleep.

Paradine had seen men in a swoon who looked like that. Yet even swooners breathed, and there was not a hair's line of motion under the dimmed brass buttons.

"Funny," thought Paradine, not meaning that he was amused. He walked on because there was nothing left to do. Just beyond that first fallen lad lay the rest of the patrol, still in the diamond-shaped formation they must have held when awake and erect. One man lay at the right side of the street, another opposite him at the left. The corporal was in the center and, to his rear, another private.

The corporal was, or had been, an excitable man. His hands clutched his musket firmly, his lips drew back from gritted teeth, his eyes were narrow instead of staring. A bit of awareness seemed to remain upon the set, stubbly face. Paradine forbore to prod him with the saber, but stooped and twitched up an eyelid. It snapped back into its squint. The corporal, too, lived but did not move.

"Wake up," Paradine urged him, as he had urged the boy. "You aren't dead." He straightened up, and stared at the more distant and numerous blue bodies in their fallen ranks. "None of you are dead!" he protested at the top of his lungs, unable to beat down his hysteria. "Wake up, Yankees!"

He was pleading with them to rise, even though he would be doomed if they did.

"Yee-hee!" he yelled. "You're all my prisoners! Up on your feet!"

"Yo're wastin' yore breath, son."

Paradine whirled like a top to face this sudden quiet rebuke.

A man stood in the front yard of a shabby house opposite, leaning on a picket fence. Paradine's first impression was of noble and vigorous old age, for a mighty cascade of white beard covered the speaker's chest, and his brow was fringed with thick cottony hair. But next moment Paradine saw that the brow was strangely narrow and sunken, that the mouth in the midst of its hoary ambush hung wryly slack, and that the eyes were bright but empty, like cheap imitation jewels.

The stranger moved slowly along the fence until he came to a gate. He pushed it creakily open, and moved across the dusty road toward Paradine. His body and legs were meager, even for an old man, and he shook and shuffled as though extremely feeble. His clothing was a hodgepodge of filthy tatters.

At any rate, he was no soldier foe. Paradine holstered his revolver, and leaned on his saber. The bearded one came close, making slow circuit of two fallen soldiers that lay in his path. Close at hand, he appeared as tall and gaunt as a flagstaff, and his beard was a fluttering white flag, but not for truce.

"I spoke to 'em," he said, quietly but definitely, "an' they dozed off like they was drunk."

"You mean these troops?"

"Who else, son? They come marchin' from them hills to the north. The folks scattered outa here like rabbits—all but me. I waited. An'—I put these here Yanks to sleep."

He reached under his veil of beard, apparently fumbling in the bosom of his ruined shirt. His brown old fork of a hand produced a dingy book, bound in gray paper.

"This does it," he said.

Paradine looked at the front cover. It bore the woodcut of an owl against a round moon.

The title was in black capitals:

JOHN GEORGE HOHMAN'S
POW-WOWS

OR

LONG LOST FRIEND

"Got it a long time back, from a Pennsylvany witch-man."

Paradine did not understand, and was not sure that he wanted to. He still wondered how so many fighting-men could lie stunned.

"I thought ye was a Yank, an' I'd missed ye somehow," the quiet old voice informed him. "That's a Yank sojer suit, hain't it? I was goin' to read ye some sleep words, but ye give the yell, an' I knew ye was secesh."

Paradine made a gesture, as though to brush away a troublesome fly. He must investigate further. Up the street he walked, among the prone soldiers.

It took him half an hour to complete his survey, walking from end to end of that unconscious host. He saw infantry, men and officers sprawling together in slack comradeship; three batteries of Parrott guns, still coupled to their limbers, with horses slumped in their harness and riders and drivers fallen in the dust beneath the wheels; a body of cavalry—it should have been scouting out front, thought Paradine professionally—all down and still, like a whole parkful of equestrian statues overturned; wagons; and finally, last of the procession save for a prudently placed rearguard, a little clutter of men in gold braid. He approached the oldest and stoutest of these, noting the two stars on the shoulder straps—a major general.

Paradine knelt, unbuttoned the frock coat, and felt in the pockets. Here were papers. The first he unfolded was the copy of an order:

General T. F. Kottler,
Commanding———Division, USA.

General:
    You will move immediately, with your entire force, taking up a
strong defensive position in the Channow Valley. . . .

This, then, was Kottler's Division. Paradine estimated the force as five thousand bluecoats, all veterans by the look of them, but nothing that his own comrades would have feared. He studied the wagon-train hungrily. It was packed with food and clothing, badly needed by the Confederacy. He would do well to get back and report his find. He turned, and saw that the old man with the white beard had followed him along the street.

"I reckon," he said to Paradine, in tones of mild reproach, "ye think I'm a-lyin' about puttin' these here Yanks to sleep."

Paradine smiled at him, as he might have smiled at an importunate child. "I didn't call you a liar," he temporized, "and the Yankees are certainly in dreamland. But I think there must be some natural explanation for—"

"Happen I kin show ye better'n tell ye," cut in the dotard. His paper-bound book was open in his scrawny hands. Stooping close to it, he began rapidly to mumble something. His voice suddenly rose, sounded almost young:

"Now, stand there till I tell ye to move!"

Paradine, standing, fought for explanations. What was happening to him could be believed, was even logical. Mesmerism, scholars called it, or a newer name, hypnotism.

As a boy he, Paradine, had amused himself by holding a hen's beak to the floor and drawing a chalk line therefrom. The hen could never move until he lifted it away from that mock tether. That was what now befell him, he was sure. His muscles were slack, or perhaps tense; he could not say by the feel. In any case, they were immovable. He could not move an eye. He could not loosen grip on his saber-hilt. Yes, hypnotism. If only he rationalized it, he could break the spell.

But he remained motionless, as though he were the little iron figure to which his horse was tethered, yonder at the foot of the street.

The old man surveyed him with a flicker of shrewdness in those bright eyes that had seemed foolish.

"I used only half power. Happen ye kin still hear me. So listen:

"My name's Teague. I live down yon by the crick. I'm a witch-man, an' my pappy was a witch-man afore me. He was the seventh son of a seventh son—an' I was *his* seventh son. I know conjer stuff—black an' white, forrard an' back'ard. It's my livin'.

"Folks in Channow make fun o' me, like they did o' my pappy when he was livin', but they buy my charms. Things to bring love or hate, if they hanker fer 'em. Cures fer sick hogs an' calves. Sayin's to drive away fever. All them things. I done it fer Channow folks all my life."

It was a proud pronouncement, Paradine realized. Here was the man diligent in business, who could stand before kings. So might speak a statesman who had long served his constituency, or the editor of a paper that had built respectful traditions, or a doctor who guarded a town's health for decades, or a blacksmith who took pride in his lifetime of skilled toil. This gaffer who called himself a witch-man considered that he had done service, and was entitled to respect and gratitude. The narrator went on, more grimly:

"Sometimes I been laffed at, an' told to mind my own bizness. Young 'uns has hooted, an' throwed stones. I coulda cursed 'em—but I didn't. Nossir. They's my friends an' neighbors—Channow folks. I kep' back evil from 'em."

The old figure straightened, the white beard jutted forward. An exultant note crept in.

"But when the Yanks come an' everybody run afore 'em but me, I didn't have no scruples! Invaders! Tyrants! Thievin' skunks in blue!" Teague sounded like a recruiting officer for a Texas regiment. "I didn't owe them nothin'—an' here in the street I faced 'em. I dug out this here little book, an' I read the sleep words to 'em. See," and the old hands gestured sweepingly, "they sleep till I tell 'em to wake. *If* I ever tell 'em!"

Paradine had to believe this tale of occult patriotism. There was nothing else to believe in its place. The old man who called himself Teague smiled twinklingly.

"Yo're secesh. Ye fight the Yanks. If ye'll be good, an' not gimme no argyments, blink yore left eye."

Power of blinking returned to that lid, and Paradine lowered it submissively.

"Now ye kin move again—I'll say the words."

He leafed through the book once more, and read out: "Ye horsemen an' footmen, conjered here at this time, ye may pass on in the name of . . ." Paradine did not catch the name, but it had a sound that chilled him. Next instant, motion was restored to his arms and legs. The blood tingled sharply in them, as if they had been asleep.

Teague offered him a hand, and Paradine took it. That hand was froggy cold and soft, for all its boniness.

"After this," decreed Teague, "do what I tell ye, or I'll read ye somethin' ye'll like less." And he held out the open book significantly.

Paradine saw the page—it bore the number 60 in one corner, and at its top was a heading in capitals: TO RELEASE SPELLBOUND PERSONS. Beneath were the lines with which Teague had set him in motion again, and among them were smudged inky marks.

"You've crossed out some words," Paradine said at once.

"Yep. An' wrote in others." Teague held the book closer to him.

Paradine felt yet another chill, and beat down a desire to turn away. He spoke again, because he felt that he should.

"It's the name of God that you've cut out, Teague. Not once, but three times. Isn't that blasphemy? And you've written in—"

"The name of somebody else." Teague's beard ruffled into a grin. "Young feller, ye don't understand. This book was wrote full of the name of God. That name is good—fer some things. But fer curses an' deaths an' overthrows, sech as this 'un— well, I changed the names an' spells by puttin' in that other name ye saw. An' it works fine." He grinned wider as he surveyed the tumbled thousands around them, then shut the book and put it away.

Paradine had been well educated. He had read Marlowe's *Dr. Faustus*, at the University of Virginia, and some accounts of the New England witchcraft cases. He could grasp, though he had never been called upon to consider, the idea of an alliance with evil. All he could reply was:

"I don't see more than five thousand Yankees in this town. Our boys can whip that many and more, without any spells."

Teague shook his old head. "Come on, let's go an' set on them steps," he invited, pointing.

The two walked back down the street, entered a yard and dropped down upon a porch. The shady leaves above them hung as silent as chips of stone. Through the fence-pickets showed the blue lumps of quiet that had been a fighting division of Federals. There was no voice, except Teague's.

"Ye don't grasp what war means, young feller. Sure, the South is winnin' now— but to win, men must die. Powder must burn. An' the South hain't got men an' powder enough to keep it up."

If Paradine had never thought of that before, neither had his superiors, except possibly General Lee. Yet it was plainly true.

Teague extended the argument:

"But if every Yank army was put to sleep, fast's it got in reach—what then? How'd ye like to lead yore own army into Washington an' grab ole Abe Lincoln right outen the White House? How'd ye like to be the second greatest man o' the South?"

"Second greatest man?" echoed Paradine breathlessly, forgetting to fear. He was being tempted as few chivalric idealists can endure. "Second only to—Robert E. Lee!"

The name of his general trembled on his lips. It trembles to this day, on the lips of those who remember. But Teague only snickered, and combed his beard with fingers like skinny sticks.

"Ye don't ketch on yet. Second man, not to Lee, but to—me, Teague! Fer I'd be a-runnin' things!"

Paradine, who had seen and heard so much to amaze him during the past hour, had yet the capacity to gasp. His saber was between his knees, and his hands tightened on the hilt until the knuckles turned pale. Teague gave no sign. He went on:

"I hain't never got no respect here in Channow. Happen it's time I showed 'em what I can do." His eyes studied the windrows of men he had caused to drop down like sickled wheat. Creases of proud triumph deepened around his eyes. "We'll do all the Yanks this way, son. Yore gen'rals hain't never done nothing like it, have they?"

His generals—Paradine had seen them on occasion. Jackson, named Stonewall for invincibility, kneeling in unashamed public prayer; Jeb Stuart, with his plume and his brown beard, listening to the clang of Sweeney's banjo; Hood, who outcharged even his wild Texans; Polk blessing the soldiers in the dawn before battle, like a prophet of brave old days; and Lee, the gray knight, at whom Teague had laughed. No, they had never done anything like it. And, if they could, they would not.

"Teague," said Paradine, "this isn't right."

"Not right? Oh, I know what ye mean. Ye don't like them names I wrote into the *Pow-Wows*, do ye? But ain't everything fair in love an' war?"

Teague laid a persuasive claw on the sleeve of Paradine's looted jacket. "Listen this oncet. Yore idee is to win with sword an' gun. Mine's to win by conjurin'. Which is the quickest way? The easiest way? The only way?"

"To my way of thinking, the only way is by fair fight. God," pronounced Paradine, as stiffly as Leonidas Polk himself, "watches armies."

"An' so does somebody else," responded Teague. "Watches—an' listens. Happen he's listenin' this minit. Well, lad, I need a sojer to figger army things fer me. You joinin' me?"

Not only Teague waited for Paradine's answer. . . . The young trooper remembered, from *Pilgrim's Progress*, what sort of dealings might be fatal. Slowly he got to his feet.

"The South doesn't need that kind of help," he said flatly.

"Too late to back out," Teague told him.

"What do you mean?"

"The help's been asked fer already, son. An' it's been given. A contract, ye might call it. If the contract's broke—well, happen the other party'll get mad. They can be worse enemies 'n Yanks."

Teague, too, rose to his feet. "Too late," he said again.

"That power can sweep armies away fer us. But if we say no—well, it's been roused up, it'll still sweep away armies—Southern armies. Ye think I shouldn't have started sech a thing? But I've started it. Can't turn back now."

Victory through evil—what would it become in the end? Faust's story told, and so did the legend of Gilles de Retz, and the play about Macbeth. But there was also the tale of the sorcerer's apprentice, and of what befell him when he tried to reject the force he had thoughtlessly evoked.

"What do you want me to do?" he asked, through lips that muddled the words.

"Good lad, I thought ye'd see sense. First off, I want yore name to the bargain. Then me 'n' you can lick the Yanks."

Lick the Yankees! Paradine remembered a gayly profane catch-phrase of the Confederate camp: "Don't say Yankee, say damned Yankee." But what about a damned Confederacy? Teague spoke of the day of victory; what of the day of reckoning?

What payment would this ally ask in the end?

Again Faust popped into his mind. He imagined the Confederacy as a Faust among the nations, devil-lifted, devil-nurtured—and devil-doomed, by the connivance of one Joseph Paradine.

Better disaster, in the way of man's warfare.

The bargain was offered him for all the South. For all the South he must reject, completely and finally.

Aloud he said: "My name? Signed to something?"

"Right here'll do."

Once more Teague brought forth the *Pow-Wows* book which he had edited so strangely. "Here, son, on this back page—in blood."

Paradine bowed his head. It was to conceal the look in his eyes, and he hoped to look as though he acquiesced. He drew his saber, passed it to his left hand. Upon its tip he pressed his right forefinger. A spot of dull pain, and a drop of blood creeping forth, as had appeared on the wrist of the ensorcelled boy lying yonder among the Yankees in the street.

"That'll be enough to sign with," approved Teague.

He flattened out the book, exposing the rear flyleaf. Paradine extended his reddened forefinger. It stained the rough white paper.

"J for Joseph," dictated Teague. "Yep, like that—"

Paradine galvanized into action. His bloody right hand seized the book, wrenching it from the trembling fingers. With the saber in his left hand, he struck.

A pretty stroke for even a practiced swordsman; the honed edge of the steel found the shaggy side of Teague's scrawny neck. Paradine felt bone impeding his powerful drawing slash. Then he felt it no longer. The neck had sliced in two, and for a moment Teague's head hung free in the air, like a lantern on a wire.

The bright eyes fixed Paradine's, the mouth fell open in the midst of the beard, trying to speak a word that would not come. Then it fell, bounced like a ball, and rolled away. The headless trunk stood on braced feet, crumpling slowly. Paradine stepped away from it, and it collapsed upon the steps of the house.

Again there was utter silence in the town and valley of Channow. The blue soldiers did not budge where they lay, Paradine knew that he alone moved and breathed and saw—no, not entirely alone. His horse was tethered at the end of the street.

He flung away his saber and ran, ashamed no more of his dread. Reaching the gray, he found his fingers shaky, but he wrenched loose the knotted reins. Flinging himself into the saddle, he rode away across the level and up the slope.

The pines sighed gently, and that sound gave him comfort after so much soundlessness.

He dismounted, his knees swaying as though their tendons had been cut, and studied the earth. Here were the footprints of Dauger's horse. Here also was a cleft stick, and in it a folded scrap of paper, a note. He lifted it, and read the penciled scrawl:

Dear frend Joe, you ant come back so I left like you said to bring up the boys. I hope your alright N if the Yankies have got you well get you back.

L. DAUGER

His comrades were coming, then, with gun and sword. They expected to meet Union soldiers. Paradine gazed back into the silence-brimmed valley, then at what he still held in his right hand. It was the *Pow-Wows* book, marked with a wet capital J in his own blood.

What had Teague insisted? The one whose name had been invoked would be fatally angry if his help were refused. But Paradine was going to refuse it.

He turned to Page 60. His voice was shaky, but he managed to read aloud:

"Ye horsemen and footmen, conjured here at this time, ye may pass on in the name of"—he faltered, but disregarded the ink-blotting, and the substituted names—"of Jesus Christ, and through the word of God."

Again he gulped, and finished. "Ye may now ride on and pass."

From under his feet burst a dry, startling thunder of sound, a partridge rising to the sky. Farther down the slope a crow took wing, cawing querulously. Wind wakened in the Channow Valley; Paradine saw the distant trees of the town stir with it. Then a confused din came to his ears, as though something besides wind was wakening.

After a moment he heard the notes of a bugle, shrill and tremulous, sounding an alarm.

Paradine struck fire, and built it up with fallen twigs. Into the hottest heart of it he thrust Teague's book of charms. The flame gnawed eagerly at it, the pages crumpled and fanned and blackened with the heat. For a moment he saw, standing out among charred fragments, a blood-red J, his writing, as though it fought for life. Then it, too, was consumed, and there were only ashes. Before the last red tongue subsided, his ears picked up a faint rebel yell, and afar into the valley rode Confederate cavalry.

He put his gray to the gallop, got down the slope and joined his regiment before it reached the town. On the street a Union line was forming. There was hot, fierce fighting, such as had scattered and routed many a Northern force.

But, at the end of it, the Southerners ran like foxes before hounds, and those who escaped counted themselves lucky.

IN HIS LATER GARRULOUS YEARS, Joseph Paradine was apt to say that the war was lost, not at Antietam or Gettysburg, but at a little valley hamlet called Channow. Refusal of a certain alliance, he would insist, was the cause; that offered ally fought thenceforth against the South.

But nobody paid attention, except to laugh or to pity. So many veterans go crazy.

THE HOWLING MAN

BY CHARLES BEAUMONT

LIKE WELLMAN BEFORE HIM, CHARLES BEAUMONT ALSO SAW A CERTAIN AMOUNT OF SUCCESS THROUGH ADAPTIONS OF HIS WORK ON *TWILIGHT ZONE*. BEAUMONT'S DOUBTING AMERICAN PROTAGONIST IS A DIRECT ANCESTOR OF KING'S SKEPTICS ON A COLLISION COURSE WITH TRUE EVIL. IN "THE HOWLING MAN" THE DEVIL IS ONCE AGAIN GIVEN HIS DUE, NAMELY ALL OF THE SUFFERING AND INHUMANITY OF MAN AGAINST MAN IN THE TWENTIETH CENTURY.

The Germany of that time was a land of valleys and mountains and swift dark rivers, a green and fertile land where everything grew tall and straight out of the earth. There was no other country like it. Stepping across the border from Belgium, where the rain-caped, mustached guards saluted, grinning, like operetta soldiers, you entered a different world entirely. Here the grass became as rich and smooth as velvet; deep, thick woods appeared; the air itself, which had been heavy with the French perfume of wines and sauces, changed: the clean, fresh smell of lakes and pines and boulders came into your lungs. You stood a moment, then, at the border, watching the circling hawks above and wondering, a little fearfully, how such a thing could happen. In less than a minute you had passed from a musty, ancient room, through an invisible door, into a kingdom of winds and light. Unbelievable! But there, at your heels, clearly in view, is Belgium, like all the rest of Europe, a faded tapestry from some forgotten mansion.

In that time, before I had heard of St. Wulfran's, of the wretch who clawed the stones of a locked cell, wailing in the midnight hours, or of the daft Brothers and their mad Abbot, I had strong legs and a mind on its last search, and I preferred to be alone. A while and I'll come back to this spot. We will ride and feel the sickness, fall, and hover on the edge of death, together. But I am not a writer, only one who loves wild, unhousebroken words; I must have a real beginning.

Paris beckoned in my youth. I heeded, for the reason most young men just out of college heed, although they would never admit it: to lie with mysterious beautiful women. A solid, traditional upbringing among the corseted ruins of Boston had succeeded, as such upbringings generally do, in honing the urge to a keen edge. My nightly dreams of beaded bagnios and dusky writhing houris, skilled beyond imagining, reached, finally, the unbearable stage beyond which lies either madness or respectability. Fancying neither, I managed to convince my parents that a year abroad would add exactly the right amount of seasoning to my maturity, like a dash of curry in an otherwise bland, if not altogether tasteless, chowder. I'm afraid that Father caught the hot glint in my eye, but he was kind. Describing, in detail, and with immense effect, the hideous consequences of profligacy, telling of men he knew who'd gone to Europe, innocently, and fallen into dissolutions so profound they'd not been heard of since, he begged me at all times to remember that I was an Ellington and turned me loose. Paris, of course, was enchanting and terrifying, as a jungle must be to a zoo-born monkey. Out of respect to the honored dead, and Dad, I did a quick trot through the Tuileries, the Louvre, and down the Champs-Elysées to the Arc de Triomphe; then, with the fall of night, I cannoned off to Montmartre and the Rue Pigalle, embarking on the Grand Adventure. Synoptically, it did not prove to be so grand as I'd imagined; nor was it, after the fourth week, so terribly adventurous. Still: important to what followed, for what followed doubtless wouldn't have but for the sweet complaisant girls.

Boston's Straights and Narrows don't, I fear, prepare one—except psychologically—for the Wild Life. My health broke in due course and, as my thirst had been well and truly slaked, I was not awfully discontent to sink back into the contemplative cocoon to which I was, apparently, more suited. Abed for a month I lay, in celibate silence and almost total inactivity. Then, no doubt as a final gesture of rebellion, I got my idea—got? or had my concentrated sins received it, like a signal from a failing tower?—and I made my strange, un-Ellingtonian decision. I would explore Europe. But not as a tourist, safe and fat in his fat, safe bus, insulated against the beauty and the ugliness of changing cultures by a pane of glass and a room at the English-speaking hotel. No. I would go like an unprotected wind, a seven-league-booted leaf, a nestless bird, and I would see this dark strange land with the vision of a boy on the last legs of his dreams. I would go by bicycle, poor and lonely and questing—as poor and lonely and questing, anyway, as one can be with a hundred thousand in the bank and a partnership in Ellington, Carruthers & Blake waiting.

So it was. New England blood and muscles wilted on that first day's pumping, but New England spirit toughened as the miles dropped back. Like an ant crawling over a once-lovely, now decayed and somewhat seedy Duchess, I rode over the body of Europe. I dined at restaurants where boars' heads hung, all vicious-tusked and blind; I slept at country inns and breathed the musty age, and sometimes girls came to the door and knocked and asked if I had everything I needed ("Well . . .") and they were better than the girls in Paris, though I can't imagine why. No matter. Out of France I pedaled, into Belgium, out, and to the place of cows and forests, mountains, brooks, and laughing people: Germany. (I've rhapsodized on purpose for I feel it's quite important to remember how completely Paradisical the land was then, at that time.)

I looked odd, standing there. The border guard asked what was loose with me, I answered Nothing—grateful for the German, and the French, Miss Finch had drummed into me—and set off along the smallest, darkest path. It serpentined through forests, cities, towns, villages, and always I followed its least likely appendages. Unreasonably, I pedaled as if toward a destination: into the Moselle Valley country, up into the desolate hills of emerald.

By a ferry, fallen to desuetude, the reptile drew me through a bosky wood. The trees closed in at once. I drank the fragrant air and pumped and kept on pumping, but a heat began to grow inside my body. My head began to ache. I felt weak. Two more miles and I was obliged to stop, for perspiration filmed my skin. You know the signs of pneumonia: a sapping of the strength, a trembling, flashes of heat and of cold; visions. I lay in the bed of damp leaves for a time, then forced myself onto the bicycle and rode for what seemed an endless time. At last a village came to view. A thirteenth-century village, gray and narrow-streeted, cobbled to the hidden store fronts. A number of old people in peasant costumes looked up as I bumped along, and I recall one ancient tallow-colored fellow—nothing more. Only the weakness, like acid, burning off my nerves and muscles. And an intervening blackness to pillow my fall.

I awoke to the smells of urine and hay. The fever had passed, but my arms and legs lay heavy as logs, my head throbbed horribly, and there was an empty shoveled-out hole inside my stomach somewhere. For a long while I did not move or open my eyes. Breathing was a major effort. But consciousness came, eventually.

I was in a tiny room. The walls and ceiling were of rough gray stone, the single glassless window was arch-shaped, the floor was uncombed dirt. My bed was not a bed at all but a blanket thrown across a disorderly pile of crinkly straw. Beside me, a crude table; upon it, a pitcher; beneath it, a bucket. Next to the table, a stool. And seated there, asleep, his tonsured head adangle from an Everest of robe, a monk.

I must have groaned, for the shorn pate bobbed up precipitately. Two silver trails gleamed down the corners of the suddenly exposed mouth, which drooped into a frown. The slumbrous eyes blinked.

"It is God's infinite mercy," sighed the gnomelike little man. "You have recovered."

"Not as yet," I told him. Unsuccessfully, I tried to remember what had happened; then I asked questions.

"I am Brother Christophorus. This is the Abbey of St. Wulfran's. The Burgermeister of Schwartzhof, Herr Barth, brought you to us nine days ago. Father Jerome said that you would die and he sent me to watch, for I have never seen a man die, and Father Jerome holds that it is beneficial for a Brother to have seen a man die. But now I suppose that you will not die." He shook his head ruefully.

"Your disappointment," I said, "cuts me to the quick. However, don't abandon hope. The way I feel now, it's touch and go."

"No," said Brother Christophorus sadly. "You will get well. It will take time. But you will get well."

"Such ingratitude, and after all you've done. How can I express my apologies?"

He blinked again. With the innocence of a child, he said, "I beg your pardon?"

"Nothing." I grumbled about blankets, a fire, some food to eat, and then slipped back into the well of sleep. A fever dream of forests full of giant two-headed beasts came, then the sound of screaming.

I awoke. The scream shrilled on—Klaxon-loud, high, cutting, like a cry for help.

"What is that sound?" I asked.

The monk smiled. "Sound? I hear no sound," he said.

It stopped. I nodded. "Dreaming. Probably I'll hear a good deal more before I'm through. I shouldn't have left Paris in such poor condition."

"No," he said. "You shouldn't have left Paris."

Kindly now, resigned to my recovery, Brother Christophorus became attentive to a fault. Nurselike, he spooned thick soups into me, applied compresses, chanted soothing prayers, and emptied the bucket out the window. Time passed slowly. As I fought the sickness, the dreams grew less vivid—but the nightly cries did not diminish. They were as full of terror and loneliness as before, strong, real in my ears. I tried to shut them out, but they would not be shut out. Still, how could they be strong and real except in my vanishing delirium? Brother Christophorus did not hear them. I watched him closely when the sunlight faded to the gray of dusk and the screams began, but he was deaf to them—if they existed. If they existed!

"Be still, my son. It is the fever that makes you hear these noises. That is quite natural. Is that not quite natural? Sleep."

"But the fever is gone! I'm sitting up now. Listen! Do you mean to tell me you don't hear *that*?"

"I hear only you, my son."

The screams, that fourteenth night, continued until dawn. They were totally unlike any sounds in my experience. Impossible to believe they could be uttered and sustained by a human, yet they did not seem to be animal. I listened, there in the gloom, my hands balled into fists, and knew, suddenly, that one of two things must be true. Either someone or something was making these ghastly sounds, and Brother Christophorus was lying, or—I was going mad. Hearing-voices mad, climbing-walls and frothing mad. I'd have to find the answer: that I knew. And by myself.

I listened with a new ear to the howls. Razoring under the door, they rose to operatic pitch, subsided, resumed, like the cries of a surly, hysterical child. To test their reality, I hummed beneath my breath, I covered my head with a blanketing, scratched at the straw, coughed. No difference. The quality of substance, of existence, was there. I tried, then, to localize the screams; and, on the fifteenth night, felt sure that they were coming from a spot not far along the hall.

"The sounds that maniacs hear seem quite real to them."

I know. I know!

The monk was by my side, he had not left it from the start, keeping steady vigil even through Matins. He joined his tremulous soprano to the distant chants, and prayed excessively. But nothing could tempt him away. The food we ate was brought to us, as were all other needs. I'd see the Abbot, Father Jerome, once I was recovered. Meanwhile . . .

"I'm feeling better, Brother. Perhaps you'd care to show me about the grounds. I've seen nothing of St. Wulfran's except this little room."

"There is only this little room multiplied. Ours is a rigorous order. The Franciscans, now, they permit themselves esthetic pleasure; we do not. It is, for us, a luxury. We have a single, most unusual job. There is nothing to see."

"But surely the Abbey is very old."

"Yes, that is true."

"As an antiquarian—"

"Mr. Ellington—"

"What is it you don't want me to see? What are you afraid of, Brother?"

"Mr. Ellington? I do not have the authority to grant your request. When you are well enough to leave, Father Jerome will no doubt be happy to accommodate you."

"Will he also be happy to explain the screams I've heard each night since I've been here?"

"Rest, my son. Rest."

The unholy, hackle-raising shriek burst loose and bounded off the hard stone walls. Brother Christophorus crossed himself, apropos of nothing, and sat like an ancient Indian on the weary stool. I knew he liked me. Especially, perhaps. We'd got along quite well in all our talks. But this—*verboten*.

I closed my eyes. I counted to three hundred. I opened my eyes.

The good monk was asleep. I blasphemed, softly, but he did not stir, so I swung my legs over the side of the straw bed and made my way across the dirt floor to the heavy wooden door. I rested there a time, in the candleless dark, listening to the howls; then, with Bostonian discretion, raised the bolt. The rusted hinges creaked, but Brother Christophorus was deep in celestial marble: his head drooped low upon his chest.

Panting, weak as a landlocked fish, I stumbled out into the corridor. The screams became impossibly loud. I put my hands to my ears, instinctively, and wondered how anyone could sleep with such a furor going on. It *was* a furor. In my mind? No. Real. The monastery shook with these shrill cries. You could feel their realness with your teeth.

I passed a Brother's cell and listened, then another; then I paused. A thick door, made of oak or pine, was locked before me. Behind it were the screams.

A chill went through me on the edge of those unutterable shrieks of hopeless, helpless anguish, and for a moment I considered turning back—not to my room, not to my bed of straw, but back into the open world. But duty held me. I took a breath and walked up to the narrow bar-crossed window and looked in.

A man was in the cell. On all fours, circling like a beast, his head thrown back, a man. The moonlight showed his face. It cannot be described—not, at least, by me. A man past death might look like this, a victim of the Inquisition rack, the stake, the pincers: not a human in the third decade of the twentieth century, surely. I had never seen such suffering within two eyes, such lost, mad suffering. Naked, he crawled about the dirt, cried, leaped up to his feet and clawed the hard stone walls in fury.

Then he saw me.

The screaming ceased. He huddled, blinking, in the corner of his cell. And then, as though unsure of what he saw, he walked right to the door.

In German, hissing: "Who are you?"

"David Ellington," I said. "Are you locked in? Why have they locked you in?"

He shook his head. "Be still, be still. You are not German?"

"No." I told him how I came to be at St. Wulfran's.

"Ah!" Trembling, his horny fingers closing on the bars, the naked man said: "Listen to me, we have only moments. They are mad. You hear? All mad. I was in the village, lying with my woman, when their crazy Abbot burst into the house and hit me with his heavy cross. I woke up here. They flogged me. I asked for food, they would not give it to me. They took my clothes. They threw me in this filthy room. They locked the door."

"Why?"

"Why?" He moaned. "I wish I knew. That's been the worst of it. Five years imprisoned, beaten, tortured, starved, and not a reason given, not a word to guess from— Mr. Ellington! I have sinned, but who has not? With my woman, quietly, alone with my woman, my love. And this God-drunk lunatic, Jerome, cannot stand it. Help me!"

His breath splashed on my face. I took a backward step and tried to think. I couldn't quite believe that in this century a thing so frightening could happen. Yet, the Abbey was secluded, above the world, timeless. What could not transpire here, secretly?

"I'll speak to the Abbot."

"No! I tell you, he's the maddest of them all. Say nothing to him."

"Then how can I help you?"

He pressed his mouth against the bars. "In one way only. Around Jerome's neck, there is a key. It fits this lock. If—"

"Mr. Ellington!"

I turned and faced a fierce El Greco painting of a man. White-bearded, prow-nosed, regal as an Emperor beneath the gray peaked robe, he came out of the darkness. "Mr. Ellington, I did not know that you were well enough to walk. Come with me, please."

The naked man began to weep hysterically. I felt a grip of steel about my arm. Through corridors, past snore-filled cells, the echoes of the weeping dying, we continued to a room.

"I must ask you to leave St. Wulfran's," the Abbot said. "We lack the proper facilities for care of the ill. Arrangements will be made in Schwartzhof—"

"One moment," I said. "While it's probably true that Brother Christophorus's ministrations saved my life—and certainly true that I owe you all a debt of gratitude—I've got to ask for an explanation of that man in the cell."

"What man?" the Abbot said softly.

"The one we just left, the one who's screamed all night long every night."

"No man has been screaming, Mr. Ellington."

Feeling suddenly very weak, I sat down and rested a few breaths' worth. Then I said, "Father Jerome—you are he? I am not necessarily an irreligious person, but neither could I be considered particularly religious. I know nothing of monasteries, what is permitted, what isn't. But I seriously doubt that you have the authority to imprison a man against his will."

"That is quite true. We have no such authority."

"Then why have you done so?"

The Abbot looked at me steadily. In a firm, inflexible voice, he said: "No man has been imprisoned at St. Wulfran's."

"He claims otherwise."

"Who claims otherwise?"

"The man in the cell at the end of the corridor."

"There is no man in the cell at the end of the corridor."

"I was talking with him!"

"You were talking with no man."

The conviction in his voice shocked me into momentary silence. I gripped the arms of the chair.

"You are ill, Mr. Ellington," the bearded holy man said. "You have suffered from delirium. You have heard and seen things which do not exist."

"That's true," I said. "But the man in the cell—whose voice I can hear now!—is not one of those things."

The Abbot shrugged. "Dreams can seem very real, my son."

I glanced at the leather thong about his turkey-gobbler neck, all but hidden beneath the beard. "Honest men make unconvincing liars," I lied convincingly. "Brother Christophorus has a way of looking at the floor whenever he denies the cries in the night. You look at me, but your voice loses its command. I can't imagine why, but you are both very intent upon keeping me away from the truth. Which is not only poor Christianity, but also poor psychology. For now I am quite curious indeed. You might as well tell me, Father; I'll find out eventually."

"What do you mean?"

"Only that. I'm sure the police will be interested to hear of a man imprisoned at the Abbey."

"I tell you, *there is no man!*"

"Very well. Let's forget the matter."

"Mr. Ellington—" The Abbot put his hands behind him. "The person in the cell is, ah, one of the Brothers. Yes. He is subject to . . . seizures, fits. You know fits? At these times, he becomes intractable. Violent. Dangerous! We're obliged to lock him in his cell, which you can surely understand."

"I understand," I said, "that you're still lying to me. If the answer were as simple as that, you'd not have gone through the elaborate business of pretending I was delirious. There'd have been no need. There's something more to it, but I can wait. Shall we go on to Schwartzhof?"

Father Jerome tugged at his beard viciously, as if it were some feathered demon come to taunt him. "Would you truly go to the police?" he asked.

"Would you?" I said. "In my position?"

He considered that for a long time, tugging the beard, nodding the prowed head; and the screams went on, so distant, so real. I thought of the naked man clawing in his filth.

"Well, Father?"

"Mr. Ellington, I see that I shall have to be honest with you—which is a great pity," he said. "Had I followed my original instinct and refused to allow you in the Abbey to begin with . . . but, I had no choice. You were near death. No physician was available. You would have perished. Still, perhaps that would have been better."

"My recovery seems to have disappointed a lot of people," I commented, "I assure you it was inadvertent."

The old man took no notice of this remark. Stuffing his mandarin hands into the sleeves of his robe, he spoke with great deliberation. "When I said that there was no man in the cell at the end of the corridor, I was telling the truth. Sit down, sir! Please! Now." He closed his eyes. "There is much to the story, much that you will not understand or believe. You are sophisticated, or feel that you are. You regard our life here, no doubt, as primitive—"

"In fact, I—"

"In fact, you do. I know the current theories. Monks are misfits, neurotics, sexual frustrates, and aberrants. They retreat from the world because they cannot cope with the world. Et cetera. You are surprised I know these things? My son, I was told by the one who began the theories!" He raised his head upward, revealing more of the leather thong. "Five years ago, Mr. Ellington, there were no screams at St. Wulfran's. This was an undistinguished little Abbey in the wild Black Mountain region, and its inmates' job was quite simply to serve God, to save what souls they could by constant prayer. At that time, not very long after the great war, the world was in chaos. Schwartzhof was not the happy village you see now. It was, my son, a resort for the sinful, a hive of vice and corruption, a pit for the unwary—and the wary also, if they had not strength. A Godless place! Forsaken, fornicators paraded the streets. Gambling was done. Robbery and murder, drunkenness, and evils so profound I cannot put them into words. In all the universe you could not have found a fouler pesthole, Mr. Ellington! The Abbots and the Brothers at St. Wulfran's succumbed for years to

Schwartzhof, I regret to say. Good men, lovers of God, chaste good men came here and fought but could not win against the black temptations. Finally it was decided that the Abbey should be closed. I heard of this and argued. 'Is that not surrender?' I said. 'Are we to bow before the strength of evil? Let me try, I beg you. Let me try to amplify the word of God that all in Schwartzhof shall hear and see their dark transgressions and repent!' "

The old man stood at the window, a trembling shade. His hands were now clutched together in a fervency of remembrance. "They asked," he said, "if I considered myself more virtuous than my predecessors that I should hope for success where they had failed. I answered that I did not, but that I had an advantage. I was a convert. Earlier I had walked with evil, and knew its face. My wish was granted. For a year. One year only. Rejoicing, Mr. Ellington, I came here; and one night, incognito, walked the streets of the village. The smell of evil was strong. Too strong, I thought—and I had reveled in the alleys of Morocco, I had seen the dens of Hong Kong, Paris, Spain. The orgies were too wild, the drunkards much too drunk, the profanities a great deal too profane. It was as if the evil of the world had been distilled and centered here, as if a pagan tribal chief, in hiding, had assembled all his rituals about him . . ." The Abbot nodded his head. "I thought of Rome, in her last days; of Byzantium; of—Eden. That was the first of many hints to come. No matter what they were. I returned to the Abbey and donned my holy robes and went back into Schwartzhof. I made myself conspicuous. Some jeered, some shrank away, a voice cried, 'Damn your foolish God!' And then a hand thrust out from darkness, touched my shoulder, and I heard: 'Now, Father, are you lost?' "

The Abbot brought his tightly clenched hands to his forehead and tapped his forehead.

"Mr. Ellington, I have some poor wine here. Please have some."

I drank, gratefully. Then the priest continued.

"I faced a man of average appearance. So average, indeed, that I felt I knew, then. 'No,' I told him, 'but you are lost!' He laughed a foul laugh. 'Are we not all, Father?' Then he said a most peculiar thing. He said his wife was dying and begged me to give her Extreme Unction. 'Please,' he said, 'in God's sweet name!' I was confused. We hurried to his house. A woman lay upon a bed, her body nude. 'It is a different Extreme Unction that I have in mind,' he whispered, laughing. 'It's the only kind, dear Father, that she understands. No other will have her! Pity! Pity on the poor soul lying there in all her suffering. Give her your Sceptre!' And the woman's arms came snaking, supplicating toward me, round and sensuous and hot . . .''

Father Jerome shuddered and paused. The shrieks, I thought, were growing louder from the hall. "Enough of that," he said. "I was quite sure then. I raised my cross and told the words I'd learned, and it was over. He screamed—as he's doing now—and fell upon his knees. He had not expected to be recognized, nor should he have been normally. But in my life, I'd seen him many times, in many guises. I brought him to the Abbey. I locked him in the cell. We chant his chains each day. And so, my son, you see why you must not speak of the things you've seen and heard?"

I shook my head, as if afraid the dream would end, as if reality would suddenly explode upon me. "Father Jerome," I said, "I haven't the vaguest idea of what you're talking about. Who is the man?"

"Are you such a fool, Mr. Ellington? That you must be told?"

"Yes!"

"Very well," said the Abbot. "He is Satan. Otherwise known as the Dark Angel, Asmodeus, Belial, Ahriman, Diabolus—the Devil."

I opened my mouth.

"I see you doubt me. That is bad. Think, Mr. Ellington, of the peace of the world in these five years. Of the prosperity, of the happiness. Think of this country, Germany, now. Is there another country like it? Since we caught the Devil and locked him up here, there have been no great wars, no overwhelming pestilences: only the sufferings man was meant to endure. Believe what I say, my son: I beg you. Try very hard to believe that the creature you spoke with is Satan himself. Fight your cynicism, for it is born of him; he is the father of cynicism, Mr. Ellington! His plan was to defeat God by implanting doubt in the minds of Heaven's subjects!" The Abbot cleared his throat. "Of course," he said, "we could never release anyone from St. Wulfran's who had any part of the Devil in him."

I stared at the old fanatic and thought of him prowling the streets, looking for sin; saw him standing outraged at the bold fornicator's bed, wheedling him into an invitation to the Abbey, closing that heavy door and locking it, and, because of the world's temporary postwar peace, clinging to his fantasy. What greater dream for a holy man than actually capturing the Devil!

"I believe you," I said.

"Truly?"

"Yes. I hesitated only because it seemed a trifle odd that Satan should have picked a little German village for his home."

"He moves around," the Abbot said. "Schwartzhof attracted him as lovely virgins attract perverts."

"I see."

"Do you? My son, do you?"

"Yes. I swear it. As a matter of fact, I thought he looked familiar, but I simply couldn't place him."

"Are you lying?"

"Father, I am a Bostonian."

"And you promise not to mention this to anyone?"

"I promise."

"Very well." The old man sighed. "I suppose," he said, "that you would not consider joining us as a Brother at the Abbey?"

"Believe me, Father, no one could admire the vocation more than I. But I am not worthy. No; it's quite out of the question. However, you have my word that your secret is safe with me."

He was very tired. Sound had, in these years, reversed for him: the screams had become silence, the sudden cessation of them, noise. The prisoner's quiet talk with me had awakened him from deep slumber. Now he nodded wearily, and I saw that what I had to do would not be difficult after all. Indeed, no more difficult than fetching the authorities.

I walked back to my cell, where Brother Christophorus still slept, and lay down. Two hours passed. I rose again and returned to the Abbot's quarters.

The door was closed but unlocked.

I eased it open, timing the creaks of the hinges with the screams of the prisoner. I tiptoed in. Father Jerome lay snoring in his bed.

Slowly, cautiously, I lifted out the leather thong, and was a bit astounded at my technique. No Ellington had ever burgled. Yet a force, not like experience, but like it, ruled my fingers. I found the knot. I worked it loose.

The warm iron key slid off into my hand.

The Abbot stirred, then settled, and I made my way into the hall.

The prisoner, when he saw me, rushed the bars. "He's told you lies, I'm sure of that!" he whispered hoarsely. "Disregard the filthy madman!"

"Don't stop screaming," I said.

"What?" He saw the key and nodded, then, and made his awful sounds. I thought at first the lock had rusted, but I worked the metal slowly and in time the key turned over.

Howling still, in a most dreadful way, the man stepped out into the corridor. I felt a momentary fright as his clawed hand reached up and touched my shoulder; but it passed. "Come on!" We ran insanely to the outer door, across the frosted ground, down toward the village.

The night was very black.

A terrible aching came into my legs. My throat went dry. I thought my heart would tear loose from its moorings. But I ran on.

"Wait."

Now the heat began.

"Wait."

By a row of shops I fell. My chest was full of pain, my head of fear: I knew the madmen would come swooping from their dark asylum on the hill. I cried out to the naked hairy man: "Stop! Help me!"

"Help you?" He laughed once, a high-pitched sound more awful than the screams had been; and then he turned and vanished in the moonless night.

I found a door, somehow.

The pounding brought a rifled burgher. Policemen came at last and listened to my story. But of course it was denied by Father Jerome and the Brothers of the Abbey.

"This poor traveler has suffered from the visions of pneumonia. There was no howling man at St. Wulfran's. No, no, certainly not. Absurd! Now, if Mr. Ellington would care to stay with us, we'd happily—no? Very well. I fear that you will be delirious a while, my son. The things you see will be quite real. Most real. You'll think—how quaint!—that you have loosed the Devil on the world and that the war to come—what war? But aren't there always wars? Of course!—you'll think that it's your fault"—those old eyes burning condemnation! Beak-nosed, bearded head atremble, rage in every word!—"that you'll have caused the misery and suffering and death. And nights you'll spend, awake, unsure, afraid. How foolish!"

Gnome of God, Christophorus, looked terrified and sad. He said to me, when Father Jerome swept furiously out: "My son, don't blame yourself. Your weakness was *his* lever. Doubt unlocked that door. Be comforted: we'll hunt *him* with our nets, and one day . . ."

One day, what?

I looked up at the Abbey of St. Wulfran's, framed by dawn, and started wondering, as I have wondered since ten thousand times, if it weren't true. Pneumonia breeds delirium; delirium breeds visions. Was it possible that I'd imagined all of this?

No. Not even back in Boston, growing dewlaps, paunches, wrinkles, sacks and money, at Ellington, Carruthers & Blake, could I accept that answer.

The monks were mad, I thought. Or: The howling man was mad. Or: The whole thing was a joke.

I went about my daily work, as every man must do, if sane, although he may have seen the dead rise up or freed a bottled djinn or fought a dragon, once, quite long ago.

But I could not forget. When the pictures of the carpenter from Braunau-am-Inn began to appear in all the papers, I grew uneasy; for I felt I'd seen this man before. When the carpenter invaded Poland, I was sure. And when the world was plunged into war and cities had their entrails blown asunder and that pleasant land I'd visited became a place of hate and death, I dreamed each night.

Each night I dreamed, until this week.

A card arrived. From Germany. A picture of the Moselle Valley is on one side, showing mountains fat with grapes and the dark Moselle, wine of these grapes.

On the other side of the card is a message. It is signed *"Brother Christophorus"* and reads (and reads and reads!):

"Rest now, my son. We have him back with us again."

TWENTY-THREE

BY AVRAM DAVIDSON

DESPITE NUMEROUS AWARDS (INCLUDING BOTH THE WORLD FANTASY AND EDGAR AWARDS), AVRAM DAVIDSON WAS NEVER CONSIDERED A HIGH-PROFILE WRITER BEFORE HIS DEATH IN 1993. PERHAPS THIS WAS BECAUSE HE SEEMED TO DO SO MANY THINGS WELL, FROM MYSTERY TO HIGH FANTASY TO ORIENTAL TALE, AND AS A RESULT HE WAS JUST TOO DIFFICULT TO PIGEONHOLE FOR SUCCESS.

IN "TWENTY-THREE" HE HAS A LITTLE FUN WITH A TWIST ON A LOVE-CRAFTIAN WEIRD TALE AS TEMPERED BY CERTAIN BITS OF AMERICANA, INCLUDING CERTAIN SECRET TEXTS OF COTTON MATHER.

Breakfast one day at the Sutters. Ellis looked up. "Say, do we have an Uncle Zachary?" he asked. Sound dies away, save for Samuel at an egg in its shell and Lewis clattering a coffee-spoon. Louise Sutter, their mother, slightly clears her throat. "Uncle Zachary had a weakness of the chest and his doctors thought he should go and live in the West where the air is dry. Samuel, don't fiddle. Lewis." If Ellis observes the difference between *Uncle Zachary has* and *Uncle Zachary had*, Ellis does not say so.

"Sidney Coolidge claims," is what Ellis next says.

"Sidney *Cool*idge!"—his sister Lucinda—"dirty-mouthed boy. Dirty-faced, too," she says.

Ellis emphatically agrees. "Dirty in lots of other places, too, say, you wouldn't believe—" His brother Lewis advises him to finish his fish-cake. His brother Samuel wants to know why they don't more often have bacon for breakfast, and Uncle Abel Sawyer, as though he had been waiting for the chance, says that bacon is *fourteen cents a pound!* Farmers never had it so good. Uncle Sawyer says. Aunt Effie (Sutter) Sawyer, pouring skim milk over something arid called Breakfast Food, declares, "The less pig, the more pie." Aunt Harriet Sutter looks at her nephews with perhaps something like foreboding. Perhaps not. What she says is not overheard. Aunt Sarah Sutter is looking at her plate. And the discussion as to what Aunt Effie Sawyer's saying means causes Uncle Zachary and Sidney Coolidge to be forgotten.

Agnes brings in the pie. The real and not the proverbial one. There is always pie. And always Agnes. Not always the same ones, of course.

Aunt Sarah eats well enough. And, as usual, she is silent.

AUNT SARAH IS USUALLY IN the same chair in the library and doesn't talk much, but saying this is not to describe a woman in rusty black with massive hands on ivory-headed walking-stick: no. Sarah is really quite slender, has been becomingly grey-haired since memory runs, wears something quite too chic to be called a pants-suit: and besides, pants-suits are yet to be invented. It is called *Aunt Sarah's house-costume* and she does not wear it out of doors. Usually the costume is grey, sometimes it has a small black checked pattern. Sarah reads a lot. There is no television in the world, the radio yet has ear-phones, and would it still had. If one asks, and few do, "What are you reading, Sarah?" one is quietly and quickly told the name of the author. Never the title. Once in a long while someone ventures to ask, "What's it about?" Really, what is Emerson, for example, *about?* A brief and level stare, and her eyes return to her book. Sarah does not suffer fools gladly.

Once, at least, Aunt Sarah tries to revive the pleasant old-fashioned custom of reading aloud to the family circle. Her choice is Longfellow's lovely poem *The Aftermath.*

When the summer fields are mown,
When the birds are fledged and flown,
  And the dry leaves strew the path,

With the falling of the snow,
With the cawing of the crow,
Once again the fields we mow
  And gather in the aftermath.

Not the sweet new grass with flowers
Is this harvesting of ours;
  Not the upland clover bloom;

But the rowan mixed with weeds,
Tangled tufts from marsh and meads,
Where the poppy drops its seeds,
  In the silence and the gloom.

The very brief silence at the poem's end is not broken by a murmur of pleasure; but by an alto, a tenor, and a baritone, guffaw. A voice says, "How well he knows—!" Says? Sneers?

Directly after this short poem comes by far a longer, beginning, *Should you ask me, whence these stories?* Nobody asks her, nobody at all. Aunt Sarah quietly closes the book. And—publically, at least—never opens it again. The custom is not revived.

She reads, too, things unpublished. Family histories, letters, journals, diaries: these things she reads downstairs in the library.

Aunt Sarah knows all about, for instance, the question of the twenty-two and a half acres of good meadow-land on which the good fortunes of the Sutter family (*of the County of Berne in the Switzers Land*) are founded. Well, the good fortunes of one part of the Sutter family. Some say that land is rightfully the property of another part of that family. It is more than twenty-two and a half acres, some say. A bit more, some say, a good bit more. Ill feelings are often caused in families by the division of property. Or by its non-division.

Upstairs or down Aunt Sarah plays solitaire, or sets out what is understood to be the Tarot.

Mostly she is silent. One tends to leave her alone.

Sutter sisters and daughters are quiet and almost plain: very well, then: *plain*. Sutter brothers and sons are something else, and although there are older Sutter women at home, there are no older Sutter men. Wars consume them, they go to far-off places and do not return and neither do they write. There are in these days only three young Sutter brothers at home, and then there are none. Of the older set, Gerald is generally understood to be somewhere very far off where he wears a burnoose or a turban and perhaps it is not true that a foreign ruler places a price upon his head. Kingston's name is on a cross in France in a place of many crosses row on row. Woodruff's name is not, although he, too, goes to France and never returns. Unless his mother's belief, seldom expressed aloud, is true. And that it *is* Woodruff Sutter who is buried in the Tomb of the Unknown Soldier.

And if the older brothers do leave some memories of unfortunate *incidents* at home, surely their heroic deeds abroad, one year apart, redeem them. And more. And more. *Valiant and courageous* (official). *Reckless and suicidal in bravery* (unofficial). *Come on, you sons of bitches, do you want to live forever?* . . . echoes . . . echoes . . . dying, dying, dying. . . .

The younger set of this generation of young men Sutters at home consists of Lewis, Ellis, and Samuel, boys of great charm and rascal beauty and of, one hears, increasingly devilish behavior. So the Headmaster of Afton says (this last phrase). For a while they are away at school or college; one by one (again and again) are expelled . . . run off . . . invited not to return from vacation . . . suspended . . . dismissed. . . . Uncle Sawyer, the non-Sutter who actually runs the business, thinks it is time they settle down and learn something about running it themselves. So one hears. Uncle Sawyer is perhaps an optimist.

They all live together in a large, an immense, wooden house overlooking a river with an American Indian name, the river which (with all its rights) is sometimes described as "a wholly-owned subsidiary of the Sutter family." Its waters are imponded by a series of dams and by each dam is a dirty brick building wherein wool from far and wide is washed . . . spun . . . woven . . . made into rugs and blankets said to wear like iron: these both perhaps more sought after formerly than presently.

The water, thus collected, washes and scours the wool and carries away the effluents of everything from sheep-dung to caustic soda and solute suint or wool-sweat and overwashes of stinking dyestuffs: it is long since the alewife or the shad are found in these streams. The Sutter Corporation collects the waters in its pens and ponds, releases them at times and between times to turn its wheels and fill its vats and, of later days, kindle its electricity. And if the river, restive, overflows its pent-up backwaters, converting tillable fields or sites for houses into sog and bog, nourishing on others' lands instead of hay or potatoes the coarse and uncommercial cat-tail, the rank and profitless goldenrod and purple milkweed, and the frail, pale wild white rose which cannot be cut and sold: why, what is this to the Corporation? nothing and less than nothing; let the former freeholders, if they will, take the Pauper's Oath and receive fifty cents a day viaticum and forfeit their suffrage: *root, hog, or die* is a saying worthy of the saints, and *pecunia non olet*, of the sages.

COUSIN CHESTER BOSWELL LIVES in a small house the other side of the Village green. This, and shares in the Sutter Corporation, constitute the larger part of his patrimony. Well . . . anyway, a *large* part. And a large part consists of an intense interest in local and familial history, and he shares this with Aunt Sarah. They also share a cousin

Waldo Sutter who lives in an even smaller house by a smaller river which has yet to know its place, unlike Waldo Sutter, who does not choose to get around much. Very rarely does Someone ask, "What does Waldo Sutter do?" and the answer is that *He* minds his own business. A . . . well . . . not exactly a message and not exactly a present but Something of Interest has come from him. As it has about once a year. Bridey has come in bearing a large brown paper bag, made in the days before paper bags were made by machinery. It is thick and heavy. And it is old. She says, "Waldo Sutter sends John Kelly with this to drop off if he's coming this way." And adds, "Waldo wants the bag back. And could you let him have a little kerosene in a bottle." The words and deeds are invariable. So is Aunt Sarah's nod as she empties the contents into a shallow wicker basket and hands over the bag. Bridey takes it and goes out.

Invariably, too, the bag (and now the basket) contains some old papers and an old book, which they all know the cousin (not a first cousin and not even a second) has had delivered at the back door. There is no other reason in the world why he would have been coming "this way," but John Kelly is Waldo Sutter's (only) tenant and no longer employable at the mill. Not for money or any other consideration would their conjoint cousin dispose of any books or papers to a historical society or a college library, a dealer, or collector; but month by month as they work their way out of the disintegrating boxes in his closely packed little house (it smells strongly of many things and the rare callers are perhaps grateful for the kerosene) he drops them in the old brown paper bag, its smell now too faint than to more than guess if it had once contained say fresh whole nutmegs or macouboy snuff or pigtail twist chewing tobacco. Candied ginger. Something for old man Waldo Sutter to smell now and then besides his rancid socks. And once a year he sends these fragments to the large house which he himself never enters by the back door *or* the front.

Bridey or Agnes or Katie is even now handing over the kerosene in a gallon-jug as per instructions . . . a *full* gallon jug. And giving Old Man Kelly a doughnut. Or a piece of johnnycake.

"Well, what have we here?" asks Chester Boswell. Lame, pensioned. Part of the patrimony. A patriot, Chester, even if *he* is not left for dead two days at Chickamauga; but merely breaks his leg in camp at Tampa before he can get to Cuba; Chester Boswell never hears the bugle-call at Kettle Hill, the bone has not healed well and there is always talk that it will have to be re-broken and re-set. When Chester Boswell comes to visit the large house—which is fairly often—he stays put for the whole day. "What have we *here?*" He adds, "This time."

Here, and Chester handles it ver-ry carefully, is a sadly broken old book, pages worn and foxed and stained with candle-grease (to Old Sutter, kerosene is a modern invention). He points the title out to his cousin Sarah. *Wonders of the Invisible World/by the Revd Mr Cotton Mather*, they exchange glances, she turns some soiled leaves, indicates with a finger the marginal notations; they nod. Out of the book slips a piece of flowered wallpaper, evidently trimmed with a knife. "Waste not, want not," Chester Boswell says. "Use it up. Wear it out. Make it do. Or do without." Part of the wisdom of their fathers. On the back of the wallpaper something is written with a lead-pencil made in the days when lead-pencils had lead in them and not graphite. He and she bend their heads to read. *Kin deamons marry?* "That's Crossley's writing. —Crossley's kind of question, too." The next question leaps across a vast sea of supposition. *Is the divorc leagle?* Crossley's spelling is not meticulous. But it is clear. *How are thes leagel and ill liegal children told apart?* How indeed; like someone better-known, Crossley Sutter does not stop for an answer: in smaller letters writes *prepar y° The* feast. Beneath that begins a list

 frsh Porke
 Samp

"When is the last time *I* ate samp?" asks Chester Boswell. "Boy," he answers. "Makes a rougher mush than regular hominy grits. *Well.* Taste and scent? No argument. Eh? Sal?" Aunt Sarah's part of the conversation is made chiefly by little motions of her mouth and brows. Though now and then she gestures. Slightly. *Feast?* Slattern hog and half-cracked corn? Crossley Sutter, their great-grandfather's half-brother, has not been known as a delicate eater. Has not been *deli*cate. Lines from his will are long repeated by generations of children when adults are not present. *To my Bastard son Nathaneal five pounds. To my basterd Son Slatheal Five pounds. To my imprudent dauhgther Prudence born in christain wedlock but most UnGreatful slutt Three cents and a buckit of ashes.*

 Still . . .

And what have they *here?* Prudence's long-missing will they have *here* and she has made many dispositions and someone's heavy hand has printed DIED INTE-STATE, for her will is not signed, impetuous death does not wait for that. Prudence is Waldo Sutter's grandmother. She has never married. Its presence here signifies that he has at last given up all hope of getting any of those bolts of cloth, that cherrywood furniture (is it anything like this cherrywood furniture), those cases of pewter plates, sets of best blue chinaware. *A little kerosene in a bottle.* Last time he sends sixteen Old Farmers Almanacs, 1810–1826, and a straight razor in a flaking case; the boys, amused, use it in turn.

 Old John Kelly is his only tenant, a gallon of lamp oil will last Waldo a long while, and the jugs are worth a penny apiece in trade. Pork. Samp. Chickamauga does not kill Waldo Sutter. Neither do the floods drown him. Certainly not the Spring freshets. Even if the Sutter company will not adjust its river-level to his comfort.

 What else is *here?* An old pamphlet on growing pot-herbs, an old booklet on raising silkworms (the smell is soon got used to), and exactly twenty small empty envelopes from a Department of Agriculture once generous with new types of seeds. All very old. But no doubt useful. And here is a note in age-browned ink on a part of a page torn from, it might be, one of those small bound "pocket-books" in which thrifty goodwives record sales of Best Brown Eggs in terms of shillings, for complete change-over to dollars and cents has to await the later 1850s; on it a short note:

 Salatheal Sutter
 old and mauger
 torn a part by wolves

And a note upon the note, in somewhat darker ink, the iron nib biting deep into the page NOT WOLVES
 No more.
 And also just such a tiny volume and Aunt Sarah at once finds the half-torn page

to match the torn-out note; in a tiny hand is neatly written, *John Q. Adams dead today.*

No more.

BUT ENOUGH OF ANCIENT HISTORY. Lewis, Ellis, and Samuel Sutter. "Charm and rascal beauty"? Yes. Increasingly "devilish behavior"? Yes. As children they are as sprightly and nimble as goat-kids. There is, later, something fawn-like (fa*u*n-like?) about the young Sutter boys, indeed devilishly bad as their behavior is sometimes said to be, eh? *their childish presences disarm*, eh? At twenty a growing heaviness becomes apparent, not fat, nothing like that, something immensely strong seems coming; the early wildness is replaced by a more deliberate quality, quite beyond description. And now they get into fights, fights—reports go about of a brutality which is not to be explained—though sometimes it has to be explained away.

Does Helen Sutter have a palsy? Dr. Brainert says no. Then what is the reason for the frequent trembling? Dr. Brainert prescribes this and suggests that. But Helen Sutter Woodruff Sutter continues so often to tremble. Aunt Harriet proposes a trip south. South Carolina. Northern Florida. "I will go with you," Aunt Harriet offers. "And Effie."

"There isn't enough money," Aunt Sawyer (Effie) says at once.

"There is enough money for that," her niece Lucinda insists. Cinda's sister Amy has married, and moved away to Portland, Oregon, which is about as far as she can move away and still keep her feet dry.

"Since Abel died," says her aunt, she means Uncle Sawyer, "there hasn't been enough money for anything." And, it is true that things seem shabbier in the very big house. Katie has died, and Mary, grown old, is retired. Neither has been replaced. Often there is talk of "having the carpenters in," but so far they are not being had. "I *wish* that the boys would set aside the nonsense. I *wish* that the boys would *take hold.*"

Aunt Harriet leaves for a moment the subject of Aiken or Vero Beach. "It is The Prohibition," she says. "The Volstead Act. It doesn't prevent. It *encourages.*"

Helen says that she hoped It would skip another generation. "I know that people blame Henry and me for marrying although we are cousins. But it had skipped two generations. And I had hoped It would skip this one, too." Tremble. Tremble. "If Kingston or Woodruff had lived. If Gerald . . ." Aunt Sarah's mouth moves. But she remains silent.

"Does no one hear from Gerald?" asks Chester Boswell.

A universal silence. *No* one hears from Gerald.

Aunt Harriet looks all around. Almost furtively. As though she knows she should not ask, she asks. "How much money was settled on the De Sousa family?"

Aunt Effie Sawyer is a lady, and ladies do not glare. Almost, though, she glares. "You know very well how much. One. Hundred. Thousand. *Dollars.* Taken out of capital." She does gasp, however, and she rolls up her eyes: tightens, but does not clench, her fists. "Out of *cap*ital."

Lucinda reminds them (yet again) of the condition of Harry De Sousa's body. Witnesses report how the red touring-car (is there another custom-painted red touring-car in all the world?) backs up and runs over Harry De Sousa again and again. "There are five small children," Lucinda says. "If there is ever a prosecution . . ." Her mother trembles, trembles. Perhaps she remembers other . . . *incidents*. . . . Before. *And* since. And other settlements.

It is long since that a settlement can be made (thus leaving Zachary free to ab-souatulate for Teckshus. *Free? Zachary? free?*) by giving someone a ninety-nine-year lease on an ice-house for ninety-nine dollars a year. And, anyway, there is only one ice-house, for

scarcely flows
the frozen Tanais
through a waste of snows

Talk, before that, of giving Waldo Sutter the lease? Talk.

Lucinda does not now remind them that she herself witnesses the near-death on North Main Street of the Universalist minister. She screams and screams, warnings to the Rev. Mr. Showalter, appeals to her brothers. Mr. Showalter, after stoically refusing to acknowledge danger in the red touring-car's furious approach, finally with a squeak of fear barely flings himself to safety; a contemporary—Dr. Nickolson the homeopath—extends shaking hands to hold the trembling cleric up; cries, "Don't tell *me* those boys don't have the witch-bump!" The Nickolsons have lived here almost as long as the Sutters: no love lost.

The red touring-car continues to tear along the street like a whirlwind, madcap yells, howls, and cries coming from the front seat: Lewis at the Wheel. Mr. Showalter has suffered such a shock that he must retire; will place charges: *duty!*—doesn't care about himself but cares about the public safety. Uncle Sawyer speaks soothingly and speaks and speaks and gives directions for a new roof to be put on the Meetinghouse. Mr. Showalter shakes his head. And on the Manse. Mr. Showalter slackens, but feels that someone must be taught a lesson. Uncle Sawyer mentions faith and hope. Uncle Sawyer settles a ten-year endowment on the Universalist pulpit's ever-faltering income. Mr. Showalter takes a vacation in the White Mountains, returns to preach with renewed vigor the doctrines of James Relly and Hosea Ballou (" *'No Hell! No Hell! No Hell! No Hell!' rings out the Universalist bell!"*)—But even Uncle Sawyer cannot keep this up forever. And, it turns out, neither can Lewis.

IF AUNT HARRIET PRETENDS to believe that her nephews' troubles stem from drink alone, *let* her. Does no one point out that Samuel, for example, does not drink. He is certainly never seen in any of the local saloons, but he is certainly talked about in them. "Sam Sutter? Know what they say about what his motto is? 'Women and children *first*,' that's what they say his motto is." People laugh at this. But their laughs are not nice ones.

Does Samuel suffer from amnesia? Sometimes people make references to the recent past, and his expression is a blank . . . that is if there can be a troubled blank. Can there be?

One afternoon in the early spring the ladies of the family are in the music room listening to the victrola. All, that is, save for Aunt Sarah, who is, as usual, in her place in the library wearing her neat house-costume; as usual, silent. Chester Boswell is, as usual, talking . . . perhaps in a lower tone of voice, even, than usual. "Gone upstairs to wash my hands," he says. "Samuel's door. Open." Everyone knows how such things are. One has *no* intention of looking. At all. But there is a slight movement and it catches one's attention, Chester's head turns automatically. Samuel is sitting at his desk, holding his head in his hands, motionless save for a slight fidget of the fingers in the hair, slight but incessant. Aunt Sarah looks up and at her cousin Chester when he says this, and he imitates for her this slight (but steady) motion, somehow restless, somehow steady, of Samuel's fingers as he holds his head in his hands.

"I don't like to see this," Chester Boswell murmurs. "That's how it all started with Lew . . ." That's how it *started* with Lew? And how does it end with Lew? For it does end. At the age of only twenty-three, Lewis takes up a heavy old Colt Navy revolver, once the property of Selah Sutter, Waldo's elder brother, and shoots himself. Fatally.

No note. As Samuel murmurs to Ellis at the service, "Not even a forwarding address."

Mother Sutter (Helen) "takes it better than we would have thought." How, better? Does she not have practice? Never mind about Zachary, she is only a child when Zachary so hastily lights out for the Territories . . . and for oblivion. He is her uncle . . . *great* uncle. Hardly counts . . . Uncle Zachary . . . though he lives on in local memory, in the minds and mouths of Sidney Coolidge and the like. Is Sid's an august name in these days? in this place? Less. Llewellyn in Wales. Cohen in Tel Aviv. *But.*

Kingston, Woodruff, Gerald. She doesn't see Kingston and Woodruff dead? She doesn't know for sure that Gerald—? She knows for sure. In her mind she sees them each dead a hundred thousand times. Perhaps there is even some comfort about Lewis. At least she touches the coffin. At least she stands by the grave. *She tries to live a little while without him, likes it not, and dies.* Waldo Sutter, he whom Chickamauga cannot kill, he whom none of them have seen in *years*, puts on his old Union uniform and attends the funeral. Stands apart, speaks to no one, is covertly observed by those curious to see if they can observe traces of the alleged blood of the Narragansetts . . . or even of a darker and more vigorous tribe. He speaks to no one; on his way home, whom Chickamauga does not kill or the wolves tear apart, collapses by the side of the road. Old John Kelly, hopefully skulking (he who should have known better than hope) to see if Waldo perhaps goes to the postfuneral feast, returning with victuals in his pocket, finds him dead.

His will: *Them as gotten everthing else as ought to ben mine, let them git all I have to leave. . . .*

And, one year later, one year and some months, Samuel at twenty-three, after something not less horrible for being less describable, Samuel rushes, roaring, naked, through the woods and dives into the water and swims outward with powerful strokes until vanishing from sight. This is shortly after Chester Boswell sees Samuel in the room with his head in his hands, motionless save for that fidget of the fingers. The rains have been heavy, the river is high, surely Samuel *knows* this? Surely Samuel knows that he is swimming *toward* the dam? They find him dead at the foot of it, drowned, and with many bones broken.

Ellis's once-high spirits, slackened when Lewis dies, seem now suddenly and entirely checked. There are no more stories told about him. One sees him no more at meals even; Agnes brings him up a tray: reports that he sits with head in hands, fingers trembling. Chester Boswell, Cousin Chester? His bad leg? It *is* re-broken and it is re-set. A room on the first floor in the large house is cleared up for him: the office of *Henry*, lost and forgotten *Henry*, husband to Helen, father of Kingston, Woodruff, Gerald, Lucinda, Amy, Lewis, Samuel, Ellis. And there Chester sleeps— what formal sleep he gets—although he spends most of his time in the library with his leg in its cast up on an ottoman; Chester still suffers from the sinking of the *Maine*, on which he never sets eyes, sometimes murmuring to silent Aunt Sarah, sometimes dozing, to awaken abruptly with a little groan. There is perhaps a slightly warmer relation between Ellis and Chester than with the other boys, has he been more like an uncle than a cousin? Ellis never comes down to see him, sends him no general or especial messages. *His* door is open only to Agnes, and, twice a day, the tray.

Down below, they wait. And wait. As each day lengthens, so the tension. Yes, even so, a dreadful shock when, one morning, a great crash. And a quite frightful human sound, part scream, and—"What the devil—" cries Chester Boswell. And now another and rather lesser crash, and the scene is one as long prepared for some set piece, for a second all gape, then a wild rush up the stairs, somehow today the carpenters have been gotten in at last, large strong men—the thud of shoulders against a shuddering door. Voices cry out in horror, there are screams and shouts and—

Silent Aunt Sarah sits silently; unmoving, her neatly trousered legs in the grey with the small black check. Trembling Chester Boswell sits, too, a prisoner of his patriot leg in its heavy cast. Turmoil, terror, tragedy. Ellis has been shaving, pauses in mid-stroke and cries out and pushes over the heavy piece of cherrywood furniture with the mirror and the basin, slashes his throat. *Deeply.* Doctor Brainert is summoned, can do nothing.

Perhaps an hour or so later when there is something more like quiet once again, Chester Boswell, "*Why*," he asks, in a trembling voice, "*Why* do all these devilish tragedies always seem to happen when they are twenty-three? Don't they always seem to happen when—"

Aunt Sarah breaks her silence. Her long, long silence. "Of course," she says. "That is when the horns begin to grow."

She leans forward and she begins to talk. And talk.

The "new" family burying-grounds make up part of the original property of twenty-two and a half acres. Some say, it is a bit more than that. A good bit more than that, some say.

WE ARE THE DEAD

BY HENRY KUTTNER

HENRY KUTTNER WAS A MASTER OF THE SCIENCE FICTION AND FANTASY PULPS. MANY MIGHT ARGUE THAT MOST OF HIS FANTASTIC WORKS WIND UP WITH RATIONALIST AND PSEUDOSCIENTIFIC EXPLANATIONS THAT TAKE THEM OUT OF THE REALM OF FANTASY AND INTO THE REALM OF SCIENCE FICTION IN THE LAST FEW PAGES OF THE STORY. IN "WE ARE THE DEAD," HOWEVER, HIS SUBJECT MATTER IS DECIDEDLY MORE DOWN TO EARTH.

Senator Kennicott was grateful for the cool night wind on his flushed face. He wished Hobson, walking slowly at his side, would stop his interminable argument about the bill. The man's high-pitched, rather unpleasant voice seemed out of place, incongruous in the peaceful hush of Arlington Cemetery.

Hobson was panting a little, his fleshy, well-massaged face creased in annoyance. The walk through the cemetery had been no hardship to the slim, whipcord body of the Senator, but Hobson was not used to walking. Kennicott had felt that a stroll homeward from the banquet would calm his turbulent thoughts, excited by the innumerable activities of Memorial Day; and Hobson, anxious to settle the matter of the bill, had rather unwillingly decided to accompany him.

"It may bring us closer to war," the Senator said, breaking in sharply on Hobson's involved explanation.

"Not at all. It's merely preparedness." Hobson's sharp little eyes searched the other's face. "We must protect American interests in foreign countries. Surely—"

"But this is very—aggressive," Kennicott objected. "After all, we don't want the hatred of other countries."

"Oh, come now! That's going it a bit strong. I've already explained how—"

"But—war," the Senator said, looking absently at a tombstone in the distance.

"There'll be no war," Hobson insisted somewhat shrilly. "If I thought this bill were really dangerous I'd be the first to demand its withdrawal."

"How much do you stand to make out of it?" the Senator asked abruptly. "Well—never mind. That's scarcely a fair question. Can't we let this go till tomorrow, Hobson? I'm so utterly tired!"

Hobson stared at him for a moment. Then, choosing his words with care, he said, "The bill really should go through, Senator. I think it will—assure your securing the nomination next year."

Kennicott looked at him keenly, little lines bracketing his mouth. Hobson's support was valuable—in fact, indispensable. If he were to withdraw it—

Glancing sideways at his companion, the Senator almost walked into a shadowy, slim figure that stood quietly in the darkness beneath a tall elm.

A drawn, white face was turned to Kennicott, and he felt a sudden sense of shock at the agony in the dark, brooding eyes. It was a young man, almost a boy, with deep lines of pain etched in his face.

"I'm sorry," the Senator said quickly, glancing at the boy's faded, worn khaki uniform. "I didn't see you."

The boy made no answer, and the Senator made a tentative movement to pass on. Abruptly the youthful, haggard face was turned away, and the boy said in a muffled tone, "I can't sleep."

"Eh?" Kennicott stared.

"I say I can't sleep," the boy repeated, his voice dull with pain.

Hobson made a clucking sound of commiseration and glanced at the Senator.

Kennicott felt a surge of sympathy. The obvious youthfulness of the boy was so incongruous with his taut face, the white tortured line of his lips.

"I know," Kennicott said. "It can be terrible. I had insomnia for almost a week once."

"A week," the other said scornfully. "That's nothing. It's been ages—"

Kennicott was scribbling something on the back of an envelope. "Be with you in a minute," he said under his breath to Hobson, who was chafing at the delay. "Here— any druggist can fill this," he said, giving the paper to the boy. "It will fix you up if anything can. I know how you feel," he ended sympathetically.

The youth took it skeptically and thrust it into a pocket. "Thanks just the same," he said oddly. "It's always like this on Memorial Day—it's worse then, you know."

HOBSON MOVED IMPATIENTLY, his pale eyes flickering uneasily over the boy's form.

"Oh," the Senator said understandingly. "I see—but—look here, aren't you rather young to—"

"Am I?" the youth asked. "I'm not so young as I look. I was in the war, all right."

Hobson gave a grunt of disbelief. Even the Senator felt that the boy was lying. True, his face was worn, haggard—but he couldn't be over twenty-five at most. Probably he didn't mean the World War. There were always battles going on—Manchuria, South America, Africa.

"Well—you get those powders," the Senator said after an awkward pause. "I'm sure they'll do the trick." He cleared his throat. "Can you use—" He drew out his wallet rather hesitantly, but the boy was not offended.

"No, thanks," he said, a boyish grin suddenly appearing on his face. Then it was gone, replaced by that strained expression of pain. He suddenly seemed to notice a low, gray tombstone nearby, and took a few slow steps toward it. "Poor fool," he murmured very softly.

The Senator looked away quickly. It was a shock to hear Hobson's high-pitched, rasping voice. Had the man no intelligence, no decency? Kennicott put up a restraining hand, but it was too late.

"Oh—come, come," Hobson was saying. "Don't say a thing like that, son. It isn't right."

"Come on," Kennicott urged under his breath, but the boy interrupted him.

"Why not?" he asked, a sharp note in his tired young voice. "Wasn't he a fool?"

Hobson would try to argue with the boy, the Senator thought hopelessly. Couldn't he see that—

"You're too young. You don't understand what he died for—what his comrades died for," Hobson said, his plump face very earnest.

"Does it matter?" the boy asked very quietly. "They—died."

"They died for something very real," Hobson plowed on. "If they could—"

"For God's sake, come on," Kennicott snapped, grasping Hobson's arm. "Leave him alone. Can't you see—"

"All right," the boy said suddenly. "Maybe you're right. But—let me tell you a little story." He came closer, his eyes dark and tortured. "About a fellow who went over to France in '17. Just an ordinary fellow, I guess—who was scared stiff when the shells started bursting around, and the machine-guns were making their racket in the dark. But he was like the rest of the fellows. He didn't dare show how much he was afraid. A sniper got him in '18."

The Senator was uncomfortable and showed it, but to his disgust he saw that Hobson was preparing to answer the boy.

"Wait—let me finish. A sniper got him, I said, and that was fine. He didn't hear the bullets screaming over the trench, or the groaning of dying men; all the horrors were gone, and he was resting, forgetting. The darkness was kind . . . and then one day he awoke."

"Eh?" That was Hobson, frankly staring.

"I say he woke up. Glory woke him up—splendor and a stone monument that was very heavy. Bitter glory and squalid splendor," the boy went on fiercely. "They tortured and shamed him. You see, he was awake now, and he wanted—God!—how he wanted to *forget!*"

There were tears in the tortured eyes, and the boy brushed them away roughly with his sleeve. Then, catching his breath in a little gasp, he turned suddenly and began to walk quickly away.

For a heartbeat the Senator stood silent, unmoving, staring at that slim khaki figure receding into the gloom. "Wait," he called.

"Let him go," Hobson said, an angry undercurrent in his voice. "You can't—"

But Kennicott was remembering that white, drawn face, those brooding eyes from which all the youthfulness had been drained. "No—I've got to—" he said in an inarticulate aside to Hobson and took a few hasty steps forward. He saw the pale blur that was the boy's face turned toward him briefly, and the slender figure increased its pace. Ignoring Hobson's remonstrances, the Senator began to hurry after the boy.

KENNICOTT HAD TO EXERT HIMSELF to overtake his quarry, and was glad that his muscles were still firm and elastic. He saw the boy turn hastily down a side path, and broke into a run. For a hundred feet or so the path was very dark, and then it broadened out into a large clearing. At its edge Kennicott swept a searching glance around, and jerked abruptly to a halt. His jaw dropped.

A moment later Hobson pounded up, wheezing a little. He paused, scrutinizing Kennicott's face. "What's the matter?" he asked quickly.

The Senator did not answer, and Hobson repeated his question. Then Kennicott turned a startled, almost frightened face to his companion. "Did—did you see that?" he asked unsteadily.

"What?" Hobson glanced around. "The boy? He's gone."

"He's—yes, he's gone. Hobson, I—I saw—" He brushed a hand across his eyes. "Hobson—can a man *vanish?*"

"What?" Hobson stared, his mouth open. "A—a man—"

"But I saw it!" the Senator said earnestly, as though pleading for belief. "That boy—wasn't—" He pointed toward a great white block in the center of the clearing. "It was right there—I—I—saw—" He could not finish.

"What are you talking about?" Hobson's voice was purposely crisp and peremptory. "You're all unnerved. Come on—the boy's gone. We can't stay here."

"You go on," Kennicott said suddenly. "I'm going to—stay here for a while."

Hobson hesitated. Then, making up his mind, he drew a paper from his pocket, held it out. "Here's the bill, then. I'll phone you tomorrow."

Kennicott made no move. He said dully, "The bill. No, no, I can't—"

"Look here," Hobson said furiously. "You're not going to act like a damned fool, are you? What the devil's the matter?"

The Senator turned to him a face of white marble and said nothing.

Hobson hesitated, and then his rage pushed aside his diplomacy, his caution. "Because—by Heaven, I can break you," he snarled. "You're not President yet! I can ruin your career, and you know it."

"I know it," the Senator said quietly. "But that bill won't pass while I'm in the Senate." He turned his back on Hobson and stood silently gazing at the gaunt white mausoleum in the clearing. He had spoken patriotically and at length there not six hours before.

It was the tomb of the Unknown Soldier.

WHERE THE SUMMER ENDS

BY KARL EDWARD WAGNER

LIKE DAVID DRAKE, KARL EDWARD WAGNER WAS ALSO A LITERARY DISCIPLE OF MANLY WADE WELLMAN'S, THOUGH HIS OWN SIGNATURE WORKS WERE OF A MUCH DARKER VARIETY. IN ADDITION TO FOLLOWING IN THE CONAN TRADITION OF ROBERT HOWARD (AS WELL AS IN HIS OWN KANE SERIES), WAGNER WAS A MASTER OF CONVEYING DREAD AND THE ANTICIPATION OF DOOM IN HIS DARK FANTASIES AND HORROR TALES. IN "WHERE THE SUMMER ENDS" WAGNER TREATS THE READER TO A DEADLY HORROR THAT LIES JUST BENEATH THE ORDINARY SURFACE, OR IN THIS CASE, THE EVER-PRESENT KUDZU OF AMERICA.

A long Grand Avenue they've torn the houses down, and left emptiness in their place. On one side a tangle of viaducts, railroad yards, and expressways—a scar of concrete and cinder and iron that divides black slum from student ghetto in downtown Knoxville. On the other side, ascending the ridge, shabby relics of Victorian and Edwardian elegance, slowly decaying beneath too many layers of cheap paint and soot and squalor. Most were broken into tawdry apartments—housing for the students at the university that sprawled across the next ridge. Closer to the university, sections had been razed to make room for featureless emplacements of asphalt and imitation used-brick—apartments for the wealthier students. But along Grand Avenue they tore the houses down and left only vacant weed-lots in their place.

Shouldered by the encroaching kudzu, the sidewalks still ran along one side of Grand Avenue, passing beside the tracks and the decrepit shells of disused warehouses. Across the street, against the foot of the ridge, the long blocks of empty lots rotted beneath a jungle of rampant vine—the buried house sites marked by ragged stumps of blackened timbers and low depressions of tumbled-in cellars. Discarded refrigerators and gutted hulks of television sets rusted amidst the weeds and omnipresent litter of beer cans and broken bottles. A green pall over the dismal ruin, the relentless tide of kudzu claimed Grand Avenue.

Once it had been a "grand avenue," Mercer reflected, although those years had passed long before his time. He paused on the cracked pavement to consider the forlorn row of electroliers with their antique lozenge-paned lamps that still lined this block of Grand Avenue. Only the sidewalk and the forgotten electroliers—curiously spared by vandals—remained as evidence that this kudzu-festooned wasteland had ever been an elegant downtown neighborhood.

Mercer wiped his perspiring face and shifted the half-gallon jug of cheap burgundy to his other hand. Cold beer would go better today, but Gradie liked wine. The late-afternoon sun struck a shimmering haze from the expanses of black pavement and riotous weed-lots, reminding Mercer of the whorled distortions viewed through antique windowpanes. The air was heavy with the hot stench of asphalt and decaying refuse and Knoxville's greasy smog. Like the murmur of fretful surf, afternoon traffic grumbled along the nearby expressway.

As he trudged along the skewed paving, he could smell a breath of magnolia through the urban miasma. That would be the sickly tree in the vacant lot across from Gradie's—somehow overlooked when the house there had been pulled down and the shrubbery uprooted—now poisoned by smog and strangled beneath the consuming masses of kudzu. Increasing his pace as he neared Gradie's refuge, Mercer reminded himself that he had less than twenty bucks for the rest of this month, and that there was a matter of groceries.

Traffic on the Western Avenue Viaduct snarled overhead as he passed in the gloom beneath—watchful for the winos who often huddled beneath the concrete arches. He kept his free hand stuffed in his jeans pocket over the double-barreled .357-Magnum derringer—carried habitually since a mugging a year ago. The area was deserted at this time of day, and Mercer climbed unchallenged past the railyards and along the unfrequented street to Gradie's house. Here as well, the weeds buried abandoned lots, and the kudzu was denser than he remembered from his previous visit. Trailing vines and smothered trees arcaded the sidewalk, forcing him into the street. Mercer heard a sudden rustle deep beneath the verdant tangle as he crossed to Gradie's gate, and he thought unpleasantly of the gargantuan rats he had glimpsed lying dead in gutters near here.

Gradie's house was one of the last few dwellings left standing in this waste—certainly it was the only one to be regularly inhabited. The other sagging shells of gaping windows and rotting board were almost too dilapidated even to shelter the winos and vagrants who squatted hereabouts.

The gate resisted his hand for an instant—mired over with the fast-growing kudzu that had so overwhelmed the low fence, until Mercer had no impression whether it was of wire or pickets. Chickens flopped and scattered as he shoved past the gate. A brown and yellow dog, whose ancestry might once have contained a trace of German shepherd, growled from his post beneath the wooden porch steps. A cluster of silver maples threw a moth-eaten blanket of shade over the yard. Eyes still dazzled from the glare of the pavement, Mercer needed a moment to adjust his vision to the sooty gloom within. By then Gradie was leaning the shotgun back amidst the deeper shadows of the doorway, stepping onto the low porch to greet him.

"Goddamn winos," Gradie muttered, watching Mercer's eyes.

"Much trouble with stealing?" the younger man asked.

"Some," Gradie grunted. "And the goddamn kids. Hush up that growling, Sheriff!"

He glanced protectively across the enclosed yard and its ramshackle dwelling. Beneath the trees, in crates and barrels, crude stands and disordered heaps, lying against the flimsy walls of the house, stuffed into the outbuildings: the plunder of the junk piles of another era.

It was a private junkyard of the sort found throughout any urban slum, smaller than some, perhaps a fraction more tawdry. Certainly it was as out-of-the-way as any. Mercer, who lived in the nearby student quarter, had stumbled upon it quite by accident only a few months before—during an afternoon's hike along the railroad tracks. He had gleaned two rather nice blue-green insulators and a brown-glass Coke bottle by the time he caught sight of Gradie's patch of stunted vegetables between the tracks and the house that Mercer had never noticed from the street. A closer look had disclosed the yard with its moraine of cast-off salvage, and a badly weathered sign that evidently had once read "Red's Second Hand" before a later hand had overpainted "Antiques."

A few purchases—very minor, but then Mercer had never seen another customer here—and several afternoons of digging through Gradie's trove, had spurred that sort of casual friendship that exists between collector and dealer. Mercer's interest in "collectibles" far outstripped his budget; Gradie seemed lonely, liked to talk, very much liked to drink wine. Mercer had hopes of talking the older man down to a reasonable figure on the mahogany mantel he coveted.

"I'll get some glasses." Gradie acknowledged the jug of burgundy. He disappeared into the cluttered interior. From the direction of the kitchen came a clatter and sputter of the tap.

Mercer was examining a stand of old bottles, arrayed on their warped and unpainted shelves like a row of targets balanced on a fence for execution by boys and a new .22. Gradie, two jelly glasses sloshing with burgundy, reappeared at the murkiness of the doorway, squinting blindly against the sun's glare. Mercer thought of a greying groundhog, or a narrow-eyed packrat, crawling out of its burrow—an image tinted grey and green through the shimmering curvatures of the bottles, iridescently filmed with a patina of age and cinder.

He had the thin, worn features that would have been thin and watchful as a child, would only get thinner and more watchful with the years. The limp sandy hair might have been red before the sun bleached it and the years leeched it to a yellow-grey. Gradie was tall, probably had been taller than Mercer before his stance froze into a slouch and then into a stoop, and had a dirty sparseness to his frame that called to mind the scarred mongrel dog that growled from beneath the steps. Mercer guessed he was probably no younger than fifty and probably not much older than eighty.

Reaching between two opalescent-sheened whiskey bottles, Mercer accepted a glass of wine. Distorted through the rows of bottles Gradie's face was watchful. His bright slits of colorless eyes flicked to follow the other's every motion—this through force of habit: Gradie trusted the student well enough.

"Got some more of those over by the fence." Gradie pointed. "In that box there. Got some good ones. This old boy dug them, some place in Vestal, traded the whole lot to me for that R.C. Cola thermometer you was looking at once before." The last with a slight sly smile, flicked lizard-quick across his thin lips: Mercer had argued that the price on the thermometer was too high.

Mercer grunted noncommittally, dutifully followed Gradie's gesture. There might be something in the half-collapsed box. It was a mistake to show interest in any item you really wanted, he had learned—as he had learned that Gradie's eyes were quick to discern the faintest show of interest. The too-quick reach for a certain item, the wrong inflection in a casual "How much?" might make the difference between two bits and two bucks for a dusty book or a rusted skillet. The matter of the mahogany mantelpiece wanted careful handling.

Mercer squatted beside the carton, stirring the bottles gingerly. He was heavyset, too young and too well-muscled to be called beefy. Sporadic employment on construction jobs and a more-or-less adhered-to program of workouts kept any beer gut from spilling over his wide belt, and his jeans and tank top fitted him as snugly as the older man's faded work clothes hung shapelessly. Mercer had a neatly trimmed beard and subtly receding hairline to his longish black hair that suggested an older grad student as he walked across campus, although he was still working for his bachelor's—in a major that had started out in psychology and eventually meandered into fine arts.

The bottles had been hastily washed. Crusts of cinder and dirt obscured the cracked and chipped exteriors and, within, mats of spider-web and moldy moss. A cobalt-blue bitters bottle might clean up nicely, catch the sun on the hallway window ledge, if Gradie would take less than a buck.

Mercer nudged a lavender-hued whiskey bottle. "How much for these?"

"I'll sell you those big ones for two, those little ones for one-fifty."

"I could dig them myself for free," Mercer scoffed. "These weed-lots along Grand are full of old junk heaps."

"Take anything in the box for a buck then," Gradie urged him. "Only don't go poking around those goddamn weed-lots. Under that kudzu. I wouldn't crawl into that goddamn vine for any money!"

"Snakes?" Mercer inquired politely.

Gradie shrugged, gulped the rest of his wine. "Snakes or worse. It was in the kudzu they found old Morny."

Mercer tilted his glass. In the afternoon sun the burgundy had a heady reek of hot alcohol, glinted like bright blood. "The cops ever find out who killed him?"

Gradie spat. "Who gives a damn what happens to old winos."

"When they start slicing each other up like that, the cops had damn well better do something."

"Shit!" Gradie contemplated his empty glass, glanced toward the bottle on the porch. "What do they know about knives. You cut a man if you're just fighting; you stab him if you want him dead. You don't slice a man up so there's not a whole strip of skin left on him."

II

"But it had to have been a gang of winos," Linda decided. She selected another yellow flower from the dried bouquet, inserted it into the bitters bottle.

"I think that red one," Mercer suggested.

"Don't you remember that poor old man they found last spring? All beaten to death in an abandoned house. And they caught the creeps who did it to him—they were a couple of his old drinking buddies, and they never did find out why."

"That was over in Lonsdale," Mercer told her. "Around here the pigs decided it was the work of hippy-dope-fiends, hassled a few street people, forgot the whole deal."

Linda trimmed an inch from the dried stalk, jabbed the red straw-flower into the narrow neck. Stretching from her bare toes, she reached the bitters bottle to the window shelf. The morning sun, spilling into the foyer of the old house, pierced the cobalt-blue glass in an azure star.

"How much did you say it cost, Jon?" She had spent an hour scrubbing at the bottle with the test tube brushes a former roommate had left behind.

"Fifty cents," Mercer lied. "I think what probably happened was that old Morny got mugged, and the rats got to him before they found his body."

"That's really nice," Linda judged. "I mean, the bottle." Freckled arms akimbo, sleeves rolled up on old blue workshirt, faded blue jeans, morning sun a nimbus through her whiskey-colored close curls, eyes two shades darker than the azure star.

Mercer remembered the half-smoked joint on the hall balustrade, struck a match. "God knows, there are rats big enough to do that to a body down under the kudzu. I'm sure it was rats that killed Midnight last spring."

"Poor old tomcat," Linda mourned. She had moved in with Mercer about a month before it happened, remembered his stony grief when their search had turned up the mutilated cat. "The city ought to clear off those weed-lots."

"All they ever do is knock down the houses," Mercer got out, between puffs. "Condemn them so you can't fix them up again. Tear them down so the winos can't crash inside."

"Wasn't that what Morny was doing? Tearing them down, I mean?"

"Sort of." Mercer coughed. "He and Gradie were partners. Gradie used to run a second-hand store back before the neighborhood had rotted much past the edges. He used to buy and sell salvage from the old houses when they started to go to seed. The last ten years or so, after the neighborhood had completely deteriorated, he started working the condemned houses. Once a house is condemned, you pretty well have to pull it down, and that costs a bundle—either to the owner or, since usually it's abandoned property, to the city. Gradie would work a deal where they'd pay him something to pull a house down—not very much, but he could have whatever he could salvage.

"Gradie would go over the place with Morny, haul off anything Gradie figured was worth saving—and by the time he got the place, there usually wasn't much. Then Gradie would pay Morny maybe five or ten bucks a day to pull the place down—taking it out of whatever he'd been paid to do the job. Morny would make a show of it, spend a couple weeks tearing out scrap timber and the like. Then, when they figured they'd done enough, Morny would set fire to the shell. By the time the fire trucks got there, there'd just be a basement full of coals. Firemen would spray some water, blame it on the winos, forget about it. The house would be down, so Gradie was clear of the deal—and the kudzu would spread over the empty lot in another year."

Linda considered the roach, snuffed it out, and swallowed it. Waste not, want not. "Lucky they never burned the whole neighborhood down. Is that how Gradie got that mantel you've been talking about?"

"Probably." Mercer followed her into the front parlor. The mantel had reminded Linda that she wanted to listen to a record.

The parlor—they used it as a living room—was heavy with stale smoke and flat beer and the pungent odor of Brother Jack's barbeque. Mercer scowled at the litter of empty Rolling Rock bottles, crumpled napkins and sauce-stained rinds of bread. He ought to clean up the house today, while Linda was in a domestic mood—but that meant they'd have to tackle the kitchen, and that was an all-day job—and he'd wanted to get her to pose while the sun was right in his upstairs studio.

Linda was having problems deciding on a record. It would be one of hers, Mercer knew, and hoped it wouldn't be Dylan again. She had called his own record library one of the wildest collections of curiosa ever put on vinyl. After half a year of living together, Linda still thought resurrected radio broadcasts of *The Shadow* were a camp joke; Mercer continued to argue that Dylan couldn't sing a note. Withal, she always paid her half of the rent on time. Mercer reflected that he got along with her better than with any previous roommate, and while the house was subdivided into a three-bedroom apartment, they never advertised for a third party.

The speakers, bunched on either side of the hearth, came to life with a scratchy Fleetwood Mac album. It drew Mercer's attention once more to the ravaged fireplace. Some Philistine landlord, in the process of remodeling the dilapidated Edwardian mansion into student apartments, had ripped out the mantel and boarded over the grate with a panel of cheap plywood. In defiance of landlord and fire laws, Mercer had torn away the pane and unblocked the chimney. The fireplace was small, with a grate designed for coal fires, but Mercer found it pleasant on winter nights. The hearth was of chipped ceramic tiles of a blue and white pattern—someone had told him they were Dresden. Mercer had scraped away the grime from the tiles, found an ornate brass grille in a flea market near Seymour. It remained to replace the mantel. Behind the plywood panel, where the original mantel had stood, was an ugly smear of bare brick and lathing. And Gradie had such a mantel.

"We ought to straighten up in here," Linda told him. She was doing a sort of half-dance around the room, scooping up debris and singing a line to the record every now and then.

"I was wondering if I could get you to pose for me this morning?"

"Hell, it's too nice a day to stand around your messy old studio."

"Just for a while. While the sun's right. If I don't get my figure studies handed in by the end of the month, I'll lose my incomplete."

"Christ, you've only had all spring to finish them."

"We can run down to Gradie's afterward. You've been wanting to see the place."

"And the famous mantel."

"Perhaps if the two of us work on him?"

THE STUDIO—SO MERCER dignified it—was an upstairs front room, thrust outward from the face of the house and onto the roof of the veranda, as a sort of cold-weather porch. Three-quarter-length casement windows with diamond panes had at one time swung outward on three sides, giving access onto the tiled porch roof. An enterprising landlord had blocked over the windows on either side, converting it into a small bedroom. The front wall remained a latticed expanse through which the morning sun flooded the room. Mercer had adopted it for his studio, and now Linda's houseplants bunched through his litter of canvases and drawing tables.

"Jesus, it's a nice day!"

Mercer halted his charcoal, scowled at the sheet. "You moved your shoulder again," he accused her.

"Lord, can't you hurry it?"

"Genius can never be hurried."

"Genius, my ass." Linda resumed her pose. She was lean, high-breasted, and thin-hipped, with a suggestion of freckles under her light tan. A bit taller, and she would have had a career as a fashion model. She had taken enough dance to pose quite well—did accept an occasional modeling assignment at the art school when cash was short.

"Going to be a *good* summer." It was that sort of morning.

"Of course." Mercer studied his drawing. Not particularly inspired, but then he never did like to work in charcoal. The sun picked bronze highlights through her helmet of curls, the feathery patches of her mons and axillae. Mercer's charcoal poked dark blotches at his sketch's crotch and armpits. He resisted the impulse to crumple it and start over.

Part of the problem was that she persisted in twitching to the beat of the music that echoed lazily from downstairs. She was playing that Fleetwood Mac album to death—had left the changer arm askew so that the record would repeat until someone changed it. It didn't help him concentrate—although he'd memorized the record to the point he no longer needed to listen to the words:

I been alone
All the years
So many ways to count the tears
I never change
I never will
I'm so afraid the way I feel
Days when the rain and the sun are gone
Black as night
Agony's torn at my heart too long
So afraid
Slip and I fall and I die

When he glanced at her again, something was wrong. Linda's pose was no longer relaxed. Her body was rigid, her expression tense.

"What is it?"

She twisted her face toward the windows, brought one arm across her breasts. "Someone's watching me."

With an angry grunt, Mercer tossed aside the charcoal, shouldered through the open casement to glare down at the street.

The sidewalks were deserted. Only the usual trickle of Saturday morning traffic drifted past. Mercer continued to scowl balefully as he studied the parked cars, the vacant weed-lot across the street, the tangle of kudzu in his front yard. Nothing.

"There's nothing out there."

Linda had shrugged into a paint-specked fatigue jacket. Her eyes were worried as she joined him at the window.

"There's something. I felt all crawly all of a sudden."

The roof of the veranda cut off view on the windows from the near sidewalk, and from the far sidewalk it was impossible to see into the studio by day. Across the street, the houses directly opposite had been pulled down. The kudzu-covered lots pitched steeply across more kudzu-covered slope, to the roofs of warehouses along the railyard a block below. If Linda were standing directly at the window, someone on the far sidewalk might look up to see her; otherwise there was no vantage from which a curious eye could peer into the room. It was one of the room's attractions as a studio.

"See. No one's out there."

Linda made a squirming motion with her shoulders. "They walked on then," she insisted.

Mercer snorted, suspecting an excuse to cut short the session. "They'd have had to run. Don't see anyone hiding out there in the weeds, do you?"

She stared out across the tangled heaps of kudzu, waving faintly in the last of the morning's breeze. "Well, there *might* be someone hiding under all that tangle." Mercer's levity annoyed her. "Why can't the city clear off those damn jungles!"

"When enough people raise a stink, they sometimes do—or make the owners clear away the weeds. The trouble is that you can't kill kudzu once the damn vines take over a lot. Gradie and Morny used to try. The stuff grows back as fast as you cut it—impossible to get all the roots and runners. Morny used to try to burn it out—crawl under and set fire to the dead vines and debris underneath the growing surface. But he could never keep a fire going under all the green stuff, and after a few spectacular failures using gasoline on the weed-lots, they made him stick to grubbing it out by hand."

"Awful stuff!" Linda grimaced. "Some of it's started growing up the back of the house."

"I'll have to get to it before it gets started. There's islands in the TVA lakes where nothing grows but kudzu. Stuff ran wild after the reservoir was filled, smothered out everything else."

"I'm surprised it hasn't covered the whole world."

"Dies down after the frost. Besides, it's not a native vine. It's from Japan. Some genius came up with the idea of using it as an ornamental groundcover on highway cuts and such. You've seen old highway embankments where the stuff has taken over the woods behind. It's spread all over the Southeast."

"Hmmm, yeah? So who's the genius who plants the crap all over the city then?"

"Get dressed, wise-ass."

III

The afternoon was hot and sodden. The sun made the air above the pavement scintillate with heat and the thick odor of tar. In the vacant lots, the kudzu leaves drooped like half-furled umbrellas. The vines stirred somnolently in the murky haze, although the air was stagnant.

Linda had changed into a halter top and a pair of patched cutoffs. "Bet I'll get some tan today."

"And maybe get soaked," Mercer remarked. "Air's got the feel of a thunderstorm."

"Where's the clouds?"

"Just feels heavy."

"That's just the goddamn pollution."

The kudzu vines had overrun the sidewalk, forcing them into the street. Tattered strands of vine crept across the gutter into the street, their tips crushed by the infrequent traffic. Vines along Gradie's fence completely obscured the yard beyond, waved curling tendrils aimlessly upward. In weather like this, Mercer reflected, you could just about see the stuff grow.

The gate hung again at first push. Mercer shoved harder, tore through the coils of vine that clung there.

"Who's that!" The tone was harsh as a saw blade hitting a nail.

"Jon Mercer, Mr. Gradie. I've brought a friend along."

He led the way into the yard. Linda, who had heard him talk about the place, followed with eyes bright for adventure. "This is Linda Wentworth, Mr. Gradie."

Mercer's voice trailed off as Gradie stumbled out onto the porch. He had the rolling slouch of a man who could carry a lot of liquor and was carrying more liquor than he could. His khakis were the same he'd had on when Mercer last saw him, and had the stains and wrinkles that clothes get when they're slept in by someone who hasn't slept well.

Red-rimmed eyes focused on the half-gallon of burgundy Mercer carried. "Guess I was taking a little nap." Gradie's tongue was muddy. "Come on up."

"Where's Sheriff?" Mercer asked. The dog usually warned his master of trespassers.

"Run off," Gradie told him gruffly. "Let me get you a glass." He lurched back into the darkness.

"Owow!" breathed Linda in one syllable. "He looks like something you see sitting hunched over on a bench talking to a bottle in a bag."

"Old Gradie has been hitting the sauce pretty hard last few times I've been by," Mercer allowed.

"I don't think I care for any wine just now," Linda decided, as Gradie reappeared, fingers speared into three damp glasses like a bunch of mismatched bananas. "Too hot."

"Had some beer in the Frigidaire, but it's all gone."

"That's all right." She was still fascinated with the enclosed yard. "What a lovely garden!" Linda was into organic foods.

Gradie frowned at the patch of anemic vegetables, beleaguered by encroaching walls of kudzu. "It's not much, but I get a little from it. Damn kudzu is just about to take it all. It's took the whole damn neighborhood—everything but me. Guess they figure to starve me out once the vines crawl over my little garden patch."

"Can't you keep it hoed?"

"Hoe kudzu, miss? No damn way. The vines grow a foot between breakfast and dinner. Can't get to the roots, and it just keeps spreading till the frost; then come spring it starts all over again where the frost left it. I used to keep it back by spraying it regular with 2,4-D. But then the government took 2,4-D off the market, and I can't find nothing else to touch it."

"Herbicides kill other things than weeds," Linda told him righteously.

Gradie's laugh was bitter. "Well, you folks just look all around as you like."

"Do you have any old clothes?" Linda was fond of creating costumes.

"Got some inside there with the books." Gradie indicated a shed that shouldered against his house. "I'll unlock it."

Mercer raised a mental eyebrow as Gradie dragged open the door of the shed, then shuffled back onto the porch. The old man was more interesting in punishing the half-gallon than in watching his customers. He left Linda to poke through the dusty jumble of warped books and faded clothes, stacked and shelved and hung and heaped within the tin-roofed musty darkness.

Instead he made a desultory tour about the yard—pausing now and again to examine a heap of old hubcaps, a stack of salvaged window frames, or a clutter of plumbing and porcelain fixtures. His deviousness seemed wasted on Gradie today. The old man remained slumped in a broken-down rocker on his porch, staring at nothing. It occurred to Mercer that the loss of Sheriff was bothering Gradie. The old yellow watchdog was about his only companion after Morny's death. Mercer reminded himself to look for the dog around campus.

He ambled back to the porch. A glance into the shed caught Linda trying on an oversized slouch hat. Mercer refilled his glass, noted that Gradie had gone through half the jug in his absence. "All right if I look at some of the stuff inside?"

Gradie nodded, rocked carefully to his feet, followed him in. The doorway opened into the living room of the small frame house. The living room had long since become a warehouse and museum for all of Gradie's choice items. There were a few chairs left to sit on, but the rest of the room had been totally taken over by the treasures of a lifetime of scavenging. Gradie himself had long ago been reduced to the kitchen and back bedroom for his own living quarters.

China closets crouched on lion paws against the wall, showing their treasures behind curved-glass bellies. Paintings and prints in ornate frames crowded the spiderwebs for space along the walls. Mounted deer's heads and stuffed owls gazed fixedly from their moth-eaten poses. Threadbare Oriental carpets lay in a great mound of bright-colored sausages. Mahogany dinner chairs were stacked atop oak and walnut tables. An extravagant brass bed reared from behind a gigantic Victorian buffet. A walnut bookcase displayed choice volumes and bric-a-brac beneath a signed Tiffany lamp. Another bedroom and the dining room were virtually impenetrable with similar storage.

Not everything was for sale. Mercer studied the magnificent walnut china cabinet that Gradie reserved as a showcase for his personal museum. Surrounded by the curving glass sides, the mementos of the junk dealer's lost years of glory reposed in dustless grandeur. Faded photographs of men in uniforms, inscribed snapshots of girls with pompadours and padded-shoulder dresses. Odd items of military uniform, medals and insignia, a brittle silk square emblazoned with the Rising Sun. Gradie was proud of his wartime service in the Pacific.

There were several hara-kiri knives—so Gradie said they were—a Nambu automatic and holster, and a Samurai sword that Gradie swore was five hundred years old. Clippings and souvenirs and odd bits of memorabilia of the Pacific theater, most bearing yellowed labels with painstakingly typed legends. A fist-sized skull—obviously some species of monkey—bore the label: "Jap General's Skull."

"That general would have had a muzzle like a possum." Mercer laughed. "Did you find it in Japan?"

"Bought it during the Occupation," Gradie muttered. "From one little Nip, said it come from a mountain-devil."

Despite the heroic-sounding labels throughout the display—"Flag Taken from Captured Jap Officer"—Mercer guessed that most of the mementos had indeed been purchased while Gradie was stationed in Japan during the Occupation.

Mercer sipped his wine and let his eyes drift about the room. Against one wall leaned the mahogany mantel, and he must have let his interest flicker in his eyes.

"I see you're still interested in the mantel," Gradie slurred, mercantile instincts rising through his alcoholic lethargy.

"Well, I see you haven't sold it yet."

Gradie wiped a trickle of wine from his stubbled chin. "I'll get me a hundred-fifty for that, or I'll keep it until I can get me more. Seen one like it, not half as nice, going for two hundred—place off Chapman Pike."

"They catch the tourists from Gatlinburg," Mercer sneered.

The mantel was of African mahogany, Mercer judged—darker than the reddish Philippine variety. For a miracle only a film of age-blackened lacquer obscured the natural grain—Mercer had spent untold hours stripping layers of cheap paint from the mahogany panel doors of his house.

It was solid mahogany, not a veneer. The broad panels that framed the fireplace were matched from the same log, so that their grains formed a mirror image. The mantelpiece itself was wide and sturdy, bordered by a tiny balustrade. Above that stretched a fine beveled mirror, still perfectly silvered, flanked by lozenge-shaped mirrors on either side. Ornately carved mahogany candlesticks jutted from either side of the mantelpiece, so that a candle flame would reflect against the beveled lozenges. More matched-grain panels continued ceilingward above the mirrors, framed by a second balustraded mantelshelf across the top. Mercer could just about touch it at fullest stretch.

Exquisite, and easily worth Gradie's price. Mercer might raise a hundred of it—if he gave up eating and paying rent for a month or three.

"Well, I won't argue it's a beauty," he said. "But a mantel isn't just something you can buy and take home under your arm, brush it off and stick it in your living room. You can always sell a table or a china closet—that's furniture. Thing like this mantel is only useful if you got a fireplace to match it with."

"You think so," Gradie scoffed. "Had a lady in here last spring, fine big house out in west Knoxville. Said she'd like to antique it with one of those paint kits, fasten it against a wall for a stand to display her plants. Wanted to talk me down to one twenty-five though, and I said 'no, ma'am.' "

Linda's scream ripped like tearing glass.

Mercer spun, was out the door and off the porch before he quite knew he was moving. "Linda!"

She was scrambling backward from the shed, silent now but her face ugly with panic. Stumbling, she tore a wrinkled flannel jacket from her shoulders, with revulsion threw it back into the shed.

"Rats!" She shuddered, wiping her hands on her shorts. "In there under the clothes! A great *big* one! Oh, Jesus!"

But Gradie had already burst out of his house, shoved past Mercer—who had pulled short to laugh. The shotgun was a rust-and-blue blur as he lunged past Linda. The shed door slammed to behind him.

"Oh, Jesus!"

The boom of each barrel, megaphoned by the confines of the shed, and in the finger-twitch between each blast, the shrill chitter of pain.

"Jon!"

Then the hysterical cursing from within, and a muffled stomping.

Linda, who had never gotten used to Mercer's guns, was clawing free of his re-assuring arm. "Let's go! Let's go!" She was kicking at the gate, as Gradie slid back out of the shed, closing the door on his heel.

"Goddamn big rat, miss." He grinned crookedly. "But I sure done for him."

"Jon, I'm going!"

"Catch you later, Mr. Gradie," Mercer yelled, grimacing in embarrassment. "Linda's just a bit freaked."

If Gradie called after him, Mercer didn't hear. Linda was walking as fast as anyone could without breaking into a run, as close to panic as need be. He loped after her.

"Hey, Linda! Everything's cool! Wait up!"

She didn't seem to hear. Mercer cut across the corner of a weed-lot to intercept her. "Hey! Wait!"

A vine tangled his feet. With a curse, he sprawled headlong. Flinching at the fear of broken glass, he dropped to his hands and knees in the tangle of kudzu. His flailing hands slid on something bulky and foul, and a great swarm of flies choked him.

"Jon!" At his yell, Linda turned about. As he dove into the knee-deep kudzu, she forgot her own near panic and started toward him.

"I'm okay!" he shouted. "Just stay there. Wait for me."

Wiping his hands on the leaves, he heaved himself to his feet, hid the revulsion from his face. He swallowed the rush of bile and grinned.

Let her see Sheriff's flayed carcass just now, and she *would* flip out.

IV

Mercer had drawn the curtains across the casement windows, but Linda was still reluctant to pose for him. Mercer decided she had not quite recovered from her trip to Gradie's.

She sneered at the unshaded floor lamp. "You and your morning sunlight."

Mercer batted at a moth. "In the morning we'll be off for the mountains." This, the bribe for her posing. "I want to finish these damn figure studies while I'm in the mood."

She shivered, listened to the nocturnal insects beat against the curtained panes. Mercer thought it was stuffy, but enough of the evening breeze penetrated the cracked casements to draw her nipples taut. From the stairwell arose the scratchy echoes of the Fleetwood Mac album—Mercer wished Linda wouldn't play an album to death when she bought it.

"Why don't we move into the mountains?"

"Be nice." This sketch was worse than the one this morning.

"No." Her tone was sharp. "I'm serious."

The idea was too fanciful, and he was in no mood to argue over another of her whims tonight. "The bears would get us."

"We could fix up an old place maybe. Or put up a log cabin."

"You've been reading *Foxfire Book* too much."

"No, I mean it! Let's get out of here!"

Mercer looked up. Yes, she did seem to mean it. "I'm up for it. But it would be a bit rough for getting to class. And I don't think they just let you homestead anymore."

"Screw classes!" she groaned. "Screw this grungy old dump! Screw this dirty goddamn city!"

"I've got plans to fix this place up into a damn nice townhouse," Mercer reminded her patiently. "Thought this summer I'd open up the side windows in here—tear out this lousy sheetrock they nailed over the openings. Gradie's got his eye out for some casement windows to match the ones we've got left."

"Oh, Jesus! Why don't you just stay the hell away from Gradie's!"

"Oh, for Christ's sake!" Mercer groaned. "You freak out over a rat, and Gradie blows it away."

"It wasn't just a rat."

"It was the Easter bunny in drag."

"It had paws like a monkey."

Mercer laughed. "I told you this grass was well worth the forty bucks an ounce."

"It wasn't the grass we smoked before going over."

"Wish we didn't have to split the bag with Ron," he mused, wondering if there was any way they might raise the other twenty.

"Oh, screw you!"

Mercer adjusted a fresh sheet onto his easel, started again. This one would be "Pouting Model," or maybe "Uneasy Girl." He sketched in silence for a while. Silence, except for the patter of insects on the windows, and the tireless repetitions of the record downstairs.

"I just want to get away from here," Linda said at last.

In the darkness downstairs, the needle caught on the scratched grooves, and the stereo mindlessly repeated:

"So afraid . . . So afraid . . . So afraid . . . So afraid . . ."

By 1:00 A.M., the heat lightning was close enough to suggest a ghost of thunder, and the night breeze was gusting enough to billow the curtains. His sketches finished— at least, as far as he cared—Mercer rubbed his eyes and debated closing the windows before going to bed. If a storm came up, he'd have to get out of bed in a hurry. If he closed them and it didn't rain, it would be too muggy to sleep. Mechanically he reached for his coffee cup, frowned glumly at the drowned moth that floated there.

The phone was ringing.

Linda was in the shower. Mercer trudged downstairs and scooped up the receiver. It was Gradie, and from his tone he hadn't been drinking milk.

"Jon, I'm sure as hell sorry about giving your little lady a fright this afternoon."

"No problem, Mr. Gradie. Linda was laughing about it by the time we got home."

"Well, that's good to hear, Jon. I'm sure glad to hear she wasn't scared bad."

"That's quite all right, Mr. Gradie."

"Just a goddamn old rat, wasn't it?"

"Just a rat, Mr. Gradie."

"Well, I'm sure glad to hear that."

"Right you are, Mr. Gradie." He started to hang up.

"Jon, what else I was wanting to talk to you about, though, was to ask you if you really wanted that mantel we was talking about today."

"Well, Mr. Gradie, I'd sure as hell like to buy it, but it's a little too rich for my pocketbook."

"Jon, you're a good old boy. I'll sell it to you for a hundred even."

"Well now, sir—that's a fair enough price, but a hundred dollars is just too much money for a fellow who has maybe ten bucks a week left to buy groceries."

"If you really want that mantel—and I'd sure like for you to have it—I'd take seventy-five for it right now tonight."

"Seventy-five?"

"I got to have it right now, tonight. Cash."

Mercer tried to think. He hadn't paid rent this month. "Mr. Gradie, it's one in the morning. I don't have seventy-five bucks in my pocket."

"How much can you raise, then?"

"I don't know. Maybe fifty."

"You bring me fifty dollars cash tonight, and take that mantel home."

"Tonight?"

"You bring it tonight. I got to have it right now."

"All right, Mr. Gradie. See you in an hour."

"You hurry now," Gradie advised him. There was a clattering fumble, and the third try he managed to hang up.

"Who was that?"

Mercer was going through his billfold. "Gradie. Drunk as a skunk. He needs liquor money, I guess. Says he'll sell me the mantel for fifty bucks."

"Is that a bargain?" She toweled her hair petulantly.

"He's been asking one-fifty. I got to give him the money tonight. How much money do you have on you?"

"Jesus, you're not going down to that place tonight?"

"By morning he may have sobered up, forgotten the whole deal."

"Oh, Jesus. You're *not* going to go down there."

Mercer was digging through the litter of his dresser for loose change. "Thirty-eight is all I've got on me. Can you loan me twelve?"

"All I've got is a ten and some change."

"How much change? There's a bunch of bottles in the kitchen—I can return them for the deposit. Who's still open?"

"Hugh's is until two. Jon, we'll be broke for the weekend. How will we get to the mountains?"

"Ron owes us twenty for his half of the ounce. I'll get it from him when I borrow his truck to haul the mantel. Monday I'll dip into the rent money—we can stall."

"You can't get his truck until morning. Ron's working graveyard tonight."

"He's off in six hours. I'll pay Gradie now and get a receipt. I'll pick up the mantel first thing."

Linda rummaged through her shoulder bag. "Just don't forget that we're going to the mountains tomorrow."

"It's probably going to rain anyway."

V

The storm was holding off as Mercer loped toward Gradie's house, but heat lightning fretted behind reefs of cloud. It was a dark night between the filtered flares of lightning, and he was very conscious that this was a bad neighborhood to be out walking with fifty dollars in your pocket. He kept one hand shoved into his jeans pocket, closed over the double-barreled derringer, and walked on the edge of the street, well away from the concealing mounds of kudzu. Once something scrambled noisily through the vines; startled, Mercer almost shot his foot off.

"Who's there!" The voice was cracked with drunken fear.

"Jon Mercer, Mr. Gradie! Jon Mercer."

"Come on into the light. You bring the money?"

"Right here." Mercer dug a crumpled wad of bills and coins from his pocket. The derringer flashed in his fist.

"Two shots, huh," Gradie observed. "Not enough to do you much good. There's too many of them."

"Just having it to show has pulled me out of a couple bad moments," Mercer explained. He dumped the money onto Gradie's shaky palm. "That's fifty. Better count it, and give me a receipt. I'll be back in the morning for the mantel."

"Take it now. I'll be gone in the morning."

Mercer glanced sharply at the other man. Gradie had never been known to leave his yard unattended for longer than a quick trip to the store. "I'll need a truck. I can't borrow the truck until in the morning."

Gradie carelessly shoved the money into a pocket, bent over a lamp-lit end table to scribble out a receipt. In the dusty glare, his face was haggard with shadowy lines. DT's, Mercer guessed: he needs money bad to buy more booze.

"This is traveling money—I'm leaving tonight," Gradie insisted. His breath was stale with wine. "Talked to an old boy who says he'll give me a good price for my stock. He's coming by in the morning. You're a good old boy, Jon—and I wanted you to have that mantel if you wanted it."

"It's two a.m.," Mercer suggested carefully. "I can be here just after seven."

"I'm leaving tonight."

Mercer swore under his breath. There was no arguing with Gradie in his present state, and by morning the old man might have forgotten the entire transaction. Selling out and leaving? Impossible. This yard was Gradie's world, his life. Once he crawled up out of this binge, he'd get over the willies and not remember a thing from the past week.

"How about if I borrow your truck?"

"I'm taking it."

"I won't be ten minutes with it." Mercer cringed to think of Gradie behind the wheel just now.

Eventually he secured Gradie's key to the aged Studebaker pickup in return for his promise to return immediately upon unloading the mantel. Together they worked the heavy mahogany piece onto the truck bed—Mercer fretting at each threatened scrape against the rusted metal.

"Care to come along to help unload?" Mercer invited. "I got a bottle at the house."

Gradie refused the bait. "I got things to do before I go. You just get back here soon as you're finished."

Grinding dry gears, Mercer edged the pickup out of the kudzu-walled yard, and clattered away into the night.

———

THE MANTEL WAS really too heavy for the two of them to move—Mercer could handle the weight easily enough, but the bulky piece needed two people. Linda struggled gamely with her end, but the mantel scraped and scuffed as they lowered it from the truck bed and hauled it into the house. By the time they had finished, they both were sticky and exhausted from the effort.

Mercer remembered his watch. "Christ, it's two-thirty. I've got to get this heap back to Gradie."

"Why don't you wait till morning? He's probably passed out cold by now."

"I promised to get right back to him."

Linda hesitated at the doorway. "Wait a second. I'm coming."

"Thought you'd had enough of Gradie's place."

"I don't like waiting here alone this late."

"Since when?" Mercer laughed, climbing into the pickup.

"I don't like the way the kudzu crawls all up the back of the house. Something might be hiding . . ."

GRADIE DIDN'T POP out of his burrow when they rattled into his yard. Linda had been right, Mercer reflected—the old man was sleeping it off. With a pang of guilt, he hoped his fifty bucks wouldn't go toward extending this binge; Gradie had really looked bad tonight. Maybe he should look in on him tomorrow afternoon, get him to eat something.

"I'll just look in to see if he's okay," Mercer told her. "If he's asleep, I'll just leave the keys beside him."

"Leave them in the ignition," Linda argued. "Let's just go."

"Won't take a minute."

Linda swung down from the cab and scrambled after him. Fitful gushes of heat lightning spilled across the crowded yard—picking out the junk-laden stacks and shelves, crouched in fantastic distortions like a Daliesque vision of Hell. The darkness in between bursts was hot and oily, heavy with moisture, and the subdued rumble of thunder seemed like gargantuan breathing.

"Be lucky to make it back before this hits," Mercer grumbled.

The screen door was unlatched. Mercer pushed it open. "Mr. Gradie?" he called softly—not wishing to wake the old man, but remembering the shotgun. "Mr. Gradie? It's Jon."

Within, the table lamps shed a dusty glow across the cluttered room. Without, the sporadic glare of heat lightning popped on and off like a defective neon sign. Mercer squinted into the pools of shadow between cabinets and shelves. Bellies of curved glass, shoulders of polished mahogany smoldered in the flickering light. From the walls, glass eyes glinted watchfully from the mounted deers' heads and stuffed birds.

"Mr. Gradie?"

"Jon. Leave the keys, and let's go."

"I'd better see if he's all right."

Mercer started toward the rear of the house, then paused a moment. One of the glass-fronted cabinets stood open; it had been closed when he was here before. Its door snagged out into the cramped aisle-space; Mercer made to close it as he edged past. It was the walnut cabinet that housed Gradie's wartime memorabilia, and Mercer paused as he closed it because one exhibit was noticeably missing: that of the monkey-like skull that was whimsically labeled "Jap General's Skull."

"Mr. Gradie?"

"Phew!" Linda crinkled her nose. "He's got something scorching on the stove!"

Mercer turned into the kitchen. An overhead bulb glared down upon a squalid confusion of mismatched kitchen furnishings, stacks of chipped, unwashed dishes, empty cans and bottles, scattered remnants of desiccated meals. Mercer winced at the thought of having drunk from these same grimy glasses. The kitchen was deserted. On the stove an overheated saucepan boiled gouts of sour steam, but for the moment Mercer's attention was on the kitchen table.

A space had been cleared by pushing away the debris of dirty dishes and stale food. In that space reposed a possum-jawed monkey's skull, with the yellow label: "Jap General's Skull."

There was a second skull beside it on the table. Except for a few clinging tatters of dried flesh and greenish fur—the other was bleached white by the sun—this skull was identical to Gradie's Japanese souvenir: a high-domed skull the size of a large, clenched fist, with a jutting, sharp-toothed muzzle. A baboon of sort, Mercer judged, picking it up.

A neatly typed label was affixed to the occiput: "Unknown Animal Skull. Found by Fred Morny on Grand Ave. Knoxville, Tenn. 1976."

"Someone lost a pet," Mercer mused, replacing the skull and reaching for the loose paper label that lay beside the two relics.

Linda had gone to the stove to turn off its burner. "Oh, *God!*" she said, recoiling from the steaming saucepan.

Mercer stepped across to the stove, followed her sickened gaze. The water had boiled low in the large saucepan, scorching the repellent broth in which the skull simmered. It was a third skull, baboon-like, identical to the others.

"He's *eating* rats!" Linda retched.

"No," Mercer said dully, glancing at the freshly typed label he had scooped from the table. "He's boiling off the flesh so he can exhibit the skull." For the carefully prepared label in his hand read: "Kudzu Devil Skull. Shot by Red Gradie in Yard, Knoxville, Tenn., June 1977."

Jon, I'm going. This man's stark crazy!"

Just let me see if he's all right," Mercer insisted. "Or go back by yourself."

"God, no!"

He's probably in his bedroom then. Fell asleep while he was working on this . . . this . . ." Mercer wasn't sure what to call it. The old man *had* seemed a bit unhinged these last few days.

The bedroom was in the other rear corner of the house, leading off from the small dining room in between. Leaving the glare of the kitchen light, the dining room was lost in shadow. No one had dined here in years obviously, for the area was another of Gradie's storerooms—stacked and double-stacked with tables, chairs, and bulky items of furniture. Threading his way between the half-seen obstructions, Mercer gingerly approached the bedroom door—a darker blotch against the opposite wall.

"Mr. Gradie? It's Jon Mercer."

He thought he heard a weak groan from the darkness within.

"It's Jon Mercer, Mr. Gradie." He called more loudly, "I've brought your keys back. Are you all right?"

"Jon, let's *go!*"

"Shut up, damn it! I thought I heard him try to answer."

He stepped toward the doorway. An object rolled and crumpled under his foot. It was an empty shotgun shell. There was a strange sweet-sour stench that tugged at Mercer's belly, and he thought he could make out the shape of a body sprawled half out of the bed.

"Mr. Gradie?"

This time a soughing gasp, too liquid for a snore.

Mercer groped for a wall switch, located it, snapped it back and forth. No light came on.

"Mr. Gradie?"

Again a bubbling sigh.

"Get a lamp! Quick!" he told Linda.

"Let him alone, for Christ's sake!"

"Damn it, he's passed out and thrown up! He'll strangle in his own vomit if we don't help him!"

"He had a big flashlight in the kitchen!" Linda whirled to get it, anxious to get away.

Mercer cautiously made his way into the bedroom—treading with care, for broken glass crunched under his foot. The outside shades were drawn, and the room was swallowed in inky blackness, but he was certain he could pick out Gradie's comatose form lying across the bed. Then Linda was back with the flashlight.

Gradie sprawled on his back, skinny legs flung onto the floor, the rest crosswise on the unmade bed. The flashlight beam shimmered on the spreading splotches of blood that soaked the sheets and mattress. Someone had spent a lot of time with him, using a small knife—small-bladed, for if the wounds that all but flayed him had not been shallow, he could not be yet alive.

Mercer flung the flashlight beam about the bedroom. The cluttered furnishings were overturned, smashed. He recognized the charge pattern of a shotgun blast low against one wall, spattered with bits of fur and gore. The shotgun, broken open, lay on the floor; its barrel and stock were matted with bloody fur—Gradie had clubbed it when he had no chance to reload. The flashlight beam probed the blackness at the base of the corner wall, where the termite-riddled floorboards had been torn away. A trail of blood crawled into the darkness beneath.

Then Mercer crouched beside Gradie, shining the light into the tortured face. The eyes opened at the light—one eye was past seeing, the other stared dully. "That you, Jon?"

"It's Jon, Mr. Gradie. You take it easy—we're getting you to the hospital. Did you recognize who did this to you?"

Linda had already caught up the telephone from where it had fallen beneath an overturned nightstand. It seemed impossible that he had survived the blood loss, but Mercer had seen drunks run off after a gut-shot that would have killed a sober man from shock.

Gradie laughed horribly. "It was the little green men. Do you think I could have told anybody about the little green men?"

"Take it easy, Mr. Gradie."

"Jon! The phone's dead!"

"Busted in the fall. Help me carry him to the truck." Mercer prodded clumsily with a wad of torn sheets, trying to remember first aid for bleeding. Pressure points? Where? The old man was cut to tatters.

"They're little green devils," Gradie raved weakly. "And they ain't no animals— they're clever as you or me. They *live* under the kudzu. That's what the Nip was trying to tell me when he sold me the skull. Hiding down there beneath the damn vines, living off the roots and whatever they can scavenge. They nurture the goddamn stuff, he said, help spread it around, care for it just like a man looks after his garden. Winter comes, they burrow down underneath the soil and hibernate."

"Shouldn't we make a litter?"

"How? Just grab his feet."

"Let me lie! Don't you see, Jon? Kudzu was brought over here from Japan, and these damn little devils came with it. I started to put it all together when Morny found the skull—started piecing together all the little hints and suspicions. They like it here, John—they're taking over all the waste-lots, got more food than out in the wild, multiplying like rats over here, and nobody knows about them."

Gradie's hysterical voice was growing weaker. Mercer gave up trying to bandage the torn limbs. "Just take it easy, Mr. Gradie. We're getting you to a doctor."

"Too late for a doctor. You scared them off, but they've done for me. Just like they done for old Morny. They're smart, Jon—that's what I didn't understand in time— smart as devils. They knew that I was figuring on them—started spying on me, creeping in to see what I knew—then came to shut me up. They don't want nobody to know about them, Jon! Now they'll come after . . ."

Whatever else Gradie said was swallowed in the crimson froth that bubbled from his lips. The tortured body went rigid for an instant, then Mercer cradled a dead weight in his arms. Clumsily, he felt for a pulse, realized the blood was no longer flowing in weak spurts.

"I think he's gone."

"Oh God, Jon. The police will think we did this!"

"Not if we report it first. Come on! We'll take the truck."

"And just leave him here?"

"He's dead. This is a murder. Best not to disturb things any more than we have."

"Oh, God! Jon, whoever did this may still be around!"

Mercer pulled his derringer from his pocket, flicked back the safety. His chest and arms were covered with Gradie's blood, he noticed. This was not going to be pleasant when they got to the police station. Thank God the cops never patrolled this slum, or else the shotgun blasts would have brought a squad car by now.

Warily he led the way out of the house and into the yard. Wind was whipping the leaves now, and a few spatters of rain were starting to hit the pavement. The erratic light peopled each grotesque shadow with lurking murderers, and against the rush of the wind, Mercer seemed to hear a thousand stealthy assassins.

A flash of electric blue highlighted the yard.

"Jon! Look at the truck!"

All four tires were flat. Slashed.

"Get in! We'll run on the rims!"

Another glare of heat lightning.

All about then, the kudzu erupted from a hundred hidden lairs.

Mercer fired twice.

SHOELESS JOE JACKSON COMES TO IOWA

BY W. P. KINSELLA

CANADA'S OWN W. P. KINSELLA IS WITHOUT A DOUBT THE SHORT STORY EQUIVALENT OF POET LAUREATE FOR AMERICA'S FAVORITE PASTIME. "IF YOU BUILD IT, HE WILL COME" OPENS THE DOOR FOR AN ENCOUNTER WITH THE PAST IN A HUMBLE IOWA CORNFIELD WHERE DREAMS OF BASEBALL'S GLORIOUS GOLDEN AGE CAN COME ALIVE FOR THOSE WHO TRULY BELIEVE. . . . AND AS A RESULT, AN AMERICAN DISGRACED BY A CHEATING SCANDAL, "SHOELESS JOE" JACKSON, HAS ACHIEVED A PLACE AMONG AMERICA'S PANTHEON OF HEROES. (HIS NOVEL *SHOELESS JOE* IS PROBABLY THE BEST MODERN BASEBALL FANTASY OF THE LATTER PART OF THE TWENTIETH CENTURY.)

My father said he saw him years later playing in a tenth-rate commercial league in a textile town in Carolina, wearing shoes and an assumed name.

"He'd put on fifty pounds and the spring was gone from his step in the outfield, but he could still hit. Oh, how that man could hit. No one has ever been able to hit like Shoeless Joe."

Three years ago at dusk on a spring evening, when the sky was a robin's-egg blue and the wind as soft as a day-old chick, I was sitting on the verandah of my farm home in eastern Iowa when a voice very clearly said to me, "If you build it, he will come."

The voice was that of a ballpark announcer. As he spoke, I instantly envisioned the finished product I knew I was being asked to conceive. I could see the dark, squarish speakers, like ancient sailors' hats, attached to aluminum-painted light standards that glowed down into a baseball field, my present position being directly behind home plate.

In reality, all anyone else could see out there in front of me was a tattered lawn of mostly dandelions and quack grass that petered out at the edge of a cornfield perhaps fifty yards from the house.

Anyone else was my wife Annie, my daughter Karin, a corn-colored collie named Carmeletia Pope, and a cinnamon and white guinea pig named Junior who ate spaghetti and sang each time the fridge door opened. Karin and the dog were not quite two years old.

"If you build it, he will come," the announcer repeated in scratchy Middle American, as if his voice had been recorded on an old 78-r.p.m. record.

A three-hour lecture or a 500-page guide book could not have given me clearer directions: Dimensions of ballparks jumped over and around me like fleas, cost figures for light standards and floodlights whirled around my head like the moths that dusted against the porch light above me.

That was all the instruction I ever received: two announcements and a vision of a baseball field. I sat on the verandah until the satiny dark was complete. A few curdly clouds striped the moon, and it became so silent I could hear my eyes blink.

Our house is one of those massive old farm homes, square as a biscuit box with a sagging verandah on three sides. The floor of the verandah slopes so that marbles, baseballs, tennis balls, and ball bearings all accumulate in a corner like a herd of cattle clustered with their backs to a storm. On the north verandah is a wooden porch swing where Annie and I sit on humid August nights, sip lemonade from teary glasses, and dream.

When I finally went to bed, and after Annie inched into my arms in that way she has, like a cat that you suddenly find sound asleep in your lap, I told her about the voice and I told her that I knew what it wanted me to do.

"Oh love," she said, "if it makes you happy you should do it," and she found my lips with hers. I shivered involuntarily as her tongue touched mine.

Annie: She has never once called me crazy. Just before I started the first landscape work, as I stood looking out at the lawn and the cornfield, wondering how it could look so different in daylight, considering the notion of accepting it all as a dream and abandoning it, Annie appeared at my side and her arm circled my waist. She leaned against me and looked up, cocking her head like one of the red squirrels that scamper along the power lines from the highway to the house. "Do it, love," she said as I looked down at her, that slip of a girl with hair the color of cayenne pepper and at least a million freckles on her face and arms, that girl who lives in blue jeans and T-shirts and at twenty-four could still pass for sixteen.

I thought back to when I first knew her. I came to Iowa to study. She was the child of my landlady. I heard her one afternoon outside my window as she told her girl friends, "When I grow up I'm going to marry . . ." and she named me. The others were going to be nurses, teachers, pilots, or movie stars, but Annie chose me as her occupation. Eight years later we were married. I chose willingly, lovingly, to stay in Iowa. Eventually I rented this farm, then bought it, operating it one inch from bank-ruptcy. I don't seem meant to farm, but I want to be close to this precious land, for Annie and me to be able to say, "This is ours."

Now I stand ready to cut into the cornfield, to chisel away a piece of our livelihood to use as dream currency, and Annie says, "Oh, love, if it makes you happy you should do it." I carry her words in the back of my mind, stored the way a maiden aunt might wrap a brooch, a remembrance of a long-lost love. I understand how hard that was for her to say and how it got harder as the project advanced. How she must have told her family not to ask me about the baseball field I was building, because they stared at me dumb-eyed, a row of silent, thickset peasants with red faces. Not an imagination among them except to forecast the wrath of God that will fall on the heads of pagans such as I.

"If you build it, he will come."

He, of course, was Shoeless Joe Jackson.

Joseph Jefferson (Shoeless Joe) Jackson
Born: Brandon Mills, South Carolina, July 16, 1887
Died: Greenville, South Carolina, December 5, 1951

In April 1945, Ty Cobb picked Shoeless Joe as the best left fielder of all time. A famous sportswriter once called Joe's glove "the place where triples go to die." He never learned to read or write. He created legends with a bat and a glove.

Was it really a voice I heard? Or was it perhaps something inside me making a statement that I did not hear with my ears but with my heart? Why should I want to follow this command? But as I ask, I already know the answer. I count the loves in my life: Annie, Karin, Iowa, Baseball. The great god Baseball.

My birthstone is a diamond. When asked, I say my astrological sign is hit and run, which draws a lot of blank stares here in Iowa where 50,000 people go to see the University of Iowa Hawkeyes football team while 500 regulars, including me, watch the baseball team perform.

My father, I've been told, talked baseball statistics to my mother's belly while waiting for me to be born.

My father: born, Glen Ullin, North Dakota, April 14, 1896. Another diamond birthstone. Never saw a professional baseball game until 1919 when he came back from World War I where he had been gassed at Passchendaele. He settled in Chicago, inhabited a room above a bar across from Comiskey Park, and quickly learned to live and die with the White Sox. Died a little when, as prohibitive favorites, they lost the 1919 World Series to Cincinnati, died a lot the next summer when eight members of the team were accused of throwing that World Series.

Before I knew what baseball was, I knew of Connie Mack, John McGraw, Grover Cleveland Alexander, Ty Cobb, Babe Ruth, Tris Speaker, Tinker-to-Evers-to-Chance, and, of course, Shoeless Joe Jackson. My father loved underdogs, cheered for the Brooklyn Dodgers and the hapless St. Louis Browns, loathed the Yankees—an inherited trait, I believe—and insisted that Shoeless Joe was innocent, a victim of big business and crooked gamblers.

That first night, immediately after the voice and the vision, I did nothing except sip my lemonade a little faster and rattle the ice cubes in my glass. The vision of the baseball park lingered—swimming, swaying, seeming to be made of red steam, though perhaps it was only the sunset. And there was a vision within the vision: one of Shoeless Joe Jackson playing left field. Shoeless Joe Jackson who last played major league baseball in 1920 and was suspended for life, along with seven of his compatriots, by Commissioner Kenesaw Mountain Landis, for his part in throwing the 1919 World Series.

Instead of nursery rhymes, I was raised on the story of the Black Sox Scandal, and instead of Tom Thumb or Rumpelstiltskin, I grew up hearing of the eight disgraced ballplayers: Weaver, Cicotte, Risberg, Felsch, Gandil, Williams, McMullin, and, always, Shoeless Joe Jackson.

"He hit .375 against the Reds in the 1919 World Series and played errorless ball," my father would say, scratching his head in wonder. "Twelve hits in an eight-game series. And *they* suspended *him*," Father would cry. Shoeless Joe became a symbol of the tyranny of the powerful over the powerless. The name Kenesaw Mountain Landis became synonymous with the Devil.

Building a baseball field is more work than you might imagine. I laid out a whole field, but it was there in spirit only. It was really only left field that concerned me. Home plate was made from pieces of cracked two-by-four embedded in the earth. The pitcher's rubber rocked like a cradle when I stood on it. The bases were stray blocks of wood, unanchored. There was no backstop or grandstand, only one shaky bleacher beyond the left-field wall. There was a left-field wall, but only about fifty feet of it, twelve feet high, stained dark green and braced from the rear. And the left-field grass. My intuition told me that it was the grass that was important. It took me three seasons to hone that grass to its proper texture, to its proper color. I made trips to Minneapolis and one or two other cities where the stadiums still have natural-grass infields and outfields. I would arrive hours before a game and watch the groundskeepers groom the field like a prize animal, then stay after the game when in the cool of the night the same groundsmen appeared with hoses, hoes, and rakes, and patched the grasses like medics attending to wounded soldiers.

I pretended to be building a Little League ballfield and asked their secrets and sometimes was told. I took interest in the total operation; they wouldn't understand if I told them I was building only a left field.

Three seasons I've spent seeding, watering, fussing, praying, coddling that field like a sick child. Now it glows parrot-green, cool as mint, soft as moss, lying there like a cashmere blanket. I've begun watching it in the evenings, sitting on the rickety bleacher just beyond the fence. A bleacher I constructed for an audience of one.

My father played some baseball, Class B teams in Florida and California. I found his statistics in a dusty minor-league record book. In Florida he played for a team called the Angels and, according to his records, was a better-than-average catcher. He claimed to have visited all forty-eight states and every major-league ballpark before, at forty, he married and settled down in Montana, a two-day drive from the nearest major-league team. I tried to play, but ground balls bounced off my chest and fly balls dropped between my hands. I might have been a fair designated hitter, but the rule was too late in coming.

There is the story of the urchin who, tugging at Shoeless Joe Jackson's sleeve as he emerged from a Chicago courthouse, said, "Say it ain't so, Joe."

Jackson's reply reportedly was, "I'm afraid it is, kid."

When he comes, I won't put him on the spot by asking. The less said the better. It is likely that he did accept money from gamblers. But throw the Series? Never! Shoeless Joe Jackson led both teams in hitting in that 1919 Series. It was the circumstances. The circumstances. The players were paid peasant salaries while the owners became rich. The infamous Ten Day Clause, which voided contracts, could end any player's career without compensation, pension, or even a ticket home.

The second spring, on a toothachy May evening, a covering of black clouds lumbered off westward like ghosts of buffalo, and the sky became the cold color of a silver coin. The forecast was for frost.

The left-field grass was like green angora, soft as a baby's cheek. In my mind I could see it dull and crisp, bleached by frost, and my chest tightened.

But I used a trick a groundskeeper in Minneapolis had taught me, saying he learned it from grape farmers in California. I carried out a hose, and, making the spray so fine it was scarcely more than fog, I sprayed the soft, shaggy spring grass all that chilled night. My hands ached and my face became wet and cold, but, as I watched, the spray froze on the grass, enclosing each blade in a gossamer-crystal coating of ice. A covering that served like a coat of armor to dispel the real frost that was set like a weasel upon killing in the night. I seemed to stand taller than ever before as the sun rose, turning the ice to eye-dazzling droplets, each a prism, making the field an orgy of rainbows.

Annie and Karin were at breakfast when I came in, the bacon and coffee smells and their laughter pulling me like a magnet.

"Did it work, love?" Annie asked, and I knew she knew by the look on my face that it had. And Karin, clapping her hands and complaining of how cold my face was when she kissed me, loved every second of it.

"And how did he get a name like Shoeless Joe?" I would ask my father, knowing the story full well but wanting to hear it again. And no matter how many times I heard it, I would still picture a lithe ballplayer, his great bare feet white as baseballs sinking into the outfield grass as he sprinted for a line drive. Then, after the catch, his toes gripping the grass like claws, he would brace and throw to the infield.

"It wasn't the least bit romantic," my dad would say. "When he was still in the minor leagues he bought a new pair of spikes and they hurt his feet. About the sixth inning he took them off and played the outfield in just his socks. The other players kidded him, called him Shoeless Joe, and the name stuck for all time."

It was hard for me to imagine that a sore-footed young outfielder taking off his shoes one afternoon not long after the turn of the century could generate a legend.

I came to Iowa to study, one of the thousands of faceless students who pass through large universities, but I fell in love with the state. Fell in love with the land, the people, the sky, the cornfields, and Annie. Couldn't find work in my field, took what I could get. For years, I bathed each morning, frosted my cheeks with Aqua Velva, donned a three-piece suit and snap-brim hat, and, feeling like Superman emerging from a telephone booth, set forth to save the world from a lack of life insurance. I loathed the job so much that I did it quickly, urgently, almost violently. It was Annie who got me to rent the farm. It was Annie who got me to buy it. I operate it the way a child fits together his first puzzle—awkwardly, slowly, but, when a piece slips into the proper slot, with pride and relief and joy.

I built the field and waited, and waited, and waited.

"It will happen, honey," Annie would say when I stood shaking my head at my folly. People looked at me. I must have had a nickname in town. But I could feel the magic building like a gathering storm. It felt as if small animals were scurrying through my veins. I knew it was going to happen soon.

One night I watch Annie looking out the window. She is soft as a butterfly, Annie is, with an evil grin and a tongue that travels at the speed of light. Her jeans are painted to her body, and her pointy little nipples poke at the front of a black T-shirt that has the single word RAH! emblazoned in waspish yellow capitals. Her red hair is short and curly. She has the green eyes of a cat.

Annie understands, though it is me she understands and not always what is happening. She attends ballgames with me and squeezes my arm when there's a hit, but her heart isn't in it and she would just as soon be at home. She loses interest if the score isn't close, or the weather's not warm, or the pace isn't fast enough. To me it is baseball, and that is all that matters. It is the game that's important—the tension, the strategy, the ballet of the fielders, the angle of the bat.

"There's someone on your lawn," Annie says to me, staring out into the orange-tinted dusk. "I can't see him clearly, but I can tell someone is there." She was quite right, at least about it being *my* lawn, although it is not in the strictest sense of the word a lawn; it is a *left field*.

I have been more restless than usual this night. I have sensed the magic drawing closer, hovering somewhere out in the night like a zeppelin, silky and silent, floating like the moon until the time is right.

Annie peeks through the drapes. "There *is* a man out there; I can see his silhouette. He's wearing a baseball uniform, an old-fashioned one."

"It's Shoeless Joe Jackson," I say. My heart sounds like someone flicking a balloon with his index finger.

"Oh," she says. Annie stays very calm in emergencies. She Band-Aids bleeding fingers and toes, and patches the plumbing with gum and good wishes. Staying calm makes her able to live with me. The French have the right words for Annie—she has a good heart.

"Is he the Jackson on TV? The one you yell 'Drop it, Jackson' at?"

Annie's sense of baseball history is not highly developed.

"No, that's Reggie. This is Shoeless Joe Jackson. He hasn't played major-league baseball since 1920."

"Well, Ray, aren't you going to go out and chase him off your lawn, or something?"

Yes. What am I going to do? I wish someone else understood. Perhaps my daughter will. She has an evil grin and bewitching eyes and loves to climb into my lap and watch television baseball with me. There is a magic about her.

"I think I'll go upstairs and read for a while," Annie says. "Why don't you invite Shoeless Jack in for coffee?" I feel the greatest tenderness toward her then, something akin to the rush of love I felt the first time I held my daughter in my arms. Annie senses that magic is about to happen. She knows she is not part of it. My impulse is to pull her to me as she walks by, the denim of her thighs making a tiny music. But I don't. She will be waiting for me.

As I step out onto the verandah, I can hear the steady drone of the crowd, like bees humming on a white afternoon, and the voices of the vendors, like crows cawing.

A ground mist, like wisps of gauze, snakes in slow circular motions just above the grass.

"The grass is soft as a child's breath," I say to the moonlight. On the porch wall I find the switch, and the single battery of floodlights I have erected behind the left-field fence sputters to life. "I've tended it like I would my own baby. It has been powdered and lotioned and loved. It is ready."

Moonlight butters the whole Iowa night. Clover and corn smells are thick as syrup. I experience a tingling like the tiniest of electric wires touching the back of my neck, sending warm sensations through me. Then, as the lights flare, a scar against the blue-black sky, I see Shoeless Joe Jackson standing out in left field. His feet spread wide, body bent forward from the waist, hands on hips, he waits. I hear the sharp crack of the bat, and Shoeless Joe drifts effortlessly a few steps to his left, raises his right hand to signal for the ball, camps under it for a second or two, catches it, at the same time transferring it to his throwing hand, and fires it to the infield.

I make my way to left field, walking in the darkness far outside the third-base line, behind where the third-base stands would be. I climb up on the wobbly bleacher behind the fence. I can look right down on Shoeless Joe. He fields a single on one hop and pegs the ball to third.

"How does it play?" I holler down.

"The ball bounces true," he replies.

"I know." I am smiling with pride, and my heart thumps mightily against my ribs. "I've hit a thousand line drives and as many grounders. It's true as a felt-top table."

"It is," says Shoeless Joe. "It is true."

I lean back and watch the game. From where I sit the scene is as complete as in any of the major-league baseball parks I have ever visited: the two teams, the stands, the fans, the lights, the vendors, the scoreboard. The only difference is that I sit alone in the left-field bleacher and the only player who seems to have substance is Shoeless Joe Jackson. When Joe's team is at bat, the left fielder below me is transparent, as if he were made of vapor. He performs mechanically but seems not to have facial features. We do not converse.

A great amphitheater of grandstand looms dark against the sky, the park is surrounded by decks of floodlights making it brighter than day, the crowd buzzes, the vendors hawk their wares, and I cannot keep the promise I made myself not to ask Shoeless Joe Jackson about his suspension and what it means to him.

While the pitcher warms up for the third inning we talk.

"It must have been . . . It must have been like . . ." But I can't find the words.

"Like having a part of me amputated, slick and smooth and painless." Joe looks up at me and his dark eyes seem about to burst with the pain of it. "A friend of mine used to tell about the war, how him and a buddy was running across a field when a piece of shrapnel took his friend's head off, and how the friend ran, headless, for several strides before he fell. I'm told that old men wake in the night and scratch itchy legs that have been dust for fifty years. That was me. Years and years later, I'd wake in the night with the smell of the ballpark in my nose and the cool of the grass on my feet. The thrill of the grass . . ."

How I wish my father could be here with me. If he'd lasted just a few months longer, he could have watched our grainy black-and-white TV as Bill Mazeroski homered in the bottom of the ninth to beat the Yankees 10–9. We would have joined hands and danced around the kitchen like madmen. "The Yankees lose so seldom you have to celebrate every single time," he used to say. We were always going to go to a major-league baseball game, he and I. But the time was never right, the money always needed for something else. One of the last days of his life, late in the night while I sat with him because the pain wouldn't let him sleep, the radio picked up a static-y station broadcasting a White Sox game. We hunched over the radio and cheered them on, but they lost. Dad told the story of the Black Sox Scandal for the last time. Told of seeing two of those World Series games, told of the way Shoeless Joe Jackson hit, told the dimensions of Comiskey Park, and how, during the series, the mobsters in striped suits sat in the box seats with their colorful women, watching the game and perhaps making plans to go out later and kill a rival.

"You must go," Dad said. "I've been in all sixteen major-league parks. I want you to do it too. The summers belong to somebody else now, have for a long time." I nodded agreement.

"Hell, you know what I mean," he said, shaking his head. I did indeed.

"I LOVED THE GAME," Shoeless Joe went on. "I'd have played for food money. I'd have played free and worked for food. It was the game, the parks, the smells, the sounds. Have you ever held a bat or a baseball to your face? The varnish, the leather. And it was the crowd, the excitement of them rising as one when the ball was hit deep. The sound was like a chorus. Then there was the chug-a-lug of the tin lizzies in the parking lots, and the hotels with their brass spittoons in the lobbies and brass beds in the rooms. It makes me tingle all over like a kid on his way to his first doubleheader, just to talk about it."

The year after Annie and I were married, the year we first rented this farm, I dug Annie's garden for her; dug it by hand, stepping a spade into the soft black soil, ruining my salesman's hands. After I finished, it rained, an Iowa spring rain as soft as spray from a warm hose. The clods of earth I had dug seemed to melt until the garden leveled out, looking like a patch of black ocean. It was near noon on a gentle Sunday when I walked out to that garden. The soil was soft and my shoes disappeared as I plodded until I was near the center. There I knelt, the soil cool on my knees. I looked up at the low gray sky; the rain had stopped and the only sound was the surrounding trees dripping fragrantly. Suddenly I thrust my hands wrist-deep into the snuffy-black earth. The air was pure. All around me the clean smell of earth and water. Keeping my hands buried I stirred the earth with my fingers and knew I loved Iowa as much as a man could love a piece of earth.

When I came back to the house Annie stopped me at the door, made me wait on the verandah and then hosed me down as if I were a door with too many handprints on it, while I tried to explain my epiphany. It is very difficult to describe an experience of religious significance while you are being sprayed with a garden hose by a laughing, loving woman.

"What happened to the sun?" Shoeless Joe says to me, waving his hand toward the banks of floodlights that surround the park.

"Only stadium in the big leagues that doesn't have them is Wrigley Field," I say. "The owners found that more people could attend night games. They even play the World Series at night now."

Joe purses his lips, considering.

"It's harder to see the ball, especially at the plate."

"When there are breaks, they usually go against the ballplayers, right? But I notice you're three-for-three so far," I add, looking down at his uniform, the only identifying marks a large *S* with an O in the top crook, an X in the bottom, and an American flag with forty-eight stars on his left sleeve near the elbow.

Joe grins. "I'd play for the Devil's own team just for the touch of a baseball. Hell, I'd play in the dark if I had to."

I want to ask about that day in December 1951. If he'd lived another few years things might have been different. There was a move afoot to have his record cleared, but it died with him. I wanted to ask, but my instinct told me not to. There are things it is better not to know.

It is one of those nights when the sky is close enough to touch, so close that looking up is like seeing my own eyes reflected in a rain barrel. I sit in the bleacher just outside the left-field fence. I clutch in my hand a hot dog with mustard, onions, and green relish. The voice of the crowd roars in my ears. Chords of "The Star-Spangled Banner" and "Take Me Out to the Ballgame" float across the field. A Coke bottle is propped against my thigh, squat, greenish, the ice-cream-haired elf grinning conspiratorially from the cap.

Below me in left field, Shoeless Joe Jackson glides over the plush velvet grass, silent as a jungle cat. He prowls and paces, crouches ready to spring as, nearly 300 feet away, the ball is pitched. At the sound of the bat he wafts in whatever direction is required, as if he were on ball bearings.

Then the intrusive sound of a slamming screen door reaches me, and I blink and start. I recognize it as the sound of the door to my house, and, looking into the distance, I can see a shape that I know is my daughter, toddling down the back steps. Perhaps the lights or the crowd have awakened her and she has somehow eluded Annie. I judge the distance to the steps. I am just to the inside of the foul pole, which is exactly 330 feet from home plate. I tense. Karin will surely be drawn to the lights and the emerald dazzle of the infield. If she touches anything, I fear it will all disappear, perhaps forever. Then, as if she senses my discomfort, she stumbles away from the lights, walking in the ragged fringe of darkness well outside the third-base line. She trails a blanket behind her, one tiny fist rubbing a sleepy eye. She is barefoot and wears a white flannelette nightgown covered in an explosion of daisies.

She climbs up the bleacher, alternating a knee and a foot on each step, and crawls into my lap silently, like a kitten. I hold her close and wrap the blanket around her feet. The play goes on; her innocence has not disturbed the balance. "What is it?" she says shyly, her eyes indicating she means all that she sees.

"Just watch the left fielder," I say. "He'll tell you all you ever need to know about a baseball game. Watch his feet as the pitcher accepts the sign and gets ready to pitch. A good left fielder knows what pitch is coming, and he can tell from the angle of the bat where the ball is going to be hit, and, if he's good, how hard."

I look down at Karin. She cocks one green eye at me, wrinkling her nose, then snuggles into my chest, the index finger of her right hand tracing tiny circles around her nose.

The crack of the bat is sharp as the yelp of a kicked cur. Shoeless Joe whirls, takes five loping strides directly toward us, turns again, reaches up, and the ball smacks into his glove. The final batter dawdles in the on-deck circle.

"Can I come back again?" Joe asks.

"I built this left field for you. It's yours anytime you want to use it. They play one hundred sixty-two games a season now."

"There are others," he says. "If you were to finish the infield, why, old Chick Gandil could play first base, and we'd have the Swede at shortstop and Buck Weaver at third." I can feel his excitement rising. "We could stick McMullin in at second, and Eddie Cicotte and Lefty Williams would like to pitch again. Do you think you could finish center field? It would mean a lot to Happy Felsch."

"Consider it done," I say, hardly thinking of the time, the money, the backbreaking labor it would entail. "Consider it done," I say again, then stop suddenly as an idea creeps into my brain like a runner inching off first base.

"I know a catcher," I say. "He never made the majors, but in his prime he was good. Really good. Played Class B ball in Florida and California . . ."

"We could give him a try," says Shoeless Joe. "You give us a place to play and we'll look at your catcher."

I swear the stars have moved in close enough to eavesdrop as I sit in this single rickety bleacher that I built with my unskilled hands, looking down at Shoeless Joe Jackson. A breath of clover travels on the summer wind. Behind me, just yards away, brook water plashes softly in the darkness, a frog shrills, fireflies dazzle the night like red pepper. A petal falls.

"God what an outfield," he says. "What a left field." He looks up at me and I look down at him. "This must be heaven," he says.

"No. It's Iowa," I reply automatically. But then I feel the night rubbing softly against my face like cherry blossoms; look at the sleeping girl-child in my arms, her small hand curled around one of my fingers; think of the fierce warmth of the woman waiting for me in the house; inhale the fresh-cut grass smell that seems locked in the air like permanent incense; and listen to the drone of the crowd, as below me Shoeless Joe Jackson tenses, watching the angle of the distant bat for a clue as to where the ball will be hit.

"I think you're right, Joe," I say, but softly enough not to disturb his concentration.

HATRACK RIVER

BY ORSON SCOTT CARD

In his mammoth multivolume fantasy series featuring the Seventh Son of a Seventh Son named Alvin Maker, Orson Scott card has undertaken the writing of an American frontier history that might have been had such things as hexes, knacks, second sights, etc., really existed in the manner that superstitious folk thought they did.

... And it all began at "Hatrack River."

Little Peggy was very careful with the eggs. She rooted her hand through the straw till her fingers bumped something hard and heavy. She gave no never mind to the chicken drips. After all, Mama never even crinkled her face to open up Cally's most spetackler diapers. Even when the chicken drips were wet and stringy and made her fingers stick together, little Peggy gave no never mind. She just pushed the straw apart, wrapped her hand around the egg, and lifted it out of the brood box. All this while standing tip-toe on a wobbly stool, reaching high above her head. Mama said she was too young for egging, but little Peggy showed her. Every day she felt in every brood box and brought in every egg, every single one, that's what she did.

Every one, she said in her mind, over and over: I got to reach into every one.

Then little Peggy looked back into the northeast corner, the darkest place in the whole coop, and there sat Bloody Mary in her brood box, looking like the devil's own bad dream, hatefulness shining out of her nasty eyes, saying Come here little girl and give me nips. I want nips of finger and nips of thumb and if you come real close and try to take my egg I'll get a nip of eye from you.

Most animals didn't have much heartfire, but Bloody Mary's was strong and made a poison smoke. Nobody else could see it, but little Peggy could. Bloody Mary dreamed of death for all folks, but most specially for a certain little girl five years old, and little Peggy had the marks on her fingers to prove it. At least one mark, anyway, and even if Papa said he couldn't see it, little Peggy remembered how she got it and nobody could blame her none if she sometimes forgot to reach under Bloody Mary who sat there like a bushwhacker waiting to kill the first folks that just tried to come by. Nobody'd get mad if she just sometimes forgot to look there.

I forgot forgot forgot. I looked in every brood box, every one, and if one got missed then I forgot forgot forgot.

Everybody knew Bloody Mary was a lowdown chicken and too mean to give any eggs that wasn't rotten anyway.

I forgot.

She got the egg basket inside before Mama even had the fire het, and Mama was so pleased she let little Peggy put the eggs one by one into the cold water. Then Mama put the pot on the hook and swung it right on over the fire. Boiling eggs you didn't have to wait for the fire to slack, you could do it smoke and all.

"Peg," said Papa.

That was Mama's name, but Papa didn't say it in his Mama voice. He said it in his little-Peggy-you're-in-dutch voice, and little Peggy knew she was completely found out, and so she turned right around and yelled what she'd been planning to say all along.

"I forgot, Papa!"

Mama turned and looked at little Peggy in surprise. Papa wasn't surprised though. He just raised an eyebrow. He was holding his hand behind his back. Little Peggy knew there was an egg in that hand. Bloody Mary's nasty egg.

"What did you forget, little Peggy?" asked Papa, talking soft.

Right that minute little Peggy reckoned she was the stupidest girl ever born on the face of the earth. Here she was denying before anybody accused her of anything.

But she wasn't going to give up, not right off like that. She couldn't stand to have them mad at her and she just wanted them to let her go away and live in England. So she put on her innocent face and said, "I don't know, Papa."

She figgered England was the best place to go live, cause England had a Lord Protector. From the look in Papa's eye, a Lord Protector was pretty much what she needed just now.

"What did you forget?" Papa asked again.

"Just say it and be done, Horace," said Mama. "If she's done wrong then she's done wrong."

"I forgot one time, Papa," said little Peggy. "She's a mean old chicken and she hates me."

Papa answered soft and slow. "One time," he said.

Then he took his hand from behind him. Only it wasn't no single egg he held, it was a whole basket. And that basket was filled with a clot of straw—most likely all the straw from Bloody Mary's box—and that straw was mashed together and glued tight with dried-up raw egg and shell bits, mixed up with about three or four chewed-up baby chicken bodies.

"Did you have to bring that in the house before breakfast, Horace?" said Mama.

"I don't know what makes me madder," said Horace. "What she done wrong or her studying up to lie about it."

"I didn't study and I didn't lie!" shouted little Peggy. Or anyways she meant to shout. What came out sounded espiciously like crying even though little Peggy had decided only yesterday that she was done with crying for the rest of her life.

"See?" said Mama. "She already feels bad."

"She feels bad being caught," said Horace. "You're too slack on her, Peg. She's got a lying spirit. I don't want my daughter growing up wicked. I'd rather see her dead like her baby sister before I see her grow up wicked."

Little Peggy saw Mama's heartfire flare up with memory, and in front of her eyes she could see a baby laid out pretty in a little box, and then another one only not so pretty cause it was the second baby Missy, the one what died of pox so nobody'd touch her but her own Mama, who was still so feeble from the pox herself that she couldn't do much. Little Peggy saw that scene, and she knew Papa had made a mistake to say what he said cause Mama's face went cold even though her heartfire was hot.

"That's the wickedest thing anybody ever said in my presence," said Mama. Then she took up the basket of corruption from the table and took it outside.

"Bloody Mary bites my hand," said little Peggy.

"We'll see what bites," said Papa. "For leaving the eggs I give you one whack, because I reckon that lunatic hen looks fearsome to a frog-size girl like you. But for telling lies I give you ten whacks."

Little Peggy cried in earnest at that news. Papa gave an honest count and full measure in everything, but most especially in whacks.

Papa took the hazel rod off the high shelf. He kept it up there ever since little Peggy put the old one in the fire and burnt it right up.

"I'd rather hear a thousand hard and bitter truths from you, Daughter, than one soft and easy lie," said he, and then he bent over and laid on with the rod across her thighs. Whick whick whick, she counted every one, they stung her to the heart, each one of them, they were so full of anger. Worst of all she knew it was all unfair because his heartfire raged for a different cause altogether, and it always did. Papa's hate for wickedness always came from his most secret memory. Little Peggy didn't understand it all, because it was twisted up and confused and Papa didn't remember it right well himself. All little Peggy ever saw plain was that it was a lady and it wasn't Mama. Papa thought of that lady whenever something went wrong. When baby Missy died of nothing at all, and then the next baby also named Missy died of pox, and then the barn burnt down once, and a cow died, everything that went wrong made him think of that lady and he began to talk about how much he hated wickedness and at those times the hazel rod flew hard and sharp.

I'd rather hear a thousand hard and bitter truths, that's what he said, but little Peggy knew that there was one truth he didn't ever want to hear, and so she kept it to herself. She'd never shout it at him, even if it made him break the hazel rod, cause whenever she thought of saying aught about that lady, she kept picturing her father dead, and that was a thing she never hoped to see for real. Besides, the lady that haunted his heartfire, she didn't have no clothes on, and little Peggy knew that she'd be whipped for sure if she talked about people being naked.

So she took the whacks and cried till she could taste that her nose was running. Papa left the room right away, and Mama came back to fix up breakfast for the blacksmith and the visitors and the hands, but neither one said boo to her, just as if they didn't even notice. She cried even harder and louder for a minute, but it didn't help. Finally she picked up her Bugy from the sewing basket and walked all stiff-legged out to Oldpappy's cabin and woke him right up.

He listened to her story like he always did.

"I know about Bloody Mary," he said, "and I told your papa fifty times if I told him once, wring that chicken's neck and be done. She's a crazy bird. Every week or so she gets crazy and breaks all her own eggs, even the ones ready to hatch. Kills her own chicks. It's a lunatic what kills its own."

"Papa like to killed me," said little Peggy.

"I reckon if you can walk somewhat it ain't so bad altogether."

"I can't walk much."

"No, I can see you're nigh crippled forever," said Oldpappy. "But I tell you what, the way I see it your mama and your papa's mostly mad at each other. So why don't you just disappear for a couple of hours?"

"I wish I could turn into a bird and fly."

"Next best thing, though," said Pappy, "is to have a secret place where nobody knows to look for you. Do you have a place like that? No, don't tell me—it wrecks it if you tell even a single other person. You just go to that place for a while. As long as it's a safe place, not out in the woods where a Red might take your pretty hair, and not a high place where you might fall off, and not a tiny place where you might get stuck."

"It's big and it's low and it ain't in the woods," said little Peggy.

"Then you go there, Maggie."

Little Peggy made the face she always made when Oldpappy called her that. And she held up Bugy and in Bugy's squeaky high voice she said, "Her name is Peggy."

"You go there, *Piggy*, if you like that better—"

Little Peggy slapped Bugy right across Oldpappy's knee.

"Someday Bugy'll do that once too often and have a rupture and die," said Old-pappy.

But Bugy just danced right in his face and insisted, "Not piggy, *Peggy!*"

"That's right, Puggy, you go to that secret place and if anybody says, We got to go find that girl, I'll say, I know where she is and she'll come back when she's good and ready."

Little Peggy ran for the cabin door and then stopped and turned. "Oldpappy, you're the nicest grown-up in the whole world."

"Your papa has a different view of me, but that's all tied up with another hazel rod that I laid hand on much too often. Now run along."

She stopped again right before she closed the door. "You're the *only* nice grown-up!" She shouted it real loud, halfway hoping that they could hear it clear inside the house. Then she was gone, right across the garden, out past the cow pasture, up the hill into the woods, and along the path to the spring house.

THEY HAD ONE GOOD WAGON, these folks did, and two good horses pulling it. One might even suppose they was prosperous, considering they had six big boys, from mansize on down to twins that had wrestled each other into being a good deal stronger than their dozen years. Not to mention one big daughter and a whole passel of little girls. A big family. Right prosperous if you didn't know that not even a year ago they had owned a mill and lived in a big house on a streambank in west New Hampshire. Come down far in the world, they had, and this wagon was all they had left of everything. But they were hopeful, trekking west along the roads that crossed the Hio, heading for open land that was free for the taking. If you were a family with plenty of strong backs and clever hands, it'd be good land, too, as long as the weather was with them and the Reds didn't raid them and all the lawyers and bankers stayed in New England.

The father was a big man, a little run to fat, which was no surprise since millers mostly stood around all day. That softness in the belly wouldn't last a year on a deepwoods homestead. He didn't care much about that, anyway—he had no fear of hard work. What worried him today was his wife, Faith. It was her time for that baby, he knew it. Not that she'd ever talk about it direct. Women just don't speak about things like that with men. But he knew how big she was and how many months it had been. Besides, at the noon stop she murmured to him, "Alvin Miller, if there's a road house along this way, or even a little broke-down cabin, I reckon I could use a bit of rest." A man didn't have to be a philosopher to understand her. And after six sons and six daughters, he'd have to have the brains of a brick not to get the drift of how things stood with her.

So he sent the oldest boy, Vigor, to run ahead on the road and see the lay of the land.

You could tell they were from New England, cause the boy didn't take no gun. If there'd been a bushwhacker the young man never would've made it back, and the fact he came back with all his hair was proof no Red had spotted him—the French up Detroit way were paying for English scalps with liquor and if a Red saw a white man alone in the woods with no rifle he'd own that white man's scalp. So maybe a man could think that luck was with the family at last. But since these Yankees had no notion that the road wasn't safe, Alvin Miller didn't think for a minute of his good luck.

Vigor's word was of a road house three miles on. That was good news, except that between them and that road house was a river. Kind of a scrawny river, and the ford was shallow, but Alvin Miller had learned never to trust water. No matter how peaceful it looks, it'll reach and try to take you. He was halfway minded to tell Faith that they'd spend the night this side of the river, but she gave just the tiniest groan and at that moment he knew that there was no chance of that. Faith had borne him a dozen living children, but it was four years since the last one and a lot of women took it bad, having a baby so late. A lot of women died. A good road house meant women to help with the birthing, so they'd have to chance the river.

And Vigor did say the river wasn't much.

THE AIR IN THE SPRING HOUSE was cool and heavy, dark and wet. Sometimes when little Peggy caught a nap here, she woke up gasping like as if the whole place was under water. She had dreams of water even when she wasn't here—that was one of the things that made some folks say she was a seeper instead of a torch. But when she dreamed outside, she always knew she was dreaming. Here the water was real.

Real in the drips that formed like sweat on the milkjars setting in the stream. Real in the cold damp clay of the spring house floor. Real in the swallowing sound of the stream as it hurried through the middle of the house.

Keeping it cool all summer long, cold water spilling right out of the hill and into this place, shaded all the way by trees so old the moon made a point of passing through their branches just to hear some good old tales. That was what little Peggy always came here for, even when Papa didn't hate her. Not the wetness of the air, she could do just fine without that. It was the way the fire went right out of her and she didn't have to be a torch. Didn't have to see into all the dark places where folks hid theirselfs.

From her they hid theirselfs as if it would do some good. Whatever they didn't like most about theirself they tried to tuck away in some dark corner but they didn't know how all them dark places burned in little Peggy's eyes. Even when she was so little that she spit out her corn mash cause she was still hoping for a suck, she knew all the stories that the folks around her kept all hid. She saw the bits of their past that they most wished they could bury, and she saw the bits of their future that they most feared.

And that was why she took to coming up here to the spring house. Here she didn't have to see those things. Not even the lady in Papa's memory. There was nothing here but the heavy wet dark cool air to quench the fire and dim the light so she could be—just for a few minutes in the day—a little five-year-old girl with a straw puppet named Bugy and not even have to *think* about any of them grown-up secrets.

I'm not wicked, she told herself. Again and again but it didn't work because she knew she was.

All right then, she said to herself, I *am* wicked. But I won't be wicked anymore. I'll tell the truth like Papa says, or I'll say nothing at all.

Even at five years old, little Peggy knew that if she kept that vow, she'd be better off saying nothing.

So she said nothing, not even to herself, just lay there on a mossy damp table with Bugy clenched tight enough to strangle in her fist.

Ching ching ching.

Little Peggy woke up and got mad for just a minute.

Ching ching ching.

Made her mad because nobody said to her, Little Peggy, you don't mind if we talk this young blacksmith feller into settling down here, do you?

Not at all, Papa, she would've said if they'd asked. She knew what it meant to have a smithy. It meant your village would thrive, and folks from other places would come, and when they came there'd be trade, and when there was trade then her father's big house could be a forest inn, and when there was a forest inn all the roads would kind of bend a little just to pass the place, if it wasn't too far out of the way—little Peggy knew all that, as sure as the children of farmers knew the rhythms of the farm. A road house by a smithy was a road house that would prosper. So she would've said, sure enough, let him stay, deed him land, brick his chimney, feed him free, let him have my bed so I have to double up with Cousin Peter who keeps trying to peek under my nightgown, I'll put up with all that—just as long as you don't put him near the spring house so that all the time, even when I want to be alone with the water, there's that whack thump hiss roar, noise all the time, and a fire burning up the sky to turn it black, and the smell of charcoal burning. It was enough to make a body wish to follow the stream right back into the mountain just to get some peace.

Of course the stream was the smart place to put the blacksmith. Except for water, he could've put his smithy anywheres at all. The iron came to him in the shipper's wagon clear from New Netherland, and the charcoal—well, there were plenty of farmers willing to trade charcoal for a good shoe. But water, that's what the smith needed that nobody'd bring him, so of course they put him right down the hill from the spring house where his ching ching ching could wake her up and put the fire back into her in the one place where she had used to be able to let it burn low and go almost to cold wet ash.

A roar of thunder.

She was at the door in a second. Had to see the lightning. Caught just the last shadow of the light but she knew that there'd be more. It wasn't much after noon, surely, or had she slept all day? What with all these blackbelly clouds she couldn't tell—it might as well be the last minutes of dusk. The air was all a-prickle with lightning just waiting to flash. She knew that feeling, knew it meant the lightning'd hit close.

She looked down to see if the blacksmith's stable was still full of horses. It was. The shoeing wasn't done, the road would turn to muck, and so the farmer with his two sons from out West Fork way was stuck here. Not a chance they'd head home in *this*, with lightning ready to put a fire in the woods, or knock a tree down on them, or maybe just smack them a good one and lay them all out dead in a circle like them five Quakers they still was talking about and here it happened back in '90 when the first white folks came to settle here. People talked still about the Circle of Five and all that, some people wondering if God up and smashed them flat so as to shut the Quakers up, seeing how nothing else ever could, while other people was wondering if God took them up into heaven like the first Lord Protector Oliver Cromwell who was smote by lightning at the age of ninety-seven and just disappeared.

No, that farmer and his big old boys'd stay another night. Little Peggy was an innkeeper's daughter, wasn't she? Papooses learnt to hunt, pickaninnies learnt to tote, farmer children learnt the weather, and an innkeeper's daughter learnt which folks would stay the night, even before they knew it right theirselfs.

Their horses were champing in the stable, snorting and warning each other about the storm. In every group of horses, little Peggy figgered, there must be one that's remarkable dumb, so all the others have to tell him what all's going on. Bad storm, they were saying. We're going to get a soaking, if the lightning don't smack us first. And the dumb one kept nickering and saying. What's the noise, what's that noise.

Then the sky just opened right up and dumped water on the earth. Stripped leaves right off the trees, it came down so hard. Came down so thick, too, that little Peggy didn't even see the smithy for a minute and she thought maybe it got washed right away into the stream. Oldpappy told her how that stream led right down to the Hatrack River, and the Hatrack poured right into the Hio, and the Hio shoved itself on through the woods to the Mizzipy, which went on down to the sea, and Oldpappy said how the sea drank so much water that it got indigestion and gave off the biggest old belches you ever heard, and what came up was clouds. Belches from the sea, and now the smithy would float all that way, get swallered up and belched out, and someday she'd just be minding her own business and some cloud would break up and plop that smithy down as neat as you please, old Makepeace Smith still ching ching chinging away.

Then the rain slacked off a mite and she looked down to see the smithy still there. But that wasn't what she saw at all. No, what she saw was sparks of fire way off in the forest, downstream toward the Hatrack, down where the ford was, only there wasn't a chance of taking the ford today, with this rain. Sparks, lots of sparks, and she knew every one of them was folks. She didn't hardly think of doing it anymore, she only had to see their heartfires and she was looking close. Maybe future, maybe past, all the visions lived together in the heartfire.

What she saw right now was the same in all their hearts. A wagon in the middle of the Hatrack, with the water rising and everything they owned in all the world in that wagon.

Little Peggy didn't talk much, but everybody knew she was a torch, so they listened whenever she spoke up about trouble. Specially this kind of trouble. Sure the settlements in these parts were pretty old now, a fair bit older than little Peggy herself, but they hadn't forgotten yet that anybody's wagon caught in a flood is everybody's loss.

She fair to flew down that grassy hill, jumping gopher holes and sliding the steep places, so it wasn't twenty seconds from seeing those far-off heartfires till she was speaking right up in the smithy's shop. That farmer from West Fork at first wanted to make her wait till he was done with telling stories about worse storms he'd seen. But Makepeace knew all about little Peggy. He just listened right up and then told those boys to saddle them horses, shoes or no shoes, there was folks caught in the Hatrack ford and there was no time for foolishness. Little Peggy didn't even get a chance to see them go—Makepeace had already sent her off to the big house to fetch her father and all the hands and visitors there. Wasn't a one of them who hadn't once put all they owned in the world into a wagon and dragged it west across the mountain roads and down into the forest. Wasn't a one of them who hadn't felt a river sucking at that wagon, wanting to steal it away. They all got right to it. That's the way it was then, you see. Folks noticed other people's trouble every bit as quick as if it was their own.

VIGOR LED THE BOYS in trying to push the wagon, while Eleanor hawed the horses. Alvin Miller spent his time carrying the little girls one by one to safety on the far shore. The current was a devil clawing at him, whispering, "I'll have your babies, I'll have them all," but Alvin said no, with every muscle in his body as he strained shoreward he said no to that whisper, till his girls stood all bedraggled on the bank with rain streaming down their faces like the tears from all the grief in the world.

He would have carried Faith, too, baby in her belly and all, but she wouldn't budge. Just sat inside that wagon, bracing herself against the trunks and furniture as the wagon tipped and rocked. Lightning crashed and branches broke; one of them tore the canvas and the water poured into the wagon but Faith held on with white knuckles and her eyes staring out. Alvin knew from her eyes there wasn't a thing he could say to make her let go. There was only one way to get Faith and her unborn baby out of that river, and that was to get the wagon out.

"Horses can't get no purchase, Papa," Vigor shouted. "They're just stumbling and bound to break a leg."

"Well we can't pull out without the horses!"

"The horses are *something*, Papa. We leave 'em in here and we'll lose wagon and horses too!"

"Your mama won't leave that wagon."

And he saw understanding in Vigor's eyes. The *things* in the wagon weren't worth a risk of death to save them. But Mama was.

"Still," he said. "On shore the team could pull strong. Here in the water they can't do a thing."

"Set the boys to unhitching them. But first tie a line to a tree to hold that wagon!"

It wasn't two minutes before the twins Wastenot and Wantnot were on the shore making the rope fast to a stout tree. David and Measure made another line fast to the rig that held the horses, while Calm cut the strands that held them to the wagon. Good boys, doing their work just right, Vigor shouting directions while Alvin could only watch helpless at the back of the wagon, looking now at Faith who was trying not to have the baby, now at the Hatrack River that was trying to push them all down to hell.

Not much of a river, Vigor had said, but then the clouds came up and the rain came down and the Hatrack became something after all. Even so it looked passable when they got to it. The horses strode in strong, and Alvin was just saying to Calm, who had the reins, "Well, we made it not a minute to spare," when the river went insane. It doubled in speed and strength all in a moment, and the horses got panicky and lost direction and started pulling against each other. The boys all hopped into the river and tried to lead them to shore but by then the wagon's momentum had been lost and the wheels were mired up and stuck fast. Almost as if the river knew they were coming and saved up its worst fury till they were already in it and couldn't get away.

"Look out! Look out!" screamed Measure from the shore.

Alvin looked upstream to see what devilment the river had in mind, and there was a whole tree floating down the river, endwise like a battering ram, the root end pointed at the center of the wagon, straight at the place where Faith was sitting, her baby on the verge of birth. Alvin couldn't think of anything to do, couldn't think at all, just screamed his wife's name with all his strength. Maybe in his heart he thought that by holding her name on his lips he could keep her alive, but there was no hope of that, no hope at all.

Except that Vigor didn't know there was no hope. Vigor leapt out when the tree was no more than a rod away, his body falling against it just above the root. The momentum of his leap turned it a little, then rolled it over, rolled it and turned it away from the wagon. Of course Vigor rolled with it, pulled right under the water— but it worked, the root end of the tree missed the wagon entirely, and the shaft of the trunk struck it a sidewise blow.

The tree bounded across the stream and smashed up against a boulder on the bank. Alvin was five rods off, but in his memory from then on, he always saw it like as if he'd been right there. The tree crashing into the boulder, and Vigor between them. Just a split second that lasted a lifetime, Vigor's eyes wide with surprise, blood already leaping out of his mouth, spattering out onto the tree that killed him. Then the Hatrack River swept the tree out into the current. Vigor slipped under the water, all except his arm, all tangled in the roots, which stuck up into the air for all the world like a neighbor waving good-bye after a visit.

Alvin was so intent on watching his dying son that he didn't even notice what was happening to his own self. The blow from the tree was enough to dislodge the mired wheels, and the current picked up the wagon, carried it downstream, Alvin clinging to the tailgate, Faith weeping inside, Eleanor screaming her lungs out from the driver's seat, and the boys on the bank shouting something. Shouting "Hold! Hold! Hold!"

The rope held, one end tied to a strong tree, the other end tied to the wagon, it held. The river couldn't tumble the wagon downstream; instead it swung the wagon to shore the way a boy swings a rock on a string, and when it came to a shuddering stop it was right against the bank, the front end facing upstream.

"It held!" cried the boys.

"Thank God!" shouted Eleanor.

"The baby's coming," whispered Faith.

But Alvin, all he could hear was the single faint cry that had been the last sound from the throat of his firstborn son, all he could see was the way his boy clung to the tree as it rolled and rolled in the water, and all he could say was a single word, a single command. "Live," he murmured. Vigor had always obeyed him before. Hard worker, willing companion, more a friend or brother than a son. But this time he knew his son would disobey. Still he whispered it. "Live."

"Are we safe?" said Faith, her voice trembling.

Alvin turned to face her, tried to strike the grief from his face. No sense her knowing the price that Vigor paid to save her and the baby. Time enough to learn of that after the baby was born. "Can you climb out of the wagon?"

"What's wrong?" asked Faith, looking at his face.

"I took a fright. Tree could have killed us. Can you climb out, now that we're up against the bank?"

Eleanor leaned in from the front of the wagon. "David and Calm are on the bank, they can help you up. The rope's holding, Mama, but who can say how long?"

"Go on, Mother, just a step," said Alvin. "We'll do better with the wagon if we know you're safe on shore."

"The baby's coming," said Faith.

"Better on shore than here," said Alvin sharply. "Go now."

Faith stood up, clambered awkwardly to the front. Alvin climbed through the wagon behind her, to help her if she should stumble. Even he could see how her belly had dropped. The baby must be grabbing for air already.

On the bank it wasn't just David and Calm, now. There were strangers, big men, and several horses. Even one small wagon, and that was a welcome sight. Alvin had no notion who these men were, or how they knew to come and help, but there wasn't a moment to waste on introductions. "You men! Is there a midwife in the road house?"

"Goody Guester does with birthing," said a man. A big man, with arms like oxlegs. A blacksmith, surely.

"Can you take my wife in that wagon? There's not a moment to spare." Alvin knew it was a shameful thing, for men to speak so openly of birthing, right in front of the woman who was set to bear. But Faith was no fool—she knew what mattered most, and getting her to a bed and a competent midwife was more important than pussyfooting around about it.

David and Calm were careful as they helped their mother toward the waiting wagon. Faith was staggering with pain. Women in labor shouldn't have to step from a wagon seat up onto a riverbank, that was sure. Eleanor was right behind her, taking charge as if she wasn't younger than all the boys except the twins. "Measure! Get the girls together. They're riding in the wagon with us. You too, Wastenot and Wantnot! I know you can help the big boys but I need you to watch the girls while I'm with Mother." Eleanor was never one to be trifled with, and the gravity of the situation was such that they didn't even call her Eleanor of Aquitaine as they obeyed. Even the little girls mostly gave over their squabbling and got right in.

Eleanor paused a moment on the bank and looked back to where her father stood on the wagon seat. She glanced downstream, then looked back at him. Alvin understood the question, and he shook his head no. Faith was not to know of Vigor's sacrifice. Tears came unwelcome to Alvin's eyes, but not to Eleanor's. Eleanor was only fourteen, but when she didn't want to cry, she didn't cry.

Wastenot hawed the horse and the little wagon lurched forward, Faith wincing as the girls patted her and the rain poured. Faith's gaze was somber as a cow's, and as mindless, looking back at her husband, back at the river. At times like birthing, Alvin thought, a woman becomes a beast, slack-minded as her body takes over and does its work. How else could she bear the pain? As if the soul of the earth possessed her the way it owns the souls of animals, making her part of the life of the whole world, unhitching her from family, from husband, from all the reins of the human race, leading her into the valley of ripeness and harvest and reaping and bloody death.

"She'll be safe now," the blacksmith said. "And we have horses here to pull your wagon out."

"It's slacking off," said Measure. "The rain is less, and the current's not so strong."

"As soon as your wife stepped ashore, it eased up," said the farmer-looking feller. "The rain's dying, that's sure."

"You took the worst of it in the water," said the blacksmith. "But you're all right now. Get hold of yourself, man, there's work to do."

Only then did Alvin come to himself enough to realize that he was crying. Work to do, that's right, get hold of yourself, Alvin Miller. You're no weakling, to bawl like a baby. Other men have lost a dozen children and still live their lives. You've had twelve, and Vigor lived to be a man, though he never did get to marry and have children of his own. Maybe Alvin had to weep because Vigor died so nobly; maybe he cried because it was so sudden.

David touched the blacksmith's arm. "Leave him be for a minute," he said softly. "Our oldest brother was carried off not ten minutes back. He got tangled in a tree floating down."

"It wasn't no *tangle*," Alvin said sharply. "He jumped that tree and saved our wagon, and your mother inside it! That river paid him back, that's what it did, it punished him."

Calm spoke quietly to the local men. "It run up against that boulder there." They all looked. There was a smear of blood on the rock.

"The Hatrack has a mean streak in it," said the blacksmith, "but I never seen this river so riled up before. I'm sorry about your boy. There's a slow, flat place downstream where he's bound to fetch up. Everything the river catches ends up there. When the storm lets up, we can go down and bring back the—bring him back."

Alvin wiped his eyes on his sleeve, but since his sleeve was soaking wet it didn't do much good. "Give me a minute more and I can pull my weight," said Alvin.

They hitched two more horses and the four beasts had no trouble pulling the wagon out against the much weakened current. By the time the wagon was set to rights again on the road, the sun was even breaking through.

"Wouldn't you know," said the blacksmith. "If you ever don't like the weather hereabouts, you just set a spell, cause it'll change."

"Not this one," said Alvin. "This storm was laid in wait for us."

The blacksmith put an arm across Alvin's shoulder, and spoke real gentle. "No offense, mister, but that's crazy talk."

Alvin shrugged him off. "That storm and that river wanted us."

"Papa," said David, "you're tired and grieving. Best be still till we get to the road house and see how Mama is."

"My baby is a boy," said Papa. "You'll see. He would have been the seventh son of a seventh son."

That got their attention, right enough, that blacksmith and the other men as well. Everybody knew a seventh son had certain gifts, but the seventh son of a seventh son was about as powerful a birth as you could have.

"That makes a difference," said the blacksmith. "He'd have been a born douser, sure, and water hates that." The others nodded sagely.

"The water had its way," said Alvin. "Had its way, and all done. It would've killed Faith and the baby, if it could. But since it couldn't, why, it killed my boy Vigor. And now when the baby comes, he'll be the sixth son, cause I'll only have five living."

"Some says it makes no difference if the first six be alive or not," said a farmer.

Alvin said nothing, but he knew it made all the difference. He had thought this baby would be a miracle child, but the river had taken care of that. If water don't stop you one way, it stops you another. He shouldn't have hoped for a miracle child. The cost was too high. All his eyes could see, all the way home, was Vigor dangling in the grasp of the roots, tumbling through the current like a leaf caught up in a dust devil, with the blood seeping from his mouth to slake the murderous thirst of the Hatrack.

LITTLE PEGGY STOOD in the window, looking out into the storm. She could see all those heartfires, especially one, one so bright it was like the sun when she looked at it. But there was a blackness all around them. No, not even black—a nothingness, like a part of the universe God hadn't finished making, and it swept around those lights as if to tear them from each other, sweep them away, swallow them up. Little Peggy knew what that nothingness was. Those times when her eyes saw the hot yellow heartfires, there were three other colors, too. The rich dark orange of the earth. The thin gray color of the air. And the deep black emptiness of water. It was the water that tore at them now. The river, only she had never seen it so black, so strong, so terrible. The heartfires were so tiny in the night.

"What do you see, child?" asked Oldpappy.

"The river's going to carry them away," said little Peggy.

"I hope not."

Little Peggy began to cry.

"There, child," said Oldpappy. "It ain't always such a grand thing to see afar off like that, is it."

She shook her head.

"But maybe it won't happen as bad as you think."

Just at that moment, she saw one of the heartfires break away and tumble off into the dark. "Oh!" she cried out, reaching as if her hand could snatch the light and put it back. But of course she couldn't. Her vision was long and clear, but her reach was short.

"Are they lost?" asked Oldpappy.

"One," whispered little Peggy.

"Haven't Makepeace and the others got there yet?"

"Just now," she said. "The rope held. They're safe now."

Oldpappy didn't ask her how she knew, or what she saw. Just patted her shoulder.

"Because you told them. Remember that, Margaret. One was lost, but if you hadn't seen and sent help, they might all have died."

She shook her head. "I should've seen them sooner, Oldpappy, but I fell asleep."

"And you blame yourself?" asked Oldpappy.

"I should've let Bloody Mary nip me, and then father wouldn't've been mad, and then I wouldn't've been in the spring house, and then I wouldn't've been asleep, and then I would've sent help in time—"

"We can all make daisy chains of blame like that, Maggie. It don't mean a thing."

But she knew it meant something. You don't blame blind people cause they don't warn you you're about to step on a snake—but you sure blame somebody with eyes who doesn't say a word about it. She knew her duty ever since she first realized that other folks couldn't see all that she could see. God gave her special eyes, so she'd better see and give warning, or the devil would take her soul. The devil or the deep black sea.

"Don't mean a thing," Oldpappy murmured. Then, like he just been poked in the behind with a ramrod, he went all straight and said, "Spring house! Spring house, of course." He pulled her close. "Listen to me, little Peggy. It wasn't none of your fault, and that's the truth. The same water that runs in the Hatrack flows in the spring house brook, it's all the same water, all through the world. The same water that wanted them dead, it knew you could give warning and send help. So it sang to you and sent you off to sleep."

It made a kind of sense to her, it sure did. "How can that be, Oldpappy?"

"Oh, that's just in the nature of it. The whole universe is made of only four kinds of stuff, little Peggy, and each one wants to have its own way." Peggy thought of the four colors that she saw when the heartfires glowed, and she knew what all four were even as Oldpappy named them. "Fire makes things hot and bright and uses them up. Air makes things cool and sneaks in everywhere. Earth makes things solid and sturdy, so they'll last. But water, it tears things down, it falls from the sky and carries off everything it can, carries it off and down to the sea. If the water had its way, the whole world would be smooth, just a big ocean with nothing out of the water's reach. All dead and smooth. That's why you slept. The water wants to tear down these strangers, whoever they are, tear them down and kill them. It's a miracle you woke up at all."

"The blacksmith's hammer woke me," said little Peggy.

"That's it, then, you see? The blacksmith was working with iron, the hardest earth, and with a fierce blast of air from the bellows, and with a fire so hot it burns the grass outside the chimney. The water couldn't touch him to keep him still."

Little Peggy could hardly believe it, but it must be so. The blacksmith had drawn her from a watery sleep. The smith had *helped* her. Why, it was enough to make you laugh, to know the blacksmith was her friend this time.

There was shouting on the porch downstairs, and doors opened and closed. "Some folks is here already," said Oldpappy.

Little Peggy saw the heartfires downstairs, and found the one with the strongest fear and pain. "It's their Mama," said little Peggy. "She's got a baby coming."

"Well, if that ain't the luck of it. Lose one, and here already is a baby to replace death with life." Oldpappy shambled on out to go downstairs and help.

Little Peggy, though, she just stood there, looking at what she saw in the distance. That lost heartfire wasn't lost at all, and that was sure. She could see it burning away far off, despite how the darkness of the river tried to cover it. He wasn't dead, just carried off, and maybe somebody could help him. She ran out then, passed Oldpappy all in a rush, clattered down the stairs.

Mama caught her by the arm as she was running into the great room. "There's a birthing," Mama said, "and we need you."

"But Mama, the one that went downriver, he's still alive!"

"Peggy, we got no time for—"

Two boys with the same face pushed their way into the conversation. "The one downriver!" cried one.

"Still alive!" cried another.

"How do you know!"

"He can't be!"

They spoke so all on top of each other that Mama had to hush them up just to hear them. "It was Vigor, our big brother, he got swept away—"

"Well he's alive," said little Peggy, "but the river's got him."

The twins looked to Mama for confirmation. "She know what she's talking about, Goody Guester?"

Mama nodded, and the boys raced for the door, shouting, "He's alive! He's still alive!"

"Are you sure?" asked Mama fiercely. "It's a cruel thing, to put hope in their hearts like that, if it ain't so."

Mama's flashing eyes made little Peggy afraid, and she couldn't think what to say.

By then, though, Oldpappy had come up from behind. "Now Peg," he said, "how would she know one was taken by the river, lessun she saw?"

"I know," said Mama. "But this woman's been holding off birth too long, and I got a care for the baby, so come on now, little Peggy, I need you to tell me what you see."

She led little Peggy into the bedroom off the kitchen, the place where Papa and Mama slept whenever there were visitors. The woman lay on the bed, holding tight to the hand of a tall girl with deep and solemn eyes. Little Peggy didn't know their faces, but she recognized their fires, especially the mother's pain and fear.

"Someone was shouting," whispered the mother.

"Hush now," said Mama.

"About him still alive."

The solemn girl raised her eyebrows, looked at Mama. "Is that so, Goody Guester?"

"My daughter is a torch. That's why I brung her here in this room. To see the baby."

"Did she see my boy? Is he alive?"

"I thought you didn't tell her, Eleanor," said Mama.

The solemn girl shook her head.

"Saw from the wagon. Is he alive?"

"Tell her, Margaret," said Mama.

Little Peggy turned and looked for his heartfire. There were no walls when it came to this kind of seeing. His flame was still there, though she knew it was afar off. This time, though, she drew near in the way she had, took a close look. "He's in the water. He's all tangled in the roots."

"Vigor!" cried the mother on the bed.

"The river wants him. The river says, Die, die."

Mama touched the woman's arm. "The twins have gone off to tell the others. There'll be a search party."

"In the dark!" whispered the woman scornfully.

Little Peggy spoke again. "He's saying a prayer, I think. He's saying—seventh son."

"Seventh son," whispered Eleanor.

"What does that mean?" asked Mama.

"If this baby's a boy," said Eleanor, "and he's born while Vigor's still alive, then he's the seventh son of a seventh son, and all of them alive."

Mama gasped. "No wonder the river—" she said. No need to finish the thought. Instead she took little Peggy's hands and led her to the woman on the bed. "Look at this baby, and see what you see."

Little Peggy had done this before, of course. It was the chief use they had for torches, to have them look at an unborn baby just at the birthing time. Partly to see how it lay in the womb, but also because sometimes a torch could see who the baby was, what it would be, could tell stories of times to come. Even before she touched the woman's belly, she could see the baby's heartfire. It was the one that she had seen before, that burned so hot and bright that it was like the sun and the moon, to compare it to the mother's fire. "It's a boy," she said.

"Then let me bear this baby," said the mother. "Let him breathe while Vigor still breathes!"

"How's the baby set?" asked Mama.

"Just right," said little Peggy.

"Head first? Face down?"

Little Peggy nodded.

"Then why won't it come?" demanded Mama.

"She's been telling him not to," said Little Peggy, looking at the mother.

"In the wagon," the mother said. "He was coming, and I did a beseeching."

"Well, you should have told me right off," said Mama sharply. "Speck me to help you and you don't even tell me he's got a beseeching on him. You, girl!"

Several young ones were standing near the wall, wide-eyed, and they didn't know which one she meant.

"Any of you, I need that iron key from the ring on the wall."

The biggest of them took it clumsily from the hook and brought it, ring and all. Mama dangled the large ring and the key over the mother's belly, chanting softly,

"Here's the circle, open wide,
Here's the key to get outside,
Earth be iron, flame be fair,
Fall from water into air."

The mother cried out in sudden agony. Mama tossed away the key, cast back the sheet, lifted the woman's knees, and ordered little Peggy fiercely to *see*.

Little Peggy touched the woman's womb. The boy's mind was empty, except for a feeling of pressure and gathering cold as he emerged into the air. But the very emptiness of his mind let her see things that would never be clearly visible again. The billion billion paths of his life lay open before him, waiting for his first choices, for the first changes in the world around him to eliminate a million futures every second. The future was there in everyone, a flickering shadow that was never visible behind the thoughts of the present moment; but here, for a few precious moments, little Peggy could see them clearly.

And what she saw was death down every path. Drowning, drowning, every path of his future led this child to a watery death.

"Why do you hate him so!" cried little Peggy.

"What?" demanded Eleanor.

"Hush," said Mama. "Let her see what she sees."

Inside the unborn child, the dark blot of water that surrounded his heartfire seemed so terribly strong that little Peggy was afraid he would be swallowed up.

"Get him out to breathe!" shouted little Peggy.

Mama reached in, even though it tore the mother something dreadful, and hooked the baby by the neck with strong fingers, drawing him out.

In that moment, the dark water retreated inside the child's mind, and just before the first breath came, little Peggy saw ten million deaths by water disappear. Now, for the first time, there were some paths open, some paths leading to a dazzling future. And all the paths that did not end in early death had one thing in common. On all those paths, little Peggy saw herself doing one simple thing.

So she did that thing. She took her hands from the slackening belly and ducked under her mother's arm. The baby's head had just emerged, and it was still covered with a bloody caul, a scrap of the sac of soft skin in which he had floated in his mother's womb.

His mouth was open, sucking inward on the caul, but it didn't break, and he couldn't breathe.

Little Peggy did what she had seen herself do in the baby's future. She reached out, took the caul from under the baby's chin, and pulled it away from his face. It came whole, in one moist piece, and in the moment it came away, the baby's mouth cleared, he sucked in a great breath, and then gave that mewling cry that birthing mothers hear as the song of life.

Little Peggy folded the caul, her mind still full of the visions she had seen down the pathways of this baby's life. She did not know yet what the visions meant, but they made such clear pictures in her mind that she knew she would never forget them. They made her afraid, because so much would depend on her, and how she used the birth caul that was still warm in her hands.

"A boy," said Mama.

"Is he," whispered the mother. "Seventh son?"

Mama was tying the cord, so she couldn't spare a glance at little Peggy. "Look," she whispered.

Little Peggy looked for the single heartfire on the distant river. "Yes," she said, for the heartfire was still burning.

Even as she watched, it flickered, died.

"Now he's gone," said little Peggy.

The woman on the bed wept bitterly, her birth-wracked body shuddering.

"Grieving at the baby's birth," said Mama. "It's a dreadful thing."

"Hush," whispered Eleanor to her mother. "Be joyous, or it'll darken the baby all his life!"

"Vigor," murmured the woman.

"Better nothing at all than tears," said Mama. She held out the crying baby, and Eleanor took it in competent arms—she had cradled many a babe before, it was plain. Mama went to the table in the corner and took the scarf that had been blacked in the wool, so it was night-colored clear through. She dragged it slowly across the weeping woman's face, saying, "Sleep, Mother, sleep."

When the cloth came away, the weeping was done, and the woman slept, her strength spent.

"Take the baby from the room," said Mama.

"Don't he need to start his sucking?" asked Eleanor.

"She'll never nurse this babe," said Mama. "Not unless you want him to suck hate."

"She can't hate him," said Eleanor. "It ain't his fault."

"I reckon her milk don't know that," said Mama. "That right, little Peggy? What teat did the baby suck?"

"His mama's," said little Peggy.

Mama looked sharp at her. "You sure of that?"

She nodded.

"Well, then, we'll bring the baby in when she wakes up. He doesn't need to eat anything for the first night, anyway." So Eleanor carried the baby out into the great room, where the fire burned to dry the men, who stopped trading stories about rains and floods worse than this one long enough to look at the baby and admire.

Inside the room, though, Mama took little Peggy by the chin and stared hard into her eyes. "You tell me the truth, Margaret. It's a serious thing, for a baby to suck on its mama and drink up hate."

"She won't hate him, Mama," said little Peggy.

"What did you see?"

Little Peggy would have answered, but she didn't know the words to tell most of the things she saw. So she looked at the floor. She could tell from Mama's quick draw of breath that she was ripe for a tongue-lashing. But Mama waited, and then her hand came soft, stroking across little Peggy's cheek. "Ah, child, what a day you've had. The baby might have died, except you told me to pull it out. You even reached in and opened up its mouth—that's what you did, isn't it?"

Little Peggy nodded.

"Enough for a little girl, enough for one day." Mama turned to the other girls, the ones in wet dresses, leaning against the wall. "And you, too, you've had enough of a day. Come out of here, let your mama sleep, come out and get dry by the fire. I'll start a supper for you, I will."

But Oldpappy was already in the kitchen, fussing around, and refused to hear of Mama doing a thing. Soon enough she was out with the baby, shooing the men away so she could rock it to sleep, letting it suck her finger.

Little Peggy figured after a while that she wouldn't be missed, and so she snuck up the stairs to the attic ladder, and up the ladder into the lightless, musty space. The spiders didn't bother her much, and the cats mostly kept the mice away, so she wasn't afraid. She crawled right to her secret hiding place and took out the carven box that Oldpappy had given her, the one he said his own papa brought from Ulster when he came to the colonies. It was full of the precious scraps of childhood—stones, strings, buttons—but now she knew that these were nothing compared to the work before her all the rest of her life. She dumped them right out, and blew into the box to clear away dust. Then she laid the folded caul inside and closed the lid.

She knew that in the future she would open that box a dozen times. That it would call to her, wake her from her sleep, tear her from her friends, and steal from her all her dreams. All because a baby boy downstairs had no future at all, except a death from the dark water, excepting if she used that caul to keep him safe, the way it once protected him in the womb.

For a moment she was angry, to have her own life so changed. Worse than the blacksmith coming, it was, worse than Papa and the hazel wand he whupped her with, worse than Mama when her eyes were angry. Everything would be different forever and it wasn't fair. Just for a baby she never invited, never asked to come here, what did she care about any old baby?

She reached out and opened the box, planning to take the caul and cast it into a dark corner of the attic. But even in the darkness, she could see a place where it was darker still: near her heartfire, where the emptiness of the deep black river was all set to make a murderer out of her.

Not me, she said to the water. You ain't part of me.

Yes I am, whispered the water. I'm all through you, and you'd dry up and die without me.

You ain't the boss of me, anyway, she retorted.

She closed the lid on the box and skidded her way down the ladder. Papa always said that she'd get splinters in her butt doing that. This time he was right. It stung something fierce, so she walked kind of sideways into the kitchen where Oldpappy was. Sure enough, he stopped his cooking long enough to pry the splinters out.

"My eyes ain't sharp enough for this, Maggie," he complained.

"You got the eyes of an eagle. Papa says so."

Oldpappy chuckled. "Does he now."

"What's for dinner?"

"Oh, you'll like this dinner, Maggie."

Little Peggy wrinkled up her nose. "Smells like chicken."

"That's right."

"I don't like chicken soup."

"Not just soup, Maggie. This one's a-roasting, except the neck and wings."

"I hate *roast* chicken, too."

"Does your Oldpappy ever lie to you?"

"Nope."

"Then you best believe me when I tell you this is one chicken dinner that'll make you *glad*. Can't you think of any way that a partickler chicken dinner could make you glad?"

Little Peggy thought and thought, and then she smiled. "Bloody Mary?"

Oldpappy winked. "I always said that was a hen born to make gravy."

Little Peggy hugged him so tight that he made choking sounds, and then they laughed and laughed.

Later that night, long after little Peggy was in bed, they brought Vigor's body home, and Papa and Makepeace set to making a box for him. Alvin Miller hardly looked alive, even when Eleanor showed him the baby. Until she said, "That torch girl. She says that this baby is the seventh son of a seventh son."

Alvin looked around for someone to tell him if it was true.

"Oh, you can trust her," said Mama.

Tears came fresh to Alvin's eyes. "That boy hung on," he said. "There in the water, he hung on long enough."

"He knowed what store you set by that," said Eleanor.

Then Alvin reached for the baby, held him tight, looked down into his eyes. "Nobody named him yet, did they?" he asked.

"Course not," said Eleanor. "Mama named all the other boys, but you always said the seventh son'd have—"

"My own name. Alvin. Seventh son of a seventh son, with the same name as his father. Alvin Junior." He looked around him, then turned to face toward the river, way off in the nighttime forest. "Hear that, you Hatrack River? His name is Alvin, and you didn't kill him after all."

Soon they brought in the box, and laid out Vigor's body with candles, to stand for the fire of life that had left him. Alvin held up the baby, over the coffin. "Look on your brother," he whispered to the infant.

"That baby can't see nothing yet, Papa," said David.

"That ain't so, David," said Alvin. "He don't *know* what he's seeing, but his eyes can see. And when he gets old enough to hear the story of his birth, I'm going to tell him that his own eyes saw his brother Vigor, who gave his life for this baby's sake."

It was two weeks before Faith was well enough to travel. But Alvin saw to it that he and his boys worked hard for their keep. They cleared a good spot of land, chopped the winter's firewood, set some charcoal heaps for Makepeace Smith, and widened the road. They also felled four big trees and made a strong bridge across the Hatrack River, a covered bridge so that even in a rainstorm people could cross that river without a drop of water touching them.

Vigor's grave was the third one there, beside little Peggy's two dead sisters. The family paid respects and prayed there on the morning that they left. Then they got in their wagon and rode off westward, "But we leave a part of ourselves here always," said Faith, and Alvin nodded.

Little Peggy watched them go, then ran up into the attic, opened the box, and held little Alvin's caul in her hand. No danger, for now at least. Safe for now. She put the caul away and closed the lid. You better be something, baby Alvin, she said, or else you caused a powerful lot of trouble for nothing.

THE HERO OF THE NIGHT

BY BRADLEY DENTON

As much as the everyman hero is a staple of American fiction, the American everyman martyr has unfortunately been a staple of American history. From the Boston Massacre to Kent State, individuals have been thrust into the limelight by their tragic and unnecessary deaths. Bradley Denton personifies this tragic side of the American spirit in his peculiar tale of a spirit (called "Crispus" after Crispus Attucks, the first man shot at the Boston Massacre and arguably the first martyr of the American Revolution) who lives out the last few hours of those who fate has chosen to follow in his footsteps.

Crispus usually dies so soon after awakening that he has no time for reflection, but this life is different. He awoke in this new place as dawn broke, and now, in the brightness of a spring day, he still lives.

As he walks to the university library, though, he sees the signs of what is coming and knows that this incarnation will end as the others have. Already he feels the first tug of his host's urge to meet the fusillade.

His host is a young white woman this time, a child only a little older than poor Sam Maverick was. Crispus wants to pray for her; but the Lord is punishing him, and he cannot expect to be heard.

Even so, as he enters the library he cannot help asking again: *Is it my fault that I was born with such pride and anger? Is it my fault that a thousand deaths have not quenched their flames?*

There is no response, so Crispus must search for an answer on his own. He flips through the card catalog until he finds a title with the phrase his host knows: *The Boston Massacre.*

The book stands on its shelf as if it has been waiting for him. The young woman's body trembles as Crispus takes the volume to an empty carrel—*all* the carrels are empty, he notices—to discover what history has to say about him.

His host is a rapid reader. Her intelligence will only make her loss all the worse for those who love her.

Crispus has her memories as well as his own, and knows her more thoroughly than she has known herself. He mourns for the beauty of who she is and for the beauty she might have become. He probes for her consciousness and cannot find it, so he hopes that the Lord has already taken her soul.

He does not want her to feel the bullets.

———

WHAT CRISPUS FINDS in the book makes him clench his host's teeth. Incredibly, John Adams, lawyer of Boston, defended Crispus's killers against the charge of murder, saying:

> "This Crispus Attucks appears to have undertaken to be the hero of the night; and to lead this army with banners, to form them in the first place in Dock Square, and march them up to King Street with their clubs. If this was not an unlawful assembly, there never was one . . .
>
> Now to have this reinforcement coming down under the command of a stout mulatto fellow, whose very looks were enough to terrify any person, what had not the soldiers then to fear? He had hardiness enough to fall in upon them, and with one hand took hold of a bayonet, and with the other knocked the man down. This was the behavior of Attucks, to whose mad proceedings in probability the dreadful carnage of that night was chiefly to be ascribed."

Crispus slams the book shut, and the sound echoes through the deserted stacks.

What did his parentage or looks have to do with anything? Did the fact that his mother was black and his father Natick give the redcoats the right to shoot him?

To return for his thousand-and-first death, and to find himself accused of his own murder—

If you were here today, Mister John Adams, Crispus thinks, *I would split your lying tongue.*

He cannot recall every detail of every death . . . but of that first, he has no doubts.

HE WAS BORN a slave in Framingham and ran away at the age of twenty-seven. His master advertised a reward, but Crispus avoided capture by hiring on with a vessel in Boston. He sailed from there to the West Indies, settling on New Providence, and continued to work on various whaling and trading ships.

Eventually, he realized that his old master must be dead and that no one would remember Crispus Attucks as being the property of another. So, two decades after leaving as a runaway slave, he returned to Boston as a free man.

But the city itself was no longer free, for the lobsterbacks had come to enforce the king's taxes and to harass free men and slaves alike.

Crispus could not hold his anger in check at the soldiers' bullying. Years before, he had struggled for his own freedom; now, he would struggle for Boston's. Or, at the very least, he would help give back to the lobsters some of what they had already given out.

He did *not* seduce his comrades of the fifth of March into following him. Each man joined the others of his own will.

The ropemaker, Sam Gray, was a prime example. As the mob approached King Street, Gray told Crispus that three days earlier a soldier had come to the ropewalk where Gray had been working and had demanded that he be hired.

"So you will work, will you?" Gray had asked him.

"I have said so, haven't I?" the soldier had snapped back.

"Then you may go clean my shithouse," Gray had said, turning back to his cable.

The furious redcoat had left then, but had returned with a gang of his fellows. The soldiers had started a fight, but the boys at the ropewalk had beaten them even though some of the lobsters had brandished cutlasses.

Crispus clapped Gray's back upon hearing the tale, and they went on together, shaking their staves above their heads.

Yes, Mister Adams, Crispus thinks, *some of us carried clubs that night. But the British carried muskets. Which weapon causes the more "dreadful carnage"?*

"Come on, you bloody lobsters!" the crowd cried, throwing ice and stones. "Put down your guns, and we're your men!"

Crispus lunged forward through the darkness to grasp a musket barrel, and the soldier jerked the gun up, cutting Crispus's hand with the bayonet. Crispus stumbled back, staring down at his wounded palm—

And then two sharp pains speared into his chest with a heat so great that he was forced to his knees. His comrades panicked, and he was knocked onto his back. Young Sam Maverick staggered past with his mouth agape.

The pain rose up like a storm swell, hurting so much that Crispus could not even cry out. Then it engulfed him, and that was all.

That is the truth of that night, Mister Adams. If you still believe me to be the cause of it, then you may kiss my ass.

CRISPUS REOPENS THE BOOK and learns of the death of a man named James Caldwell, whom he did not know, and of the other victims who died later. As he reads, his anger fades and is replaced by a dull sadness.

If he was *not* wrong to do as he did in Boston, then why is he being punished? Why must he suffer death after death after death?

He lowers his host's head onto the book, pressing her cheek flat against the pages. One slender hand lies on the desktop as if already drained of life.

Crispus searches the young woman's mind and finds nothing there of evil. She does not deserve to die.

But neither did any of the others.

AFTER FALLING to the cobblestones in King Street, Crispus awoke as a small boy. He did not have time to become awe-stricken at the miracle of his resurrection, though, for his second death came swiftly.

His host was shivering, so cold that he could hardly think, huddling with a cluster of women and children. They were mourning the defeat of their tribe by the long-knives.

Crispus had been alive for less than a minute when a huge mass of strangely clothed soldiers on horseback charged into the camp with their swords drawn and their guns thundering. The air filled with smoke and screams. Crispus tried to run away through the snow, but even in his panic he knew that his frostbitten, wasted body could not escape.

He felt the vibration of the horse coming up fast behind him and tried to dodge, but his host's feet and legs were too cold. The horse ran him down, crushing his spine. The soldier rode on, leaving Crispus to suffer white spikes of agony, but another came soon after and put a bullet into his head.

Even with that wound, Crispus lived long enough to feel something worse than what he had felt in Boston. This time, his pain was steeped in despair.

THE VEINS IN the young woman's hand stand out in blue relief as Crispus knots the fingers into a fist. He hates being her, hates knowing that her mind will soon be dead and empty. A few of her memories will stay with him, but none of them will ever be hers again.

He closes her eyes and sees buildings of glass and steel so high that their tops seem to shrink to nothing. He sees winged ships carrying people into the sky and around the world. He sees men in thick white suits standing on the moon.

Yet as wondrous as these things are, they do not surprise him, for he has caught glimpses of their approach over the decades. They are simply part of the changing world, the world that he saw changing even during the forty-seven years of his first life.

He looks at his host's wristwatch and sees that he has lived for more than six hours. The Lord is giving him extra time to examine and repent of his sins.

But the longer he stays alive, the more deaths he remembers; and with each of these memories, he asks, *Why must there be such pain in the world?*

And why must I feel so much of it, over and over again?

It is so . . . lonely.

CRISPUS PRESSES HIS host's face hard against the book as he remembers the death he experienced immediately before becoming her. Its sting is fresh.

He was a child for at least the hundredth time—a little girl who knew only hunger, mud, and fear. Her life up to the point that he became her had been nothing but misery, and he knew that it would get no better.

The wild-eyed soldiers who came into the village wore filthy clothing of green and brown. Crispus did not know how many there were, because as they arrived his host's mother picked up the child and held her tight. Crispus found himself covered with a conical grass hat, enclosed as though he were in a tent.

Shouting and shoving, the soldiers herded everyone into a ditch, and then the explosive rattling noises started. Crispus, responding to an imperative built into his host, began to weep.

The mother's body jerked, pushing him down.

"Bloody *lobsters!*" he tried to cry, but his host's mouth filled with mud.

Then came the pain, razor-keen but quick, and he awoke as a college student.

CRISPUS OPENS THE FIST as his host's head rises from the book. He is startled for an instant at the touch of her long hair on her cheek.

He wants to continue reading, but the young woman's death-urge comes in full force now, overwhelming him. As she stands, he can hear the shouts and chants and threats beginning outside. He wishes the noises were as far away as they sound.

His host's thoughts flood in and mix with his. He sees her as she was yesterday, walking past a Guardsman who had a flower stuck in his rifle barrel.

Flowers are better than bullets.

They leave the library stacks. Crispus knows that his host is not planning to take part in the demonstration, and for a moment he clings to the useless hope that she will survive after all.

She blinks as she comes out into the sunshine. Crispus is a mere passenger now;

he can do nothing more than watch as they move toward the mob, toward the Guards-
men, toward the guns.

It hurts a lot this time.

CRISPUS AWAKENS WITH THE KNOWLEDGE that only eleven days have passed since
his previous death. Never before has so little time elapsed between incarnations.

He is outside in the sun again, but the day is hotter, more humid. His host, a young
black man, is sweating. The demonstration has already begun.

Brothers dying for nothing.

A voice bellows, sounding as though it has come from the sky, and orders them
to disperse. The white cops move toward them.

The man beside Crispus throws a rock.

Then the familiar gunfire comes, and the rock-thrower falls. Crispus leans down
to help, and his host's insides become an inferno.

He falls too, living just long enough to hear someone shout, "Goddamn *niggers!*"

TWENTY-THREE MORE LIVES come in quick succession, some of them so brief that
Crispus cannot even breathe before the bullets hit. He begins to long for a true death,
for oblivion . . . for anything that will make it stop.

Then he awakens as a woman whose mind is so self-controlled and serene that he
cannot help but share her calm. The blood of three races courses through her veins,
and despite her sex, Crispus feels almost like himself.

The woman is alone in her one-room apartment, her golden fingers resting on the
keyboard of a portable computer. Crispus has seen such machines in the minds of his
most recent hosts, but this is the first time that he has been close to one.

The words on the flat blue monitor glow a soft amber, and Crispus reads what his
host has just written:

> *That our government cannot comprehend the reasons for our anger should come
> as no surprise; thirty years ago, the official response to the uprisings of that
> era was much the same. For example, after armed "peace officers" killed two
> members of a protest rally, the president was heard to ask the head of the
> victims' college, "Look, what are we going to do to get more respect for the
> police from our young people?"*

Crispus remembers being told of similar questions from Governor Hutchinson in
Boston: "What has happened to respect for the soldiers of the Crown? What are we
to do about the young ruffians who roam the streets at night?"

Drawing on the skill of his host to operate the keyboard, Crispus writes,

> *Why do the people still allow Tories to hold positions of power? And why do
> these same Tories always blame dissent on the rebelliousness of the young? I
> was in my forty-eighth year when I challenged the red-coated bastards in King
> Street, and I am almost three hundred years old now. Yet despite all that God
> and man have done to me, I am ever angry, ever rebellious, ever*

He stops writing as he sees the face of his host reflected in the monitor. Her hair
is long and dark; her mouth is firm and strong; her eyes are piercing and clear.

Crispus stands and walks to the narrow bed on the other side of the room. It is true that he is still angry, rebellious, and proud . . . but it is even more true that he has become sick of death.

He sits cross-legged on the mattress. A single translucent window in the west wall catches the last light of the day, warming the woman's skin as Crispus looks around at the room. The walls are covered with photographs, and the faces of girls and boys smile out everywhere. The woman works with children who have been hurt by their parents, teaching them that they are valuable, that they matter.

She lives simply. All of her clothes fit into a chipped four-drawer bureau. All of her cooking is done with a tiny microwave oven. Her bicycle, which leans against the foot of the bed, is her sole means of transportation. The room has no shelves, so her books are stacked against the walls, reaching up to the photographs like towers of words.

Crispus feels something like love for this woman. He wants her to live.

What would happen, he wonders, if he were to trap her so that she could not go out to meet her doom? Would she die anyway? If she survived, would Crispus survive as well? Could they live together, sharing one body, one brain?

Crispus decides to find out.

HE PROBES THE WOMAN'S MIND for possible methods, hurrying for fear that the death-urge will come soon. It takes him less than a second to find something that might work.

He walks into the doorless, closet-sized bathroom and searches through the jumble of tools in the cabinet under the sink until he finds the spray can labeled INSTANT EPOXY. Then he returns to the main room, locks the hollow steel door, and sprays the doorknob and lock until they are encased in a thick, clear coat. The fumes give his host a headache.

As soon as he has finished with the door, he goes to the window and sprays its lock as well, emptying the can. The windowpane is made of stiff, heavy plastic, and he does not think his host could break it—but to make it tougher still, he fetches a roll of metallic tape from the bathroom and covers the pane with silver strips.

The light that had filled the room fades with each strip of tape, and by the time Crispus is finished, the only illumination in the apartment comes from the amber glow of the computer monitor.

Crispus drops the empty cardboard ring and crosses back to the door. The knob and lock will not budge.

But he is still not satisfied, for this host is strong and clever. He wants to immobilize her.

A chain with an electronic combination lock is wrapped around part of the bicycle frame, but the woman knows the combination. As Crispus racks her brain, though, he discovers that she keeps a metal box containing legal documents under the bed. The box is secured by an old-fashioned padlock whose key is hidden in the bureau's bottom drawer.

Once Crispus has opened the padlock, he slides the key out under the glued door and makes certain that his host cannot reach it. Then he goes into the bathroom and empties her bladder and bowels. When he comes out, he switches on the ceiling light and moves the computer table over to the bed. That done, he goes to the stacks of books and selects several volumes at random, tossing them onto the mattress.

Finally, he unwraps the chain from the bicycle frame. Then he sits on the edge of the bed and loops the chain around the woman's right ankle.

When he is certain that the chain cannot be slid off the bed frame and that it is pulled so tight that his host cannot work herself free, he slips the padlock through the end links and snaps it shut.

Then he waits.

ONE OF THE BOOKS on the bed is a thick paperback anthology on civil disobedience. For a moment, Crispus considers tossing it back to its stack against the wall; but then, assuring himself that the woman is safe no matter what he reads, he picks it up and turns to an essay on the Massacre.

He is surprised to find himself referred to as "the first martyr of the American Revolution," but what surprises him even more is an excerpt from the diary of John Adams, dated July 1773, that is in the form of a letter to Governor Hutchinson:

To Tho. Hutchinson/Sir:
You will hear from Us with Astonishment.
You ought to hear from Us with Horror. You are chargeable before God and Man, with our Blood.
The soldiers were but passive Instruments, were Machines, neither moral nor voluntary Agents in our Destruction more than the leaden Pellets, with which we were wounded.
You were a free Agent.
You acted, coolly, deliberately, with all that premeditated Malice, not against Us in Particular but against the People in general, which in the Sight of the Law is an ingredient in the Composition of Murder. You will hear further from Us hereafter.

Adams has signed the letter *Chrispus Attucks.*

Crispus takes a tremulous breath. It is infinitely strange to know that these words came from the pen of the man who condemned him at the soldiers' trial. Their meaning, however, is clear: By 1773, John Adams blamed Governor Hutchinson, not the mulatto Attucks, for the Boston Massacre.

With that in mind, Crispus decides that he must forgive Adams for the lawyer's earlier remarks. But as he does so, he realizes that he must then also forgive the men who shot him on that cold March night.

The thought is troubling, for it suggests that he must in turn forgive everyone who has killed him in each of his incarnations.

He lies back on the mattress, painfully aware of the ankle chained to the bedpost, and covers the woman's eyes with one hand. Adams he can forgive, and perhaps even the soldiers at the Custom House . . .

The Soldiers were but passive Instruments . . .

You were a free Agent.

Is it so in every case? Crispus wonders. Is there always a Governor Hutchinson in a mansion somewhere, staying safe and pampered while his Machines commit his murders?

He thinks back over his many deaths and remembers seeing a horrible kind of lust in the eyes of some of his killers. Those men he can never forgive, even if it means that the Lord will punish him for all eternity. But he can also remember the faces of other killers—some who seemed tortured or frightened to the point of wildness, and some who seemed empty of all emotion, as if their blood had been drained and replaced with water.

Those frightened or empty ones, Crispus concludes, could not have been in possession of their own souls. Their souls, then, he will forgive.

The Hutchinsons of the world are another matter.

He damns their invisible faces.

CRISPUS IS READING in the book again when he feels the first tremors of his host's urge to escape and die. Her ankle twists inside the tight loops of chain, chafing the skin so badly that he is afraid she will bleed.

Listen to me, he thinks fiercely. *If you leave this room tonight, you will not live to see the morning.*

The twisting and pulling weaken slightly, but in the woman's heart Crispus can still feel her desire to join her friends. He thinks again that he should not have selected this particular book . . . but he cannot stop reading yet, for he has found another passage about himself:

A "Crispus Attucks Day" was first held in Boston in 1858. The primary speaker, Wendell Phillips, claimed that the shot heard round the world was not fired at Lexington. Rather, Phillips asserted, that shot was fired in Boston.

"Who set the example of guns?" Phillips asked. "Who taught the British soldier that he might be defeated? Who first dared look into his eyes? The 5th of March, 1770, was the baptism of blood. I place, therefore, this Crispus Attucks in the foremost rank of the men that dared. When we talk of courage, he rises, with his dark face, in the clothes of the laborer, his head uncovered, his arm raised above him defying bayonets.

Crispus closes the book, wishing that he had done so earlier. He knows that he is no hero, no personification of courage. He is simply a man who was unwilling to take a blow without striking back.

His host's body quivers, then shakes violently, jerking at the chain.

Crispus flings the book across the room. Its words have made the woman's desire to sacrifice herself stronger than ever.

As he throws the book, he sees his bitter questions about Tories glowing in the computer screen. He turns away, afraid to face their bright rage.

CRISPUS PICKS UP another book, an old volume of stories and essays about the future. This, he thinks, should provide some distraction. Dreams and fantasies are what he and his host need.

But the book is not what he expects, for most of the pieces are about war and injustice. His host's chained ankle begins to bleed.

He curses aloud and hears the woman's voice for the first time. Even in cursing, it is gentle.

Despite himself, Crispus continues reading, and his eyes light upon an essayist's list of "Commandments for Survival." The first of these Commandments says, NEVER THROW THINGS AT MEN WITH GUNS.

The woman struggles harder, and Crispus finds himself wanting to struggle with her.

A corollary to the Commandment says, NEVER STAND BESIDE SOMEONE WHO IS THROWING THINGS AT MEN WITH GUNS.

Crispus rips the page from the book and crumples it. Then he reaches for the computer keyboard and writes:

If armed men wrong you, whether of their own wills or at the bidding of another, then you must fight them. Though they have muskets and you have only stones and ice, I say throw what you have and Survival be damned. And if armed men wrong your friend instead, then I say stand beside your friend and throw stones and ice together.

Crispus hesitates, realizing that with every word, he slips closer toward defeat in the battle he has set out to fight today.

But he cannot stop himself. *If you do not do these things*, he writes, *then I say you are a coward and undeserving of Survival, or of the title of Free Man.*

"Or Free Woman," his host's voice says.

Crispus sits as if frozen for a long moment. Then, tentatively, he probes through the woman's mind and finds her, awake and alive.

"I throw words," she tells him. "The targets react as though the words were stones or ice, but I will not stop."

Crispus stares at his host's reflection in the monitor. *I do not even know what you are fighting for.*

She gives him a vision of fire, blood, and pain in a small, faraway country.

Crispus's anger flares. The name of the small country does not matter; what matters is that he has seen all this before, and that he hates it.

"Free me," his host says.

CRISPUS KNOWS what will happen—and since the woman can see his thoughts, she knows too. She knows everything, and yet she wants to go. She wants to fight despite the fact that the fight will kill her.

Crispus decides that he does not have the right to save her.

As for himself . . .

He is a strong man, and can stand another painful transition into the future.

He has seen the colonies become a nation, and the nation become a mighty power. Perhaps, if he continues hurtling onward through the years, propelled by the burning sting of bullets, he will see something even greater come to pass.

Perhaps he isn't being punished after all. Perhaps he is being rewarded with the chance to see the day when Death is finally defeated.

He stretches his host's body out along the bed until her hands are able to grasp a bicycle spoke. It takes all of the woman's strength and costs her more blood, but the spoke breaks free from the rim.

Crispus unhooks the spoke from the wheel hub, then lowers his host to the floor and crawls to the door, dragging the bed behind him. After several minutes of trying, he is able to snag the padlock key with the spoke and to pull it back inside.

When the woman's leg is free of the chain, Crispus limps into the bathroom and finds a screwdriver in the cabinet. The apartment door has three hinges, but he discovers that he only has to unfasten two before the door leans far enough to allow an escape.

Satisfied? Crispus asks. But his host has said all that is necessary, and remains silent.

Crispus takes a short, thick candle from the top of the bureau and lights it with a match. He begins to leave then, but stops with one foot outside the narrow passage.

He turns and walks back to the computer. There, in amber, are his last words, to which he adds two final sentences:

Though I die, I, Crispus Attucks, am a Free Man and have no need of your mourning or prayers. Mourn and pray instead for the Tories, for they will indeed hear further from me hereafter.

He hits the SAVE button and leaves the apartment.

In the moonless night, a flurry of snow creates white halos around the street lamps. Crispus shields his small flame with his host's palm, and as he walks he sees hundreds of other flames converging at the foot of a dark hill at the edge of the city. There the flames become one tremendous dancing light, and the men and women inside that light begin singing an insistent song of protest.

Crispus feels outrage heating the winter air as he joins the crowd, and he knows he is home.

An inhuman voice shouts down from the top of the hill. "YOU ARE TRESPASSING ON GOVERNMENT PROPERTY. DISPERSE AT ONCE."

"*We* are the government!" the man beside Crispus cries, and the words ripple out from person to person until the chant shakes the earth.

Crispus grins. *Put down those muskets, you bloody lobsters, and we're your men and women.*

Then, feeling a joy that he has not felt for almost two and a half centuries, he links arms with his friends and ascends the hill, his fire defying the darkness ahead.

THE WHIMPER OF WHIPPED DOGS

BY HARLAN ELLISON

HARLAN ELLISON IS ONE OF THE MOST CRITICALLY ACCLAIMED FANTASISTS OF THE LATTER HALF OF THE TWENTIETH CENTURY, EQUALLY ADEPT WITH THE TOOLS OF WHIMSICAL WORDPLAY AND WITH THE STONE-COLD INSTRUMENTS OF BRUTAL REALITY. A YOUNG WOMAN IN NEW YORK WAS BRUTALLY MURDERED OUTSIDE OF HER HOME WHILE HER NEIGHBORS, SAFELY ENSCONCED INSIDE THEIR HOMES WELL WITHIN SIGHT AND EARSHOT OF HER STRUGGLES, FAILED TO INTER-CEDE OR CALL FOR HELP. THE WOMAN'S NAME WAS KITTY GENOVESE . . .

. . . AND FROM THIS SHAMEFUL INCIDENT OF AN UNFEELING CITY, ELLISON MASTERFULLY BRINGS TO LIFE A TALE OF AN EVEN DARKER SPIRIT THAT RULES OUR CITY STREETS.

On the night after the day she had stained the louvered window shutters of her new apartment on East 52nd Street, Beth saw a woman slowly and hideously knifed to death in the courtyard of her building. She was one of twenty-six witnesses to the ghoulish scene, and, like them, she did nothing to stop it.

She saw it all, every moment of it, without break and with no impediment to her view. Quite madly, the thought crossed her mind as she watched in horrified fasci-nation, that she had the sort of marvelous line of observation Napoleon had sought when he caused to have constructed, at the *Comédie-Française* theaters, a curtained box at the rear, so he could watch the audience as well as the stage. The night was clear, the moon was full, she had just turned off the 11:30 movie on Channel 2 after the second commercial break, realizing she had already seen Robert Taylor in *West-ward the Women*, and had disliked it the first time; and the apartment was quite dark.

She went to the window, to raise it six inches for the night's sleep, and she saw the woman stumble into the courtyard. She was sliding along the wall, clutching her left arm with her right hand. Con Ed had installed mercury-vapor lamps on the poles; there had been sixteen assaults in seven months; the courtyard was illuminated with a chill purple glow that made the blood streaming down the woman's left arm look black and shiny. Beth saw every detail with utter clarity, as though magnified a thou-sand power under a microscope, solarized as if it had been a television commercial.

The woman threw back her head, as if she were trying to scream, but there was no sound. Only the traffic on First Avenue, late cabs foraging for singles paired for the night at Maxwell's Plum and Friday's and Adam's Apple. But that was over there, beyond. Where *she* was, down there seven floors below, in the courtyard, everything seemed silently suspended in an invisible force-field.

Beth stood in the darkness of her apartment, and realized she had raised the window completely. A tiny balcony lay just over the low sill; now not even glass separated her from the sight; just the wrought-iron balcony railing and seven floors to the courtyard below.

The woman staggered away from the wall, her head still thrown back, and Beth could see she was in her mid-thirties, with dark hair cut in a shag; it was impossible to tell if she was pretty: terror had contorted her features, and her mouth was a twisted black slash, opened but emitting no sound. Cords stood out in her neck. She had lost one shoe, and her steps were uneven, threatening to dump her to the pavement.

The man came around the corner of the building, into the courtyard. The knife he held was enormous—or perhaps it only seemed so: Beth remembered a bone-handled fish knife her father had used one summer at the lake in Maine: it folded back on itself and locked, revealing eight inches of serrated blade. The knife in the hand of the dark man in the courtyard seemed to be similar.

The woman saw him and tried to run, but he leaped across the distance between them and grabbed her by the hair and pulled her head back as though he would slash her throat in the next reaper-motion.

Then the woman screamed.

The sound skirled up into the courtyard like bats trapped in an echo chamber, unable to find a way out, driven mad. It went on and on . . .

The man struggled with her and she drove her elbows into his sides and he tried to protect himself, spinning her around by her hair, the terrible scream going up and up and never stopping. She came loose and he was left with a fistful of hair torn out by the roots. As she spun out, he slashed straight across and opened her up just below the breasts. Blood sprayed through her clothing and the man was soaked; it seemed to drive him even more berserk. He went at her again, as she tried to hold herself together, the blood pouring down over her arms.

She tried to run, teetered against the wall, slid sidewise, and the man struck the brick surface. She was away, stumbling over a flower bed, falling, getting to her knees as he threw himself on her again. The knife came up in a flashing arc that illuminated the blade strangely with purple light. And still she screamed.

Lights came on in dozens of apartments and people appeared at windows.

He drove the knife to the hilt into her back, high on the right shoulder. He used both hands.

Beth caught it all in jagged flashes—the man, the woman, the knife, the blood, the expressions on the faces of those watching from the windows. Then lights clicked off in the windows, but they still stood there, watching.

She wanted to yell, to scream, "What are you doing to that woman?" But her throat was frozen, two iron hands that had been immersed in dry ice for ten thousand years clamped around her neck. She could feel the blade sliding into her own body.

Somehow—it seemed impossible but there it was down there, happening somehow—the woman struggled erect and *pulled* herself off the knife. Three steps, she took three steps and fell into the flower bed again. The man was howling now, like a great beast, the sounds inarticulate, bubbling up from his stomach. He fell on her and the knife went up and came down, then again, and again, and finally it was all a blur of motion, and her scream of lunatic bats went on till it faded off and was gone.

Beth stood in the darkness, trembling and crying, the sight filling her eyes with horror. And when she could no longer bear to look at what he was doing down there to the unmoving piece of meat over which he worked, she looked up and around at the windows of darkness where the others still stood—even as she stood—and somehow she could see their faces, bruise-purple with the dim light from the mercury lamps, and there was a universal sameness to their expressions. The women stood with their nails biting into the upper arms of their men, their tongues edging from the corners of their mouths; the men were wild-eyed and smiling. They all looked as though they were at cock fights. Breathing deeply. Drawing some sustenance from the grisly scene below. An exhalation of sound, deep, deep, as though from caverns beneath the earth. Flesh pale and moist.

And it was then that she realized the courtyard had grown foggy, as though mist off the East River had rolled up 52nd Street in a veil that would obscure the details of what the knife and the man were still doing . . . endlessly doing it . . . long after there was any joy in it . . . still doing it . . . again and again . . .

But the fog was unnatural, thick and gray and filled with tiny scintillas of light. She stared at it, rising up in the empty space of the courtyard. Bach in the cathedral, stardust in a vacuum chamber.

Beth saw eyes.

There, up there, at the ninth floor and higher, two great eyes, as surely as night and the moon, there were *eyes*. And—a face? Was that a face, could she be sure, was she imagining it . . . a face? In the roiling vapors of chill fog something lived, something brooding and patient and utterly malevolent had been summoned up to witness what was happening down there in the flower bed. Beth tried to look away, but could not. The eyes, those primal burning eyes, filled with an abysmal antiquity yet frighteningly bright and anxious like the eyes of a child; eyes filled with tomb depths, ancient and new, chasm-filled, burning, gigantic and deep as an abyss, holding her, compelling her. The shadow play was being staged not only for the tenants in their windows, watching and drinking of the scene, but for some *other*. Not on frigid tundra or waste moors, not in subterranean caverns or on some faraway world circling a dying sun, but here, in the city, here the eyes of that *other* watched.

Shaking with the effort, Beth wrenched her eyes from those burning depths up there beyond the ninth floor, only to see again the horror that had brought that *other*. And she was struck for the first time by the awfulness of what she was witnessing, she was released from the immobility that had held her like a coelacanth in shale, she was filled with the blood thunder pounding against the membranes of her mind: she had *stood* there! She had done nothing, nothing! A woman had been butchered and she had said nothing, done nothing. Tears had been useless, tremblings had been pointless, she *had done nothing*!

Then she heard hysterical sounds midway between laughter and giggling, and as she stared up into that great face rising in the fog and chimneysmoke of the night, she heard *herself* making those deranged gibbon noises and, from the man below, a pathetic, trapped sound, like the whimper of whipped dogs.

She was staring up into that face again. She hadn't wanted to see it again—ever. But she was locked with those smoldering eyes, overcome with the feeling that they were childlike, though she *knew* they were incalculably ancient.

Then the butcher below did an unspeakable thing and Beth reeled with dizziness and caught the edge of the window before she could tumble out onto the balcony; she steadied herself and fought for breath.

She felt herself being looked at, and for a long moment of frozen terror she feared she might have caught the attention of that face up there in the fog. She clung to the window, feeling everything growing faraway and dim, and stared straight across the court. She *was* being watched. Intently. By the young man in the seventh-floor window across from her own apartment. Steadily, he was looking at her. Through the strange fog with its burning eyes feasting on the sight below, he was staring at her.

As she felt herself blacking out, in the moment before unconsciousness, the thought flickered and fled that there was something terribly familiar about his face.

IT RAINED THE NEXT DAY. East 52nd Street was slick and shining with the oil rain-bows. The rain washed the dog turds into the gutters and nudged them down and down to the catch-basin openings. People bent against the slanting rain, hidden beneath umbrellas, looking like enormous, scurrying black mushrooms. Beth went out to get the newspapers after the police had come and gone.

The news reports dwelled with loving emphasis on the twenty-six tenants of the building who had watched in cold interest as Leona Ciarelli, 37, of 455 Fort Washington Avenue, Manhattan, had been systematically stabbed to death by Burton H. Wells, 41, an unemployed electrician, who had been subsequently shot to death by two off-duty police officers when he burst into Michael's Pub on 55th Street, covered with blood and brandishing a knife that authorities later identified as the murder weapon.

She had thrown up twice that day. Her stomach seemed incapable of retaining anything solid, and the taste of bile lay along the back of her tongue. She could not blot the scenes of the night before from her mind; she re-ran them again and again, every movement of that reaper arm playing over and over as though on a short loop of memory. The woman's head thrown back for silent screams. The blood. Those eyes in the fog.

She was drawn again and again to the window, to stare down into the courtyard and the street. She tried to superimpose over the bleak Manhattan concrete the view from her window in Swann House at Bennington: the little yard and another white, frame dormitory; the fantastic apple trees; and from the other window, the rolling hills and gorgeous Vermont countryside; her memory skittered through the change of seasons. But there was always concrete and the rain-slick streets; the rain on the pavement was black and shiny as blood.

She tried to work, rolling up the tambour closure of the old rolltop desk she had bought on Lexington Avenue and hunching over the graph sheet of choreographer's charts. But Labanotation was merely a Jackson Pollock jumble of arcane hieroglyphics to her today, instead of the careful representation of eurhythmics she had studied four years to perfect. And before that, Farmington.

The phone rang. It was the secretary from the Taylor Dance Company, asking when she would be free. She had to beg off. She looked at her hand, lying on the graph sheets of figures Laban had devised, and she saw her fingers trembling. She had to beg off. Then she called Guzman at the Downtown Ballet Company, to tell him she would be late with the charts.

"My God, lady, I have ten dancers sitting around in a rehearsal hall getting their leotards sweaty! What do you expect me to do?"

She explained what had happened the night before. And as she told him, she realized the newspapers had been justified in holding that tone against the twenty-six witnesses to the death of Leona Ciarelli. Paschal Guzman listened, and when he spoke again, his voice was several octaves lower, and he spoke more slowly. He said he understood and she could take a little longer to prepare the charts. But there was a distance in his voice, and he hung up while she was thanking him.

She dressed in an argyle sweater vest in shades of dark purple, and a pair of fitted khaki gabardine trousers. She had to go out, to walk around. To do what? To think about other things. As she pulled on the Fred Braun chunky heels, she idly wondered if that heavy silver bracelet was still in the window of Georg Jensen's. In the elevator, the young man from the window across the courtyard stared at her. Beth felt her body begin to tremble again. She went deep into the corner of the box when he entered behind her.

Between the fifth and fourth floors, he hit the *off* switch and the elevator jerked to a halt.

Beth stared at him and he smiled innocently.

"Hi. My name's Gleeson, Ray Gleeson, I'm in 714."

She wanted to demand he turn the elevator back on, by what right did he *presume* to do such a thing, what did he mean by this, turn it on at once or suffer the consequences. That was what she *wanted* to do. Instead, from the same place she had heard the gibbering laughter the night before, she heard her voice, much smaller and much less possessed than she had trained it to be, saying, "Beth O'Neill, I live in 701."

The thing about it was that *the elevator was stopped*. And she was frightened. But he leaned against the paneled wall, very well dressed, shoes polished, hair combed and probably blown dry with a hand dryer, and he *talked* to her as if they were across a table at L'Argenteuil. "You just moved in, huh?"

"About two months ago."

"Where did you go to school? Bennington or Sarah Lawrence?"

"Bennington. How did you know?"

He laughed, and it was a nice laugh. "I'm an editor at a religious book publisher; every year we get half a dozen Bennington, Sarah Lawrence, Smith girls. They come hopping in like grasshoppers, ready to revolutionize the publishing industry."

"What's wrong with that? You sound like you don't care for them."

"Oh, I *love* them, they're marvelous. They think they know how to write better than the authors we publish. Had one darlin' little item who was given galleys of three books to proof, and she rewrote all three. I think she's working as a table-swabber in a Horn & Hardart's now."

She didn't reply to that. She would have pegged him as an antifeminist, ordinarily, if it had been anyone else speaking. But the eyes. There was something terribly familiar about his face. She was enjoying the conversation; she rather liked him.

"What's the nearest big city to Bennington?"

"Albany, New York. About sixty miles."

"How long does it take to drive there?"

"From Bennington? About an hour and a half."

"Must be a nice drive, that Vermont country, really pretty. They went coed, I understand. How's that working out?"

"I don't know, really."

"You don't know?"

"It happened around the time I was graduating."

"What did you major in?"

"I was a dance major, specializing in Labanotation. That's the way you write choreography."

"It's all electives, I gather. You don't have to take anything required, like sciences, for example." He didn't change tone as he said, "That was a terrible thing last night. I saw you watching. I guess a lot of us were watching. It was a really terrible thing."

She nodded dumbly. Fear came back.

"I understand the cops got him. Some nut, they don't even know why he killed her, or why he went charging into that bar. It was really an awful thing. I'd very much like to have dinner with you one night soon, if you're not attached."

"That would be all right."

"Maybe Wednesday. There's an Argentinian place I know. You might like it."

"That would be all right."

"Why don't you turn on the elevator, and we can go," he said, and smiled again. She did it, wondering why she had stopped the elevator in the first place.

ON HER THIRD DATE WITH HIM, they had their first fight. It was at a party thrown by a director of television commercials. He lived on the ninth floor of their building. He had just done a series of spots for *Sesame Street* (the letters "U" for Underpass, "T" for Tunnel, lower-case "b" for boats, "c" for cars; the numbers 1 to 6 and the numbers 1 to 20; the words *light* and *dark*) and was celebrating his move from the arena of commercial tawdriness (and its attendant $75,000 a year) to the sweet fields of educational programming (and its accompanying descent into low-pay respectability). There was a logic in his joy Beth could not quite understand, and when she talked with him about it, in a far corner of the kitchen, his arguments didn't seem to parse. But he seemed happy, and his girlfriend, a long-legged ex-model from Philadelphia, continued to drift to him and away from him, like some exquisite undersea plant, touching his hair and kissing his neck, murmuring words of pride and barely submerged sexuality. Beth found it bewildering, though the celebrants were all bright and lively.

In the living room, Ray was sitting on the arm of the sofa, hustling a stewardess named Luanne. Beth could tell he was hustling; he was trying to look casual. When he *wasn't* hustling, he was always intense, about everything. She decided to ignore it, and wandered around the apartment, sipping at a Tanqueray and tonic.

There were framed prints of abstract shapes clipped from a calendar printed in Germany. They were in metal Bonniers frames.

In the dining room a huge door from a demolished building somewhere in the city had been handsomely stripped, teaked and refinished. It was now the dinner table.

A Lightolier fixture attached to the wall over the bed swung out, levered up and down, tipped, and its burnished globe-head revolved a full three hundred and sixty degrees.

She was standing in the bedroom, looking out the window, when she realized *this* had been one of the rooms in which light had gone on, gone off; one of the rooms that had contained a silent watcher at the death of Leona Ciarelli.

When she returned to the living room, she looked around more carefully. With only three or four exceptions—the stewardess, a young married couple from the second floor, a stockbroker from Hemphill, Noyes—*everyone* at the party had been a witness to the slaying.

"I'd like to go," she told him.

"Why, aren't you having a good time?" asked the stewardess, a mocking smile crossing her perfect little face.

"Like all Bennington ladies," Ray said, answering for Beth, "she is enjoying herself most by not enjoying herself at all. It's a trait of the anal retentive. Being here in someone else's apartment, she can't empty ashtrays or rewind the toilet paper roll so it doesn't hang a tongue, and being tightassed, her nature demands we go.

"All right, Beth, let's say our goodbyes and take off. The Phantom Rectum strikes again."

She slapped him and the stewardess's eyes widened. But the smile remained frozen where it had appeared.

He grabbed her wrist before she could do it again. "Garbanzo beans, baby," he said, holding her wrist tighter than necessary.

They went back to her apartment, and after sparring silently with kitchen cabinet doors slammed and the television being tuned too loud, they got to her bed, and he tried to perpetuate the metaphor by fucking her in the ass. He had her on elbows and knees before she realized what he was doing; she struggled to turn over and he rode her bucking and tossing without a sound. And when it was clear to him that she would never permit it, he grabbed her breast from underneath and squeezed so hard she howled in pain. He dumped her on her back, rubbed himself between her legs a dozen times, and came on her stomach.

Beth lay with her eyes closed and an arm thrown across her face. She wanted to cry, but found she could not. Ray lay on her and said nothing. She wanted to rush to the bathroom and shower, but he did not move, till long after his semen had dried on their bodies.

"Who did you date at college?" he asked.

"I didn't date anyone very much." Sullen.

"No heavy makeouts with wealthy lads from Williams and Dartmouth . . . no Amherst intellectuals begging you to save them from creeping faggotry by permitting them to stick their carrots in your sticky little slit?"

"Stop it!"

"Come on, baby, it couldn't all have been knee socks and little round circle-pins. You don't expect me to believe you didn't get a little mouthful of cock from time to time. It's only, what? about fifteen miles to Williamstown? I'm sure the Williams werewolves were down burning the highway to your cunt on weekends; you can level with old Uncle Ray . . ."

"Why are you like this?!" She started to move, to get away from him, and he grabbed her by the shoulder, forced her to lie down again. Then he rose up over her and said, "I'm like this because I'm a New Yorker, baby. Because I live in this fucking city every day. Because I have to play patty-cake with the ministers and other sanctified holy-joe assholes who want their goodness and lightness tracts published by the Blessed Sacrament Publishing and Storm Window Company of 277 Park Avenue, when what I *really* want to do is toss the stupid psalmsuckers out the thirty-seventh-floor window and listen to them quote chapter-and-worse all the way down. Because

I've lived in this great big snapping dog of a city all my life and I'm mad as a mudfly, for chrissakes!"

She lay unable to move, breathing shallowly, filled with a sudden pity and affection for him. His face was white and strained, and she knew he was saying things to her that only a bit too much Almadén and exact timing would have let him say.

"What do you expect from me," he said, his voice softer now, but no less intense, "do you expect kindness and gentility and understanding and a hand on *your* hand when the smog burns your eyes? I can't do it, I haven't got it. No one has it in this cesspool of a city. Look around you; what do you think is happening here? They take rats and they put them in boxes and when there are too many of them, some of the little fuckers go out of their minds and start gnawing the rest to death. *It ain't no different here, baby!* It's rat time for everybody in this madhouse. You can't expect to jam as many people into this stone thing as we do, with buses and taxis and dogs shitting themselves scrawny and noise night and day and no money and not enough places to live and no place to go to have a decent think . . . you can't do it without making the time right for some godforsaken other kind of thing to be born! You can't hate everyone around you, and kick every beggar and nigger and *mestizo* shithead, you can't have cabbies stealing from you and taking tips they don't deserve, and then cursing you, you can't walk in the soot till your collar turns black, and your body stinks with the smell of flaking brick and decaying brains, you can't do it without calling up some kind of awful—"

He stopped.

His face bore the expression of a man who has just received brutal word of the death of a loved one. He suddenly lay down, rolled over, and turned off.

She lay beside him, trembling, trying desperately to remember where she had seen his face before.

HE DIDN'T CALL HER AGAIN, after the night of the party. And when they met in the hall, he pointedly turned away, as though he had given her some obscure chance and she had refused to take it. Beth thought she understood: though Ray Gleeson had not been her first affair, he had been the first to reject her so completely. The first to put her not only out of his bed and his life, but even out of his world. It was as though she were invisible, not even beneath contempt, simply not there.

She busied herself with other things.

She took on three new charting jobs for Guzman and a new group that had formed on Staten Island, of all places. She worked furiously and they gave her new assignments; they even paid her.

She tried to decorate the apartment with a less precise touch. Huge poster blowups of Merce Cunningham and Martha Graham replaced the Brueghel prints that had reminded her of the view looking down the hill toward Williams. The tiny balcony outside her window, the balcony she had steadfastly refused to stand upon since the night of the slaughter, the night of the fog with eyes, that balcony she swept and set about with little flower boxes in which she planted geraniums, petunias, dwarf zinnias, and other hardy perennials. Then, closing the window, she went to give herself, to involve herself in this city to which she had brought her ordered life.

And the city responded to her overtures:

Seeing off an old friend from Bennington, at Kennedy International, she stopped at the terminal coffee shop to have a sandwich. The counter—like a moat—surrounded a center service island that had huge advertising cubes rising above it on burnished poles. The cubes proclaimed the delights of Fun City. *New York Is a Summer Festival*, they said, and *Joseph Papp Presents Shakespeare in Central Park* and *Visit the Bronx Zoo* and *You'll Adore Our Contentious but Lovable Cabbies*. The food emerged from a window far down the service area and moved slowly on a conveyor belt through the hordes of screaming waitresses who slathered the counter with redolent washcloths. The lunchroom had all the charm and dignity of a steel-rolling mill, and approximately the same noise level. Beth ordered a cheeseburger that cost a dollar and a quarter, and a glass of milk.

When it came, it was cold, the cheese unmelted, and the patty of meat resembling nothing so much as a dirty scouring pad. The bun was cold and untoasted. There was no lettuce under the patty.

Beth managed to catch the waitress's eye. The girl approached with an annoyed look. "Please toast the bun, and may I have a piece of lettuce?" Beth said.

"We dun' do that," the waitress said, turning half away as though she would walk in a moment.

"You don't do what?"

"We dun' toass the bun here."

"Yes, but I *want* the bun toasted," Beth said firmly.

"An' you got to pay for extra lettuce."

"If I was asking for *extra* lettuce," Beth said, getting annoyed, "I would pay for it, but since there's *no* lettuce here, I don't think I should be charged extra for the first piece."

"We dun' do that."

The waitress started to walk away. "Hold it," Beth said, raising her voice just enough so the assembly-line eaters on either side stared at her. "You mean to tell me I have to pay a dollar and a quarter and I can't get a piece of lettuce or even get the bun toasted?"

"Ef you dun' like it . . ."

"Take it back."

"You gotta pay for it, you order it."

"I said take it back, I don't want the fucking thing!"

The waitress scratched it off the check. The milk cost 27¢ and tasted going-sour. It was the first time in her life that Beth had said *that* word aloud.

At the cashier's stand, Beth said to the sweating man with the felt-tip pens in his shirt pocket, "Just out of curiosity, are you interested in complaints?"

"No!" he said, snarling, quite literally snarling. He did not look up as he punched out 73¢ and it came rolling down the chute.

The city responded to her overtures:

It was raining again. She was trying to cross Second Avenue, with the light. She stepped off the curb and a car came sliding through the red and splashed her. "Hey!" she yelled.

"Eat shit, sister!" the driver yelled back, turning the corner.

Her boots, her legs and her overcoat were splattered with mud. She stood trembling on the curb.

The city responded to her overtures:

She emerged from the building at One Astor Place with her big briefcase full of Laban charts; she was adjusting her rain scarf about her head. A well-dressed man with an attaché case thrust the handle of his umbrella up between her legs from the rear. She gasped and dropped her case.

The city responded and responded and responded.

Her overtures altered quickly.

The old drunk with the stippled cheeks extended his hand and mumbled words. She cursed him and walked on up Broadway past the beaver film houses.

She crossed against the lights on Park Avenue, making hackies slam their brakes to avoid hitting her; she used *that* word frequently now.

When she found herself having a drink with a man who had elbowed up beside her in the singles' bar, she felt faint and knew she should go home.

But Vermont was so far away.

NIGHTS LATER. She had come home from the Lincoln Center ballet, and gone straight to bed. Lying half-asleep in her bedroom, she heard an alien sound. One room away, in the living room, in the dark, there was a sound. She slipped out of bed and went to the door between the rooms. She fumbled silently for the switch on the lamp just inside the living room, and found it, and clicked it on. A black man in a leather car coat was trying to get *out* of the apartment. In that first flash of light filling the room, she noticed the television set beside him on the floor as he struggled with the door, she noticed the police lock and bar had been broken in a new and clever manner *New York* magazine had not yet reported in a feature article on apartment ripoffs, she noticed that he had gotten his foot tangled in the telephone cord that she had requested be extra-long so she could carry the instrument into the bathroom, I don't want to miss any business calls when the shower is running; she noticed all things in perspective and one thing with sharpest clarity: the expression on the burglar's face.

There was something familiar in that expression.

He almost had the door open, but now he closed it, and slipped the police lock. He took a step toward her.

Beth went back, into the darkened bedroom.

The city responded to her overtures.

She backed against the wall at the head of the bed. Her hand fumbled in the shadows for the telephone. His shape filled the doorway, light, all light behind him.

In silhouette it should not have been possible to tell, but somehow she knew he was wearing gloves and the only marks he would leave would be deep bruises, very blue, almost black, with the tinge under them of blood that had been stopped in its course.

He came for her, arms hanging casually at his sides. She tried to climb over the bed, and he grabbed her from behind, ripping her nightgown. Then he had a hand around her neck and he pulled her backward. She fell off the bed, landed at his feet and his hold was broken. She scuttled across the floor and for a moment she had the respite to feel terror. She was going to die, and she was frightened.

He trapped her in the corner between the closet and the bureau and kicked her. His foot caught her in the thigh as she folded tighter, smaller, drawing her legs up. She was cold.

Then he reached down with both hands and pulled her erect by her hair. He slammed her head against the wall. Everything slid up in her sight as though running off the edge of the world. He slammed her head against the wall again, and she felt something go soft over her right ear.

When he tried to slam her a third time she reached out blindly for his face and ripped down with her nails. He howled in pain and she hurled herself forward, arms wrapping themselves around his waist. He stumbled backward and, in a tangle of thrashing arms and legs, they fell out onto the little balcony.

Beth landed on the bottom, feeling the window boxes jammed up against her spine and legs. She fought to get to her feet, and her nails hooked into his shirt under the open jacket, ripping. Then she was on her feet again and they struggled silently.

He whirled her around, bent her backward across the wrought-iron railing. Her face was turned outward.

They were standing in their windows, watching.

Through the fog she could see them watching. Through the fog she recognized their expressions. Through the fog she heard them breathing in unison, bellows breathing of expectation and wonder. Through the fog.

And the black man punched her in the throat. She gagged and started to black out and could not draw air into her lungs. Back, back, he bent her farther back, and she was looking up, straight up, toward the ninth floor and higher . . .

Up there: eyes.

The words Ray Gleeson had said in a moment filled with what he had become, with the utter hopelessness and finality of the choice the city had forced on him, the words came back. *You can't live in this city and survive unless you have protection . . . you can't live this way, like rats driven mad, without making the time right for some godforsaken other kind of thing to be born . . . you can't do it without calling up some kind of awful . . .*

God! A new God, an ancient God come again with the eyes and hunger of a child, a deranged blood God of fog and street violence. A God who needed worshippers and offered the choices of death as a victim or life as an eternal witness to the deaths of *other* chosen victims. A God to fit the times, a God of streets and people.

She tried to shriek, to appeal to Ray, to the director in the bedroom window of his ninth-floor apartment with his long-legged Philadelphia model beside him and his fingers inside her as they worshipped in their holiest of ways, to the others who had been at the party that had been Ray's offer of a chance to join their congregation. She wanted to be saved from having to make that choice.

But the black man had punched her in the throat, and now his hands were on her, one on her chest, the other in her face, the smell of leather filling her where the nausea could not. And she understood Ray had *cared*, had wanted her to take the chance offered; but she had come from a world of little white dormitories and Vermont countryside; it was not a real world. *This* was the real world and up there was the God who ruled this world, and she had rejected him, had said no to one of his priests and servitors. *Save me! Don't make me do it!*

She knew she had to call out, to make appeal, to try and win the approbation of that God. *I can't . . . save me!*

She struggled and made terrible little mewling sounds trying to summon the words to cry out, and suddenly she crossed a line, and screamed up into the echoing courtyard with a voice Leona Ciarelli had never known enough to use.

"Him! Take him! Not me! I'm yours, I love you, I'm yours! Take him, not me, please not me, take him, take him, I'm yours!"

And the black man was suddenly lifted away, wrenched off her, and off the balcony, whirled straight up into the fog-thick air in the courtyard, as Beth sank to her knees on the ruined flower boxes.

She was half-conscious, and could not be sure she saw it just that way, but up he went, end over end, whirling and spinning like a charred leaf.

And the form took firmer shape. Enormous paws with claws and shapes that no animal she had ever seen had ever possessed, and the burglar, black, poor, terrified, whimpering like a whipped dog, was stripped of his flesh. His body was opened with a thin incision, and there was a rush as all the blood poured from him like a sudden cloudburst, and yet he was still alive, twitching with the involuntary horror of a frog's leg shocked with an electric current. Twitched, and twitched again as he was torn piece by piece to shreds. Pieces of flesh and bone and half a face with an eye blinking furiously, cascaded down past Beth, and hit the cement below with sodden thuds. And still he was alive, as his organs were squeezed and musculature and bile and shit and skin were rubbed, sandpapered together and let fall. It went on and on, as the death of Leona Ciarelli had gone on and on, and she understood with the blood-knowledge of survivors *at any cost* that the reason the witnesses to the death of Leona Ciarelli had done nothing was not that they had been frozen with horror, that they didn't want to get involved, or that they were inured to death by years of television slaughter.

They were worshippers at a black mass the city had demanded be staged; not once, but a thousand times a day in this insane asylum of steel and stone.

Now she was on her feet, standing half-naked in her ripped nightgown, her hand tightening on the wrought-iron railing, begging to see more, to drink deeper.

Now she was one of them, as the pieces of the night's sacrifice fell past her, bleeding and screaming.

Tomorrow the police would come again, and they would question her, and she would say how terrible it had been, that burglar, and how she had fought, afraid he would rape her and kill her, and how he had fallen, and she had no idea how he had been so hideously mangled and ripped apart, but a seven-storey fall, after all . . .

Tomorrow she would not have to worry about walking in the streets, because no harm could come to her. Tomorrow she could even remove the police lock. Nothing in the city could do her any further evil, because she had made the only choice. She was now a dweller in the city, now wholly and richly a part of it. Now she was taken to the bosom of her God.

She felt Ray beside her, standing beside her, holding her, protecting her, his hand on her naked backside, and she watched the fog swirl up and fill the courtyard, fill the city, fill her eyes and her soul and her heart with its power. As Ray's naked body pressed tightly inside her, she drank deeply of the night, knowing whatever voices she heard from this moment forward would be the voices not of whipped dogs, but those of strong, meat-eating beasts.

At last she was unafraid, and it was so good, so very good *not* to be afraid.

When inward life dries up, when feeling decreases and apathy increases, when one cannot affect or even genuinely touch another person, violence flares up as a daimonic necessity for contact, a mad drive forcing touch in the most direct way possible.

Rollo May,
LOVE AND WILL

PART THREE

LANDS OF ENCHANTMENT AND EVERYDAY LIFE

THE GRIFFIN AND
THE MINOR CANON

BY FRANK STOCKTON

FRANK STOCKTON ONCE TOLD AN INTERVIEWER THAT WHEN HE WAS VERY YOUNG HE DETERMINED THAT HE WANTED TO WRITE SOME FAIRY TALES BECAUSE HIS MIND WAS SO FULL OF THEM . . . BUT THESE FAIRY TALES WERE GOING TO BE DIFFERENT BECAUSE HE DESIRED THAT THEY ACT "AS FAR AS POSSIBLE . . . AS IF THEY WERE INHABITANTS OF THE REAL WORLD." IN DOING SO HE EARNED HIMSELF AN HONORED PLACE IN THE PANTHEON OF CHILDREN'S AUTHORS (THOUGH MOST ADULTS TODAY PRIMARILY REMEMBER HIM FOR HIS FAMOUS CLIFFHANGER SHORT STORY "THE LADY OR THE TIGER").

THOUGH SET IN A NONDESCRIPT RURAL SETTING (PROBABLY AT A MEDIEVAL TIME), "THE GRIFFIN AND THE MINOR CANON" MAKES WONDERFULLY FANTASTIC USE OF AN ENCROACHING MONSTER, THE GRIFFIN, AS A MEANS OF INSTIGATING SOCIAL CHANGE IN A MANNER THAT CAPTAIN JOHN SMITH OF JAMESTOWN (WHO IS CREDITED WITH DECLARING THAT IF "YOU DON'T WORK, YOU DON'T EAT") MIGHT HAVE BEEN PROUD OF.

. . . AND ALL BECAUSE A GRIFFIN HAPPENED BY TO ADMIRE A GARGOYLE ON THE CANON'S CHURCH.

Over the great door of an old, old church, which stood in a quiet town of a faraway land, there was carved in stone the figure of a large griffin. The old-time sculptor had done his work with great care, but the image he had made was not a pleasant one to look at. It had a large head, with enormous open mouth and savage teeth. From its back arose great wings, armed with sharp hooks and prongs. It had stout legs in front, with projecting claws, but there were no legs behind, the body running out into a long and powerful tail, finished off at the end with a barbed point. This tail was coiled up under him, the end sticking up just back of his wings.

The sculptor, or the people who had ordered this stone figure, had evidently been very much pleased with it, for little copies of it, also in stone, had been placed here and there along the sides of the church, not very far from the ground, so that people could easily look at them and ponder on their curious forms. There were a great many other sculptures on the outside of this church—saints, martyrs, grotesque heads of men, beasts, and birds, as well as those of other creatures which cannot be named, because nobody knows exactly what they were. But none were so curious and interesting as the great griffin over the door and the little griffins on the sides of the church.

A long, long distance from the town, in the midst of dreadful wilds scarcely known to man, there dwelt the Griffin whose image had been put up over the church door. In some way or other the old-time sculptor had seen him, and afterwards, to the best of his memory, had copied his figure in stone. The Griffin had never known this until, hundreds of years afterwards, he heard from a bird, from a wild animal, or in some manner which it is not easy to find out, that there was a likeness of him on the old church in the distant town.

Now, this Griffin had no idea whatever how he looked. He had never seen a mirror, and the streams where he lived were so turbulent and violent that a quiet piece of water, which would reflect the image of anything looking into it, could not be found. Being, as far as could be ascertained, the very last of his race, he had never seen another griffin. Therefore it was that, when he heard of this stone image of himself, he became very anxious to know what he looked like, and at last he determined to go to the old church and see for himself what manner of being he was. So he started off from the dreadful wilds, and flew on and on until he came to the countries inhabited by men, where his appearance in the air created great consternation. But he alighted nowhere, keeping up a steady flight until he reached the suburbs of the town which had his image on its church. Here, late in the afternoon, he alighted in a green meadow by the side of a brook, and stretched himself on the grass to rest. His great wings were tired, for he had not made such a long flight in a century or more.

The news of his coming spread quickly over the town, and the people, frightened nearly out of their wits by the arrival of so extraordinary a visitor, fled into their houses and shut themselves up. The Griffin called loudly for some one to come to him; but the more he called, the more afraid the people were to show themselves. At length he saw two laborers hurrying to their homes through the fields, and in a terrible voice he commanded them to stop. Not daring to disobey, the men stood, trembling.

"What is the matter with you all?" cried the Griffin. "Is there not a man in your town who is brave enough to speak to me?"

"I think," said one of the laborers, his voice shaking so that his words could hardly be understood, "that—perhaps—the Minor Canon—would come."

"Go, call him, then!" said the Griffin. "I want to see him."

The Minor Canon, who filled a subordinate position in the old church, had just finished the afternoon service, and was coming out of a side door, with three aged women who had formed the weekday congregation. He was a young man of a kind disposition, and very anxious to do good to the people of the town. Apart from his duties in the church, where he conducted services every weekday, he visited the sick and the poor, counselled and assisted persons who were in trouble, and taught a school composed entirely of the bad children in the town, with whom nobody else would have anything to do. Whenever the people wanted something difficult done for them, they always went to the Minor Canon. Thus it was that the laborer thought of the young priest when he found that some one must come and speak to the Griffin.

The Minor Canon had not heard of the strange event, which was known to the whole town except himself and the three old women, and when he was informed of it, and was told that the Griffin had asked to see him, he was greatly amazed and frightened.

"Me!" he exclaimed. "He has never heard of me! What should he want with *me*?"

"Oh, you must go instantly!" cried the two men. "He is very angry now because he has been kept waiting so long, and nobody knows what may happen if you don't hurry to him."

The poor Minor Canon would rather have had his hand cut off than to go out to meet an angry griffin; but he felt that it was his duty to go, for it would be a woeful thing if injury should come to the people of the town because he was not brave enough to obey the summons of the Griffin; so, pale and frightened, he started off.

"Well," said the Griffin, as soon as the young man came near, "I am glad to see that there is some one who has the courage to come to me."

The Minor Canon did not feel very courageous, but he bowed his head.

"Is this the town," said the Griffin, "where there is a church with a likeness of myself over one of the doors?"

The Minor Canon looked at the frightful creature before him, and saw that it was, without doubt, exactly like the stone image on the church. "Yes," he said, "you are right."

"Well, then," said the Griffin, "will you take me to it? I wish very much to see it."

The Minor Canon instantly thought that if the Griffin entered the town without the people knowing what he came for, some of them would probably be frightened to death, and so he sought to gain time to prepare their minds.

"It is growing dark now," he said, very much afraid, as he spoke, that his words might enrage the Griffin, "and objects on the front of the church cannot be seen clearly. It will be better to wait until morning, if you wish to get a good view of the stone image of yourself."

"That will suit me very well," said the Griffin. "I see you are a man of good sense. I am tired, and I will take a nap here on this soft grass, while I cool my tail in the little stream that runs near me. The end of my tail gets red-hot when I am angry or excited, and it is quite warm now. So you may go, but be sure and come early tomorrow morning, and show me the way to the church."

The Minor Canon was glad enough to take his leave, and hurried into the town. In front of the church he found a great many people assembled to hear his report of his interview with the Griffin. When they found that he had not come to spread ruin and devastation, but simply to see his stony likeness on the church, they showed neither relief nor gratification, but began to upbraid the Minor Canon for consenting to conduct the creature into the town.

"What could I do?" cried the young man. "If I should not bring him he would come himself, and perhaps end by setting fire to the town with his red-hot tail."

Still the people were not satisfied, and a great many plans were proposed to prevent the Griffin from coming into the town. Some elderly persons urged that the young men should go out and kill him. But the young men scoffed at such a ridiculous idea. Then some one said that it would be a good thing to destroy the stone image, so that the Griffin would have no excuse for entering the town. This proposal was received with such favor that many of the people ran for hammers, chisels, and crowbars with which to tear down and break up the stone griffin. But the Minor Canon resisted this plan with all the strength of his mind and body. He assured the people that this action would enrage the Griffin beyond measure, for it would be impossible to conceal from him that his image had been destroyed during the night.

But they were so determined to break up the stone griffin that the Minor Canon saw that there was nothing for him to do but to stay there and protect it. All night he walked up and down in front of the church door, keeping away the men who brought ladders by which they might mount to the great stone griffin and knock it to pieces with their hammers and crowbars. After many hours the people were obliged to give up their attempts, and went home to sleep. But the Minor Canon remained at his post till early morning, and then he hurried away to the field where he had left the Griffin.

The monster had just awakened, and rising to his fore legs and shaking himself, he said that he was ready to go into the town. The Minor Canon, therefore, walked back, the Griffin flying slowly through the air at a short distance above the head of his guide. Not a person was to be seen in the streets, and they proceeded directly to the front of the church, where the Minor Canon pointed out the stone griffin.

The real Griffin settled down in the little square before the church and gazed earnestly at his sculptured likeness. For a long time he looked at it. First he put his head on one side, and then he put it on the other. Then he shut his right eye and gazed with his left, after which he shut his left eye and gazed with his right. Then he moved a little to one side and looked at the image, then he moved the other way. After a while he said to the Minor Canon, who had been standing by all this time:

"It is, it must be, an excellent likeness! That breadth between his eyes, that expansive forehead those massive jaws! I feel that it must resemble me. If there is any fault to find with it, it is that the neck seems a little stiff. But that is nothing. It is an admirable likeness—admirable!"

The Griffin sat looking at his image all the morning and all the afternoon. The Minor Canon had been afraid to go away and leave him, and had hoped all through the day that he would soon be satisfied with his inspection and fly away home. But by evening the poor young man was utterly exhausted, and felt that he must eat and sleep. He frankly admitted this fact to the Griffin, and asked him if he would not like something to eat. He said this because he felt obliged in politeness to do so; but as soon as he had spoken the words, he was seized with dread lest the monster should demand half a dozen babies, or some tempting repast of that kind.

"Oh, no," said the Griffin, "I never eat between the equinoxes. At the vernal and at the autumnal equinox I take a good meal, and that lasts me for half a year. I am extremely regular in my habits, and do not think it healthful to eat at odd times. But if you need food, go and get it, and I will return to the soft grass where I slept last night, and take another nap."

The next day the Griffin came again to the little square before the church, and remained there until evening, steadfastly regarding the stone griffin over the door. The Minor Canon came once or twice to look at him, and the Griffin seemed very glad to see him. But the young clergyman could not stay as he had done before, for he had many duties to perform. Nobody went to the church, but the people came to the Minor Canon's house, and anxiously asked him how long the Griffin was going to stay.

"I do not know," he answered, "but I think he will soon be satisfied with looking at his stone likeness, and then he will go away."

But the Griffin did not go away. Morning after morning he went to the church, but after a time he did not stay there all day. He seemed to have taken a great fancy to the Minor Canon, and followed him about as he pursued his various avocations. He would wait for him at the side door of the church, for the Minor Canon held services every day, morning and evening, though nobody came now. "If any one should come," he said to himself, "I must be found at my post." When the young man came out, the Griffin would accompany him in his visits to the sick and the poor, and would often look into the windows of the school-house where the Minor Canon was teaching his unruly scholars. All the other schools were closed, but the parents of the Minor Canon's scholars forced them to go to school, because they were so bad they could not endure them at home—griffin or no griffin. But it must be said they generally behaved very well when that great monster sat up on his tail and looked in at the school-room window.

When it was perceived that the Griffin showed no sign of going away, all the people who were able to do so, left the town. The canons and the higher officers of the church had fled away during the first day of the Griffin's visit, leaving behind only the Minor Canon and some of the men who opened the doors and swept the church. All the citizens who could afford it shut up their houses and travelled to distant parts, and only the working-people and the poor were left behind. After some days these ventured to go about and attend to their business, for if they did not work they would starve. They were getting a little used to seeing the Griffin, and having been told that he did not eat between equinoxes, they did not feel so much afraid of him as before.

Day by day the Griffin became more and more attached to the Minor Canon. He kept near him a great part of the time, and often spent the night in front of the little house where the young clergyman lived alone. This strange companionship was often burdensome to the Minor Canon. But, on the other hand, he could not deny that he derived a great deal of benefit and instruction from it. The Griffin had lived for hundreds of years, and had seen much, and he told the Minor Canon many wonderful things.

"It is like reading an old book," said the young clergyman to himself. "But how many books I would have had to read before I would have found out what the Griffin has told me about the earth, the air, the water, about minerals, and metals, and growing things, and all the wonders of the world!"

Thus the summer went on, and drew toward its close. And now the people of the town began to be very much troubled again.

"It will not be long," they said, "before the autumnal equinox is here, and then that monster will want to eat. He will be dreadfully hungry, for he has taken so much exercise since his last meal. He will devour our children. Without doubt, he will eat them all. What is to be done?"

To this question no one could give an answer, but all agreed that the Griffin must not be allowed to remain until the approaching equinox. After talking over the matter a great deal, a crowd of the people went to the Minor Canon, at a time when the Griffin was not with him.

"It is your fault," they said, "that the monster is among us. You brought him here, and you ought to see that he goes away. It is only on your account that he stays here at all, for, although he visits his image every day, he is with you the greater part of the time. If you were not here he would not stay. It is your duty to go away, and then he will follow you, and we shall be free from the dreadful danger which hangs over us."

"Go away!" cried the Minor Canon, greatly grieved at being spoken to in such a way. "Where shall I go? If I go to some other town, shall I not take this trouble there? Have I a right to do that?"

"No," said the people, "you must not go to any other town. There is no town far enough away. You must go to the dreadful wilds where the Griffin lives, and then he will follow you and stay there."

They did not say whether or not they expected the Minor Canon to stay there also, and he did not ask them anything about it. He bowed his head, and went into his house to think. The more he thought, the more clear it became to his mind that it was his duty to go away, and thus free the town from the presence of the Griffin.

That evening he packed a leather bag full of bread and meat, and early the next morning he set out on his journey to the dreadful wilds. It was a long, weary, and doleful journey, especially after he had gone beyond the habitations of men; but the Minor Canon kept on bravely, and never faltered. The way was longer than he had expected, and his provisions soon grew so scanty that he was obliged to eat but a little every day; but he kept up his courage, and pressed on, and after many days of toilsome travel he reached the dreadful wilds.

When the Griffin found that the Minor Canon had left the town, he seemed sorry, but showed no disposition to go and look for him. After a few days had passed, he became much annoyed, and asked some of the people where the Minor Canon had gone. But although the citizens had been so anxious that the young clergyman should go to the dreadful wilds, thinking that the Griffin would immediately follow him, they were now afraid to mention the Minor Canon's destination, for the monster seemed angry already, and if he should suspect their trick, he would doubtless become very much enraged. So every one said he did not know, and the Griffin wandered about disconsolate. One morning he looked into the Minor Canon's school-house, which was always empty now, and thought that it was a shame that everything should suffer on account of the young man's absence.

"It does not matter so much about the church," he said, "for nobody went there. But it is a pity about the school. I think I will teach it myself until he returns."

It was the hour for opening the school, and the Griffin went inside and pulled the rope which rang the school bell. Some of the children who heard the bell ran in to see what was the matter, supposing it to be a joke of one of their companions. But when they saw the Griffin they stood astonished and scared.

"Go tell the other scholars," said the monster, "that school is about to open, and that if they are not all here in ten minutes I shall come after them."

In seven minutes every scholar was in place.

Never was seen such an orderly school. Not a boy or girl moved or uttered a whisper. The Griffin climbed into the master's seat; his wide wings spread on each side of him, because he could not lean back in his chair while they stuck out behind, and his great tail coiled around in front of the desk, the barbed end sticking up, ready to tap any boy or girl who might misbehave. The Griffin now addressed the scholars, telling them that he intended to teach them while their master was away. In speaking he endeavored to imitate, as far as possible, the mild and gentle tones of the Minor Canon, but it must be admitted that in this he was not very successful. He had paid a good deal of attention to the studies of the school, and he determined not to attempt to teach them anything new, but to review them in what they had been studying. So he called up the various classes, and questioned them upon their previous lessons. The children racked their brains to remember what they had learned. They were so afraid of the Griffin's displeasure that they recited as they had never recited before.

One of the boys, far down in his class, answered so well that the Griffin was astonished.

"I should think you would be at the head," said he. "I am sure you have never been in the habit of reciting so well. Why is this?"

"Because I did not choose to take the trouble," said the boy, trembling in his boots. He felt obliged to speak the truth, for all the children thought that the great eyes of the Griffin could see right through them, and that he would know when they told a falsehood.

"You ought to be ashamed of yourself," said the Griffin. "Go down to the very tail of the class, and if you are not at the head in two days, I shall know the reason why."

The next afternoon this boy was number one.

It was astonishing how much these children now learned of what they had been studying. It was as if they had been educated over again. The Griffin used no severity toward them, but there was a look about him which made them unwilling to go to bed until they were sure they knew their lessons for the next day.

The Griffin now thought that he ought to visit the sick and the poor, and he began to go about the town for this purpose. The effect upon the sick was miraculous. All, except those who were very ill indeed, jumped from their beds when they heard he was coming, and declared themselves quite well. To those who could not get up he gave herbs and root which none of them had ever before thought of as medicines, but which the Griffin had seen used in various parts of the world, and most of them recovered. But, for all that, they afterwards said that no matter what happened to them, they hoped that they should never again have such a doctor coming to their bedsides, feeling their pulses and looking at their tongues.

As for the poor, they seemed to have utterly disappeared. All those who had depended upon charity for their daily bread were now at work in some way or other, many of them offering to do odd jobs for their neighbors just for the sake of their meals—a thing which before had been seldom heard of in the town. The Griffin could find no one who needed his assistance.

The summer now passed, and the autumnal equinox was rapidly approaching. The citizens were in a state of great alarm and anxiety. The Griffin showed no signs of going away, but seemed to have settled himself permanently among them. In a short time the day for his semi-annual meal would arrive, and then what would happen? The monster would certainly be very hungry, and would devour all their children.

Now they greatly regretted and lamented that they had sent away the Minor Canon. He was the only one on whom they could have depended in this trouble, for he could talk freely with the Griffin, and so find out what could be done. But it would not do to be inactive. Some step must be taken immediately. A meeting of the citizens was called, and two old men were appointed to go and talk to the Griffin. They were instructed to offer to prepare a splendid dinner for him on equinox day—one which would entirely satisfy his hunger. They would offer him the fattest mutton, the most tender beef, fish and game of various sorts, and anything of the kind he might fancy. If none of these suited, they were to mention that there was an orphan asylum in the next town.

"Anything would be better," said the citizens, "than to have our dear children devoured."

The old men went to the Griffin, but their propositions were not received with favor.

"From what I have seen of the people of this town," said the monster, "I do not think I could relish anything which was prepared by them. They appear to be all cowards, and, therefore, mean and selfish. As for eating one of them, old or young, I could not think of it for a moment. In fact, there was only one creature in the whole place for whom I could have had an appetite, and that is the Minor Canon, who has gone away. He was brave, and good, and honest, and I think I should have relished him."

"Ah!" said one of the old men, very politely, "in that case I wish we had not sent him to the dreadful wilds!"

"What!" cried the Griffin. "What do you mean? Explain instantly what you are talking about!"

The old man, terribly frightened at what he had said, was obliged to tell how the Minor Canon had been sent away by the people, in the hope that the Griffin might be induced to follow him.

When the monster heard this he became furiously angry. He dashed away from the old men and, spreading his wings, flew backward and forward over the town. He was so much excited that his tail became red-hot, and glowed like a meteor against the evening sky. When at last he settled down in the little field where he usually rested, and thrust his tail into the brook; the steam arose like a cloud, and the water of the stream ran hot through the town. The citizens were greatly frightened, and bitterly blamed the old man for telling about the Minor Canon.

"It is plain," they said, "that the Griffin intended at last to go and look for him, and we should have been saved. Now who can tell what misery you have brought upon us?"

The Griffin did not remain long in the little field. As soon as his tail was cool he flew to the town hall and rang the bell. The citizens knew that they were expected to come there, and although they were afraid to go, they were still more afraid to stay away, and they crowded into the hall. The Griffin was on the platform at one end, flapping his wings and walking up and down, and the end of his tail was still so warm that it slightly scorched the boards as he dragged it after him.

When everybody who was able to come was there, the Griffin stood still and addressed the meeting.

"I have had a contemptible opinion of you," he said, "ever since I discovered what cowards you are, but I had no idea that you were so ungrateful, selfish, and cruel as I now find you to be. Here was your Minor Canon, who labored day and night for your good, and thought of nothing else but how he might benefit you and make you happy, and as soon as you imagine yourselves threatened with a danger,—for well I know you are dreadfully afraid of me,—you send him off, caring not whether he returns or perishes, hoping thereby to save yourselves. Now, I had conceived a great liking for that young man, and had intended, in a day or two, to go and look him up. But I have changed my mind about him. I shall go and find him, but I shall send him back here to live among you, and I intend that he shall enjoy the reward of his labor and his sacrifices. Go, some of you, to the officers of the church, who so cowardly ran away when I first came here, and tell them never to return to this town under penalty of death. And if, when your Minor Canon comes back to you, you do not bow yourselves before him, put him in the highest place among you, and serve and honor him all his life, beware of my terrible vengeance! There were only two good things in this town: the Minor Canon and the stone image of myself over your church door. One of these you have sent away, and the other I shall carry away myself."

With these words he dismissed the meeting and it was time, for the end of his tail had become so hot that there was danger of its setting fire to the building.

The next morning the Griffin came to the church, and tearing the stone image of himself from its fastenings over the great door, he grasped it with his powerful fore-legs and flew up into the air. Then, after hovering over the town for a moment, he gave his tail an angry shake, and took up his flight to the dreadful wilds. When he reached this desolate region, he set the stone griffin upon a ledge of a rock which rose in front of the dismal cave he called his home. There the image occupied a position somewhat similar to that it had had over the church door; and the Griffin, panting with the exertion of carrying such an enormous load to so great a distance, lay down upon the ground, and regarded it with much satisfaction. When he felt somewhat rested he went to look for the Minor Canon. He found the young man, weak and half starved, lying under the shadow of a rock. After picking him up and carrying him to his cave, the Griffin flew away to a distant marsh, where he procured some roots and herbs which he well knew were strengthening and beneficial to man, though he had never tasted them himself. After eating these the Minor Canon was greatly revived, and sat up and listened while the Griffin told him what had happened in the town.

"Do you know," said the monster, when he had finished, "that I have had, and still have, a great liking for you?"

"I am very glad to hear it," said the Minor Canon, with his usual politeness.

"I am not at all sure that you would be," said the Griffin, "if you thoroughly understood the state of the case, but we will not consider that now. If some things were different, other things would be otherwise. I have been so enraged by discovering the manner in which you have been treated that I have determined that you shall at last enjoy the rewards and honors to which you are entitled. Lie down and have a good sleep, and then I will take you back to the town."

As he heard these words, a look of trouble came over the young man's face.

"You need not give yourself any anxiety," said the Griffin, "about my return to the town. I shall not remain there. Now that I have that admirable likeness of myself in front of my cave, where I can sit at my leisure and gaze upon its noble features and magnificent proportions, I have no wish to see that abode of cowardly and selfish people."

The Minor Canon, relieved from his fears, lay back, and dropped into a doze, and when he was sound asleep, the Griffin took him up and carried him back to the town. He arrived just before daybreak, and putting the young man gently on the grass in the little field where he himself used to rest, the monster, without having been seen by any of the people, flew back to his home.

When the Minor Canon made his appearance in the morning among the citizens, the enthusiasm and cordiality with which he was received were truly wonderful. He was taken to a house which had been occupied by one of the banished high officers of the place, and every one was anxious to do all that could be done for his health and comfort. The people crowded into the church when he held services, so that the three old women who used to be his week-day congregation could not get to the best seats, which they had always been in the habit of taking; and the parents of the bad children determined to reform them at home, in order that he might be spared the trouble of keeping up his former school. The Minor Canon was appointed to the highest office of the old church, and before he died he became a bishop.

During the first years after his return from the dreadful wilds, the people of the town looked up to him as a man to whom they were bound to do honor and reverence. But they often, also, looked up to the sky to see if there were any signs of the Griffin coming back. However, in course of time they learned to honor and reverence their former Minor Canon without the fear of being punished if they did not do so.

But they need never have been afraid of the Griffin. The autumnal equinox day came round, and the monster ate nothing. If he could not have the Minor Canon, he did not care for anything. So, lying down with his eyes fixed upon the great stone griffin, he gradually declined, and died. It was a good thing for some of the people of the town that they did not know this.

If you should ever visit the old town, you would still see the little griffins on the sides of the church, but the great stone griffin that was over the door is gone.

THE ENCHANTED BUFFALO

BY L. FRANK BAUM

THOUGH PRIMARILY KNOWN AS THE CREATOR OF OZ, THE MAGICAL KINGDOM THAT EXISTS JUST OVER THE RAINBOW FROM KANSAS, L. FRANK BAUM WAS A FANTASIST OF MANY TALENTS AND MIGHT EVEN BE DESERVING OF THE TITLE "FATHER OF CONTEMPORARY AMERICAN FANTASY" (INDEED, THE YEAR AFTER HE PUBLISHED HIS FIRST OZ BOOK HE FOLLOWED IT WITH A COLLECTION ENTITLED "AMERICAN FAIRY TALES"). ONE OF THE THINGS HE TOOK GREAT PAINS IN DOING WAS USING REAL-LIFE AMERICAN SETTINGS SUCH AS KANSAS OR EVEN CHICAGO (AS HE DID IN "THE GLASS DOG") AS EITHER HIS JUMPING-OFF POINT OR AS THE BASIS FOR HIS IMAGINED WORLD. IN "THE ENCHANTED BUFFALO," HE SETS HIS SIGHTS ON THE PLAINS WITH A MAGICAL LOOK AT ONE OF ITS DENIZENS.

This is a tale of the Royal Tribe of Okolom—those mighty buffaloes that once dominated all the Western prairies. Seven hundred strong were the Okolom—great, shaggy creatures herding together and defying all enemies. Their range was well known to the Indians, to lesser herds of bisons and to all the wild animals that roamed in the open; but none cared to molest or interfere with the Royal Tribe.

Dakt was the first King of the Okolom. By odds the fiercest and most intelligent of his race, he founded the Tribe, made the Laws that directed their actions and led his subjects through wars and dangers until they were acknowledged masters of the prairie.

Dakt had enemies, of course; even in the Royal Tribe. As he grew old it was whispered he was in league with Pagshat, the Evil Genius of the prairies; yet few really believed the lying tale, and those who did but feared King Dakt the more.

The days of this monarch were prosperous days for the Okolom. In Summer their feeding grounds were ever rich in succulent grasses; in Winter Dakt led them to fertile valleys in the shelter of the mountains.

But in time the great leader grew old and gray. He ceased quarreling and fighting and began to love peace—a sure sign that his days were numbered. Sometimes he would stand motionless for hours, apparently in deep thought. His dignity relaxed; he became peevish; his eye, once shrewd and compelling, grew dim and glazed.

Many of the younger bulls, who coveted his Kingship, waited for Dakt to die; some patiently, and some impatiently. Throughout the herd there was an undercurrent of excitement. Then, one bright Spring morning, as the Tribe wandered in single file toward new feeding grounds, the old King lagged behind. They missed him, presently, and sent Barrag the Bull back over the hills to look for him. It was an hour before this messenger returned, coming into view above the swell of the prairie.

"The King is dead," said Barrag the Bull, as he walked calmly into the midst of the tribe. "Old age has at last overtaken him."

The members of the Okolom looked upon him curiously. Then one said: "There is blood upon your horns, Barrag. You did not wipe them well upon the grass."

Barrag turned fiercely. "The old King is dead," he repeated. "Hereafter, I am the King!"

No one answered in words; but, as the Tribe pressed backward into a dense mass, four young bulls remained standing before Barrag, quietly facing the would-be King. He looked upon them sternly. He had expected to contend for his royal office. It was the Law that any of the Tribe might fight for the right to rule the Okolom. But it surprised him to find there were four who dared dispute his assertion that he was King.

Barrag the Bull had doubtless been guilty of a cowardly act in goring the feeble old King to his death. But he could fight; and fight he did. One after another the powerful young bulls were overthrown, while every member of the Tribe watched the great tournament with eager interest. Barrag was not popular with them, but they could not fail to marvel at his prowess. To the onlookers he seemed inspired by unseen powers that lent him a strength fairly miraculous. They murmured together in awed tones, and the name of the dread Pagshat was whispered more than once.

As the last of the four bulls—the pride of half the Tribe—lay at the feet of the triumphant Barrag, the victor turned and cried aloud: "I am King of the Okolom! Who dares dispute my right to rule?"

For a moment there was silence. Then a fresh young voice exclaimed: "I dare!" and a handsome bull calf marched slowly into the space before Barrag and proudly faced him. A muttered protest swelled from the assemblage until it became a roar. Before it had subsided the young one's mother rushed to his side with a wail of mingled love and fear.

"No, no, Oknu!" she pleaded, desperately. "Do not fight, my child. It is death! See—Barrag is twice thy size. Let him rule the Okolom!"

"But I myself am the son of Dakt the King, and fit to rule in his place," answered Oknu, tossing his head with pride. "This Barrag is an interloper! There is no drop of royal blood in his veins."

"But he is nearly twice thy size!" moaned the mother, nearly frantic with terror. "He is leagued with the Evil Genius. To fight him means defeat and death!"

"He is a murderer!" returned the young bull, glaring upon Barrag. "He has killed his King, my father!"

"Enough!" roared the accused. "I am ready to silence this king's cub. Let us fight."

"No!" said an old bull, advancing from the herd. "Oknu shall not fight to-day. He is too young to face the mighty Barrag. But he will grow, both in size and strength; and then, when he is equal to the contest, he may fight for his father's place among the Okolom. In the meantime we acknowledge Barrag our King!"

A shout of approval went up from all the Tribe, and in the confusion that followed the old Queen thrust her bold son out of sight amidst the throng.

Barrag was King. Proudly he accepted the acclaims of the Okolom—the most powerful tribe in his race. His ambition was at last fulfilled; his plotting had met with success. The unnatural strength he had displayed had vanquished every opponent. Barrag was King.

Yet as the new ruler led his followers away from the field of conflict and into fresh pastures, his heart was heavy within him. He had not thought of Prince Oknu, the son of the terrible old King he had assisted to meet death. Oknu was a mere youth, half-grown and untried. Yet the look in his dark eyes as he had faced his father's murderer filled Barrag with a vague uneasiness. The youth would grow, and bade fair to become as powerful in time as old Dakt himself. And when he was grown he would fight for the leadership of the Okolom.

Barrag had not reckoned upon that.

When the moon came up, and the prairie was dotted with the reclining forms of the hosts of the Royal Tribe, the new King rose softly to his feet and moved away with silent tread. His pace was slow and stealthy until he had crossed the first rolling swell of prairie; then he set off at a brisk trot that covered many leagues within the next two hours.

At length Barrag reached a huge rock that towered above the plain. It was jagged and full of rents and fissures, and after a moment's hesitation the King selected an opening and stalked fearlessly into the black shadows. Presently the rift became a tunnel; but Barrag kept on, feeling his way in the darkness with his fore feet. Then a tiny light glimmered ahead, guiding him, and soon after he came into a vast cave hollowed in the centre of the rock. The rough walls were black as ink, yet glistened with an unseen light that shed its mellow but awesome rays throughout the cavern.

Here Barrag paused, saying in a loud voice:

"To thee, O Pagshat, Evil Genius of the Prairies, I give greeting! All has occurred as thou didst predict. The great Dakt is dead, and I, Barrag the Bull, am ruler of the Tribe of Okolom."

For a moment after he ceased the stillness was intense. Then a Voice, grave and deep, answered in the language of the buffaloes: "It is well!"

"But all difficulties are not yet swept aside," continued Barrag. "The old King left a son, an audacious young bull not half grown, who wished to fight me. But the patriarchs of the Tribe bade him wait until he had size and strength. Tell me, can the young Prince Oknu defeat me then?"

"He can," responded the Voice.

"Then what shall I do?" demanded the King. "Thou hast promised to make me secure in my power."

"I promised only to make you King of the Tribe—and you are King. Farther than that, you must protect yourself," the Voice of the Evil Genius made answer. "But, since you are hereafter my slave, I will grant you one more favor—the power to remove your enemy by enchantment."

"And how may I do that?" asked Barrag, eagerly.

"I will give you the means," was the reply. "Bow low thine head, and between the horns I will sprinkle a magical powder."

Barrag obeyed. "And now?" said he, inquiringly.

"Now," responded the unseen Voice, "mark well my injunctions. You must enchant the young Prince and transform him from a buffalo into some small and insignificant animal. Therefore, to-morrow you must choose a spring, and before any of the Tribe has drunk therein, shake well your head above the water, that the powder may sift down into the spring. At the same time centre your thoughts intently upon the animal into which you wish the Prince transformed. Then let him drink of the water in the spring, and the transformation on the instant will be accomplished."

"That is very simple," said Barrag. "Is the powder between my horns?"

"It is," answered the Voice.

"Then farewell, O Pagshat!"

From the cavern of the Evil Genius the King felt his way through the passages until he emerged upon the prairie. Then, softly—that he might not disturb the powder of enchantment—he trotted back to the sleeping herd.

Just before he reached it a panther, slender, lithe and black as coal, bounded across his path, and with a quick blow of his hoof Barrag crushed in the animal's skull. "Panthers are miserable creatures," mused the King, as he sought his place among the slumbering buffaloes. "I think I shall transform young Oknu into a black panther."

Secure in his great strength, he forgot that a full-grown panther is the most terrible foe known to his race.

AT SUNRISE THE KING LED THE ROYAL TRIBE of Okolom to a tiny spring that welled clear and refreshing from the centre of a fertile valley.

It is the King's right to drink first, but after bending his head above the spring and shaking it vigorously Barrag drew back and turned to the others.

"Come! I will prove that I bear no ill will," said he, treacherously. "Prince Oknu is the eldest son of our dead but venerated King Dakt. It is not for me to usurp his right. Prince Oknu shall drink first."

Hearing this, the patriarchs looked upon one another in surprise. It was not like Barrag the Bull to give way to another. But the Queen-mother was delighted at the favor shown her son, and eagerly pushed him forward. So Oknu advanced proudly to the spring and drank, while Barrag bent his thought intently upon the black panther.

An instant later a roar of horror and consternation came from the Royal Tribe; for the form of Prince Oknu had vanished, and in its place crouched the dark form of a trembling, terrified panther.

Barrag sprang forward. "Death to the vermin!" he cried, and raised his cloven hoof to crush in the panther's skull.

A sudden spring, a flash through the air, and the black panther alighted upon Barrag's shoulders. Then its powerful jaws closed over the buffalo's neck, pressing the sharp teeth far into the flesh.

With a cry of pain and terror the King reared upright, striving to shake off his tormentor; but the panther held fast. Again Barrag reared, whirling this way and that, his eyes staring, his breath quick and short, his great body trembling convulsively.

The others looked on fearfully. They saw the King kneel and roll upon the grass; they saw him arise with his foe still clinging to his back with claw and tooth; they heard the moan of despair that burst from their stricken leader, and the next instant Barrag was speeding away across the prairie like an arrow fresh from a bow, and his bellows of terror grew gradually fainter as he passed from their sight.

The prairie is vast. It is lonely, as well. A vulture, resting on outstretched wings, watched anxiously the flight of Barrag the Bull as hour by hour he sped away to the southward—the one moving thing on all that great expanse.

The sun sank low and buried itself in the prairie's edge. Twilight succeeded, and faded into night. And still a black shadow, leap by leap, sprang madly through the gloom. The jackals paused, listening to the short, quick pants of breath—the irregular hoof-beats of the galloping bull. But while they hesitated the buffalo passed on, with the silent panther still crouched upon its shoulders.

In the black night Barrag suddenly lifted up his voice. "Come to me, O Pagshat—Evil Genius that thou art—come to my rescue!" he cried.

And presently it seemed that another dark form rushed along beside his own.

"Save me, Pagshat!" he moaned. "Crush thou mine enemy, and set me free!"

A cold whisper reached him in reply: "I cannot!"

"Change him again into his own form," panted Barrag; "hark ye, Pagshat: 'tis the King's son—the cub—the weakling! Disenchant him, ere he proves my death!"

Again came the calm reply, like a breath of Winter sending a chill to his very bones: "I cannot."

Barrag groaned, dashing onward—ever onward.

"When you are dead," continued the Voice, "Prince Oknu will resume his own form. But not before."

"Did we not make a compact?" questioned Barrag, in despairing tone.

"We did," said the Evil Genius, "and I have kept my pact. But you have still to fulfill a pledge to me."

"At my death—only at my death, Pagshat!" cried the bull, trembling violently.

A cruel laugh was the only response. The moon broke through a rift in the clouds, flooding the prairie with silver light. The Evil Genius had disappeared, and the form of the solitary buffalo, with its clinging, silent foe, stumbled blindly across the endless plains.

Barrag had bargained with the Evil One for strength, and the strength of ten bulls was his. The legends do not say how many days and nights the great buffalo fled across the prairies with the black panther upon his shoulders. We know that the Utes saw him, and the Apaches, for their legends tell of it. Far to the south, hundreds of miles away, lived the tribe of the Comanches; and those Indians for many years told their children of Barrag the Bull, and how the Evil Genius of the Prairies, having tempted him to sin, betrayed the self-made King and abandoned him to the vengeance of the Black Panther, who was the enchanted son of the murdered King Dakt.

The strength of ten bulls was in Barrag; but even that could not endure forever. The end of the wild run came at last, and as Barrag fell lifeless upon the prairie the black panther relaxed its hold and was transformed into its original shape. For the enchantment of the Evil Genius was broken, and, restored to his own proper form, Prince Oknu cast one last glance upon his fallen enemy and then turned his head to the north.

It would be many moons before he could rejoin the Royal Tribe of the Okolom.

SINCE KING BARRAG had left them in his mad dash to the southward the Royal Tribe had wandered without a leader. They knew Oknu, as the black panther, would never relax his hold on his father's murderer; but how the strange adventure might end all were unable to guess.

So they remained in their well-known feeding grounds and patiently awaited news of the absent ones.

A full year had passed when a buffalo bull was discovered one day crossing the prairie in the direction of the Okolom. Dignity and pride was in his step; his glance was fearless, but full of wisdom. As he stalked majestically to the very centre of the herd his gigantic form towered far above that of any buffalo among them.

A stillness fraught with awe settled upon the Royal Tribe.

"It is old King Dakt, come to life again!" finally exclaimed one of the patriarchs.

"Not so," answered the newcomer, in a clear voice; "but it is the son of Dakt— who has avenged his father's death. Look upon me! I am Oknu, King of the Royal Tribe of Okolom. Dares any dispute my right to rule?"

No voice answered the challenge. Instead, every head of the seven hundred was bowed in silent homage to Oknu, the son of Dakt, the first King of the Okolom.

THE YELLOW WALLPAPER

BY CHARLOTTE PERKINS GILMAN

PIONEER FEMINIST AND REFORMER, CHARLOTTE PERKINS GILMAN USED HER FICTION AS A MEANS TO PROMULGATE HER MESSAGE, AND HER ALLEGORICAL NOVEL *HERLAND* RANKS WITH *EREWHON* AND *LOOKING BACKWARD* AS MASTERWORKS OF UTOPIAN FICTION. TO MY KNOWLEDGE, "THE YELLOW WALLPAPER" IS HER ONLY STORY OF THE FANTASTIC, THOUGH WHETHER IT IS A STORY OF THE SUPERNATURAL SUBJUGATION OF WOMEN BY MEN OR A CLASSIC TRADITIONAL GHOST STORY IN THE TRADITION OF "THE JOLLY CORNER" IS LEFT UP TO THE READER TO DECIDE.

It is very seldom that mere ordinary people like John and myself secure ancestral halls for the summer.

A colonial mansion, a hereditary estate, I would say a haunted house, and reach the height of romantic felicity—but that would be asking too much of fate!

Still I will proudly declare that there is something queer about it.

Else, why should it be let so cheaply? And why have stood so long untenanted.

John laughs at me, of course, but one expects that in marriage.

John is practical in the extreme. He has no patience with faith, an intense horror of superstition, and he scoffs openly at any talk of things not to be felt and seen and put down in figures.

John is a physician, and *perhaps*—(I would not say it to a living soul, of course, but this is dead paper and a great relief to my mind)—*perhaps* that is one reason I do not get well faster.

You see he does not believe I am sick!

And what can one do?

If a physician of high standing, and one's own husband, assures friends and relatives that there is really nothing the matter with one but temporary nervous depression—a slight hysterical tendency—what is one to do?

My brother is also a physician, and also of high standing, and he says the same thing.

So I take phosphates or phosphites—whichever it is, and tonics, and journeys, and air, and exercise, and am absolutely forbidden to "work" until I am well again.

Personally, I disagree with their idea.

Personally, I believe that congenial work, with excitement and change, would do me good.

But what is one to do?

I did write for a while in spite of them: but it *does* exhaust me a good deal—having to be so sly about it, or else meet with heavy opposition.

I sometimes fancy that in my condition if I had less opposition and more society and stimulus—but John says the very worst thing I can do is to think about my condition, and I confess it always makes me feel bad.

So I will let it alone and talk about the house.

The most beautiful place! It is quite alone, standing well back from the road, quite three miles from the village. It makes me think of English places that you read about, for there are hedges and walls and gates that lock, and lots of separate little houses for the gardeners and people.

There is a *delicious* garden! I never saw such a garden—large and shady, full of box-bordered paths, and lined with long grape-covered arbors with seats under them.

There were greenhouses, too, but they are all broken now.

There was some legal trouble, I believe, something about the heirs and coheirs; anyhow, the place has been empty for years.

That spoils my ghostliness, I am afraid, but I don't care—there is something strange about the house—I can feel it.

I even said so to John one moonlight evening but he said what I felt was a *draught,* and shut the window.

I get unreasonably angry with John sometimes. I'm sure I never used to be so sensitive. I think it is due to this nervous condition.

But John says if I feel so, I shall neglect proper self-control; so I take pains to control myself—before him, at least, and that makes me very tired.

I don't like our room a bit. I wanted one downstairs that opened on the piazza and had roses all over the window, and such pretty old-fashioned chintz hangings! But John would not hear of it.

He said there was only one window and not room for two beds, and no near room for him if he took another.

He is very careful and loving, and hardly lets me stir without special direction.

I have a schedule prescription for each hour in the day; he takes all care from me, and so I feel basely ungrateful not to value it more.

He said we came here solely on my account, that I was to have perfect rest and all the air I could get. "Your exercise depends on your strength, my dear," said he, "and your food somewhat on your appetite; but air you can absorb all the time." So we took the nursery at the top of the house.

It is a big, airy room, the whole floor nearly, with windows that look all ways, and air and sunshine galore. It was nursery first and then playroom and gymnasium. I should judge; for the windows are barred for little children, and there are rings and things in the walls.

The paint and paper look as if a boy's school had used it. It is stripped off—the paper—in great patches all around the head of my bed, about as far as I can reach, and in a great place on the other side of the room low down. I never saw a worse paper in my life.

One of those sprawling flamboyant patterns committing every artistic sin.

It is dull enough to confuse the eye in following, pronounced enough to constantly irritate and provoke study, and when you follow the lame uncertain curves for a little distance they suddenly commit suicide—plunge off at outrageous angles, destroy themselves in unheard of contradictions.

The color is repellent, almost revolting; a smoldering unclean yellow, strangely faded by the slow-turning sunlight.

It was a dull yet livid orange in some places, a sickly sulphur tint in others.

No wonder the children hated it! I should hate it myself if I had to live in this room long.

There comes John, and I must put this away—he hates to have me write a word.

WE HAVE BEEN HERE TWO WEEKS, and I haven't felt like writing before, since that first day.

I am sitting by the window now, up in this atrocious nursery, and there is nothing to hinder my writing as much as I please, save lack of strength.

John is away all day, and even some nights when his cases are serious.

I am glad my case is not serious!

But these nervous troubles are dreadfully depressing.

John does not know how much I really suffer. He knows there is no *reason* to suffer, and that satisfies him.

Of course it is only nervousness. It does weigh on me so not to do my duty in any way!

I meant to be such a help to John, such a real rest and comfort, and here I am a comparative burden already!

Nobody would believe what an effort it is to do what little I am able—to dress and entertain, and order things.

It is fortunate Mary is so good with the baby. Such a dear baby!

And yet I *cannot* be with him, it makes me so nervous.

I suppose John never was nervous in his life. He laughs at me so about this wallpaper!

At first he meant to repaper the room, but afterward he said that I was letting it get the better of me, and that nothing was worse for a nervous patient than to give way to such fancies.

He said that after the wallpaper was changed it would be the heavy bedstead, and then the barred windows, and then that gate at the head of the stairs, and so on.

"You know the place is doing you good," he said, "and really, dear, I don't care to renovate the house just for three months' rental."

"Then do let us go downstairs," I said, "there are such pretty rooms there."

Then he took me in his arms and called me a blessed little goose, and said he would go down to the cellar, if I wished, and have it whitewashed into the bargain.

But he is right enough about the beds and windows and things.

It is an airy and comfortable room as any one need wish, and, of course, I would not be so silly as to make him uncomfortable just for a whim.

I'm really getting quite fond of the big room, all but that horrid paper.

Out of one window I can see the garden, those mysterious deepshaded arbors, the riotous old-fashioned flowers, and bushes and gnarly trees.

Out of another I get a lovely view of the bay and a little private wharf belonging to the estate. There is a beautiful shaded lane that runs down there from the house. I always fancy I see people walking in these numerous paths and arbors, but John has cautioned me not to give way to fancy in the least. He says that with my imaginative power and habit of story-making, a nervous weakness like mine is sure to lead to all manner of excited fancies, and that I ought to use my will and good sense to check the tendency. So I try.

I think sometimes that if I were only well enough to write a little it would relieve the press of ideas and rest me.

But I find I get pretty tired when I try.

It is so discouraging not to have any advice and companionship about my work. When I get really well, John says we will ask Cousin Henry and Julia down for a long visit; but he says he would as soon put fireworks in my pillowcase as to let me have those stimulating people about now.

I wish I could get well faster.

But I must not think about that. This paper looks to me as if it *knew* what a vicious influence it had!

There is a recurrent spot where the pattern lolls like a broken neck and two bulbous eyes stare at you upside down.

I get positively angry with the impertinence of it and the everlastingness. Up and down and sideways they crawl, and those absurd, unblinking eyes are everywhere. There is one place where two breadths didn't match, and the eyes go all up and down the line, one a little higher than the other.

I never saw so much expression in an inanimate thing before, and we all know how much expression they have! I used to lie awake as a child and get more entertainment and terror out of blank walls and plain furniture than most children could find in a toy-store.

I remember what a kindly wink the knobs of our big, old bureau used to have, and there was one chair that always seemed like a strong friend.

I used to feel that if any of the other things looked too fierce I could always hop into the chair and be safe.

The furniture in this room is no worse than inharmonious, however, for we had to bring it all from downstairs. I suppose when this was used as a playroom they had to take the nursery things out, and no wonder! I never saw such ravages as the children have made here.

The wallpaper, as I said before, is torn off in spots, and it sticketh closer than a brother—they must have had perseverance as well as hatred.

Then the floor is scratched and gouged and splintered, the plaster itself is dug out here and there, and this great heavy bed which is all we found in the room, looks as if it had been through the wars.

But I don't mind it a bit—only the paper.

There comes John's sister. Such a dear girl as she is, and so careful of me! I must not let her find me writing.

She is a perfect and enthusiastic housekeeper, and hopes for no better profession. I verily believe she thinks it is the writing which made me sick!

But I can write when she is out, and see her a long way off from these windows.

There is one that commands the road, a lovely shaded winding road, and one that just looks off over the country. A lovely country, too, full of great elms and velvet meadows.

This wallpaper has a kind of sub-pattern in a different shade, a particularly irritating one, for you can only see it in certain lights, and not clearly then.

But in the places where it isn't faded and where the sun is just so—I can see a strange, provoking, formless sort of figure, that seems to skulk about that silly and conspicuous front design.

There's sister on the stairs!

WELL, THE FOURTH OF JULY IS OVER! The people are all gone and I am tired out. John thought it might do me good to see a little company, so we just had mother and Nellie and the children down for a week.

Of course I didn't do a thing. Jennie sees to everything now.

But it tired me all the same.

John says if I don't pick up faster he shall send me to Weir Mitchell in the fall.

But I don't want to go there at all. I had a friend who was in his hands once, and she says he is just like John and my brother, only more so!

Besides, it is such an undertaking to go so far.

I don't feel as if it was worthwhile to turn my hand over for anything, and I'm getting dreadfully fretful and querulous.

I cry at nothing, and cry most of the time.

Of course I don't when John is here, or anybody else, but when I am alone.

And I am alone a good deal just now. John is kept in town very often by serious cases, and Jennie is good and lets me alone when I want her to.

So I walk a little in the garden or down that lovely lane, sit on the porch under the roses, and lie down up here a good deal.

I'm getting really fond of the room in spite of the wallpaper. Perhaps *because* of the wallpaper.

It dwells in my mind so!

I lie here on this great immovable bed—it is nailed down, I believe—and follow that pattern about by the hour. It is as good as gymnastics, I assure you. I start, we'll say, at the bottom, down in the corner over there where it has not been touched, and I determine for the thousandth time that I *will* follow that pointless pattern to some sort of conclusion.

I know a little of the principle of design, and I know this thing was not arranged on any laws of radiation, or alternation, or repetition, or symmetry, or anything else that I never heard of.

It is repeated, of course, by the breadths, but not otherwise.

Looked at in one way each breadth stands alone, the bloated curves and flourishes—a kind of "debased Romanesque" with *delirium tremens*—go waddling up and down in isolated columns of fatuity.

But, on the other hand, they connect diagonally, and the sprawling outlines run off in great slanting waves of optic horror, like a lot of wallowing seaweeds in full chase.

The whole thing goes horizontally, too, at least it seems so, and I exhaust myself in trying to distinguish the order of its going in that direction.

They have used a horizontal breadth for a frieze, and that adds wonderfully to the confusion.

There is one end of the room where it is almost intact, and there, when the crosslights fade and the low sun shines directly upon it, I can almost fancy radiation after all—the interminable grotesques seem to form around a common center and rush off in headlong plunges of equal distraction.

It makes me tired to follow it. I will take a nap I guess.

I don't know why I should write this.

I don't want to.

I don't feel able.

And I know John would think it absurd. But I *must* say what I feel and think in some way—it is such a relief!

But the effort is getting to be greater than the relief.

Half the time now I am awfully lazy and lie down ever so much.

John says I mustn't lose my strength, and has me take cod liver oil and lots of tonics and things, to say nothing of ale and wine and rare meat.

Dear John! He loves me very dearly, and hates to have me sick. I tried to have a real earnest reasonable talk with him the other day, and tell him how I wish he would let me go and make a visit to Cousin Henry and Julia.

But he said I wasn't able to go, nor able to stand it after I got there; and I did not make out a very good case for myself, for I was crying before I had finished.

It is getting to be a great effort for me to think straight. Just this nervous weakness I suppose.

And dear John gathered me up in his arms, and just carried me upstairs and laid me on the bed, and sat by me and read to me till it tired my head.

He said I was his darling and his comfort and all he had, and that I must take care of myself for his sake, and keep well.

He says no one but myself can help me out of it, that I must use my will and self-control and not let any silly fancies run away with me.

There's one comfort, the baby is well and happy, and does not have to occupy this nursery with the horrid wallpaper.

If we had not used it, that blessed child would have! What a fortunate escape! Why, I wouldn't have a child of mine, an impressionable little thing live in such a room for worlds.

I never thought of it before, but it is lucky that John kept me here after all. I can stand it so much easier than a baby, you see.

Of course I never mention it to them any more—I am too wise—but I keep watch of it all the same.

There are things in that paper that nobody knows but me, or ever will.

Behind that outside pattern the dim shapes get clearer every day.

It is always the same shape, only numerous.

And it is like a woman stooping down and creeping about behind that pattern. I don't like it a bit. I wonder—I begin to think—I wish John would take me away from here!

It is so hard to talk with John about my case, because he is so wise, and because he loves me so.

But I tried it last night.

It was moonlight. The moon shines in all around just as the sun does.

I hate to see it sometimes, it creeps so slowly, and always comes in by one window or another.

John was asleep and I hated to wake him, so I kept still and watched the moonlight on the undulating wallpaper till I felt creepy.

The faint figure behind seemed to shake the pattern, just as if she wanted to get out.

I got up softly and went to feel and see if the paper *did* move, and when I came back John was awake.

"What is it, little girl?" he said. "Don't go walking about like that—you'll get cold."

I thought it was a good time to talk, so I told him that I really was not gaining here, and that I wished he would take me away.

"Why darling!" said he, "our lease will be up in three weeks, and I can't see how to leave before.

"The repairs are not done at home, and I cannot possibly leave town just now. Of course if you were in any danger, I could and would, but you really are better dear, whether you see it or not. I am a doctor, dear, and I know. You are gaining flesh and color, your appetite is better, I feel really much easier about you."

"I don't weigh a bit more," said I, "nor as much; and my appetite may be better in the evening when you are here, but it is worse in the morning when you are away!"

"Bless her little heart!" said he with a big hug, "she shall be as sick as she pleases! But now let's improve the shining hours by going to sleep, and talk about it in the morning!"

"And you won't go away?" I asked gloomily.

"Why, how can I, dear? It is only three weeks more and then we will take a nice little trip of a few days while Jennie is getting the house ready. Really, dear, you are better!"

"Better in body perhaps—" I began, and stopped short, for he sat up straight and looked at me with such a stern, reproachful look that I could not say another word.

"My darling," said he, "I beg of you, for my sake and for our child's sake, as well as for your own, that you will never for one instant let that idea enter your mind! There is nothing so dangerous, so fascinating, to a temperament like yours. It is a false and foolish fancy. Can you not trust me as a physician when I tell you so?"

So of course I said no more on that score, and we went to sleep before long. He thought I was asleep first, but I wasn't and lay there for hours trying to decide whether that front pattern and the back pattern really did move together or separately.

ON A PATTERN LIKE THIS, by daylight, there is a lack of sequence, a defiance of law, that is a constant irritant to a normal mind.

The color is hideous enough, and unreliable enough, and infuriating enough, but the pattern is torturing.

You think you have mastered it, but just as you get well underway in following, it turns a back-somersault and there you are. It slaps you in the face, knocks you down, and tramples upon you. It is like a bad dream.

The outside pattern is a florid arabesque, reminding one of a fungus. If you can imagine a toadstool in joints, an interminable string of toadstools, budding and sprouting in endless convolutions—why, that is something like it.

That is, sometimes!

There is one marked peculiarity about this paper, a thing nobody seems to notice but myself, and that is that it changes as the light changes.

When the sun shoots in through the east window—I always watch for that first long, straight ray—it changes so quickly that I never can quite believe it.

That is why I watch it always.

By moonlight—the moon shines in all night when there is a moon—I wouldn't know it was the same paper.

At night in any kind of light, in twilight, candle light, lamplight, and worst of all by moonlight, it becomes bars! The outside pattern I mean, and the woman behind it is as plain as can be.

I didn't realize for a long time what the thing was that showed behind, that dim sub-pattern, but now I am quite sure it is a woman.

By daylight she is subdued, quiet. I fancy it is the pattern that keeps her so still. It is so puzzling. It keeps me quiet by the hour.

I lie down so much now. John says it is good for me, and to sleep all I can.

Indeed he started the habit by making me lie down for an hour after each meal.

It is a very bad habit I am convinced, for you see I don't sleep.

And that cultivated deceit, for I don't tell them I'm awake—O no!

The fact is I am getting a little afraid of John.

He seems very queer sometimes, and even Jennie has an inexplicable look.

It strikes me occasionally, just as a scientific hypothesis—that perhaps it is the paper!

I have watched John when he did not know I was looking, and come into the room suddenly on the most innocent excuses, and I've caught him several times *looking at the paper!* And Jennie too. I caught Jennie with her hand on it once.

She didn't know I was in the room, and when I asked her in a quiet, a very quiet voice, with the most restrained manner possible, what she was doing with the paper— she turned around as if she had been caught stealing, and looked quite angry—asked me why I should frighten her so!

Then she said that the paper stained everything it touched, that she had found yellow smooches on all my clothes and John's, and she wished we would be more careful!

Did not that sound innocent? But I know she was studying that pattern, and I am determined that nobody shall find it out but myself!

LIFE IS VERY MUCH MORE EXCITING NOW than it used to be. You see I have something more to expect, to look forward to, to watch. I really do eat better, and am more quiet than I was.

John is so pleased to see me improve! He laughed a little the other day, and said I seemed to be flourishing in spite of my wallpaper.

I turned it off with a laugh. I had no intention of telling him it was *because* of the wallpaper—he would make fun of me. He might even want to take me away.

I don't want to leave now until I have found out. There is a week more, and I think that will be enough.

I'm feeling ever so much better! I don't sleep much at night, for it is so interesting to watch developments; but I sleep a good deal in the daytime.

In the daytime it is tiresome and perplexing.

There are always new shoots on the fungus, and new shades of yellow all over it. I cannot keep count of them, though I have tried conscientiously.

It is the strangest yellow, that wallpaper! It makes me think of all the yellow things I ever saw—not beautiful ones like buttercups, but old foul, bad yellow things.

But there is something else about that paper—the smell! I noticed it the moment we came into the room, but with so much air and sun it was not bad. Now we have had a week of fog and rain, and whether the windows are open or not, the smell is here.

It creeps all over the house.

I find it hovering in the dining room, skulking in the parlor, hiding in the hall, lying in wait for me on the stairs.

It gets into my hair.

Even when I go to ride, if I turn my head suddenly and surprise it—there is that smell!

Such a peculiar odor, too! I have spent hours in trying to analyze it, to find what it smelled like.

It is not bad—at first, and very gentle, but quite the subtlest, most enduring odor I ever met.

In this damp weather it is awful, I wake up in the night and find it hanging over me.

It used to disturb me at first. I thought seriously of burning the house—to reach the smell.

But now I am used to it. The only thing I can think of that it is like is the *color* of the paper! A yellow smell.

There is a very funny mark on this wall, low down, near the mopboard. A streak that runs round the room. It goes behind every piece of furniture, except the bed, a long, straight, even *smooch*, as if it had been rubbed over and over.

I wonder how it was done and who did it, and what they did it for. Round and round and round—round and round and round—it makes me dizzy!

I REALLY HAVE DISCOVERED SOMETHING at last.

Through watching so much at night, when it changes so, I have finally found out.

The front pattern *does* move—and no wonder! The woman behind shakes it!

Sometimes I think there are a great many women behind, and sometimes only one, and she crawls around fast, and her crawling shakes it all over.

Then in the very bright spots she keeps still, and in the very shady spots she just takes hold of the bars and shakes them hard.

And she is all the time trying to climb through. But nobody could climb through that pattern—it strangles so; I think that is why it has so many heads.

They get through, and then the pattern strangles them off and turns them upside down, and makes their eyes white!

If those heads were covered or taken off it would not be half so bad.

I think that woman gets out in the daytime!

And I'll tell you why—privately—I've seen her!

I can see her out of every one of my windows!

It is the same woman, I know, for she is always creeping, and most women do not creep by daylight.

I see her on the long road under the trees, creeping along, and when a carriage comes she hides under the blackberry vines.

I don't blame her a bit. It must be very humiliating to be caught creeping by daylight!

I always lock the door when I creep by daylight. I can't do it at night, for I know John would suspect something at once.

And John is so queer now, that I don't want to irritate him. I wish he would take another room! Besides, I don't want anybody to get that woman out at night but myself.

I often wonder if I could see her out of all the windows at once.

But, turn as fast as I can, I can only see out of one at one time.

And though I always see her, she *may* be able to creep faster than I can turn!

I have watched her sometimes away off in the open country, creeping as fast as a cloud shadow in a high wind.

IF ONLY THAT TOP PATTERN could be gotten off from the under one! I mean to try it, little by little.

I have found out another funny thing, but I shan't tell it this time! It does not do to trust people too much.

There are only two more days to get this paper off, and I believe John is beginning to notice. I don't like the look in his eyes.

And I heard him ask Jennie a lot of professional questions about me. She had a very good report to give.

She said I slept a good deal in the daytime.

John knows I don't sleep very well at night, for all I'm so quiet!

He asked me all sorts of questions, too, and pretended to be very loving and kind. As if I couldn't see through him!

Still, I don't wonder he acts so, sleeping under this paper for three months.

It only interests me, but I feel sure John and Jennie are secretly affected by it.

HURRAH! THIS IS THE LAST DAY, but it is enough. John had to stay in town overnight, and won't be out until this evening.

Jennie wanted to sleep with me—the sly thing! but I told her I should undoubtedly rest better for a night all alone.

That was clever, for really I wasn't alone a bit! As soon as it was moonlight and that poor thing began to crawl and shake the pattern, I got up and ran to help her.

I pulled and she shook, I shook and she pulled, and before morning we had peeled off yards of that paper.

A strip about as high as my head and half around the room.

And then when the sun came and that awful pattern began to laugh at me, I declared I would finish it today!

We go away tomorrow, and they are moving all my furniture down again to leave things as they were before.

Jennie looked at the wall in amazement but I told her merrily that I did it out of pure spite at the vicious thing.

She laughed and said she wouldn't mind doing it herself, but I must not get tired. How she betrayed herself that time!

But I am here, and no person touches this paper but me—not *alive!*

She tried to get me out of the room—it was too patent! But I said it was so quiet and empty and clean now that I believed I would lie down again and sleep all I could; and not to wake me even for dinner—I would call when I woke.

So now she is gone, and the servants are gone, and the things are gone, and there is nothing left but that great bedstead nailed down, with the canvas mattress we found on it.

We shall sleep downstairs tonight, and take the boat home tomorrow.

I quite enjoy the room, now it is bare again.

How those children did tear about there!

This bedstead is fairly gnawed!

But I must get to work.

I have locked the door and thrown the key down into the front path.

I don't want to go out, and I don't want to have anybody come in, till John comes. I want to astonish him.

I've got a rope up here that even Jennie did not find. If that woman does get out, and tries to get away, I can tie her!

But I forgot I could not reach far without anything to stand on!

This bed will *not* move!

I tried to lift and push it until I was lame, and then I got so angry I bit off a little piece at one corner—but it hurt my teeth.

Then I peeled off all the paper I could reach standing on the floor. It sticks horribly and the pattern just enjoys it! All those strangled heads and bulbous eyes and waddling fungus growths just shriek with derision!

I am getting angry enough to do something desperate. To jump out of the window would be admirable exercise, but the bars are too strong even to try.

Besides I wouldn't do it. Of course not. I know well enough that a step like that is improper and might be misconstrued.

I don't like to *look* out of the windows even—there are so many of those creeping women and they creep so fast.

I wonder if they all come out of that wallpaper as I did?

But I am securely fastened now by my well-hidden rope—you don't get *me* out in the road there!

I suppose I shall have to get back behind the pattern when it comes night, and that is hard!

It is so pleasant to be out in this great room and creep around as I please!

I don't want to go outside. I won't, even if Jennie asks me to.

For outside you have to creep on the ground, and everything is green instead of yellow.

But here I can creep smoothly on the floor, and my shoulder just fits in that long smooch around the wall, so I cannot lose my way.

Why there's John at the door!

It is no use, young man, you can't open it!

How he does call and pound!

Now he's crying for an axe.

It would be a shame to break down that beautiful door!

"John dear!" said I in the gentlest voice, "the key is down by the front steps, under a plantain leaf!"

That silenced him for a few moments.

Then he said—very quietly indeed, "Open the door, my darling!"

"I can't," said I. "The key is down by the front door under a plantain leaf!"

And then I said it again, several times, very gently and slowly, and said it so often that he had to go and see, and he got it of course, and came in. He stopped short by the door.

"What is the matter?" he cried. "For God's sake, what are you doing!"

I kept on creeping just the same, but I looked at him over my shoulder.

"I've got out at last," said I, "in spite of you and Jennie. And I've pulled off most of the paper, so you can't put me back!"

Now why should that man have fainted? But he did, and right across my path by the wall, so that I had to creep over him every time!

THE MOVING FINGER

BY EDITH WHARTON

EDITH WHARTON WAS PROBABLY AMERICA'S MOST SUCCESSFUL FEMALE GHOST-STORY WRITER OF THE TURN OF THE CENTURY EVEN THOUGH TODAY SHE IS MORE WIDELY RECALLED FOR HER NOVELS OF MANNERS AND SOCIETY SUCH AS *THE HOUSE OF MIRTH*. IN "THE MOVING FINGER" THERE ARE FLASHES OF HAWTHORNE IN HER SOCIETAL TALE OF ART AND INSPIRATION AND INFLUENCE FROM BEYOND THE GRAVE IN A SUBTLY "IS IT OR ISN'T IT" FANTASTIC MANNER.

The news of Mrs. Grancy's death came to me with the shock of an immense blunder—one of fate's most irretrievable acts of vandalism. It was as though all sorts of renovating forces had been checked by the clogging of that one wheel. Not that Mrs. Grancy contributed any perceptible momentum to the social machine: Her unique distinction was that of filling to perfection her special place in the world. There are so many people like badly composed statues, overlapping their niches at one point and leaving them vacant at another. Mrs. Grancy's niche was her husband's life; and if it be argued that the space was not large enough for its vacancy to leave a very big gap, I can only say that, at the last resort, such dimensions must be determined by finer instruments than any ready-made standard of utility. Ralph Grancy's was, in short, a kind of disembodied usefulness—one of those constructive influences that, instead of crystallizing into definite forms, remains as it were a medium for the development of clear thinking and fine feeling. He faithfully irrigated his own dusty patch of life, and the fruitful moisture stole far beyond his boundaries. If, to carry on the metaphor, Grancy's life was a sedulously cultivated enclosure, his wife was the flower he had planted in its midst—the embowering tree, rather, which gave him rest and shade at its foot and the wind of dreams in its upper branches.

We had all—his small but devoted band of followers—known a moment when it seemed likely that Grancy would fail us. We had watched him pitted against one stupid obstacle after another—ill health, poverty, misunderstanding and, worst of all for a man of his texture, his first wife's soft insidious egotism. We had seen him sinking under the leaden embrace of her affection like a swimmer in a drowning clutch; but just as we despaired he had always come to the surface again, blinded, panting, but striking out fiercely for the shore. When at last her death released him, it became a question as to how much of the man she had carried with her. Left alone, he revealed numb withered patches, like a tree from which a parasite has been stripped. But gradually he began to put out new leaves; and when he met the lady who was to become his second wife—his one *real* wife, as his friends reckoned—the whole man burst into flower.

The second Mrs. Grancy was past thirty when he married her, and it was clear that she had harvested that crop of middle joy which is rooted in young despair. But if she had lost the surface of eighteen, she had kept its inner light; if her cheek lacked the gloss of immaturity, her eyes were young with the stored youth of half a lifetime. Grancy had first known her somewhere in the East—I believe she was the sister of one of our consuls out there—and when he brought her home to New York she came among us as a stranger. The idea of Grancy's remarriage had been a shock to us all. After one such calcining most men would have kept out of the fire; but we agreed that he was predestined to sentimental blunders and we awaited with resignation the embodiment of his latest mistake. Then Mrs. Grancy came—and we understood. She was the most beautiful and the most complete of explanations. We shuffled our defeated omniscience out of sight, and gave it hasty burial under a prodigality of welcome. For the first time in years we had Grancy off our minds. "He'll do something great now!" the least sanguine of us prophesied; and our sentimentalist emended, "He *has* done it—in marrying her!"

It was Claydon, the portrait-painter, who risked this hyperbole, and who soon afterward, at the happy husband's request, prepared to defend it in a portrait of Mrs. Grancy. We were all—even Claydon—ready to concede that Mrs. Grancy's unwontedness was in some degree a matter of environment. Her graces were complementary and it needed the mate's call to reveal the flash of color beneath her neutral-tinted wings. But if she needed Grancy to interpret her, how much greater was the service she rendered him! Claydon professionally described her as the right frame for him; but if she defined, she also enlarged; if she threw the whole into perspective, she also cleared new ground, opened fresh vistas, reclaimed whole areas of activity that had run to waste under the harsh husbandry of privation. This interaction of sympathies was not without its visible expression. Claydon was not alone in maintaining that Grancy's presence—or indeed the mere mention of his name—had a perceptible effect on his wife's appearance. It was as though a light were shifted, a curtain drawn back; as though, to borrow another of Claydon's metaphors, Love, the indefatigable artist, were his model. In this interpretative light Mrs. Grancy acquired the charm which makes some women's faces like a book of which the last page is never turned. There was always something new to read in her eyes. What Claydon read there—or at least such scattered hints of the ritual as reached him through the sanctuary doors—his portrait in due course declared to us. When the picture was exhibited, it was at once acclaimed as his masterpiece; but the people who knew Mrs. Grancy smiled and said it was flattered. Claydon, however, had not set out to paint *their* Mrs. Grancy—or ours, even—but Ralph's; and Ralph knew his own at a glance. At the first confrontation he saw that Claydon had understood. As for Mrs. Grancy, when the finished picture was shown to her she turned to the painter and said simply, "Ah, you've done me facing the east!"

The picture, then, for all its value, seemed a mere incident in the unfolding of their double destiny—a footnote to the illuminated text of their lives. It was not till afterward that it acquired the significance of last words spoken on a threshold never to be recrossed. Grancy, a year after his marriage, had given up his town house and carried his bliss an hour's journey away, to a little place among the hills. His various duties and interests brought him frequently to New York, but we necessarily saw him less often than when his house had served as the rallying-point of kindred enthusiasms. It seemed a pity that such an influence should be withdrawn, but we all felt that his long arrears of happiness should be paid in whatever coin he chose. The distance from which the fortunate couple radiated warmth on us was not too great for friendship to traverse; and our conception of a glorified leisure took the form of Sundays spent in the Grancys' library, with its sedative rural outlook, and the portrait of Mrs. Grancy illuminating its studious walls. The picture was at its best in that setting; and we used to accuse Claydon of visiting Mrs. Grancy in order to see her portrait. He met this by declaring that the portrait *was* Mrs. Grancy; and there were moments when the statement seemed unanswerable. One of us, indeed—I think it must have been the novelist—said that Claydon had been saved from falling in love with Mrs. Grancy only by falling in love with his picture of her; and it was noticeable that he, to whom his finished work was no more than the shed husk of future effort, showed a perennial tenderness for this one achievement. We smiled afterward to think how often, when Mrs. Grancy was in the room, her presence reflecting itself in our talk like a gleam of sky in a hurrying current, Claydon, averted from the real woman, would sit as if he were listening to the picture. His attitude, at the time, seemed only a part of the unusualness of those picturesque afternoons, when the most familiar combinations of life underwent a magical change. Some human happiness is a land-locked lake; but the Grancys' was an open sea, stretching a buoyant and illimitable surface to the voyaging interests of life. There was room and to spare on those waters for all our separate ventures; and always, beyond the sunset, a mirage of the fortunate isles toward which our prows were bent.

II

It was in Rome that, three years later I heard of her death. The notice said "suddenly"; I was glad of that. I was glad, too—basely, perhaps—to be away from Grancy at a time when silence must have seemed obtuse and speech derisive.

I was still in Rome when, a few months afterward, he suddenly arrived there. He had been appointed secretary of legation at Constantinople, and was on the way to his post. He had taken the place, he said frankly, "to get away." Our relations with the Porte held out a prospect of hard work, and that, he explained, was what he needed. He could never be satisfied to sit down among the ruins. I saw that, like most of us in moments of extreme moral tension, he was playing a part, behaving as he thought it became a man to behave in the eye of disaster. The instinctive posture of grief is a shuffling compromise between defiance and prostration; and pride feels the need of striking a worthier attitude in face of such a foe. Grancy, by nature musing and retrospective, had chosen the role of the man of action, who answers blow for blow and opposes a mailed front to the thrusts of destiny; and the completeness of the equipment testified to his inner weakness. We talked only of what we were not thinking of, and parted, after a few days, with a sense of relief that proved the inadequacy of friendship to perform in such cases the office assigned to it by tradition.

Soon afterward my own work called me home, but Grancy remained several years in Europe. International diplomacy kept its promise of giving him work to do, and during the year in which he acted as *charge d'affaires* he acquitted himself, under trying conditions, with conspicuous zeal and discretion. A political redistribution of matter removed him from office just as he had proved his usefulness to the government; and the following summer I heard that he had come home and was down at his place in the country.

On my return to town I wrote him, and his reply came by the next post. He answered as it were in his natural voice, urging me to spend the following Sunday with him and suggesting that I should bring down any of the old set who could be persuaded to join me. I thought this a good sign, and yet—shall I own it?—I was vaguely disappointed. Perhaps we are apt to feel that our friends' sorrows should be kept like those historic monuments from which the encroaching ivy is periodically removed.

That very evening at the club I ran across Claydon. I told him of Grancy's invitation and proposed that we should go down together; but he pleaded an engagement. I was sorry, for I had always felt that he and I stood nearer Ralph than the others, and if the old Sundays were to be renewed, I should have preferred that we two should spend the first alone with him. I said as much to Claydon, and offered to fit my time to his; but he met this by a general refusal.

"I don't want to go to Grancy's," he said bluntly.

I waited a moment, but he appended no qualifying clause.

"You've seen him since he came back?" I finally ventured.

Claydon nodded.

"And is he so awfully bad?"

"Bad? No; he's all right."

"All right? How can he be, unless he's changed beyond all recognition?"

"Oh, you'll recognize *him*," said Claydon, with a puzzling deflection of emphasis.

His ambiguity was beginning to exasperate me, and I felt myself shut out from some knowledge to which I had as good a right as he.

"You've been down there already, I suppose?"

"Yes, I've been down there."

"And you've done with each other—the partnership is dissolved?"

"Done with each other? I wish to God we had!" He rose nervously and tossed aside the review from which my approach had diverted him. "Look here," he said, standing before me, "Ralph's the best fellow going and there's nothing under heaven I wouldn't do for him—short of going down there again." And with that he walked out of the room.

Claydon was incalculable enough for me to read a dozen different meanings into his words; but none of my interpretations satisfied me. I determined, at any rate, to seek no further for a companion; and the next Sunday I travelled down to Grancy's alone. He met me at the station and I saw at once that he had changed since our last meeting. Then he had been in fighting array, but now if he and grief still housed together it was no longer as enemies. Physically the transformation was as marked, but less reassuring. If the spirit triumphed, the body showed its scars. At five-and-forty he was gray and stooping, with the tired gait of an old man. His serenity, however, was not the resignation of age. I saw that he did not mean to drop out of the game. Almost immediately he began to speak of our old interests, not with an effort, as at our former meeting, but simply and naturally, in the tone of a man whose life has flowed back into its normal channels. I remembered, with a touch of self-reproach, how I had distrusted his reconstructive powers; but my admiration for his reserved force was now tinged by the sense that, after all, such happiness as his ought to have been paid with his last coin. The feeling grew as we neared the house, and I found how inextricably his wife was interwoven with my remembrance of the place; how the whole scene was but an extension of that vivid presence.

Within-doors nothing was changed, and my hand would have dropped without surprise into her welcoming clasp. It was luncheon-time, and Grancy led me at once to the dining-room, where the walls, the furniture, the very plate and porcelain, seemed a mirror in which a moment since her face had been reflected. I wondered whether Grancy, under the recovered tranquillity of his smile, concealed the same sense of her nearness, saw perpetually between himself and the actual her bright unappeasable ghost. He spoke of her once or twice in an easy incidental way, and her name seemed to hang in the air after he had uttered it, like a chord that continues to vibrate. If he felt her presence it was evidently as an enveloping medium, the moral atmosphere in which he breathed. I had never before known how completely the dead may survive.

After luncheon we went for a long walk through the autumnal fields and woods, and dusk was falling when we re-entered the house. Grancy led the way to the library, where at this hour his wife had always welcomed us back to a bright fire and a cup of tea. The room faced the west and held a clear light of its own after the rest of the house had grown dark. I remembered how young she had looked in this pale gold light, which irradiated her eyes and hair, or silhouetted her girlish outline as she passed before the windows. Of all the rooms the library was most peculiarly hers; and here I felt that her nearness might take visible shape. Then, all in a moment, as Grancy opened the door, the feeling vanished, and a kind of resistance met me on the threshold. I looked about me. Was the room changed? Had some desecrating hand effaced the traces of her presence? No; here too the setting was undisturbed. My feet sank into the same deep-piled Daghestan; the bookshelves took the firelight on the same rows of rich subdued bindings; her arm-chair stood in its old place near the tea-table; and from the opposite wall her face confronted me.

Her face—but *was* it hers? I moved nearer and stood looking up at the portrait. Grancy's glance had followed mine and I heard him move to my side.

"You see a change in it?" he said.

"What does it mean?" I asked.

"It means—that five years have passed."

"Over *her?*"

"Why not? Look at me!" He pointed to his gray hair and furrowed temples. "What do you think kept *her* so young? It was happiness! But now—" he looked up at her with infinite tenderness. "I like her better so," he said. "It's what she would have wished."

"Have wished?"

"That we should grow old together. Do you think she would have wanted to be left behind?"

I stood speechless, my gaze travelling from his worn grief-beaten features to the painted face above. It was not furrowed like his; but a veil of years seemed to have descended on it. The bright hair had lost its elasticity, the cheek its clearness, the brow its light—the whole woman had waned.

Grancy laid his hand on my arm. "You don't like it?" he said sadly.

"Like it? I—I've lost her!" I burst out.

"And I've found her," he answered.

"In *that?*" I cried, with a reproachful gesture.

"Yes, in that." He swung round on me almost defiantly. "The other had become a sham, a lie! This is the way she would have looked—does look, I mean. Claydon ought to know, oughtn't he?"

I turned suddenly. "Did Claydon do this for you?"

Grancy nodded.

"Since your return?"

"Yes; I sent for him after I'd been back a week—"

He turned away and gave a thrust to the smouldering fire. I followed, glad to leave the picture behind me. Grancy threw himself into a chair near the hearth, so that the light fell on his sensitive variable face. He leaned his head back, shading his eyes with his hand, and began to speak.

III

"You fellows knew enough of my early history to guess what my second marriage meant to me. I say guess, because no one could understand—really. I've always had a feminine streak in me, I suppose—the need of a pair of eyes that should see with me, of a pulse that should keep time with mine. Life is a big thing, of course; a magnificent spectacle; but I got so tired of looking at it alone! Still, it's always good to live, and I had plenty of happiness—of the evolved kind. What I'd never had a taste of was the simple inconscient sort that one breathes in like the air. . . .

"Well—I met her. It was like finding the climate in which I was meant to live. You know what she was—how infinitely she multiplied one's points of contact with life, how she lit up the caverns and bridged the abysses. Well, I swear to you (though I suppose the sense of all that was latent in me) that what I used to think of on my way home at the end of the day was simply that when I opened this door she'd be sitting over there, with the lamplight falling in a particular way on one little curl in her neck. . . . When Claydon painted her he caught just the look she used to lift to mine when I came in—I've wondered, sometimes, at his knowing how she looked when she and I were alone. How I rejoiced in that picture! I used to say to her: 'You're my prisoner now—I shall never lose you. If you grew tired of me and left me, you'd leave your real self there on the wall!' It was always one of our jokes that she was going to grow tired of me—

"Three years of it—and then she died. It was so sudden that there was no change, no diminution. It was as if she had suddenly become fixed, immovable, like her own portrait; as if Time had ceased at its happiest hour, just as Claydon had thrown down his brush one day and said, 'I can't do better than that.'

"I went away, as you know, and stayed over there five years. I worked as hard as I knew how, and after the first black months a little light stole in on me. From thinking that she would have been interested in what I was doing, I came to feel that she *was* interested—that she was there and that she knew. I'm not talking any psychical jargon—I'm simply trying to express the sense I had that an influence so full, so abounding as hers couldn't pass like a spring shower. We had so lived into each other's hearts and minds that the consciousness of what she would have thought and felt illuminated all I did. At first she used to come back shyly, tentatively, as though not sure of finding me; then she stayed longer and longer, till at last she became again the very air I breathed. . . . There were bad moments, of course, when her nearness mocked me with the loss of the real woman; but gradually the distinction between the two was effaced and the mere thought of her grew warm as flesh and blood.

"Then I came home. I landed in the morning and came straight down here. The thought of seeing her portrait possessed me, and my heart beat like a lover's as I opened the library door. It was in the afternoon and the room was full of light. It fell on her picture—the picture of a young and radiant woman. She smiled at me coldly across the distance that divided us. I had the feeling that she didn't even recognize me. And then I caught sight of myself in the mirror over there—a gray-haired broken man whom she had never known!

"For a week we two lived together—the strange woman and the strange man. I used to sit night after night and question her smiling face; but no answer ever came. What did she know of me, after all? We were irrevocably separated by the five years of life that lay between us. At times, as I sat here, I almost grew to hate her; for her presence had driven away my gentle ghost—the real wife who had wept, aged, struggled with me during those awful years. . . . It was the worst loneliness I've ever known. Then, gradually, I began to notice a look of sadness in the picture's eyes; a look that seemed to say, 'Don't you see that *I* am lonely too?' And all at once it came over me how she would have hated to be left behind! I remembered her comparing life to a heavy book that could not be read with ease unless two people held it together; and I thought how impatiently her hand would have turned the pages that divided us! So the idea came to me: 'It's the picture that stands between us; the picture that is dead, and not my wife. To sit in this room is to keep watch beside a corpse.' As this feeling grew on me the portrait became like a beautiful mausoleum in which she had been buried alive; I could hear her beating against the painted walls and crying to me faintly for help. . . .

"One day I found I couldn't stand it any longer and I sent for Claydon. He came down, and I told him what I'd been through and what I wanted him to do. At first he refused point-blank to touch the picture. The next morning I went off for a long tramp and when I came home I found him sitting here alone. He looked at me sharply for a moment and then he said, 'I've changed my mind; I'll do it.' I arranged one of the north rooms as a studio and he shut himself up there for a day; then he sent for me. The picture stood there as you see it now—it was as though she'd met me on the threshold and taken me in her arms! I tried to thank him, to tell him what it meant to me, but he cut me short.

" 'There's an up train at five, isn't there?' he asked. 'I'm booked for a dinner tonight. I shall just have time to make a bolt for the station and you can send my traps after me.' I haven't seen him since. . . .

"I can guess what it cost him to lay hands on his masterpiece; but, after all, to him it was only a picture lost; to me it was my wife regained!"

IV

After that, for ten years or more, I watched the strange spectacle of a life of hopeful and productive effort based on the structure of a dream. There could be no doubt to those who saw Grancy during this period that he drew his strength and courage from the sense of his wife's mystic participation in his task. When I went back to see him a few months later I found the portrait had been removed from the library and placed in a small study upstairs, to which he had transferred his desk and a few books. He told me he always sat there when he was alone, keeping the library for his Sunday visitors. Those who missed the portrait of course made no comment on its absence, and the few who were in his secret respected it. Gradually all his old friends had gathered about him and our Sunday afternoons regained something of their former character; but Claydon never reappeared among us.

As I look back now I see that Grancy must have been failing from the time of his return home. His invincible spirit belied and disguised the signs of weakness that afterward asserted themselves in my remembrance of him. He seemed to have an inexhaustible fund of life to draw on, and more than one of us was a pensioner on his superfluity.

Nevertheless, when I came back one summer from my European holiday and heard that he had been at the point of death, I understood at once that we had believed him well only because he wished us to.

I hastened down to the country and found him midway in a slow convalescence. I felt then that he was lost to us and he read my thought at a glance.

"Ah," he said, "I'm an old man now and no mistake. I suppose we shall have to go half-speed after this; but we sha'n't need towing just yet!"

The plural pronoun struck me, and involuntarily I looked up at Mrs. Grancy's portrait. Line by line I saw my fear reflected in it. It was the face of a woman *who knows that her husband is dying.*

My heart stood still at the thought of what Claydon had done.

Grancy had followed my glance. "Yes, it's changed her," he said quietly. "For months, you know, it was touch and go with me—we had a long fight of it and it was worse for her than for me." After a pause he added "Claydon has been very kind; he's so busy nowadays that I seldom see him, but when I sent for him the other day he came down at once."

I was silent, and we spoke no more of Grancy's illness; but when I took leave it seemed like shutting him in alone with his death-warrant.

The next time I went down to see him he looked much better. It was a Sunday and he received me in the library, so that I did not see the portrait again. He continued to improve and toward spring we began to feel that, as he had said, he might yet travel a long way without being towed.

One evening, on returning to town after a visit which had confirmed my sense of reassurance, I found Claydon dining alone at the club. He asked me to join him, and over the coffee our talk turned to his work.

"If you're not too busy," I said at length, "you ought to make time to go down to Grancy's again."

He looked up quickly. "Why?" he asked.

"Because he's quite well again," I returned with a touch of cruelty. "His wife's prognostications were mistaken."

Claydon stared at me a moment. "Oh, *she* knows," he affirmed with a smile that chilled me.

"You mean to leave the portrait as it is, then?" I persisted.

He shrugged his shoulders. "He hasn't sent for me yet!" A waiter came up with the cigars, and Claydon rose and joined another group.

It was just a fortnight later that Grancy's housekeeper telegraphed for me. She met me at the station with the news that he had been "taken bad" and that the doctors were with him.

I had to wait for some time in the deserted library before the medical men appeared. They had the baffled manner of empirics who have been superseded by the great Healer, and I lingered only long enough to hear that Grancy was not suffering and that my presence could do him no harm.

I found him seated in his arm-chair in the little study. He held out his hand with a smile.

"You see she was right, after all," he said.

"She?" I repeated, perplexed for the moment.

"My wife." He indicated the picture. "Of course I knew she had no hope from the first. I saw that"—he lowered his voice—"after Claydon had been here. But I wouldn't believe it at first!"

I caught his hands in mine. "For God's sake don't believe it now!" I adjured him.

He shook his head gently. "It's too late," he said. "I might have known that she knew."

"But, Grancy, listen to me," I began; and then I stopped. What could I say that would convince him! There was no common ground of argument on which we could meet; and after all it would be easier for him to die feeling that she *had* known. Strangely enough, I saw that Claydon had missed his mark. . . .

V

Grancy's will named me as one of his executors; and my associate, having other duties on his hands, begged me to assume the task of carrying out our friend's wishes. This placed me under the necessity of informing Claydon that the portrait of Mrs. Grancy had been bequeathed to him; and he replied by the next post that he would send for the picture at once. I was staying in the deserted house when the portrait was taken away; and as the door closed on it I felt that Grancy's presence had vanished too. Was it his turn to follow her now, and could one ghost haunt another?

After that, for a year or two, I heard nothing more of the picture, and though I met Claydon from time to time we had little to say to each other. I had no definable grievance against the man and I tried to remember that he had done a fine thing in sacrificing his best picture to a friend; but my resentment had all the tenacity of unreason.

One day, however, a lady whose portrait he had just finished begged me to go with her to see it. To refuse was impossible, and I went with the less reluctance that I knew I was not the only person invited. The others were all grouped around the easel when I entered, and after contributing my share to the chorus of approval I turned away and began to stroll about the studio. Claydon was something of a collector and his things were generally worth looking at. The studio was a long tapestried room with a curtained archway at one end. The curtains were looped back, showing a smaller apartment, with books and flowers and a few fine bits of bronze and porcelain. The tea-table standing in this inner room proclaimed that it was open to inspection, and I wandered in. A *bleu poudre* vase first attracted me; then I turned to examine a slender bronze Ganymede, and in so doing found myself face to face with Mrs. Grancy's portrait. I stared up at it blankly and the face smiled back at me in all the recovered radiance of youth. The artist had effaced every trace of his later touches and the original picture had reappeared. It throned alone on the panelled wall, asserting a brilliant supremacy over its carefully chosen surroundings. I felt in an instant that the whole room was tributary to it—that Claydon had heaped his treasures at the feet of the woman he loved. Yes—it was the woman he had loved, and not the picture; and my instinctive resentment was explained.

Suddenly I felt a hand on my shoulder.

"Ah, how could you?" I cried, turning on him.

"How could I?" he retorted. "How could I *not*? Doesn't she belong to me now?"

I moved away impatiently.

"Wait a moment," he said with a detaining gesture. "The others have gone and I want to say a word to you—Oh, I know what you've thought of me—I can guess! You think I killed Grancy, I suppose?"

I was startled by his sudden vehemence. "I think you tried to do a cruel thing," I said slowly.

"Ah—what a little way you others see into life!" he murmured. "Sit down a moment—here, where we can look at her—and I'll tell you."

He threw himself on the ottoman beside me and sat gazing up at the picture, with his hands clasped about his knee.

"Pygmalion," he began slowly, "turned his statue into a real woman; *I* turned my real woman into a picture. Small compensation, you think—but you don't know how much of a woman belongs to you after you've painted her! Well, I made the best of it, at any rate—I gave her the best I had in me; and she gave me in return what such a woman gives by merely being. And after all she rewarded me enough by making me paint as I shall never paint again. There was one side of her, though that was mine alone, and that was her beauty, for no one else understood it. To Grancy, even, it was the mere expression of herself—what language is to thought. Even when he saw the picture he didn't guess my secret—he was so sure she was all his! As though a man should think he owned the moon because it was reflected in the pool at his door—

"Well—when he came home and sent for me to change the picture, it was like asking me to commit murder. He wanted me to make an old woman of her—of her who had been so divinely, unchangeably young! As if any man who really loved a woman would ask her to sacrifice her youth and beauty for his sake! At first I told him I couldn't do it—but afterward, when he left me alone with the picture, something queer happened. I suppose it was because I was always so confoundedly fond of Grancy that it went against me to refuse what he asked. . . . Anyhow, as I sat looking up at her, she seemed to say, 'I'm not yours, but his, and I want you to make me what he wishes.' And so I did it. I could have cut my hand off when the work was done—I dare say he told you I never would go back and look at it. He thought I was too busy—he never understood. . . .

"Well—and then last year he sent for me again—you remember. It was after his illness, and he told me he'd grown twenty years older and that he wanted her to grow older too—he didn't want her to be left behind. The doctors all thought he was going to get well at that time, and he thought so too; and so did I when I first looked at him. But when I turned to the picture—ah! now I don't ask you to believe me, but I swear it was *her* face that told me he was dying, and that she wanted him to know it! She had a message for him and she made me deliver it."

He rose abruptly and walked toward the portrait; then he sat down beside me again.

"Cruel? Yes, it seemed so to me at first; and this time, if I resisted, it was for *his* sake and not for mine. But all the while I felt her eyes drawing me, and gradually she made me understand. If she'd been there in the flesh (she seemed to say) wouldn't she have seen before any of us that he was dying? Wouldn't he have read the news first in her face? And wouldn't it be horrible if now he should discover it instead in strange eyes? Well—that was what she wanted of me and I did it. I kept them together to the last!" He looked up at the picture again. "But now she belongs to me," he repeated.

SLOW SCULPTURE

BY THEODORE STURGEON

THEODORE STURGEON WAS A MASTER STUDENT OF THE HUMAN CONDITION. HE HAD INSIGHT INTO PSYCHES FROM HIS OBSERVATIONS AND AN ALMOST EMPATHIC RESONANCE WITH FEELINGS . . . AND IT SHOWS IN HIS CHARACTERIZATIONS.

MOST OF HIS FANTASY STORIES HAVE AT THEIR CENTER A VERY BASIC PREMISE—AN INDIVIDUAL IS CONFRONTED WITH AN UNBELIEVABLE SITUATION OR BEING AND IS FORCED TO REACT. USUALLY THAT CONFRONTATION INVOLVES CERTAIN MATTERS THAT ARE BEYOND THE INDIVIDUALS' COMPREHENSION, WHERE INDEED ADVANCED SCIENCE MIGHT BE CONSTRUED AS ITS OWN FORM OF MAGIC. AND IN STURGEON'S CASE, THE SCIENCE IS BESIDE THE POINT; IT IS THE PEOPLE THAT MATTER.

He didn't know who he was when she met him—well, not many people did. He was in the high orchard doing something under a pear tree. The land smelled of late summer and wind—bronze, it smelled bronze.

He looked up at a compact girl in her mid-twenties, at a fearless face and eyes the same color as her hair, which was extraordinary because her hair was red-gold. She looked down at a leather-skinned man in his forties, at a gold-leaf electroscope in his hand, and felt she was an intruder.

She said, "Oh—" in what was apparently the right way.

Because he nodded once and said, "Hold this—" and there could then be no thought of intrusion.

She kneeled down beside him and took the instrument, holding it exactly where he positioned her hand. He moved away a little and struck a tuning fork against his kneecap.

"What's it doing?"

He had a good voice, the kind of voice strangers notice and listen to.

She looked at the delicate leaves of gold in the glass shield of the electroscope. "They're moving apart."

He struck the tuning fork again and the leaves pressed away from one another. "Much?"

"About forty-five degrees when you hit the fork."

"Good—that's about the most we'll get." From a pocket of his bush jacket he drew a sack of chalk dust and dropped a small handful on the ground. "I'll move now. You stay right there and tell me how much the leaves separate."

He traveled around the pear tree in a zigzag course, striking his tuning fork while she called out numbers—ten degrees, thirty, five, twenty, nothing. Whenever the gold foil pressed apart to maximum—forty degrees or more—he dropped more chalk. When he was finished the tree was surrounded by a rough oval of white dots. He took out a notebook and diagramed them and the tree, put away the book and took the electroscope out of her hands.

"Were you looking for something?" he asked her.

"No," she said. "Yes."

He could smile. Though it did not last long she found the expression surprising in a face like his.

"That's not what is called, in a court of law, a responsive answer."

She glanced across the hillside, metallic in that late light. There wasn't much on it—rocks, weeds the summer was done with, a tree or so, the orchard. Anyone present had come a long way to get here.

"It wasn't a simple question," she said, tried to smile and burst into tears.

She was sorry and said so.

"Why?" he asked.

This was the first time she was to experience this ask-the-next-question thing of his. It was unsettling. It always would be—never less, sometimes a great deal more.

"Well—one doesn't have emotional explosions in public."

"You do. I don't know this 'one' you're talking about."

"I—guess I don't either, now that you mention it."

"Tell the truth then. No sense in going around and around about it. *He'll think that I* . . . and the like. I'll think what I think, whatever you say. Or—go down the mountain and just don't say any more." She did not turn to go, so he added: "Try the truth, then. If it's important, it's simple. And if it's simple it's easy to say."

"I'm going to die!" she cried.

"So am I."

"I have a lump in my breast."

"Come up to the house and I'll fix it."

WITHOUT ANOTHER WORD he turned away and started through the orchard. Startled half out of her wits, indignant and full of insane hope, experiencing, even, a quick curl of astonished laughter, she stood for a moment watching him go and then found herself (at what point did I decide?) running after him.

She caught up with him on the uphill margin of the orchard.

"Are you a doctor?"

He appeared not to notice that she had waited, had run.

"No," he said and, walking on, appeared not to see her stand again pulling at her lower lip, then run again to catch up.

"I must be out of my mind," she said, joining him on a garden path.

She said it to herself. He must have known because he did not answer. The garden was alive with defiant chrysanthemums and a pond in which she saw the flicker of a pair of redcap imperials—silver, not gold fish—the largest she had ever seen. Then—the house.

First it was part of the garden with its colonnaded terrace—and then, with its rock walls (too massive to be called fieldstone) part of the mountain. It was on and in the hillside. Its roofs paralleled the skylines, front and sides; and part of it was backed against an outjutting cliff face. The door, beamed and studded and featuring two archers' slits, was opened for them (but there was no one there) and when it closed it was silent, a far more solid exclusion of things outside than any click or clang of latch or bolt.

She stood with her back against it watching him cross what seemed to be the central well of the house, or at least this part of it. It was a kind of small court in the center of which was an atrium, glazed on all of its five sides and open to the sky at the top. In it was a tree, a cypress or juniper, gnarled and twisted and with the turnedback, paralleled, sculptured appearance of what the Japanese call bonsai.

"Aren't you coming?" he called, holding open a door behind the atrium.

"Bonsai just aren't fifteen feet tall," she said.

"This one is."

She walked past it slowly, looking.

"How long have you had it?"

His tone of voice said he was immensely pleased. It is a clumsiness to ask the owner of a bonsai how old it is—you are then demanding to know if it is his work or if he has acquired and continued the concept of another; you are tempting him to claim for his own the concept and the meticulous labor of someone else and it becomes rude to tell a man he is being tested. Hence, *How long have you had it?* is polite, forbearing, profoundly courteous.

He answered, "Half my life."

She looked at the tree. Trees can be found, sometimes, not quite discarded, not quite forgotten, potted in rusty gallon cans in not quite successful nurseries, unsold because they are shaped oddly or have dead branches here and there, or because they have grown too slowly in whole or part. These are the ones which develop interesting trunks and a resistance to misfortune that makes them flourish if given the least excuse for living. This one was far older than half this man's life, or all of it. Looking at it, she was terrified by the unbidden thought that a fire, a family of squirrels, some subterranean worm or termite could end this beauty—something working outside any concept of rightness or justice or—of respect.

She looked at the tree. She looked at the man.

"Coming?"

"Yes," she said and went with him into his laboratory. "Sit down over there and relax," he told her. "This might take a little while."

"Over there" was a big leather chair by the bookcase. The books were right across the spectrum—reference works in medicine and engineering, nuclear physics, chemistry, biology, psychiatry. Also tennis, gymnastics, chess, the oriental war game Go, and golf. And then drama, the techniques of fiction, *Modern English Usage, The American Language* and supplement, Wood's and Walker's *Rhyming Dictionaries* and an array of other dictionaries and encyclopedias. A whole long shelf of biographies.

"You have quite a library."

He answered her rather shortly—clearly he did not want to talk. Just now, for he was very busy.

He said only, "Yes I have—perhaps you'll see it some time—" which left her to pick away at his words to find out what on earth he meant by them.

He could only have meant, she decided, that the books beside her chair were what he kept handy for his work—that his real library was elsewhere. She looked at him with a certain awe.

AND SHE WATCHED HIM. She liked the way he moved—swiftly, decisively. Clearly he knew what he was doing. He used some equipment that she recognized—a glass still, titration equipment, a centrifuge. There were two refrigerators, one of which was not a refrigerator at all, for she could see the large indicator on the door. It stood at 70°F. It came to her that a modern refrigerator is perfectly adaptable to the demand for controlled environment, even a warm one.

But all that—and the equipment she did not recognize—was only furniture. It was the man who was worth watching, the man who kept her occupied so that not once in all the long time she sat there was she tempted toward the bookshelves.

At last he finished a long sequence at the bench, threw some switches, picked up a tall stool and came over to her. He perched on the stool, hung his heels on the cross-spoke and lay a pair of long brown hands over his knees.

"Scared."

He made it a statement.

"I suppose I am."

"You don't have to stay."

"Considering the alternative—" she began bravely but the courage-sound somehow oozed out. "It can't matter much."

"Very sound," he said almost cheerfully. "I remember when I was a kid there was a fire scare in the apartment house where we lived. It was a wild scramble to get out and my ten-year-old brother found himself outside in the street with an alarm clock in his hand. It was an old one and it didn't work—but of all the things in the place he might have snatched up at a time like that, it turned out to be the clock. He's never been able to figure out why."

"Have you?"

"Not why he picked that particular thing—no. But I think I know why he did something obviously irrational. You see, panic is a very special state. Like fear and flight, or fury and attack, it's a pretty primitive reaction to extreme danger. It's one of the expressions of the will to survive. What makes it so special is that it's irrational. Now, why would the abandonment of reason be a survival mechanism?"

She thought about this seriously. There was that about this man which made serious thought imperative.

"I can't imagine," she said finally. "Unless it's because, in some situations, reason just doesn't work."

"You can imagine," he said, again radiating that huge approval, making her glow. "And you just did. If you are in danger and you try reason and reason doesn't work—you abandon it. You can't say it's unintelligent to abandon what doesn't work, right? So then you are in panic. You start to perform random acts. Most of them—far and away most—will be useless. Some might even be dangerous. But that doesn't matter—you're in danger already. Where the survival factor comes in is that away down deep you know that one chance in a million is better than no chance at all. So—here you sit—you're scared and you could run. Something says you should run but you won't."

She nodded.

He went on: "You found a lump. You went to a doctor and he made some tests and gave you the bad news. Maybe you went to another doctor and he confirmed it.

You then did some research and found out what was to happen next—the exploratory, the radical, the questionable recovery, the whole long agonizing procedure of being what they call a terminal case. You then flipped out. Did some things you hope I won't ask you about. Took a trip somewhere, anywhere, wound up in my orchard for no reason." He spread the good hands and let them go back to their kind of sleep. "Panic. The reason for little boys in their pajamas standing at midnight with a broken alarm clock in their arms—and for the existence of quacks." Something chimed over on the bench and he gave her a quick smile and went back to work, saying over his shoulder, "I'm not a quack, by the way. To qualify as a quack you have to claim to be a doctor. I don't."

She watched him switch off, switch on, stir, measure and calculate. A little orchestra of equipment chorused and soloed around him as he conducted, whirring, hissing, clicking, flickering. She wanted to laugh, to cry and to scream. She did not one of these things for fear of not stopping, ever.

When he came over again, the conflict was not raging within her but was exerting steady and opposed tensions. The result was a terrible stasis and all she could do when she saw the instrument in his hand was to widen her eyes. She quite forgot to breathe.

"Yes, it's a needle," he said, his tone almost bantering. "A long shiny sharp needle. Don't tell me you are one of those needle-shy people." He flipped the long power cord that trailed from the black housing around the hypodermic to get some slack, straddled the stool. "Want something to steady your nerves?"

She was afraid to speak. The membrane containing her sane self was very thin, stretched very tight.

He said, "I'd rather you didn't, because this pharmaceutical stew is complex enough as it is. But if you need it—"

She managed to shake her head a little and again felt the wave of approval from him. There were a thousand questions she wanted to ask—had meant to ask—needed to ask. What was in the needle? How many treatments must she have? What would they be like? How long must she stay and where? And most of all—oh, could she live, could she live?

II

He seemed concerned with the answer to only one of these.

"It's mostly built around an isotope of potassium. If I told you all I know about it and how I came on it in the first place it would take—well, more time than we've got. But here's the general idea. Theoretically, every atom is electrically balanced—never mind ordinary exceptions. Likewise all electrical charges in the molecule are supposed to be balanced—so much plus, so much minus, total zero. I happened on the fact that the balance of charges in a wild cell is not zero—not quite. It's as if there were a submicroscopic thunderstorm going on at the molecular level, with little lightning bolts flashing back and forth and changing the signs. Interfering with communications—static—and that," he said, gesturing with the shielded hypo in his hand, "is what this is all about. When something interferes with communications—especially the RNA mechanism that says, *Read this blueprint, build accordingly and stop when it's done*—when that message gets garbled lopsided things get built. Off balance things. Things that do almost what they should, do it almost right—they're wild cells and the messages they pass on are even worse.

"Okay. Whether these thunderstorms are caused by viruses or chemicals or radiation or physical trauma or even anxiety—and don't think anxiety can't do it—is secondary. The important thing is to fix it so the thunderstorm can't happen. If you can do that the cells have plenty of ability all by themselves to repair and replace what's gone wrong. And biological systems aren't like ping-pong balls with static charges waiting for the charge to leak away or to discharge into a grounded wire. They have a kind of resilience—I call it forgiveness—that enables them to take on a little more charge, or a little less, and do all right. Well, then—say a certain clump of cells is wild and say it carries an aggregate of a hundred units extra on the positive side. Cells immediately around it are affected—but not the next layer or the next.

"If they could be opened to the extra charge—if they could help to drain it off— they would, well, *cure* the wild cells of the surplus. You see what I mean? And they would be able to handle that little overage themselves or pass it on to other cells and still others who could deal with it. In other words, if I can flood your body with a medium that can drain off and distribute a concentration of this unbalanced charge, the ordinary bodily processes will be free to move in and clear up the wild-cell damage. And that's what I have here."

He held the shielded needle between his knees and from a side pocket of his lab coat he took a plastic box, opened it and drew out an alcohol swab. Still cheerfully talking, he took her terror-numbed arm and scrubbed at the inside of her elbow.

"I am not for one second implying that nuclear charges in the atom are the same thing as static electricity. They're in a different league altogether. But the analogy holds. I could use another analogy. I could liken the charge in the wild cells to accumulations of fat. And this gunk of mine to a detergent that would break it up and spread it so far it couldn't be detected any more. But I'm led to the static analogy by an odd side effect—organisms injected with this stuff do build up one hell of a static charge. It's a byproduct and, for reasons I can only theorize about at the moment, it seems to be keyed to the audio spectrum. Tuning forks and the like. That's what I was playing with when I met you. That tree is drenched with this stuff. It used to have a whorl of wild-cell growth. It hasn't any more."

He gave her the quick, surprising smile and let it flicker away as he held the needle point upward and squirted it. With his other hand wrapped around her left bicep he squeezed gently and firmly. The needle was lowered and placed and slid into the big vein so deftly that she gasped—not because it hurt but because it did not. Attentively he watched the bit of glass barrel protruding from the black housing as he withdrew the plunger a fraction and saw the puff of red into the colorless fluid inside.

Then he bore steadily on the plunger again.

"PLEASE DON'T MOVE. I'm sorry, this will take a little time. I have to get quite a lot of this into you. Which is fine, you know," he said, resuming the tone of his previous remarks about audio spectra, "because side effect or no, it's consistent. Healthy bio systems develop a strong electrostatic field, unhealthy ones a weak one or none at all. With an instrument as primitive and simple as that little electroscope you can tell if any part of the organism has a community of wild cells and if so, where it is and how big and how wild." Deftly he shifted his grip on the encased hypodermic without moving the point or varying the plunger pressure. It was beginning to be uncomfortable—an ache turning into a bruise. "And if you're wondering why this mosquito has a housing on it with a wire attached (although I'll bet you're not and that you know as well as I do that I'm doing all this talking just to keep your mind occupied) I'll tell you. It's nothing but a coil carrying a high-frequency alternating current. The alternating field sees to it that the fluid is magnetically and electrostatically neutral right from the start."

He withdrew the needle suddenly and smoothly, bent an arm and trapped in the inside of her elbow a cotton swab.

"Nobody ever told me that after a treatment," she said.

"What?"

"No charge," she said.

Again that wave of approval, this time with words: "I like your style. How do you feel?"

She cast about for accurate phrases.

"Like the owner of a large sleeping hysteria begging someone not to wake it up."

He laughed.

"In a little while you are going to feel so weird you won't have time for hysteria."

He got up and returned the needle to the bench, looping up the cable as he went. He turned off the AC field and returned with a large glass bowl and a square of plywood. He inverted the bowl on the floor near her and placed the wood on its broad base.

"I remember something like that," she said. "When I was in—in junior high school. They were generating artificial lightning with a—let me see—well, it had a long, endless belt running over pulleys and some little wires scraping on it and a big copper ball on top."

"Van de Graaf generator."

"Right. And they did all sorts of things with it. But what I specially remember is standing on a piece of wood on a bowl like that and they charged me up with the generator. I didn't feel much of anything except all my hair stood out from my head. Everyone laughed. I looked like a golliwog. They said I was carrying forty thousand volts."

"Good. I'm glad you remember that. This'll be a little different, though. By roughly another forty thousand."

"Oh!"

"Don't worry. As long as you're insulated and as long as grounded or comparatively grounded objects—me, for example—stay well away from you, there won't be any fireworks."

"Are you going to use a generator like that?"

"Not like that—and I already did. You're the generator."

"I'm—oh!" She had raised her hand from the upholstered chair arm and there was a crackle of sparks and the faint smell of ozone.

"You sure are and more than I thought—and quicker. Get up."

She started up slowly. She finished the maneuver with speed. As her body separated from the chair she was, for a fractional second, seated in a tangle of spitting blue-white threads. They, or she, propelled her a yard and a half away, standing. Literally shocked half out of her wits, she almost fell.

"Stay on your feet," he snapped and she recovered, gasping. He stepped back a pace. "Get up on the board. Quickly now."

She did as she was told, leaving, for the two paces she traveled, two brief footprints of fire. She teetered on the board. Visibly, her hair began to stir.

"What's happening to me?" she cried.

"You're getting charged after all," he said jovially but at this point she failed to appreciate the extension of even her own witticism.

She cried again, "What's happening to me?"

"It's all right," he said consolingly.

He went to the bench and turned on a tone generator. It moaned deep in the one to three hundred cycle range. He increased the volume and turned the pitch control. It howled upward and, as it did so, her red-gold hair shivered and swept up and out, each hair attempting frantically to get away from all the others. He ran the tone up above ten thousand cycles and all the way back to a belly-bumping inaudible eleven. At the extremes her hair slumped but at around eleven hundred it stood out in, as she had described it, golliwog style. She could feel it.

He turned down the gain to a more or less bearable level and picked up the electroscope. He came toward her, smiling.

"You are an electroscope, you know that? And a living Van de Graaf generator as well. And a golliwog."

"Let me down," was all she could say.

"Not yet. Please hang tight. The differential between you and everything else here is so high that if you got near any of it you'd discharge into it. It wouldn't harm you—it isn't current electricity—but you might get a burn and a nervous shock out of it." He held out the electroscope. Even at that distance—and in her distress—she could see the gold leaves writhe apart. He circled her, watching the leaves attentively, moving the instrument forward and back and from side to side. Once he went to the tone generator and turned it down some more. "You're sending such a strong field I can't pick up the variations," he explained and returned to her, coming closer now.

"I can't—much more—I can't," she murmured.

He did not hear or he did not care. He moved the electroscope near her abdomen, up and from side to side.

"Yup. There you are," he said cheerfully, moving the instrument close to her right breast.

"What?" she whimpered.

"Your cancer. Right breast, low, around toward the armpit." He whistled. "A mean one, too. Malignant as hell."

She swayed and then collapsed forward and down. A sick blackness swept down on her, receded explosively in a glare of agonizing blue-white and then crashed down on her like a mountain falling.

Place where wall meets ceiling. Another wall, another ceiling. Hadn't seen it before. Didn't matter. Don't care.

Sleep.

Place where wall meets ceiling. Something in the way. His face, close, drawn, tired—eyes awake, though, and penetrating. Doesn't matter. Don't care.
Sleep.

Place where wall meets ceiling. Down a bit, late sunlight. Over a little, rusty-gold chrysanthemums in a gold-green glass cornucopia. Something in the way again—his face.
"Can you hear me?"
Yes, but don't answer. Don't move. Don't speak.
Sleep.

It's a room, a wall, a table, a man pacing—a nighttime window and mums you'd think were alive but don't you know they're cut right off and dying?
Do they know that?
"How are you?"
Urgent, urgent.
"Thirsty."

COLD AND A BITE TO it that aches the hinges of the jaws. Grapefruit juice. Lying back on his arm while he holds the glass in the other hand.
Oh, no, that's not . . .
"Thank you. Thanks very—"
Try to sit up. The sheet—my clothes!
"Sorry about that," he said, the mindreader-almost. "Some things that have to be done just aren't consistent with pantyhose and a minidress. All washed and dried and ready for you, though—any time. Over there."
The brown wool and the pantyhose and the shoes, on the chair.
He's respectful, standing back, putting the glass next to an insulated carafe on the night table.
"What things?"
"Throwing up. Bedpans," he said candidly.
Protective with the sheet, which can hide bodies but—oh—not embarrassment.
"Oh, I'm sorry. Oh. I must have—"
Shake head and he slides back and forth in the vision.
"You went into shock and then you just didn't come out of it."
He hesitated. It was the first time she had ever seen him hesitate over anything. She became for a moment an almost-mindreader.
Should I tell her what's in my mind?
Sure, he should. And he did.
"You didn't want to come out of it."
"It's all gone out of my head."
"The pear tree, the electroscope. The injection, the electrostatic response."
"No," she said, not knowing. Then, knowing: "No!"
"Hang on," he rapped and next thing she knew he was by the bed, over her, his two hands hard on her cheeks. "Don't slip off again. You can handle it. You can handle it because it's all right now, do you understand that? You're all right."
"You told me I had cancer."

She sounded pouty, accusing.

He laughed at her, actually laughed.

"You told me you had it."

"Oh, but I didn't know."

"That explains it, then," he said in a load-off-my-back tone. "There wasn't anything in what I did that could cause a three-day withdrawal like that. It had to be something in you."

"Three days!"

He simply nodded and went on with what he was saying.

"I get a little pompous once in a while," he said engagingly. "Comes from being right so much of the time. Took a bit more for granted than I should have, didn't I? When I assumed you'd been to a doctor, maybe even had a biopsy? You hadn't, had you?"

"I was afraid," she admitted. She looked at him. "My mother died of it—and my aunt—and my sister had a radical mastectomy. I couldn't bear it. And when you—"

"When I told you what you already knew and what you never wanted to hear—you couldn't take it. You blacked right out, you know. Fainted away. And it had nothing to do with the seventy-odd thousand volts of static you were carrying. I caught you." He put out his arms where they were, on display, until she looked at them and saw the angry red scorch marks on his forearms and heavy biceps, as much of them as she could see from under his shortsleeved shirt. "About nine-tenths knocked me out too," he said. "But at least you didn't crack your head or anything."

"Thank you," she said reflexively and then began to cry. "What am I going to do?"

"Do? Go back home, wherever that is—pick up your life again, whatever that might mean."

"But you said—"

"When are you going to get it into your head that what I did was not a diagnostic?"

"Are you—did you—you mean you cured it?"

"I mean you're curing it right now. I explained it all to you before. You remember that now, don't you?"

"Not altogether but—yes." Surreptitiously (but not enough, because he saw her) she felt under the sheet for the lump. "It's still there."

"If I bopped you over the head with a bat," he said with slightly exaggerated simplicity, "there would be a lump on it. It would be there tomorrow and the next day. The day after that it might be smaller. In a week you'd still be able to feel it but it would be gone. Same thing here."

At last she let the enormity of it touch her. "A one-shot cure for cancer—"

"Oh, God," he said harshly. "I can tell by looking at you that I am going to have to listen to that speech again. Well, I won't."

STARTLED, SHE ASKED "What speech?"

"The one about my duty to humanity. It comes in two phases and many textures. Phase one has to do with my duty to humanity and really means we could make a classic buck with it. Phase two deals solely with my duty to humanity and I don't hear that one very often. Phase two utterly overlooks the reluctance humanity has to accept good things unless they arrive from accepted and respectable sources. Phase one is fully aware of this but gets rat shrewd in figuring ways around it."

She said, "I don't—" but could get no farther.

"The textures," he overrode her, "are accompanied by the light of revelation, with or without religion and/or mysticism. Or they are cast sternly in the ethical-philosophy mold and aim to force me to surrender through guilt mixed—to some degree all the way up to total—with compassion."

"But I only—"

"You," he said, aiming a long index finger at her, "have robbed yourself of the choicest example of everything I have just said. If my assumptions had been right and you had gone to your friendly local sawbones—and he had diagnosed cancer and referred you to a specialist and he had done likewise and sent you to a colleague for consultation and, in random panic, you had fallen into my hands and been cured— and had gone back to your various doctors to report a miracle, do you know what you'd have gotten from them? 'Spontaneous remission,' that's what you'd have gotten. And it wouldn't be only doctors," he went on with a sudden renewal of passion, under which she quailed in her bed. "Everybody has his own commercial. Your nutritionist would have nodded over his wheat germ or his macrobiotic rice cakes, your priest would have dropped to his knees and looked at the sky, your geneticist would have a pet theory about generation-skipping and would assure you that your grandparents probably had spontaneous remissions, too, and never knew it."

"Please!" she cried but he shouted at her.

"Do you know what I am? I am an engineer twice over, mechanical and electrical— and I have a law degree. If you were foolish enough to tell anyone about what has happened here (which I hope you aren't—but if you are I know how to protect myself) I could be jailed for practicing medicine without a license. You could have me up for assault because I stuck a needle into you and even for kidnaping if you could prove I carried you in here from the lab. Nobody would give a damn that I had cured your cancer. You don't know who I am, do you?"

"No. I don't even know your name."

"And I won't tell you. I don't know your name either—"

"Oh! It's—"

"Don't tell me! Don't tell me! I don't want to hear it. I wanted to be involved with your lump and I was. I want it and you to be gone as soon as you're both up to it. Have I made myself absolutely clear?"

"Just let me get dressed," she said tightly, "and I'll leave right now."

"Without making a speech?"

"Without making a speech." And in a flash her anger turned to misery and she added: "I was going to say I was grateful. Would that have been all right, sir!"

And his anger underwent a change too, for he came close to the bed and sat down on his heel, bringing their faces to a level, and said quite gently, "That would be fine. Although—you won't really be grateful for another ten days, when you get your 'spontaneous remission' reports—or maybe for six months or a year or two or five, when examinations keep on testing out negative."

She detected such a wealth of sadness behind this that she found herself reaching for the hand with which he steadied himself against the edge of the bed. He did not recoil but he didn't seem to welcome her touch either.

"Why can't I be grateful right now?"

"That would be an act of faith," he said bitterly, "and that just doesn't happen any more—if it ever did." He rose and went toward the door. "Please don't go tonight," he said. "It's dark and you don't know the way. I'll see you in the morning."

When he came back in the morning the door was open. The bed was made and the sheets were folded neatly on the chair, together with the pillow slips and the towels she had used. She wasn't there.

HE CAME OUT into the entrance court and contemplated his bonsai.

Early sun gold-frosted the horizontal upper foliage of the old tree and brought its gnarled limbs into sharp relief, tough brown-gray creviced in velvet. Only the companion of a bonsai (there are owners of bonsai but they are a lesser breed) fully understands the relationship. There is an exclusive and individual treeness to the tree because it is a living thing and living things change—and there are definite ways in which the tree desires to change. A man sees the tree and in his mind makes certain extensions and extrapolations of what he sees and sets about making them happen. The tree in turn will do only what a tree can do, will resist to the death any attempt to do what it cannot do or to do it in less time than it needs. The shaping of a bonsai is therefore always a compromise and always a cooperation. A man cannot create bonsai, nor can a tree. It takes both and they must understand one another. It takes a long time to do that. One memorizes one's bonsai, every twig, the angle of every crevice and needle and, lying awake at night or in a pause a thousand miles away, one recalls this or that line or mass, one makes one's plans. With wire and water and light, with tilting and with the planting of water-robbing weeds or heavy, root-shading ground cover, one explains to the tree what one wants. And if the explanation is well enough made and there is great enough understanding the tree will respond and obey—almost.

Always there will be its own self-respecting, highly individual variation: *Very well, I shall do what you want, but I will do it my way.* And for these variations the tree is always willing to present a clear and logical explanation and, more often than not (almost smiling), it will make clear to the man that he could have avoided it if his understanding had been better.

It is the slowest sculpture in the world, and there is, at times, doubt as to which is being sculpted, man or tree.

So he stood for perhaps ten minutes, watching the flow of gold over the upper branches, and then went to a carved wooden chest, opened it, shook out a length of disreputable cotton duck. He opened the hinged glass at one side of the atrium and spread the canvas over the roots and all the earth to one side of the trunk, leaving the rest open to wind and water. Perhaps in a while—a month or two—a certain shoot in the topmost branch would take the hint and the uneven flow of moisture up through the cambium layer would nudge it away from that upward reach and persuade it to continue the horizontal passage. And perhaps not—and it would need the harsher language of binding and wire. But then it might have something to say, too, about the rightness of an upward trend and would perhaps say it persuasively enough to convince the man—altogether, a patient, meaningful, and rewarding dialogue.

"Good morning."

"Oh, goddam!" he barked. "You made me bite my tongue. I thought you'd gone."

"I had." She kneeled in the shadows, her back against the inner wall, facing the atrium. "But then I stopped to be with the tree for a while."

"Then what?"

"I thought a lot."

"What about?"

"You."

"Did you now?"

"Look," she said firmly. "I'm not going to any doctor to get this thing checked out. I didn't want to leave until I had told you that and until I was sure you believed me."

"Come on in and we'll get something to eat."

Foolishly, she giggled.

"I can't. My feet are asleep."

Without hesitation he scooped her up in his arms and carried her around the atrium.

She asked, her arm around his shoulders and their faces close, "Do you believe me?"

He continued around until they reached the wooden chest, then stopped and looked into her eyes.

"I believe you. I don't know why you decided as you did but I'm willing to believe you."

He set her down on the chest and stood back.

"It's that act of faith you mentioned," she said gravely. "I thought you ought to have it at least once in your life—so you can never say again what you said." She tapped her heels gingerly against the slate floor. "Ow!" She made a pained smile. "Pins and needles."

"You must have been thinking for a long time."

"Yes. Want more?"

"Sure."

"You are an angry, frightened man."

He seemed delighted.

"Tell me about all that!"

"No," she said quietly. "You tell me. I'm very serious about this. Why are you angry?

"I'm not."

"Why are you so angry?"

"I tell you I'm not. Although," he added good-naturedly, "you're pushing me in that direction."

"Well then, why?"

HE GAZED AT HER for what to her seemed a very long time indeed.

"You really want to know, don't you?"

She nodded.

He waved a sudden hand, up and out.

"Where do you suppose all this came from—the house, the land, the equipment?"

She waited.

"An exhaust system," he said, with a thickening of his voice she was coming to know. "A way of guiding exhaust gases out of internal combustion engines in such a way that they are given a spin. Unburned solids are embedded in the walls of the muffler in a glass-wool liner that slips out in one piece and can be replaced by a clean one every couple of thousand miles. The rest of the exhaust is fired by its own spark plug and what will burn, burns. The heat is used to preheat the fuel. The rest is spun again through a five-thousand mile cartridge. What finally gets out is, by today's standards at least, pretty clean. And because of the preheating it actually gets better mileage out of the engine."

"So you've made a lot of money."

"I made a lot of money," he echoed. "But not because the thing is being used to cut down air pollution. I got the money because an automobile company bought it and buried it in a vault. They don't like it because it costs something to install in new cars. Some friends of theirs in the refining business don't like it because it gets high performance out of crude fuels. Well, all right—I didn't know any better and I won't make the same mistake again. But yes—I'm angry. I was angry when I was a kid on a tankship and we were set to washing down a bulkhead with chipped brown soap and canvas. I went ashore and bought a detergent and tried it and it was better, faster and cheaper, so I took it to the bos'n, who gave me a punch in the mouth for pretending to know his job better than he did. Well, he was drunk at the time but the rough part came when the old shellbacks in the crew ganged up on me for being what they called a 'company man'—that's a dirty name in a ship. I just couldn't understand why people got in the way of something better.

"I've been up against that all my life. I have something in my head that just won't quit. It's a way I have of asking the next question: why is so-and-so the way it is? Why can't it be such-and-such instead? There is always another question to be asked about anything or any situation—especially you shouldn't quit when you like an answer because there's always another one after it. And we live in a world where people just don't want to ask the next question!

"I've been paid all my stomach will take for things people won't use and if I'm mad all the time it's really my fault—I admit it—because I just can't stop asking that next question and coming up with answers. There are a half-dozen real block-busters in that lab that nobody will ever see and half a hundred more in my head. But what can you do in a world where people would rather kill each other in a desert, even when they're shown it can turn green and bloom—where they'll fall all over themselves to pour billions into developing a new oil strike when it's been proved over and over again that the fossil fuels will kill us all? "Yes, I'm angry. Shouldn't I be?"

She let the echoes of his voice swirl around the court and out through the hole in the top of the atrium and waited a little longer to let him know he was here with her and not beside himself and his fury. He grinned at her sheepishly when he came to this.

And she said, "Maybe you're asking the next question instead of asking the right question. I think people who live by wise old sayings are trying not to think—but I know one worth paying some attention to. It's this: If you ask a question the right way, you've just given the answer." She paused to see if he was paying real attention. He was. She went on, "I mean, if you put your hand on a hot stove you might ask yourself, how can I stop my hand from burning? And the answer is pretty clear, isn't it? If the world keeps rejecting what you have to give—there's some way of asking why that contains the answer."

"It's a simple answer," he said shortly. "People are stupid."

"That isn't the answer and you know it," she said.

"What is?"

"Oh, I can't tell you that! All I know is that the way you do something, where people are concerned, is more important than what you do. If you want results. I mean—you already know how to get what you want with the tree, don't you?"

"I'll be damned."

"People are living, growing things, too. I don't know a hundredth part of what you do about bonsai but I do know this—when you start one, it isn't often the strong straight healthy ones you take. It's the twisted sick ones that can be made the most beautiful. When you get to shaping humanity, you might remember that."

"Of all the—I don't know whether to laugh in your face or punch you right in the mouth!"

She rose. He hadn't realized she was quite this tall.

"I'd better go."

"Come on now. You know a figure of speech when you hear one."

"Oh, I didn't feel threatened. But—I'd better go, all the same."

Shrewdly he asked her, "Are you afraid to ask the next question?"

"Terrified."

"Ask it anyway."

"No."

"Then I'll do it for you. You said I was angry—and afraid. You want to know what I'm afraid of."

"Yes."

"You. I am scared to death of you."

"Are you really?"

"You have a way of provoking honesty," he said with some difficulty. "I'll say what I know you're thinking: I'm afraid of any close human relationship. I'm afraid of something I can't take apart with a screwdriver or a mass spectroscope or a table of cosines and tangents. I don't know how to handle it."

His voice was jocular but his hands were shaking.

"You do it by watering one side," she said softly, "or by turning it just so in the sun. You handle it as if it were a living thing, like a species or a woman or a bonsai. It will be what you want it to be if you let it be itself and take the time and the care."

"I think," he said, "that you are making me some kind of offer. Why?"

"Sitting there most of the night," she said, "I had a crazy kind of image. Do you think two sick twisted trees ever made bonsai out of one another?"

"What's your name?" he asked her.

THE COIN COLLECTOR

BY JACK FINNEY

JACK FINNEY LIKES TO PLAY WITH CASUAL ENCOUNTERS WITH THE UNUSUAL FOR AN EVERYMAN PROTAGONIST, WHETHER IT HAS TO DO WITH A TRAVEL AGENCY THAT HAS A SPECIAL PACKAGE FOR CLIENTS WHO CAN KEEP THEIR MOUTHS SHUT OR A SECRET LEVEL IN GRAND CENTRAL TERMINAL WHERE A VERY SPECIAL SET OF TRAIN LINES RUN OR A STRANGE COIN THAT IS APPARENTLY NOT MINTED IN OUR WORLD (LIKE OUR DIMES BUT WITH A DIFFERENT PRESIDENT ON THEM). FINNEY IS PRIMARILY KNOWN FOR HIS TIME-TRAVEL NOVELS *TIME AND AGAIN*, AND *TIME AFTER TIME*, BUT *THE WOODROW WILSON DIME* (WHICH IS BASED ON THIS STORY) PROBABLY COMES IN A CLOSE THIRD.

"**. . .** Will let me know the number of the pattern," my wife was saying, following me down the hall toward our bedroom, "and I can knit it myself if I get the blocking done."

I think she said blocking, anyway—whatever that means. And I nodded, unbuttoning my shirt as I walked; it had been hot out today, and I was eager to get out of my office clothes. I began thinking about a dark-green eight-thousand-dollar sports car I'd seen during noon hour in that big showroom on Park Avenue.

". . . kind of a ribbed pattern with a matching freggel-heggis," my wife seemed to be saying as I stopped at my dresser. I tossed my shirt on the bed and turned to the mirror, arching my chest.

". . . middy collar, batten-barton sleeves with sixteen rows of smeddlycup balderdashes. . . ." Pretty good chest and shoulders, I thought, staring in the mirror, I'm twenty-six years old, kind of thin faced, not bad-looking, not good-looking.

". . . dropped hem, doppelganger waist, maroon-green, and a sort of frimbleframble daisystitch. . . ." Probably want two or three thousand bucks down on a car like that, I thought; the payments'd be more than the rent on this whole apartment. I began emptying the change out of my pants pockets, glancing at each of the coins. When I was a kid there used to be an ad in a boys' magazine; "Coin collecting can be PROFITABLE," it read, "and FUN too! Why don't you start TODAY!" It explained that a 1913 Liberty-head nickel—"And many others!"—was worth thousands, and I guess I'm still looking for one.

"So what do you think?" Marion was saying. "You think they'd go well together?"

"Sure." I nodded at her reflection in my dresser mirror; she stood leaning in the bedroom doorway, arms folded, staring at the back of my head. "They'd look fine." I brought a dime up to my eyes for a closer look; it was minted in 1958 and had a profile of Woodrow Wilson, and I turned to Marion. "Hey, look," I said, "here's a new kind of dime—Woodrow Wilson." But she wouldn't look at my hand. She just stood there with her arms folded, glaring at me; and I said, "Now, what? What have I done wrong now?" Marion wouldn't answer, and I walked to my closet and began looking for some wash pants. After a moment I said coaxingly, "Come on, Sweetfeet, what'd I do wrong?"

"Oh, Al!" she wailed. "You don't listen to me; you really don't! Half the time you don't hear a word I say!"

"Why, sure I do, honey," I was rattling the hangers, hunting for my pants. "You were talking about knitting."

"An orange sweater, I said, Al—orange. I *knew* you weren't listening and asked you how an orange sweater would go with—Close your eyes."

"What?"

"No, don't turn around! And close your eyes." I closed them, and Marion said, "Now, without any peeking, because I'll see you, tell me what I'm wearing right now."

It was ridiculous. In the last five minutes, since I'd come home from the office, I must have glanced at Marion maybe two or three times. I'd kissed her when I walked into the apartment, or I was pretty sure I had. Yet standing at my closet now, eyes closed, I couldn't for the life of me say what she was wearing. I worked at it; I could actually hear the sound of her breathing just behind me and could picture her standing there, a small girl five feet three inches tall, weighing just over a hundred pounds, twenty-four years old, nice complexion, pretty face, honey-blond hair, and wearing— wearing—

"Well, am I wearing a dress, slacks, medieval armor, or standing here stark naked?"

"A dress."

"What color?"

"Ah—dark green?"

"Am I wearing stockings?"

"Yes."

"Is my hair done up; shaved off or in a pony tail?"

"Done up."

"O.K., you can look now."

Of course the instant I turned around to look, I remembered. There she stood, eyes blazing, her bare foot angrily tapping the floor, and she was wearing sky-blue wash slacks and a white cotton blouse. As she swung away to walk out of the room and down the hall, her pony tail was bobbing furiously.

Well, brother—and you, too, sister—unless the rice is still in your hair, you know what came next: the hurt, indignant silence. I got into slacks, short-sleeved shirt and huarachos, strolled into the living room, and there on the davenport sat Madame Defarge grimly studying the list, disguised as a magazine, of next day's guillotine victims. I knew whose name headed the list; and I walked straight to the kitchen, mixed up some booze in tall glasses and found a screw driver in a kitchen drawer.

In the living room, coldly ignored by what had once been my radiant, laughing bride, I set the drinks on the coffee table, reached behind Marion's magazine and gripped her chin between thumb and forefinger. The magazine dropped, and I instantly inserted the tip of the screw driver between her front teeth, pried open her mouth, picked up a glass and tried to pour in some booze. She started to laugh, spilling some down her front, and I grinned, handing her the glass, and picked up mine. Sitting down beside her, I saluted Marion with my glass, then took a delightful sip; and as it hurried to my sluggish blood stream, I could feel the happy corpuscles dive in, laughing and shouting, and felt able to cope with the next item on the agenda, which followed immediately.

"You don't love me any more," said Marion.

"Oh, yes, I do." I leaned over to kiss her neck, glancing around the room over her shoulder.

"Oh, no, you don't; not really."

"Oh, yes, I do; really. Honey, where's that book I was reading last night?"

"There! You see! All you want to do is read all the time! You never want to go out! The honeymoon's certainly over around here, all right!"

"No, it isn't, Sweetknees; not at all, I feel exactly the way I did the day I proposed to you: I honestly do. Was there any mail?"

"Just some ads and a bill. You used to listen to every word I said before we were married and you always noticed what I wore and you complimented me and you sent me flowers and you brought me little surprises and"—suddenly she sat bolt upright— "remember those cute little notes you used to send me! I'd find them all the time," she said sadly, staring past my shoulder, her eyes widening wistfully. "Tucked in my purse maybe"—she smiled mournfully—"or in a glove. Or they'd come to the office on post cards, even in telegrams a couple times. All the other girls used to say they were just darling." She swung to face me. "Honey, why don't you ever—"

"Help!" I said. "Help, help!"

"What do you mean?" Marion demanded coolly, and I tried to explain.

"Look, honey," I said briskly, putting an arm companionably around her shoulders, "we've been married four years. Of course the honeymoon's over! What kind of imbeciles," I asked with complete reasonableness, "would we be if it weren't? I love you, sure," I assured her, shrugging a shoulder. "Of course. You bet. Always glad to see you: any wife of old Al Pullen is a wife of mine! But after four years I walk up the stairs when I come home; I no longer run up three at a time. That's life," I said, clapping her cheerfully on the back. "Even four-alarm fires eventually die down, you know." I smiled at her fondly. "And as for cute little notes tucked in your purse— help, help!" I should have known better, I guess; there are certain things you just can't seem to explain to a woman.

I had trouble getting to sleep that night—the davenport is much too short for me— and it was around two-forty-five before I finally sank into a kind of exhausted and broken-backed coma. Breakfast next morning, you can believe me, was a glum affair at the town home of Mr. and Mrs. Alfred E. Pullen, devoted couple.

Who can say whether the events of the night before affected those which now followed? I certainly couldn't; I was too tired, dragging home from the office along Third Avenue, heading uptown from Thirty-fourth Street about five-thirty the next evening. I was tired, depressed, irritated and in no hurry at all to get home. It was hot and muggy outside, and I was certain Marion would give me cold cuts for sup- per—and all evening long, for that matter. My tie was pulled down, my collar open, hat shoved back, coat slung over one shoulder, and trudging along the sidewalk there I got to wishing things were different.

I didn't care how, exactly—just different. For example, how would things be right now, it occurred to me, if I'd majored in creative botany at college instead of physical ed? Or what would I be doing at this very moment if I'd gone to Siam with Tom Biehler that time? Or if I'd got the job with Enterprises, Incorporated, instead of Serv-Eez? Or if I hadn't broken off with what's-her-name, that big, black-haired girl who could sing *Japanese Sandman* through her nose?

At Thirty-sixth Street I stopped at the corner newsstand, planking my dime down on the counter before the man who ran it; we knew each other long since, though I don't think we've ever actually spoken. Glancing at me, he scooped up my dime, grabbed a paper from one of the slacks and folded it as he handed it to me; and I nodded my thanks, tucking it under my arm, and walked on. And that's when it happened: I glanced up at a brick building kitty-corner across the street, and there on a blank side wall three or four stories up was a painted advertisement—a narrow-waisted bottle filled with a reddish-brown beverage and lying half buried in a bed of blue-white ice. Painted just over the bottle in a familiar script were the words, "Drink Coco-Coola."

Do you see? It didn't say "Coca-Cola"; not quite. And staring up at that painted sign, I knew it was no sign painters' mistake. They don't make mistakes like that; not on great big outdoor signs that take a couple of men several days to paint. I knew it couldn't possibly be a rival soft drink either; the spelling and entire appearance of this ad were too close to those of Coca-Cola. No, I knew that sign was meant to read "Coco-Coola," and turning to walk on finally—well, it may strike you as insane what I felt certain I knew from just the sight of that painted sign high above a New York street.

But within two steps that feeling was confirmed. I glanced out at the street beside me; it was rush hour and the cars streamed past, clean cars and dirty ones, old and new. But every one of them was painted a single color only, mostly black, and there wasn't a tail fin or strip of chromium in sight. These were modern, fast, good-looking cars, you understand, but utterly different in design from any I'd ever before seen. The traffic lights on Third Avenue clicked to red, the cars slowed and stopped, and now as I walked along past them I was able to read some of their names. There were a Ford, a Buick, two Wintons, a Stutz, a Cadillac, a Dort, a Kissel, an Oldsmobile and at least four or five small Pierce-Arrows. Then, glancing down Thirty-seventh Street as I passed it. I saw a billboard advertising Picayune Cigarettes; "America's Largest-Selling Brand." And now a Third Avenue bus dragged past me, crammed with people as usual this time of day, but it was shaped a little differently and it was painted blue and white.

I spun suddenly around on the walk, looking frantically for the Empire State Building. But it was there, all right, just where it was supposed to be; and I actually sighed with relief. It was shorter, though—by a good ten stories at least. When had all this happened? I wondered dazedly and opened my paper, but there was nothing unusual in it—till I noticed the name at the top of the page. *New York Sun*, it said, and I stood on the sidewalk gaping at it: because the *Sun* hasn't been published in New York for years.

Do you understand now? I did, finally, but of course I like to read—when I get the chance, that is—and I'm extremely well grounded in science from all the science-fiction I've read. So I was certain, presently, that I knew what had happened: maybe you've figured it out too.

Years ago someone had to decide on a name for a new soft drink and finally picked "Coca-Cola." But certainly he considered other possible alternatives; and if the truth could be known, I'll bet one of them was "Coco-Coola." It's not a bad name—sounds cool and refreshing—and he may have come very close to deciding on it.

And how come Ford, Buick, Chevrolet and Oldsmobile survived while the Moon, Willys-Knight, Hupmobile and Kissel didn't? Well, at some point or other maybe a decision was made by the men who ran the Kissel Company, for example, which might just as easily have been made another way. If it had, maybe Kissel would have survived and be a familiar sight today.

Instead of Lucky Strikes, Camels and Chesterfields, we might be buying chiefly Picayunes, Sweet Caporals and Piedmonts. We might not have the Japanese beetle or the atom bomb. While the biggest newspaper in New York could be the *Sun*, and George Coopernagel might be President. If—what would the world be like right now, what would you or I be doing?—if only things in the past had happened just a tiny bit differently. There are thousands of possibilities, of course; there are millions and trillions. There is every conceivable kind of world, in fact; and a theory of considerable scientific standing—Einstein believed it—is that these other possible worlds actually exist; all of them, side by side and simultaneously with the one we happen to be familiar with.

I believed it too now, naturally; I knew what had happened all right. Walking along Third Avenue through the late afternoon on my way home from the office, I had come to one of the tiny points where two of these alternate worlds intersected somehow. And I had walked off out of one into another slightly altered, somewhat different world of "If" that was every bit as real, and which existed quite as much, as the one I'd just left.

For maybe a block I walked on, stunned, but with a growing curiosity and excitement—because it had occurred to me to wonder where I was going. I was walking on with a definite purpose and destination, I realized; and when a traffic light beside me clicked to green, I took the opportunity to cross La Guardia Avenue, as it was labeled now, and then continue west along Thirty-ninth Street. I was going somewhere, no doubt about that; and in the instant of wondering where, I felt a chill along my spine. Because suddenly I knew.

All the memories of my life in another world, you understand, still existed in my mind; from distant past to the present. But beginning with the moment that I had turned from the newsstand to glance up at that pointed sign, another set of memories— an alternate set of memories of my other life in this alternate world—began stirring to life underneath the first. But they were dim and faint yet, out of focus. I knew where I was going—vaguely, and I no more had to think how to get there than any other man on his way home from work. My legs simply moved in an old familiar pattern, carrying me up to the double glass doors of a big apartment building, and the doorman said, "Evening, Mr. Pullen, Hot today."

"You said it, Charley," I answered and walked on into the lobby; and then my legs were carrying me up the stairs to the second floor, then down a corridor to an apartment door which stood open. And just as I did every night, I realized, I walked into the living room, tossing my copy of the *Sun* to the davenport. I was wearing a suit I'd never seen before, I noticed, but it fitted me perfectly, of course, and was a little worn.

"Hi, I'm home," I heard my voice call out as always; and at one and the same time I knew, with complete and time-dulled familiarity—and also wondered with intense and fascinated curiosity—who in the world was going to answer: who in *this* world?

An oven door slammed in the kitchen as I turned to hang up my suit coat in the hall closet as always, then footsteps sounded on the wood floor between the kitchen and the living room. And as she said, "Hi, darling." I turned to see my wife walking toward me.

I had to admire my taste in this world. She was a big girl, tall and not quite slim; black-haired and with a very fair complexion; quite a pretty face with a single vertical frown line between her brows; and she had an absolutely gorgeous figure with long handsome legs. "Why, hel-lo," I said slowly. "What a preposterously good-looking female you are!"

Her jaw dropped in simple astonishment, her blue eyes narrowing suspiciously. I held my arms wide then, walking toward her delightedly, and while she accepted my embrace, she drew back to sniff my breath. She couldn't draw back very far, though, because my embrace—I simply couldn't help this—was tight and close; this fine-looking girl was a spectacular armful. "Now I know why I go to the office every day," I was saying as I nuzzled her lovely white neck, an extremely agreeable sensation. "There had to be a reason, and now I know what it is. It's so I can come home to this."

"Al, what in the world is the matter with you!" she said. Her voice was still astonished, but she'd quit trying to draw back.

"Nothing you can't remedy," I said, "in a variety of delightful ways," and I kissed her again.

"Honey," she murmured after a considerable time, "I have to fix supper," and she made a little token effort to get away.

"Supper can wait." I answered, and my voice was a full octave deeper, "but I can't." Again I kissed her, hard and eagerly, full on the lips. Her great big beautiful blue eyes widened in amazement—then they slowly closed and she smiled languorously.

Marion's face abruptly rose up in my mind. There in the forefront of my consciousness and conscience suddenly, was her betrayed and indignant face, every bit as vivid as though she'd actually walked in through the door to discover this sultry brunette in my arms; and I could feel my face flame with guilt. Because I couldn't kid myself. I couldn't possibly deny the intensity of the pleasure I'd felt at this girl in my arms. I knew how very close I'd come to betraying Marion, and I felt terribly ashamed, and stood wondering—this long length of glorious girlhood still in my arms—how to end the situation, and with charm and grace. Now a moment later, her eyes opened, and she looked up at me questioningly, those full ripe moist lips slightly apart. "Hate to say this," I said then, sniffing the air thoughtfully, "but seems to me I smell something burning—besides me."

"Oh!"—she let out a little shriek, and as she ran to the kitchen I actually closed my eyes and sighed with a terrible relief. I didn't know how I'd walked into this other alternate world, or how I could leave it; but Marion was alive in my mind, while the world around me seemed unreal. In the kitchen I heard the oven door open, heard water run in the sink, then the momentary sizzle of cooking meat; and I walked quickly to the davenport and snatched up my copy of the *Sun*.

As I raised it to my face, the tap of high heels sounded on the wood floor just outside the kitchen door. There was silence as they crossed the rug toward me, then the davenport cushion beside me sank; I felt a deliciously warm breath on my cheek, and I had to lower my trembling, rattling newspaper, turn and manage to smile into the sloe eyes of the creature beside me.

Once again—my head slowly shaking in involuntary approval—I had to admire my own good taste; this was not a homely woman. "I turned the oven down," she murmured. "It might be better to have dinner a little later. When it gets cooler," she added softly.

I nodded quickly. "Good idea. Paper says it's the hottest day in five hundred years." I babbled. "Doctors advise complete immobility."

But the long-legged beauty beside me wasn't listening. "So I'm the reason you like to come home, am I?" she breathed into my ear. "It's been a long time, darling, since you said anything like that."

"H'm'm," I murmured and nodded frantically at the paper in my hands. "I see they're going to tear down City Hall," I muttered wildly, but she was blowing gently in my ear now, then she pulled the *Sun* from my paralyzed fingers, tossed it over her shoulder and leaned toward me. *Marion!* I was shrieking silently. *Help!* Then the raven-haired girl beside me had her arms around my neck, and I simply did not know what to do; I thought of pretending to faint, claiming sunstroke.

Then with the blinding force of a revelation it came to me. Through no fault of my own, I was in another world, another life. The girl in my arms—somehow that's where she was now—was singing softly, almost inaudibly. It took me a moment to recognize the tune: then finally I knew, finally I recognized this magnificent girl. "Just a Japanese Sand—man," she was singing softly through her lovely nose, and now I remembered fully everything about the alternate world I was in. 'I hadn't broken off with this girl at all—not in this particular world! Matter of fact, I suddenly realized. I'd never even met Marion in this world. It was even possible, it occurred to me now, that she'd never been born. In any case, this was the girl I'd married in this world. No denying it, this was my wife here beside me with her arms around my neck; we'd been married three years, in fact. And now I knew what to do—perfectly well.

Oh, boy! What a wonderful time Vera and I had in the months that followed. My work at the office was easy—no strain at all. I seemed to have an aptitude for it and, just as I'd always suspected, I made rather more money at Enterprises, Incorporated, than that Serv-Eez outfit ever paid in their lives. More than once, too, I left the office early, since no one seemed to mind, just to hurry back home—leaping up the stairs three at a time—to that lovely big old Vera again. And at least once every week I'd bring home a load of books under my arm, because she loved to read, just like me; and I'd made a wonderful discovery about this alternate world.

Life, you understand, was different in its details. The San Francisco Giants had won the 'Fifty-eight Series, for example; the Second Avenue El was still up; Yucatan gum was the big favorite; television was good; and several extremely prominent people whose names would astound you were in jail. But basically the two worlds were much the same. Drugstores, for example, looked and smelled just about the same; and one night on the way home from work I stopped in at a big drugstore to look over the racks of paper-back books and made a marvelous discovery.

There on the revolving metal racks were the familiar rows of glossy little books, every one of which, judging from the covers, seemed to be about an abnormally well-developed girl. Turning the rack slowly I saw books by William Faulkner, Bernard Glemser, Agatha Christie, and Charles Einstein, which I'd read and liked. Then, down near the bottom of the rack my eye was caught by the words, "By Mark Twain." The cover showed an old side-wheeler steamboat, and the title was *South From Cairo*. A reprint fitted out with a new title, I thought, feeling annoyed; and I picked up the book to see just which of Mark Twain's it really was. I've read every book he wrote—*Huckleberry Finn* at least a dozen times since I discovered it when I was eleven years-old.

But the text of this book was new to me. It seemed to be an account, told in the first person by a young man of twenty, of his application for a job on a Mississippi steamboat. And then, from the bottom of a page, a name leaped out at me, " 'Finn, sir,' I answered the captain," the text read, " 'but mostly they call me Huckleberry.' "

For a moment I just stood there in the drugstore with my mouth hanging open; then I turned the little book in my hands. On the back cover was a photograph of Mark Twain; the familiar shock of white hair, the mustache, that wise old face. But underneath this the brief familiar account of his life ended with saying that he had died in 1918 in Mill Valley, California. Mark Twain had lived eight years longer in this alternate world, and had written—well, I didn't yet know how many more books he had written in this wonderful world, but I knew I was going to find out. And my hand was trembling as I walked up to the cashier and gave her two bits for my priceless copy of *South From Cairo*.

I love reading in bed, and that night I read a good half of my new Mark Twain in bed with Vera, and then afterward—well, afterward she fixed me a nice cool Tom Collins. And oh, boy, this was the life all right.

In the weeks that followed—that lanky length of violet-eyed womanhood cuddled up beside me, singing softly through her nose—I read a new novel by Ernest Hemingway: the best yet, I think. I read a serious, wonderfully good novel by James Thurber, and something else I'd been hoping to find for years—the sequel to a marvelous book called *Delilah,* by Marcus Goodrich. In fact, I read some of the best reading since Gutenberg kicked things off—a good deal of it aloud to Vera, who enjoyed it as much as I did. I read *Mistress Murder* a hilarious detective story by George S. Kaufman: *The Queen Is Dead,* by George Bernard Shaw; *The Third Level*, a collection of short stories by someone or other I never heard of, but not too bad: a wonderful novel by Allen Marple: a group of fine stories about the advertising business by Alfred Eichter; a terrific play by Orson Welles; and a whole new volume of Sherlock Holmes stories by A. Conan Doyle.

For four or five months, as Vera rather aptly remarked, I thought, it was like a second honeymoon. I did all the wonderful little things, she said, that I used to do on our honeymoon and before we were married; I even thought up some new ones. And then—all of a sudden one night—I wanted to go to a night club.

All of a sudden I wanted to get out of the house in the evening, and do something else for a change. Vera was astonished—wanted to know what was the matter with me, which is typical of a woman. If you don't react precisely the same way day after day after endless day, they think something must be wrong with you. They'll even insist on it. I didn't want any black-cherry ice cream for dessert. I told Vera one night at dinner. Why not, she wanted to know—which is idiotic if you stop to think about it. I didn't want any because I didn't want any, that's all! But being a woman she had to have a reason; so I said, "Because I don't like it."

"But of course you like it," she said. "You always used to like it!"

You see what I mean? Anyway, we did go to this night club, but it wasn't much fun. Vera got sleepy, and we left and were home before twelve. Then she wasn't sleepy, but I was. Couple nights later I came home from the office and was changing my clothes; she said something or other, and I didn't hear her and didn't answer, and we actually had a little argument. She wanted to know why I always looked at every coin in my pocket, like an idiot, every time I changed clothes. I explained quietly enough; told her about the ad I used to read as a kid and how I was still looking for a 1913 Liberty-head nickel worth thousands of dollars, which was the truth.

But it wasn't the whole truth. As I looked through the coins I'd collected in my pocket during the day—the Woodrow Wilson dimes, the Grover Cleveland pennies, the nickels with George Coopernagel's profile, and all the other familiar coins of the world I now lived in—I understood something that had puzzled me once.

These other alternate worlds in which we also live intersect here and there—at a corner newsstand, for example, on Third Avenue in New York and at many another place, too, no doubt. And from these intersecting places every once in a while something from one of these worlds—a Woodrow Wilson dime, for example—will stray into another one. I'd found such a dime and when I happened to plank it down on the counter of that little newsstand, there at an intersection of two alternate worlds, that dime bought a newspaper in the world it belonged in. And I walked off into that world with the *New York Sun* under my arm. I knew this now, and I'd known it long since. I understood it finally, but I didn't tell Vera. I simply told her I was looking for a 1913 Liberty-head nickel. I didn't tell her I was also looking for a Roosevelt dime.

I found one too. One night, finally, sure enough, there it lay in my palm a dime with the profile of Franklin D. Roosevelt on its face. And when I slipped it down on the counter of the little newsstand next evening, there at the intersection of two alternate worlds, I was trembling. The man snatched up a paper, folding it as he handed it to me, and I tucked it under my arm and walked on for three or four steps, hardly daring to breathe. Then I opened the paper and looked at it. *New York World-Telegram*, the masthead read, and I began to run—all the way to Forty-fourth Street, then east to First Avenue and then up three flights of stairs.

I could hardly talk I was so out of breath when I burst into the apartment, but I managed to gasp out the only word that mattered. "Marion!" I said and grabbed her to me, almost choking her, because my arms hit the back of her head about where Vera's shoulders would have been. But she managed to talk, struggling to break loose, her voice sort of muffled against my coat.

"Al!" she said. "What in the world is the matter with you?"

For her, of course, I'd been here last night and every night for the months and years past. And of course, back in this world, I remembered it, too, but dimly, mistily. I stepped back now and looked down at the marvelous tiny size of Marion, at that wonderful, petite figure, at her exquisite and fragile blond beauty. "Nothing's the matter with me," I said, grinning down at her. "It's just that I've got a beautiful wife and was in a hurry to get home to her. Anything wrong with that?"

There wasn't; not a thing, and—well, it's been wonderful, my life with Marion, ever since. It's an exciting life; we're out three and four nights a week, I guess—dancing, the theater, visiting friends, going to night clubs, having dinner out, even bowling. It's the way things used to be, as Marion has aptly said. In fact, she remarked recently, it's like a second honeymoon, and she's wonderfully happy these days and so am I.

Oh, sometimes I'm a little tired at night lately. There are times after a tough day at Serv-Eez when I'd almost rather stay home and read a good book; it's been quite a while since I did. But I don't worry about that. Because the other night, about two-thirty in the morning, just back from The Mirimba, standing at my dresser looking through the coins in my pocket, I found it—another Woodrow Wilson dime. You come across them every once in a while, I've noticed, if you just keep your eyes open; Wilson dimes, Ulysses Grant quarters, Coopernagel nickels. And I've got my Wilson dime safely tucked away, and—well, I'm sure Vera, that lithe-limbed creature, will be mighty glad to see her husband suddenly acting his old self once again. I imagine it'll be like a third honeymoon. Just as—in time—it will be for Marion.

So there you are, brother, coin collecting can be profitable. And fun too! Why don't you start—tonight!

PREY

BY RICHARD MATHESON

RICHARD MATHESON IS THE THIRD AUTHOR IN THIS ANTHOLOGY WITH SUCCESSFUL ADAPTATIONS OF HIS WORK IN ROD SERLING'S TWILIGHT ZONE, AS WELL AS IN OTHER DRAMATIC VENUES AS WELL. (HIS STORY "DUEL" WAS A HUGELY SUCCESSFUL TV MOVIE FILMED BY A VERY YOUNG DIRECTOR BY THE NAME OF SPIELBERG.)

MATHESON IS AT HIS BEST WHEN SETTING A SITUATION OF TENSION BETWEEN AN INDIVIDUAL AND THE UNKNOWN WHICH LEAVES THE PROTAGONIST WITH NO CHOICE BUT TO REACT IN ORDER TO SURVIVE. IN "DUEL" IT WAS A MALEVOLENT TRUCK DRIVER. IN "PREY" IT IS AN AFRICAN DOLL THAT COMES TO LIFE AND DECIDES TO HUNT THE VERY CONTEMPORARY WOMAN WHO PURCHASED IT.

Amelia arrived at her apartment at six-fourteen. Hanging her coat in the hall closet, she carried the small package into the living room and sat on the sofa. She nudged off her shoes while she unwrapped the package on her lap. The wooden box resembled a casket. Amelia raised its lid and smiled. It was the ugliest doll she'd ever seen. Seven inches long and carved from wood, it had a skeletal body and an oversized head. Its expression was maniacally fierce, its pointed teeth completely bared, its glaring eyes protuberant. It clutched an eight-inch spear in its right hand. A length of fine, gold chain was wrapped around its body from the shoulders to the knees. A tiny scroll was wedged between the doll and the inside wall of its box. Amelia picked it up and unrolled it. There was handwriting on it. *This is He Who Kills*, it began. *He is a deadly hunter*. Amelia smiled as she read the rest of the words. Arthur would be pleased.

The thought of Arthur made her turn to look at the telephone on the table beside her. After a while, she sighed and set the wooden box on the sofa. Lifting the telephone to her lap, she picked up the receiver and dialed a number.

Her mother answered.

"Hello, Mom," Amelia said.

"Haven't you left yet?" her mother asked.

Amelia steeled herself. "Mom, I know it's Friday night—" she started.

She couldn't finish. There was silence on the line. Amelia closed her eyes. Mom, please, she thought. She swallowed. "There's this man," she said. "His name is Arthur Breslow. He's a high-school teacher."

"You aren't coming," her mother said.

Amelia shivered. "It's his birthday," she said. She opened her eyes and looked at the doll. "I sort of promised him we'd . . . spend the evening together."

Her mother was silent. There aren't any good movies playing tonight, anyway, Amelia's mind continued. "We could go tomorrow night," she said.

Her mother was silent.

"Mom?"

"Now even Friday night's too much for you."

"Mom, I see you two, three nights a week."

"To *visit*," said her mother. "When you have your own room here."

"Mom, *let's not start on that again*," Amelia said. I'm not a child, she thought. Stop treating me as though I were a child!

"How long have you been seeing him?" her mother asked.

"A month or so."

"Without telling me," her mother said.

"I had every intention of telling you." Amelia's head was starting to throb. I will *not* get a headache, she told herself. She looked at the doll. It seemed to be glaring at her. "He's a nice man, Mom," she said.

Her mother didn't speak. Amelia felt her stomach muscles drawing taut. I won't be able to eat tonight, she thought.

She was conscious suddenly of huddling over the telephone. She forced herself to sit erect. *I'm 33 years old*, she thought. Reaching out, she lifted the doll from its box. "You should *see* what I'm giving him for his birthday," she said. "I found it in a curio shop on Third Avenue. It's a genuine Zuñi fetish doll, extremely rare. Arthur is a buff on anthropology. That's why I got it for him."

There was silence on the line. All right, *don't talk*, Amelia thought. "It's a hunting fetish," she continued, trying hard to sound untroubled. "It's supposed to have the spirit of a Zuñi hunter trapped inside it. There's a golden chain around it to prevent the spirit from"—She couldn't think of the word. She ran a shaking finger over the chain—"escaping, I guess," she said. "His name is He Who Kills. You should see his face." She felt warm tears trickling down her cheeks.

"Have a good time," said her mother, hanging up.

Amelia stared at the receiver, listening to the dial tone. Why is it always like this? she thought. She dropped the receiver onto its cradle and set aside the telephone. The darkening room looked blurred to her. She stood the doll on the coffee-table edge and pushed to her feet. I'll take my bath now, she told herself. I'll meet him and we'll have a lovely time. She walked across the living room. A lovely time, her mind repeated emptily. She knew it wasn't possible. Oh, *Mom!* she thought. She clenched her fists in helpless fury as she went into the bedroom.

In the living room, the doll fell off the table edge. It landed head down and the spear point, sticking into the carpet, braced the doll's legs in the air.

The fine, gold chain began to slither downward.

IT WAS ALMOST DARK when Amelia came back into the living room. She had taken off her clothes and was wearing her terrycloth robe. In the bathroom, water was running into the tub.

She sat on the sofa and placed the telephone on her lap. For several minutes, she stared at it. At last, with a heavy sigh, she lifted the receiver and dialed a number.

"Arthur?" she said when he answered.

"Yes?" Amelia knew the tone—pleasant but suspecting. She couldn't speak.

"Your mother," Arthur finally said.

That cold, heavy sinking in her stomach. "It's our night together," she explained. "Every Friday—" She stopped and waited. Arthur didn't speak. "I've mentioned it before," she said.

"I know you've mentioned it," he said.

Amelia rubbed at her temple.

"She's still running your life, isn't she?" he said.

Amelia tensed. "I just don't want to hurt her feelings anymore," she said. "My moving out was hard enough on her."

"I don't want to hurt her feelings either," Arthur said. "But how many birthdays a year do I have? We *planned* on this."

"I know." She felt her stomach muscles tightening again.

"Are you really going to let her do this to you?" Arthur asked. "One Friday night out of the whole year?"

Amelia closed her eyes. Her lips moved soundlessly. I just can't hurt her feelings anymore, she thought. She swallowed. "She's my mother," she said.

"Very well," he said. "I'm sorry. I was looking forward to it, but—" He paused. "I'm sorry," he said. He hung up quietly.

Amelia sat in silence for a long time, listening to the dial tone. She started when the recorded voice said loudly, "Please hang up." Putting the receiver down, she replaced the telephone on its table. So much for my birthday present, she thought. It would be pointless to give it to Arthur now. She reached out, switching on the table lamp. She'd take the doll back tomorrow.

The doll was not on the coffee table. Looking down, Amelia saw the gold chain lying on the carpet. She eased off the sofa edge onto her knees and picked it up, dropping it into the wooden box. The doll was not beneath the coffee table. Bending over, Amelia felt around underneath the sofa.

She cried out, jerking back her hand. Straightening up, she turned to the lamp and looked at her hand. There was something wedged beneath the index fingernail. She shivered as she plucked it out. It was the head of the doll's spear. She dropped it into the box and put the finger in her mouth. Bending over again, she felt around more cautiously beneath the sofa.

She couldn't find the doll. Standing with a weary groan, she started pulling one end of the sofa from the wall. It was terribly heavy. She recalled the night that she and her mother had shopped for the furniture. She'd wanted to furnish the apartment in Danish modern. Mother had insisted on this heavy, maple sofa; it had been on sale. Amelia grunted as she dragged it from the wall. She was conscious of the water running in the bathroom. She'd better turn it off soon.

She looked at the section of carpet she'd cleared, catching sight of the spear shaft. The doll was not beside it. Amelia picked it up and set it on the coffee table. The doll was caught beneath the sofa, she decided; when she'd moved the sofa, she had moved the doll as well.

She thought she heard a sound behind her—fragile, skittering. Amelia turned. The sound had stopped. She felt a chill move up the backs of her legs. "It's He Who Kills," she said with a smile. "He's taken off his chain and gone—"

She broke off suddenly. There had definitely been a noise inside the kitchen; a metallic, rasping sound. Amelia swallowed nervously. What's going on? she thought. She walked across the living room and reached into the kitchen, switching on the light. She peered inside. Everything looked normal. Her gaze moved falteringly across the stove, the pan of water on it, the table and chair, the drawers and cabinet doors all shut, the electric clock, the small refrigerator with the cookbook lying on top of it, the picture on the wall, the knife rack fastened to the cabinet side—

—its small knife missing.

Amelia stared at the knife rack. Don't be silly, she told herself. She'd put the knife in the drawer, that's all. Stepping into the kitchen, she pulled out the silverware drawer. The knife was not inside it.

Another sound made her look down quickly at the floor. She gasped in shock. For several moments, she could not react; then, stepping to the doorway, she looked into the living room, her heartbeat thudding. Had it been imagination? She was sure she'd seen a movement.

"Oh, come on," she said. She made a disparaging sound. She hadn't seen a thing.

Across the room, the lamp went out.

Amelia jumped so startledly, she rammed her right elbow against the doorjamb. Crying out, she clutched the elbow with her left hand, eyes closed momentarily, her face a mask of pain.

She opened her eyes and looked into the darkened living room. "Come on," she told herself in aggravation. Three sounds plus a burned-out bulb did not add up to anything as idiotic as—

She willed away the thought. She had to turn the water off. Leaving the kitchen, she started for the hall. She rubbed her elbow, grimacing.

There was another sound. Amelia froze. Something was coming across the carpet toward her. She looked down dumbly. No, she thought.

She saw it then—a rapid movement near the floor. There was a glint of metal, instantly, a stabbing pain in her right calf. Amelia gasped. She kicked out blindly. Pain again. She felt warm blood running down her skin. She turned and lunged into the hall. The throw rug slipped beneath her and she fell against the wall, hot pain lancing through her right ankle. She clutched at the wall to keep from falling, then went sprawling on her side. She thrashed around with a sob of fear.

More movement, dark on dark. Pain in her left calf, then her right again. Amelia cried out. Something brushed along her thigh. She scrabbled back, then lurched up blindly, almost falling again. She fought for balance, reaching out convulsively. The heel of her left hand rammed against the wall, supporting her. She twisted around and rushed into the darkened bedroom. Slamming the door, she fell against it, panting. Something banged against it on the other side, something small and near the floor.

Amelia listened, trying not to breathe so loudly. She pulled carefully at the knob to make sure the latch had caught. When there were no further sounds outside the door, she backed toward the bed. She started as she bumped against the mattress edge. Slumping down, she grabbed at the extension phone and pulled it to her lap. Whom could she call? The police? They'd think her mad. Mother? She was too far off.

She was dialing Arthur's number by the light from the bathroom when the door-knob started turning. Suddenly, her fingers couldn't move. She stared across the dark-ened room. The door latch clicked. The telephone slipped off her lap. She heard it thudding onto the carpet as the door swung open. Something dropped from the outside knob.

Amelia jerked back, pulling up her legs. A shadowy form was scurrying across the carpet toward the bed. She gaped at it. It isn't true, she thought. She stiffened at the tugging on her bedspread. *It was climbing up to get her.* No, she thought; *it isn't true.* She couldn't move. She stared at the edge of the mattress.

Something that looked like a tiny head appeared. Amelia twisted around with a cry of shock, flung herself across the bed and jumped to the floor. Plunging into the bathroom, she spun around and slammed the door, gasping at the pain in her ankle. She had barely thumbed in the button on the doorknob when something banged against the bottom of the door. Amelia heard a noise like the scratching of a rat. Then it was still.

She turned and leaned across the tub. The level of the water was almost to the overflow drain. As she twisted shut the faucets, she saw drops of blood falling into the water. Straightening up, she turned to the medicine-cabinet mirror above the sink.

She caught her breath in horror as she saw the gash across her neck. She pressed a shaking hand against it. Abruptly, she became aware of pain in her legs and looked down. She'd been slashed along the calves of both legs. Blood was running down her ankles, dripping off the edges of her feet. Amelia started crying. Blood ran between the fingers of the hand against her neck. It trickled down her wrist. She looked at her reflection through a glaze of tears.

Something in her face aroused her, a wretchedness, a look of terrified surrender. No, she thought. She reached out for the medicine-cabinet door. Opening it, she pulled out iodine, gauze and tape. She dropped the cover of the toilet seat and sank down gingerly. It was a struggle to remove the stopper of the iodine bottle. She had to rap it hard against the sink three times before it opened.

The burning of the antiseptic on her calves made her gasp. Amelia clenched her teeth as she wrapped gauze around her right leg.

A sound made her twist toward the door. She saw the knife blade being jabbed beneath it. It's trying to stab my feet, she thought; it thinks I'm standing there. She felt unreal to be considering its thoughts. *This is He Who Kills*; the scroll flashed suddenly across her mind. *He is a deadly hunter.* Amelia stared at the poking knife blade. God, she thought.

Hastily, she bandaged both her legs, then stood and, looking into the mirror, cleaned the blood from her neck with a washrag. She swabbed some iodine along the edges of the gash, hissing at the fiery pain.

She whirled at the new sound, heartbeat leaping. Stepping to the door, she leaned down, listening hard. There was a faint, metallic noise inside the knob.

The doll was trying to unlock it.

Amelia backed off slowly, staring at the knob. She tried to visualize the doll. Was it hanging from the knob by one arm, using the other to probe inside the knob lock with the knife? The vision was insane. She felt an icy prickling on the back of her neck. *I mustn't let it in,* she thought.

A hoarse cry pulled her lips back as the doorknob button popped out. Reaching out impulsively, she dragged a bath towel off its rack. The doorknob turned, the latch clicked free. The door began to open.

Suddenly the doll came darting in. It moved so quickly that its figure blurred before Amelia's eyes. She swung the towel down hard, as though it were a huge bug rushing at her. The doll was knocked against the wall. Amelia heaved the towel on top of it and lurched across the floor, gasping at the pain in her ankle. Flinging open the door, she lunged into the bedroom.

She was almost to the hall door when her ankle gave. She pitched across the carpet with a cry of shock. There was a noise behind her. Twisting around, she saw the doll come through the bathroom doorway like a jumping spider. She saw the knife blade glinting in the light. Then the doll was in the shadows, coming at her fast. Amelia scrabbled back. She glanced over her shoulder, saw the closet and backed into its darkness, clawing for the doorknob.

Pain again, an icy slashing at her foot. Amelia screamed and heaved back. Reaching up, she yanked a topcoat down. It fell across the doll. She jerked down everything in reach. The doll was buried underneath a mound of blouses, skirts and dresses. Amelia pitched across the moving pile of clothes. She forced herself to stand and limped into the hall as quickly as she could. The sound of thrashing underneath the clothes faded from her hearing. She hobbled to the door. Unlocking it, she pulled the knob.

The door was held. Amelia reached up quickly to the bolt. It had been shot. She tried to pull it free. It wouldn't budge. She clawed at it with sudden terror. It was twisted out of shape. "No," she muttered. *She was trapped.* "Oh, God." She started pounding on the door. "Please help me! *Help* me!"

Sound in the bedroom. Amelia whirled and lurched across the living room. She dropped to her knees beside the sofa, feeling for the telephone, but her fingers trembled so much that she couldn't dial the numbers. She began to sob, then twisted around with a strangled cry. The doll was rushing at her from the hallway.

Amelia grabbed an ashtray from the coffee table and hurled it at the doll. She threw a vase, a wooden box, a figurine. She couldn't hit the doll. It reached her, started jabbing at her legs. Amelia reared up blindly and fell across the coffee table. Rolling to her knees, she stood again. She staggered toward the hall, shoving over furniture to stop the doll. She toppled a chair, a table. Picking up a lamp, she hurled it at the floor. She backed into the hall and, spinning, rushed into the closet, slammed the door shut.

She held the knob with rigid fingers. Waves of hot breath pulsed against her face. She cried out as the knife was jabbed beneath the door, its sharp point sticking into one of her toes. She shuffled back, shifting her grip on the knob. Her robe hung open. She could feel a trickle of blood between her breasts. Her legs felt numb with pain. She closed her eyes. Please, someone help, she thought.

She stiffened as the doorknob started turning in her grasp. Her flesh went cold. It couldn't be stronger than she: it *couldn't* be. Amelia tightened her grip. *Please*, she thought. The side of her head bumped against the front edge of her suitcase on the shelf.

The thought exploded in her mind. Holding the knob with her right hand, she reached up, fumbling, with her left. The suitcase clasps were open. With a sudden wrench, she turned the doorknob, shoving at the door as hard as possible. It rushed away from her. She heard it bang against the wall. The doll thumped down.

Amelia reached up, hauling down her suitcase. Yanking open the lid, she fell to her knees in the closet doorway, holding the suitcase like an open book. She braced herself, eyes wide, teeth clenched together. She felt the doll's weight as it banged against the suitcase bottom. Instantly, she slammed the lid and threw the suitcase flat. Falling across it, she held it shut until her shaking hands could fasten the clasps. The sound of them clicking into place made her sob with relief. She shoved away the suitcase. It slid across the hall and bumped against the wall. Amelia struggled to her feet, trying not to listen to the frenzied kicking and scratching inside the suitcase.

She switched on the hall light and tried to open the bolt. It was hopelessly wedged. She turned and limped across the living room, glancing at her legs. The bandages were hanging loose. Both legs were streaked with caking blood, some of the gashes still bleeding. She felt at her throat. The cut was still wet. Amelia pressed her shaking lips together. She'd get to a doctor soon now.

Removing the ice pick from its kitchen drawer, she returned to the hall. A cutting sound made her look toward the suitcase. She caught her breath. The knife blade was protruding from the suitcase wall, moving up and down with a sawing motion. Amelia stared at it. She felt as though her body had been turned to stone.

She limped to the suitcase and knelt beside it, looking, with revulsion, at the sawing blade. It was smeared with blood. She tried to pinch it with the fingers of her left hand, pull it out. The blade was twisted, jerked down, and she cried out, snatching back her hand. There was a deep slice in her thumb. Blood ran down across her palm. Amelia pressed the finger to her robe. She felt as though her mind were going blank.

Pushing to her feet, she limped back to the door and started prying at the bolt. She couldn't get it loose. Her thumb began to ache. She pushed the ice pick underneath the bolt socket and tried to force it off the wall. The ice pick point broke off. Amelia slipped and almost fell. She pushed up, whimpering. There was no time, no time. She looked around in desperation.

The window! She could throw the suitcase out! She visualized it tumbling through the darkness. Hastily, she dropped the ice pick, turning toward the suitcase.

She froze. The doll had forced its head and shoulders through the rent in the suitcase wall. Amelia watched it struggling to get out. She felt paralyzed. The twisting doll was staring at her. No, she thought, it isn't true. The doll jerked free its legs and jumped to the floor.

Amelia jerked around and ran into the living room. Her right foot landed on a shard of broken crockery. She felt it cutting deep into her heel and lost her balance. Landing on her side, she thrashed around. The doll came leaping at her. She could see the knife blade glint. She kicked out wildly, knocking back the doll. Lunging to her feet, she reeled into the kitchen, whirled, and started pushing shut the door.

Something kept it from closing. Amelia thought she heard a screaming in her mind. Looking down, she saw the knife and a tiny wooden hand. The doll's arm was wedged between the door and the jamb! Amelia shoved against the door with all her might, aghast at the strength with which the door was pushed the other way. There was a cracking noise. A fierce smile pulled her lips back and she pushed berserkly at the door. The screaming in her mind grew louder, drowning out the sound of splintering wood.

The knife blade sagged. Amelia dropped to her knees and tugged at it. She pulled the knife into the kitchen, seeing the wooden hand and wrist fall from the handle of the knife. With a gagging noise, she struggled to her feet and dropped the knife into the sink. The door slammed hard against her side; the doll rushed in.

Amelia jerked away from it. Picking up the chair, she slung it toward the doll. It jumped aside, then ran around the fallen chair. Amelia snatched the pan of water off the stove and hurled it down. The pan clanged loudly off the floor, spraying water on the doll.

She stared at the doll. It wasn't coming after her. It was trying to climb the sink, leaping up and clutching at the counter side with one hand. It wants the knife, she thought. It has to have its weapon.

She knew abruptly what to do. Stepping over to the stove, she pulled down the broiler door and twisted the knob on all the way. She heard the puffing detonation of the gas as she turned to grab the doll.

She cried out as the doll began to kick and twist, its maddened thrashing flinging her from one side of the kitchen to the other. The screaming filled her mind again and suddenly she knew it was the spirit in the doll that screamed. She slid and crashed against the table, wrenched herself around and, dropping to her knees before the stove, flung the doll inside. She slammed the door and fell against it.

The door was almost driven out. Amelia pressed her shoulder, then her back against it, turning to brace her legs against the wall. She tried to ignore the pounding scrabble of the doll inside the broiler. She watched the red blood pulsing from her heel. The smell of burning wood began to reach her and she closed her eyes. The door was getting hot. She shifted carefully. The kicking and pounding filled her ears. The screaming flooded through her mind. She knew her back would get burned, but she didn't dare to move. The smell of burning wood grew worse. Her foot ached terribly.

Amelia looked up at the electric clock on the wall. It was four minutes to seven. She watched the red second hand revolving slowly. A minute passed. The screaming in her mind was fading now. She shifted uncomfortably, gritting her teeth against the burning heat on her back.

Another minute passed. The kicking and the pounding stopped. The screaming faded more and more. The smell of burning wood had filled the kitchen. There was a pall of gray smoke in the air. That they'll see, Amelia thought. Now that it's over, they'll come and help. That's the way it always is.

She started to ease herself away from the broiler door, ready to throw her weight back against it if she had to. She turned around and got on her knees. The reek of charred wood made her nauseated. She had to know, though. Reaching out, she pulled down the door.

Something dark and stifling rushed across her and she heard the screaming in her mind once more as hotness flooded over her and into her. It was a scream of victory now.

Amelia stood and turned off the broiler. She took a pair of ice tongs from its drawer and lifted out the blackened twist of wood. She dropped it into the sink and ran water over it until the smoke had stopped. Then she went into the bedroom, picked up the telephone and depressed its cradle. After a moment, she released the cradle and dialed her mother's number.

"This is Amelia, Mom," she said. "I'm sorry I acted the way I did. I want us to spend the evening together. It's a little late, though. Can you come by my place and we'll go from here?" She listened. "Good," she said. "I'll wait for you."

Hanging up, she walked into the kitchen, where she slid the longest carving knife from its place in the rack. She went to the front door and pushed back its bolt, which now moved freely. She carried the knife into the living room, took off her bathrobe and danced a dance of hunting, of the joy of hunting, of the joy of the impending kill.

Then she sat down, cross-legged, in the corner. He Who Kills sat, cross-legged, in the corner, in the darkness, waiting for the prey to come.

THE GEEZENSTACKS

BY FREDRIC BROWN

FREDRIC BROWN IS THE MASTER OF THE SHORT SHORT WITH A MULTITUDE OF STORIES TO HIS CREDIT THAT ARE LESS THAN A SINGLE PAGE IN LENGTH (MANY OF WHICH HAVE PUNCH-LINE ENDINGS) . . . BUT IN ORDER TO BE TRULY SCARY A READER NEEDS TO BE DRAWN INTO A CERTAIN DEGREE OF NORMALCY BEFORE THE TRAP IS SPRUNG. "THE GEEZENSTACKS" IS SUCH A STORY. THE CHARACTERS ARE NORMAL PEOPLE, LEADING NORMAL LIVES, UNTIL THEIR CAREFUL ROUTINES AND THE CONTROL OF THEIR OWN LIVES SEEM TO SLIP OUT OF THEIR HANDS AFTER THE ARRIVAL OF YET ANOTHER SEEMINGLY HARMLESS DOLL, OR IN THIS CASE, A WHOLE FAMILY OF THEM.

One of the strange things about it was that Aubrey Walters wasn't at all a strange little girl. She was quite as ordinary as her father and mother, who lived in an apartment on Otis Street, and who played bridge one night a week, went out somewhere another night, and spent the other evenings quietly at home.

Aubrey was nine, and had rather stringy hair and freckles, but at nine one never worries about such things. She got along quite well in the not-too-expensive private school to which her parents sent her, she made friends easily and readily with other children, and she took lessons on a three-quarter-size violin and played it abominably.

Her greatest fault, possibly, was her predeliction for staying up late of nights, and that was the fault of her parents, really, for letting her stay up and dressed until she felt sleepy and wanted to go to bed. Even at five and six, she seldom went to bed before ten o'clock in the evening. And if, during a period of maternal concern, she was put to bed earlier, she never went to sleep anyway. So why not let the child stay up?

Now, at nine years, she stayed up quite as late as her parents did, which was about eleven o'clock on ordinary nights and later when they had company for bridge, or went out for the evening. Then it was later, for they usually took her along. Aubrey enjoyed it, whatever it was. She'd sit still as a mouse in a seat at the theater, or regard them with little-girl seriousness over the rim of a glass of ginger ale while they had a cocktail or two at a night club. She took the noise and the music and the dancing with big-eyed wonder and enjoyed every minute of it.

Sometimes Uncle Richard, her mother's brother, went along with them. She and Uncle Richard were good friends. It was Uncle Richard who gave her the dolls.

"Funny thing happened today," he'd said. "I'm walking down Rodgers Place, past the Mariner Building—you know, Edith; it's where Doc Howard used to have his office—and something thudded on the sidewalk right behind me. And I turned around, and there was this package."

"This package" was a white box a little larger than a shoe box, and it was rather strangely tied with gray ribbon. Sam Walters, Aubrey's father, looked at it curiously.

"Doesn't look dented," he said. "Couldn't have fallen out of a very high window. Was it tied up like that?"

"Just like that. I put the ribbon back on after I opened it and looked in. Oh, I don't mean I opened it then or there. I just stopped and looked up to see who'd dropped it—thinking I'd see somebody looking out of a window. But nobody was, and I picked up the box. It had something in it, not very heavy, and the box and the ribbon looked like—well, not like something somebody'd throw away on purpose. So I stood looking up, and nothing happened, so I shook the box a little and—"

"All right, all right," said Sam Walters. "Spare us the blow-by-blow. You didn't find out who dropped it?"

"Right. And I went up as high as the fourth floor, asking the people whose windows were over the place where I picked it up. They were all home, as it happened, and none of them had ever seen it. I thought it might have fallen off a window ledge. But—"

"What's in it, Dick?" Edith asked.

"Dolls. Four of them. I brought them over this evening for Aubrey. If she wants them."

He untied the package, and Aubrey said, "Oooo, Uncle Richard. They're—they're *lovely*."

Sam said, "Hm. Those look almost more like manikins than dolls, Dick. The way they're dressed, I mean. Must have cost several dollars apiece. Are you sure the owner won't turn up?"

Richard shrugged. "Don't see how he can. As I told you, I went up four floors, asking. Thought from the look of the box and the sound of the thud, it couldn't have come from even that high. And after I opened it, well—look—" He picked up one of the dolls and held it out for Sam Walters' inspection.

"Wax. The heads and hands, I mean. And not one of them cracked. It couldn't have fallen from higher than the second story. Even then, I don't see how—" He shrugged again.

"They're the Geezenstacks," said Aubrey.

"Huh?" Sam asked.

"I'm going to call them the Geezenstacks," Aubrey said. "Look, this one is Papa Geezenstack and this one is Mama Geezenstack, and the little girl one—that's—that's Aubrey Geezenstack. And the other man one, we'll call him Uncle Geezenstack. The little girl's uncle."

Sam chuckled. "Like us, eh? But if Uncle—uh—Geezenstack is Mama Geezenstack's brother, like Uncle Richard is Mama's brother, then his name wouldn't be Geezenstack."

"Just the same, it is," Aubrey said. "They're all Geezenstacks. Papa, will you buy me a house for them?"

"A doll house? Why—" He'd started to say, "Why, sure," but caught his wife's eye and remembered. Aubrey's birthday was only a week off and they'd been wondering what to get her. He changed it hastily to "Why, I don't know. I'll think about it."

IT WAS A BEAUTIFUL DOLL HOUSE. Only one-story high, but quite elaborate, and with a roof that lifted off so one could rearrange the furniture and move the dolls from room to room. It scaled well with the manikins Uncle Richard had brought.

Aubrey was rapturous. All her other playthings went into eclipse and the doings of the Geezenstacks occupied most of her waking thoughts.

It wasn't for quite a while that Sam Walters began to notice, and to think about, the strange aspect of the doings of the Geezenstacks. At first, with a quiet chuckle at the coincidences that followed one another.

And then, with a puzzled look in his eyes.

It wasn't until quite a while later that he got Richard off into a corner. The four of them had just returned from a play. He said, "Uh—Dick."

"Yeah, Sam?"

"These dolls, Dick. Where *did* you get them?"

Richard's eyes stared at him blankly. "What do you mean, Sam? I told you where I got them."

"Yes, but—you weren't kidding, or anything? I mean, maybe you bought them for Aubrey, and thought we'd object if you gave her such an expensive present, so you—uh—"

"No, honest, I didn't."

"But dammit, Dick, they couldn't have fallen out of a window, or dropped out, and not broken. They're wax. Couldn't someone walking behind you—or going by in an auto or something—?"

"There wasn't anyone around, Sam. Nobody at all. I've wondered about it myself. But if I was lying, I wouldn't make up a screwy story like that, would I? I'd just say I found them on a park bench or a seat in a movie. But why are you curious?"

"I—uh—I just got to wondering."

Sam Walters kept on wondering, too.

They were little things, most of them. Like the time Aubrey had said, "Papa Geezenstack didn't go to work this morning. He's in bed, sick."

"So?" Sam had asked. "And what is wrong with the gentleman?"

"Something he ate, I guess."

And the next morning, at breakfast, "And how is Mr. Geezenstack, Aubrey?"

"A little better, but he isn't going to work today yet, the doctor said. Tomorrow, maybe."

And the next day, Mr. Geezenstack went back to work. That, as it happened, was the day Sam Walters came home feeling quite ill, as a result of something he'd eaten for lunch. Yes, he'd missed two days from work. The first time he'd missed work on account of illness in several years.

And some things were quicker than that, and some slower. You couldn't put your finger on it and say, "Well, if this happens to the Geezenstacks, it will happen to us in twenty-four hours." Sometimes it was less than an hour. Sometimes as long as a week.

"Mama and Papa Geezenstack had a quarrel today."

And Sam had tried to avoid that quarrel with Edith, but it seemed he just couldn't.

He'd been quite late getting home, through no fault of his own. It had happened often, but this time Edith took exception. Soft answers failed to turn away wrath, and at last he'd lost his own temper.

"Uncle Geezenstack is going away for a visit." Richard hadn't been out of town for years, but the next week he took a sudden notion to run down to New York. "Pete and Amy, you know. Got a letter from them asking me—"

"When?" Sam asked, almost sharply. "When did you get the letter?"

"Yesterday."

"Then last week you weren't—This sounds like a silly question, Dick, but last week were you thinking about going anywhere? Did you say anything to—to anyone about the possibility of your visiting someone?"

"Lord, no. Hadn't even thought about Pete and Amy for months, till I got their letter yesterday. Want me to stay a week."

"You'll be back in three days—maybe," Sam had said. He wouldn't explain, even when Richard did come back in three days. It sounded just too damn' silly to say that he'd known how long Richard was going to be gone, because that was how long Uncle Geezenstack had been away.

Sam Walters began to watch his daughter, and to wonder. She, of course, was the one who made the Geezenstacks do whatever they did. Was it possible that Aubrey had some strange preternatural insight which caused her, unconsciously, to predict things that were going to happen to the Walters and to Richard?

He didn't, of course, believe in clairvoyance. But was Aubrey clairvoyant?

"Mrs. Geezenstack's going shopping today. She's going to buy a new coat."

That one almost sounded like a put-up job. Edith had smiled at Aubrey and then looked at Sam. "That reminds me, Sam. Tomorrow I'll be downtown, and there's a sale at—"

"But, Edith, these are war times. And you don't *need* a coat."

He'd argued so earnestly that he made himself late for work. Arguing uphill, because he really could afford the coat and she really hadn't bought one for two years. But he couldn't explain that the real reason he didn't want her to buy one was that Mrs. Geezen—Why, it was too silly to say, even to himself.

Edith bought the coat.

Strange, Sam thought, that nobody else noticed those coincidences. But Richard wasn't around all the time, and Edith—well, Edith had the knack of listening to Aubrey's prattle without hearing nine-tenths of it.

"Aubrey Geezenstack brought home her report card today, Papa. She got ninety in arithmetic and eighty in spelling and—"

And two days later, Sam was calling up the headmaster of the school. Calling from a pay station, of course, so nobody would hear him. "Mr. Bradley, I'd like to ask a question that I have a—uh—rather peculiar, but important, reason for asking. Would it be possible for a student at your school to know in advance exactly what grades . . ."

No, not possible. The teachers themselves didn't know, until they'd figured averages, and that hadn't been done until the morning the report cards were made out, and sent home. Yes, yesterday morning, while the children had their play period.

"Sam," Richard said, "you're looking kind of seedy. Business worries? Look, things are going to get better from now on, and with your company, you got nothing to worry about anyway."

"That isn't it, Dick. It—I mean, there isn't anything I'm worrying about. Not exactly. I mean—" And he'd had to wriggle out of the cross-examination by inventing a worry or two for Richard to talk him out of.

He thought about the Geezenstacks a lot. Too much. If only he'd been superstitious, or credulous, it might not have been so bad. But he *wasn't*. That's why each succeeding coincidence hit him a little harder than the last.

Edith and her brother noticed it, and talked about it when Sam wasn't around.

"He *has* been acting queer lately, Dick. I'm—I'm really worried. He acts so— Do you think we could talk him into seeing a doctor or a—"

"A psychiatrist? Um, if we could. But I can't see him doing it, Edith. Something's eating him, and I've tried to pump him about it, but he won't open up. Y'know—I think it's got something to do with those damn' dolls."

"Dolls? You mean Aubrey's dolls? The ones you gave her?"

"Yes, the Geezenstacks. He sits and stares at the doll house. I've heard him ask the kid questions about them, and he was *serious*. I think he's got some delusion or something about them. Or centering on them."

"But, Dick, that's—*awful*."

"Look, Edie, Aubrey isn't as interested in them as she used to be, and— Is there anything she wants very badly?"

"Dancing lessons. But she's already studying violin and I don't think we can let her—"

"Do you think if you promised her dancing lessons if she gave up those dolls, she'd be willing? I think we've got to get them out of the apartment. And I don't want to hurt Aubrey, so—"

"Well—but what would we tell Aubrey?"

"Tell *her* I know a poor family with children who haven't any dolls at all. And—I think she'll agree, if you make it strong enough."

"But, Dick, what will we tell Sam? He'll know better than that."

"Tell Sam, when Aubrey isn't around, that you think she's getting too old for dolls, and that—tell him she's taking an unhealthy interest in them, and that the doctor advises— That sort of stuff."

Aubrey wasn't enthusiastic. She was not as engrossed in the Geezenstacks as she'd been when they were newer, but couldn't she have both the dolls *and* the dancing lessons?

"I don't think you'd have time for both, honey. And there are those poor children who haven't *any* dolls to play with, and you ought to feel sorry for them."

And Aubrey weakened, eventually. Dancing school didn't open for ten days, though, and she wanted to keep the dolls until she could start her lessons. There was argument, but to no avail.

"That's all right, Edie," Richard told her. "Ten days is better than not at all, and— well, if she doesn't give them up voluntarily, it'll start a rumpus and Sam'll find out what we're up to. You haven't mentioned anything to him at all, have you?"

"No. But maybe it would make him feel better to know they were—"

"I wouldn't. We don't know just what it is about them that fascinates or repels him. Wait till it happens, and then tell him. Aubrey has already given them away. Or *he* might raise some objection or want to keep them. If I get them out of the place first, he can't."

"You're right, Dick. And Aubrey won't tell him, because I told her the dancing lessons are going to be a surprise for her father, and she can't tell him what's going to happen to the dolls without telling the other side of the deal."

"Swell, Edith."

It might have been better if Sam had known. Or maybe everything would have happened just the same, if he had.

Poor Sam. He had a bad moment the very next evening. One of Aubrey's friends from school was there, and they were playing with the doll house. Sam watching them, trying to look less interested than he was. Edith was knitting and Richard, who had just come in, was reading the paper.

Only Sam was listening to the children and heard the suggestion.

". . . and then let's have a play funeral, Aubrey. Just pretend one of them is—"

Sam Walters let out a sort of strangled cry and almost fell getting across the room.

There was a bad moment, then, but Edith and Richard managed to pass it off casually enough, outwardly. Edith discovered it was time for Aubrey's little friend to leave, and she exchanged a significant glance with Richard and they both escorted the girl to the door.

Whispered, "Dick, did you *see*—"

"Something is wrong, Edie. Maybe we shouldn't wait. After all, Aubrey has agreed to give them up, and—"

Back in the living room, Sam was still breathing a bit hard. Aubrey looked at him almost as though she was afraid of him. It was the first time she'd ever looked at him like that, and Sam felt ashamed. He said, "Honey, I'm sorry I—But listen, you'll promise me you'll *never* have a play funeral for one of your dolls? Or pretend one of them is badly sick or has an accident or anything bad at all? Promise?"

"Sure, Papa. I'm—I'm going to put them away for tonight."

She put the lid on the doll house and went back toward the kitchen.

In the hallway, Edie said, "I'll—I'll get Aubrey alone and fix it with her. You talk to Sam. Tell him—look, let's go out tonight, go somewhere and get him away from everything. See if he will."

Sam was still staring at the doll house.

"Let's get some excitement, Sam," Richard said. "How's about going out somewhere? We've been sticking too close to home. It'll do us good."

Sam took a deep breath. "Okay, Dick. If you say so. I—I could use a little fun, I guess."

Edie came back with Aubrey, and she winked at her brother. "You men go on downstairs and get a cab from the stand around the corner. Aubrey and I'll be down by the time you bring it."

Behind Sam's back, as the men were putting on their coats, Richard gave Edith an inquiring look and she nodded.

Outside, there was a heavy fog; one could see only a few yards ahead. Sam insisted that Richard wait at the door for Edith and Aubrey while he went to bring the cab. The woman and girl came down just before Sam got back.

Richard asked, "Did you—?"

"Yes, Dick. I was going to throw them away, but I gave them away instead. That way they're *gone*; he might have wanted to hunt in the rubbish and find them if I'd just thrown—"

"Gave them away? To whom?"

"Funniest thing, Dick. I opened the door and there was an old woman going by in the back hall. Don't know which of the apartments she came from, but she must be a scrubwoman or something, although she looked like a witch really, but when she saw those dolls I had in my hands—"

"Here comes the cab," Dick said. "You gave them to her?"

"Yes, it was funny. She said, *'Mine? To Keep? Forever?'* Wasn't that a strange way of asking it? But I laughed and said, 'Yes, ma'am. Yours forev—' "

She broke off, for the shadowy outline of the taxi was at the curb, and Sam opened the door and called out, "Come on, folks!"

Aubrey skipped across the sidewalk into the cab, and the others followed. It started.

The fog was thicker now. They could not see out the windows at all. It was as though a gray wall pressed against the glass, as though the world outside was gone, completely and utterly. Even the windshield, from where they sat, was a gray blank.

"How can he drive so fast?" Richard asked, and there was an edge of nervousness in his voice. "By the way, where are we going, Sam?"

"By George," Sam said, "I forgot to tell her."

"Her?"

"Yeah. Woman driver. They've got them all over now. I'll—"

He leaned forward and tapped on the glass, and the woman turned.

Edith saw her face, and screamed.

PALADIN OF THE LOST HOUR

BY HARLAN ELLISON

In "The Whimper of Whipped Dogs" we saw Harlan Ellison at his darkest. In "Paladin of the Lost Hour" we see him masterfully moving us from despair to hope and maybe to optimism. It is a story about loss and regret and an enchanted watch that controls the existence of time as we know it, and how real magic can exist in our lives if we just give it a chance. (Like its predecessor, this too, was yet another of Harlan's award-winning tales of the fantastic.)

This was an old man. Not an incredibly old man: obsolete, spavined; not as worn as the sway-backed stone steps ascending the Pyramid of the Sun to an ancient temple; not yet a relic. But even so, a *very* old man, this old man perched on an antique shooting stick, its handles opened to form a seat, its spike thrust at an angle into the soft ground and trimmed grass of the cemetery. Gray, thin rain misted down at almost the same angle as that at which the spike pierced the ground. The winter-barren trees lay flat and black against an aluminum sky, unmoving in the chill wind. An old man sitting at the foot of a grave mound whose headstone had tilted slightly when the earth had settled; sitting in the rain and speaking to someone below.

"They tore it down, Minna.

"I tell you, they must have bought off a councilman.

"Came in with bulldozers at six o'clock in the morning, and you *know* that's not legal. There's a Municipal Code. Supposed to hold off till at least seven on weekdays, eight on the weekend; but there they were at six, even *before* six, barely light for godsakes. Thought they'd sneak in and do it before the neighborhood got wind of it and called the landmarks committee. Sneaks: they come on *holidays*, can you imagine!

"But I was out there waiting for them, and I told them, 'You can't do it, that's Code number 91.3002, sub-section E,' and they lied and said they had special permission, so I said to the big muckymuck in charge, 'Let's see your waiver permit,' and he said the Code didn't apply in this case because it was supposed to be only for grading, and since they were demolishing and not grading, they could start whenever they felt like it. So I told him I'd call the police, then, because it came under the heading of Disturbing the Peace, and he said . . . well, I know you hate that kind of language, old girl, so I won't tell you what he said, but you can imagine.

"So I called the police, and gave them my name, and of course they didn't get there till almost quarter after seven (which is what makes me think they bought off a councilman), and by then those 'dozers had leveled most of it. Doesn't take long, you know that.

"And I don't suppose it's as great a loss as, maybe, say, the Great Library of Alexandria, but it was the last of the authentic Deco design drive-ins, and the carhops still served you on roller skates, and it was a landmark, and just about the only place left in the city where you could still get a decent grilled cheese sandwich pressed very flat on the grill by one of those weights they used to use, made with real cheese and not that rancid plastic they cut into squares and call it 'cheese food.'

"Come, old dear, gone and mourned. And I understand they plan to put up another one of those mini-malls on the site, just ten blocks away from one that's already there, and you know what's going to happen: this new one will drain off the traffic from the older one, and then that one will fail the way they all do when the next one gets built, you'd think they'd see some history in it; but no, they never learn. And you should have seen the crowd by seven-thirty. All ages, even some of those kids painted like aborigines, with torn leather clothing. Even they came to protest. Terrible language, but at least they were concerned. And nothing could stop it. They just whammed it, and down it went.

"I do so miss you today, Minna. No more good grilled cheese." Said the *very* old man to the ground. And now he was crying softly, and now the wind rose, and the mist rain stippled his overcoat.

Nearby, yet at a distance, Billy Kinetta stared down at another grave. He could see the old man over there off to his left, but he took no further notice. The wind whipped the vent of his trenchcoat. His collar was up but rain trickled down his neck. This was a younger man, not yet thirty-five. Unlike the old man, Billy Kinetta neither cried nor spoke to memories of someone who had once listened. He might have been a geomancer, so silently did he stand, eyes toward the ground.

One of these men was black; the other was white.

BEYOND THE HIGH, spiked-iron fence surrounding the cemetery two boys crouched, staring through the bars, through the rain; at the men absorbed by grave matters, by matters of graves. These were not really boys. They were legally young men. One was nineteen, the other two months beyond twenty. Both were legally old enough to vote, to drink alcoholic beverages, to drive a car. Neither would reach the age of Billy Kinetta.

One of them said, "Let's take the old man."

The other responded, "You think the guy in the trenchcoat'll get in the way?"

The first one smiled; and a mean little laugh. "I sure as shit hope so." He wore, on his right hand, a leather carnaby glove with the fingers cut off, small round metal studs in a pattern along the line of his knuckles. He made a fist, flexed, did it again.

They went under the spiked fence at a point where erosion had created a shallow gully. "Sonofabitch!" one of them said, as he slid through on his stomach. It was muddy. The front of his sateen roadie jacket was filthy. "Sonofabitch!" He was speaking in general of the fence, the sliding under, the muddy ground, the universe in total. And the old man, who would now *really* get the crap kicked out of him for making this fine sateen roadie jacket filthy.

They sneaked up on him from the left, as far from the young guy in the trenchcoat as they could. The first one kicked out the shooting stick with a short, sharp, downward movement he had learned in his Tae Kwon Do class. It was called the *yup-chagi*. The old man went over backward.

Then they were on him, the one with the filthy sonofabitch sateen roadie jacket punching at the old man's neck and the side of his face as he dragged him around by the collar of the overcoat. The other one began ransacking the coat pockets, ripping the fabric to get his hand inside.

The old man commenced to scream. "Protect me! You've got to protect me . . . it's necessary to protect me!"

The one pillaging pockets froze momentarily. What the hell kind of thing is that for this old fucker to be saying? Who the hell does he think'll protect him? Is he asking *us* to protect him? I'll protect you, scumbag! I'll kick in your fuckin' lung! "Shut 'im up!" he whispered urgently to his friend. "Stick a fist in his mouth!" Then his hand, wedged in an inside jacket pocket, closed over something. He tried to get his hand loose, but the jacket and coat and the old man's body had wound around his wrist. "C'mon loose, motherfuckah!" he said to the very old man, who was still screaming for protection. The other young man was making huffing sounds, as dark as mud, as he slapped at the rain-soaked hair of his victim. "I can't . . . he's all twisted 'round . . . getcher hand outta there so's I can . . ." Screaming, the old man had doubled under, locking their hands on his person.

And then the pillager's fist came loose, and he was clutching—for an instant—a gorgeous pocket watch.

What used to be called a turnip watch.

The dial face was *cloisonné*, exquisite beyond the telling.

The case was of silver, so bright it seemed blue.

The hands, cast as arrows of time, were gold. They formed a shallow V at precisely eleven o'clock. This was happening at 3:45 in the afternoon, with rain and wind.

The timepiece made no sound, no sound at all.

Then: there was space all around the watch, and in that space in the palm of the hand, there was heat. Intense heat for just a moment, just long enough for the hand to open.

The watch glided out of the boy's palm and levitated.

"Help me! You *must* protect me!"

Billy Kinetta heard the shrieking, but did not see the pocket watch floating in the air above the astonished young man. It was silver, and it was end-on toward him, and the rain was silver and slanting; and he did not see the watch hanging free in the air, even when the furious young man disentangled himself and leaped for it. Billy did not see the watch rise just so much, out of reach of the mugger.

Billy Kinetta saw two boys, two young men of ratpack age, beating someone much older; and he went for them. Pow, like that!

Thrashing his legs, the old man twisted around—over, under—as the boy holding him by the collar tried to land a punch to put him away. Who would have thought the old man to have had so much battle in him?

A flapping shape, screaming something unintelligible, hit the center of the group at full speed. The carnaby-gloved hand reaching for the watch grasped at empty air one moment, and the next was buried under its owner as the boy was struck a crack-back block that threw him face-first into the soggy ground. He tried to rise, but something stomped him at the base of his spine; something kicked him twice in the kidneys; something rolled over him like a flash flood.

Twisting, twisting, the very old man put his thumb in the right eye of the boy clutching his collar.

The great trenchcoated maelstrom that was Billy Kinetta whirled into the boy as he let loose of the old man on the ground and, howling, slapped a palm against his stinging eye. Billy locked his fingers and delivered a roundhouse wallop that sent the boy reeling backward to fall over Minna's tilted headstone.

Billy's back was to the old man. He did not see the miraculous pocket watch smoothly descend through rain that did not touch it, to hover in front of the old man. He did not see the old man reach up, did not see the timepiece snuggle into an arthritic hand, did not see the old man return the turnip to an inside jacket pocket.

Wind, rain and Billy Kinetta pummeled two young men of a legal age that made them accountable for their actions. There was no thought of the knife stuck down in one boot, no chance to reach it, no moment when the wild thing let them rise. So they crawled. They scrabbled across the muddy ground, the slippery grass, over graves and out of his reach. They ran; falling, rising, falling again; away, without looking back.

Billy Kinetta, breathing heavily, knees trembling, turned to help the old man to his feet; and found him standing, brushing dirt from his overcoat, snorting in anger and mumbling to himself.

"Are you all right?"

For a moment the old man's recitation of annoyance continued, then he snapped his chin down sharply as if marking end to the situation, and looked at his cavalry to the rescue. "That was very good, young fella. Considerable style you've got there."

Billy Kinetta stared at him wide-eyed. "Are you sure you're okay?" He reached over and flicked several blades of wet grass from the shoulder of the old man's overcoat.

"I'm fine. I'm fine but I'm wet and I'm cranky. Let's go somewhere and have a nice cup of Earl Grey."

There had been a look on Billy Kinetta's face as he stood with lowered eyes, staring at the grave he had come to visit. The emergency had removed that look. Now it returned.

"No, thanks. If you're okay. I've got to do some things."

The old man felt himself all over, meticulously, as he replied, "I'm only superficially bruised. Now if I were an old woman, instead of a spunky old man, same age though, I'd have lost considerable of the calcium in my bones, and those two would have done me some mischief. Did you know that women lose a considerable part of their calcium when they reach my age? I read a report." Then he paused, and said shyly, "Come on, why don't you and I sit and chew the fat over a nice cup of tea?"

Billy shook his head with bemusement, smiling despite himself. "You're something else, Dad. I don't even know you."

"I like that."

"What: that I don't know you?"

"No, that you called me 'Dad' and not 'Pop.' I *hate* 'Pop.' Always makes me think the wise-apple wants to snap off my cap with a bottle opener. Now *Dad* has a ring of respect to it. I like that right down to the ground. Yes, I believe we should find someplace warm and quiet to sit and get to know each other. After all, you saved my life. And you know what that means in the Orient."

Billy was smiling continuously now. "In the first place, I doubt very much I saved your life. Your wallet, maybe. And in the second place, I don't even know your name; what would we have to talk about?"

"Gaspar," he said, extending his hand. "That's a first name. Gaspar. Know what it means?"

Billy shook his head.

"See, already we have something to talk about."

So Billy, still smiling, began walking Gaspar out of the cemetery. "Where do you live? I'll take you home."

They were on the street, approaching Billy Kinetta's 1979 Cutlass. "Where I live is too far for now. I'm beginning to feel a bit peaky. I'd like to lie down for a minute. We can just go on over to your place, if that doesn't bother you. For a few minutes. A cup of tea. Is that all right?"

He was standing beside the Cutlass, looking at Billy with an old man's expectant smile, waiting for him to unlock the door and hold it for him till he'd placed his still-calcium-rich but nonetheless old bones in the passenger seat. Billy stared at him, trying to figure out what was at risk if he unlocked that door. Then he snorted a tiny laugh, unlocked the door, held it for Gaspar as he seated himself, slammed it and went around to unlock the other side and get in. Gaspar reached across and thumbed up the door lock knob. And they drove off together in the rain.

Through all of this the timepiece made no sound, no sound at all.

LIKE GASPAR, Billy Kinetta was alone in the world.

His three-room apartment was the vacuum in which he existed. It was furnished, but if one stepped out into the hallway and, for all the money in all the numbered accounts in all the banks in Switzerland, one were asked to describe those furnishings, one would come away no richer than before. The apartment was charisma poor. It was a place to come when all other possibilities had been expended. Nothing green, nothing alive, existed in those boxes. No eyes looked back from the walls. Neither warmth nor chill marked those spaces. It was a place to wait.

Gaspar leaned his closed shooting stick, now a walking stick with handles, against the bookcase. He studied the titles of the paperbacks stacked haphazardly on the shelves.

From the kitchenette came the sound of water running into a metal pan. Then tin on cast iron. Then the hiss of gas and the flaring of a match as it was struck; and the pop of the gas being lit.

"Many years ago," Gaspar said, taking out a copy of Moravia's *The Adolescents* and thumbing it as he spoke, "I had a library of books, oh, thousands of books— never could bear to toss one out, not even the bad ones—and when folks would come to the house to visit they'd look around at all the nooks and crannies stuffed with books; and if they were the sort of folks who don't snuggle with books, they'd always ask the same dumb question." He waited a moment for a response and when none was forthcoming (the sound of china cups on sink tile), he said, "Guess what the question was."

From the kitchen, without much interest: "No idea."

"They'd always ask it with the kind of voice people use in the presence of large sculptures in museums. They'd ask me, 'Have you read all these books?' " He waited again, but Billy Kinetta was not playing the game. "Well, young fella, after a while the same dumb question gets asked a million times, you get sorta snappish about it. And it came to annoy me more than a little bit. Till I finally figured out the right answer.

"And you know what that answer was? Go ahead, take a guess."

Billy appeared in the kitchenette doorway. "I suppose you told them you'd read a lot of them but not all of them."

Gaspar waved the guess away with a flapping hand. "Now what good would that have done? They wouldn't know they'd asked a dumb question, but I didn't want to insult them, either. So when they'd ask if I'd read all those books, I'd say, 'Hell, no. Who wants a library full of books you've already read?' "

Billy laughed despite himself. He scratched at his hair with idle pleasure, and shook his head at the old man's verve. "Gaspar, you are a wild old man. You retired?"

The old man walked carefully to the most comfortable chair in the room, an over-stuffed Thirties-style lounge that had been reupholstered many times before Billy Kinetta had purchased it at the American Cancer Society Thrift Shop. He sank into it with a sigh. "No sir, I am not by any means retired. Still very active."

"Doing what, if I'm not prying?"

"Doing ombudsman."

"You mean, like a consumer advocate? Like Ralph Nader?"

"Exactly. I watch out for things. I listen, I pay some attention; and if I do it right, sometimes I can even make a little difference. Yes, like Mr. Nader. A very fine man."

"And you were at the cemetery to see a relative?"

Gaspar's face settled into an expression of loss. "My dear old girl. My wife, Minna. She's been gone, well, it was twenty years in January." He sat silently staring inward for a while, then: "She was everything to me. The nice part was that I knew how important we were to each other; we discussed, well, just *everything*. I miss that the most, telling her what's going on.

"I go to see her every other day.

"I used to go every day. But. It. Hurt. Too much."

They had tea. Gaspar sipped and said it was very nice, but had Billy ever tried Earl Grey? Billy said he didn't know what that was, and Gaspar said he would bring him a tin, that it was splendid. And they chatted. Finally, Gaspar asked, "And who were you visiting?"

Billy pressed his lips together. "Just a friend." And would say no more. Then he sighed and said, "Well, listen, I have to go to work."

"Oh? What do you do?"

The answer came slowly. As if Billy Kinetta wanted to be able to say that he was in computers, or owned his own business, or held a position of import. "I'm night manager at a 7-Eleven."

"I'll bet you meet some fascinating people coming in late for milk or one of those slushies," Gaspar said gently. He seemed to understand.

Billy smiled. He took the kindness as it was intended. "Yeah, the cream of high society. That is, when they're not threatening to shoot me through the head if I don't open the safe."

"Let me ask you a favor," Gaspar said. "I'd like a little sanctuary, if you think it's all right. Just a little rest. I could lie down on the sofa for a bit. Would that be all right? You trust me to stay here while you're gone, young fella?"

Billy hesitated only a moment. The very old man seemed okay, not a crazy, certainly not a thief. And what was there to steal? Some tea that wasn't even Earl Grey?

"Sure. That'll be okay. But I won't be coming back till two A.M. So just close the door behind you when you go; it'll lock automatically."

They shook hands, Billy shrugged into his still-wet trenchcoat, and he went to the door. He paused to look back at Gaspar sitting in the lengthening shadows as evening came on. "It was nice getting to know you, Gaspar."

"You can make that a mutual pleasure, Billy. You're a nice young fella."

And Billy went to work, alone as always.

WHEN HE CAME HOME AT TWO, prepared to open a can of Hormel chili, he found the table set for dinner; with the scent of an elegant beef stew enriching the apartment. There were new potatoes and stir-fried carrots and zucchini that had been lightly battered to delicate crispness. And cupcakes. White cake with chocolate frosting. From a bakery.

And in that way, as gently as that, Gaspar insinuated himself into Billy Kinetta's apartment and his life.

As they sat with tea and cupcakes, Billy said, "You don't have anyplace to go, do you?"

The old man smiled and made one of those deprecating movements of the head. "Well, I'm not the sort of fella who can bear to be homeless, but at the moment I'm what vaudevillians used to call 'at liberty.' "

"If you want to stay on a time, that would be okay," Billy said. "It's not very roomy here, but we seem to get on all right."

"That's strongly kind of you, Billy. Yes, I'd like to be your roommate for a while. Won't be too long, though. My doctor tells me I'm not long for this world." He paused, looked into the teacup and said softly, "I have to confess . . . I'm a little frightened. To go. Having someone to talk to would be a great comfort."

And Billy said, without preparation, "I was visiting the grave of a man who was in my rifle company in Viet Nam. I go there sometimes." But there was such pain in his words that Gaspar did not press him for details.

So the hours passed, as they will with or without permission, and when Gaspar asked Billy if they could watch the television, to catch an early newscast, and Billy tuned in the old set just in time to pick up dire reports of another aborted disarmament talk, and Billy shook his head and observed that it wasn't only Gaspar who was frightened of something like death, Gaspar chuckled, patted Billy on the knee and said, with unassailable assurance, "Take my word for it, Billy . . . it isn't going to happen. No nuclear holocaust. Trust me, when I tell you this: it'll never happen. Never, never, not ever."

Billy smiled wanly. "And why not? What makes *you* so sure . . . got some special inside information?"

And Gaspar pulled out the magnificent timepiece, which Billy was seeing for the first time, and he said. "It's not going to happen because it's only eleven o'clock."

Billy stared at the watch, which read 11:00 precisely. He consulted his wristwatch. "Hate to tell you this, but your watch has stopped. It's almost five-thirty."

Gaspar smiled his own certain smile. "No, it's eleven."

And they made up the sofa for the very old man, who placed his pocket change and his fountain pen and the sumptuous turnip watch on the now-silent television set, and they went to sleep.

ONE DAY BILLY WENT OFF while Gaspar was washing the lunch dishes, and when he came back, he had a large paper bag from Toys R Us.

Gaspar came out of the kitchenette rubbing a plate with a souvenir dish towel from Niagara Falls, New York. He stared at Billy and the bag. "What's in the bag?" Billy inclined his head, and indicated the very old man should join him in the middle of the room. Then he sat down crosslegged on the floor, and dumped the contents of the bag. Gaspar stared with startlement, and sat down beside him.

So for two hours they played with tiny cars that turned into robots when the sections were unfolded.

Gaspar was excellent at figuring out all the permutations of the Transformers, Starriors and GoBots. He played well.

Then they went for a walk. "I'll treat you to a matinee," Gaspar said. "But no films with Karen Black, Sandy Dennis or Meryl Streep. They're always crying. Their noses are always red. I can't stand that."

They started to cross the avenue. Stopped at the light was this year's Cadillac Brougham, vanity license plates, ten coats of acrylic lacquer and two coats of clear (with a little retarder in the final "color coat" for a slow dry) of a magenta hue so rich that it approximated the shade of light shining through a decanter filled with Château Lafite-Rothschild 1945.

The man driving the Cadillac had no neck. His head sat thumped down hard on the shoulders. He stared straight ahead, took one last deep pull on the cigar, and threw it out the window. The still-smoking butt landed directly in front of Gaspar as he passed the car. The old man stopped, stared down at this coprolitic metaphor, and then stared at the driver. The eyes behind the wheel, the eyes of a macaque, did not waver from the stoplight's red circle. Just outside the window, someone was looking in, but the eyes of the rhesus were on the red circle.

A line of cars stopped behind the Brougham.

Gaspar continued to stare at the man in the Cadillac for a moment, and then, with creaking difficulty, he bent and picked up the smoldering butt of stogie.

The old man walked the two steps to the car—as Billy watched in confusion—thrust his face forward till it was mere inches from the driver's profile, and said with extreme sweetness, "I think you dropped this in our living room."

And as the glazed simian eyes turned to stare directly into the pedestrian's face, nearly nose-to-nose, Gaspar casually flipped the butt with its red glowing tip, into the back seat of the Cadillac, where it began to burn a hole in the fine Corinthian leather.

Three things happened simultaneously:

The driver let out a howl, tried to see the butt in his rearview mirror, could not get the angle, tried to look over his shoulder into the back seat but without a neck could not perform that feat of agility, put the car into neutral, opened his door and stormed into the street trying to grab Gaspar. "You fuckin' bastid, whaddaya think you're doin' tuh my car you asshole bastid, I'll kill ya . . ."

Billy's hair stood on end as he saw what Gaspar was doing; he rushed back the short distance in the crosswalk to grab the old man; Gaspar would not be dragged away, stood smiling with unconcealed pleasure at the mad bull rampaging and screaming of the hysterical driver. Billy yanked as hard as he could and Gaspar began to move away, around the front of the Cadillac, toward the far curb. Still grinning with octogeneric charm.

The light changed.

These three things happened in the space of five seconds, abetted by the impatient honking of the cars behind the Brougham; as the light turned green.

Screaming, dragging, honking, as the driver found he could not do three things at once: he could not go after Gaspar while the traffic was clanging at him; could not let go of the car door to crawl into the back seat from which now came the stench of charring leather that could not be rectified by an inexpensive Tijuana tuck-'n-roll; could not save his back seat and at the same time stave off the hostility of a dozen drivers cursing and honking. He trembled there, torn three ways, doing nothing.

Billy dragged Gaspar.

Out of the crosswalk. Out of the street. Onto the curb. Up the side street. Into the alley. Through a backyard. To the next street over away from the avenue.

Puffing with the exertion, Billy stopped at last, five houses up the street. Gaspar was still grinning, chuckling softly with unconcealed pleasure at his puckish ways. Billy turned on him with wild gesticulations and babble.

"You're *nuts*!"

"How about that?" the old man said, giving Billy an affectionate poke in the bicep.

"Nuts! Looney! That guy would've torn off your head! What the hell's wrong with you, old man? Are you out of your boots?"

"I'm not crazy. I'm responsible."

"Responsible!?! Responsible, fer chrissakes? For what? For all the butts every yotz throws into the street?"

The old man nodded. "For butts, and trash, and pollution, and toxic waste dumping in the dead of night; for bushes, and cactus, and the baobab tree; for pippin apples and even lima beans, which I despise. You show me someone who'll eat lima beans without being at gun-point, I'll show you a pervert!"

Billy was screaming. "What the hell are you talking about?"

"I'm also responsible for dogs and cats and guppies and cockroaches and the President of the United States and Jonas Salk and your mother and the entire chorus line at the Sands Hotel in Las Vegas. Also their choreographer."

"Who do you think you are? God?"

"Don't be sacrilegious. I'm too old to wash your mouth out with laundry soap. Of course, I'm not God. I'm just an old man. *But I'm responsible*."

Gaspar started to walk away, toward the corner and the avenue, and a resumption of their route. Billy stood where the old man's words had pinned him.

"Come on, young fella," Gaspar said, walking backward to speak to him, "we'll miss the beginning of the movie. I hate that."

BILLY HAD FINISHED EATING, and they were sitting in the dimness of the apartment, only the lamp in the corner lit. The old man had gone to the County Art Museum and had bought inexpensive prints—Max Ernst, Gérôme, Richard Dadd, a subtle Feininger—which he had mounted in Insta-Frames. They sat in silence for a time, relaxing; then murmuring trivialities in a pleasant undertone.

Finally, Gaspar said, "I've been thinking a lot about my dying. I like what Woody Allen said."

Billy slid to a more comfortable position in the lounger. "What was that?"

"He said: I don't mind dying, I just don't want to be there when it happens."

Billy snickered.

"I feel something like that, Billy. I'm not afraid to go, but I don't want to leave Minna entirely. The times I spend with her, talking to her, well, it gives me the feeling we're still in touch. When I go, that's the end of Minna. She'll be well and truly dead. We never had any children, almost everyone who knew us is gone, no relatives. And we never did anything important that anyone would put in a record book, so that's the end of us. For me, I don't mind; but I wish there was someone who knew about Minna . . . she was a remarkable person."

So Billy said, "Tell me. I'll remember for you."

MEMORIES IN NO PARTICULAR ORDER. Some as strong as ropes that could pull the ocean ashore. Some that shimmered and swayed in the faintest breeze like spiderwebs. The entire person, all the little movements, that dimple that appeared when she was amused at something foolish he had said. Their youth together, their love, the procession of their days toward middle age. The small cheers and the pain of dreams never realized. So much about *him*, as he spoke of *her*. His voice soft and warm and filled with a longing so deep and true that he had to stop frequently because the words broke and would not come out till he had thought away some of the passion. He thought of her and was glad. He had gathered her together, all her dowry of love and taking care of him, her clothes and the way she wore them, her favorite knickknacks, a few clever remarks: and he packed it all up and delivered it to a new repository.

The very old man gave Minna to Billy Kinetta for safekeeping.

DAWN HAD COME. The light filtering in through the blinds was saffron. "Thank you, Dad," Billy said. He could not name the feeling that had taken him hours earlier. But he said this: "I've never had to be responsible for anything, or anyone, in my whole life. I never belonged to anybody . . . I don't know why. It didn't bother me, because I didn't know any other way to be."

Then his position changed, there in the lounger. He sat up in a way that Gaspar thought was important. As if Billy were about to open the secret box buried at his center. And Billy spoke so softly the old man had to strain to hear him.

"I didn't even know him.

"We were defending the airfield at Danang. Did I tell you we were 1st Battalion, 9th Marines? Charlie was massing for a big push out of Quang Ngai province, south of us. Looked as if they were going to try to take the provincial capital. My rifle company was assigned to protect the perimeter. They kept sending in patrols to bite us. Every day we'd lose some poor bastard who scratched his head when he shouldn't of. It was June, late in June, cold and a lot of rain. The foxholes were hip-deep in water.

"Flares first. Our howitzers started firing. Then the sky was full of tracers, and I started to turn toward the bushes when I heard something coming, and these two main-force regulars in dark blue uniforms came toward me. I could see them so clearly. Long black hair. All crouched over. And they started firing. And that goddam carbine seized up, wouldn't fire; and I pulled out the banana clip, tried to slap in another, but they saw me and just turned a couple of AK-47s on me . . . God, I remember everything slowed down . . . I looked at those things, seven-point-six-two-millimeter assault rifles they were . . . I got crazy for a second, tried to figure out in my own mind if they were Russian-made, or Chinese, or Czech, or North Korean. And it was so bright from the flares I could see them starting to squeeze off the rounds, and then from out of nowhere this lance corporal jumped out at them and yelled somedamnthing like, 'Hey, you VC fucks, looka here!' except it wasn't that . . . I never could recall what he said actually . . . and they turned to brace him . . . and they opened him up like a Baggie full of blood . . . and he was all over me, and the bushes, and oh god there was pieces of him floating on the water I was standing . . ."

Billy was heaving breath with impossible weight. His hands moved in the air before his face without pattern or goal. He kept looking into far corners of the dawn-lit room as if special facts might present themselves to fill out the reasons behind what he was saying.

"Aw, geezus, he was *floating* on the water . . . aw, christ, *he got in my boots*!" Then a wail of pain so loud it blotted out the sound of traffic beyond the apartment; and he began to moan, but not cry; and the moaning kept on; and Gaspar came from the sofa and held him and said such words as *it's all right*, but they might not have been those words, or *any* words.

And pressed against the old man's shoulder, Billy Kinetta ran on only half sane: "He wasn't my friend, I never knew him, I'd never talked to him, but I'd seen him, he was just this guy, and there wasn't any reason to do that, he didn't know whether I was a good guy or a shit or anything, so why did he do that? He didn't need to do that. They wouldn't of seen him. He was dead before I killed them. He was gone already. I never got to say thank you or thank you or . . . *anything!*

"Now he's in that grave, so I came here to live, so I can go there, but I try and try to say thank you, and he's dead, and he can't hear me, he can't hear nothin', he's just down there, down in the ground, and I can't say thank you . . . oh, geezus, geezus, why don't he hear me, I just want to say thanks . . ."

Billy Kinetta wanted to assume the responsibility for saying thanks, but that was possible only on a night that would never come again; and this was the day.

Gaspar took him to the bedroom and put him down to sleep in exactly the same way he would soothe an old, sick dog.

Then he went to his sofa, and because it was the only thing he could imagine saying, he murmured, "He'll be all right, Minna. Really he will."

WHEN BILLY LEFT for the 7-Eleven the next evening, Gaspar was gone. It was an alternate day, and that meant he was out at the cemetery. Billy fretted that he shouldn't be there alone, but the old man had a way of taking care of himself. Billy was not smiling as he thought of his friend, and the word *friend* echoed as he realized that, yes, this was his friend, truly and really his friend. He wondered how old Gaspar was, and how soon Billy Kinetta would be once again what he had always been: alone.

When he returned to the apartment at two-thirty, Gaspar was asleep, cocooned in his blanket on the sofa. Billy went in and tried to sleep, but hours later, when sleep would not come, when thoughts of murky water and calcium night light on dark foliage kept him staring at the bedroom ceiling, he came out of the room for a drink of water. He wandered around the living room, not wanting to be by himself even if the only companionship in this sleepless night was breathing heavily, himself in sleep.

He stared out the window. Clouds lay in chiffon strips across the sky. The squealing of tires from the street.

Sighing, idle in his movement around the room, he saw the old man's pocket watch lying on the coffee table beside the sofa. He walked to the table. If the watch was still stopped at eleven o'clock, perhaps he would borrow it and have it repaired. It would be a nice thing to do for Gaspar. The old man loved that beautiful timepiece.

Billy bent to pick it up.

The watch, stopped at the V of eleven precisely, levitated at an angle, floating away from him.

Billy Kinetta felt a shiver travel down his back to burrow in at the base of his spine. He reached for the watch hanging in air before him. It floated away just enough that his fingers massaged empty space. He tried to catch it. The watch eluded him, lazily turning away like an opponent who knows he is in no danger of being struck from behind.

Then Billy realized Gaspar was awake. Turned away from the sofa, nonetheless he knew the old man was observing him. And the blissful floating watch.

He looked at Gaspar.

They did not speak for a long time.

Then: "I'm going back to sleep," Billy said. Quietly.

"I think you have some questions," Gaspar replied.

"Questions? No, of course not, Dad. Why in the world would I have questions? I'm still asleep." But that was not the truth, because he had not been asleep that night.

"Do you know what 'Gaspar' means? Do you remember the three wise men of the Bible, the Magi?"

"I don't want any frankincense and myrrh. I'm going back to bed. I'm going now. You see, I'm going right now."

" 'Gaspar' means master of the treasure, keeper of the secrets, paladin of the palace." Billy was staring at him, not walking into the bedroom; just staring at him. As the elegant timepiece floated to the old man, who extended his hand palm-up to receive it. The watch nestled in his hand, unmoving, and it made no sound, no sound at all.

"You go back to bed. But will you go out to the cemetery with me tomorrow? It's important."

"Why?"

"Because I believe I'll be dying tomorrow."

It was a nice day, cool and clear. Not at all a day for dying, but neither had been many such days in Southeast Asia, and death had not been deterred.

They stood at Minna's gravesite, and Gaspar opened his shooting stick to form a seat; and he thrust the spike into the ground; and he settled onto it, and sighed, and said to Billy Kinetta, "I'm growing cold as that stone."

"Do you want my jacket?"

"No, I'm cold inside." He looked around at the sky, at the grass, at the rows of markers. "I've been responsible, for all of this, and more."

"You've said that before."

"Young fella, are you by any chance familiar, in your reading, with an old novel by James Hilton called *Lost Horizon*? Perhaps you saw the movie. It was a wonderful movie, actually much better than the book. Mr. Capra's greatest achievement. A human testament. Ronald Colman was superb. Do you know the story?"

"Yes."

"Do you remember the High Lama, played by Sam Jaffe? His name was Father Perrault?"

"Yes."

"Do you remember how he passed on the caretakership of that magical hidden world, Shangri-La, to Ronald Colman?"

"Yes, I remember that." Billy paused. "Then he died. He was very old, and he died."

Gaspar smiled up at him. "Very good, Billy. I knew you were a good boy. So now, if you remember all that, may I tell you a story? It's not a very long story."

Billy nodded, smiling at his friend.

"In 1582 Pope Gregory XIII decreed that the civilized world would no longer observe the Julian calendar. October 4th, 1582 was followed, the next day, by October 15th. Eleven days vanished from the world. One hundred and seventy years later, the British Parliament followed suit, and September 2nd, 1752 was followed, the next day, by September 14th. Why did he do that, the Pope?"

Billy was bewildered by the conversation. "Because he was bringing it into synch with the real world. The solstices and equinoxes. When to plant, when to harvest."

Gaspar waggled a finger at him with pleasure. "Excellent, young fella. And you're correct when you say Gregory abolished the Julian calendar because its error of one day in every one hundred and twenty-eight years had moved the vernal equinox to March 11th. That's what the history books say. It's what *every* history book says. But what if?"

"What if *what*? I don't know what you're talking about."

"What if: Pope Gregory had the knowledge revealed to him that he *must* readjust time in the minds of men? What if: the excess time in 1582 was eleven days and one hour? What if: the accounted for those eleven days, vanished those eleven days, but that one hour slipped free, was left loose to bounce through eternity? A very special hour . . . an hour that must *never* be used . . . an hour that must never toll. What if?"

Billy spread his hands. "What if, what if, what if! It's all just philosophy. It doesn't mean anything. Hours aren't real, time isn't something that you can bottle up. So what if there is an hour out there somewhere that . . ."

And he stopped.

He grew tense, and leaned down to the old man. "The watch. Your watch. It doesn't work. It's stopped."

Gaspar nodded. "At eleven o'clock. My watch works; it keeps very special time, for one very special hour."

Billy touched Gaspar's shoulder. Carefully he asked, "Who are you, Dad?"

The old man did not smile as he said, "Gaspar. Keeper. Paladin. Guardian."

"Father Perrault was hundreds of years old."

Gaspar shook his head with a wistful expression on his old face. "I'm eighty-six years old, Billy. You asked me if I thought I was God. Not God, not Father Perrault, not an immortal, just an old man who will die too soon. Are you Ronald Colman?"

Billy nervously touched his lower lip with a finger. He looked at Gaspar as long as he could, then turned away. He walked off a few paces, stared at the barren trees. It seemed suddenly much chillier here in this place of entombed remembrances. From a distance he said, "But it's only . . . what? A chronological convenience. Like daylight saving time; Spring forward, Fall back. We don't actually *lose* an hour; we get it back."

Gaspar stared at Minna's grave. "At the end of April I lost an hour. If I die now, I'll die an hour short in my life. I'll have been cheated out of one hour I want, Billy." He swayed toward all he had left of Minna. "One last hour I could have with my old girl. That's what I'm afraid of, Billy. I have that hour in my possession. I'm afraid I'll use it, god help me, I want so much to use it."

Billy came to him. Tense, and chilled, he said, "Why must that hour never toll?"

Gaspar drew a deep breath and tore his eyes away from the grave. His gaze locked with Billy's. And he told him.

The years, all the days and hours, exist. As solid and as real as mountains and oceans and men and women and the baobab tree. Look, he said, at the lines in my face and deny that time is real. Consider these dead weeds that were once alive and try to believe it's all just vapor or the mutual agreement of Popes and Caesars and young men like you.

"The lost hour must never come, Billy, for in that hour it all ends. The light, the wind, the stars, this magnificent open place we call the universe. It all ends, and in its place—waiting, always waiting—is eternal darkness. No new beginnings, no world without end, just the infinite emptiness."

And he opened his hand, which had been lying in his lap, and there, in his palm, rested the watch, making no sound at all, and stopped dead at eleven o'clock. "Should it strike twelve, Billy, eternal night falls; from which there is no recall."

There he sat, this very old man, just a perfectly normal old man. The most recent in the endless chain of keepers of the lost hour, descended in possession from Caesar and Pope Gregory XIII, down through the centuries of men and women who had served as caretakers of the excellent timepiece. And now he was dying, and now he wanted to cling to life as every man and woman clings to life no matter how awful or painful or empty, even if it is for one more hour. The suicide, falling from the bridge, at the final instant, tries to fly, tries to climb back up the sky. This weary old man, who only wanted to stay one brief hour more with Minna. Who was afraid that his love would cost the universe.

He looked at Billy, and he extended his hand with the watch waiting for its next paladin. So softly Billy could barely hear him, knowing that he was denying himself what he most wanted at this last place in his life, he whispered, "If I die without passing it on . . . it will begin to tick."

"Not me," Billy said. "Why did you pick me? I'm no one special. I'm not someone like you. I run an all-night service mart. There's nothing special about me the way there is about you! I'm *not* Ronald Colman! I don't want to be responsible, I've *never* been responsible!"

Gaspar smiled gently. "You've been responsible for me."

Billy's rage vanished. He looked wounded.

"Look at us, Billy. Look at what color you are; and look at what color I am. You took me in as a friend. I think of you as worthy, Billy. Worthy."

They remained there that way, in silence, as the wind rose. And finally, in a timeless time, Billy nodded.

Then the young man said, "You won't be losing Minna, Dad. Now you'll go to the place where she's been waiting for you, just as she was when you first met her. There's a place where we find everything we've ever lost through the years."

"That's good, Billy, that you tell me that. I'd like to believe it, too. But I'm a pragmatist. I believe in what exists . . . like rain and Minna's grave and the hours that pass that we can't see, but they *are*. I'm afraid, Billy. I'm afraid this will be the last time I can speak to her. So I ask a favor. As payment, in return for my life spent protecting the watch.

"I ask for one minute of the hour, Billy. One minute to call her back, so we can stand face-to-face and I can touch her and say goodbye. You'll be the new protector of this watch, Billy, so I ask you please, just let me steal one minute."

Billy could not speak. The look on Gaspar's face was without horizon, empty as tundra, bottomless. The child left alone in darkness; the pain of eternal waiting. He knew he could never deny this old man, no matter what he asked, and in the silence he heard a voice say: *"No!"* And it was his own.

He had spoken without conscious volition. Strong and determined, and without the slightest room for reversal. If a part of his heart had been swayed by compassion, that part had been instantly overridden. No. A final, unshakeable no.

For an instant Gaspar looked crestfallen. His eyes clouded with tears; and Billy felt something twist and break within himself at the sight. He knew he had hurt the old man. Quickly, but softly, he said urgently, "You know that would be wrong, Dad. We mustn't . . ."

Gaspar said nothing. Then he reached out with his free hand and took Billy's. It was an affectionate touch. "That was the last test, young fella. Oh, you know I've been testing you, don't you? This important item couldn't go to just anyone.

"And you passed the test, my friend: my last, best friend. When I said I could bring her back from where she's gone, here in this place we've both come to so often, to talk to someone lost to us, I knew you would understand that *anyone* could be brought back in that stolen minute. I knew you wouldn't use it for yourself, no matter how much you wanted it; but I wasn't sure that as much as you like me, it might not sway you. But you wouldn't even give it to *me*, Billy."

He smiled up at him, his eyes now clear and steady.

"I'm content, Billy. You needn't have worried. Minna and I don't need that minute. But if you're to carry on for me, I think you *do* need it. You're in pain, and that's no good for someone who carries this watch. You've got to heal, Billy.

"So I give you something you would never take for yourself. I give you a going-away present . . ."

And he started the watch, whose ticking was as loud and as clear as a baby's first sound; and the sweep-second hand began to move away from eleven o'clock.

Then the wind rose, and the sky seemed to cloud over, and it grew colder, with a remarkable silver-blue mist that rolled across the cemetery; and though he did not see it emerge from that grave at a distance far to the right, Billy Kinetta saw a shape move toward him. A soldier in the uniform of a day past, and his rank was Lance Corporal. He came toward Billy Kinetta, and Billy went to meet him as Gaspar watched.

They stood together and Billy spoke to him. And the man whose name Billy had never known when he was alive, answered. And then he faded, as the seconds ticked away. Faded, and faded, and was gone. And the silver-blue mist rolled through them, and past them, and was gone; and the soldier was gone.

Billy stood alone.

When he turned back to look across the grounds to his friend, he saw that Gaspar had fallen from the shooting-stick. He lay on the ground. Billy rushed to him, and fell to his knees and lifted him onto his lap. Gaspar was still.

"Oh, god, Dad, you should have heard what he said. Oh, geez, he let me go. He let me go so I didn't even have to say I was sorry. He told me he didn't even *see* me in that foxhole. He never knew he'd saved my life. I said thank you and he said no, thank *you*, that he hadn't died for nothing. Oh, please, Dad, please don't be dead yet. I want to tell you . . ."

And, as it sometimes happens, rarely but wonderfully, sometimes they come back for a moment, for an instant before they go, the old man, this very old man, opened his eyes, just before going on his way, and he looked through the dimming light at his friend, and he said, "May I remember you to my old girl, Billy?"

And his eyes closed again, after only a moment; and his caretakership was at an end; as his hand opened and the most excellent timepiece, now stopped again at one minute past eleven, floated from his palm and waited till Billy Kinetta extended his hand; and then it floated down and lay there silently, making no sound, no sound at all. Safe. Protected.

There in the place where all lost things returned, the young man sat on the cold ground, rocking the body of his friend. And he was in no hurry to leave. There was time.

A blessing of the 18th Egyptian Dynasty;

God be between you and harm in
all the empty places you walk.

The author gratefully acknowledges the importance of a discussion with Ms. Ellie Grossman in the creation of this work of fiction.

THE BLACK FERRIS

BY RAY BRADBURY

Ray Bradbury knows about small-town life, childhood friendships and the wonders that exist on the shelves of a library. He also knows how to draw a reader in by threatening this ideal setting with outsiders who, like Benét's Scratch, offer the everyman his heart's desire. . . . And moreover, Bradbury knows that sometimes adults as well as children really don't know any better.

"The Black Ferris" deals with a mysterious carnival that comes to town with rides and attractions that may be more than they seem (it was also the basis for his fantasy *Something Wicked This Way Comes*).

The carnival had come to town like an October wind, like a dark bat flying over the cold lake, bones rattling in the night, mourning, sighing, whispering up the tents in the dark rain. It stayed on for a month by the gray, restless lake of October, in the black weather and increasing storms and leaden skies.

During the third week, at twilight on a Thursday, the two small boys walked along the lake shore in the cold wind.

"Aw, I don't believe you," said Peter.

"Come on, and I'll show you," said Hank.

They left wads of spit behind them all along the moist brown sand of the crashing shore. They ran to the lonely carnival grounds. It had been raining. The carnival lay by the sounding lake with nobody buying tickets from the flaky black booths, nobody hoping to get the salted hams from the whining roulette wheels, and none of the thin-fat freaks on the big platforms. The midway was silent, all the gray tents hissing on the wind like gigantic prehistoric wings. At eight o'clock perhaps, ghastly lights would flash on, voices would shout, music would go out over the lake. Now there was only a blind hunchback sitting on a black booth, feeling of the cracked china cup from which he was drinking some perfumed brew.

"There," said Hank, pointing.

The black Ferris wheel rose like an immense light-bulbed constellation against the cloudy sky, silent.

"I still don't believe what you said about it," said Peter.

"You wait, I saw it happen. I don't know how, but it did. You know how carnivals are; all funny. Okay; this one's even *funnier*."

Peter let himself be led to the high green hiding place of a tree.

Suddenly, Hank stiffened. "*Hist!* There's Mr. Cooger, the carnival man, now!" Hidden, they watched.

Mr. Cooger, a man of some thirty-five years, dressed in sharp, bright clothes, a lapel carnation, hair greased with oil, drifted under the tree, a brown derby hat on his head. He had arrived in town three weeks before, shaking his brown derby hat at people on the street from inside his shiny red Ford, tooting the horn.

Now Mr. Cooger nodded at the little blind hunchback, spoke a word. The hunchback blindly, fumbling, locked Mr. Cooger into a black seat and sent him whirling up into the ominous twilight sky. Machinery hummed.

"See!" whispered Hank. "The Ferris wheel's going the wrong way. Backwards instead of forwards!"

"So what?" said Peter.

"Watch!"

The black Ferris wheel whirled twenty-five times around. Then the blind hunchback put out his pale hands and halted the machinery. The Ferris wheel stopped, gently swaying, at a certain black seat.

A ten-year-old boy stepped out. He walked off across the whispering carnival ground, in the shadows.

Peter almost fell from his limb. He searched the Ferris wheel with his eyes. "Where's Mr. Cooger!"

Hank poked him. "You wouldn't believe! Now *see!*"

"Where's Mr. Cooger at!"

"Come on, quick, run!" Hank dropped and was sprinting before he hit the ground.

UNDER GIANT CHESTNUT TREES, next to the ravine, the lights were burning in Mrs. Foley's white mansion. Piano music tinkled. Within the warm windows, people moved. Outside, it began to rain, despondently, irrevocably, forever and ever.

"I'm *so* wet," grieved Peter, crouching in the bushes. "Like someone squirted me with a hose. How much longer do we wait?"

"Sh!" said Hank, cloaked in wet mystery.

They had followed the little boy from the Ferris wheel up through town, down dark streets to Mrs. Foley's ravine house. Now, inside the warm dining room of the house the strange little boy sat at dinner, forking and spooning rich lamb chops and mashed potatoes.

"I know his name," whispered Hank, quickly. "My Mom told me about him the other day. She said, 'Hank, you hear about the li'l orphan boy moved in Mrs. Foley's? Well, his name is Joseph Pikes and he just came to Mrs. Foley's one day about two weeks ago and said how he was an orphan run away and could he have something to eat, and him and Mrs. Foley been getting on like hot apple pie ever since.' That's what my Mom said," finished Hank, peering through the steamy Foley window. Water dripped from his nose. He held onto Peter who was twitching with cold. "Pete, I didn't like his looks from the first, I didn't. He looked—mean."

"I'm scared," said Peter, frankly wailing. "I'm cold and hungry and I don't know what this's all about."

"Gosh, you're dumb!" Hank shook his head, eyes shut in disgust. "Don't you see; three weeks ago the carnival came. And about the same time this little ole orphan shows up at Mrs. Foley's. And Mrs. Foley's son died a long time ago one night one winter, and she's never been the same, so here's this little ole orphan boy who butters her all around."

"Oh," said Peter, shaking.

"Come on," said Hank. They marched to the front door and banged the lion knocker.

After awhile the door opened and Mrs. Foley looked out.

"You're all wet, come in," she said. "My land," she herded them into the hall. "What do you want?" she said, bending over them, a tall lady with lace on her full bosom and a pale thin face with white hair over it. "You're Henry Walterson, aren't you?"

Hank nodded, glancing fearfully at the dining room where the strange little boy looked up from his eating. "Can we see you alone, ma'am?" And when the old lady looked palely surprised, Hank crept over and shut the hall door and whispered at her. "We got to warn you about something, it's about that boy come to live with you, that orphan?"

The hall grew suddenly cold. Mrs. Foley drew herself high and stiff. "Well?"

"He's from the carnival, and he ain't a boy, he's a man, and he's planning on living here with you until he finds where your money is and then run off with it some night, and people will look for him but because they'll be looking for a little ten-year-old boy they won't recognize him when he walks by a thirty-five-year man, named Mr. Cooger!" cried Hank.

"What *are* you talking about?" declared Mrs. Foley.

"The carnival and the Ferris wheel and this strange man, Mr. Cooger, the Ferris wheel going backward and making him younger, I don't know how, and him coming here as a boy, and you can't trust him, because when he has your money he'll get on the Ferris wheel and it'll go *forward*, and he'll be thirty-five years old again, and the boy'll be gone forever!"

"Good night, Henry Walterson, don't *ever* come back!" shouted Mrs. Foley.

The door slammed. Peter and Hank found themselves in the rain once more. It soaked into and into them, cold and complete.

"Smart guy," snorted Peter. "Now you fixed it. Suppose he heard us, suppose he comes and *kills* us in our beds tonight, to shut us all up for keeps!"

"He wouldn't do that," said Hank.

"Wouldn't he?" Peter seized Hank's arm. "Look."

In the big bay window of the dining room now the mesh curtain pulled aside. Standing there in the pink light, his hand made into a menacing fist, was the little orphan boy. His face was horrible to see, the teeth bared, the eyes hateful, the lips mouthing out terrible words. That was all. The orphan boy was there only a second, then gone. The curtain fell into place. The rain poured down upon the house. Hank and Peter walked slowly home in the storm.

DURING SUPPER, Father looked at Hank and said, "If you don't catch pneumonia, I'll be surprised. Soaked, you were, by God! What's this about the carnival?"

Hank fussed at his mashed potatoes, occasionally looking at the rattling windows. "You know Mr. Cooger, the carnival man, Dad?"

"The one with the pink carnation in his lapel?" asked Father.

"Yes!" Hank sat up. "You've seen him around?"

"He stays down the street at Mrs. O'Leary's boarding house, got a room in back. Why?"

"Nothing," said Hank, his face glowing.

After supper Hank put through a call to Peter on the phone. At the other end of the line, Peter sounded miserable with coughing.

"Listen, Pete!" said Hank. "I see it all now. When that li'l ole orphan boy, Joseph Pikes, gets Mrs. Foley's money, he's got a good plan."

"What?"

"He'll stick around town as the carnival man, living in a room at Mrs. O'Leary's. That way nobody'll get suspicious of him. Everybody'll be looking for that nasty little boy and he'll be gone. And he'll be walking around, all disguised as the carnival man. That way, nobody'll suspect the carnival at all. It would look funny if the carnival suddenly pulled up stakes."

"Oh," said Peter, sniffling.

"So we got to act fast," said Hank.

"Nobody'll believe us, I tried to tell my folks but they said hogwash!" moaned Peter.

"We got to act tonight, anyway. Because why? Because he's gonna try to kill us! We're the only ones that know and if we tell the police to keep an eye on him, he's the one who stole Mrs. Foley's money in cahoots with the orphan boy, he won't live peaceful. I bet he just tries something tonight. So, I tell you, meet me at Mrs. Foley's in half an hour."

"Aw," said Peter.

"You wanna die?"

"No." Thoughtfully.

"Well, then. Meet me there and I bet we see that orphan boy sneaking out with the money, tonight, and running back down to the carnival grounds with it, when Mrs. Foley's asleep. I'll see you there. So long, Pete!"

"Young man," said Father, standing behind him as he hung up the phone. "You're not going anywhere. You're going straight up to bed. Here." He marched Hank upstairs. "Now hand me out everything you got on." Hank undressed. "There're no other clothes in your room are there?" asked Father.

"No, sir, they're all in the hall closet," said Hank, disconsolately.

"Good," said Dad and shut and locked the door.

Hank stood there, naked. "Holy Cow," he said.

"Go to bed," said Father.

PETER ARRIVED AT MRS. FOLEY'S HOUSE AT ABOUT NINE-THIRTY, sneezing, lost in a vast raincoat and mariner's cap. He stood like a small water hydrant on the street, mourning softly over his fate. The lights in the Foley house were warmly on upstairs. Peter waited for a half an hour, looking at the rain-drenched slick streets of night.

Finally there was a darting paleness, a rustle in wet bushes.

"Hank?" Peter questioned the bushes.

"Yeah." Hank stepped out.

"Gosh," said Peter, staring. "You're—you're *naked!*"

"I ran all the way," said Hank. "Dad wouldn't let me out."

"You'll get pneumonia," said Peter.

The lights in the house went out.

"Duck," cried Hank, bounding behind some bushes. They waited. "Pete," said Hank. "You're wearing pants, aren't you?"

"Sure," said Pete.

"Well, you're wearing a raincoat, and nobody'll know, so lend me your pants," asked Hank.

A reluctant transaction was made. Hank pulled the pants on.

The rain let up. The clouds began to break apart.

In about ten minutes a small figure emerged from the house, bearing a large paper sack filled with some enormous loot or other.

"There he is," whispered Hank.

"There he goes!" cried Peter.

The orphan boy ran swiftly.

"Get after him!" cried Hank.

They gave chase through the chestnut trees, but the orphan boy was swift, up the hill, through the night streets of town, down past the rail yards, past the factories, to the midway of the deserted carnival. Hank and Peter were poor seconds, Peter weighted as he was with the heavy raincoat, and Hank frozen with cold. The thumping of Hank's bare feet sounded through the town.

"Hurry, Pete! We can't let him get to that Ferris wheel before we do, if he changes back into a man we'll never prove anything!"

"I'm hurrying!" But Pete was left behind as Hank thudded on alone in the clearing weather.

"Yah!" mocked the orphan boy, darting away, no more than a shadow ahead, now. Now vanishing into the carnival yard.

Hank stopped at the edge of the carnival lot. The Ferris wheel was going up and up into the sky, a big nebula of stars caught on the dark earth and turning forward and forward, instead of backward, and there sat Joseph Pikes in a green painted bucket-seat, laughing up and around and down and up and around and down at little old Hank standing there, and the little blind hunchback had his hand on the roaring, oily black machine that made the Ferris wheel go ahead and ahead. The midway was deserted because of the rain. The merry-go-round was still, but its music played and crashed in the open spaces. And Joseph Pikes rode up into the cloudy sky and came down and each time he went around he was a year older, his laughing changed, grew deep, his face changed, the bones of it, the mean eyes of it, the wild hair of it, sitting there in the green bucket-seat whirling, whirling swiftly, laughing into the bleak heavens where now and again a last split of lightning showed itself.

Hank ran forward at the hunchback by the machine. On the way he picked up a tent spike. "Here, now!" yelled the hunchback. The black Ferris wheel whirled around. "You!" stormed the hunchback, fumbling out. Hank hit him in the kneecap and danced away. "Ouch!" screamed the man, falling forward. He tried to reach the machine brake to stop the Ferris wheel. When he put his hand on the brake, Hank ran in and slammed the tent spike against the fingers, mashing them. He hit them twice. The man held his hand in his other hand, howling. He kicked at Hank. Hank grabbed the foot, pulled, the man slipped in the mud and fell. Hank hit him on the head, shouting.

The Ferris wheel went around and around and around.

"Stop, stop the wheel!" cried Joseph Pikes-Mr. Cooger flung up in a stormy cold sky in the bubbled constellation of whirl and rush and wind.

"I can't move," groaned the hunchback. Hank jumped on his chest and they thrashed, biting, kicking.

"Stop, stop the wheel!" cried Mr. Cooger, a man, a different man and voice this time, coming around in panic, going up into the roaring hissing sky of the Ferris wheel. The wind blew through the high dark wheel spokes. "Stop, stop, oh, please stop the wheel!"

Hank leaped up from the sprawled hunchback. He started in on the brake mechanism, hitting it, jamming it, putting chunks of metal in it, tying it with rope, now and again hitting at the crawling weeping dwarf.

"Stop, stop, stop the wheel!" wailed a voice high in the night where the windy moon was coming out of the vaporous white clouds now. "Stop . . ." The voice faded.

Now the carnival was ablaze with sudden light. Men sprang out of tents, came running. Hank felt himself jerked into the air with oaths and beatings rained on him. From a distance there was a sound of Peter's voice and behind Peter, at full tilt, a police officer with pistol drawn.

"Stop, stop the wheel!" In the wind the voice sighed away.

The voice repeated and repeated.

The dark carnival men tried to apply the brake. Nothing happened. The machine hummed and turned the wheel around and around. The mechanism was jammed.

"Stop!" cried the voice one last time.

Silence.

WITHOUT A WORD THE FERRIS WHEEL FLEW IN A CIRCLE, a high system of electric stars and metal and seats. There was no sound now but the sound of the motor which died and stopped. The Ferris wheel coasted for a minute, all the carnival people looking up at it, the policeman looking up at it, Hank and Peter looking up at it.

The Ferris wheel stopped. A crowd had gathered at the noise. A few fishermen from the wharfhouse, a few switchmen from the rail yards. The Ferris wheel stood whining and stretching in the wind.

"Look," everybody said.

The policeman turned and the carnival people turned and the fishermen turned and they all looked at the occupant in the black-painted seat at the bottom of the ride. The wind touched and moved the black wooden seat in a gentle rocking rhythm, crooning over the occupant in the dim carnival light.

A skeleton sat there, a paper bag of money in its hands, a brown derby hat on its head.

BED & BREAKFAST

BY GENE WOLFE

GENE WOLFE IS ANOTHER FANTASIST TO COME OUT OF AMERICA'S HEARTLAND. THOUGH PRIMARILY KNOWN FOR HIS FIVE-VOLUME MASTERWORK *THE BOOK OF THE NEW SUN*, WOLFE HAS ALSO SHOWN A GREAT DEAL OF VERSATILITY IN OTHER BOOKS AND STORIES WITH SETTINGS AND PREMISES AS VARIED AS ANCIENT GREEK SOLDIERS WITH HEAD WOUNDS AND A MID-AMERICAN TOWN WHERE THE CASTLE OF MORGAN LA FEY JUST SO HAPPENS TO MAKE AN APPEARANCE.

IN "BED & BREAKFAST" WE ARE TREATED TO A COZY OVERNIGHTER FOR THOSE ON THE ROAD, THOUGH SOME OF THE GUESTS MAY NOT KNOW WHERE THEIR FINAL DESTINATION REALLY IS.

I know an old couple who live near Hell. They have a small farm, and, to supplement the meager income it provides (and to use up its bounty of chickens, ducks, and geese, of beefsteak tomatoes, bull-nose peppers, and roastin' ears), open their spare bedrooms to paying guests. From time to time, I am one of those guests.

Dinner comes with the room if one arrives before five; and leftovers, of which there are generally enough to feed two or three more persons, will be cheerfully warmed up afterward—provided that one gets there before nine, at which hour the old woman goes to bed. After nine (and I arrived long after nine last week) guests are free to forage in the kitchen and prepare whatever they choose for themselves.

My own choices were modest: coleslaw, cold chicken, fresh bread, country butter, and buttermilk. I was just sitting down to this light repast when I heard the doorbell ring. I got up, thinking to answer it and save the old man the trouble, and heard his, and hear his limping gait in the hallway. There was murmur of voices, the old man's and someone else's; the second sounded like a deep-voiced woman's, so I remained standing.

Their conversation lasted longer than I had expected; and although I could not distinguish a single word, it seemed to me that the old man was saying no, no no, and the woman proposing various alternatives.

At length he showed her into the kitchen; tall and tawny-haired, with a figure rather too voluptuous to be categorized as athletic, and one of those interesting faces that one calls beautiful only after at least half an hour of study; I guessed her age near thirty. The old man introduced us with rustic courtesy, told her to make herself at home, and went back to his book.

"He's very kind, isn't he?" she said. Her name was Eira something. I concurred, calling him a very good soul indeed.

"Are you going to eat all that?" She was looking hungrily at the chicken. I assured her I would have only a piece or two. (I never sleep well after a heavy meal.) She opened the refrigerator, found the milk, and poured herself a glass that she pressed against her cheek. "I haven't any money. I might as well tell you."

That was not my affair, and I said so.

"I don't. I saw the sign, and I thought there must be a lot of work to do around such a big house, washing windows and making beds, and I'd offer to do it for food and place to sleep."

"He agreed?" I was rather surprised.

"No." She sat down and drank half her milk, seeming to pour it down her throat with no need of swallowing. "He said I could eat and stay in the empty room— they've got an empty room tonight—if nobody else comes. But if somebody does, I'll have to leave." She found a drumstick and nipped it with strong white teeth. "I'll pay them when I get the money, but naturally he didn't believe me. I don't blame him. How much is it?"

I told her, and she said it was very cheap.

"Yes," I said, "but you have to consider the situation. They're off the highway, with no way of letting people know they're here. They get a few people on their way to Hell, and a few demons going out on assignments or returning. Regulars, as they call them. Other than that," I shrugged, "eccentrics like me and passers-by like you."

"Did you say Hell?" She put down her chicken leg.

"Yes. Certainly."

"Is there a town around here called Hell?"

I shook my head. "It has been called a city, but it's a region, actually. The infernal Empire. Hades. Gehenna, where the worm dieth not, and the fire is not quenched. You know."

She laughed, the delighted crow of a large, bored child who has been entertained at last.

I buttered a second slice of bread. The bread is always very good, but this seemed better than usual.

"Abandon hope, you who enter here. Isn't that supposed to be the sign over the door?"

"More or less," I said. "Over the gate Dante used, at any rate. It wasn't this one, so the inscription here may be quite different, if there's an inscription at all."

"You haven't been there?"

I shook my head. "Not yet."

"But you're going," she laughed again, a deep, throaty, very feminine chuckle this time, "and it's not very far."

"Three miles, I'm told, by the old country road. A little less, two perhaps, if you were to cut across the fields, which almost no one does."

"I'm not going," she said.

"Oh, but you are. So am I. Do you know what they do in Heaven?"

"Fly around playing harps?"

"There's the Celestial Choir, which sings the praises of God throughout all eternity. Everyone else beholds His face."

"That's it?" She was skeptical but amused.

"That's it. It's fine for contemplative saints. They go there, and they love it. They're the only people suited to it, and it suits them. The unbaptized go to Limbo. All the rest of us go to Hell; and for a few, this is the last stop before they arrive."

I waited for her reply, but she had a mouthful of chicken. "There are quite a number of entrances, as the ancients knew. Dodona, Ephyra, Acheron, Averno, and so forth. Dante went in through the crater of Vesuvius, or so rumor had it; to the best of my memory, he never specified the place in his poem."

"You said demons stay here."

I nodded. "If it weren't for them, the old people would have to close, I imagine."

"But you're not a demon and neither am I. Isn't it pretty dangerous for us? You certainly don't look—I don't mean to be offensive—"

"I don't look courageous." I sighed. "Nor am I. Let me concede that at once, because we need to establish it from the very beginning. I'm innately cautious, and have been accused of cowardice more than once. But don't you understand that courage has nothing to do with appearances? You must watch a great deal of television; no one would say what you did who did not. Haven't you ever seen a real hero on the news? Someone who had done something extraordinarily brave? The last one I saw looked very much like the black woman on the pancake mix used to, yet she'd run into a burning tenement to rescue three children. Not her own children, I should add."

Eira got up and poured herself a second glass of milk. "I said I didn't want to hurt your feelings, and I meant it. Just to start with, I can't afford to tick off anybody just now—I need help. I'm sorry. I really am."

"I'm not offended. I'm simply telling you the truth, that you cannot judge by appearances. One of the bravest men I've known was short and plump and inclined to be careless, not to say slovenly, about clothes and shaving and so on. A friend said that you couldn't imagine anyone less military, and he was right. Yet that fat little man had served in combat with the Navy and the Marines, and with the Israeli Army."

"But isn't it dangerous? You said you weren't brave to come here."

"In the first place, one keeps one's guard up here. There are precautions, and I take them. In the second, they're not on duty, so to speak. If they were to commit murder or set the house on fire, the old people would realize immediately who had done it and shut down; so while they are here, they're on their good behavior."

"I see." She picked up another piece of chicken. "*Nice* demons."

"Not really. But the old man tells me that they usually overpay and are, well, businesslike in their dealings. Those are the best things about evil. It generally has ready money, and doesn't expect to be trusted. There's a third reason, as well. Do you want to hear it?"

"Sure."

"Here one can discern them, and rather easily for the most part. When you've identified a demon, his ability to harm you is vastly reduced. But past this farm, identification is far more difficult; the demons vanish in the surging tide of mortal humanity that we have been taught by them to call life, and one tends to relax somewhat. Yet scarcely a week goes by in which one does not encounter a demon unaware."

"All right, what about the people on their way to Hell? They're dead, aren't they?"

"Some are, and some aren't."

"What do you mean by that?"

"Exactly what I said. Some are and some are not. It can be difficult to tell. They aren't ghosts in the conventional sense, you understand, any more than they are corpses, but the person who has left the corpse and the ghost behind."

"Would you mind if I warmed up a couple of pieces of this, and toasted some of that bread? We could share it."

I shook my head. "Not in the least, but I'm practically finished."

She rose, and I wondered whether she realized just how graceful she was. "I've got a dead brother, my brother Eric."

I said that I was sorry to hear it.

"It was a long time ago, when I was a kid. He was four, I think, and he fell off the balcony. Mother always said he was an angel now, an angel up in heaven. Do dead people really get to be angels if they're good?"

"I don't know; it's and interesting question. There's a suggestion in the book of Tobit that the Archangel Raphael is actually an ancestor of Tobit's. *Angel* means 'messenger,' as you probably know; so if God were to employ one of the blest as a messenger, he or she could be regarded as an angel, I'd think."

"Devils are fallen angels, aren't they? I mean, if they exist." She dropped three pieces of chicken into a frying pan, hesitated, and added a fourth. "So if good people really get recycled as angels, shouldn't the bad ones get to be devils or demons?"

I admitted that it seemed plausible.

She lit the stove with a kitchen match, turning the burner higher than I would have. "You sound like you come here pretty often. You must talk to them at breakfast, or whenever. You ought to know."

"Since you don't believe me, wouldn't it be logical for you to believe my admissions of ignorance?"

"No way!" She turned to face me, a forefinger upraised. "You've got to be consistent, and coming here and talking to lots of demons, you'd know."

I protested that information provided by demons could not be relied upon.

"But what do you think? What's your best guess? See, I want to find out if there's any hope for us. You said we're going to Hell, both of us, and that dude—the Italian—"

"Dante," I supplied.

"Dante says the sign over the door says don't hope. I went to a school like that for a couple years, come to think of it."

"Were they merely strict, or actually sadistic?"

"Mean. But the teachers lived better than we did—a lot better. If there's a chance of getting to be one yourself, we could always hope for that."

At that moment, we heard a knock at the front door, and her shoulders sagged. "There goes my free room. I guess I've got to be going. It was fun talking to you, it really was."

I suggested she finish her chicken first.

"Probably I should. I'll have to find another place to stay, though, and I'd like to get going before they throw me out. It's pretty late already." She hesitated. "Would you buy my wedding ring? I've got it right here." Her thumb and forefinger groped the watch pocket of her bluejeans.

I took a final bite of coleslaw and pushed back my plate. "It doesn't matter, actually, whether I want to buy your ring or not. I can't afford to. Someone in town might, perhaps."

A booming voice in the hallway drowned out the old man's; I knew that the new guest was a demon before I saw him or heard a single intelligible word.

She held up her ring, a whitegold band set with two small diamonds. "I had a job, but he never let me keep anything from it and I finally caught on—if I kept waiting till I had some money or someplace to go, I'd never get away. So I split, just walked away with nothing but the clothes I had on."

"Today?" I inquired.

"Yesterday. Last night I slept in a wrecked truck in a ditch. You probably don't believe that, but it's the truth. All night I was afraid somebody'd come to tow it away. There were furniture pads in the back, and I lay on a couple and pulled three more on top of me, and they were pretty warm."

"If you can sell your ring," I said, "there's a Holiday Inn in town. I should warn you that a great many demons stay there, just as you would expect."

The kitchen door opened. Following the old man was one of the largest I have ever seen, swag-bellied and broad-hipped; he must have stood at least six-foot-six.

"This's our kitchen." the old man told him.

"I know," the demon boomed. "I stopped off last year. Naturally you don't remember, Mr. Hopsack. But I remembered you and this wonderful place of yours. I'll scrounge around and make out all right."

The old man gave Eira a significant look and jerked his head toward the door, at which she nodded almost imperceptibly. I said, "She's going to stay with me, Ten There's plenty of room in the bed. You don't object, I trust?"

He did, of course, though he was much too diffident to say so; at last he managed, "Double's six dollars more."

I said, "Certainly," and handed him the money, at which the demon snickered.

"Just don't you let Ma find out."

When the old man had gone, the demon fished business cards from his vest pocket; I did not trouble to read the one that he handed me, knowing that nothing on it would be true. Eira read hers aloud, however, with a good simulation of admiration. "J. Gunderson Foulweather, Broker, Commodities Sales."

The demon picked up her skillet and tossed her chicken a foot into the air, catching all four pieces with remarkable dexterity. "Soap, dope, rope, or hope. If it's sold in bulk I'll buy it, and give you the best price anywhere. If it's bought in bulk, I sell it cheaper than anybody in the nation. Pleasure to meet you."

I introduced myself, pretending not to see his hand, and added, "This is Eira Mumble."

"On your way to St. Louis? Lovely city! I know it well."

I shook my head.

She said, "But you're going somewhere—home to some city—in the morning aren't you? And you've got a car. There are cars parked outside. The black Plymouth?"

My vehicle is a gray Honda Civic, and I told her so.

"If I—you know."

"Stay in my room tonight."

"Will you give me a ride in the morning? Just a ride? Let me off downtown, that's all I ask."

I do not live in St. Louis and had not intended to go there, but I said I would.

She turned to the demon. "He says this's close to Hell, and the souls of people going there stop off here, sometimes. Is that where you're going?"

His booming laugh shook the kitchen. "Not me! Davenport. Going to do a little business in feed corn if I can."

Eira looked at me as if to say, there, you see?

The demon popped the largest piece of chicken into his mouth like an hors d'oeuvre; I have never met one who did not prefer his food smoking hot. "He's giving you the straight scoop though, Eira. It is."

"How'd you do that?"

"Do what?"

"Talk around that chicken like that."

He grinned, which made him look like a portly crocodile. "Swallowed it, that's all. I'm hungry. I haven't eaten since lunch."

"Do you mind if I take the others? I was warming them up for myself, and there's more in the refrigerator."

He stood aside with a mock bow.

"You're in this together—this thing about Hell. You and him." Eira indicated me as she took the frying pan from the stove.

"We met before?" he boomed at me. I said that we had not, to the best of my memory.

"Devils—demons, are what he calls them. He says there are probably demons sleeping here right now, up on the second floor."

I put in, "I implied that, I suppose. I did not state it."

"Very likely true," the demon boomed, adding "I'm going to make coffee, if anybody wants some."

"And the—damned. They're going to Hell, but they stop off here."

He gave me a searching glance. "I've been wondering about you, to tell the truth. You seem like the type."

I declared that I was alive for the time being.

"That's the best anybody can say."

"But the cars—" Eira began.

"Some drive, some fly." He had discovered slices of ham in the refrigerator, and he slapped them into the frying pan as though he were dealing blackjack. "I used to wonder what they did with all the cars down there."

"But you don't any more." Eira was going along now, once more willing to play what she thought (or wished me to believe she thought) a rather silly game. "So you found out. What is it?"

"Nope." He pulled out one of the wooden, yellow-enameled kitchen chairs and sat down with such force I was surprised it did not break. "I quit wondering, that's all. I'll find out soon enough, or I won't. But in places this close—I guess there's others— you get four kinds of folks." He displayed thick fingers, each with a ring that looked as if it had cost a great deal more than Eira's. "There's guys that's still alive, like our friend here." He clenched one finger. "Then there's staff. You know what I mean?"

Eira looked puzzled. "Devils?"

"J. Gunderson Foulweather," the demon jerked his thumb at his vest, "doesn't call anybody racial names unless they hurt him or his, especially when there's liable to be a few eating breakfast in the morning. Staff, okay? Free angels. Some of them are business contacts of mine. They told me about this place, that's why I came the first time."

He clenched a second finger and touched third with the index finger of his free hand. "Then there's future inmates. You used a word J. Gunderson Foulweather himself wouldn't say in the presence of a lady, but since you're the only lady here, no harm done. Colonists, okay?"

"Wait a minute." Eira looked from him to me. "You both claim they stop off here." We nodded.

"On their way to Hell. So why do they go? Why don't they just go off," she hesitated, searching for the right word, and finished weakly, "back home or something?"

The demon boomed, "You want to field this one?"

I shook my head. "Your information is superior to mine, I feel certain."

"Okay, a friend of mine was born and raised in Newark, New Jersey. You ever been to Newark?"

"No," Eira said.

"Some parts are pretty nice, but it's not, like, the hub of Creation, see? He went to France when he was twenty-two and stayed twenty years, doing jobs for American magazines around Paris. Learned to speak the language better than the natives. He's a photographer, a good one."

The demon's coffee had begun to perk. He glanced around at it, sniffed appreciatively, and turned back to us, still holding up his ring and little fingers. "Twenty years, then he goes back to Newark. J. Gunderson Foulweather doesn't stick his nose into other people's business, but I asked him the same thing you did me, how come? He said he felt like he belonged there."

Eira nodded slowly.

I said, "The staff, as you call them, might hasten the process, I imagine."

The demon appeared thoughtful. "Could be. Sometimes, anyhow." He touched the fourth and final finger. "All the first three's pretty common from what I hear. Only there's another kind you don't hardly ever see. The runaways."

Eira chewed and swallowed. "You mean people escape?"

"That's what I hear. Down at the bottom, Hell's pretty rough, you know? Higher up it's not so bad."

I put in, "That's what Dante reported, too."

"You know him? Nice guy. I never been there myself, but that's what they say. Up at the top it's not so bad, sort of like one of those countryclub jails for politicians. The guys up there could jump the fence and walk out. Only they don't, because they know they'd get caught and send down where things aren't so nice. Only every so often somebody does. So you got them, too, headed out. Anybody want coffee? I made plenty."

Long before he had reached his point, I had realized what it was; I found it difficult to speak, but managed to say that I was going up to bed and coffee would keep me awake.

"You, Eira?"

She shook her head. It was at that moment that I at last concluded that she was truly beautiful, not merely attractive in an unconventional way. "I've had all I want, really. You can have my toast for your ham."

I confess that I heaved a sigh of relief when the kitchen door swung shut behind us. As we mounted the steep, carpeted stair, the house seemed so silent that I supposed for a moment that the demon had dematerialized, or whatever it is they do. He began to whistle a hymn in the kitchen, and I looked around sharply.

She said, "He scares you, doesn't he? He scares me too. I don't know why."

I did, or believed I did, though I forbore.

"You probably thought I was going to switch—spend the night with him instead of you, but I'd rather sleep outside in your car."

I said, "Thank you," or something of the kind, and Eira took my hand; it was the first physical intimacy of any sort between us.

When we reached the top of the stair, she said, "Maybe you'd like it if I waited out here in the hall till you get undressed? I won't run away."

I shook my head. "I told you I take precautions. As long as you're in my company, those precautions protect you as well to a considerable extent. Out here alone, you'd be completely vulnerable."

I unlocked the door of my room, opened it, and switched on the light. "Come in, please. There are things in here, enough protection to keep us both safe tonight, I believe. Just don't touch them. Don't touch anything you don't understand."

"You're keeping out demons?" She was no longer laughing, I noticed.

"Unwanted guests of every sort." I endeavored to sound confident, though I have had little proof of the effectiveness of those old spells. I shut and relocked the door behind us.

"I'm going to have to go out to wash up. I'd like to take a bath."

"The Hopsacks have only two rooms with private baths, but this is one of them." I pointed. "We're old friends, you see; their son and I went to Dartmouth together, and I reserved this room in advance."

"There's one other thing. Oh, God! I don't know how to say this without sounding like a jerk."

"Your period has begun."

"I'm on the pill. It's just that I'd like to rinse out my underwear and hang it up to dry overnight, and I don't have a nightie. Would you turn off the lights in here when I'm ready to come out of the bathroom?"

"Certainly."

"If you want to look you can, but I'd rather you didn't. Maybe just that little lamp on the vanity?"

"No lights at all," I told her. "You divined very quickly that I am a man of no great courage. I wish that you exhibited equal penetration with respect to my probity. I lie only when forced to, and badly as a rule; and my word is as good as any man's. I will keep any agreement we make, whether expressed or implied, as long as you do."

"You probably want to use the bathroom too."

I told her that I would wait, and that I would undress in the bedroom while she bathed, and take my own bath afterward.

Of the many things, memories as well as speculations, that passed through my mind as I waited in our darkened bedroom for her to complete her ablutions, I shall say little here; perhaps I should say nothing. I shot the nightbolt, switched off the light and undressed. Reflecting that she might readily make away with my wallet and my watch while I bathed, I considered hiding them; but I felt certain that she would not, and to tell the truth my watch is of no great value and there was less than a hundred dollars in my wallet. Under these circumstances, it seemed wise to show I trusted her, and I resolved to do so.

In the morning I would drive her to the town in which I live or to St. Louis, as she preferred. I would give her my address and telephone number, with twenty dollars, perhaps, or even thirty. And I would tell her in a friendly fashion that if she could find no better place to stay she could stay with me whenever she chose, on tonight's terms. I speculated upon a relationship (causal and even promiscuous, if you like) that would not so much spring into being as grow by the accretion of familiarity and small kindnesses. At no time have I been the sort of man women prefer, and I am whole decades past the time in life in which love is found if it is found at all, overcautious and overintellectual, little known to the world and certainly not rich.

Yet I dreamt, alone in that dark, high-ceilinged bedroom. In men such as I, the foolish fancies of boyhood are superseded only by those of manhood, unsought visions less gaudy, perhaps, but more foolish still.

Even in these the demon's shadow fell between us; I felt certain then that she had escaped, and that he had come to take her back. I heard the flushing of the toilet, heard water run in the tub, and compelled myself to listen no more.

Though it was a cold night, the room we would share was warm. I went to the window most remote from the bathroom door, raised the shade, and stood for a time staring up at the frosty stars, then stretched myself quite naked upon the bed, thinking of many things.

I STARTED WHEN THE BATHROOM DOOR OPENED; I must have been half asleep.

"I'm finished," Eira said, "you can go in now." Then, "Where are you?"

My own eyes were accommodated to the darkness, as hers were not. I could make her out, white and ghostly, in the starlight; and I thrilled at the sight. "I'm here," I told her, "on the bed. It's over this way." As I left the bed and she slipped beneath its sheets and quilt, our hands touched. I recall that moment more clearly than any of the rest.

Instructed by her lack of night vision (whether real or feigned), I pulled the dangling cord of the bathroom light before I toweled myself dry. When I opened the door, half expecting to find her gone, I could see her almost as well as I had when she had emerged from the bathroom, lying upon her back, her hair a damp-darkened aureole about her head and her arms above the quilt. I circled the bed and slid in.

"Nice bath?" Then, "How do you want to do it?"

"Slowly," I said.

At which she giggled like a schoolgirl. "You're fun. You're not like him at all, are you?"

I hoped that I was not, as I told her.

"I know—do that again—who you are! You're Larry."

I was happy to hear it; I had tired of being myself a good many years ago.

"He was the smartest boy in school—in the high school that my husband and I graduated from. He was Valedictorian, and president of the chess club and the debating team and all that. Oh, my!"

"Did you go out with him?" I was curious, I confess.

"Once or twice. No, three times. Times when there was something I wanted to go to—a dance or a game—an my husband couldn't take me, or wouldn't. So I went with Larry, dropping hints, you know that I'd like to go, then saying okay when he asked. I never did this with him, though. Just with my husband, except that he wasn't my husband then. Could you sorta run your fingers inside my knees and down the backs of my legs?"

I complied. "It might be less awkward if you employed your husband's name. Use a false one if you like. Tom, Dick, or Harry would do, or even Mortimer."

"That wouldn't be him, and I don't want to say it. Aren't you going to ask if he beat me? I went to the battered women's shelter once, and they kept coming back to that. I think they wanted me to lie."

"You said that you left home yesterday, and I've seen your face. It isn't bruised."

"Now up here. He didn't. Oh, he knocked me down a couple times, but not lately. They're supposed to get drunk and beat you up."

I said that I had heard that before, though I had never understood it.

"You don't get mean when you're drunk."

"I talk too much and too loudly," I told her, "and I can't remember names, or the word I want to use. Eventually I grow ashamed and stop talking completely, and drinking as well."

"My husband used to be happy and rowdy—that was before we got married. After, it was sort of funny, because you could see him starting to get mad before he got the top off the first bottle. Isn't that funny?"

"No one can bottle emotions," I said. "We must bring them to the bottles ourselves."

"Kiss me."

We kissed. I had always thought it absurd to speak of someone enraptured by a kiss, yet I knew a happiness that I had not thought myself capable of.

"Larry was really smart, like you. Did I say that?"

I managed to nod.

"I want to lie on top of you. Just for a minute or so. Is that all right?"

I told her truthfully that I would adore it.

"You can put your hands anyplace you want, but hold me. That's good. That's nice. He was really smart, but he wasn't good at talking to people. Socially, you know? The stuff he cared about didn't matter to us, and the stuff we wanted to talk about didn't matter to him. But I let him kiss me in his dad's car, and I always danced the first and last numbers with him. Nobody cares about that now, but then they did, where we came from. Larry and my husband and I. I think if he'd kept on drinking—he'd have maybe four or five beers every night, at first—he'd have beaten me to death, and that was why he stopped. But he used to threaten. Do you know what I mean?"

I said that I might guess, but with no great confidence.

"Like he'd pick up my big knife in the kitchen, and he'd say, I could stick this right through you—in half a minute it would all be over. Or he'd talk about how you could choke somebody with a wire till she died, and while he did he'd be running the lamp cord through his fingers, back and forth. Do you like this?"

"Don't!" I said.

"I'm sorry, I thought you'd like it."

"I like it too much. Please don't. Not now."

"He'd talk about other men, how I was playing up to them. Sometimes it was men

I hadn't even noticed. Like we'd go down to the pizza place, and when we got back he'd say, the big guy in the leather jacket—I saw you. He was eating it up, and you couldn't give him enough, could you? You just couldn't give him enough."

"And I wouldn't have seen anybody in a leather jacket. I'd be trying to remember who this was. But when we were in school he was never jealous of Larry, because he knew Larry was just a handy man to me. I kind of liked him the way I kind of liked the little kid next door."

"You got him to help you with your homework," I said.

"Yes, I did. How'd you know?"

"A flash of insight. I have them occasionally."

"I'd get him to help before a big quiz, too. When we were finishing up the semester, in Social Studies or whatever, I wouldn't have a clue about what she was going to ask on the test, but Larry always knew. He'd tell me half a dozen things, maybe, and five would be right there on the final. A flash of insight, like you said."

"Similar, perhaps."

"But the thing was—it was—was—"

She gulped and gasped so loudly that even I realized she was about to cry. I hugged her, perhaps the most percipient thing I have ever done.

"I wasn't going to tell you that, and I guess I'd better not or I'll bawl. I just wanted to say you're Larry, because my husband never minded him, not really, or anyhow not very much, and he'd kid around with him in those days, and sometimes Larry'd help him with his homework too."

"You're right," I told her, "I am Larry; and your name is Martha Williamson, although she was never half so beautiful as you are, and I had nearly forgotten her."

"Have you cooled down enough?"

"No. Another five minutes, possibly."

"I hope you don't get the aches. Do you really think I'm beautiful?"

I said I did, and that I could not tell her properly how lovely she was, because she would be sure I lied.

"My face is too square."

"Absolutely not! Besides, you mean rectangular, surely. It's not too rectangular, either. Any face less rectangular than yours is too square or too round."

"See? You are Larry."

"I know."

"This is what I was going to tell, if I hadn't gotten all weepy. Let me do it, and after that we'll . . . You know. Get together."

I nodded, and she must have sensed my nod in movement of my shoulder, or perhaps a slight motion of the mattress. She was silent for what seemed to me half a minute, if not longer. "Kiss me, then I'll tell it."

I did.

"You remember what you said in the kitchen?"

"I said far too many things in the kitchen. I'm afraid. I tend to talk too much even when I'm sober. I'm sure I couldn't recall them all.

"It was before that awful man came in and took my room. I said the people going to Hell were dead, and you said some were and some weren't. That didn't make any sense to me till later when I thought about my husband. He was alive, but it was like something was getting a tighter hold on him all the time. Like Hell was reaching right out and grabbing him. He went on so about me looking at other men that I started really doing it. I'd see who was there, trying to figure out which one he'd say when we got home. Then he started bringing up ones that hadn't been there, people from school—this was after we were out of school and married, and I hadn't seen a lot of them in years."

I said, "I understand."

"He'd been on the football team and the softball team and run track and all that, and mostly it was those boys he'd talk about, but one time it was the shop teacher. I never even took shop."

I nodded again, I think.

"But never Larry, so Larry got to be special to me. Most of those boys, well, maybe they looked, but I never looked at them. But I'd really dated Larry, and he'd had his arms around me and even kissed me a couple of times, and I danced with him. I could remember the cologne he used to wear, and that checkered wool blazer he had. After graduation most of the boys from our school got jobs with the coal company or in the tractor plant, but Larry won a scholarship to some big school, and after that I never saw him. It was like he'd gone there and died."

"It's better now," I said, and I took her hand, just as she had taken mine going upstairs.

She misunderstood, which may have been fortunate. "It is. It really is. Having you here like this makes it better." She used my name, but I am determined not to reveal it.

"Then after we'd been married about for years, I went in the drugstore, and Larry was there waiting for a prescription for his mother. We said hi, and shook hands, and talked about old times and how it was with us, and I got the stuff I'd come for and started to leave. When I got to the door, I thought Larry wouldn't' be looking any more, so I stopped and looked at him."

"He was still looking at me." She gulped. "You're smart. I bet you guessed, didn't you?"

"I would have been," I said. I doubt that she heard me.

"I'll never, ever, forget that look. He wanted me so bad, just so bad it was tearing him up. My husband starved a dog to death once. His name was Ranger, and he was a blue-tick hound. They said he was good coon dog, and I guess he was. My husband had helped this man with some work, so he gave him Ranger. But my husband used to pull on Ranger's ears till he'd yelp, and finally Ranger bit his hand. He just locked Ranger up after that and wouldn't feed him any more. He'd go out in the yard and Ranger'd be in that cage hoping for him to feed him and knowing he wouldn't, and that was the way Larry looked at me in the drugstore. It brought it all back, about the dog two years before, and Larry, and lots of other things. But the thing was—thing was—"

I stroked her hand.

"He looked at me like that, and I saw it, and when I did I knew I was looking at him that very same way. That was when I decided, except that I thought I'd save up money, and write to Larry when I had enough, and see if he'd help me. Are you all right now?"

"No," I said, because at that moment I could have cut my own throat or thrown myself through the window.

"He never answered my letters, though. I talked to his mother, and he's married with two children. I like you better anyway."

Her fingers had resumed explorations. I said, "Now, if you're ready."

And we did. I felt heavy and clumsy, and it was over far too quickly; yet if I were given what no man actually is, the opportunity to experience a bit of his life a second time, I think I might well choose those moments.

"Did you like that?"

"Yes, very much indeed. Thank you."

"You're pretty old for another one, aren't you?"

"I don't know. Wait a few minutes, and we'll see."

"We could try some other way. I like you better than Larry. Have I said that?"

I said she had not, and that she had made me wonderfully happy by saying it.

"He's married, but I never wrote him. I won't lie to you much more."

"In that case, may I ask you a question?"

"Sure."

"Or two? Perhaps three?"

"Go ahead."

"You indicated that you had gone to a school, a boarding school apparently, where you were treated badly. Was it near here?"

"I don't remember about that—I don't think I said it."

"We were talking about the inscription Dante reported. I believe it ended *Lasciate ogni speranza, voi ch'entrate!* Leave all hope, you that enter!"

"I said I wouldn't lie. It's not very far, but I can't give you the name of a town you'd know, or anything like that."

"My second—"

"Don't ask anything else about the school. I won't tell you."

"All right, I won't. Someone gave your husband a hunting dog. Did your husband hunt deer? Or quail, perhaps?"

"Sometimes. I think you're right. He'd rather have had a bird dog, but the man he helped didn't raise them."

I kissed her. "You're in danger, and I think that you must know how much. I'll help you all I can. I realize how very trite this will sound, but I would give my life to save you from going back to that school, if need be."

"Kiss me again." There was a new note in her voice, I thought, and it seemed to me that it was hope.

When we parted, she asked, "Are you going to drive me to St. Louis in the morning?"

"I'll gladly take you farther. To New York or Boston or even to San Francisco. It means Saint Francis, you know."

"You think you could again?"

At her touch, I knew the answer was yes; so did she.

Afterward she asked, "What was your last question?" and I told her I had no last question.

"You said one question then it was two, then three. So what was the last one?"

"You needn't answer."

"All right, I won't. What was it?"

"I was going to ask you in what year you and your husband graduated from high school."

"You don't mind?"

I sighed. "A hundred wise men have said in various ways that love transcends the power of death; and millions of fools have supposed that they meant nothing by it. At this late hour in my life I have learned what they meant. They meant that love transcends death. They are correct."

"Did you think that salesman was really a cop? I think you did. I did, too, almost."

"No or yes, depending upon what you mean by 'cop.' But we've already talked too much about these things."

"Would you rather I'd do this?"

"Yes," I said, and meant it with every fiber of my being. "I would a thousand times rather have you do that."

AFTER SOME GENTLE TEASING about my age and inadequacies (the sort of thing that women always do, in my experience, as anticipatory vengeance for the contempt with which they expect to be treated when the sexual act is complete), we slept. In the morning, Eira wore her wedding band to breakfast, where I introduced her to the old woman as my wife, to the old man's obvious relief. The demon sat opposite me at the table, wolfing down scrambled eggs, biscuits, and home-made sausage he did not require, and from time to time winking at me in an offensive manner that I did my best to tolerate.

Outside I spoke to him in private while Eira was upstairs searching out room for the hairbrush that I had been careful to leave behind.

"If you are here to reclaim her," I told him, "I am your debtor. Thank you for waiting until morning."

He grinned like the trap he was. "Have a nice night?"

"Very."

"Swell. You folks think we don't want you to have any fun. That's not the way it is at all." He strove to stifle his native malignancy as he said this, with the result that it showed so clearly I found it difficult not to cringe. "I do you a favor, maybe you'll do me one sometime. Right?"

"Perhaps." I hedged.

He laughed. I have heard many actors try to reproduce the hollowness and cruelty of that laugh, but not one has come close. "Isn't that what keeps you coming back here? Wanting favors? You know we don't give anything away."

"I hope to learn, and to make myself a better man."

"Touching. You and Doctor Frankenstein."

I forced myself to smile. "I owed you thanks, as I said, and I do thank you. Now I'll impose upon your good nature, if I may. Two weeks. You spoke of favors, of the possibility of accommodation. I would be greatly in your debt. I am already, as I acknowledge."

Grinning, he shook his head.

"One week, then. Today is Thursday. Let us have—the me have her until next Thursday."

"Afraid not pal."

"Three days then. I recognize that she belongs to you, but you'll have her for eternity, and she can't be an important prisoner."

"Inmate. Inmate sounds better." The demon laid his hand upon my shoulder, and I was horribly conscious of its weight and bone-crushing strength. "You think I let you jump her last night because I'm such a nice guy? You really believe that?"

"I was hoping that was the case, yes."

"Bright. Real bright. Just because I got here a little after she did, you think I was trailing her like that flea-bitten dog, and I followed her here." He sniffed, and it was precisely the sniff of a hound on the scent. The hand that held my shoulder drew me to him until I stood with the almost insuperable weight of his entire arm on my shoulders. "Listen here. I don't have to track anybody. Wherever they are, I am. See?"

"I understand."

"If I'd been after her, I'd of had her away from you as soon as I saw her. Only she's not why I came here, she's not why I'm leaving, and if I was to grab her all it would do is get me in the soup with the big boys downstairs. I don't want you either."

"I'm gratified to hear it."

"Swell. If I was to give you a promise, my solemn word of dishonor, you wouldn't think that was worth shit-paper, would you?"

"To the contrary." Although I was lying in his teeth, I persevered. "I know an angel's word is sacred, to him at least."

"Okay, then. I don't want her. You wanted a couple of weeks, and I said no deal because I'm letting you have her forever, and vice versa. You don't know what forever means, whatever you think. But I do."

"Thank you, sir," I said; and I meant it from the bottom of my soul. "Thank you very, very much."

The demon grinned and took his arm from my shoulders. "I wouldn't mess around with your or her or a single thing the two of you are going to do together, see? Word of dishonor. The boys downstairs would skin me, because you're her assignment. So be happy." He slapped me on the back so hard that he nearly knocked me down.

Still grinning, he walked around the corner of someone's camper van. I followed as quickly as I could, but he had disappeared.

LITTLE REMAINS TO TELL. I drove Eira to St. Louis, as I had promised, and she left me with a quick kiss in the parking area of the Gateway Arch; we had stopped at a McDonald's for lunch on the way, and I had scribbled my address and telephone number on a paper napkin there and watched her tuck it into a pocket of the denim shirt she wore. Since then I have had a week in which to consider my adventure, as I said on the first page of this account.

In the beginning (especially Friday night), I hoped for a telephone call or a midnight summons from my doorbell. Neither came.

On Monday I went to the library, where I perused the back issues of newspapers; and this evening, thanks to a nephew at an advertising agency, I researched the matter further, viewing twenty-five and thirty-year-old tapes of news broadcasts. The woman's name was not Eira, a name that means "snow," and the name of the husband she had slain with his own shotgun was not Tom, Dick, Harry, or even Mortimer; but I was sure I had found her. (Fairly sure, at least.) She took her own life in jail, awaiting trial.

She had been in Hell. That, I feel, is the single solid fact, the one thing on which I can rely. But did she escape? Or was she vomited forth?

All this has been brought to a head by the card I received today in the mail. It was posted on Monday from St. Louis, and has taken a disgraceful four days to make a journey that the most cautious driver can complete in a few hours. On it's front, a tall, beautiful, and astonishingly busty woman is crowding a fearful little man. The caption reads, *I want to impress one thing on you.*

Inside the card: *My body.*

Beneath that is the scrawled name *Eira*, and a telephone number. Should I call her? Dare I?

Bear in mind (as I must constantly remind myself to) that nothing the demon said can be trusted. Neither can anything that she herself said. She would have had me take her for a living woman, if she could.

Has the demon devised an excruciating torment for us both?

Or for me alone?

The telephone number is at my elbow as I write. Her card is on my desk. If I dial the number, will I be blundering into the snare, or will I have torn the snare to pieces?

Should I call her?

A final possibility remains, although I find it almost impossible to write of it.

What if I am mad?

What if Foulweather the salesman merely played up to what he assumed was an elaborate joke? What if my last conversation with him (that is to say, with the demon) was a delusion? What if Eira is in fact the living woman that almost every man in the world would take her for, save I?

She cannot have much money and may well be staying for a few days with some chance acquaintance.

Am I insane? Deluded?

Tomorrow she may be gone. One dash three one four—

Should I call?

Perhaps I may be a man of courage after all, a man who has never truly understood his own character.

Will I call her? Do I dare?

DEAD RUN

BY GREG BEAR

THOUGH THE VAST MAJORITY OF GREG BEAR'S LITERARY WORK HAS BEEN IN THE SUBGENRE OF HARD SCIENCE FICTION WITH SUCH MAJOR NOVELS AS *EON* AND *QUEEN OF ANGELS* AND AWARD-WINNING SHORT STORIES LIKE "BLOOD MUSIC" AND "TANGENTS," HE HAS ALSO WRITTEN SEVERAL VERY GENTLE WORKS OF FANTASY.

THEY SAY THE ROAD TO HELL IS PAVED WITH GOOD INTENTIONS. WELL, SOMEONE HAS TO DRIVE DOWN THOSE ROADS, AND IN "DEAD RUN," BEAR GETS TO PASS A FEW FINAL JUDGEMENTS OF HIS OWN BEFORE ARRIVING AT THE FINAL DESTINATION.

There aren't many hitchhikers on the road to Hell.

I noticed this dude from four miles away. He stood where the road is straight and level, crossing what looks like desert except it has all these little empty towns and motels and shacks. I had been on the road for about six hours, and the folks in the cattle trailers behind me had been quiet for the last three—resigned, I guess—so my nerves had settled a bit and I decided to see what the dude was up to. Maybe he was one of the employees. That would be interesting, I thought.

Truth to tell, once the wailing settled down, I got pretty bored.

The dude was on the right-hand side of the road, thumb out. I piano-keyed down the gears, and the air brakes hissed and squealed at the tap of my foot. The semi slowed and the big diesel made that gut-deep dinosaur-belch of shuddered-downness. I leaned across the cab as everything came to a halt and swung the door open.

"Where you heading?" I asked.

He laughed and shook his head, then spit on the soft shoulder. "I don't know," he said. "Hell, maybe." He was thin and tanned with long, greasy black hair and blue jeans and a vest. His straw hat was dirty and full of holes, but the feathers around the crown were bright and new-looking, pheasant, if I was any judge. A worn gold chain hung out of his vest going into his watch pocket. He wore old Frye boots with the toes turned up and soles thinner than my spare's retread. He looked an awful lot like I had when I hitchhiked out of Fresno, broke and unemployed, looking for work.

"Can I take you there?" I asked.

"Sho'." He climbed in and eased the door shut behind him, took out a kerchief and mopped his forehead, then blew his long nose and stared at me with bloodshot sleepless eyes. "What you hauling?" he asked.

"Souls," I said. "Whole shitload of them."

"What kind?" He was young, not more than twenty-five. He wanted to sound nonchalant, but I could hear the nerves.

"Usual kind," I said. "Human. Got some Hare Krishnas this time. Don't look too close anymore."

I coaxed the truck along, wondering if the engine was as bad as it sounded. When we were up to speed—eighty, eighty-five, no smokies on *this* road—he asked, "How long you been hauling?"

"Two years."

"Good pay?"

"It'll do."

"Benefits?"

"Union like everyone else."

"I heard about that," he said. "In that little dump about two miles back."

"People live there?" I asked. I didn't think anything lived along the road.

"Yeah. Real down folks. They said Teamster bosses get carried in limousines when they go."

"Don't really matter how you get there, I suppose. The trip's short, and forever is a long time."

"Getting there's all the fun?" he asked, trying to grin. I gave him a shallow one.

"What're you doing out here?" I asked a few minutes later. "You aren't dead, are you?" I'd never heard of dead folks running loose or looking quite as vital as he did, but I couldn't imagine anyone else being on the road. Dead folks—and drivers.

"No," he said. He was quiet for a bit. Then, slow, as if it embarrassed him, "I came to find my woman."

"Yeah?" Not much surprised me, but that was a new twist. "There ain't no returning, you know."

"Sherill's her name, spelled like sheriff but with two L's."

"Got a cigarette?" I asked. I didn't smoke, but I could use them later. He handed me the last three in a crush-proof pack, not just one but all, and didn't say anything.

"Haven't heard of her," I said. "But then, I don't get to converse with everybody I haul. And there are lots of trucks, lots of drivers."

"I know," he said. "But I heard about them benefits."

He had a crazy kind of sad look in his eye when he glanced at me, and that made me angry. I tightened my jaw and stared straight ahead.

"You know," he said, "back in that town they tell some crazy stories. About how they use old trains for China and India, and in Russia there's a tramline. In Mexico it's old buses along roads, always at night—"

"Listen, I don't use all the benefits," I said. "I know some do, but I don't."

"Sure, I got you," he said, nodding that exaggerated goddamn young folks' nod, his whole neck and shoulders moving along, it's all right everything's cool.

"How you gonna find her?" I asked.

"I don't know. Do the road, ask the drivers."

"How'd you get in?"

He didn't answer for a moment. "I'm coming here when I die. That's pretty sure. It's not so hard for folks like me to get in beforehand. And . . . my daddy was a driver. He told me the route. By the way, my name's Bill."

"Mine's John," I said.

"Glad to meet you."

We didn't say much after that for a while. He stared out the right window and I watched the desert and faraway shacks go by. Soon the mountains came looming up—space seems compressed on the road, especially once past the desert—and I sped up for the approach. There was some noise from the back.

"What'll you do when you get off work?" Bill asked.

"Go home and sleep."

"Nobody knows?"

"Just the union."

"That's the way it was with Daddy, until just before the end. Look, I didn't mean to make you mad or nothing. I'd just heard about the perks, and I thought . . ." He swallowed, his Adam's apple bobbing. "Thought you might be able to help. I don't know how I'll ever find Sherill. Maybe back in the annex . . ."

"Nobody in their right minds goes into the yards by choice," I said. "And you'd have to look over everybody that's died in the last four months. They're way backed up."

Bill took that like a blow across the face, and I was sorry I'd said it. "She's only been gone a week," he said.

"Well," I said.

"My mom died two years ago, just before Daddy."

"The High Road," I said.

"What?"

"Hope they both got the High Road."

"Mom, maybe. Yeah. She did. But not Daddy. He knew." Bill hawked and spit out the window. "Sherill, she's here—but she don't belong."

I couldn't help but grin.

"No, man, I mean it, I belong but not her. She was in this car wreck couple of months back. Got pretty badly messed up. I'd dealed her dope at first and then fell in love with her, and by the time she landed in the hospital, she was, you know, hooked on about four different things."

My arms stiffened on the wheel.

"I tried to tell her when I visited that it wouldn't be good for her to get anything, no more dope, but she begged me. What could I do? I loved her." He wasn't looking out the window now. He was looking down at his worn boots and nodding. "She begged me, man. So I brought her stuff. I mean she took it all when they weren't looking. She just took it *all*. They pumped her out, but her insides were just gone. I didn't hear about her being dead until two days ago, and that really burned me. I was the only one who loved her and they didn't even tell me. I had to go up to her room and find her bed empty. Jesus. I hung out at Daddy's union hall. Someone talked to someone else and I found her name on a list. The Low Road."

I hadn't known it was that easy to find out; but then, I'd never traveled in dopers' territory. Dope can loosen a lot of lips.

"I don't use any of those perks," I said, just to make it clear I couldn't help him. "Folks in back got enough trouble without me. I think the union went too far there."

"Bet they felt you'd get lonely, need company," Bill said quietly, looking at me. "It don't hurt the folks back there. Maybe give them another chance to, you know, think things over. Give 'em relief for a couple of hours, a break from the mash—"

"Listen, a couple of hours don't mean nothing in relation to eternity. I'm not so sure I won't be joining them someday, and if that's the way it is, I want it smooth, nobody pulling me out of a trailer and putting me back in."

"Yeah," he said. "Got you, man. I know where that's at. But she might be back there right now, and all you'd have to—"

"Bad enough I'm driving this rig in the first place." I wanted to change the subject.

"Yeah. How'd that happen?"

"Couple of accidents. Hot-rodding with an old fart in a Triumph. Nearly ran over some joggers on a country road. My premiums went up to where I couldn't afford payments and finally they took my truck away."

"You coulda gone without insurance."

"Not me," I said. "Anyway, some bad word got out. No companies would hire me. I went to the union to see if they could help. They told me I was a dead-ender, either get out of trucking or . . ." I shrugged. "This. I couldn't leave trucking. It's bad out there, getting work. Lots of unemployed. Couldn't see myself pushing a hack in some big city."

"No, man," Bill said, giving me that whole-body nod again. He cackled sympathetically.

"They gave me an advance, enough for a down payment on my rig." The truck was grinding a bit but maintaining. Over the mountains, through a really impressive pass like from an old engraving, and down in a rugged rocky valley, was the City. I'd deliver my cargo, get my slip, and take the rig (with Bill) back to Baker. Park it in the yard next to my cottage after letting him out someplace sane.

Get some sleep.

Start over again next Monday, two loads a week.

"I don't think I'd better go on," Bill said. "I'll hitch with some other rig, ask around."

"Well, I'd feel better if you rode with me back out of here. Want my advice?" Bad habit. "Go home—"

"No," Bill said. "Thanks anyway. I can't go home. Not without Sherill. She don't belong here." He took a deep breath. "I'll try to work up a trade. I stay, she goes to the High Road. That's the way the game runs down here, isn't it?"

I didn't tell him otherwise. I couldn't be sure he wasn't right. He'd made it this far. At the top of the pass I pulled the rig over and let him out. He waved at me, I waved back, and we went our separate ways.

Poor rotten doping son of a bitch. I'd screwed up my life half a dozen different ways—three wives, liquor, three years at Tehachapi—but I'd never done dope. I felt self-righteous just listening to the dude. I was glad to be rid of him, truth be told.

The City looks a lot like a county full of big white cathedrals. Casting against type. High wall around the perimeter, stretching as far as my eye can see. No horizon but a vanishing point, the wall looking like an endless highway turned on its side. As I geared the truck down for the decline, the noise in the trailers got irritating again. They could smell what was coming, I guess, like pigs stepping up to the man with the knife.

I pulled into the disembarkation terminal and backed the first trailer up to the holding pen. Employees let down the gates and used some weird kind of prod to herd them. These people were past mortal.

Employees unhooked the first trailer and I backed in the second.

I got down out of the cab and an employee came up to me, a big fellow with red eyes and brand-new coveralls. "Good ones this load?" he asked. His breath was like the end of a cabbage, bean and garlic dinner.

I shook my head and held a cigarette out for a light. He pressed his fingernail against the tip. The tip flared and settled down to a steady glow. He looked at it with pure lust.

"Listen," I said. "You had anyone named Sherill through here?"

"Who's asking?" he grumbled, still eyeing the cigarette. He started to do a slow dance.

"Just curious. I heard you guys knew all the names."

"So?" He stopped. He had to walk around, otherwise his shoes melted the asphalt and got stuck. He came back and stood, lifting one foot, twisting a bit, then putting it down and lifting the other.

"So," I said, with as much sense.

"Like Cherry with an L?"

"No. Sherill, like sheriff but with two L's."

"Couple of Cheryls. No Sherills," he said. "Now . . ."

I handed him the cigarette. They loved the things. "Thanks," I said. I pulled another out of the pack and gave it to him. He popped both of them into his mouth and chewed, bliss pushing over his seamed face. Tobacco smoke came out his nose and he swallowed. "Nothing to it," he said, and walked on.

The road back is shorter than the road in. Don't ask how. I'd have thought it was the other way around, but barriers are what's important, not distance. Maybe we all get our chances so the road to Hell is long. But once we're there, there's no returning. You have to save on the budget somewhere.

I took the empties back to Baker. Didn't see Bill. Eight hours later I was in bed, beer in hand, paycheck on the bureau, my eyes wide open.

Shit, I thought. Now my conscience was working. I could have sworn I was past that. But then, I didn't use the perks. I wouldn't drive without insurance.

I wasn't really cut out for the life.

THERE ARE NO NORMAL DAYS and nights on the road to Hell. No matter how long you drive, it's always the same time when you arrive as when you left, but it's not necessarily the same time from trip to trip.

The next trip, it was cool dusk, and the road didn't pass through desert and small, empty towns. Instead, it crossed a bleak flatland of skeletal trees, all the same uniform gray as if cut from paper. When I pulled over to catch a nap—never sleeping more than two hours at a stretch—the shouts of the damned in the trailers bothered me even more than usual. Silly things they said, like:

"You can take us back, mister! You really can!"

"Can he?"

"Shit no, mofuck pig."

"You can let us out! We can't hurt you!"

That was true enough. Drivers were alive, and the dead could never hurt the living. But I'd heard what happened when you let them out. There were about ninety of them in back, and in any load there was always one would make you want to use your perks.

I scratched my itches in the narrow bunk, looking at the Sierra Club calendar hanging just below the fan. The Devil's Postpile. The load became quieter as the voices gave up, one after the other. There was one last shout—some obscenity—then silence.

It was then I decided I'd let them out and see if Sherill was there, or if anyone knew her. They mingled in the annex, got their last socializing before the City. Some-one might know. Then I saw Bill again—

What? What could I do to help him? He had screwed Sherill up royally, but then, she'd had a hand in it too, and that was what Hell was all about. Poor stupid sons of bitches.

I swung out of the cab, tucking in my shirt and pulling my straw hat down on my crown. "Hey!" I said, walking alongside the trailers. Faces peered at me from the two inches between each white slat. "I'm going to let you out. Just for a while. I need some information."

"Ask!" someone screamed. "Just ask, goddammit!"

"You know you can't run away. You can't hurt me. You're all dead. Understand?"

"We know," said another voice, quieter.

"Maybe we can help."

"I'm going to open the gates one trailer at a time." I went to the rear trailer first, took out my keys and undid the Yale padlock. Then I swung the gates open, standing back a little like there was some kind of infected wound about to drain.

They were all naked, but they weren't dirty. I'd seen them in the annex yards and at the City; I knew they weren't like concentration camp prisoners. The dead can't really be unhealthy. Each just had some sort of air about him telling why he was in Hell; nothing specific but subliminal.

Like three black dudes in the rear trailer, first to step out. Why they were going to Hell was all over their faces. They weren't in the least sorry for the lives they'd led. They wanted to keep on doing what had brought them here in the first place—scav-enging, hurting, hurting *me* in particular.

"Stupid ass mofuck," one of them said, staring at me beneath thin, expressive eyebrows. He nodded and swung his fists, trying to pound the slats from the outside, but the blows hardly made them vibrate.

An old woman crawled down, hair white and neatly coifed. I couldn't be certain what she had done, but she made me uneasy. She might have been the worst in the load. And lots of others, young, old, mostly old. Quiet for the most part.

They looked me over, some defiant, most just bewildered.

"I need to know if there's anyone here named Sherill," I said, "who happens to know a fellow named Bill."

"That's my name," said a woman hidden in the crowd.

"Let me see her." I waved my hand at them. The black dudes came forward. A funny look got in their eyes and they backed away. The others parted and a young woman walked out. "How do you spell your name?" I asked.

She got a panicked expression. She spelled it, hesitating, hoping she'd make the grade. I felt horrible already. She was a Cheryl.

"Not who I'm looking for," I said.

"Don't be hasty," she said, real soft. She wasn't trying hard to be seductive, but she was succeeding. She was very pretty with medium-sized breasts, hips like a teen-ager's, legs not terrific but nice. Her black hair was clipped short and her eyes were almost Oriental. I figured maybe she was Lebanese or some other kind of Middle Eastern.

I tried to ignore her. "You can walk around a bit," I told them. "I'm letting out the first trailer now." I opened the side gates on that one and the people came down. They didn't smell, didn't look hungry, they just all looked pale. I wondered if the torment had begun already, but if so, I decided, it wasn't the physical kind.

One thing I'd learned in my two years was that all the Sunday school and horror movie crap about Hell was dead wrong.

"Woman named Sherill," I repeated. No one stepped forward. Then I felt someone close to me and I turned. It was the Cheryl woman. She smiled. "I'd like to sit up front for a while," she said.

"So would we all, sister," said the white-haired old woman. The black dudes stood off separate, talking low.

I swallowed, looking at her. Other drivers said they were real insubstantial except at one activity. That was the perk. And it was said the hottest ones always ended up in Hell.

"No," I said. I motioned for them to get back into the trailers. Whatever she was on the Low Road for, it wouldn't affect her performance in the sack, that was obvious.

It had been a dumb idea all around. They went back and I returned to the cab, lighting up a cigarette and thinking about what had made me do it.

I shook my head and started her up. Thinking on a dead run was no good. "No," I said, "goddamn," I said, "good."

Cheryl's face stayed with me.

Cheryl's body stayed with me longer than the face.

Something always comes up in life to lure a man onto the Low Road, not driving but riding in the back. We all have some weakness. I wondered what reason God had to give us each that little flaw, like a chip in crystal, you press the chip hard enough, everything splits up crazy.

At least now I knew one thing. My flaw wasn't sex, not this way. What most struck me about Cheryl was wonder. She was so pretty; how'd she end up on the Low Road?

For that matter, what had Bill's Sherill done?

I returned hauling empties and found myself this time outside a small town called Shoshone. I pulled my truck into the cafe parking lot. The weather was cold and I left the engine running. It was about eleven in the morning and the cafe was half-full. I took a seat at the counter next to an old man with maybe four teeth in his head, attacking French toast with downright solemn dignity. I ordered eggs and hash browns and juice, ate quickly, and went back to my truck.

Bill stood next to the cab. Next to him was an enormous young woman with a face like a bulldog. She was wrapped in a filthy piece of plaid fabric that might have been snatched from a trash dump somewhere. "Hey," Bill said. "Remember me?"

"Sure."

"I saw you pulling up. I thought you'd like to know . . . This is Sherill. I got her out of there." The woman stared at me with all the expression of a brick. "It's all screwy. Like a power failure or something. We just walked out on the road and nobody stopped us."

Sherill could have hid any number of weirdnesses beneath her formidable looks and gone unnoticed by ordinary folks. But I didn't have any trouble picking out the biggest thing wrong with her: she was dead. Bill had brought her out of Hell. I looked around to make sure I was in the World. I was. He wasn't lying. Something serious had happened on the Low Road.

"Trouble?" I asked.

"Lots." He grinned at me. "Pan-demon-ium." His grin broadened.

"That can't happen," I said. Sherill trembled, hearing my voice.

"He's a *driver*, Bill," she said. "He's the one takes us there. We should git out of here." She had that soul-branded air and the look of a pig that's just escaped slaughter, seeing the butcher again. She took a few steps backward. Gluttony, I thought. Gluttony and buried lust and a real ugly way of seeing life, inner eye pulled all out of shape by her bulk.

Bill hadn't had much to do with her ending up on the Low Road.

"Tell me more," I said.

"There's folks running all over down there, holing up in them towns, devils chasing them—"

"Employees," I corrected.

"Yeah. Every which way."

Sherill tugged on his arm. "We got to go, Bill."

"We got to go," he echoed. "Hey, man, thanks. I found her!" He nodded his whole-body nod and they were off down the street, Sherill's plaid wrap dragging in the dirt.

I drove back to Baker, wondering if the trouble was responsible for my being rerouted through Shoshone. I parked in front of my little house and sat inside with a beer while it got dark, checking my calendar for the next day's run and feeling very cold. I can take so much supernatural in its place, but now things were spilling over, smudging the clean-drawn line between my work and the World. Next day I was scheduled to be at the annex and take another load.

Nobody called that evening. If there was trouble on the Low Road, surely the union would let me know, I thought.

I drove to the annex early in the morning. The crossover from the World to the Low Road was normal; I followed the route and the sky muddied from blue to solder-color and I was on the first leg to the annex. I backed the rear trailer up to the yard's gate and unhitched it, then placed the forward trailer at a ramp, all the while keeping my ears tuned to pick up interesting conversation.

The employees who work the annex look human. I took my invoice from a red-faced old guy with eyes like billiard balls and looked at him like I was in the know but could use some updating. He spit smoking saliva on the pavement, returned my look slantwise and said nothing. Maybe it was all settled. I hitched up both full trailers and pulled out.

I didn't even mention Sherill and Bill. Like in most jobs, keeping one's mouth shut is good policy. That and don't volunteer.

It was the desert again this time, only now the towns and tumbledown houses looked bomb-blasted, like something big had come through flushing out game with a howitzer.

Eyes on the road. Push that rig.

Four hours in, I came to a roadblock. Nobody on it, no employees, just big carved-lava barricades cutting across all lanes, and beyond them a yellow smoke which, the driver's unwritten instructions advised, meant absolutely no entry.

I got out. The load was making noises. I suddenly hated them. Nothing beautiful there—just naked Hell-bounders shouting and screaming and threatening like it wasn't already over for them. They'd had their chance and crapped out and now they were still bullshitting the World.

Least they could do was go with dignity and spare me their misery.

That's probably what the engineers on the trains to Auschwitz thought. Yeah, yeah, except I was the fellow who might be hauling those engineers to their just deserts.

Crap, I just couldn't be one way or the other about the whole thing. I could feel mad and guilty and I could think Jesus, probably I'll be complaining just as much when my time comes. Jesus H. Twentieth Century Man Christ.

I stood by the truck, waiting for instructions or some indication what I was supposed to do. The load became quieter after a while, but I heard noises off the road, screams mostly and far away.

"There isn't anything," I said to myself, lighting up on of Bill's cigarettes even though I don't smoke and dragging deep, "*anything* worth this shit." I vowed I would quit after this run.

I heard something come up behind the trailers and I edged closer to the cab steps. High wisps of smoke obscured things at first, but a dark shape three or four yards high plunged through and stood with one hand on the top slats of the rear trailer. It was covered with naked people, crawling all over, biting and scratching and shouting obscenities. It made little grunting noises, fell to its knees, then stood again and lurched off the road. Some of the people hanging on saw me and shouted for me to come help.

"Help us get this son of a bitch down!"

"Hey, you! We've almost got 'im!"

"He's a driver—"

"Fuck 'im, then."

I'd never seen an employee so big before, nor in so much trouble. The load began to wail like banshees. I threw down my cigarette and ran after it.

Workers will tell you. Camaraderie extends even to those on the job you don't like. If they're in trouble, it's part of the mystique to help out. Besides, the unwritten instructions were very clear on such things, and I've never knowingly broken a job rule—not since getting my rig back—and couldn't see starting now.

Through the smoke and across great ridges of lava, I ran until I spotted the employee about ten yards ahead. It had shaken off the naked people and was standing with one in each hand. Its shoulders smoked and scales stood out at all angles. They'd really done a job on the bastard. Ten or twelve of the dead were picking themselves off the lava, unscraped, unbruised. They saw me.

The employee saw me.

Everyone came at me. I turned and ran for the truck, stumbling, falling, bruising and scraping myself everywhere. My hair stood on end. People grabbed me, pleading for me to haul them out, old, young, all fawning and screeching like whipped dogs.

Then the employee swung me up out of reach. Its hand was cold and hard like iron tongs kept in a freezer. It grunted and ran toward my truck, opening the door wide and throwing me roughly inside. It made clear with huge, wild gestures that I'd better turn around and go back, that waiting was no good and there was no way through.

I started the engine and turned the rig around. I rolled up my window and hoped the dead weren't substantial enough to scratch paint or tear up slats.

All rules were off now. What about the ones in my load? All the while I was doing these things, my head was full of questions, like how could souls fight back and wasn't there some inflexible order in Hell that kept such things from happening? That was what had been implied when I hired on. Safest job around.

I headed back down the road. My load screamed like no load I'd ever had before. I was afraid they might get loose, but they didn't. I got near the annex and they were quiet again, too quiet for me to hear over the diesel.

The yards were deserted. The long, white-painted cement platforms and white-washed wood-slat loading ramps were unattended. No souls in the pens.

The sky was an indefinite gray. An out-of-focus yellow sun gleamed faintly off the stark white employees' lounge. I stopped the truck and swung down to investigate.

There was no wind, only silence. The air was frosty without being particularly cold. What I wanted to do most was unload and get out of there, go back to Baker or Barstow or Shoshone.

I hoped that was still possible. Maybe all exits had been closed. Maybe the overseers had closed them to keep any more souls from getting out.

I tried the gate latches and found I could open them. I did so and returned to the truck, swinging the rear trailer around until it was flush with the ramp. Nobody made a sound. "Go on back," I said. "Go on back. You've got more time here. Don't ask me how."

"Hello, John." That was behind me. I turned and saw an older man without any clothes on. I didn't recognize him at first. His eyes finally clued me in.

"Mr. Martin?" My high school history teacher. I hadn't seen him in maybe twenty years. He didn't look much older, but then, I'd never seen him naked. He was dead, but he wasn't like the others. He didn't have that look that told me why he was here.

"This is not the sort of job I'd expect one of my students to take," Martin said. He laughed the smooth laugh he was famous for, the laugh that seemed to take everything he said in class and put it in perspective.

"You're not the first person I'd expect to find here," I responded.

"The cat's away, John. The mice are in charge now. I'm going to try to leave."

"How long you been here?" I asked.

"I died a month ago, I think," Martin said, never one to mince words.

"You can't leave," I said. Doing my job even with Mr. Martin. I felt the ice creep up my throat.

"Team player," Martin said. "Still the screwball team player, even when the team doesn't give a damn what you do."

I wanted to explain, but he waked away toward the annex and the road out. Looking back over his shoulder, he said, "Get smart, John. Things aren't what they seem. Never have been."

"Look!" I shouted after him. "I'm going to quit, honest, but this load is my responsibility." I thought I saw him shake his head as he rounded the corner of the annex.

The dead in my load had pried loose some of the ramp slats and were jumping off the rear trailer. Those in the forward trailer were screaming and carrying on, shaking the whole rig.

Responsibility, shit, I thought. As the dead followed after Mr. Martin, I unhitched both trailers. Then I got in the cab and swung away from the annex, onto the incoming road. "I'm going to quit," I said. "Sure as anything, I'm going to quit."

The road out seemed awfully long. I didn't see any of the dead, surprisingly, but then, maybe they'd been shunted away. I was taking a route I'd never been on before, and I had no way of knowing if it would put me where I wanted to be. But I hung in there for two hours, running the truck dead-out on the flats.

The air was getting grayer like somebody turning down the contrast on a TV set. I switched on the high beams, but they didn't help. By now I was shaking in the cab and saying to myself, Nobody deserves this. Nobody deserves going to Hell no matter what they did. I was scared. It was getting colder.

Three hours and I saw the annex and yards ahead of me again. The road had looped back. I swore and slowed the rig to a crawl. The loading docks had been set on fire. Dead were wandering around with no idea what to do or where to go. I sped up and drove over the few that were on the road. They'd come up and the truck's bumper would hit them and I wouldn't feel a thing, like they weren't there. I'd see them in the rearview mirror, getting up after being knocked over. Just knocked over. Then I was away from the loading docks and there was no doubt about it this time.

I was heading straight for Hell.

The disembarkation terminal was on fire, too. But beyond it, the City was bright and white and untouched. For the first time I drove past the terminal and took the road into the City.

It was either that or stay on the flats with everything screwy. Inside, I thought maybe they'd have things under control.

The truck roared through the gate between two white pillars maybe seventy or eighty feet thick and as tall as the Washington Monument. I didn't see anybody, employees or the dead. Once I was through the pillars—and it came as a shock—

There was no City, no walls, just the road winding along and countryside in all directions, even behind.

The countryside was covered with shacks, houses, little clusters and big clusters. Everything was tight-packed, people working together on one hill, people sitting on their porches, walking along paths, turning to stare at me as the rig barreled on through. No employees—no monsters. No flames. No bloody lakes or rivers.

This must be the outside part, I thought. Deeper inside it would get worse.

I kept on driving. The dog part of me was saying let's go look for authority and ask some questions and get out. But the monkey was saying let's just go look and find out what's going on, what Hell is all about.

Another hour of driving through that calm, crowded landscape and the truck ran out of fuel. I coasted to the side and stepped down from the cab, very nervous.

Again I lit up a cigarette and leaned against the fender, shaking a little. But the shaking was running down and a tight kind of calm was replacing it.

The landscape was still condensed, crowded, but nobody looked tortured. No screaming, no eternal agony. Trees and shrubs and grass hills and thousands and thousands of little houses.

It took about ten minutes for the inhabitants to get around to investigating me. Two men came over to my truck and nodded cordially. Both were middle-aged and healthy-looking. They didn't look dead. I nodded back.

"We were betting whether you're one of the drivers or not," said the first, a black-haired fellow. He wore a simple handwoven shirt and pants. "I think you are. That so?"

"I am."

"You're lost, then."

I agreed. "Maybe you can tell me where I am?"

"Hell," said the second man, younger by a few years and just wearing shorts. The way he said it was just like you might say you came from Los Angeles or Long Beach. Nothing big, nothing dramatic.

"We've heard rumors there's been problems outside," a woman said, coming up to join us. She was about sixty and skinny. She looked like she should be twitchy and nervous, but she acted rock-steady. They were all rock-steady.

"There's some kind of strike," I said. "I don't know what it is, but I'm looking for an employee to tell me."

"They don't usually come this far in," the first man said. "We run things here. Or rather, nobody tells us what to do."

"You're alive?" the woman asked, a curious hunger in her voice. Others came around to join us, a whole crowd. They didn't try to touch. They stood their ground and stared and talked.

"Look," said an old black fellow. "You ever read about the Ancient Mariner?"

I said I had in school.

"Had to tell everybody what he did," the black fellow said. The woman beside him nodded slowly. "We're all Ancient Mariners here. But there's nobody to tell it to. Would you like to know?" The way he asked was pitiful. "We're sorry. We just want everybody to know how sorry we are."

"I can't take you back," I said. "I don't know how to get there myself."

"We can't go back," the woman said. "That's not our place."

More people were coming and I was nervous again. I stood my ground, trying to seem calm, and the dead gathered around me, eager.

"I never thought of anybody but myself," one said. Another interrupted with, "Man, I fucked my whole life away, I hated everybody and everything. I was burned out—"

"I thought I was the greatest. I could pass judgment on everybody—"

"I was the stupidest goddamn woman you ever saw. I was a sow, a pig. I farrowed kids and let them run wild, without no guidance. I was stupid and cruel, too. I used to hurt things—"

"Never cared for anyone. Nobody ever cared for me. I was left to rot in the middle of a city and I wasn't good enough not to rot."

"Everything I did was a lie after I was about twelve years old—"

"Listen to me, mister, because it hurts, it hurts so bad—"

I backed up against my truck. They were lining up now, organized, not like any mob. I had a crazy thought they were behaving better than any people on Earth, but these were the damned.

I didn't hear or see anybody famous. An ex-cop told me about what he did to people in jails. A Jesus-freak told me that knowing Jesus in your heart wasn't enough. "Because I should have made it, man, I should have made it."

"A time came and I was just broken by it all, broke myself really. Just kept stepping on myself and making all the wrong decisions—"

They confessed to me, and I began to cry. Their faces were so clear and so pure, yet here they were, confessing, and except maybe for specific things—like the fellow who had killed Ukrainians after the Second World War in Russian camps—they didn't sound any worse than the crazy sons of bitches I called friends who spent their lives in trucks or bars or whorehouses.

They were all recent. I got the impression the deeper into Hell you went, the older the damned became, which made sense; Hell, just got bigger, each crop of damned got bigger, with more room on the outer circles.

"We wasted it," someone said. "You know what my greatest sin was? I was dull. Dull and cruel. I never saw beauty. I saw only dirt. I loved the dirt, and the clean just passed me by."

Pretty soon my tears were uncontrollable. I kneeled down beside the truck, hiding my head, but they kept on coming and confessing. Hundreds must have passed, talking quietly, gesturing with their hands.

Then they stopped. Someone had come and told them to back away, that they were too much for me. I took my face out of my hands and a very young-seeming fellow stood looking down on me. "You all right?" he asked.

I nodded, but my insides were like broken glass. With every confession I had seen myself, and with every tale of sin, I had felt an answering echo.

"Someday, I'm going to be here. Someone's going to drive me in a cattle car to Hell," I mumbled. The young fellow helped me to my feet and cleared a way around my truck.

"Yeah, but not now," he said. "You don't belong here yet." He opened the door to my cab and I got back inside.

"I don't have any fuel," I said.

He smiled that sad smile they all had and stood on the step, up close to my ear. "You'll be taken out of here soon anyway. One of the employees is bound to get around to you." He seemed a lot more sophisticated than the others. I looked at him maybe a little queerly, like there was some explaining in order.

"Yeah, I know all that stuff," he said. "I was a driver once. Then I got promoted. What are they all doing back there?" He gestured up the road. "They're really messing things up now, ain't they?"

"I don't know," I said, wiping my eyes and cheeks with my sleeve.

"You go back, and you tell them that all this revolt on the outer circles, it's what I expected. Tell them Charlie's here and that I warned them. Word's getting around. There's bound to be discontent.

"Word?"

"About who's in charge. Just tell them Charlie knows and I warned them. I know something else, and you shouldn't tell anybody about this . . ." He whispered an incredible fact into my ear then, something that shook me deeper than what I had already been through.

I closed my eyes. Some shadow passed over. The young fellow and everybody else seemed to recede. I felt rather than saw my truck being picked up like a toy.

Then I suppose I was asleep for a time.

In the cab in the parking lot of a truck stop in Bakersfield, I jerked awake, pulled my cap out of my eyes and looked around. It was about noon. There was a union hall in Bakersfield. I checked and my truck was full of diesel, so I started her up and drove to the union hall.

I knocked on the door of the office. I went in and recognized the fat old dude who had given me the job in the first place. I was tired and I smelled bad, but I wanted to get it all done with now.

He recognized me but didn't know my name until I told him. "I can't work the run anymore," I said. The shakes were on me again. "I'm not the one for it. I don't feel right driving them when I know I'm going to be there myself, like as not."

"Okay," he said, slow and careful, sizing me up with a knowing eye. "But you're out. You're busted then. No more driving, no more work for us, no more work for any union we support. It'll be lonely."

"I'll take that kind of lonely any day," I said.

"Okay." That was that. I headed for the door and stopped with my hand on the knob.

"One more thing," I said. "I met Charlie. He says to tell you word's getting around about who's in charge, and that's why there's so much trouble in the outer circles."

The old dude's knowing eye went sort of glassy. "You're the fellow got into the City?"

I nodded.

He got up from his seat real fast, jowls quivering and belly doing a silly dance beneath his work blues. He flicked one hand at me, come'ere. "Don't go. Just you wait a minute. Outside in the office."

I waited and heard him talking on the phone. He came out smiling and put his hand on my shoulder. "Listen, John, I'm not sure we should let you quit. I didn't know you were the one who'd gone inside. Word is, you stuck around and tried to help when everybody else ran. The company appreciates that. You've been with us a long time, reliable driver, maybe we should give you some incentive to stay. I'm sending you to Vegas to talk with a company man . . ."

The way he said it, I knew there wasn't much choice and I better not fight it. You work union long enough and you know when you keep your mouth shut and go along.

They put me up in a motel and fed me, and by late morning I was on my way to Vegas, arriving about two in the afternoon. I was in a black union car with a silent driver and air conditioning and some *Newsweek*s to keep me company.

The limo dropped me off in front of a four-floor office building, glass and stucco, with lots of divorce lawyers and a dentist and small companies with anonymous names. White plastic letters on a ribbed felt background in a glass case. There was no name on the office number I had been told to go to, but I went up and knocked anyway.

I don't know what I expected. A district supervisor opened the door and asked me a few questions and I said what I'd said before. I was adamant. He looked worried. "Look," he said. "It won't be good for you now if you quit."

I asked him what he meant by that, but he just looked unhappy and said he was going to send me to somebody higher up.

That was in Denver, nearer my God to thee. The same black car took me there, and Saturday morning, bright and early, I stood in front of a very large corporate building with no sign out front and a bank on the bottom floor. I went past the bank and up to the very top.

A secretary met me, pretty but her hair done up very tight and her jaw grimly square. She didn't like me. She let me into the next office, though.

I swear I'd seen the fellow before, but maybe it was just a passing resemblance. He wore a narrow tie and a tasteful but conservative gray suit. His shirt was pastel blue and there was a big Rembrandt Bible on his desk, sitting on the glass top next to an alabaster pen holder. He shook my hand firmly and perched on the edge of the desk.

"First, let me congratulate you on your bravery. We've had some reports from the . . . uh . . . field, and we're hearing nothing but good about you." He smiled like that fellow on TV who's always asking the audience to give him some help. Then is face got sincere and serious. I honestly believe he was sincere; he was also well trained in dealing with not-very-bright people. "I hear you have a report for me. From Charles Frick."

"He said his name was Charlie." I told him the story. "What I'm curious about, what did he mean, this thing about who's in charge?"

"Charlie was in Organization until last year. He died in a car accident. I'm shocked to hear he got the Low Road." He didn't look shocked. "Maybe I'm shocked but not surprised. To tell the truth, he was a bit of a troublemaker." He smiled brightly again and his eyes got large and there was a little too much animation in his face. He had on these MacArthur wire-rimmed glasses too big for his eyes.

"What did he mean?"

"John, I'm proud of all our drivers. You don't know how proud we all are of you folks down there doing the dirty work."

"What did Charlie mean?"

"The abortionists and pornographers, the hustlers and muggers and murderers. Atheists and heathens and idol-worshippers. Surely there must be some satisfaction in keeping the land clean. Sort of a giant sanitation squad, you people keep the scum away from the good folks. The plain good folks. Now, we know that driving's maybe the hardest job we have in the company, and that not everyone can stay on the Low Road indefinitely. Still, we'd like you to stay on. Not as a driver—unless you really wish to continue. For the satisfaction of a tough job. No, if you want to move up— and you've earned it by now, surely—we have a place for you here. A place where you'll be comfortable and—"

"I've already said I want out. You're acting like I'm hot stuff and I'm just shit. You know that, I know that. What is going on?"

His face hardened on me. "It isn't easy up here, either, buster." The "buster" bit tickled me. I laughed and got up from the chair. I'd been in enough offices, and this fancy one just made me queasy. When I stood, he held up his hand and pursed his lips as he nodded. "Sorry. There's incentive, there's certainly a reason why you should want to work here. If you're so convinced you're on your way to the Low Road, you can work it off here, you know."

"How can you say that?"

Bright smile. "Charlie told you something. He told you about who's in charge here."

Now I could smell something terribly wrong, like with the union boss. I mumbled, "He said that's why there's trouble."

"It comes every now and then. We put it down gentle. I tell you where we really need good people, compassionate people. We need them to help with the choosing."

"Choosing?"

"Surely you don't think the Boss does all the choosing directly?"

I couldn't think of a thing to say.

"Listen, the Boss . . . let me tell you. A long time ago, the Boss decided to create a new kind of worker, one with more decision-making ability. Some of the supervisors disagreed, especially when the Boss said the workers would be around for a long, long time—that they'd be indestructible. Sort of like nuclear fuel, you know. Human souls. The waste builds up after a time, those who turn out bad, turn out to be chronically unemployable. They don't go along with the scheme, or get out of line. Can't get along with their fellow workers. You know the type. What do you do with them? Can't just let them go away—they're indestructible, and that ain't no joke, so—"

"Chronically unemployable?"

"You're a union man. Think of what it must feel like to be out of work . . . *forever*. Damned. Nobody will hire you."

I knew the feeling, both the way he meant it and the way it had happened to me.

"The Boss feels the project half succeeded, so He doesn't dump it completely. But He doesn't want to be bothered with all the pluses and minutes, the bookkeeping."

"*You're* in charge," I said, my blood cooling.

And I knew where I had seen him before.

On television.

God's right-hand man.

And human. Flesh and blood.

We ran Hell.

He nodded. "Now, that's not the sort of thing we'd like to get around."

"You're in charge, and you let the drivers take their perks on the loads, you let—" I stopped, instinct telling me I would soon be on a rugged trail with no turnaround.

"I'll tell you the truth, John. I have only been in charge here for a year, and my predecessor let things get out of hand. He wasn't a religious man, John, and he thought this was a job like any other, where you could compromise now and then. I know that isn't so. There's no compromise here, and we'll straighten out those inequities and bad decisions very soon. You'll help us, I hope. You may know more about the problems than we do."

"How do you . . . how do you qualify for a job like this?" I asked. "And who offered it to you?"

"Not the Boss, if that's what you're getting at, John. It's been kind of traditional. You may have heard about me. I'm the one, when there was all this talk about after-death experiences and everyone was seeing bright light and beauty, I'm the one who wondered why no one was seeing the other side. I found people who had almost died and had seen Hell, and I turned their lives around. The management in the company decided a fellow with my ability could do good work here. And so I'm here. And I'll tell you, it isn't easy. I sometimes wish we had a little more help from the Boss, a little more guidance, but we don't, and somebody has to do it. Somebody has to clean out the stables, John." Again the smile.

I put on my mask. "Of course," I said. I hoped a gradual increase in piety would pass his sharp-eyed muster.

"And you can see how this all makes you much more valuable to the organization." I let light dawn slowly.

"We'd hate to lose you now, John. Not when there's security, so much security, working for us. I mean, here we learn the real ins and outs of salvation."

I let him talk at me until he looked at his watch, and all the time I nodded and considered and tried to think of the best ploy. Then I eased myself into a turnabout. I did some confessing until his discomfort was stretched too far—I was keeping him from an important appointment—and made my concluding statement.

"I just wouldn't feel right up here," I said. "I've driven all my life. I'd just want to keep on, working where I'm best suited."

"Keep your present job?" he said, tapping his shoe on the side of the desk.

"Lord, yes," I said, grateful as could be.

Then I asked him for his autograph. He smiled real big and gave it to me, God's right-hand man, who had prayed with presidents.

THE NEXT TIME OUT, I thought about the incredible thing that Charlie Frick had told me. Halfway to Hell, on the part of the run that he had once driven, I pulled the truck onto the gravel shoulder and walked back, hands in pockets, squinting at the faces. Young and old. Mostly old, or in their teens or twenties. Some were clearly bad news . . . But I was looking more closely this time, trying to discriminate. And sure enough, I saw a few that didn't seem to belong.

The dead hung by the slats, sticking their arms through, beseeching. I ignored as much of that as I could. "You," I said, pointing to a pale, thin fellow with a listless expression. "Why are you here?"

They wouldn't lie to me. I'd learned that inside the City. The dead don't lie.

"I kill people," the man said in a high whisper. "I kill children."

That confirmed my theory. I had *known* there was something wrong with him. I pointed to an old woman, plump and white-haired, lacking any of the signs. "You. Why are you going to Hell?"

She shook her head. "I don't know," she said. "Because I'm bad, I suppose."

"What did you do that was bad?"

"I don't know!" she said, flinging her hands up. "I really don't know. I was a librarian. When all those horrible people tried to take books out of my library, I fought them. I tried to reason with them . . . They wanted to remove Salinger and Twain and Baum . . ."

I picked out another young man. "What about you?"

"I didn't think it was possible," he said. "I didn't believe that God hated me, too."

"What did you do?" These people *didn't need to confess.*

"I loved God. I loved Jesus. But, dear Lord, I couldn't help it. I'm gay. I never had a choice. God wouldn't send me here just for being gay, would he?"

I spoke to a few more, until I was sure I had found all I had in this load. "You, you, you and you, out," I said, swinging open the rear gate. I closed the gate after them and led them away from the truck. Then I told them what Charlie Frick had told me, what he had learned on the road and in the big offices.

"Nobody's really sure where it goes," I said. "But it doesn't go to Hell, and it doesn't go back to Earth."

"Where, then?" the old woman asked plaintively. The hope in her eyes made me want to cry, because I just wasn't sure.

"Maybe it's the High Road," I said. "At least it's a chance. You light out across this stretch, go back of that hill, and I think there's some sort of trail. It's not easy to find, but if you look carefully, it's there. Follow it."

The young man who was gay took my hand. I felt like pulling away, because I've never been fond of homos. But he held on and he said, "Thank you. You must be taking a big risk."

"Yes, thank you," the librarian said. "Why are you doing it?"

I had hoped they wouldn't ask. "When I was a kid, one of my Sunday school teachers told me about Jesus going down to Hell during the three days before he rose up again. She told me Jesus went to Hell to bring out those who didn't belong. I'm certainly no Jesus, I'm not even much of a Christian, but that's what I'm doing. She called it Harrowing Hell." I shook my head. "Never mind. Just go," I said. I watched them walk across the gray flats and around the hill, then I got back into my truck and took the rest into the annex. Nobody noticed. I suppose the records just aren't that important to the employees.

None of the folks I've let loose have ever come back.

I'm staying on the road. I'm talking to people here and there, being cautious. When it looks like things are getting chancy, I'll take my rig back down to the City. And then I'm not sure what I'll do.

I don't want to let everybody loose. But I want to know who's ending up on the Low Road who shouldn't be. People unpopular with God's right-hand man.

My message is simple.

The crazy folks are running the asylum. We've corrupted Hell.

If I get caught, I'll be riding in back. And if you're reading this, chances are you'll be there, too.

Until then, I'm doing my bit. How about you?

HER PILGRIM SOUL

BY ALAN BRENNERT

HAWTHORNE WROTE AT LEAST TWO CAUTIONARY TALES ("RAPPACCINI'S DAUGHTER" AND "THE BIRTHMARK") OF SCIENTISTS WHO FELL IN LOVE WITH THEIR WORK MUCH TO THE DETRIMENT OF THOSE THEY LOVED, THUS CLEARLY SETTING THE ARCHETYPE FOR THE AMERICAN VERSION OF THE MAD SCIENTIST AS DESCRIBED IN MARY SHELLEY'S *FRANKENSTEIN*.

IN ALAN BRENNERT'S "HER PILGRIM SOUL," THE EXECUTION AND OUTCOME ARE MUCH MORE GENTLE, AND DESPITE ITS SCIENTIFIC TRAPPINGS OF THE PLOT, THE STORY IS MUCH MORE MAGICAL AND HUMANE, MUCH ALONG THE LINES OF THE EVOLUTION OF THE MAIN CHARACTER.

1

A pillar of stars stood in the center of the room: a shaft of deep violet light, perhaps three feet in diameter, rising from floor to ceiling like a Roman column—sculpted not of marble, but of light, and steel. Kevin watched, frowning, as a spiral nebula— a dusky rose in color—rotated elegantly on its axis, each spiral arm sweeping across the starfield in arcs of a billion years, revolving at its own accelerated pace . . . like a dancer, arms outstretched, growing older with each pirouette. It was lovely to watch, and when the astrophysics department saw their theoretical model so beautifully rendered, they'd surely be delighted; but there was something in it that disturbed him, and with a distracted tap on the keyboard he brought the wheeling spray of stars to a halt, then wiped it completely from the image area. In the same motion he called up another program, and now a gas giant—the same dusky rose as the nebula, its banded atmosphere merely deeper tones of the same color—appeared in the display. It arced in its vast orbit, disappearing from the column of light as the pastel rings of Saturn swung briefly into view—they too vanishing as they made way for Jupiter, the asteroid belt, Mars, and finally Earth, growing larger and larger in the display. The cloud cover scattered like smoke on water, Kevin feeling as though he were plummeting from thirty thousand feet—gaining momentum as he plunged through a second layer of clouds and the vivid topography of continents, oceans, and mountain ranges was revealed; the Earth rotated below him as he fell, then the line of horizon was lost and he was diving toward the urban gridwork of Boston, veering over the Charles River, the Yards and Commons of Cambridge looming up—

The image dispersed, scattered, dissolving back into a starfield once more. It was perfect. Every nuance of orbit and rotation taken into account; every detail of the Earth's surface reproduced to exact scale. The program had taken all the variables, all the parameters, and coordinated them without a hitch. It was the third time he'd run it today, and each time it had performed flawlessly; he should have been jubilant, he should have been giddy with triumph at the thought of three years of exhaustive research and development this near to fruition.

So why, instead, did he feel so empty . . . so depressed . . . when he looked at it? This device, once merely an abstract construct in his own imagination, now fully realized? Why couldn't he seem to take any joy in its creation, much less its completion?

Kevin sighed, ran a hand through his hair, and switched off the system. The column of violet light winked out, leaving two steel-blue cinctures on floor and ceiling; the room looked suddenly incomplete. And only when he'd pulled himself from his immersion in the strange starlight he'd conjured up did he realize that the phone was ringing; that it had, in fact, been ringing for quite some time. He crossed the lab to answer, stealing a glance at the clock, and realized he was late for his 2:00 optics class. With one hand he started shuffling papers into his briefcase; with the other he snapped up the phone. "Drayton," he said, more brusquely than he'd intended.

"Kev? Good God, the phone must've rung thirty times. You forget to put the machine on?"

Awkwardly he stripped off his white labcoat and shrugged into a suede sports jacket, juggling the receiver from hand to hand. "Carol, I can't talk just now, I'm late for class—"

"Are you okay?"

"Of course I am," he said, a bit peevishly. "I was just working. Can I call you after—"

"This won't take long." Kevin detected a certain sharpness in her tone, in response to his own. "Are we still meeting at Wirth's, at six?"

Damn. He'd forgotten to make the reservations, but he wasn't about to let Carol know that. "Right," he said, his free hand grabbing the phone book, flipping the Yellow Pages open to the restaurants section, "six o'clock, give or take a little."

"Is everything all right over there?"

"Everything's fine. I'm just late. See you at six, okay?" But it wasn't just his 2:00 class that made him anxious to end the conversation, this or a dozen others in recent months. His father would've called it ants-in-the-pants, as when the young Kevin would fidget restlessly around the house on a dull Sunday afternoon; but at least then he knew why he was anxious—for the life of him, he could not say what it was that made him so uncomfortable, so impatient, these days, around his wife.

"Okay," she said uncertainly. "See you then." He hung up, made a fast call to Jacob Wirth's in Boston, leaving his name and request for reservations on their answering machine, then hurried out of the lab, sealing the room with the palm of his hand pressed against an optical scanner—a burst of light, briefly silhouetting his splayed fingers, and then the door slid shut and locked, the room accessible now only to Kevin, or his lab assistant, Daniel.

Kevin took the stairs two at a time (spatial imaging projects were headquartered in the basement of the Wiesner Building, relatively buffered from the vibrations of ground traffic) and hurried out of the flash and dazzle of the Media Lab, cutting across Ames Street and McDermott Court to building fifty-six, where his class, accustomed to his rather rococo sense of punctuality, would be indulgently waiting for him—at least for the customary fifteen minutes' grace period, after which, also according to custom, they would bolt, run, and scatter like a flock of horny geese.

He still enjoyed them, even after ten years; these students who watched as Kevin ambled down the aisle of the classroom, who laughed as he joked with them about his own tardiness before launching into a discussion of the effects of second- and third-order nonlinear susceptibility—he liked them, liked being among them. Up here, standing at a podium or enthusiastically scribbling a Fresnel equation on the chalkboard, he felt at home in a way he did nowhere else. And at class's end, he would spend perhaps fifteen minutes talking with individual students, wondering which of them might show the kind of promise Daniel had, back when he'd been a student in one of Kevin's graduate seminars. He was an assistant professor now, and in point of fact only a year or two younger than Kevin, but though friends, they were not intimates, or confidants; as proud as he was of Daniel's achievements, and as grateful as he was to him for his help with the holography research, they rarely talked of anything but work, or campus politics.

But after class, when he returned to the lab, Daniel, as ever, was waiting for him, running through the astrophysics program again, a pale rose galaxy rotating inside the shaft of violet light; he seemed never to tire of it.

"Hi, Doc." It was a mark of the careful distance between the two men that Daniel rarely called him by his first name. "Looking good, isn't she?"

Kevin felt another pang of emptiness as he looked at the whorl of stars. At first he'd chalked it up to the stress of spending half his time in intensive research and the other half grading papers on Gaussian beams and Fourier spectroscopy; but as winter drew to a close and the pressure of finals eased, that sense of detachment, of depression, had remained. He could no longer attribute it to overwork or divided attention; but neither could he determine its cause.

All he could do was try to ignore it. He shrugged back into his labcoat. "Yes," he agreed. "Very good."

"I ran a full systems check—we should be ready for the presentation in another week, I'd guess, maybe less—"

Kevin wasn't listening. His mood had darkened as he flipped the answering machine to playback, listening to the message from Wirth's informing him that they were very sorry but they were all booked up for that evening. *Damn.* He switched off the machine, punched the autodial for his home number, and in the calmest, most measured tones he could muster, told Carol he couldn't get the reservations.

"But I thought you said you'd already gotten them."

"I'm sorry. I forgot. I tried to get them, but they were full up."

"Why didn't you just tell me you'd forgotten in the first place?" she asked.

"Look," Kevin said, impatient again, "why don't we just go to Grendel's Den? I'll call now and make a—"

"That's not important, Kevin. What's important is why you felt you had to lie to me about it."

Kevin struggled to keep his anger in check. "Look, why is this such a big deal?"

"It's not. That's what I'm trying to—"

"I've got to go," Kevin said preemptorily. "I've got some tests to run. Why don't you call wherever you want to have dinner, make the reservation, and call me back, okay?"

There was a frustrated, confused silence at the other end of the line. "Kevin, I know you don't want to have this talk tonight, but—"

"Carol, I've got to go." At the far end of the room, Daniel pretended to be engrossed in his work. "I'll see you later, okay?" Kevin hung up as though the receiver had suddenly become electrified and he couldn't bear to hold it a moment longer. Jesus. Why did every conversation with Carol end this way, these days? He turned, about to apologize to Daniel for holding things up, implicitly for making him a reluctant observer of the dispute—

And, as he turned, his eyes widened in surprise and bewilderment.

"What the hell is *that?*" he asked.

Daniel looked up from his desk and followed Kevin's gaze. Floating in the middle of the pillar of violet light was no galaxy, no tapestry of stars, but what appeared to be—a human fetus. Suspended about three feet off the ground in a halo of pinkish light, rocking gently in some invisible womb, a ropy umbilical cord trailing up and out to the very edge of the image area, where it ended abruptly—but as it moved, as it shifted position, almost as though in amniotic fluid, one could see parts of the cord appear from "outside" the shaft of light—as if it continued, somehow, beyond the parameters of the display . . .

Kevin and Daniel walked slowly around the anomaly, examining it with a mixture of amazement and irritation. "I . . . I don't know," Daniel said finally. "It's not any program of *ours* . . ."

Kevin stared at the fetus, noting the embryonic heartbeat inside its tiny chest, the way its not-fully-formed fingers moved, slightly, as a real fetus might stir in the womb. He fixed Daniel with a sober look. "If this is a joke," he said, "this would be a good time to let me in on it."

"If it's a joke, it's not mine." Daniel was already at the keyboard.

Kevin frowned. "Some clown in the Comp Sci lab is probably having fun with us. Just dump it and let's get on with our lives."

Daniel's hands moved across the keys . . . but the fetal image remained in the display. Several moments later, Daniel looked up and declared, flatly, "I can't."

"What?"

"I can't dump it."

"Then abort the program. Reset the system."

Daniel punched in the appropriate commands and the shaft of light winked out; seconds later he reactivated it, only to find the fetus still there, still suspended in midair. Worse yet, Kevin was becoming slowly aware of a dull, rhythmic beating sound coming now from the system's audio speakers . . .

Irritation turning to anger, Kevin took Daniel's place and began inputting commands into the computer—to no effect. After several minutes, Kevin finally turned and glared at the uninvited visitor to his lab.

"*Damn* it," he said softly. "That bastard Jacobi, in Life Sciences. This is just the sort of warped practical joke he'd pull." He considered his options, but only one seemed practical just now. "Okay," he sighed. "We'll have to clear the memory. Power it down and reload the system from the tape backups."

Daniel looked aghast. "It could take hours to bring it back up again."

Kevin raised an eyebrow. "You have a better suggestion?"

They powered it down. It did indeed take hours to bring the system up again, during which Kevin had the unpleasant task of calling Carol and telling her he'd be an hour or two later than planned; she accepted it with the tense silence of a woman who suspected she was being put off, and all of Kevin's protestations to the contrary couldn't convince her otherwise. After all, he *had* been putting her off, all week, about this dinner and this particular conversation; he could hardly expect her to believe him when a genuine crisis came up.

Finally, at a quarter to eight, Kevin sat at the keyboard, took a deep breath, and started punching keys. "Okay," he said. "Let's see where we are."

He keyed in the final sequence of numbers, looked up as the hologram display hummed into life—

A violet column of light, empty and clear of any images whatever, reappeared in the middle of the room. The two men let out their breaths almost simultaneously.

"Well," Kevin said, switching off the display once again. "That was interesting."

"Yeah, but where the hell did it come from?"

Kevin stood, stretched, shook off his labcoat. "Something that sophisticated has to leave tracks. If it *was* Jacobi, I'm going to nail his ass to the wall. Tomorrow. Tonight, I'm late for dinner."

Kevin was already in the doorway; Daniel lingered, staring back at the empty air in which, hours before, the image, the thing—the fetus—had floated in its dusky halo. "I don't know," he said quietly. "It almost seemed . . . *alive* . . ."

Kevin snapped off the lights, plunging the room into darkness.

"Probably was," he said. "Video of a real fetus, computer-enhanced. C'mon, Dan. Don't get weird on me."

Daniel made an uncertain, noncommittal sound and shrugged on his own jacket. The two men exited, the door sliding and locking behind them; for a full minute the lab was still and dark, the only light the faint blue nimbus of a computer readout. Then, all at once, a column of bright violet light erupted in the middle of the room— like a candle, inadequately snuffed out, flaming to life. And now, at the center of that flame, was the image not of a human fetus—but a newborn infant. An infant whose cries and squalls, reflected off walls of metal and glass, off instruments blind to its birth and indifferent to its discontent, echoed unnaturally in the empty lab; alone and afraid in its cradle of light.

THEY MISSED THEIR DINNER RESERVATIONS, couldn't get into Boston in time, and so the conversation Kevin had been so dreading occurred instead in the bedroom of their co-op on Trowbridge Street. Carol Drayton was an attractive, dark-haired woman in her early thirties, with intense dark eyes and an air of reason and calm about her; that was what had first attracted Kevin to her, that assuredness, that inner serenity. You didn't find it in most artists, even commercial artists, but Carol was atypical; even now she struggled to retain that composure, trying to fathom this man who had, so suddenly it seemed, become so much a mystery to her.

"Kev, I don't understand. You knew when we got married that I wanted children. I thought you wanted them, too."

She was sitting up in bed, several pillows between her and the headboard; Kevin sat on the edge of the mattress, weighing his words carefully. "I do," he said, sounding unconvincing even to himself. "I just don't . . . feel ready yet, that's all. There's still too much to do at the lab, and—"

"To *hell* with the lab," she said with uncharacteristic vehemence. "I barely see you anymore, and when I do, all you can talk about is the damn *lab*."

"It's three years of my life, Carol! I can't just throw that away, can I?"

Carol hesitated only a moment. "You've got four years invested in our marriage. You can't very well throw that away, either, can you?"

Kevin turned, saw the look of fear in her eyes—Good Lord, when had he ever seen Carol *afraid* of anything?—and in a gesture of conciliation put his hand on hers. "No," he said. "No, of course not . . ."

She moved over to his side of the bed, put a hand to his back, feeling the knot of tension in his neck, trying to knead it out. "Kev, what is it? What's bothering you?"

His muscles, if anything, seemed to grow tighter. "I've just been under a lot of pressure to get the project done. That's all."

"Kevin—please," she said, feeling his body belie his words. "It's not the work. You've been under job pressure before and things have never been this bad between us. What's wrong? Can't I help?"

Kevin stood, suddenly unable to bear the touch of her fingers, unable to accept either the gentle caress or the desire to understand that came with it. This whole conversation—children, babies—all seemed a mockery after what had happened today in the lab; but who could have known that they'd be discussing this tonight, who could be cruel enough to offer up such a black-humored joke? He'd told no one of the nature of his problems with Carol, not even Dan; how could anyone possibly have known enough to send that jape, that mockery, that *thing*, in the holo display?

"I'm sorry," he said, facing her, backing off. "I just can't handle this right now. I've got to be alone for a while. I'll sleep in the den; just for tonight. Okay?"

He started out, pausing in the doorway, wanting to say something but not knowing what; failing, he turned and left the room. Carol Drayton looked after—baffled, confused, frightened; worried that she was watching her husband drift slowly out of reach—and worse, not having the slightest idea why.

2

Kevin left the house the next morning before his wife had even awakened, more out of avoidance than necessity. He was seeking the sanctuary and solace of his lab, a place he understood, an environment he could control; it was only as he put his palm to the image scanner at the door that he got his first intimation that that control was, in fact, illusory. As the scanner responded with a blast of white light, Kevin heard something inside the lab—something soft, and muffled, but sounding uncannily like the cries of a small child. The door slid open and the sound became louder, more distinct; Kevin rushed in, only to stop dead a few feet from the closing door.

A little girl, no more than five years old, sat hunched over in the center of the circle of violet light, hugging her knees, crying to herself. She was wearing a frilly, old-fashioned dress, a straw bonnet adorned with a band of flowers and secured by a ribbon gathered in a bow beneath her chin; like all images in the display, she was a pale rose monochrome, though parts of her—her hair, her eyes—were darker than others.

She seemed not to notice Kevin as he stood there, too stunned to move; until he realized that of course she wouldn't notice him—she was just a video image, like the fetus, albeit far more sophisticated. Heartened by this realization, he took a step forward, more assuredly.

The little girl looked up at him and met his gaze.

With that one simple motion—that slight tilt of the head—Kevin's ordered, orderly world threatened to capsize. There were no video or audio inputs that allowed the computer to "see" or "hear" what went on in the room; it was impossible for anything inside the hologram to interact, therefore, with anything or anyone outside the display area.

Yet despite this, the girl suddenly sniffed back her tears and spoke up.

"They left me here," she announced, in a tone both wounded and affronted, "all night. All *alone*."

She started crying again, the baffled cries of an abandoned child. Maybe, Kevin thought desperately, maybe it was just a coincidence that she'd looked in his direction; perhaps whoever had designed the program had simply made a good guess as to where he would enter the room. Yes. Of course. That had to be it; a lucky guess. Encouraged, he began crossing the lab to get a closer look.

The girl's eyes tracked him across the room.

He stopped, stunned and disbelieving. She continued to look straight at him. He took a few steps backward, and to the side; but each time, the girl's gaze followed.

Jesus God, Kevin thought. Any thoughts of artificial-intelligence programs, or outside access to the computer, were quickly forgotten. The girl in the hologram simply could not *do* what she was doing.

She kept on doing it, tears flowing from translucent eyes that shouldn't—by all reason, by all sanity—be able to see.

Even her cries, though they clearly emanated from the system's audio speakers, sounded uncomfortably real, and Kevin found himself wanting to still them, somehow. He took a few slow steps forward—instinctively lowering his voice, trying to sound calm and soothing, as he squatted down beside her. "Hey," he said. "It—it's okay. Everything's okay . . ."

For the moment, all he could think of was how to quiet her, how to comfort her. Grabbing the nearest keyboard, he began punching in coordinates, selecting programs—

In the violet light above the child, a rose-colored sphere, cone, and funnel began to take shape. "Look," Kevin said. "What's that?" As she looked up, Kevin manipulated the computer-generated forms, making them spin and dip in a playful ballet. The girl stared up, fascinated, at the dancing objects, her tears momentarily forgotten; then she took a jump up and tried to touch them, succeeding in hitting the sphere a glancing blow, making it spin all the faster.

Kevin punched in another command and the sphere took on the appearance of a banded rubber ball; he wiped the cone and funnel from the image area, then allowed the ball to drop into the girl's arms.

She caught it, bounced it once on the base of the display, caught it again and laughed delightedly, her fear and loneliness apparently fled. Kevin stood slowly, eyes wide as he watched it—her—play with the ball. He barely heard the hiss of the door behind him as Daniel entered, caught one glimpse of the image in the display, and stopped short, even as Kevin had. He cast a querulous look at Kevin, but before he could respond, the girl looked up, saw Daniel, and, with a big, happy smile, said, "Hi!"

Daniel looked about ready to drop through the floor.

"Say hi," Kevin prompted, amused despite himself.

Daniel cleared his throat, looked at the girl. "Uh . . . hi," he croaked out.

Daniel glanced at Kevin. "AI program?" he asked hopefully.

Kevin shook his head. "No program in the world can mimic spontaneous reaction to unexpected stimuli."

Daniel looked at the girl again. She waved at him. He waved back.

A wan smile frozen on his face, Daniel said in a low tone, "What the hell *is* she?"

Kevin stared at her as she bounced the ball, happily, on the floor of the holo display. Under the circumstances, he could think of only one reply.

"I don't know," he said, moving toward the display. "Let's ask."

The girl looked up at his approach. "Hi," he said, as casually as he could manage. "You . . . like the ball?"

She nodded. "Yeah. Thanks, mister."

"The name's Kevin. What's yours?"

"Nola," the girl replied.

By now Daniel had joined Kevin at the display, circling it slowly, carefully. "You . . . have a last name, honey?"

She glanced over at Daniel, her face screwing up in concentration. Finally, after several moments, she announced triumphantly, "Granville."

"Nola Granville," Daniel repeated. He cast a spooked look askance at Kevin. "Pretty name. Where do you . . . live, Nola?"

Nola thought a moment, then said, "I used to live in Wesschesser."

Kevin smiled. "You mean Westchester? In New York?"

"Yeah," Nola said. "In a big green house. Across from the sprained lake."

"The what?"

"Grassy Sprain Lake," explained Daniel, a Long Island native. "It's a big reservoir in upper Yonkers . . . near Hastings-on-Hudson."

Kevin squatted down again, wondering how best to couch his question. "Nola?" he said gently. "What are you doing in here, honey?"

Panic flared in her eyes, the pupils dilating with sudden fear, then quickly covered by a little-girl bravado. "Silly," she admonished them. "Isn't this where I'm *supposed* to be?"

Kevin looked at Daniel. Daniel looked at Kevin. Her *pupils* had actually *dilated*.

"Yeah . . . sure," Daniel said, at a loss for what else to say. "Of course it is, Nola. You're . . ." He glanced helplessly at Kevin, then back to Nola. "You're *home*."

Nola broke into a wide, confident grin, bouncing the ball again, catching it with eager hands. Kevin sank into a chair and watched her. This promised to be a very long day. How long, he was scarcely able to guess.

SHE WAS AGING, it seemed, at a rate of about five months every hour; ten years each day. At eight o'clock in the morning she had been a frightened, lonely five-year-old girl; by eight that evening, she was a more mature, outgoing ten-year-old. Kevin called in sick to the dean's office, had his classes suspended indefinitely, and over the next

twelve hours watched as Nola literally grew up before his eyes. The degree of detail—
as her hair grew longer, then shorter, then long again; as her body slowly but perceptibly elongated, at just the right rate of speed for a normal child's growth—was
astonishing. The minutiae involved, from the subtle changes in weight distribution to
the larger growth in bone structure, were staggering to contemplate—they required
thousands of different "processes" running at once; even her garments would change
from hour to hour, from dress clothes to play, all of it still quite old-fashioned. Kevin
spent all day listening carefully to this shy, beguiling apparition as it went from
kindergarten to elementary school, from five to six to seven years old, speech becoming increasingly more sophisticated, reactions exactly appropriate for a girl of whatever age she was at that moment—by the time she reached six, she had outgrown the
ball, so Kevin had fashioned a holographic doll for her; at seven, a jump-rope; and
at eight, a set of jacks.

That evening, Daniel returned from Rotch Library with his research on the "big
green house" Nola had described twelve hours—or was it five years?—earlier.

"There *is* a Granville family living in that area," Daniel said, sotto voce, as they
watched Nola sitting cross-legged in the holo display, playing jacks. "The house she
described . . . It's been in the family since the turn of the century. The current owners
don't have a daughter named Nola, but . . ." He hesitated. "The woman I talked to
did recall a great-aunt of hers by that name . . . something of a black sheep, apparently;
the family never talked much about her."

Kevin put a hand to his mouth, restraining a manic laugh. This was becoming more
baroque by the minute. "Does anybody know where this . . . 'great-aunt' *is?*"

Daniel hesitated again. "She died. Quite a while back; no one knew the exact date,
and county records for the area don't reveal anything, either."

Kevin didn't reply. He got up from his work station, moved over to where Nola
was playing with her jacks; there was a faraway look in her eyes, but as soon as she
glimpsed Kevin, her face lit up with a wide smile. "Hi, Kevin." She had the shy,
guileless look of a young girl with her first crush.

"Hi, Nola." Her smitten look was not lost on him. "You, uh, want me to make you
some more toys? You must be getting tired of the jacks."

"That's okay," she said, standing. "I don't need any."

"Don't you get kind of . . . bored, Nola?" Daniel asked.

She shrugged lightly. "Sometimes. But when I do, I just . . . go somewhere else."
Kevin and Daniel exchanged puzzled looks.

"In my head," she explained. "Like just now, I was out by the sprained lake.
Remembering the time Daddy took us out for a picnic, and I walked into the water
up to my knees, and"—her face clouded over—"Daddy paddled me. Hard." She
winced. "I didn't want to remember that part."

"So when you think about places . . . people . . . things . . . it's like you're almost
there?" Kevin asked.

"Yeah," she said, then added, with a shy smile: "But I like being here, with you,
better."

Kevin couldn't help but smile back. Daniel looked at him and thought: My God,
he's actually blushing! "Nola?" he said, filling the awkward silence. "You remember
when it was your Daddy took you to the lake? What year?"

Again that endearingly sober look as she concentrated. "I think it was . . . nineteen and—seventeen. Or maybe sixteen. Yeah," she said, more confidently, "that's right. Nineteen and sixteen."

Kevin and Daniel stared at each other, dumbfounded.

Later, in Kevin's private office adjacent to the lab, Daniel sat slumped in a chair as Kevin paced. "Maybe," Daniel suggested, "we should call in Hinerman, over in AI Alley."

"No," Kevin said quickly. "He'd turn this into a sideshow. And even if she *is* an AI program—which I don't believe for a minute—how does she *see* us? Hinerman would be as incapable of explaining that as we are."

Daniel shook his head. "She's totally aware of her surroundings—even her *form*— yet seems perfectly comfortable with them. As though it were the most natural thing in the world."

"Well, despite her memories of a . . . previous existence, she's spent all her life, subjectively, in that hologram. And the older she gets, the more she remembers. It's almost as though she's existing on two different levels of consciousness—one a re-membered past that expands as she ages, the other her real-time presence here, with us."

Daniel hesitated. "Look," he said, tentatively, "I know this is going to sound pretty bizarre, but . . ." Daniel screwed up his nerve under Kevin's even gaze. "Do you suppose that somehow . . . in some way, a . . . a soul . . . a human *soul* . . . has been— reincarnated, inside that computer?"

Kevin sighed indulgently. "Daniel, I'm not even sure I believe in the human soul, much less in reincarnation."

"Why? Why is the idea of a soul any less believable than that of any of a dozen subatomic particles? We can't prove *they* exist, either."

"Yes, but that's *different*. We *can* posit their existence by the behavior of other, observable phenomena."

Daniel was silent a moment, then stood, went to the door, and opened it. He nodded in the direction of the lab. "There's your phenomenon in there, Doc," he said. "Go observe."

3

Over the course of a single night, Kevin saw Nola grow from child to woman; he saw the passing of seasons in her face and in her body, observed the transit of years in her ever-changing clothes, and marveled at the flowering of what was becoming a quick and agile mind. She went from a shy ten-year-old to a studious twelve-year-old, and together they discussed the books she'd been reading (in that other place, on that other level of consciousness manifested here only as memory): *Silas Marner, Les Miserables, A Tale of Two Cities.* At fourteen she began avidly reading poetry— Browning, Blake, Keats, Marvell; Kevin, who'd barely had time to indulge his fond-ness for literature since his undergrad days, found himself racing to keep up with her. Her appetite for literature was enormous; she was as intelligent as she was beautiful.

And she was—was becoming—very beautiful indeed. It was the beauty of a soft, sensitive face, a quick wit, and the lingering traces of girlhood shyness in her smile.

Every time she laughed, every time she smiled, it was warm, and open, and meant for him and him alone; with a dizzy sense of wonder and delight, Kevin was experiencing anew the excitement of *discovering* someone, exploring not simply shared tastes and common interests, but the delightful differences, as well—ideas and experiences he had never encountered, which made him think in new ways, consider other points of view. She was a young woman coming to maturity in the 1920s; he was a man who had reached his majority decades later, in the 1970s. They were separated by more than fifty years of progress and decline, undreamt-of war and uneasy peace; yet not only did they find common ground, they thrilled to the discovery of the other's world.

This, more than any scrutiny of data or processes, convinced him that this woman of light was just that—a woman. Not an artificial intelligence program, not a hoax or a joke. He had no idea what she was doing here, how any of this had come about, but after twelve sleepless hours, mesmerized by her intelligence, her humor, and, quite often, her pain—only intimated when she was a child, the unhappy home life which seemed to kindle her immersion in books—Kevin believed in her.

And yet *if* he believed in her, *if* she existed—there had to be a reason for her presence here. But whenever he tried broaching the subject, she just shrugged it off; this room, this place, it all seemed to be somewhere she was merely *visiting*, while living on another level . . . as though Kevin existed between the instants of her life. She did express curiosity as to what these odd machines were surrounding her, but when Kevin used the analogy of adding machines, that seemed to quell her interest: "I liked math up until trigonometry," she told him. "Does anybody really *understand* trigonometry?" He relied instead on more gentle probing—finding out about her life, her feelings, taking surreptitious notes during coffee breaks, anything that might provide raw data for Daniel to investigate.

But Kevin did not have to force himself to ask those questions. He enjoyed them; he enjoyed her.

"I remember one time," she said, a radiant twenty-year-old sitting cross-legged at the very edge of the column of light, "Daddy got hold of a book of poetry I was reading . . . William Butler Yeats? In one poem, Yeats uses the dread word, *copulate*, and Daddy—" She laughed. "—well, Daddy was neither amused nor enlightened." Kevin joined in her laughter. "I tried reading him the one that begins, 'I will arise and go now, and go to Innisfree/And a small cabin build there, of clay and wattles made—' "

Kevin picked up the rest: " 'Nine bean-rows will I have there,' " he quoted, searching for the elusive lines, " 'a hive for the honey-bee'—"

" 'And live alone in the bee-loud glade,' " they finished together. Nola laughed at their simultaneity; Kevin leaned forward on the backrest of his chair, finishing, a bit distantly, " 'And I shall have some peace there . . .' "

There was a pleased smile on Nola's face. "You know Yeats."

"I know . . . *some* Yeats," Kevin allowed. "What about your father? Did he like the poem?"

Nola's face clouded over in much the same way it had as a child, recalling the picnic at the lake. "He didn't let me finish," she said quietly. "Took the book away from me, and . . . tossed it in the fire." She looked down. " 'It's not a girl's place,' he'd say, 'to think about such things.' And whenever I'd ask questions . . . about politics, or history . . . he'd just smile a patronizing little smile, and tell me how beautiful I was."

"But it was the 1920s. Suffragettes. Flappers. Women getting the vote."

"Not in my home," Nola said flatly. "My father was holding on, desperately, to the world he knew. My mother would always take his side, do whatever he told her; and there I was, constantly questioning him, contradicting him . . ." Her voice trailed off; she shook off the bleak mood which seemed to have descended on her and looked up, trying for a gay smile. "But honestly—you must be bored silly by me and my stories," she said. "What about you? What's your life like? Tell me everything."

"Nothing much to tell, really," Kevin answered evasively. "About your parents—"

"Are you married, Kevin?"

Kevin hesitated, then reluctantly held up his ring finger. "Yes. I am."

Nola's face fell. "Oh," she said, then, quickly, to mask her disappointment: "What's her name?"

"Carol," Kevin said, and, finding the subject uncomfortable, tried again to return to Nola's life: "So how old were you when you—"

"What's she like?" Nola persisted. "Is she smart? She'd have to be, for you to marry her."

"Yes," Kevin admitted. "She's very smart. We . . . met in a night class, five years ago." He surrendered to the memory of that night, the crisp autumn breeze cutting through the auditorium during break, his first glimpse of Carol, a fan of dark shoulder-length hair whipped by the wind. "This woman, she just . . . sat down and started talking with me. Inside of five minutes we were chatting away like old friends. Inside of a week, I was in love. Not long after that, we were married." He smiled, shook his head. "I never thought it would happen that quickly, to me. I—"

He looked up and saw the feelings Nola was trying so hard to conceal. "Well. Anyway. Yes, she's a . . . very bright lady."

Nola smiled at him, and mixed with the disappointment there was a sincerity when she said, "That's . . . that's nice. I'm happy for you, Kevin." She looked at him with impossible longing. "She must be a very lucky girl."

CAROL DRAYTON WATCHED, unnerved and uncomprehending, as her husband finished packing a small suitcase with socks, shirts and underwear. The entire scene felt unreal; he seemed to be moving in strobe-motion, every other moment a blank, and in those hidden moments, she knew, was the answer, the explanation for all that was occurring. She watched him take a pair of socks from the dresser drawer, and spoke to him as though to a ghost, as though he already belonged to the realm of memory.

"Kevin," she heard herself ask, as from a distance, "what do you expect me to say? You spend all night on campus, you don't call, I can't even get through to you on the phone—"

"I explained that." Kevin did not turn. "We had the phone lines to the lab temporarily disconnected, for security reasons. And I forgot to call. I'm sorry."

"And now—" Carol got up from where she had been sitting on the bed, stood beside Kevin as he packed the last of his clothing. "What could possibly be so wrong with your project that you have to go sleep in the *lab?*"

Kevin turned to her, sighed, briefly considered the truth but quickly discarded the notion. "If I told you, you'd think I was crazy."

"We've lived this long with each other's craziness," she said gently. "I think I can stand a little more."

"For Christ's sake, Carol, it's just for—" He stopped, lowered his voice. "I don't know how long it's for. But it's only temporary. Until I can get this . . . sorted out."

Carol watched as her husband went into the bathroom to select some toiletries, his back to her. "Sorted out," she repeated. "You mean your project . . . or us?"

Kevin didn't reply. Didn't know how to reply. He returned to the suitcase, tossed the toiletries inside. Very quietly, Carol asked, "Are you leaving me, Kevin?"

The vehemence of his reply surprised him as much as it did her.

"I don't *know!*" he yelled, causing her to flinch, to shrink from him for the first time in their marriage. "I don't *know* anything anymore!"

He slammed shut the suitcase, snapped it up, and headed for the door. Carol did not turn. She refused to turn. Refused to let him see her face, the tears welling up in her eyes . . .

He paused in the doorway, looking back. He couldn't see her face, just the way her shoulders were hunched with tension. He wished he had an answer for her, something that would make sense, something she could accept; but the truth was, things had ceased making sense between them even before this business in the lab, and he could no more explain that to her than he could Nola.

"I'll call," he said lamely. "I promise."

He hurried out. Carol heard his footfalls on the steps, listened to the front door as it swung open, then slammed shut; heard the motor of their Volvo turn over as the ignition was keyed. She remained where she was, fighting the urge to go to the window and watch the car back out of her driveway, onto Trowbridge; knowing that she was losing him, that much was clear, but to whom, or to what, she had no inkling. Not an affair, that much she knew, that much she would be able to tell; but something else. Something she couldn't put a name to—and something, she knew instinctively, with which she could not compete.

4

The big green house on Grassy Sprain Road, across from a sprawling golf course that Daniel doubted had existed in Nola's time, was much as she had described it; there had been a great many coats of paints applied in the last fifty years, another couple of bedrooms added on, but it was essentially the same rambling Victorian home the young girl claimed to have grown up in. At the door, Daniel was met by a blondish woman in her mid-twenties who introduced herself as Susan Granville; Daniel had spoken to her the day before, purporting to be involved in genealogical research at MIT. He felt guilty now as she ushered him cheerfully into the house—uneasy at the ruse which had gained him entry, but fascinated by what he saw around him.

He saw, as they moved through the house, a winding staircase fanning in a lazy curve down from a spacious second story; he remembered Nola telling of how she had tripped on that staircase when she was four, chipping her tooth on the banister.

He saw two bedrooms on the upper floor, one with a view of a tall oak tree easily a hundred years old—the same tree Nola had described as being outside her own window. He saw, in that glimpse of the backyard, an old toolshed, many times restored; a toolshed in which Nola's father had repeatedly taken the strap to her, in an age long before the term "child abuse" had been coined.

"After you called," Susan was saying, "I started digging through some old trunks in the attic. Found a few family albums that might be useful. What exactly are you looking for?"

"Corroboration," Daniel answered truthfully. "We just need to confirm some birth dates, death dates, that sort of thing." He'd invented a mythical 17th-century Granville for whom, he told her, he was trying to establish a genealogical time line; he felt uncomfortable at the excitement this falsehood seemed to bring to her as she led the way up into a musty attic filled with cardboard boxes, discarded toys, overstuffed furniture, and a large steamer trunk.

"Here we go," she said, opening the trunk, taking a dozen photo albums from atop the heaped contents. She opened the oldest of the albums, carefully turning its brittle pages, eyes brightening as she came to one in particular. "Here she is," she said, as Daniel took a step forward to look; "this is Aunt Nola. When she was five years old."

It was an old sepia-toned photograph, flaking around the edges, only two of its gummed corners still in place. The background was faded but vaguely recognizable as the backyard of this very house; the girl in the picture was pretty but bashful-looking, wearing a straw bonnet gathered with a bow at her neck, a band of flowers decorating the hat.

It was, unmistakably, the same five-year-old girl who had appeared in the hologram two days before.

Jesus, Daniel thought, his discomfort ebbing as he scanned the page and Susan leafed slowly through the album. There she was, Nola at eight, at ten, at twelve . . . exactly as she had appeared, at various stages, hundreds of miles away. The sepia tones of the snapshots gave her the same ethereal quality as the dusky rose of the holo display; Daniel wasn't sure if he was awed or alarmed, filled with wonder or with fear.

"Her father—my great-great-uncle, Thomas—was a banker," Susan explained. "Snobbish, provincial old bastard . . . lost half his fortune in the stock market crash. Hated the fact that he'd been brought down to the level of the masses. They lived a comfortable life, better than most of the country during the Depression, but that wasn't enough; not for him."

As the years progressed there were fewer and fewer pictures of Nola; but those few corresponded exactly to the image of the twenty-year-old Nola Daniel had just left, hours before.

"I asked my mother about her—she says Nola and her father had some kind of falling out when she was in her twenties. That's when the family lost contact with her."

"A falling out?" Daniel asked. "Over what?"

Susan turned a page, and Daniel saw the last photograph of Nola in the album—a smiling woman in her mid-twenties sitting in the front seat of a '39 Plymouth, a man in a snap-brim hat and dark suit leaning into the picture beside her.

"Him." Susan nodded to the man. "Law student, tutoring at NYU. Her father threatened to disinherit her, but Nola didn't care; she'd always felt guilty about her family's wealth." She laughed. "Very little of which survives today. Myself, I wouldn't mind being a bit more guilty."

Daniel returned the laugh, distractedly, as he leaned in to study the man's face: angular, bespectacled, with dark, intelligent eyes and an easy smile. "I think his name was . . . Robert," Susan ventured. "Robert—"

"—GOLDMAN," Nola said. "He was nothing like the polo-playing dunderheads I grew up with . . . he saw the sorry state the world was in, wanted to *do* something about it . . ."

It was the evening of the fourth day of Nola's "life," and she sat at the base of the column of light, looking like a frosted image on amethyst crystal; but a moving, speaking, living image. She was approximately thirty years old, her youthful beauty matured and multiplied; she was wearing a V-neck dress, a string of pearls which she fingered absently as she spoke, her hair upswept in back, a high pompadour in front. Since county records had put her actual birth at 1908, at the moment she was remembering up to—but not yet beyond—1938.

"He was an attorney?" Kevin said.

She nodded. "And he *listened* to me, Kevin . . . just like you do." She smiled, and Kevin returned it, feeling an odd mix of satisfaction and guilt. He thought of Carol, told himself he was merely gathering empirical evidence, but knew better.

"We talked about . . . *everything*. Politics, religion, literature, the law, every forbidden subject on my father's list of Don'ts. Father didn't want me going to college in the first place—kept bringing round the sons of old country-club friends of his, hoping one of them would sweep me off my feet—but after a few years he gave up, relented, and let me go to NYU, to major in English. That was where I met Robert."

"This was when you were, what, twenty-three, twenty-four?"

"Twenty-four, when I started. I met Robert in my senior year—he was tutoring a classmate of mine, a pre-law student—and we . . ." She hesitated, in a rather charming reticence that was very much of her time and breeding, and Kevin found himself fighting a stab of jealousy. ". . . we began seeing one another. By the time I'd graduated, we'd decided to get married; he wanted to move to Boston, set up a law practice for the disadvantaged, and I could get my master's in literature at Boston College."

The scientist in Kevin sparked at that last part, wondering if the connection could be geographical: If Nola had lived in Boston, could her spirit have become tied to this area somehow? Could that be why she was manifesting herself here, in this computer? But if so, why the rebirth, why the aging process? And why wasn't she conscious of *all* her life, as ghosts—Good God, he couldn't believe he was actually taking all this seriously—as ghosts usually, supposedly, were?

"So you moved to Boston?" he said, trying to keep the excitement from his tone.

She nodded. "South Boston, actually. A little apartment off West Broadway. Not the best section of town, but we made do."

"Couldn't your parents have helped out?"

Nola's face darkened; she shook her head. "No," she said tersely. There was a flush of anger and hurt in that otherwise calm and composed face, and Kevin felt suddenly wary in his questioning: "What *did* your parents think of all this? The move, the marriage, grad school—?"

Nola looked down, her eyes hooded.

"Father . . . didn't approve. Of any of it." She hesitated, then added, "Especially Robert."

"Why not? Because the guy wasn't rich?"

"That, too," Nola said tonelessly. "But mainly because he was Jewish."

Kevin started. "You're kidding." Bigotry against blacks, or Asians, that was the sort of prejudice Kevin had grown up around, but anti-Semitism? It seemed positively antediluvian. Then he thought of the year in which this was all taking place—1938— and of the events that would follow in a few short years, and he began to understand . . .

"He made it quite clear," Nola continued flatly. "If I married Robert, I'd be . . . cut off. From him . . . from Mother . . . from—" Her voice broke. "From everyone," she said softly. "The whole family."

Kevin instinctively reached out to comfort her.

"Nola, I'm sor—"

His hand, outstretched to take hers, instead passed right through it—as suddenly this woman who had seemed so vibrant and alive became, for a moment, discarnate; as Kevin was abruptly reminded of her tenuous existence, her fragile purchase on this world. He quickly drew back, but the damage had been done; Nola sat, looking down at her hand, which only moments before had actually shared the same physical space as Kevin's, and when she looked up Kevin saw for the first time the true distance between them, reflected in her face—itself only a refraction, a trick of light.

"Kevin . . ." Her tone was muted but frightened. He hadn't heard or seen fear in her since she was a child, only . . . three days ago? "Kevin, why am I here? Like this, with you?"

He stared into her eyes—what color *were* they, he wondered, in real life?—and sighed wearily. "I don't know, Nola," he admitted. "That's what I've been trying to figure out."

"Why you've been asking me about my life?"

"Yes."

She hesitated a long moment. "Am I . . . dead, Kevin? Is that it? Am I a—" She didn't finish. Kevin flinched. This was the moment he'd been expecting, the moment he thought himself prepared for, and now he was adrift, floundering for words:

"Daniel . . . found a record of your birth, but not—" He hesitated, feeling as though nothing he could say would be the right thing. "We . . . don't know for sure."

But she knew. He looked at her, and he could tell: she knew. "What year is it, Kevin?" she asked.

After a moment's hesitation, he told her.

She shut her eyes briefly, then opened them again. "Then I must be dead," she said, tonelessly.

"Not necessarily," Kevin said. "Perhaps—"

"Perhaps what? Am I very old, my spirit drifting from my dying body, accidentally caught here, somehow? Or am I a . . ."

She still couldn't bring herself to say the word. She looked away; Kevin couldn't be sure, it might have been a variation in light, a fluctuation in wavelength, but there seemed to be tears in her eyes.

"I feel . . ." She looked back, and seemed as though she were trying to recall something, something urgent. "I feel like there's something I have to *do* . . . something I have to *accomplish* . . . but I can't seem to . . . remember . . ."

She held out her hands, palms up—half helplessness, half entreaty—in a gesture both touching and frustrating.

"Help me, Kevin? Help me to remember?"

Kevin hesitated—then, slowly, he reached back into the holo display, as he had minutes before . . . but this time, he placed his hands just under Nola's, as though cupping them in his. His hands were washed in rose and violet light, and for a moment, it appeared that that part of him might have been made of light, as well. Seeing what he was doing, Nola turned her own hands over, and, silently, pressed the palms close to his—their hands just barely meeting, almost overlapping; joining and not-joining. A defiant act of affirmation and union, to whatever gods had placed them here, together, like strands of a double helix: discrete yet united, entwined but never touching.

5

He watched the seasons change in her world, as spring gave way to summer—a happy, dreaming time for her and Robert, a time of mutual discovery and pleasure, despite the gathering clouds of war over Europe. She told of going down to the Haymarket to buy the day's groceries, the smell of cod and halibut just in from Long Wharf, the feel of crisp vegetables freshly picked from farms in Deerfield or Agawam; even that was remarkable to Kevin, the idea of buying groceries, fresh, each day, in those days before adequate refrigeration. She told of frequent visits to the Old Corner Book Store in the long-vanished crescent of Cornhill Street, lost forever along with neighboring Brattle Street and Scollay Square, a procession of phantom roads, like narrow Change Avenue, existing only in the memory of those who walked their paths, decades ago— and now, with their balustrades and dormer windows, conjured up for a rapt Kevin. She spoke of riding the trolley to Franklin Park, of hearing the bells of King's Chapel ringing out on Sunday walks, of stealing a kiss in the shade of Adams Square Station during a warm summer rain; she spoke of long-dead authors as though they were bright new discoveries, as indeed they were, to her, e.e. cummings, Auden, and Eliot; James Hilton's *Random Harvest*, and Robert Nathan's *Portrait of Jennie*. Often she would read aloud at night, and depending on the author they would either fall asleep in each other's arms (Robert Frost) or spend half the night making love (D. H. Lawrence).

With Pearl Harbor, of course, that short summer was brought to a jarring close. Robert tried to enlist in the Army, but his astigmatism (evidenced by all the photographs Daniel had unearthed of this intense young man wearing thick, round glasses) ranked him 4-F. Within the year, however, he had found a niche: his storefront law office became a mecca, of sorts, for hundreds of immigrants, most of them Jewish, fleeing in Hitler's wake. Robert helped them wend their way through government bureaucracy, helped find them housing, jobs, and a sense of home in an unfamiliar land. When Nola spoke of them it was not as a mass but as a collection of individuals: more than one spent a night, or two, or three, on the floor of the Goldmans' cramped apartment. There was a look to their eyes, she said, even in the oldest men, of lost children wandered far from home; a distant glaze that spoke silently of family and friends who were not as lucky as they, left behind in a land stripped of sense and gentleness; a mixture of relief at having escaped, and guilt for those remaining.

It was 1943, that morning, to judge by Nola's bobbed hair and long cloth skirt; she had been talking about their apartment in South Boston, how they loved it but had outgrown it: "My books and Robert's law texts were the real occupants," she said, grinning. "We were just boarders. But when I finally became pregnant, we knew we'd have to—"

"Wait a minute," Kevin interrupted. "*Pregnant?* You never mentioned that before."

Nola thought for a moment, then laughed, wonderingly. "I just remembered it," she said, a distant glaze to her eyes. "In an odd sort of way, Kevin, when I sit here, remembering, it's . . . almost as though it's all happening for the first time." She shook her head as though to clear it. "Anyway," she went on, "the pregnancy came as quite a surprise. My obstetrician had said I had a slight malformation of the uterus . . . warned me it might be difficult to conceive a child, but—"

For the next hour, Kevin watched in awe and fascination as Nola's slim figure filled out with the onset of pregnancy, her eyes shining with something new, an anticipation and happiness only hinted at before. As Nola rattled on almost constantly about the baby-to-be—about clothes and cribs, possible names (Sarah if a girl; Jacob if a boy), all the usual obsessions of impending motherhood—Kevin saw, if not understood, that excitement in a way he never had before. The time compression at work—five months passing in just one hour—made for a vivid cameo of joy and anticipation, exhilaration and trepidation. He was no closer to understanding that parental pride and excitement than ever, but he found himself excited for Nola's sake—pleased that someone who'd known more cold than warmth in her life would have a share of some genuine happiness.

By noon she was seven months pregnant, and talking about a vacation she and Robert had decided to take, that month. "Robert had been working twelve hours a day, seven days a week, for a solid year," she said, "and we realized that if we didn't get away now, after the baby came there was no telling when we might have time for a holiday. Robert's law partner, John Ruskin, had a small cabin in the Berkshires that he let us use . . . it was a full day's drive from Boston, way out in the country, but it was beautiful; there was a small stream in the woods where Robert did some fishing, while inside I did a little writing. I remember thinking about Yeats's lake, at Innisfree, and how it couldn't have been more peaceful than this. And then—"

Her expression went from serene to troubled. "It . . . all went wrong," she said, looking confused, frightened, as the "new" memories flooded into her, unbidden and somehow now unwanted. "After a walk in the woods, I . . . I started having contractions. First an hour apart, then half an hour, then every ten minutes. I was going into . . . premature labor." Her voice wavered; Kevin, pouring a cup of coffee, stared at her, a feeling of dread claiming him. "There were no hospitals around," Nola went on, "just a local doctor. Robert rushed me into town . . . I remember the doctor's office, in the back of his house . . . I remember him forcing my fingers open . . . I'd been writing a paper for the Poetry Review, and unconsciously I'd clutched it all the way from the cabin—"

Her left hand clenched into a fist, and as she stared at her suddenly trembling hand, her face twisted in discomfort. "He . . . he finally pried it loose as I was being lifted onto the operating—"

Nola suddenly cried out in pain. She fell to the floor, hands bracing her fall, as Kevin rushed to her side. "*Nola!* What *is* it, what's *wrong?*"

She was doubled over, clutching her stomach, her baby. "Oh, *God*, make it *stop!*" she screamed. "Make it *stop,* please, make it—"

Kevin dropped to his knees, helpless as though watching a fire on the moon. Something was horribly wrong, but whatever it was, it had happened over forty years ago; and as he knelt there, powerless to offer anything, even a hand in comfort, Kevin knew that he indeed *was* powerless—that whatever she was going through she had gone through decades before, and was merely reliving now. He wished he could jump into the hologram, become a thing of light and refraction himself—hold her, *help* her—but he couldn't; all he could do was stand by and watch her tortured face, listen to her terrible screams . . . screams so loud they brought Daniel rushing in from Kevin's office.

There were tears in her eyes now, eyes shut tight against the pain. "Kevin," she implored, aware of him for the first time in what seemed minutes, "Kevin, please, *do* something—"

Kevin's words sounded hollow and leaden. "Nola, I . . . I *can't*, I don't know *what* to—"

And then, as suddenly as it began, it stopped.

All at once, the pain in her face gave way to shock; the shock to astonishment; the astonishment to sorrow. Her cries stilled, Nola remained hunched over, continuing to clutch her stomach . . . a stomach no longer full with child, as empty as the look in her eyes, the vacant stare with which she gazed into space.

"Nola?" Kevin asked finally. "Are you—all right?"

At the sound of his voice, Nola turned, seeming to pull herself away from whatever bleak, lost place she had been, and when she looked up at him, when she spoke, there was immeasurable sorrow in her voice. "I . . . I lost it, Kevin," she said softly. "I lost the baby . . ."

Her eyes widened, and in that moment, it seemed to Kevin, there was a sudden maturity, a wisdom born of pain and grief, that had not been there before. "I remember now . . ."

Kevin felt her pain as his, felt almost as though he had lost a child of his own, and for the first time understood something of her need, her desire, her love for something yet unborn.

"I'm sorry, Nola," he said, just as softly. "I'm so sorry."

Nola nodded, but her gaze was once again remote, unfocused. "I have to . . . be by myself for a while, Kevin," she said distantly. "Just a little while. But I'll be back. I promise. I'll be back . . ."

Even as she spoke, her image turned from translucent to transparent, from dusky rose to glassy amethyst; and when she'd faded completely from the shaft of violet light, the display abruptly winked off—the system shutting down, seemingly of its own volition.

Daniel started. "I . . . didn't know she could do that."

"Neither did I." Kevin was less startled than in shock. Daniel looked at him—at his rumpled clothes, the unruly mop of hair, the dark circles under his eyes—and he felt a stab of fear, and concern. "Christ, you look awful. How much sleep are you getting?"

"Enough. Couple hours a night. I can't afford to squander my time with her, Dan."

Something in his tone disturbed Daniel even more than the way he continued to stare at the empty hologram display. Daniel tapped him, lightly, on the arm, trying to draw him out, draw him back from whatever far places he was living in, more and more, each day.

"C'mon," he said. "Let's get some air. I think we need to talk."

THEY CROSSED THE SPRAWLING GREEN of MITs Great Court as Kevin drank what Daniel estimated to be his twelfth cup of coffee that day, his hands still shaky as they held the styrofoam mug. Across Memorial Drive, up and down the Charles, white sails swept across the water like gulls; on the other side of the river, the Victorian houses of the Back Bay, though dwarfed by the gleaming towers of the John Hancock and Prudential buildings, seemed serenely comfortable with their modern neighbors, in that architectural repose of past and present so unique to Boston. It was a bright, almost preternaturally beautiful spring day, but if Kevin had any inkling of it, it didn't show in his hooded, brooding expression as he updated Daniel on events in the lab.

"Have you told her about the death certificate we found for Robert?" Daniel asked. "Does she know he died in 1953?"

Kevin hesitated. "Dan, you can't just tell someone that the man she loves, the man she still thinks of as *alive*, is long dead—*will* be dead, from her viewpoint."

Daniel felt alarmed once more. "Doc . . . this is information. We're scientists, we can't just . . . ignore relevant data because it may be too painful, or—"

"You still haven't turned up anything similar for Nola?" Kevin asked, turning the subject aside.

Daniel frowned, shook his head. "Bureau of Vital Statistics for Westchester County has a record of her birth, but not her death. Neither does Boston."

"What about the names she gave us? Robert's clients?"

Daniel took out a well-thumbed notepad, flipped it open. "Most of them were fairly well along in years when they emigrated to the U.S. Their sons and daughters, those I've contacted, may remember Robert's name, vaguely, but that's all."

"*Damn* it," Kevin muttered. "There must be someone still alive who knew them, someone who might be able to give us a clue—"

"It was a long time ago, Doc."

"No, it's not. It's happening now, across the street, in my lab, and I want to know *why*. She *needs* to know why."

"How can you figure *anything* out," Daniel said, "when you're so damn exhausted? Maybe I can spell you. Spend some time with her, while you grab a few hours' sleep."

Kevin looked almost jealous at the suggestion. He shook his head, reached into his pocket, and ripped a page from the small notebook he'd been keeping. "Not necessary, Dan. Besides, I think we may have a decent lead. Today she mentioned a partner in Robert's law firm—must've joined sometime between 1938 and 1943—named Ruskin; John Ruskin. See what you can turn up on him."

Daniel took the slip of paper reluctantly, an unvoiced concern in his eyes so plain that even Kevin, absorbed as he was, could see it. "Daniel, she's a very special person. She's as confused by all this as we are."

"Is she?"

Kevin's eyes remained hooded. "What's that supposed to mean?"

"We know she's controlling the computer. Ordering up the different processes needed to simulate her image . . ."

"Autonomous functions. She's no more conscious of doing it than we are of the way our heart pumps blood, or our blood assimilates oxygen . . ."

"She seemed awfully damned conscious of shutting down the system, just now."

"I can't explain that," Kevin said, feeling besieged and not a little helpless. "But she's not here for any . . . ill intent. I *know* it, Dan. I can *feel* it. My God, I've watched her grow *up*. I'd *know* if there were something wrong about her."

Daniel looked at him, then looked away, at the sailboats drifting up the Charles, then turned back to Kevin. "Look . . . Doc. You and I, we've never really had more than a . . . professional relationship, so maybe this is out of line, but—" No turning back now: "You're not getting yourself . . . involved . . . here, are you?"

" 'Involved'?" Kevin tried, without much success, to sound incredulous. "With a . . . a *spirit?*"

Daniel shrugged. "Some would say, that's what we fall in love with, when we fall in love. A soul . . . a spirit." He saw the telltale wince on Kevin's face, knew that his words had struck home. Hating the necessity of it, he went on, as gently as he could: "She's aging ten years for every day. At this rate, she'll be . . . gone . . . in three or four days. What do you do then?"

Kevin had no answer. To anything.

6

He waited all that day for Nola to return, but by evening the system remained shut down. Finally, he gave in to the temptation he'd been fighting all day and switched on the system himself. The display snapped on, the column of light shimmering from floor to ceiling; but it was empty. Kevin fought back his fear, telling himself that if Nola had had control enough to shut down the system, she had control enough not to manifest herself if she didn't want to; but he wasn't sure what he was afraid of, the possibility that Nola had been taken away against her will, removed for the same arbitrary reasons she had appeared, or perhaps that Daniel, in his cautions, was right, and that there was more to Nola than Kevin was allowing himself to see.

By evening his exhaustion at last claimed him; he rigged an alarm to go off once the display was reactivated, then lay down on the cot near the far wall for what he assumed—what he hoped—would be one or two hours' sleep. Within minutes his body had taken quick advantage of the opportunity.

Kevin had only one dream in that time, at least only one that he remembered, and it was of Carol. She was here, in the lab, with him—but *he* was inside the hologram. He saw her through a violet veil, and when he looked down at himself—at his hands, his legs—he saw that they were a pale, translucent rose. Carol sat outside, in his chair, weeping, but when he tried to reach out to comfort her, his hand was swallowed up as it reached the edge of the image area, and as he watched his fingers disappear, he lost all feeling in them, as well, all control, as though they had ceased to exist. Panicky, he jerked back his arm—his hand came back, and with it, his feeling and control. He flexed the fingers of one hand to prove to himself that he was real—that he had substance—

And then Carol got up, went to the control station, and turned him off.

THE ALARM SOUNDED a little after eight the next morning, a high whistling tone that brought Kevin immediately awake. He was startled to find that nearly twelve hours had passed, but at least the numbing fatigue which had dogged him these past days had abated; he felt rested, refreshed. He looked up to find the system back on, the column of light in the center of the room—and, in its center, Nola sat on a holographic stool . . . a stool, he realized later, unlike any he had conjured up for her.

"Nola?" He hurried to her side, relieved to see her, but distressed at the pace of years evident in her appearance. She looked to be about forty-four, forty-five, still very lovely but with a new maturity to her, the beginnings of which he had only glimpsed before. The small lines around her mouth and eyes, the lighter hues in her hair which Kevin took for thin streaks of gray—they did not detract from her beauty; if anything they added to it, lending her the grace of time.

"Hello, Kevin," she said, with the trace of a small smile. Her eyes, which had shone so brightly just twenty-four hours ago, seemed melancholy now. "I'm sorry I stayed away so long. I just . . . needed some time. To think."

"Are you all right?" Kevin asked, wanting to reach out and touch her, knowing he could not.

Nola nodded slowly. "It was . . . a long time ago," she said, unwittingly echoing Daniel's words of the previous day. "He was a country doctor. Didn't have the facilities they'd have had in Boston. Maybe if we hadn't gone away, if we'd stayed in town . . . but maybe not. Robert blamed himself for it."

"But there was no way he could have known. You were two months from term."

"Intent didn't matter to him," she said quietly. "Only result. Cause and effect. He was a very logical man, a good lawyer, that was the way he thought. If we'd been in the city, it might not have happened; we weren't in the city because he'd taken a vacation; therefore, it was his fault." She was silent for several long moments; then, her eyes fixed at some point far from Kevin, she said, sadly and softly, "It was a little girl, Kevin. A beautiful little girl . . ."

What could he say? All the alternatives sounded lame, and clichéd. "I'm sorry, Nola," he said finally, as he had before. "I'm so sorry."

Nola drew a deep breath and sighed. "God, Kevin—I wanted it so badly," she said wistfully. "The chance to give someone the kind of love I never had, growing up . . ."

Kevin heard in Nola's words and voice an unsettling echo of another woman, another place, a similar regret. Nola saw his disquiet; glanced at him. "Kevin? What is it?"

Kevin slowly sat down on his desk chair, poised backward as before, hands resting on the backrest.

"Carol's mother . . . my wife's mother . . . was an alcoholic," he said, staring past Nola into space. "I remember this time Carol said to me how she really wanted to have a baby . . . because she wanted to be the kind of mother *she* never had." He paused, then admitted, quietly, "I guess I never really understood what she meant . . . until now."

THE TONE OF THEIR DISCUSSIONS WAS DIFFERENT after that; it became less a chronology than a colloquy, less historical than philosophical—they spoke more and more of books they'd read, or doctrines they'd studied, favorite plays or books or movies. Kevin even created—at Nola's request—a holographic chess-board that floated, unsupported, above her lap; she moved her pieces by hand, while he used a keyboard in his lap to make the pieces rise, float across the board, and take their squares. When a piece was captured by either of them, it winked out of existence.

They talked sometimes of Robert, and the changes that came over him in the passing years—the enthusiastic young man she married turning slowly inward—but she spoke less and less of her life, presumably because she didn't wish to dwell on it, on the ways it had turned sour. Once Kevin asked if they had tried having another baby; Nola merely shook her head in a way that suggested it was no longer an option, and Kevin did not press the issue.

By the end of the day Nola was well into the autumn of her years, hair almost completely gray—as gray as anything was in her monochrome image—and cut in a Fifties style. They were deep into their fourth chess match of the day, and as Nola moved a rook, Kevin nodded admiringly.

"You're a good player," he said.

"I had a good teacher. Robert loved chess."

"However . . ." He tapped at the keyboard, moving one of his own rooks. "Check."

Nola smiled. "You're no slouch at this yourself."

"She said, having won three games in a row."

Nola interposed a knight between Kevin's rook and her king, he'd expected it and had his next move ready. He felt a pang of guilt for enjoying this—the game, her company, her presence—when he knew he should be searching for the reasons for that presence. "Nola, are you sure you want to be . . . playing games, like this . . . instead of—" He hesitated. "I mean, what about your later years with Robert? Was there anything that happened between you that might account for—"

"Oh, Lord, Kevin, I'm so tired of talking about myself," she sighed. "Let's just enjoy the game, for now, all right?"

Kevin backed off. "All right," he said, relenting. He moved his bishop along the diagonal. "Check."

Nola studied the board a long moment, and studied Kevin for perhaps even longer. She moved a pawn forward to threaten the bishop, asking, offhandedly, "Have you spoken to your wife lately? To Carol?"

Kevin took her pawn with a rook, said, "Check," but nothing more.

Nola didn't touch the board. She looked soberly at Kevin, her tone quiet. "Do you really want to lose her, Kevin?"

Kevin looked up sharply, suddenly angry—the same anger, the same irritation, he felt with Carol. "Don't talk to me about *losing* things," he snapped. "All I know is, the minute you become truly happy in this life, that's when they pull the rug out from under you! *That's* when it's all taken away."

Nola nodded. "And if you never *know* happiness . . . you never know what it's like to *lose* it. Do you?"

Her words caught him unaware; it was an idea that somehow had never occurred to him, and he groped for some easy way to rebut it.

"No. No, I wouldn't put it like . . . I mean, that's . . . that's not what I—"

He trailed off—confused, uncertain, his anger replaced by doubt and a certain . . . embarrassment. He looked at Nola—at her knowing, understanding smile—and he laughed a small, awkward laugh.

"I . . . guess it is kind of a . . . foolish way to look at things," he admitted. Embarrassed and uncomfortable, he looked down at the board; Nola moved a pawn to capture his bishop, held the captured piece between two fingers and smiled teasingly.

But Kevin merely tapped at his keyboard and pushed his queen through a gap opened by her capture. "Checkmate."

Nola looked down at the board, and when she looked up again, it was, oddly, with pleasure, and satisfaction.

"Very good," she said, approvingly. "You're learning."

7

The retirement home was just outside Brookline, in that area where Jamaica Plain and Forest Hills meet, near the Arnold Arboretum. The grounds were large and well kept, broad pathways shaded by wide beech trees; there was a scent of lilacs in the air. All in all, Daniel reflected, not a bad place to end one's days, and John Ruskin, despite everything, seemed to agree. A reedy, gentle man in his early seventies, Ruskin navigated the winding path expertly, and when Daniel offered his help rounding a bend, he just laughed quietly. "I know my way around," he assured him. He stopped at a rosebush, absently caressing the petals, assuredly avoiding the thorns; it was only in the way he held his head, free from having to look directly at someone with whom he was speaking, that one could tell he was blind.

"I appreciate your taking the time to talk with me, Mr. Ruskin," Daniel said, still a little off balance. When the Massachusetts Bar Association had given him Ruskin's current address, as well as his physical condition, Daniel had not expected to find such a spry old bird. "I haven't been having the best of luck tracking down most of Robert and Nola's friends. Most of them are—"

He caught himself, but Ruskin finished the sentence for him: "Most of them are dead?" he said with a trace of amusement.

"I'm sorry. I didn't mean to sound . . . tactless . . ."

Ruskin laughed softly. "I've spent the last fifteen years in darkness," he said, "and I've managed to enjoy life in spite of it. If it's darkness I have ahead of me, I think I can make the best of it."

Daniel began to feel more at ease. "You knew Robert and Nola for—how long?"

"Ever since Robert opened his law practice. I had the office across from his, and after two or three years, we decided to set up shop together . . . about the time the Second World War broke out. They were lovely people—Robert with his passion for justice, Nola and her love of poetry . . . she published quite a few papers, did you know that?"

"Yes. I did."

Ruskin reached out and brought down a lilac blossom to his face, breathed in its distinctive aroma, and smiled. "These must be beautiful," he said.

"Yes," Daniel agreed. "They are." He hesitated. "Did either of them . . . Robert or Nola . . . ever attend MIT, at some time in their lives?"

Ruskin seemed baffled by the question. "Not that I know of. They both graduated NYU, as I recall, but only Nola went on for further studies, and that was at—Boston College, I believe."

"Did they ever live anywhere in Cambridge?"

Ruskin laughed. "Good Lord, no. You couldn't get Robert very far from his office, or his clients."

"Did either of them"—Daniel groped to express the inexpressible—"did either of them leave behind any kind of . . . 'unfinished business'? Some goal, some dream, they never fulfilled?"

"Well, yes, of course," Ruskin said, seeming almost to regard Daniel's question as a little dense. "When someone leaves as suddenly as Nola did, there's bound to be unfinished business. He blamed himself; lost so much of that passion of his in later years." He shook his head sadly. "She was taken from him so early, you know. I don't think he ever really recovered from that."

Daniel stopped dead in his tracks, though Ruskin kept ambling along the shaded path. "Excuse me," Daniel said, trying to regain his balance, "but . . . exactly *when* did Nola die?"

Ruskin could obviously tell from Daniel's voice that the younger man had stopped, so he too paused. "In March, I believe," he said thoughtfully. "March of . . . 1943. She was only thirty-five." Ruskin shook his head ruefully. "What a waste. What a terrible waste . . ."

Daniel stood there, stunned, beginning to realize just why Nola's death certificate might never have found its way to Boston.

"*How*—did she die?"

Ruskin turned and faced him for the first time.

"I thought you knew," he said, surprised. "She died in childbirth."

THE PHONE RANG a little after nine a.m., Carol ran downstairs, hoping to God it wasn't a wrong number or a phone solicitation, and snapped it up on the third ring. "Hello?"

To her relief, the voice at the other end was Kevin's. "Carol? It's Kevin. I'm at the lab."

"Kev?" She tried to keep the fear, the uncertainty, from her tone. "Are you all right?"

"I'm fine. And I've missed you."

"I . . . I've missed you, too," she said, voice wavering only a little, her heart suddenly racing as she heard her husband say: "I'm ready to come home. Think you can swing by and give a guy a lift?"

Carol smiled. "Yeah,' she said, tears welling up in her eyes. "I think I can manage that."

"See you in a while," came the reply. "I love you."

There was a click, and then a dial tone, and Carol Drayton hurriedly put the receiver back into its cradle, grabbing her coat and crying tears of relief that whatever had happened—whatever had gone wrong—was over . . .

At the lab, the autodial on the telephone hung up the call even as the speech synthesizer switched itself off. Kevin lay sleeping on his cot, as, nearby, Nola stood in the center of the hologram—a grandmotherly, white-haired woman in her early sixties. A part of her consciousness reached out into the speech synthesis program and deleted the exact modulations of tone and pitch which she had earlier painstakingly matched to Kevin's voice. She looked down at the sleeping Kevin with a pleased, protective smile, then bent down until she was kneeling on the floor of the holo display, and said gently: "Kevin? Kevin, it's time to wake up."

Kevin stirred, not remembering when he'd fallen asleep, but certainly not prepared for what he saw as he sat up, groggily, and looked at Nola. Good God—how long had he been asleep? Her hair was a halo of pale rose light surrounding a lined and aged face; her hands, braced on her knees for support, were thin and wrinkled. And yet—

She was still beautiful, to him; still Nola. He saw in her smile the same shy affection he had seen in the ten-year-old she had once been; saw in her eyes the enthusiasm, the curiosity, the intelligence, of the twenty-year-old lover of Yeats and Byron and Browning; read, in the lines around her eyes and mouth, the sadness of past grief and disappointments, none of which had dimmed the things he'd come to love about her. For some, age became a shriven reminder of bitterness and decay; for others—for Nola—it merely confirmed that the body was but a shell to the soul, a testament of flesh to spirit.

Kevin got shakily to his feet as Nola announced, calmly, "It's time for me to go now, Kevin."

His heart pounded; he felt as though he were falling. *"No,"* he said, as though by sheer force of will he might keep her here.

"I'm afraid so," Nola said. "I accomplished what I had to, and now . . . now it's time to leave."

Kevin started; the purpose, the meaning which he had labored so to discover this past week, was now starkly evident in her tone. *She* knew, even if he did not. "What?" he demanded. *"What* did you accomplish? Why were you *here?"*

Nola laughed a small, easy laugh. "I was here for you, Kevin," she said, as though it should have been apparent all along.

"For *me?"* Kevin took a deep breath; tried to keep calm. "Look," he said, trying desperately to buy some time, "I . . . I don't understand what you're saying, but if what you say is true . . . please. Don't leave . . ."

"My time is up, Kevin," she said sadly. "I'm sorry."

Suddenly angry, Kevin snapped, "You can't! Not *yet."*

"I have no *choice."*

"No!" Kevin yelled. "Damn it, Nola, I can't lose you again!"

Nola said gently, "Like you lost me before?"

"Yes!" Kevin said. "Like before! Like—"

He stopped, suddenly aware of what he was saying. Part of him tried to deny what he was slowly coming to realize, while another part, a deeper part, knew the truth; had always known the truth. Nola smiled at him with love and sorrow.

"I left you too soon, my darling," she said, softly. "I didn't mean to, but I did."

Kevin shook his head; his voice was a hoarse whisper. "No . . . no, this isn't . . . *possible . . ."*

"But it is," Nola said. "You carried the grief with you all your life . . . and into the next."

Kevin was ashen; disbelieving.

"But I don't . . . I don't *remember* . . ."

"You remembered enough to be afraid," she said. "Afraid of love . . . afraid of losing it. I had to live out a life with you . . . to make up for the one we never had a chance to share . . . so the fear would go away."

Kevin's hands were trembling. "You knew?" he said, a trace of betrayal in his tone. "From the start?"

"No," Nola said quickly. "Only after I . . . lost the baby." She hesitated, her eyes glazed with the memory of that moment. "I wasn't just remembering my pain, Kevin . . . I was remembering my death."

Kevin shut his eyes, which he found were filled with tears. He knew, now. He may not have remembered, but he *knew*.

"After that," Nola said tonelessly, "it all became clear . . ."

Kevin put his hands to his head, holding his throbbing temples, letting the tears flow. "I don't know if I . . . can believe *any* of this . . ."

Nola nodded. "Perhaps that's just as well. You have a life to get back to." She fixed him with a sober gaze. "Don't let it slip *by*. Not *again*."

She stood, slowly, as Kevin took his hands away and stared up at her. "I have to leave now," she said again.

"No," Kevin said, and this time it wasn't an angry entreaty but a simple, respectful request; "wait. Just a minute more?"

He held up a hand, and Nola nodded her assent. Quickly he turned, went into his office, rummaged under a pile of books on his desk until he found the one he sought, as Nola watched with an amused, affectionate smile.

He came back into the room, one hand clutching the leatherbound book. He smiled. "Yeats, again," he said with a small laugh. "Do you remember the one called . . . 'When You Are Old'?"

The old woman with the child's smile nodded in recognition. " 'When you are old and grey and full of sleep—' "

"Yes," Kevin said, flipping through the book, searching for the right page. "There's this one line . . ."

He found the page, looked up at Nola, and read:

" 'How many loved your moments of glad grace,

" 'And loved your beauty with love false or true—' "

His eyes shone; his voice was clear and strong.

" 'But one man loved the pilgrim soul in you,

" 'And loved the sorrows of your changing face . . .' "

Nola smiled a soft, gentle, happy smile.

"Goodbye—Robert," she said softly. "I love you."

Her figure turned from rose to amethyst, from frosted glass to clear crystal; Kevin watched, strangely without sadness, as the last trace of her faded from the display, leaving behind a vacant shaft of violet light, a shaft that would always seem empty to him, no matter what universes might fill it in the future. And yet for the first time he felt pride in its creation, in its completion—for the first time he felt happy, and unworried that that happiness might be taken away from him.

His reverie was interrupted by the sound of the phone; still clutching the small book of poetry in his hands, he picked up the receiver, only half conscious of what he was saying. "Yes?"

"Dr. Drayton, this is security. There's a woman here; says she's your wife. Should we let her in?"

Puzzled but not displeased, Kevin told them yes, by all means, send her in. He put aside the book, feeling an unaccustomed sense of anticipation and excitement at the thought of Carol; finding himself hurrying, in fact, to the door, pressing his palmprint against the scanner, counting the seconds it took for the burst of light to register his print and disarm the lock—

The door slid open, and Carol stood there, nervous but happy, a small anxious smile on her lips.

"You called for a taxi, mister?" she said lightly.

Kevin didn't understand, but discovered that he didn't care; all that mattered was that she was here, and she was real, and he could touch her. He embraced her, held her with a longing he had not felt in many months; he kissed her tenderly, and she eagerly returned it. He stroked the side of her face, brushing aside a strand of long brown hair, and they laughed shyly at one another, like teenagers on a first date. He took her in his arms again, let his mouth find hers, then let her rest her head on his shoulder while he stroked her back with his hands. And he marveled at the happiness he felt, at the absence of the stress and uneasiness that had separated them these many long months.

Carol rested her chin on his shoulder, his muscles so relaxed, the tension vanished; she put a hand to his other shoulder, stroked it gently, opened her eyes—

And blinked at what she saw in front of her.

"Kevin?" she said wonderingly. "What's that?"

They separated, and Kevin turned to find, floating in the middle of the hologram display, a sphere . . . a striped ball, identical to the one he had created to calm the five-year-old Nola. Slowly, he and Carol made their way to it as it danced a tuneless dance, moving to a melody they could not hear; they squatted down to study it, and Kevin thought again of Yeats, of the poem composed by a spurned and angry young man, which Kevin—once so angry himself—had oddly interpreted as a thank-you, and farewell:

> *And bending down beside the glowing bars,*
> *Murmur, a little sadly, how Love fled—*

Fled but not forgotten; never forgotten. It was all right to love her, even now, because he would never love anyone else in the same way he had loved *her*—just as he would never love anyone in exactly the same way he loved Carol. He would love them both, each in their own ways, one in life and one in memory.

> *—And paced upon the mountains overhead—*

The ball suddenly dropped out of its floating dance, bounced off the floor of the display—and for the briefest of moments, its image seemed to spring *out* of the column of light, so real, so immediate, that Carol brought her hands up to catch it—but by the time she had, the afterimage had faded, like a retinal blur, a shadow at twilight—

And hid Her face amid a crowd of stars.

In the middle of the hologram display, a spiral nebula appeared once more, starry arms revolving in calm repose, and Kevin no longer felt afraid.

—for Asha

MRS. TODD'S SHORTCUT

BY STEPHEN KING

EVEN HORROR MASTER STEPHEN KING HAS A GENTLE SIDE, AND NOWHERE IS IT MORE EVIDENT THAN IN THIS DELIGHTFUL TALE OF A GOODLY, PRAGMATIC NEW ENGLAND MATRON WHO IS ALWAYS IN SEARCH OF THE LATEST SHORTCUT SO AS NOT TO WASTE ANY MORE TIME THAN SHE HAS TO.

... AND ON A REGIONAL NOTE, PERHAPS YOU CAN HEAR THE VOICE OF A NEW ENGLANDER CAPTURING THE ESSENCE OF THE STORY AS THEY TRY TO EXPLAIN TO YOU THAT SOMETIMES, "YOU JUST CAN'T GET THERE FROM HERE."

"There goes the Todd woman," I said.

Homer Buckland watched the little Jaguar go by and nodded. The woman raised her hand to Homer. Homer nodded his big, shaggy head to her but didn't raise his own hand in return. The Todd family had a big summer home on Castle Lake, and Homer had been their caretaker since time out of mind. I had an idea that he disliked Worth Todd's second wife every bit as much as he'd liked 'Phelia Todd, the first one.

This was just about two years ago and we were sitting on a bench in front of Bell's Market, me with an orange soda-pop, Homer with a glass of mineral water. It was October, which is a peaceful time in Castle Rock. Lots of the lake places still get used on the weekends, but the aggressive, boozy summer socializing is over by then and the hunters with their big guns and their expensive nonresident permits pinned to their orange caps haven't started to come into town yet. Crops have been mostly laid by. Nights are cool, good for sleeping, and old joints like mine haven't yet started to complain. In October the sky over the lake is passing fair, with those big white clouds that move so slow; I like how they seem so flat on the bottoms, and how they are a little gray there, like with a shadow of sundown foretold, and I can watch the sun sparkle on the water and not be bored for some space of minutes. It's in October, sitting on the bench in front of Bell's and watching the lake from afar off, that I still wish I was a smoking man.

"She don't drive as fast as 'Phelia," Homer said. "I swan I used to think what an old-fashion name she had for a woman that could put a car through its paces like she could."

Summer people like the Todds are nowhere near as interesting to the year-round residents of small Maine towns as they themselves believe. Year-round folk prefer their own love stories and hate stories and scandals and rumors of scandal. When that textile fellow from Amesbury shot himself, Estonia Corbridge found that after a week or so she couldn't even get invited to lunch on her story of how she found him with the pistol still in one stiffening hand. But folks are still not done talking about Joe Camber, who got killed by his own dog.

Well, it don't matter. It's just that they are different race-courses we run on. Summer people are trotters; us others that don't put on ties to do our week's work are just pacers. Even so there was quite a lot of local interest when Ophelia Todd disappeared back in 1973. Ophelia was a genuinely nice woman, and she had done a lot of things in town. She worked to raise money for the Sloan Library, helped to refurbish the war memorial, and that sort of thing. But *all* the summer people like the idea of raising money. You mention raising money and their eyes light up and commence to gleam. You mention raising money and they can get a committee together and appoint a secretary and keep an agenda. They like that. But you mention *time* (beyond, that is, one big long walloper of a combined cocktail party and committee meeting) and you're out of luck. Time seems to be what summer people mostly set a store by. They lay it by, and if they could put it up in Ball jars like preserves, why, they would. But 'Phelia Todd seemed willing to *spend* time—to do desk duty in the library as well as to raise money for it. When it got down to using scouring pads and elbow-grease on the war memorial, 'Phelia was right out there with town women who had lost sons in three different wars, wearing an overall with her hair done up in a kerchief. And when kids needed ferrying to a summer swim program, you'd be as apt to see her as anyone headed down Landing Road with the back of Worth Todd's big shiny pickup full of kids. A good woman. Not a town woman, but a good woman. And when she disappeared, there was concern. Not grieving, exactly, because a disappearance is not exactly like a death. It's not like chopping something off with a cleaver; more like something running down the sink so slow you don't know it's all gone until long after it is.

" 'Twas a Mercedes she drove," Homer said, answering the question I hadn't asked. "Two-seater sportster. Todd got it for her in sixty-four or sixty-five, I guess. You remember her taking the kids to the lake all those years they had Frogs and Tadpoles?"

"Ayuh."

"She'd drive em no more than forty, mindful they was in the back. But it chafed her. That woman had lead in her foot and a ball bearing sommers in the back of her ankle."

It used to be that Homer never talked about his summer people. But then his wife died. Five years ago it was. She was plowing a grade and the tractor tipped over on her and Homer was taken bad off about it. He grieved for two years or so and then seemed to feel better. But he was not the same. He seemed waiting for something to happen, waiting for the next thing. You'd pass his neat little house sometimes at dusk and he would be on the porch smoking a pipe with a glass of mineral water on the porch rail and the sunset would be in his eyes and pipe smoke around his head and you'd think—I did, anyway—*Homer is waiting for the next thing*. This bothered me over a wider range of my mind than I liked to admit, and at last I decided it was because if it had been me, I wouldn't have been waiting for the next thing, like a groom who has put on his morning coat and finally has his tie right and is only sitting there on a bed in the upstairs of his house and looking first at himself in the mirror and then at the clock on the mantel and waiting for it to be eleven o'clock so he can get married. If it had been me, I would not have been waiting for the next thing; I would have been waiting for the last thing.

But in that waiting period—which ended when Homer went to Vermont a year later—he sometimes talked about those people. To me, to a few others.

"She never even drove fast with her husband; s'far as I know. But when I drove with her, she made that Mercedes strut."

A fellow pulled in at the pumps and began to fill up his car. The car had a Massachusetts plate.

"It wasn't one of these new sports cars that run on unleaded gasoline and hitch every time you step on it; it was one of the old ones, and the speedometer was calibrated all the way up to a hundred and sixty. It was a funny color of brown and I ast her one time what you called that color and she said it was champagne. Ain't that *good*. I says, and she laughs fit to split. I like a woman who will laugh when you don't have to point her right at the joke, you know."

The man at the pumps had finished getting his gas.

"Afternoon, gentlemen," he says as he comes up the steps.

"A good day to you," I says, and he went inside.

" 'Phelia was always looking for a shortcut," Homer went on as if we had never been interrupted. "That woman was mad for a shortcut. I never saw the beat of it. She said if you can save enough distance, you'll save time as well. She said her father swore by that scripture. He was a salesman, always on the road, and she went with him when she could, and he was always lookin for the shortest way. So she got in the habit.

"I ast her one time if it wasn't kinda funny—here she was on the one hand, spendin her time rubbin up that old statue in the Square and takin the little ones to their swimmin lessons instead of playing tennis and swimming and getting boozed up like normal summer people, and on the other hand bein so damn set on savin fifteen minutes between here and Fryeburg that thinkin about it probably kep her up nights. It just seemed to me the two things went against each other's grain, if you see what I mean. She just looks at me and says, 'I like being helpful, Homer. I like driving, too—at least sometimes, when it's a challenge—but I don't like the *time* it takes. It's mending clothes—sometimes you take tucks and sometimes you let things out. Do you see what I mean?'

" 'I guess so, missus,' I says, kinda dubious.

" 'If sitting behind the wheel of a car was my idea of a really good time *all* the time, I would look for long-cuts,' she says, and that tickled me s'much I had to laugh."

The Massachusetts fellow came out of the store with a six-pack in one hand and some lottery tickets in the other.

"You enjoy your weekend," Homer says.

"I always do," the Massachusetts fellow says. "I only wish I could afford to live here all year round."

"Well, we'll keep it all in good order for when you *can* come," Homer says, and the fellow laughs.

We watched him drive off toward someplace, that Massachusetts plate showing. It was a green one. My Marcy says those are the ones the Massachusetts Motor Registry gives to drivers who ain't had a accident in that strange, angry, fuming state for two years. If you have, she says, you got to have a red one so people know to watch out for you when they see you on the roll.

"They was in-state people, you know, the both of them," Homer said, as if the Massachusetts fellow had reminded him of the fact.

"I guess I did know that," I said.

"The Todds are just about the only birds we got that fly north in the winter. The new one, I don't think she likes flying north too much."

He sipped his mineral water and fell silent a moment, thinking.

"She didn't mind it, though," Homer said. "At least, I *judge* she didn't although she used to complain about it something fierce. The complaining was just a way to explain why she was always lookin for a shortcut."

"And you mean her husband didn't mind her traipsing down every wood-road in tarnation between here and Bangor just so she could see if it was nine-tenths of a mile shorter?"

"He didn't care piss-all," Homer said shortly, and got up, and went in the store. There now, Owens, I told myself, you know it ain't safe to ast him questions when he's yarning, and you went right ahead and ast one, and you have buggered a story that was starting to shape up promising.

I sat there and turned my face up into the sun and after about ten minutes he come out with a boiled egg and sat down. He ate her and I took care not to say nothing and the water on Castle Lake sparkled as blue as something as might be told of in a story about treasure. When Homer had finished his egg and had a sip of mineral water, he went on. I was surprised, but still said nothing. It wouldn't have been wise.

"They had two or three different chunks of rolling iron," he said. "There was the Cadillac, and his truck, and her little Mercedes go-devil. A couple of winters he left the truck, 'case they wanted to come down and do some skiin. Mostly when the summer was over he'd drive the Caddy back up and she'd take her go-devil."

I nodded but didn't speak. In truth, I was afraid to risk another comment. Later I thought it would have taken a lot of comments to shut Homer Buckland up that day. He had been wanting to tell the story of Mrs. Todd's shortcut for a long time.

"Her little go-devil had a special odometer in it that told you how many miles was in a trip, and every time she set off from Castle Lake to Bangor she'd set it 000-point-0 and let her clock up to whatever. She had made a game of it, and she used to chafe me with it."

He paused, thinking that back over.

"No, that ain't right."

He paused more and faint lines showed up on his forehead like steps on a library ladder.

"She *made* like she made a game of it, but it was a serious business to her. Serious as anything else, anyway." He flapped a hand and I think he meant the husband. "The glovebox of the little go-devil was filled with maps, and there was a few more in the back where there would be a seat in a regular car. Some was gas station maps, and some was pages that had been pulled from the Rand-McNally Road Atlas; she had some maps from Appalachian Trail guidebooks and a whole mess of topographical survey-squares, too. It wasn't her having those maps that made me think it wa'a'nt a game; it was how she'd drawed lines on all of them, showing routes she'd taken or at least tried to take.

"She'd been stuck a few times, too, and had to get a pull from some farmer with a tractor and chain.

"I was there one day laying tile in the bathroom, sitting there with grout squittering out of every damn crack you could see—I dreamed of nothing but squares and cracks that was bleeding grout that night—and she come stood in the doorway and talked to me about it for quite a while. I used to chafe her about it, but I was also sort of interested, and not just because my brother Franklin used to live down-Bangor and I'd traveled most of the roads she was telling me of. I was interested just because a man like me is always oncommon interested in knowing the shortest way, even if he don't always want to take it. You that way too?"

"Ayuh," I said. There's something powerful about knowing the shortest way, even if you take the longer way because you know your mother-in-law is sitting home. Getting there quick is often for the birds, although no one holding a Massachusetts driver's license seems to know it. But *knowing* how to get there quick—or even knowing how to get there a way that the person sitting beside you don't know . . . that has power.

"Well, she had them roads like a Boy Scout has his knots," Homer said, and smiled his large, sunny grin. "She says, 'Wait a minute, wait a minute,' like a little girl, and I hear her through the wall rummaging through her desk; and then she comes back with a little notebook that looked like she'd had it a good long time. Cover was all rumpled, don't you know, and some of the pages had pulled loose from those little wire rings on one side.

" 'The way Worth goes—the way *most* people go—is Route 97 to Mechanic Falls, then Route 11 to Lewiston, and then the Interstate to Bangor. 156.4 miles.' "

I nodded.

" 'If you want to skip the turnpike—and save some distance—you'd go to Mechanic Falls, Route 11 to Lewiston, Route 202 to Augusta, then up Route 9 through China Lake and Unity and Haven to Bangor. That's 144.9 miles.'

" 'You won't save no time that way, missus,' I says, 'not going through Lewiston *and* Augusta. Although I will admit that drive up the Old Derry Road to Bangor is real pretty.'

" 'Save enough miles and soon enough you'll save time,' she says. 'And I didn't say that's the way I'd go, although I have a good many times; I'm just running down the routes most people use. Do you want me to go on?'

" 'No,' I says, 'just leave me in this cussed bathroom all by myself starin at all these cussed cracks until I start to rave.'

" 'There are four major routes in all,' she says. 'The one by Route 2 is 163.4 miles. I only tried it once. Too long.'

" 'That's the one I'd hosey if my wife called and told me it was leftovers,' I says, kinda low.

" 'What was that?' she says.

" 'Nothin,' I says, 'Talkin to the grout.'

" 'Oh. Well, the fourth—and there aren't too many who know about it, although they are all good roads—paved, anyway, is across Speckled Bird Mountain on 219 to 202 *beyond* Lewiston. Then, if you take Route 19, you can get around Augusta. Then you take the Old Derry Road. That way is just 129.2.'

"I didn't say nothing for a little while and p'raps she thought I was doubting her because she says, a little pert, 'I know it's hard to believe, but it's so.'

"I said I guessed that was about right, and I thought—looking back—it probably was. Because that's the way I'd usually go when I went down to Bangor to see Franklin when he was still alive. I hadn't been that way in years, though. Do you think a man could just—well—forget a road, Dave?"

I allowed it was possible. The turnpike is easy to think of. After a while it almost fills a man's mind, and you think not how could I get from here to there but how can I get from here to the turnpike ramp that's *closest* to there. And that made me think that maybe there are lots of roads all over that are just going begging; roads with rock walls beside them, real roads with blackberry bushes growing alongside them but nobody to eat the berries but the birds and gravel pits with old rusted chains hanging down in low curve in front of their entryways, the pits themselves as forgotten as a child's old toys with scrumgrass growing up their deserted unremembered sides. Roads that have just been forgot except by the people who live on them and think of the quickest way to get off them and onto the turnpike where you can pass on a hill and not fret over it. We like to joke in Maine that you can't get there from here, but maybe the joke is on us. The truth is there's about a damn thousand ways to do it and man doesn't bother.

Homer continued: "I grouted tile all afternoon in that hot little bathroom and she stood there in the doorway all that time, one foot crossed behind the other, bare-legged, wearin loafers and a khaki-colored skirt and a sweater that was some darker. Hair was drawed back in a hosstail. She must have been thirty-four or -five then, but her face was lit up with what she was tellin me and I swan she looked like a sorority girl home from school on vacation.

"After a while she musta got an idea of how long she'd been there cuttin the air around her mouth because she says, 'I must be boring the hell out of you, Homer.'

" 'Yes'm,' I says, 'you are. I druther you went away and left me to talk to this damn grout.'

" 'Don't be sma'at, Homer,' she says.

" 'No, missus, you ain't borin me,' I says.

"So she smiles and then goes back to it, pagin through her little notebook like a salesman checkin his orders. She had those four main ways—well, really three because she gave up on Route 2 right away—but she must have had forty different other ways that were play-offs on those. Roads with state numbers, roads without, roads with names, roads without. My head fair spun with em. And finally she says to me, 'You ready for the blue ribbon winner, Homer?'

" 'I guess so,' I says.

" 'At least it's the blue ribbon winner so *far*,' she says. 'Do you know, Homer, that a man wrote an article in *Science Today* in 1921 proving that no man could run a mile in under four minutes? He *proved* it, with all sorts of calculations based on the maximum length of the male thigh-muscles, maximum length of stride, maximum lung capacity, maximum heart-rate, and a whole lot more. I was *taken* with that article! I was so taken that I gave it to Worth and asked him to give it to Professor Murray in the math department at the University of Maine. I wanted those figures checked because I was sure they must have been based on the wrong postulates, or something. Worth probably thought I was being silly—"Ophelia's got a bee in her bonnet" is what he says—but he took them. Well, Professor Murray checked through the man's figures quite carefully . . . and do you know *what*, Homer?'

" 'No, missus.'

" 'Those figures were *right*. The man's criteria were *solid*. He proved, back in 1923, that a man couldn't run a mile in under four minutes. He *proved* that. But people do it all the time, and do you know what that means?'

" 'No, missus,' I said, although I had a glimmer.

" 'It means that no blue ribbon is forever,' she says. 'Someday—if the world doesn't explode itself in the meantime—someone will run a *two*-minute mile in the Olympics. It may take a hundred years or a thousand, but it will happen. Because there is no ultimate blue ribbon. There is zero, and there is eternity, and there is mortality, but there is no *ultimate*.'

"And there she stood, her face clean and scrubbed and shinin, that darkish hair of hers pulled back from her brow, as if to say 'Just you go ahead and disagree if you can.' But I couldn't. Because I believe something like that. It is much like what the minister means, I think, when he talks about grace.

" 'You ready for the blue-ribbon winner *for now*?' she says.

" 'Ayuh,' I says, and I even stopped groutin for the time bein. I'd reached the tub anyway and there wasn't nothing left but a lot of those frikkin squirrelly little corners. She drawed a deep breath and then spieled it out at me as fast as that auctioneer goes over in Gates Falls when he has been putting the whiskey to himself, and I can't remember it all, but it went something like this."

Homer Buckland shut his eyes for a moment, his big hands lying perfectly still on his long thighs, his face turned up toward the sun. Then he opened his eyes again and for a moment I swan he *looked* like her, yes he did, a seventy-year-old man looking like a woman of thirty-four who was at that moment in her time looking like a college girl of twenty, and I can't remember exactly what *he* said any more than *he* could remember exactly what *she* said, not just because it was complex but because I was so fetched by how he looked sayin it, but it went close enough like this:

" 'You set out Route 97 and then cut up Denton Street to the Old Townhouse Road and that way you get around Castle Rock downtown but back to 97. Nine miles up you can go an old logger's road a mile and a half to Town Road #6, which takes you to Big Anderson Road by Sites' Cedar Mill. There's a cut-road the old-timers call Bear Road, and that gets you to 219. Once you're on the far side of Speckled Bird Mountain you grab the Stanhouse Road, turn left onto the Bull Pine Road—there's a swampy patch there but you can spang right through it if you get up enough speed on the gravel—and so you come out on Route 106. 106 cuts through Alton's Plantation to the Old Derry Road—and there's two or three woods roads there that you follow and so come out on Route 3 just beyond Derry Hospital. From there it's only four miles to Route 2 in Etna, and so into Bangor.'

"She paused to get her breath back, then looked at me. 'Do you know how long that is, all told?'

" 'No'm' I says, thinking it sounds like about a hundred and ninety miles and four bust springs.

" 'It's 116.4 miles,' she says."

I laughed. The laugh was out of me before I thought I wasn't doing myself any favor if I wanted to hear this story to the end. But Homer grinned himself and nodded.

"I know. And you know I don't like to argue with anyone, Dave. But there's a difference between having your leg pulled and getting it shook like a damn apple-tree.

" 'You don't believe me,' she says.

" 'Well, it's *hard* to believe, missus,' I said.

" 'Leave that grout to dry and I'll show you,' she says. "You can finish behind the tub tomorrow. Come on, Homer. I'll leave a note for Worth—he may not be back tonight anyway—and you can call your wife! We'll be sitting down to dinner in the Pilot's Grille in'—she looks at her watch—'two hours and forty-five minutes from right now. And if it's a minute longer, I'll buy you a bottle of Irish Mist to take home with you. You see, my dad was right. Save enough miles and you'll save time, even if you have to go through every damn bog and sump in Kennebec County to do it. Now what do you say?'

"She was lookin at me with her brown eyes just like lamps, there was a devilish look in them that said turn your cap around back'rds, Homer, and climb aboard this hoss, I be first and you be second and let the devil take the hindmost, and there was a grin on her face that said the exact same thing, and I tell you, Dave, I wanted to *go*. I didn't even want to top that damn can of grout. And I *certain* sure didn't want to drive that go-devil of hers. I wanted just to sit in it on the shotgun side and watch her get in, see her skirt come up a little, see her pull it down over her knees or not, watch her hair shine."

He trailed off and suddenly let off a sarcastic, choked laugh. That laugh of his sounded like a shotgun loaded with rock salt.

"Just call up Megan and say, 'You know 'Phelia Todd, that woman you're halfway to being so jealous of now you can't see straight and can't ever find a good word to say about her? Well, her and me is going to make this speed-run down to Bangor in that little champagne-colored go-devil Mercedes of hers, so don't wait dinner.'

"Just call her up and say that. Oh *yes*. Oh *ayuh*."

And he laughed again with his hands lying there on his legs just as natural as ever was and I seen something in his face that was almost hateful and after a minute he took his glass of mineral water from the railing there and got outside some of it.

"You didn't go," I said.

"Not *then*."

He laughed, and this laugh was gentler.

"She must have seen something in my face, because it was like she found herself again. She stopped looking like a sorority girl and just looked like 'Phelia Todd again. She looked down at the notebook like she didn't know what it was she had been holding and put it down by her side, almost behind her skirt.

"I says, 'I'd like to do just that thing, missus, but I got to finish up here, and my wife has got a roast on for dinner.'

"She says, 'I understand, Homer—I just got a little carried away. I do that a lot. All the time, Worth says.' Then she kinda straightened up and says, 'But the offer holds, any time you want to go. You can even throw your shoulder to the back end if we get stuck somewhere. Might save me five dollars.' And she laughed.

" 'I'll take you up on it, missus,' I says, and she seen that I meant what I said and wasn't just being polite.

" 'And before you just go believing that a hundred and sixteen miles to Bangor is out of the question, get out your own map and see how many miles it would be as the crow flies.'

"I finished the tiles and went home and ate leftovers—there wa'n't no roast, and

I think 'Phelia Todd knew it—and after Megan was in bed, I got out my yardstick and a pen and my Mobil map of the state, and I did what she had told me ... because it had laid hold of my mind a bit, you see. I drew a straight line and did out the calculations accordin to the scale of miles. I was some surprised. Because if you went from Castle Rock up there to Bangor like one of those little Piper Cubs could fly on a clear day—if you didn't have to mind lakes, or stretches of lumber company woods that was chained off, or bogs, or crossing rivers where there wasn't no bridges, why, it would just be seventy-nine miles, give or take."

I jumped a little.

"Measure it yourself, if you don't believe me," Homer said. "I never knew Maine was so small until I seen that."

He had himself a drink and then looked around at me.

"There come a time the next spring when Megan was away in New Hampshire visiting with her brother. I had to go down to the Todds' house to take off the storm doors and put on the screens, and her little Mercedes go-devil was there. She was down by herself.

"She come to the door and says: 'Homer! Have you come to put on the screen doors?'

"And right off I says: 'No, missus, I come to see if you want to give me a ride down to Bangor the short way.'

"Well, she looked at me with no expression on her face at all, and I thought she had forgotten all about it. I felt my face gettin red, the way it will when you feel you just pulled one hell of a boner. Then, just when I was getting ready to pologize, her face busts into that grin again and she says, 'You just stand right there while I get my keys. And don't change your mind, Homer!'

"She come back a minute later with em in her hand. 'If we get stuck, you'll see mosquitoes just about the size of dragonflies.'

" 'I've seen em as big as English sparrows up in Rangely, missus,' I said, 'and I guess we're both a spot too heavy to be carried off.'

"She laughs. 'Well, I warned you, anyway. Come on, Homer.'

" 'And if we ain't there in two hours and forty-five minute,' I says, kinda sly, 'you was gonna buy me a bottle of Irish Mist.'

"She looks at me kinda surprised, the driver's door of the go-devil open and one foot inside. 'Hell, Homer,' she says, 'I told you that was the Blue Ribbon for *then*. I've found a way up there that's *shorter*. We'll be there in two and a half hours. Get in here, Homer. We are going to roll.' "

He paused again, hands lying calm on his thighs, his eyes dulling, perhaps seeing that champagne-colored two-seater heading up the Todds' steep driveway.

"She stood the car still at the end of it and says, 'You sure?'

" 'Let her rip,' I says. The ball-bearing in her ankle rolled and that heavy foot come down. I can't tell you nothing much about whatall happened after that. Except after a while I couldn't hardly take my eyes off her. There was somethin wild that crep into her face, Dave—somethin *wild* and something *free*, and it frightened my heart. She was beautiful, and I was took with love *for* her, anyone would have been, any man, anyway, and maybe any woman too, but I was scairt *of* her too; because she looked like she could kill you if her eye left the road and fell on you and she decided to love you back. She was wearin blue jeans and a old white shirt with the sleeves rolled up—I had a idea she was maybe fixin to paint somethin on the back deck when I came by—but after we had been goin for a while seemed like she was dressed in nothin but all this white billowy stuff like a pitcher in one of those old gods-and-goddesses books."

He thought, looking out across the lake, his face very somber.

"Like the huntress that was supposed to drive the moon across the sky."

"Diana?"

"Ayuh. Moon was her go-devil. 'Phelia looked like that to me and I just tell you fair out that I was stricken in love for her and never would have made a move, even though I was some younger then than I am now. I would not have made a move even had I been twenty, although I suppose I might of at sixteen, and been killed for it— killed if she looked at me was the way it felt.

"She was like that woman drivin the moon across the sky, halfway up over the splashboard with gossamer stoles all flyin out behind her in silver cobwebs and her hair streamin back to show the dark little hollows of her temples, lashin those horses and tellin me to get along faster and never mind how they blowed, just faster, faster, *faster.*

"We went down a lot of woods roads—the first two or three I knew, and after that I didn't know none of them. We must have been a sight to those trees that had never seen nothing with a motor in it before but big old pulp-trucks and snowmobiles; that little go-devil that would most likely have looked more at home on the Sunset Boulevard than shooting through those woods, spitting and bulling its way up one hill and then slamming down the next through those dusty green bars of afternoon sunlight— she had the top down and I could smell everything in those woods, and you know what an old fine smell that is, like something which has been mostly left alone and is not much troubled. We went on across corduroy which had been laid over some of the boggiest parts, and black sand squelched up between some of those cut logs and she laughed like a kid. Some of the logs was old and rotted, because there hadn't been nobody down a couple of those roads—except for her, that is—in I'm going to say five or ten years. We was *alone*, except for the birds and whatever animals seen us. The sound of that go-devil's engine, first buzzin along and then windin up high and fierce when she punched in the clutch and shifted down . . . that was the only motor-sound I could hear. And although I knew we had to be close to *someplace* all the time—I mean, these days you always are—I started to feel like we had gone back in time, and there wasn't *nothing*. That if we stopped and I climbed a high tree, I wouldn't see nothing in any direction but woods and woods and more woods. And all the time she's just *hammering* that thing along, her hair all out behind her, smilin, her eyes flashin. So we come out on the Speckled Bird Mountain Road and for a while I known where we were again, and then she turned off and for just a little bit I *thought* I knew, and then I didn't even bother to kid myself no more. We went cut-slam down another woods road, and then we come out—I swear it—on a nice paved road with a sign that said MOTORWAY B. You ever heard of a road in the state of Maine that was called MOTORWAY B?"

"No," I says. "Sounds English."

"Ayuh. *Looked* English. These trees like willows overhung the road. 'Now watch out here, Homer,' she says, 'one of those nearly grabbed me a month ago and gave me an Indian burn.'

"I didn't know what she was talkin about and started to say so, and then I seen that even though there was no wind, the branches of those trees was dippin down— they was *waverin* down. They looked black and wet inside the fuzz of green on them. I couldn't believe what I was seein. Then one of em snatched off my cap and I knew I wasn't asleep. 'Hi!' I shouts, 'Give that back!'

" 'Too late now, Homer,' she says, and laughs. 'There's daylight, just up ahead . . . we're okay.'

"Then another one of 'em comes down, on her side this time, and snatches at her— I swear it did. She ducked, and it caught in her hair and pulled a lock of it out. 'Ouch, dammit that *hurts!*' she yells, but she was laughin, too. The car swerved a little when she ducked and I got a look into the woods and holy God, Dave! *Everythin* in there was movin. There was grass wavin and plants that was all knotted together so it seemed like they made faces, and I seen somethin sittin in a squat on top of a stump, and it looked like tree-toad, only it was as big as a full-growed cat.

"Then we come out of the shade to the top of a hill and she says, 'There! That was exciting, wasn't it?' as if she was talkin about no more than a walk through the Haunted House at the Fryeburg Fair.

"About five minutes later we swung onto another of her woods roads. I didn't want no more woods right then—I can tell you that for sure—but these were just plain old woods. Half an hour after that, we was pulling into the parking lot of the Pilot's Grille in Bangor. She points to that little odometer for trips and says, 'Take a gander, Homer.' I did, and it said 111.6. 'What do you think now? Do you believe in my shortcut?'

"That wild look had mostly faded out of her, and she was just 'Phelia Todd again. But that other look wasn't entirely gone. It was like she was two women, 'Pehlia and Diana, and the part of her that was Diana was so much in control when she was driving the back roads that the part that was 'Phelia didn't have no idea that her shortcut was taking her through places . . . places that ain't on any map of Maine, not even on those survey-squares.

"She says again, 'What do you think of my shortcut, Homer?'

"And I says the first thing to come into my mind, which ain't something you'd usually say to a lady like 'Phelia Todd. 'It's a real piss-cutter, missus,' I says.

"She laughs, just as pleased as punch, and I seen it then, just as clear as glass: She didn't remember none of the funny stuff. Not the willow-branches—except they weren't willows, not at all, not really anything like em, or anything else—that grabbed off m'hat, not that MOTORWAY B sign, or that awful-lookin toad-thing. *She didn't remember none of that funny stuff!* Either I had dreamed it was there or she had dreamed it wasn't. All I knew for sure, Dave, was that we had rolled only a hundred and eleven miles and gotten to Bangor, and that wasn't no daydream; it was right there on the little go-devil's odometer, in black and white.

" 'Well, it is,' she says. 'It *is* a piss-cutter. I only wish I could get Worth to give it a go sometime . . . but he'll never get out of his rut unless someone blasts him out of it, and it would probably take a Titan II missile to do that, because I believe he has built himself a fallout shelter at the bottom of that rut. Come on in, Homer, and let's dump some dinner into you.'

"And she bought me one hell of a dinner, Dave, but I couldn't eat very much of it. I kep thinkin about what the ride back might be like, now that it was drawing down dark. Then, about halfway through the meal, she excused herself and made a telephone call. When she came back she ast me if I would mind drivin the go-devil back to Castle Rock for her. She said she had talked to some woman who was on the same school committee as her, and the woman said they had some kind of problem about somethin or other. She said she'd grab herself a Hertz car if Worth couldn't see her back down. 'Do you mind awfully driving back in the dark?' she ast me.

"She looked at me, kinda smilin, and I knew she remembered *some* of it all right— Christ knows how much, but she remembered enough to know I wouldn't want to try her way after dark, if ever at all . . . although I seen by the light in her eyes that it wouldn't have bothered her a bit.

"So I said it wouldn't bother me, and I finished my meal better than when I started it. It was drawin down dark by the time we was done, and she run us over to the house of the woman she'd called. And when she gets out she looks at me with that same light in her eyes and says, 'Now, you're *sure* you don't want to wait, Homer? I saw a couple of side roads just today, and although I can't find them on my maps, I think they might chop a few miles.'

"I says, 'Well, missus, I would, but at my age the best bed to sleep in is my own, I've found. I'll take your car back and never put a ding in her . . . although I guess I'll probably put on some more miles than you did.'

"Then she laughed, kind of soft, and she give me a kiss. That was the best kiss I ever had in my whole life, Dave. It was just on the cheek, and it was the chaste kiss of a married woman, but it was as ripe as a peach, or like those flowers that open in the dark, and when her lips touched my skin I felt like . . . I don't know exactly what I felt like, because a man can't easily hold on to those things that happened to him with a girl who was ripe when the world was young or how those things felt—I'm talking around what I mean, but I think you understand. Those things all get a red cast to them in your memory and you cannot see through it at all.

" 'You're a sweet man, Homer, and I love you for listening to me and riding with me,' she says. 'Drive safe.'

"Then in she went, to that woman's house. Me, I drove home."

"How did you go?" I asked.

He laughed softly. "By the turnpike, you damned fool," he said, and I never seen so many wrinkles in his face before as I did then.

He sat there, looking into the sky.

"Came the summer she disappeared. I didn't see much of her . . . that was the summer we had the fire, you'll remember, and then the big storm that knocked down all the trees. A busy time for caretakers. Oh, I *thought* about her from time to time, and about that day, and about that kiss, and it started to seem like a dream to me. Like one time, when I was out plowing George Bascomb's west field, the one that looks acrost the lake at the mountains, dreamin about what teenage boys dream of. And I pulled up this rock with the harrow blades, and it split open, and it *bled*. At least, it looked to me like it bled. Red stuff come runnin out of the cleft in the rock and soaked into the soil. And I never told no one but my mother, and I never told her what it meant to me, or what happened to me, although she washed my drawers and maybe she knew. Anyway, she suggested I ought to pray on it. Which I did, but I never got no enlightenment, and after a while something started to suggest to my mind that it had been a dream. It's that way, sometimes. There is holes in the *middle*, Dave. Do you know that?"

"Yes," I says, thinking of one one night when I'd seen something. That was in '59, a bad year for us, but my kids didn't know it was a bad year; all they knew was that they wanted to eat just like always. I'd seen a bunch of whitetail in Henry Brugger's back field, and I was out there after dark with a jacklight in August. You can shoot two when they're summer-fat; the second'll come back and sniff at the first as if to say *What the hell? Is it fall already?* and you can pop him like a bowlin pin. You can hack off enough meat to feed yowwens for six weeks and bury what's left. Those are two whitetails the hunters who come in November don't get a shot at, but kids have to eat. Like the man from Massachusetts said, *he'd* like to be able to afford to live here the year around, and all I can say is sometimes you pay for the privilege after dark. So there I was, and I seen this big orange light in the sky; it comes down and down, and I stood and watched it with my mouth hung on down to my breastbone and when it hit the lake the whole of it was lit up for a minute a purple-orange that seemed to go right up to the sky in rays. Wasn't nobody ever said nothing to me about that light, and I never said nothing to nobody myself, partly because I was afraid they'd laugh, but also because they'd wonder what the hell I'd been doing out there after dark to start with. And after a while it was like Homer said—it seemed like a dream I had once had, and it didn't signify to me because I couldn't make nothing of it which would turn under my hand. It was like a moonbeam. It didn't have no handle and it didn't have no blade. I couldn't make it work so I left it alone, like a man does when he knows the day is going to come up nevertheless.

"There are *holes* in the middle of things," Homer said, and he sat up straighter, like he was mad. "Right in the damn *middle* of things, not even to the left or right where your p'riph'ral vision is and you could say 'Well, but hell—' They are there and you go around them like you'd go around a pothole in the road that would break an axle. You know? And you forget it. Or like if you are plowin, you can plow a dip. But if there's somethin like a *break* in the earth, where you see darkness, like a cave might be there, you say 'Go around, old hoss. Leave that alone! I got a good shot over here to the left 'ards.' Because it wasn't a cave you was lookin for, or some kind of college excitement, but good plowin.

"*Holes* in the *middle* of things."

He fell still a long time then and I let him be still. Didn't have no urge to move him. And at last he says:

"She disappeared in August. I seen her for the first time in early July, and she looked . . ." Homer turned to me and spoke each word with careful spaced emphasis. "Dave Owens, she looked *gorgeous!* Gorgeous and wild and almost untamed. The little wrinkles I'd started to notice around her eyes all seemed to be gone. Worth Todd, he was at some conference or something in Boston. And she stands there at the edge of the deck—I was out in the middle with my shirt off—and she says 'Homer, you'll never believe it.'

" 'No, missus, but I'll try,' I says.

" 'I found two new roads,' she says, 'and I got to Bangor this last time in just sixty-seven miles.'

"I remembered what she said before and I says, 'That's not possible, missus. Beggin your pardon, but I did the mileage on the map myself, and seventy-nine is tops . . . as the crow flies.'

"She laughed, and she looked prettier than ever. Like a goddess in the sun, on one of those hills in a story where there's nothing but green grass and fountains and no puckies to tear at a man's forearms at all. 'That's right,' she says, 'and you can't run a mile in under four minutes. It's been mathematically *proved*.'

" 'It ain't the same,' I says.

" 'It's the same,' she says. 'Fold the map and see how many miles it is then, Homer. It can be a little less than a straight line if you fold it a little, or it can be a lot less if you fold it a lot.'

"I remembered our ride then, the way you remember a dream, and I says, 'Missus, you can fold a map on paper but you can't fold *land*. Or at least you shouldn't ought to try. You want to leave it alone.'

" 'No, sir,' she says. 'It's the one thing right now in my life that I won't leave alone, because it's *there*, and it's *mine*.'

"Three weeks later—this would be about two weeks before she disappeared—she give me a call from Bangor. She says, 'Worth has gone to New York, and I am coming down. I've misplaced my damn key, Homer. I'd like you to open the house so I can get in.'

"Well, that call come at eight o'clock, just when it was starting to come down dark. I had a sanwidge and a beer before leaving—about twenty minutes. Then I took a ride down there. All in all, I'd say I was forty-five minutes. When I got down there to the Todds', I seen there was a light on in the pantry I didn't leave on while I was comin down the driveway. I was lookin at that, and I almost run right into her little go-devil. It was parked kind of on a slant, the way a drunk would park it, and it was splashed with muck all the way up to the windows, and there was this stuff stuck in that mud along the body that looked like seaweed . . . only when my lights hit it, it seemed to be *movin*. I parked behind it and got out of my truck. That stuff wasn't seaweed, but it *was* weeds, and it *was* movin . . . kinda slow and sluggish, like it was dyin. I touched a piece of it, and it tried to wrap itself around my hand. It felt nasty and awful. I drug my hand away and wiped it on my pants. I went around to the front of the car. It looked like it had come through about ninety miles of splash and low country. Looked *tired*, it did. Bugs was splashed all over the windshield—only they didn't look like no kind of bugs *I* ever seen before. There was a moth that was about the size of a sparrow, its wings still flappin a little, feeble and dyin. There are things like mosquitoes, only they had real eyes that you could see—and they seemed to be seein *me*. I could hear those weeds scrapin against the body of the go-devil, dyin, tryin to get a hold on somethin. And all I could think was Where in the hell has she been? And how did she get here in only three-quarters of an hour? Then I seen somethin else. There was some kind of a animal half-smashed onto the radiator grille, just under where that Mercedes ornament is—the one that looks kinda like a star looped up into a circle? Now most small animals you kill on the road is bore right under the car, because they are crouching when it hits them, hoping it'll just go over and leave them with their hide still attached to their meat. But every now and then one will jump, not away, but right at the damn car, as if to get in one good bite of whatever the buggardly thing is that's going to kill it—I have known that to happen. This thing had maybe done that. And it looked mean enough to jump a Sherman tank. It looked like something which come of a mating between a woodchuck and weasel, but there was other stuff thrown in that a body didn't even want to look at. It hurt your eyes, Dave; worse'n that, it hurt your *mind*. Its pelt was matted with blood, and there was claws sprung out of the pads on its feet like a cat's claws, only longer. It had big yellowy eyes, only they was glazed. When I was a kid I had a porcelain marble—a croaker—that looked like that. And teeth. Long thin needle teeth that looked almost like darning needles, stickin out of its mouth. Some of them was sunk right into that steel grillwork. That's why it was still hanging on; it had hung its *own* self on by the teeth. I looked at it and knowed it had a headful of poison just like a rattlesnake, and it jumped at that go-devil when it saw it was about to be run down, trying to bite it to death. And I wouldn't be the one to try and yonk it offa there because I had cuts on my hands—hay-cuts—and I thought it would kill me as dead as a stone parker if some of that poison seeped into the cuts.

"I went around to the driver's door and opened it. The inside light come on, and I looked at that special odometer that she set for trips . . . and what I seen there was 31.6.

"I looked at that for a bit, and then I went to the back door. She'd forced the screen and broke the glass by the lock so she could get her hand through and let herself in. There was a note that said: 'Dear Homer—got here a little sooner than I thought I would. Found a shortcut, and it is a dilly! You hadn't come yet so I let myself in like a burglar. Worth is coming day after tomorrow. Can you get the screen fixed and the door reglazed by then? Hope so. Things like that always bother him. If I don't come out to say hello, you'll know I'm asleep. The drive was very tiring, but I was here in no time! Ophelia.'

"*Tirin!* I took another look at that bogey-thing hangin offa the grille of her car, and I thought Yessir, it *must* have been tiring. By God, *yes.*"

He paused again, and cracked a restless knuckle.

"I seen her only once more. About a week later. Worth was there, but he was swimmin out in the lake, back and forth, back and forth, like he was sawin wood or signin papers. More like he was signin papers, I guess.

" 'Missus,' I says, 'this ain't my business, but you ought to leave well enough alone. That night you come back and broke the glass of the door to come in, I seen somethin hangin off the front of your car—'

" 'Oh, the chuck! I took care of that,' she says.

" 'Christ!' I says. 'I hope you took some care!'

" 'I wore Worth's gardening gloves,' she said. 'It wasn't anything anyway, Homer, but a jumped-up woodchuck with a little poison in it.'

" 'But missus,' I says, 'where there's woodchucks there's bears. And if that's what the woodchucks look like along your shortcut, what's going to happen to you if a bear shows up?'

"She looked at me, and I seen that other woman in her—that Diana-woman. She says, 'If things are different along those roads, Homer, maybe I am different, too. Look at this.'

"Her hair was done up in a clip at the back, looked sort of like a butterfly and had a stick through it. She let it down. It was the kind of hair that would make a man wonder what it would look like spread out over a pillow. She says, 'It was coming in gray, Homer. Do you see any gray?' And she spread it with her fingers so the sun could shine on it.

" 'No'm,' I says.

"She looks at me, her eyes all a-sparkle, and she says, 'Your wife is a good woman,

Homer Buckland, but she has seen me in the store and in the post office, and we've passed the odd word or two, and I have seen her looking at my hair in a kind of satisfied way that only women know. I know what she says, and what she tells her friends . . . that Ophelia Todd has started dyeing her hair. But I have not. I have lost my way looking for a shortcut more than once . . . lost my way . . . and lost my gray.' And she laughed, not like a college girl but like a girl in high school. I admired her and longed for her beauty, but I seen that other beauty in her face as well just then . . . and I felt afraid again. Afraid *for* her, and afraid *of* her.

" 'Missus,' I says, 'you stand to lose more than a little sta'ch in your hair.'

" 'No,' she said. 'I tell you I am different over there . . . I am *all myself* over there. When I am going along that road in my little car I am not Ophelia Todd, Worth Todd's wife who could never carry a child to term, or that woman who tried to write poetry and failed at it, or the woman who sits and takes notes in committee meetings, or anything or anyone else. When I am on that road I am in the heart of myself, and I feel like—'

" '*Diana*,' I said.

"She looked at me kind of funny and kind of surprised, and then she laughed. 'O like some goddess, I suppose,' she said. 'She will do better than most because I am a night person—I love to stay up until my book is done or until the National Anthem comes on the TV, and because I am very pale, like the moon—Worth is always saying I need a tonic, or blood tests or some sort of similar bosh. But in her heart what every woman wants to be is some kind of goddess, I think—men pick up a ruined echo of that thought and try to put them on pedestals (a woman, who will pee down her own leg if she does not squat! It's funny when you stop to think of it)—but what a man senses is not what a woman wants. A woman wants to be in the clear, is all. To stand if she will, or walk . . .' Her eyes turned toward that little go-devil in the driveway, and narrowed. Then she smiled. 'Or to *drive*, Homer. A man will not see that. He thinks a goddess wants to loll on a slope somewhere on the foothills of Olympus and eat fruit, but there is no god or goddess in that. All a woman wants is what a man wants—a woman wants to *drive*.'

" 'Be careful where you drive, missus, is all,' I says, and she laughs and give me a kiss spang in the middle of the forehead.

"She says, 'I will, Homer,' but it didn't mean nothing, and I known it, because she said it like a man who says he'll be careful to his wife or his girl when he knows he won't . . . can't.

"I went back to my truck and waved to her once, and it was a week later that Worth reported her missing. Her and that go-devil both. Todd waited seven years and had her declared legally dead, and then he waited another year for good measure— I'll give the sucker that much—and then he married the second Missus Todd, the one that just went by. And I don't expect you'll believe a single damn word of the whole yarn."

In the sky one of those big flat-bottomed clouds moved enough to disclose the ghost of the moon—half-full and pale as milk. And something in my heart leaped up at the sight, half in fright, half in love.

"I do though," I said. "Every frigging damned word. And even if it ain't true, Homer, it ought to be."

He give me a hug around the neck with his forearm, which is all men can do since the world don't let them kiss but only women, and laughed, and got up.

"Even if it *shouldn't* ought to be, it is," he said. He got his watch out of his pants and looked at it. "I got to go down the road and check on the Scott place. You want to come?"

"I believe I'll sit here for a while," I said, "and think."

He went to the steps, then turned back and looked at me, half-smiling. "I believe she was right," he said. "She *was* different along those roads she found . . . wasn't nothing that would dare touch her. You or me, maybe, but not her.

"And I believe she's young."

Then he got in his truck and set off to check the Scott place.

THAT WAS TWO YEARS AGO, and Homer has since gone to Vermont, as I think I told you. One night he come over to see me. His hair was combed, he had a shave, and he smelled of some nice lotion. His face was clear and his eyes were alive. That night he looked sixty instead of seventy, and I was glad for him and I envied him and I hated him a little, too. Arthritis is one buggardly great old fisherman, and that night Homer didn't look like arthritis had any fishhooks sunk into his hands the way they were sunk into mine.

"I'm going," he said.

"Ayuh?"

"Ayuh."

"All right; did you see to forwarding your mail?"

"Don't want none forwarded," he said. "My bills are paid. I am going to make a clean break."

"Well, give me your address. I'll drop you a line from one time to the another, old hoss." Already I could feel loneliness settling over me like a cloak . . . and looking at him, I knew that things were not quite what they seemed.

"Don't have none yet," he said.

"All right," I said "*Is* it Vermont, Homer?"

"Well," he said, "It'll do for people who want to know."

I almost didn't say it and then I did. "What does she look like now?"

"Like Diana," he said. "But she is kinder."

"I envy you, Homer," I said, and I did.

I stood at the door. It was twilight in that deep part of summer when the fields fill with perfume and Queen Anne's Lace. A full moon was beating a silver track across the lake. He went across my porch and down the steps. A car was standing on the soft shoulder of the road, its engine idling heavy, the way the old ones do that still run full bore straight ahead and damn the torpedoes. Now that I think of it, that car *looked* like a torpedo. It looked beat up some, but as if it could go the ton without breathin hard. He stopped at the foot of my steps and picked something up—it was his gas-can, the big one that holds ten gallons. He went down my walk to the passenger side of the car. She leaned over and opened the door. The inside light came on and just for a moment I saw her, long red hair around her face, her forehead shining like a lamp. Shining like the *moon*. He got in and she drove away. I stood out on my porch and watched the taillights of her little go-devil twinkling red in the dark . . . getting smaller and smaller. They were like embers, then they were like flickerflies, and then they were gone.

Vermont, I tell the folks from town, and Vermont they believe, because it's as far as most of them can see inside their heads. Sometimes I almost believe it myself, mostly when I'm tired and done up. Other times I think about them, though—all this October I have done so, it seems, because October is the time when men think mostly about far places and the roads which might get them there. I sit on the bench in front of Bell's Market and think about Homer Buckland and about the beautiful girl who leaned over to open his door when he come down that path with the full red gasoline can in his right hand—she looked like a girl of no more than sixteen, a girl on her learner's permit, and her beauty *was* terrible, but I believe it would no longer kill the man it turned itself on; for a moment her eyes lit on me, I was not killed, although part of me died at her feet.

Olympus must be a glory to the eyes and the heart, and there are those who crave it and those who find a clear way to it, mayhap, but I know Castle Rock like the back of my hand and I could never leave it for no shortcuts where the roads may go; in October the sky over the lake is no glory but it is passing fair, with those big white clouds that move so slow; I sit here on the bench, and think about 'Phelia Todd and Homer Buckland, and I don't necessarily wish I was where they are . . . but I still wish I a smoking man.

AMONG THE HANDLERS OR, THE MARK 16 HANDS-ON ASSEMBLY OF JESUS RISEN, FORMERLY SNAKE-O-RAMA

BY MICHAEL BISHOP

MICHAEL BISHOP IS A MARVELOUSLY VERSATILE FANTASIST WHO HAS WRITTEN THE SECOND-BEST BASEBALL FANTASY NOVEL OF THE LATTER HALF OF THE TWENTIETH CENTURY. IT'S TITLE IS *BRITTLE INNINGS* AND IT INVOLVES A MINOR-LEAGUE TEAM WHO HAS MARY SHELLEY'S BOY VICTOR'S FAVORITE CREATION AS ONE OF ITS ROOKIES.

IN "AMONG THE HANDLERS" HE TAKES US DOWN SOUTH TO VISIT THE OFF-SHOOTS OF CHRISTIAN FUNDAMENTALISM WHERE CONCEPTS LIKE FIGHTING THE DEVIL AND GOD'S PROTECTION ARE TAKEN QUITE LITERALLY.

And He said to them, "Go into all the world and preach the gospel to every creature . . . And these signs will follow those who believe: In My name they will cast out demons; they will speak with new tongues; they will take up serpents; and if they drink anything deadly, it will by no means hurt them; they will lay hands on the sick, and they will recover."

—Mark 16: 15, 17-18

Men in soiled workclothes occupied the cracked red leather booths. Some pointed at their cronies with wrist-twisted forks. Two or three ate alone, a folded newspaper at hand or a scowl of wary dragged-out blankness protecting or maybe legitimating their aloneness. None of them any longer took heed of the smells saturating Deaton's Bar-B-Q: scalded grease, boiled collards, sauce-drowned pork. And the sinuous anglings of the sandyhaired kid waiting their tables drew the notice of only one or two.

Becknell, a hulking thirty-two-year-old in a filthy ballcap, said: So how you like a peckerwood that lifts up snakes handlin yore vittles?

His boothmate, Greg Maharry, said: You mean Pilcher?

Course I mean him. Anyways, it ain't my idea of telligent ressraunt policy.

Criminy, Maharry said, who're you to bellyache bout young Pilcher's cleanliness?

Who am I? Becknell squinted at Maharry.

You spend most days up to yore butt in axle grease.

So?

I reckon Hoke knows as well as you to wersh his hands.

Mebbe. But grease's clean gainst them slitherin canebrakes thet Sixteener bunch of his favors.

You ever lifted a snake? I bet you never.

Think I ain't got the sand? Greg, thet's—

Hoke Pilcher eased around the honeycombed divider from the kitchen with his tray aloft. Becknell, bigger than Maharry by a head, released a long sibilant breath while Maharry gave Hoke a queasy smile. Hoke lowered the tray to waistheight so that he could remove to the table the loaded barbecue platters, two sweaty amber longnecks, and two heavyweight mugs bearing icy white fur from Mr. Deaton's walk-in freezer. Holding the tray against the table edge, Hoke began to rearrange the items on it for easier transfer.

Mr. Becknell, he said, I aint been to an assembly out to Frye's Mill Road in moren a month.

Becknell said: You blong to thet bunch, don't you?

Yessir. But I've never lifted a snake there. He wanted to add, Either, but swallowed the impulse.

How come you not to've?

No anointin's ever come on me. So far I've mostly just shouted and raised my hands. Waitin and prayin, I guess. Hoke reached the longnecks onto the table, then the mugs with their dire chiseled coldness.

Becknell said: My golly. Yo're a Mark Sixteener thout the balls to do what you say you blieve.

Leave him go, Albert, Maharry said.

Why?

Minit ago you was blastin him for bein a Jesus Only. Now yo're chewin on him for the contrary.

Thet's where yo're flat wrong, Greg.

Okay. Tell me how.

I'm chewin on him for claimin one thing then actin somethin allover yellowbelly else.

Hoke set Maharry's hubcapsized pork platter in front of him and shifted the tray to unload Becknell's wheel of shrimp and chicken, with onion rings and hot slaw around them for pungent garnish.

Becknell said: And if you really blong to thet bunch, whyn hell don't you go to their services?

It's sorter complicated, Mr. Becknell.

You aint turned heathen?

Nosir. I'm tryin—

A heathen's shore as Judas lost, but a Mark Sixteener thet acts like what he sez mebbe has a chanst. Mebbe.

Hoke felt his grip loosen and the tray tilt. Becknell's chicken, scarletbrown in its breathtaking sauce, slid down his mattress-striped overall bib along with an avalanche of slaw and shrimp pellets. The onion rings flipped ceilingward and dropped about Becknell and Maharry like mudcaked nematodes. A longneck toppled. A razorthin tide of beer sluiced across the table and off it into Becknell's lap. He roared and jumped, catching a falling onion ring on one ear and nearly upsetting Maharry's bottle.

Maharry grabbed it in a trembling fist and held it down. Hoke's tray, which had hit the floor, rattled from edge to edge.

My cryin cripes! Becknell said. You summabitch!

It was an accydent, Maharry said. Go easy now.

Using the towel on his belt, Hoke picked chicken and slaw off Becknell. He righted the fallen longneck, daubed at the beer, and turned this way and that between the unbroken platter under the table and the reverberating plastic tray. His boss, Mr. Deaton, burst into the diningroom with so many wrinkles on his forehead's pale dome that Hoke could not help thinking of a wadded pile of linen outside a unit of the Beulah Fork Motel. Deaton, stooped from working under the greaseguard that hooded his stove, unfolded to full height.

Hoke, what you done now?

Ruint my clothes, Becknell said. Ruint my meal. Stole my peace of mind.

It wasn't apurpose, Maharry said.

Thet's the second spill you've had today, Deaton said. The second.

See, Maharry said. He didn't mean it personal.

Albert, Deaton said, I'll bring you replacement eats in ten minutes. He thought about that. No, seven.

Free?

Awright. Spruce up in the ressroom. I'll pay for either yore drycleanin or a new pair of overalls. He turned to Hoke. Criminy, boy. My Lord.

My mind's gone off, Mr. Deaton. I cain't focus.

S thet right? Well. I cain't afford to keep you till you git it right. Ast Maltilda Jack to pay you off.

I'm fired?

Yore word, not mine. Just git yore money and beat it on out of here.

Sir, I need this job.

Mebbe you can git you somethin out to the sawmill.

I done ast.

Ast again. Now git. Have mercy.

Hoke tossed the filthy sodden towel onto the table, amazed that the disaster had scarcely dirtied his hands, much less his clothes. He strode through Deaton's Bar-B-Q under the mirthful or slipeyed gazes of maybe a dozen other customers and wrenched back the frontdoor.

From airconditioning to pitiless summer swelter. Hoke hiked straight across Deaton's parkinglot, filched a cigarette from his shirtpocket. The sky pulsed so starwebbed that the neon sign winking Bar-B-Q, Bar-B-Q, could neither sponge those stars away nor make Beulah Fork's maindrag look like anything other than a gaudy podunk road.

Hoke lit up. Smoke curled past his eyes, settled in lazy helices into his lungs.

THIRTY MINUTES LATER, still afoot, Hoke stopped on the edge of Twyla Glanton's place, a clearing off Frye's Mill Road. He registered the insult of the jacked-up candyapple-red pickup with chromium rollbars parked alongside the deck of Twyla's doublewide. The truck belonged to Johnny Mark Carnes, a deacon in the Mark 16 Hands-On Assembly of Jesus Risen, a congregation whose tumbledown stone meeting center lay farther along this blacktopped strip. Like Albert Becknell, Carnes had ten years and maybe forty pounds on Hoke.

Almost aloud, Hoke said: Pox on yore hide, Carnes. Then waded through fragrant redclover and sticky Queen Anne's lace toward the deck. He felt gut-knotted in a way reminiscent of the cramps after a dose of paregoric. What did he plan to do? No clear notion. None.

His tennis shoes carried him up the treated plank steps of Twyla's deck, anyway, and before he could compute the likely outcome of this showdown, his fist began to pound the flimsy aluminum stormdoor over the cheap wooden one that was supposed to keep Twyla Glanton safe from burglars, conartists, and escaped murderers out here in the honeysuckle-drenched boonies of Hothlepoya County. Yeah.

Carnes himself opened the door, then stood in it like the sentry that Hoke would have hoped for, except that Hoke wanted someone else in the role and took no pleasure in any detail of Carnes' manifestation there but the fact that he still had his britches on. Unless of course . . .

Pilcher, Carnes said. Kinda late to come callin on a lady, ain't it?

You've just said so.

I been here a while. Somethin we can do you for?

Even with the light behind him, Carnes presented a handsome silhouette: narrowheaded, wideshouldered, almost oaken in the stolidity of his planting. Actually, the light's fanning from behind improved his looks, dropping a darkness over his sunken piggy eyes and also the waffleironlike acne scars below and off to one side of his bottom lip.

Could I just talk to Twyla a minit, Johnny Mark?

From somewhere in the doublewide's livingroom, Twyla said: Let him in.

Some folks you let em in, it's nigh-on the War tween the States to git em out again. Carnes stood stockstill, unmoving as a capsized tractor.

Twyla appeared behind him. Her look surprised Hoke. She wore a swallowing purple sweatshirt, luminous green and purple windsuit pants with a band of Navajo brocade down each leg, and pennyloafers. Her sorrel hair had a mahogany nimbus from the backglow, and strands floated about her teased-out helmet like charged spidersilk. Hoke, looking past Carnes at Twyla, felt the pilotlight in his gut igniting, warming him from that point outward.

A pearl onion of sweat pipped out on his forehead.

Never before had he seen a Mark Sixteener woman in any garb but ankle-length skirts or dresses. Certainly not Twyla, whose daddy had lifted serpents, and who called out His name at every assembly, and who, at Li'l People Day Care in Beulah Fork, had a steady job, where she so staunchly refused to wear jeans that she often got the other workers' goat. Hoke, though, had given her a private pledge of fidelity.

He said: Colby Deaton fired me tonight.

The jerk, Twyla said. Babes, I'm so sorry.

Tough way for a guy to git him some sympathy, Carnes said.

We've missed you out to church, Twyla said. You orter not stopped comin cuz of me. I'm still yore friend.

Thet ain't it, Carnes said. He's afraid to come.

Not of snakes, though. I wunst saw him grab a pygmyrattler with a stick and a gloved hand.

No, not of snakes, Carnes said. Thisere wiseboy's scairt of me. Cause I'm even more pyzon than they are.

Wadn't afraid to come up here with yore showoffy truck out front. Or to knock on Twyla's door.

Yall stop yore headbuttin! Twyla pushed Carnes aside and the stormdoor out. She laid a cool hand on Hoke's shoulder, bridging him into the doublewide, beckoning him out of the dark to either self-extinguishment or redemption—if these options did not, in fact, mesh or cancel. Go on home, babes. Sleep on it. Tomorry's got to have a perter face.

I'm footsore, Twyla. Bout wore out.

I'll wear you out, Carnes said.

What you'll do, Johnny Mark, is none of the sort.

Then praytell what?

Yo're gonna carry him home. In yore truck.

Play chauffeur for puley Mr. Pilcher here? Dream on.

No dream to it. And do it now. S bout time for me to turn in anyways.

So Hoke sat hugging the passengerside door of the jacked-up candyapple-red truck as Carnes accelerated through the woods and flung back under his tires long humming stretches of asphalt. Possum eyes caught fire in the headlamps. An owl stooped in cascades through a picketing of trees, and a fieldmouse, or a rabbit, or some other fourlegged hider in the leafmulch was rolled to its back and taloned insensate.

Past this kill, through some roadside cane that loblollies deeper in over-towered, a quartet of ghostly deer—two does, two fawns—made Carnes brake. The deer negotiated a quicksilver singlefile crossing. The truck fishtailed hearts-toppingly and squealed to juddering rest on the shoulder in time for Hoke to watch the flags on the deer's rumps bounce into the pines' mazy sanctuary.

Carnes muttered, strangled the steeringwheel, exhaled hard.

Nice job, Hoke said.

Don't talk to me. Carnes took an audible breath.

We could've died if we'd hit just one of em. Hoke spoke the truth. In this part of Hothlepoya County deer on the road comprised an often deadly, year-round hazard. Hoke knew—had known—a highschool girl cut to ribbons by a buck attempting to leap the hood of her boyfriend's car. The buck had landed on the hood and, asprawl there, struggled to free itself from the windshield glass, one bloody leg kicking repeatedly through the glittery hole.

Don't compliment me, Pilcher. Ever.

Awright. I won't.

You aint got the right to tell me nothin. Cept mebbe yo're a sorry excuse for a Sixteener.

Hold it a minit.

And mebbe not even thet. Speak when spoken to. Otherwise, hush it the hell up.

Who made you God?

Carnes pointed a finger, holding its tip less than a wasp's body from Hoke's nose and staring down it like a man sighting a rifle.

I did speak to you, pissant, but I didn't ast you a blessed thing. He dropped the point.

Hoke wanted to say, Up yores, but leaned back against his door instead, shrinking from the despisal in Carnes' face. Who would know or care if Carnes killed him out here on this road, then rolled his body into the cane? Twyla. Thank God for Twyla Glanton.

And thank God Carnes didn't have a row of snakeboxes in the bed of his truck or, even worse, a solitary crate here in the passengerside footwell. Hoke could imagine sitting over an irritated pitviper—copperhead, rattler, whatever—with one foot to either side of the box, the rotting vegetable smell of its scales using alien and humid to gag him, its heartshaped head searching for a way out. Meantime, though, he had Johnny Mark Carnes less than a yard away, still wired from their close call with the deer, still palpably resentful of Hoke's presence in his truckcab.

Whym I drivin you home, pissant?

Hoke set his teeth and stared.

I ast you a question. You can answer. You better.

Twyla told you to.

Ast me to. Nobody tells me to do anythin, Pilcher, least of all a outtake from the flank of Adam.

Hoke thought a moment. Then he said: You got no bidnus movin in on her. I had my eye on her first. From all the way back in school, even.

I beg yore pardon.

You heard me.

Losers weepers, huh?

I love her, Johnny Mark.

God loves her. You just got yore hormones in high gear.

I spose you got yores set on idle?

You wisht. Look, pissant, what can you give the lady but puppydog looks and a fat double handful of air?

Somethin thet counts.

Deaton canned you tonight from yore waitressin. You live in a verbital cave. It's not a cave. Don't say waitressing. Men do it too.

Yore mama died of a lack o faith drinkin strychnine.

No, Hoke said. The Spirit went off her cause strife had fallen mongst the people. She had faith aplenty.

And yore daddy hightailed it to who knows where, Minnesota mebbe. No wonder Twyla took her a second look at you.

Like yo're a prize.

Got me balls enough to uplift serpents to the Lord and make us babies in the marriage bed.

Hoke shut his eyes. Yo're already married.

Not for long. Carnes smiled. Comparisons're hateful, aint they, pissant? Least you've got yore faith, though.

Yes, said Hoke quietly.

Which gives you a family in Jesus. Protection from slings and arrows, snakebites and poison. Right?

Right.

So come on to meetin this Friday. Forgit Twyla's migrated affections. Us Mark Sixteeners want you mongst us. Whcrc clsc you got to go, Pilcher?

Nowhere.

Aint thet the truth. So come on Friday. I got someone you need to meet here.

Like who?

S name's Judas, Pilcher. He's a longboy. Called for the betrayer cause they aint no trustin when or who he next might bite.

Hoke put his hands on his knees and squeezed. Carnes had him a new diamondback, name of Judas. Well, of course he did. Subtlety had never much appealed to Carnes, else he would have linked with Methodists and driven a white twodoor coupe off a Detroit assemblyline.

Now git out, he said.

Yo're sposed to take me home.

Carried you far as I aim to. You aint but a mile from thet crayfish den of yores anyways. Out.

Hoke got out. Carnes put the boxy truck in gear, flung sod and gravel backing off the shoulder, and shouted out the window after a screechy turnaround: Don't I deserve a nice thanks for totin you this far?

Thank you. Hoke eyed Carnes blankly, then stared away down the blacktop at dwindling taillights and the broken ramparts of pines bracketing it. Shithead, Hoke said, turning to foot it the rest of the way home, morosely aware that he had no idea which of them, Carnes or himself, he had just cursed. Nor did the incessant burring of the cicadas among the cane afford him any clue or solace.

HE HAD NEVER LIVED IN A CAVE. He lived with Ferlin Rodale, a former schoolmate now doing construction work, in a dugout of bulldozed earth, old automobile tires hardpacked with clay, and plastered-over walls strengthened with empty aluminum softdrink cans. Ferlin had seen such houses on a hitchhiking trip to New Mexico, then brought back to Hothlepoya County—whose director of Department of Community Development had never even heard of such structures—an obsession to build one locally, despite the higher watertable and wetter climate. Anyway, to Hoke's mind, Ferlin's dugout qualified as a house. Even the head of Community Development had allowed as much by issuing Ferlin a building permit even though his tirehouse lay outside every local engineering code. It wasn't finished, though, and wouldn't be for another six to eight months, if that soon, and so Ferlin and Hoke lived in the shell of the place, sleeping in a U-shaped room that faced south under a roof of plywood, black felt, and grimy plastic sheeting.

Mebbe it is a kinda cave, Hoke said, limping home through the woods. Carnes is sorta right, the bastid.

Well, so what? Ferlin had wired it for lights, sunk a well, and laid PVC piping so that both sinks and the cracked and resealed commode had water. Hoke paid fifty dollars a month for a pallet in the lone bedroom and split the electric bill with Ferlin. His own folks had never had so nice a place, only a rented fourroom shack, aboveground, with pebbled green shingles on the walls and a tarpaper roof. If Ferlin's house struck some ornery people as cavelike, well, better a cave than a windbuffeted shanty on lopsided fieldstone pillars. Mama and Daddy Pilcher should've enjoyed such luck—even with the beer cans, bottlecaps, cigarette packages, candywrappers, clamlike fastfood cartons, and other junk littering Ferlin's clayey grounds.

In a footsore trance Hoke shuffled over the murderously potholed drive leading in, a drive lined about its full length with blackberry brambles, dogwoods and pines. He had only starlight and lichenglow to guide him, just those undependable helps and the somewhat less fickle guyings of nightly habit. At length he approached a sycamore, a striated ghost among the scaly conifers, on which Ferlin had hammered up a hand-lettered placard:

TRESPAsERS!!!—
WE AIM to PLEZE But SHOT to KILL!

Hoke stopped, perplexed. Did that mean him? Ferlin had prepared the sign to secure them solitude, even down to the premeditated detail of its misspellings, working on the already frequently borne-out surmise that the image of a surly cracker with a shotgun would scare off uninvited visitors better than a store-bought KEEP OUT notice. Hoke, shambling by, gave the sign a fresh twist out of true and chuckled bitterly.

Half the people in Beulah Fork probably thought that Ferlin and he, not to mention every Mark Sixteener in the county, were ignorant sisterswyving moon-calves. Well, damn them too, along with Carnes.

I know a thing or two the President don't, Hoke said. Or a perfessor up to Athens, even.

Like what? he wondered.

Aloud he said: Like I love Twyla and don't want to die in front of her with a snakefang in my flesh.

This saying stirred Ferlin's dogs, a redbone hound named Sackett and a mongrel terrier named Rag that began barking in echoey relay. They came hurtling through the dark to meet the intruder and possibly to turn him.

Hush, Hoke said. S only me.

Sackett took Hoke's hand in the webbing between thumb and forefinger and led him up the trail, his whole ribby fuselage atremble. Rag pelted along behind, kinking and unkinking like an earthworm on a hot paving stone.

From the dugout—doors wide open, plastic scrolled back to the clocking stars—Hoke heard a breathy female voice singing mournfully from Ferlin's totable CD player. It sang about a blockbusted blonde with a disconnected plug at the Last Chance Texaco. Ferlin sang along, overriding the soft female voice, his screechy updown falsetto an insult to his dogs, to Hoke, to the very notion of singing.

Thank God the Last Chance Texaco cut was fading, drifting like a car whose driver has nodded asleep. But as Hoke crossed the dugout's threshold, into earthen coolness and the glare of one electric bulb swinging on a tarnished chain, the next song began and Ferlin ignored Hoke's arrival to play airguitar and hoot along with Rickie Lee Jones, albeit out of sync and out of tune, the words in his throat (*Cmon, Cecil, take some money! Cmon, Ceece, take you a ten*) like cogs mangled and flung from the strident clockwork coming-apart of his lungs and throat. Ferlin wore a jockstrap and flipflops, nothing else, and when he finally looked at Hoke, he checked his wrist, which bore no watch, raised his eyebrows, and kept on screeching, his stance hip-cocked, showbizzy and questioning at once. At the end of Rickie Lee's cut, he mouthed, *But, baby, don' dish it ovah if he don' preciate it. . . .*

Then Ferlin turned off the player and came over to Hoke with a look of almost daddyish concern on his freckled hatchet face. Squinting and grinning, he said, Home a mite early, aint you?

Deaton canned me. Hoke told Ferlin the whole story, even the parts about stopping at Twyla's and catching a spooky ride in Johnny Mark Carnes' pickup. But you don't like Carnes, said Ferlin.

I don't like walkin neither.

You walkt in. I didn't hear nothin stop out on 18.

Hoke crumpled into a lawnchair Ferlin had salvaged from the county landfill. Carnes got him a new snake he's callin Judas, he said. Wants me to make the next service out to the assembly so's I can charm it.

Ferlin whistled, a sound like a mortar shell rainbowing in. You aint handled with em yet, and he wants you to lift a serpent name of Judas right out the gate?

Looks thet way.

S why my religion don't include handlin, less a course it's women. Them I'll handle. Devotedly. Ferlin never attended services anywhere, but to willing females he tithed regularly the selfalleged five inflated to ten percent of himself that at this moment he had pouched in his jockstrap.

Such talk. Eddie Moomaw told me to git a new roommate if I planned to stay on a Sixteener.

Ferlin played airguitar. *O mean Mark Sixteener, he sang: Climb outta yore rut!*

Hush thet, Hoke said.

But Ferlin kept singing: *You don't like my wiener, So you show me yore butt!*

Didn't I ask you polite to stop it?

Ferlin threw his airguitar at the wall and paced away from Hoke. You got to watch yore fanny. Some of them Sixteeners'll drag you down for pure selfrighteous spite.

Meanin Johnny Mark Carnes?

Him, ol Moomaw, and anyone else over there thet cain't pray a blessing thout first tearin the world a new a-hole.

The world hates us Mark Sixteeners.

It don't understand yall, Ferlin said. Neither do I.

So I shouldn't go this Friday?

You hear me say thet? I just said to watch yore fanny.

So mebbe I orter go?

Ferlin said: I wouldn't visit thet stonecold snakeranch of yall's thout a direct order from God Hisself.

Groaning, Hoke pulled off his tennis shoes and claystained sweatsocks. His feet sang their relief, his anxiety over his lost job, the more judgmental Mark Sixteeners, and Carnes' new diamondback a smidgen allayed by the night air and his roomy's profane straightforward banter.

Then he said: Ferlin, I have to go.

Nigh-on to hatchling naked, Ferlin squatted over his svelte black CD player. Balancing on the spongy toes of his flipflops he punched up a song about Weasel and the White Boys Cool, his wide chocolate irises reflecting a crimson 9 backward from the control console. Ditchfrogs, a cicada chorus and Ferlin all crooned along with the disc (*Likes it rare but gits it well, A weasel on a shoadohdah flo*), but this time so low and softly that Hoke did not feel slighted. Ferlin had heard him, and as soon as cut number nine ended, and before number ten began, Ferlin said:

What would happen if you didn't?

I'm not rightly shore. The Holy Ghost'd probably go off me for good.

Meanin what?

I'd send my soul to perdition for aye and awways.

Better go then, Ferlin said, knobbing down the volume on cut ten. Hell's a damned serious bidnus and forever's a smart jot longern Monday.

Hoke gave him back a forlorn chuckle.

Answer me one thing: Why would a fella with half a brain and a workin pecker take up a pyzonous snake?

To git Spiritjumped and throughblest totally. You won't never know, Ferlin, till you've gone puppetdancin in Jesus' grace yoreself.

Sounds like really rollickin sex.

S a billion times better.

The expert speaks, Ferlin said. Hothlepoya County's Only Still Cherry Stud.

They's moren one kinda virgin, Hoke said. Not bein married I've never slept with a woman. But not being sanctified you've never come under the Spirit's caress.

Ooooooo, Ferlin said. Got me. Got me good. He fell over next to his CD player, writhing as if gutshot. When Rickie Lee finished singing about her gang's all going home, leaving her abandoned on a streetcorner, Ferlin stopped thrashing and lay motionless: a rangy unclad departmentstore dummy, flung supine into a junkroom.

Hoke struggled out of the lawnchair. He hobbled over to Ferlin and around the CD player on whose console a red O had brilliantly digitized. He nudged Ferlin in the armpit with his toe. When Ferlin persisted in his willful unflinchingness Hoke said, Thanks for the words of wisdom, dead man, and retreated to their U-shaped bedroom to dream of Twyla and climbing knots of sullen upraised snakes.

FERLIN DROVE HOKE in his customized '54 Ford, a bequeathment from Ferlin's daddy, to the Friday-night meeting of the Mark 16 Hands-On Assembly of Jesus Risen farther down Frye's Mill Road, on an island between that road and a twolane branch going who knows where. Ferlin dropped Hoke off near a private cemetery about fifty yards from the church itself, with a nod and a last cry of advice:

Be careful, Pilcher, who you take a rattlesnake from!

Hoke recognized the saying as one of the shibboleths of a wellknown Alabama handler selfbilled the EndTime Evangelist, a big amiable man who preached a foursquare Jesus Only doctrine heavier on redemption than judgment. A year ago he had visited their hall, blessing it with both his message and his serpent handling; and when a longtime Mark Sixteener upbraided an older teenager near the front for wearing a T-shirt printed with the profane logo of a rocknroll band, the evangelist helped avert a nasty dustup, saying: Leave him go, Brother Eddie. You've got to catch the fish before you can clean em.

Hoke remembered that saying and also the preacher's caution against accepting a pitviper from just anybody. Anyway, even should an anointing drop on him like a garment of spiritwoven armor, Hoke would steer clear of Johnny Mark Carnes. A spirit of deceitfulness and envy in a house of worship could undo even an honest-to-Christ mantling of the Holy Ghost, as his own mama had learned too late to prevent her from dying of a pintjar of strychnine so polluted.

Polluted pyzon? Ferlin had said once, reacting to Hoke's story. Aint thet redundant?

A child of the world would think so, but a Sixteener would know from experience that it wasn't. It wasn't that such petty feelings could defeat God, but rather that the Spirit generally chose not to consort with folks nastily prey to them. If it withdrew when you had fifteen pounds of diamondback looped in your hands, of course, you would probably find beside the point the distinction between a defeated Spirit and just a particular One. . . .

Dented pickups and rattletrap jalopies surrounded the stone church. Years ago—a couple of decades, in fact—it had housed a country grocery and a fillingstation. Then it had closed. It had reopened for three or four summer reasons as a roadside produce market, setting out wicker baskets of peaches, grapes and tomatoes, along with two hulking smokeblackened cauldrons for boiling peanuts. Then the place had closed again. An oil company removed the gaspumps. The owner died, and the owner's family sold out.

A Mark Sixteener from Cottonton, Alabama, purchased the building and turned it into a touristtrap herpetology museum called Snake-O-Rama. This entrepreneur equipped the interior with several long trestletables, furnished the trestletables with three or four glasswalled aquariums apiece, and stocked the aquariums with serpents. For two bucks (for grownups) or fifty cents (for kids), you could go in and ogle diamondbacks, copperheads, cottonmouths, water-moccasins, pygmyrattlers, timber-rattlers, kingsnakes, greensnakes, racers, coralsnakes, gartersnakes, one sleepy boa-constrictor, and, for variety's sake, geckos, chameleons, newts, an aquatic salamander called a hellbender that resembled a knobby strip of bark with legs, and an ugly stuffed gilamonster.

Hoke had visited Snake-O-Rama on an eighthgrade fieldtrip with Mr. Nyeland's science class, the year before he laid out of school for good. But tourist traffic on Frye's Mill Road was light to nonexistent, and the number of subsidized trips from the Hothlepoya County schools fell so dramatically during Snake-O-Rama's second year that the welloff Mark Sixteener who ran the place—most members of the Assembly were collardpoor—arranged to sell the building and land, not including the old family graveyard nextdoor, to a dispossessed offshoot of his church from west of Beulah Fork.

The Pilchers began attending the new Assembly as a family. Hoke's mama died only months later—a death the coroner ruled an accidental poisoning—and his daddy soon thereafter fled such crazy piety. Hoke, though, had hung on, convinced that these handlers, poisondrinkers, and ecstatic babblers were now kin and that one day Jesus would bless him if he lifted up and chanted over a handful of coiling snakes. For the most part, Hoke had found that belief fulfilled in his association with the Sixteeners, especially in his friendships with Twyla, an elderly couple called the Loomises, and the family of the black preacher C. K. Sermons, whose surname jibed so exactly with his calling that even a few in their Assembly wrongly figured it a pulpit alias.

In fact, of all the twentyodd folks who met regularly in the former Snake-O-Rama, only Johnny Mark Carnes and two other men in their thirties, Ron Strock and Eddie Moomaw, had ever shown him anything other than acceptance and aid. Their help had included shoemoney, a Bible, and Sam Loomis' appeal to Colby Deaton to give Hoke a job at Deaton's Bar-B-Q.

The trio of Carnes, Strock, and Moomaw, though, saw him as a pretender, a pain in the buttocks, and, in Carnes' case, a misbegotten rival for Twyla Glanton, even though Carnes already had a wife from whom he had separated over her disenchantment with hazardous church practices and his evergrowing inventory of scaly pets. Eddie Moomaw called Hoke the orphan and, in a service not long after Hoke moved into the tirehouse, rebuked Hoke for living with an unredeemed heathen, taking as his text the prophetic recriminations of *Ezekiel* 16:

Then I wershed you in water; yes, I thoroughly wershed off yore blood, and I anointed you with oil! Moomaw had said, his eyes not on Hoke but instead on a wildeyed portrait of Jesus on the Snake-O-Rama's rear wall.

Amen! said many of the unwary Sixteeners, Hoke included *Tell it, Brother Eddie!*

Brother Eddie told it, at last bringing his eyes down on the target of his rant: You offered yourself to everyone who passed by, and multiplied yore acts of harlotry!

Amen! Woe to all sinners!

Hoke stayed silent, but his napehair rose.

Yet you were not like a harlot, Moomaw said, because you scorned payment! Sicm, Brother Eddie! Hie on!

Men make payment to awl harlots, but you made yore payment to awl yore lovers, and hired em to come to you from awl aroun for yore harlotry!

Amen! Go, Brother Eddie! At this point, only Carnes and Ron Strock were seconding Moomaw's quoted accusations. No one else understood the reasons for such condemnation. No one else could follow the argument.

I will bring blood upon you in fury and jealousy! Moomaw said, pointing the whole top half of his body at Hoke, snakily twisting shoulders, neck, and head.

At that point C. K. Sermons rose from his altarchair. His skin the purple of a decaying eggplant, he clapped his enormous hands as if slamming shut a thousandpage book.

I will be quiet n be angry no more, he said. The boy you scold does not deserve such upbraision, Brother Eddie. He goes where he muss to put shelter over his head.

Amen! Twyla said. *Amen!* said the Loomises. *Amen!* said a dozen other Sixteeners.

A course he's a orphan. He's done long since lost his mama n daddy. But didn't Jesus say, I will not leave you orphans, I will come to you?

He said it! Deed He did!

So what if the Pilchers come to us stead of vice versa? So what? They's moren one way fo the body of Jesus to surroun this worl's orphans! Moren one way to stretch comfort to the comfortless!

Amen! Praise God!

Thus rebuked, Eddie Moomaw retreated to his own altarchair grimfaced and blanched, his tongue so thick on the inside of his cheek that its bulge looked like a tumor. And only C. K. Sermons raised snakes heavenward that night. Of course, he had also—alone among the evening's worshipers—tossed back a small mayonnaise jar of strychnine (making a comical pucker at its bitterness), retold in tongues, and restored Brother Eddie to concord with their fold by exorcising from his body a demon of resentment named Rathcor.

Rathcor! Sermons shouted, one hand hard on Moomaw's chest, the other shoving downward on his head. Rathcor, come ye forth in shame n wretchedess! *Now!*

And Rathcor had departed Moomaw, half its vileness in a sulfurous breeze from Moomaw's mouth and half in a startling report from his backside. These smells had lingered in the stone building, a stench that Hoke recalled as burnt cinnamon, bad eggs, and decomposed pintobeans.

S awright, Sermons told everyone. Just means the demon's done hightailed it. Means Brother Eddie's free.

Brother Eddie had smiled, lifting his hands into cobwebby shadow and praising the Lord. But his hostility toward Hoke, not to say that of Carnes and Strock, never fully evaporated, and Hoke could only wonder if a portion of Rathcor had lodged in the most secret passages of Moomaw's anatomy—his nose, his ears, his anus, his dick—because Hoke could not imagine, from Moomaw's present behavior, that Sermons had cast Rathcor out of him entire.

Greet one another with a holy kiss.

—*Romans* 16:16

The closer Hoke drew to the kudzu-filigreed building the louder grew the buzzing syncopated music leaking through its mortared joins. He heard tambourines, trap drums, an electric guitar, a trumpet. This music, pulsing like strobes in the grimy windows, told him he had arrived late, the service had already begun. The stolid rockwalls and the roof of steeply pitched shakes seemed almost to expand and contract with the singing and its jangly backup, like a jukejoint roadhouse in an old Krazy Kat cartoon.

The people crooned: *Oh, weary soul, the gate is neah. In sin why still abide? Both peace n rest are waiting heah, And you are just outside.*

And a fervent chorus: *Just outside the door, just outside the door, Behold it stands ajar! Just outside the door, just outside the door—So neah n yet so far!*

Hoke halted, clammy with the cold suspicion that through this old gospel hymn the Sixteeners were addressing and jeering his tardiness:

Just outside the door, just outside the door—So neah n yet so far!

Then go on in, he told himself. Walk through the gate and face em like one of their forever own.

He did, pushing in more like a gunslinger entering a saloon than a believer in search of his sweet Jesus Only. The ruckus from the toothache-imparting guitar and trumpet, not to mention the rattle of drums and tambourines, smacked him like a falling wall. The handclapping, pogojumping Mark Sixteeners—men to the left of the pewless sanctuary, women to the right—ladled a soupy nausea into Hoke's gut. Usually, such motionful devotion wired him for most of the fiercest God frequencies, but tonight a fretfulness lay on the people, a catching mood of upset, even derangement.

At the end of Just Outside the Door, Sermons leapt to the altardeck from between his wife, Betty, and their thirteen-year-old daughter, Regina, already a jivy trumpeter. The only black male in the building, Sermons wore a sweated-out Sunday shirt and a bolo tie with a turquoise cross on its ceramic slide. He harangued the sweltering room:

I grew up wi the cutaway eyes n the sad caloomniation o folks who figgered me n my kin just a lucky step up from the monkeys.

We hear you, Brother C. K.!

Caw it bigotry, peoples. Caw it hate or ignorance. Caw it puft-up delusion.

Amen!

Whatever anybody caws it, peoples, it hurt—like stones n flails. Sometimes, Lawd Lawd, it still lays me out, even me, faithful servant to our Risen Jesus thet I long since become in my rebornin.

Glory!

Now the chilrens of this worl done started comin after our own. Mockin, name-cawin, greedy to troublemake.

Satan has em, C. K.! Satan!

Lissen what they done to Sister Twyla—to make her move off our Risen Jesus to the dead Christ they socawed churches strive to burry eyebrow deep in works n talk!

Preach it!

They bite like unprayed-over snakes! They want to pyzon the chilrens of the light!

God'll repay!

Sister Twyla, cmon up here! Testify to what the heathen n them lukewarm Christians of Beulah Fork's sitdown churches done to knock back yore faith!

C. K. Sermons reached out a hand, and Twyla, modest in a lightyellow anklelength poplin dress, emerged redeyed from the women. She floated across the floor to the platform. She did not mount it, but pivoted to face everyone with a sweet timid smile. People upfront parted to make her visible to worshipers farther back.

Hoke stood admiring. Three nights ago she'd worn her hair in an unrighteous teased-up globe. Now it hung long, reddish streaks flashing in the sorrel every time she moved her head, a small ivory barrette for ornament. Hoke could tell, though, that she'd had a monster bout with tears: Her eyesockets looked scoured, shiny with knuckling.

Bless yall, she said. Praise God.

Praise God!

Yall notice, please, thet Hoke Pilcher's come in. It'd be good if you men greeted him with a holy kiss, like Paul sez to do, and you womenfolk guv him sisterly nod.

Hoke felt an abrupt heat climb from his chest and settle in his cheeks. The women to his right nodded or curtsied while in their half of the sanctuary the men milled into ranks to bestow on him the holy kiss spelled out in Romans 16. Sermons, Eddie Moomaw and Hugh Bexton leapt down from the altardeck to greet him—mechanically in Moomaw's case, it seemed to Hoke—and Ron Strock and Johnny Mark Carnes used their go-bys to pinch one of Hoke reddened earlobes or to razz him about the irregularity of Twyla's appeal.

I need to remember this tactic, Carnes said, nudging Hoke's cheek: Big entrance, ten minits late.

Ferlin couldn't git his Ford cranked. I wadn't—

Stifle it, Pilcher, Carnes said. Lady's gonna talk.

Twyla absentmindedly rubbed her palms together. Early Wednesday mornin, she said, I had my car tires slashed and my deck strewn with toy rubber snakes. My trees got toiletpapered and my trailer aigged.

Cry out to God, said Camille Loomis, the Sixteener nearly everyone called Prophetess Camille.

That's not all. On Wednesday I went to Li'l People, where I've done worked three years now, and Miss Victoria let me go. Said some of her parents don't want their babies tended to by a known snake handler.

C. K. Sermons said: Christian parents, no doubt.

Sposedly. Anyways, I'm a known handler. Like a known car thief or a known ax murderer.

Yo're a known blessed friend, said Sam Loomis.

I cain't work a minit longer cause I might feed somebody's darlin a bowl of baby rattlers. I might wrap a watermoccasin up in the poor kid's didy.

We'll hep you, said Angela Bexton.

I know yall will. Like Brother C. K. sez, it hurts—this persecution by the world.

Somebody suggested a love offering.

Wait, Twyla said. The world thinks we've gone crazy cause we abide in and by the Word. Thet's what the silly children of this world've come to.

Amen!

But much as I love them little ones I seen to awmost ever day for three years, I love the Word—I love the Lord—more. I won't walk outta the light to satisfy any false Christian I many offend by abidin true.

Praise God!

And as Moses lifted up the serpent in the wilderness, even so must the Son of Man be lifted up.

Amen! Praise God!

Jesus sez thet in the Book. Which is to affirm thet I will lift serpents myself at ever pure anointin.

In His name! Amen!

I will do it to lift up the Word thet is also Jesus Risen, else this brief life will fall out in ashes and I myself blow away like so much outworn dust.

Twyla's speech, carrying news of her persecution and the witness of her resolve, stunned Hoke. He could not move. His embarrassment had drained away, though, and in its place welled pride. His love streamed over and then from Twyla like a flood of rich silt. Others among the Sixteeners did move in response to her testimony, reclaiming their instruments, cranking up a gospel shout, swaying to the acid caterwauling of Ron Strock's guitar and the ripple blasts of young Regina's trumpet, leaping about like stifflegged colts, footstomping and handclapping not in unison but in a great cheerful boil that somehow melded them in faith and triumph. Finally, Hoke absorbed through his pores their backasswards confederating spirit. And then he too began to move.

The bite of the serpent is nothing compared to the bite of your fellow man.
        —Charles McGlocklin, the End Time Evangelist

Later C. K. Sermons leapt again to the altardeck. His wife, Sister Betty, a light-skinned African American with the figure and selfpossession of a teenaged gymnast, broke out a video camera. She shouldered it like an infantryman shouldering a bazooka. Hoke had noticed such cameras at other Jesus Risen services, usually in the hands of local TV crews looking for two or three filler minutes for an 11:00 P.M. news broadcast. The red light on Sister Betty's camera glowed like a coal, or a serpent's eye.

Sister Twyla did no preachin tonight, said Sermons. She testified. You see, I just heard some wayward mumblin bout how womens don't blong up here preachin.

They don't, said Leonard Callender.

Nobody disputes it, said Sermons. I know they got no caw to make mens subject to they preachments n foretellins. And Sister Twyla knows it. Futhamore, nothin like thet's happened here tonight. Yall unnerstand?

Praise God we do!

Good. We got new bidnus to tend to, new praises to lift. And none of it'll go Jesus Risen smooth if they's wrong thinkin or foolish resentments mongst us.

A fiftyish man named Darren DeVore bumped Hoke's shoulder. S mazin to me, he whispered, how we got us a nigger preacherman and female testifiers.

Thet so? said Hoke, stepping away.

My daddy woulda cut the fig off thetere fella and led the uppity women outside to catch some rocks.

Whynt you tell it so everybody can hear you?

I ain't my daddy, Brother Hoke. I've changed wi the times. Grinning, he angled off through the other men toward the altar platform.

We need some prayin music, Sermons told the band. We got to pray over these pernicious snakes.

The band struck up a hardrock hymn, Regina Sermons cocking her elbows and blowing out her cheeks like a swampfrog. Twyla, Hoke noticed, had a tambourine. She hipbanged it in proximate time to the hymn's rhythm. Only the women sang:

When Judah played the harlot,
When proud Judah mocked her God,
God stripped her of her garments,
Nor did He spare the rod.

Yet His love was such, O mighty such,
Judah He toiled to save:
He proffered her His Jesus touch,
And with sweet rue forgave.

As the women sang, C. K. Sermons, Eddie Moomaw, and Hugh Bexton prayed over the snakeboxes against the church's rear wall. The boxes showed bright hand-painted portraits of Jesus, Mary and the disciples. The men prayed with their eyes shut, hands palm upward at shoulderheight or squeezed into juddering fists at their bellies, their voices either high monotone pleas or low gruff summonses.

Shan-pwei-koloh-toshi-monha-plezia-klek! shouted Prophetess Camille, her head thrown back as if inviting a knife to unhinge it at her wattled throat. *Fehzhka-skraiiii*! Camille sez they's a demon in here, Sam Loomis told Hoke over the tubthumping music.

A demon? Rathcor?

A betrayer. A worker of hoodoo what'll drag hypocrites and baby blievers straight to hellfire.

Camille turned in a slow circle, her arms hanging down like rusty windowsash weights. *Auvlih-daks-bel-woh-oh-vehm-ah-pih!* she cried. *Neh-hyat-skraiiii!*

Camille sez we got moren one in here! said Loomis. But the betrayer he's done fell to pitdiggin!

Sermons did a solitary congadance from the snakeboxes to the edge of the altardeck with three or four serpents in each hand. He dipped from side to side in an ecstatic crouch as the Jesus Risen band veered into a rave-up of Higher Ground. Eddie Moomaw and Hugh Bexton slid forward to bookend Sermons, the way the thieves on Golgotha had flanked the crucified Jesus, Bexton with canebrakes and pygmyrattlers squirming about his wrists like overboiled spaghetti, Moomaw with only a single snake but that one a silky diamondback of such length that it looped his forearms in countergliding coils.

Hoke knew this snake for Judas even before Carnes took it from Moomaw. Carnes began to handle it in an orgasmic frenzy. He may have even moaned glory in his upright congress with Judas, but the rattle and blare of the Sixteener combo, along with the worshipers' continuing babel, drowned even the loudest utterances of the chief three handlers.

In spite of Prophetess Camille's warning, Hoke could feel a benevolent essence—the Holy Ghost—seeping from overhead and even sideways through the stones into the former Snake-O-Rama. He half expected everyone to sprout plumelike flames from the crowns of their heads, like so many outsized cigarette lighters snapping to radiant point.

It entered Hoke, this Spirit, and, amid the crazy din, he too began to dance, jitterbugging in place, barking praise, reconnecting with his dead mama and his absconded daddy as well as with the raptured majority of the Sixteeners. This was what it was like to open to and be tenanted by the Comforter, Jesus Risen at His ghostliest and most tender.

Yes. It was like a blessed fit.

Hoke began to stutterstep diagonally through the other happy epileptics, a chess piece on a mission. He could smell the Holy Ghost, Who had now so totally saturated the room that C. K. Sermons and the other handlers pranced about veiled in a haze thick as woodsmoke. The smell was not woodsmoke, though, but cinnamon sourdough and overripe juiceapples, offerings to eat and drink, not to laud. Hoke elbowed through this fragrant haze, seeking its source. He suspected that it had its focus somewhere near C. K. Sermons.

Sermons gave Regina—the band now lacked a trumpetplayer—two snakes; and Regina, more child than woman, lifted them through the layered gauze of the Spirit, to the Spirit, one snake climbing as the other twisted back to flick her pugnose with its quick split tongue. Sister Betty videotaped Regina's performance.

Other Sixteeners began to handle, one man thrusting a snake into his shirt, another tiptoeing over a diamondback as if it were a tightrope, enacting Jesus' promise, Behold, I give you authority to trample on serpents.

Sister Camille fell down ranting. Twyla, Polly DeVore and Angela Bexton knelt beside her with prayercloths and stoppered bottles of oliveoil, dimestore items with which to minister to her as holy paramedics.

Hoke, still dancing, had reached the front, hungry for the boon of a serpent from C. K. Sermons. For the first time since joining the Sixteeners, he knew the Holy Ghost had anointed him to handle, as it had anointed nearly every other person in the church tonight. But Sermons had already distributed his entire allotment of snakes. He stood on the platform with a masonjar of strychine, praying over it, preparing to drink.

Hoke floated past Sermons and many others . . . to Eddie Moomaw, who still had three or four living bracelets to hand out. He looked peeved that no one had yet come to relieve him of them. Sister Betty, Hoke noted sidelong, recorded the chaos with her video camera, paying as much heed to him and the other congregants as to her own husband and child.

Then Hoke went flatfooted and reached out to Moomaw, his face helplessly mimacing. He mewled aloud. Moomaw handed him a canebrake, a pinkishbeige timberrattler not quite a yard long, a satinback that winched itself up to his chin, shaking its rattles like maracas.

Hoke was anointed, fearless. Gripping the canebrake with both hands, he inscribed 8s with it in the air before him. He slipped into a floating whiteness where the rattler focused his whole attention and no other material body in the Snake-O-Rama impinged on him at all.

Furiously, the snake continued to rattle warning, but Hoke had surrounded and entered it just as the Spirit had done him, and it would not strike. Hoke knew this with the same kind of bodyborne knowledge that made real to him its possession of ears, elbows, knees, even if he made no effort to touch them. He and the snake shared one spellbound mind. In fact, he felt so loose, so brainfree, that he imagined the serpent an extract from his own person: his spinalcord and brainstem in a sleeve of patterned velvet.

Then something in the immaterial sanctuary of Hoke's trance bumped him. *Bumped* him. Someone in the Hands-On Assembly was shouting louder than anyone else, louder even than the scouring racket of the Jesus Only band.

Hoke sensed the soft white pocket of his trance blurring at the edges, breaking down. Forms and voices began to intrude upon him. The timberrattler in his hands separated out of the albino plasma that had sheltered them, taking on the outline and bulk of a realworld menace. Hoke finally understood that the loudest screaming in the room was his own. He clamped his mouth shut, thinning out the sound, and turned to Moomaw to rid himself of the agitated canebrake.

Regina Sermons, still powerfully anointed, stood handling beside him, but even without looking at Hoke, she edged away to allow him to make the transfer.

Eddie Moomaw took the snake from Hoke, smiling mysteriously sidelong. Why the smile? Was he disappointed that Hoke had escaped unbit? sorry that snake had already come back to him? peeved that no one else had returned one? Hoke shook his head and retreated a step.

C. K. Sermons, holding his masonjar, wiped the back of his hand across his mouth. Good to the last drop! he said. Praise God! He beamed at Sister Betty's camera, spread his arms wide, revolved on the deck like a musicbox figurine.

Hoke decided he had to get some air. He turned to thread his way doorward.

Carnes blocked his path. Welcome back, Pilcher, he said. Here. Have you another. . . .

JUDAS FOLDED INTO HOKE'S ARMS LIKE EIGHT FEET OF BURDENSOME FIREHOSE. Hoke had no time to sidestep the handoff. To keep from dropping it he shifted the diamondback and, as he did, saw on Carnes' face a look of combined glee and despisal. More from surprise than fear, Hoke lost his grip. Judas, suddenly alert and coiling, dropped. Hoke went to one knee to catch the snake, managed a partial grab, and found himself eye to yellow eye with Judas. Fear washed through him, a quickacting venom, and he shielded his face with the edge of his hand. The snake struck, spiking him just below the knuckles of his pinkie and his ringfinger, a puncture that toppled him.

Somebody screamed piercingly, and this time the rising sirenlike wail belonged not to him but to Twyla Glanton. Judas crawled over Hoke's fallen body. It bit him again, this time in the upperarm, then rippled over the concrete in a beautiful coiling glide.

Help him! shouted Twyla, arrowing in. Hush thet racket and help him, else he's bound to die!

Not if he's got faith! said Carnes.

The band stopped playing, the prophets stopped babbling, and Sermons, Bexton and Moomaw hopped down from the altardeck to see about Hoke. He could hear the cicadas outside, whirring dryly, the sad bellyaching of ditchfrogs, and the faraway hum and buzz of pickup tires rolling on asphalt and ratcheting over a cattleguard.

Git him a doctor, somebody!

Now, Twyla, if we do thet, Carnes said, aint we sayin the Word's not the Word? Before Twyla could answer, Carnes looked down at Hoke. Boy, you want a doctor?

Nosir. Just some kinda ease. Hoke sprawled, burning where Judas had fanged him.

He'd say thet, Twyla said. Just to fit in better here at th Assembly.

He won't ever fit in better if he truckles to this world's medicine, said Carnes.

Sermons knelt beside Hoke. He don't want a doctor, Sister Twyla, cause he knows from whence comes his hep.

Praise God!

Look here, said Twyla. Thet's a big Judas of a snake. It spiked him twyst. Thet much venom'd drop a buffalo, much less a peaked skinny boy.

Faith can toss mountains into the sea, Carnes said.

Twyla grimaced. When was the last time yore faith tossed a mountain into the sea?

Kept me safe handlin thatere serpent, Carnes said. S moren anybody can say for Brother Hoke.

Hoke'd done handled, Sermons said. You caught m when the Spirit'd gone off him.

Hugh Bexton returned with Judas around one shoulder like a great drooping epaulette braid. He stood directly over Hoke, and Hoke could see Bexton and the snake looming like paradefloats against the cracked ceiling. Judas seemed to probe about for a baseboard chink or a skylight, a way to escape. Occasionally, though, it coiled the upper portion of its length floorward and flicked its tongue, swimming over Hoke with the airy loveliness of a saltwater eel.

If Brother Hoke dies faithless, said Camille Loomis, he'll go straight to—hellfire, Sam Loomis finished for her.

It was told me from on high, said Camille.

What happens to the hoodoo workers here amongst us? Twyla said. Do those betrayers go to hellfire too?

Not till they die, Camille said.

But they laid the hoodoo on Judas and got poor Hoke bit.

Camille sounded sad or embarrassed: No, missy, them hoodoo workers just showed up his weakness.

What garbage, Twyla said. What backasswards crap.

The Loomises looked at each other and backed away. Hoke watched Judas swimming, climbing, loopsliding in dimensionless emptiness. The Loomises' curse—*straight to hellfire*—rang in his head. The faces of those still hovering over him revealed a peculiar range of passions, Twyla's running from cajolery to outrage, Carnes' from amusement to satisfaction. Sermons made a series of increasingly sluggish peacemaking gestures. Judas bobbed down in a slowmotion arc and once again laid its yellow gaze on Hoke.

Somewhere beyond the diamondback's scrutiny glowed a single pulsing red dot.

Hoke thought: I'm going straight to hellfire.

LIKE JESUS, HOKE RISES FROM HIMSELF and strides out of the cooling tomb of his own bones.

He leaves Twyla, Carnes, Moonaw, Sermons, and all the other Sixteeners and ambles into the quiet darkness—no cicadas, no frogs, no trucks—outside the Hands-On Assembly of Jesus Risen, formerly Snake-O-Rama. He walks and walks. In less time than it takes to leap a ditch he comes to a steeppitched road lined with blackberry brambles, dogwoods, pines.

A sycamore almost concealed by this other foliage bears a handlettered sign:

TRESPAsERS!!!—
WE AIM to PLEZE But SHOT to KILL!

He has come home to his roommate Ferlin's tirehouse in a hard-to-reach pocket of Hothlepoya County. Neither Sackett nor Rag rushes out to greet him. The house itself blazes like a firebombed tiredump, turbulent coalback smoke billowing away, climbing into the sky's midnight fade.

The conflagration does not devour the house, but surrounds, dances on, and leaps from it. Pungent smoke skirls ceaselessly from the twoply radials and the halfburied whitewalls. Hoke calmy observes the fire, then cuts painlessly through its pall, and enters the dugout's U-shaped livingroom.

Ferlin! he shouts. You to home?

The interior startles him. It looks like an immense tiled lavatory. The walls glitter like scrubbed kitchen appliances, even if their white enamel faintly reflects the movement of fire and rippling smoke. Although he has no trouble breathing here, he must hike forever—longer than it takes to leap a ditch—to reach the glass cage, a bullet-shaped capsule, across from Ferlin's frontdoor.

Hoke rides the capsule down. Flames twist in the glass or clear hardplastic shaping it, flickering from side to side as well as up and down. Beyond these flames the countryside (yes, countryside) looks infinitely hilly. Figures—faceless sticks dwarfed by the buttes and spires in the brickbrown landscape—cower in halfhidden rock niches or flee over plains like fiery icefloes.

Occasionally a longnosed fish, or a mutant parrot, or a parachuting man-of-war drifts past the capsule, each with some raw disfigurement: a gash, an extraneous growth, an unhealthy purpling of its visible membranes. Hoke wants to pull these wounded critters inside the capsule and heal their wounds with hands-on prayer.

Can God dwell in any of these freaks? In any part of this infernal canyon? Hoke thinks so. How could he have trespassed here without help?

In the subbasement the capsule halts. Hoke emerges, and an ordinarylooking man in a chambray shirt and a pair of designer jeans meets him. The man does not speak.

His sunglasses lenses betray neither friendliness nor hostility. Hoke discovers his name only because it is stitched in flowing script—JUDAS—over his heartside shirtpocket (if he has a heart). He greets Hoke with a crooked thrifty bow.

This man, this Judas, leads Hoke through a tunnel lit at distant intervals with baseboard lights fashioned to resemble lifesized Old and New World serpents: cobras, mambas, pythons, shieldtails, eggeaters, rattlesnakes, vipers and so on, each of these sinuous devices plugged in at ankleheight and aglow with an icy radiance that both animates and eerily Xrays the shaped light. Hoke can see the skull, vertebrae, and tubelike organs of each makebelieve serpent.

Leading the way, Judas lists to one side or the other of the tunnel, but Hoke walks straight down its middle, trying to ignore the threat implicit in the baseboard lamps. The tunnel—itself a hollow, kinking serpent—goes on and on. Sometimes its twisty floor and curved walls seem to tremble, as if bombs have fallen close to hand.

At length the tunnel opens into a chamber—Hoke regards it as a satanic chapel— with a crooked wingless caduceus where the cross would hang in most decent Prot- estant churches. Ringing the chamber's squat dome are bleak stainedglass windows whose cames outline serpents in a stew of motifs, all colored in deep brown, indigo, or slumbering purple, with intermittent shards of crimson or yellow to accent the snakes' hooded or bulgingly naked eyes.

In these cames Hoke sees the same kinds of snakes in two dimensions that he saw rendered in the tunnel in three, except that here the serpents are all venomous cobras or pitvipers. The conflagration outside the chamber inflicts a sullen glitter on the dome's glass, but Hoke draws some comfort from it, as he would from a fire on a stone hearth.

Unlike the church on Frye's Mill Road, Judas' antichapel has pews. Three rows of benches face the pulpit, each one covered in snakeskin. Behind the pulpit, a choir loft made of long white bones and ornate ivory knobs faces outward beneath a stainedglass triptych.

With a gesture, Judas urges Hoke to find a place among the pews. Hoke chooses the curved middle pew and sits halfway along its scaly length. Judas mounts to the pulpit, growing two feet in height as he uncoils from a deceptive stoop. For the first time since arriving down here, Hoke can study Judas' face.

It is the machinemolded face of a departmentstore dummy, with just enough play in the blockfoam to permit the creature to smile faintly or to twitch a lip corner. When he removes his sunglasses, he reveals yellow eyes like a diamondback's and his face deforms into the soft triangle of a pitviper's head, with severe dents, in the cheeks and a smile that has widened alarmingly. The rest of Judas' body maintains a human cast, and, hands gripping the pulpit's sides, he leans forward to regale Hoke, his lone congregant, with a stemwinding sermon. Outside, bombs or depth charges continue to explode, and Judas responds to the tremblors by rubbernecking his head around and whiteknuckling the lectern that seems to hold him erect. Hoke pays close heed.

Judas' sermon has no words. It issues from the creature's smile as hisses and sighs. Flickers of a doubletipped tongue break the sibilance, and at each pause Judas seems to rethink the next segment of his message. Then, as the crux of his text demands, a quiet or a vigorous hissing resumes, along with more tongueflickers and sighs. Some- times Judas pounds the lectern or ambles briefly and shakily away from it. Hoke can make no sense of any of it, but Judas' voiceless sermonizing continues without relent.

Hoke would like to make a getaway back through the tunnel, but his dead mama taught him never to walk out on a preacher and so he sits longsufferingly in place. Maybe Judas wants to torment him the way Carnes and the handlers tormented their spiritdrugged snakes.

Long into this sermon, a blue film creeps over Judas' eyes, turning them a sickly green. This milky film thickens. As it does, Judas' eyes go from green to seagreen to turquoise to a dreamy cobalt. These cobalt veils blind Judas, but he goes on hissing his wordless rant.

When Hoke thinks he can take no more, Judas stops hissing and rubs his snout with his human hands. The skin over his snout loosens all the way back to his capped eyes. Judas grabs this scaly layer and peels it back. Then the skin on his hands splits, and the new hands beneath these glovelike husks break through to peel away the old skin, including his chambray shirt and designer jeans.

With one reborn hand on the pulpit for support, Judas steps out of this old covering and sets it aside. The husk rocks on its feet like a display mannikin fit only for junking. The new Judas, meanwhile, clings to the pulpit in the guise of a human female: another mannikin, but an animated one for the women's department. With chestnut hair that cascades down and trembles over her shoulders, this female version of Judas picks up her discarded skin by the shoulders, carries it to the choir loft, and places it in one of the five chairs there. The integument of this molt rattles dryly, its snaky head deforming again into something recognizably human, as if its serpentshape had never really taken.

Hoke sits mesmerized. He no longer wants to run, simply to understand. At the lectern again, the female snakeperson goes on changing, her face shrinking and triangulating, her tresses pulling back into her skull and weaving into satiny snakeskin. Looking past her, Hoke sees that the molt in the choir has come to resemble his daddy, who ran out on his mama and him shortly after she had yoked them with the Sixteeners.

You bastid! Hoke shouts at the thing.

Outside, very near, a bomb falls. The explosion rocks the domed chamber, audibly warping the stainedglass in its cames, swaying the pulpit and rattling the hollow imago of his daddy, which totters in its chair. The imago has no eyes, only gaping vents, but it stares at Hoke without love, remorse, or any plea for understanding. It sits, merely sits, teetering whenever ordnance detonates.

The snakeperson at the pulpit ignores Hoke's daddy and launches into another harangue—a hissyfit, Hoke things—that expands and expands. Usually Hoke's bladder, given the length of these speeches, would expand too, threatening rupture and flood, but here in Ferlin's subbasement his bladder has lots of stretch and he too much endurance.

At last, though, the second Judas' eyes grow a milky film and a second shedding occurs, revealing a new snakeperson and leaving behind a female husk that the third version of Hoke's guide places in the choir loft next to his daddy. The face of this shell takes on the features of his mama, while the third snaky preacher begins a brandnew tirade.

Hoke nods. At length, a third molt puts a fresh male husk in the loft with his folks. This tedious process occurs twice more. By the end of the diamondback's fifth hissyfit, every seat in the choir is occupied. The choir now comprises five false human beings whom Hoke sees as wicked likenesses of his daddy, his mama, Johnny Mark Carnes, Twyla Glanton and Ferlin Rodale. They rustle to their feet, and the sixth Judas sheds its preacherly garments to join them in the loft as an immense coiled rattler.

How can they sing an anthem when they have no voices? Why does the sixth Judas lace her long anatomy among the other five betrayers, then raise her triangular head above the zombie face of Johnny Mark Carnes?

Ulo-shan-pwei-koloh-ehlo-scraiiii! says the sixth Judas in a female voice familiar to Hoke. *Neh-hyat-kolotosh-mona-ho!* Her split tongue flits among these syllables like a hummingbird sampling morningglory blossoms. Then, on her warning rattle, the choir, once mute, joins her in pealing out a hymn that Hoke well knows:

O for a thousand tongues to sing. . . .

HANDS PRESSED AGAINST HIM, their warm palms on his chest, upperarms, forehead. One pair had a viselike grip on his temples, flattening his ears and struggling to touch fingertips behind his head.

Here he comes, a voice said. Glory.

Bring m out, Jesus. Bring m on out.

Hoke let the faces surrounding him clarify in the glare of a ceilinglamp. As his pupils narrowed, even the darker faces among the four took on definition. He recognized Twyla Glanton and then every member of the Sermons family.

Praise God.

Twyla's face came toward him, and she placed one ear less than an inch from his lips. Say again, she said. Her sorrel hair touched his face.

Lift him from the pit n set him upright midst us, said C. K. Sermons. Bless his ever goin forth in comin home.

Say again, Twyla said again.

Hoke tried—no sound, but his lips quirked.

Looky there, said Regina Sermons. He be smilin.

HOKE STAYED WITH the Sermonses the next three days. They prayed with and over him, often laying on hands. They fed him unsalted rice, applesauce, bananas, and tea made of chamomile flowers, passionflower leaves, and crushed rosebuds. With no other medical attention but this food and prayer ("Antivenin is the antichrist and doctors are its antifaith disciples," Carnes had liked to say), Hoke recovered quickly.

On Sunday morning, the Sermonses held an outdoor service on the decks of the splitlevel gazebo in their backyard. No one brought snakes into it, although Hoke knew that the Sermonses kept a dozen or more in crates along the rear of their double garage. Twyla, Ferlin Rodale, and Sam and Camille Loomis (who had forgiven Twyla her words at the Friday-night snakehandling service) attended this informal gathering. Oddly, though, no other member of the congregation showed up, and Hoke began to suspect that something more dire than his own rattlerbites had disrupted Friday's worship.

The Sermonses refused to talk about such matters while his body went about healing itself. When not praying or reading the Bible with him, they gave him his space, including free run of their house and grounds.

Their brick house sat on an acre off White Cow Creek Road, ten miles west of

Beulah Fork. It appeared to have been lifted from a hightone suburban subdivision and set down again in the sharecropper boonies. It had three bedrooms, a study, and a den with a hightech entertainment center: largescreen TV and VCR combo, multideck stereophonic CD soundsystem, and, because none of the Mark Sixteeners were teetotalers, a wellsupplied wetbar. The Sermonses could afford such a place because C. K. sold insurance as well as preached, and Betty worked a deskjob in the Hothlepoya Country Health Department, even if her job struck Hoke as peculiarly at odds with the noninterventionist doctrines of their Hands-On Assembly.

On Monday evening, Twyla, Ferlin, and the Loonises came for another call. This time, though, C. K. herded everyone into the den to watch the videotape that Betty had shot three evenings earlier. Hoke understood that C. K. had organized the gathering as a small party in honor of his recovery. If it had any other purpose, beyond showing off Betty's skills as a camerawoman, he could not have named it.

This past Friday a true anointin came on Brother Hoke, C. K. said. Yall watch n see.

Somebody had wound the tape exactly to the point at which Eddie Moomaw passed Hoke a timberrattler. The tape showed Hoke handling, there among the other Sixteeners. The hopping and stutterstepping of the worshipers, the clangy music, the scary inscrutability of the snakes—everything on the tape united to make Hoke see himself and his friends as part of an outlandish spectacle, separate somehow from their everyday selves. He recognized himself, and he didn't. He recognized Twyla and the Sermonses, and he didn't. Betty's tape tweaked the familiar old church and the ordinary folks inside it into a gaudy circus tent, with jugglers, acrobats and clowns.

My Lord, Ferlin said.

You know you'da loved to been there, Twyla said.

F yall think this's gonna work on me like a recruitin film, yall just don't know Ferlin Rodale.

Where is it? Hoke said. I don't see it.

Betty Sermons leaned over and patted his forearm. Where's what, baby?

The Spirit, Hoke said. Thet night it was so thick in there you could bottled it.

It don't tape, Betty said. Never has.

Hush, Prophetess Camille said. This's where Brother Hoke passes his serpent on back to Eddie Moomaw.

Hoke watched himself hand off the timberrattler. Then he watched C. K. take a hearty swig of poison and Carnes explode into view to unload an even bigger snake on the video image of himself. On the Sermonses' largescreen, Hoke accepted and then almost dropped the diamondback.

Yall're flakier than a deadman's dandruff, Ferlin said.

From a threestage recliner, Sam Loomis leveled a hard gaze on Ferlin. Who taught you yore manners, young man?

Beg yore pardon, sir. I've just never liked snakes.

They've always spoken well of you, Twyla said.

The videotape continued to unspool, flickering and jumping in testimony to Betty's active camera technique.

Here comes the bites! Regina said.

Hoke flinched. So did Ferlin, who looked off at the framed underwriter certificates on the wall. Hoke kept watching and soon saw himself sprawled on the concrete floor, surrounded by Twyla, the Loomises, Sermons, Moomaw, Bexton, and two bigeyed little boys—the Strock twins—who had wriggled free of their mama's restraining arms to hunker next to Hoke and gawk at him in cheerful expectation of his demise.

Brats, thought Hoke.

Aloud he said: This's where I died. Then walked home to Ferlin's. And rode a elevator straight to hell.

Except, of course, the largescreen showed no sequence of events like that at all. Instead they saw Judas writhing above Hoke in Hugh Bexton's arms, and Twyla saying, *What backasswards crap,* and the Loomises moving stiffly out of view. Then the screen showed a dozen worshipers milling, smoke rolling over the floor from beneath the altardeck, a painted churchwindow shattering, and a fractured brick tumbling end over end on the concrete.

Sermons and the others raised their heads to register the broken-out window. Smoke began to rise through the church from baseboards, closets, windowsills, and the junk-rooms behind the altar. The pictures of the outbreaking fire careened even more madly than Betty's earlier shots. Folks scrambled to flee the building. A sound like the amplified crumpling of Styrofoam dominated the audio; shouts, children crying, and the slamming of car and pickup doors echoed in the background.

C. K., Darren DeVore, Leonard Callender, and Ron Strock—there to shoo away his twins as much as to assist Hoke—picked Hoke up and hustled him in a hammockcarry to the door. Other men crated up and rescued their snakes, sometimes appearing to put their decorated boxes and the creatures inside them before their own wives and kids. The tape's last poorly exposed shots included a pan from the church's burning facade to the gleaming asphalt road going past it.

What was thet all about? Hoke said.

A fire got goin in the dry kudzu behind the church, Twyla said. It burnt us out, comin through the back.

How? Why?

Somebody done set it, C. K. Sermons said. A enemy like unto them cropburners in the gospel.

Only part standin today is walls, Betty said.

Twyla allowed that the fire could have started from a flungaway cigarette, but that C. K.'s investigation on Saturday morning did make it look that somebody had piled dry brush and maybe even two or three wheelbarrows of waste lumber, ends and pieces, against the church's rear wall. Then the sleazes had soaked the piles with kerosene, covered them with kudzu leaves and evergreen branches, and sneaked up during the snakehandling to drag the brush away and light the kindling.

Why'd anybody try to kill yall? Ferlin said. Yall're in a damnfool hurry to do it yoreselves.

Rathcor had his claws in it, said Camille. And whilst them snakes were out, I bet you cash money thet Carnes, Moomaw and DeVore awl played divil's innkeeper.

You don't know thet, Twyla said.

She sez it she's nigh-on certain, Sam Loomis said.

Plus it looks like Carnes's done skedaddled outta thisere county, C. K. said.

Hoke cavecrawled into himself. The Mark Sixteeners had lost their meeting-hall, Johnny Mark Carnes had vamoosed without a faretheewell, and a disagreement of fierce consequence had split the Assembly—Eddie Moomaw and his cronies arguing that the fire bespoke a judgment for allowing a descendant of Ham to preach and handle snakes amongst them; the Loomises, Twyla, and their friends adamant that Moomaw had laid a vile scapegoatment on the Sermonses for reasons having less to do with theology than with low blood, covetousness, and whitetrash pride. There had been no full Mark Sixteener fellowship on Sunday morning not merely because their church had burnt, but because a schism along skewed racial and maybe even economic lines had cleft the Assembly.

Why'd Johnny Mark run? Hoke said.

I tracked him, Betty Sermons said. Taped his ever step wi thet big Judas snake of his. He figgered if you died, we'd put it out to Sheriff Ott thet he murdered you.

Then the bigger fool he, C. K. said. Law aint gonna squash no Sixteener for killin a Sixteener.

Why not? Regina said.

Same reason it aint like to vestigate our church fire as a arson, said C. K. dyspeptically, as if the strychnine he'd drunk had soured his stomach.

Or look too hard at the mischief out my way, said Twyla.

Rewind, said Regina.

Mam? said C. K. Sermons.

Rewind. Show me playin wi them ol snakes again.

Betty Sermons rewound the tape, and everyone watched Regina handle her rattlers again. Then the TV rescreened Hoke's work with the canebrake. Was that Hoke Pilcher? he wondered. Yes, but Hoke Pilcher under a throughblest anointing. In spite of everything else—snakebite, hellfire, schism—the sight of this miracle poured a tart joy into him, and Hoke perched before it, utterly rapt, oblivious to his surroundings.

THAT AUTUMN TWYLA GLANTON MOVED FROM HOTHLEPOYA COUNTY TO COTTONTON, Alabama. There she found a job as assistant city clerk and joined a small offshoot of the Hands-On Assembly of Jesus Risen. In early October Hoke got Ferlin to drive him to Cottonton to see her, but Twyla had begun to date a surveyor in the Alabama highway department, and Hoke's visit brought down embarrassment on everyone but Ferlin.

Johnny Mark Carnes, according to Eddie Moomaw, had opened an upholstery shop near Waycross. In this shop, he recovered easychairs, divans, carseats, footstools, threestage recliners, and a variety of other items from pewcushions to the padded lids of jewelryboxes. Occasionally, according to Moomaw, he used snakeskin, for which reason he made frequent unauthorized jaunts into the Okefenokee Swamp.

The Mark Sixteeners in Hothlepoya County remained divided. The Moomaw faction held brush arbor services on New Loyd Hill until the first frost in October. The Sermons family met with the Loomises, the Callenders, and the Bextons in either their garage or the splitdeck gazebo in their backyard, depending on the weather. Both groups suffered snakebites over these weeks, but no one died. Neither faction attracted anyone new to its meetings except the occasional media reporter and GBI agents in scruffy but futile disguise.

Hoke attended the services of neither group. He had gone to hell in a disorienting feverdream, but the conflicts among the local Sixteeners, especially in the absence of Twyla, had tormented him a thousand times worse than either his snakebite or his resultant delirious trip to the sheol tucked away under Ferlin Rodale's tirehouse. Why attend services if a spirit of feud and persnicketiness held the real Spirit at bay? Hell had nothing on a holeful of serpents or an assembly of quarrelsome believers. Hoke would gladly risk eternal judgment if he could avoid the latter two kinds of snakes.

Aside from spiritual issues and Twyla's leavetaking, Hoke's biggest worry was putting money in his pockets. Ferlin forgave him rent shortfalls and overdue payments for the electric bill, but Hoke cringed to impose and even in his exile from Deaton's Bar-B-Q often ventured into Beulah Fork to prune shrubbery, cut grass, sweep parkinglots, or carry out groceries. Sometimes he went with Ferlin on roofing or carpentry jobs, earning his hire by toting shingles, bracing ladders, and sorting nails into the pockets of canvas aprons.

In December, Colby Deaton rehired him to bus tables, wash dishes, and run errands, and Hoke stayed with this job—despite the ragging of halfwit good ol boys like Albert Becknell—until early March, when he quit to begin a new line of work, catching and selling poisonous snakes.

A JAPANESE TULIPTREE had flowered in the wilderness among dogwoods and redbuds still under winter's spell. Hoke stopped with his crokersack to marvel at it. The tuliptree had set out its pink blossoms on whitespotted grey limbs altogether bare of leaves. These flowers danced like ballerinas against the naked boughs. Another coldsnap, no matter how brief, would kill the flowers; a violent rainstorm would knock them to the leafmulch, and no one would ever guess that they had bloomed.

At the base of an uglier tree nearby—Hoke took it for a blighted elm—a timberrattler slithered languidly up into the day from a hole down among the tree's roots. Hoke had come for just this event, the emergence of a congregation of snakes from their hibernating place. Because it was still early, he could expect more snakes to follow this one to the surface. Dens in which to pass safely an entire winter commanded allegiance, and snakes that had successfully hibernated returned to them fall after fall. Many serpents slept coiled together in the same den, moccasins with cottonmouths, diamondbacks with canebrakes, an immobile scrum of pitvipers in cold-blooded wintersleep. And this first rattler, Hoke knew, signaled like a robin the coming of even more of its kind.

In his lowcut tennis shoes he crept up to the elm, seized the canebrake behind its head, and quickly bagged it. Then he crouched and waited. This strategy brought results. In an hour, with the latewinter sun steadily climbing to the south, he caught four more snakes, bagging them as efficiently as he had the first.

Even this small early haul promised a decent payoff. He could get ten dollars a snake from some of the Sixteeners and possibly as much as fifty if he captured a rattler longer than six feet. Snakes died over the winter, or escaped, or emerged from their crates bent like fishhooks from clumsy handling. Conscientious handlers would replace and retire their injured snakes. That turnover meant a career of sorts, if Ferlin would allow him to breed members of like species inside or near the tirehouse. And Sam Loomis had told Hoke of a research center in Atlanta that bought pitvipers for their venom, yet another likely customer and income source.

Hoke caught three more emerging snakes, and then there was a lull. Well, fine. All work and no lolligagging made Hoke a dull dude. His gaze wandered to the tuliptree again and to the pink chalicelike blossoms fluttering in it—pretty, so pretty. Then Hoke started. A human figure sat in an upper crook of the tuliptree, balanced there as shakily as an egg on an upended coffeecup. The figure shifted, and Hoke recognized her as his dead mama, Jillrae Evans Pilcher. He stood up.

Good to see you again, Hoke.

You too, Hoke told his mama. He meant it.

What day is it, honey?

Sunday, he said.

Well. You orter have yore tail over to the Sermonses then, shouldn't you?

Hoke explained about Rathcor and Carnes and Judas and the schism that had come to the Mark Sixteeners in the aftermath of the fire at the former Snake-O-Rama. He explained why he would never encounter the Holy Spirit among either of the church's contending factions and how attending the services of one or the other turned him into an angry uptight nitpicker, a heathen nearlybout. God, he said, would more likely happen to him here in the woods.

My me, said Jillrae Pilcher. The classic copout.

Mama, I cain't do everthin the same blest way you would.

Look quick, she said. They's more comin.

Hoke looked. A halfdozen pitvipers had boiled up through the tunnel from their den. They burst forth into the dappled noon in a slithery tangle. Hoke chuckled to see them, but made no sudden grab to catch one. He glanced back at the tuliptree, his awkwardly perched mama, and the pink blossoms stark against the reawakening woods. His mama faded a little, but because he held his glance, the pink grew lovelier, the sunlight crisper, and the separate trees beyond the tuliptree both more distinct and more mysterious, a pleasant contradiction. Then a snake raced over Hoke's instep. He had no need to look away from the tuliptree at the escaping serpents because their touch told him nearly everything and the woods into which he continued to peer told him the rest.

What is it? said his mama, clinging to the forking branches over her head.

Hoke smiled and blew her a kiss.

The woods behind the tuliptree filled with a haze like a cottony pollen, and this haze drifted through the dogwoods, redbuds, and conifer pillars until it hung from every limb of every tree within a hundredfoot radius of Hoke's dying elm. The awakening snakes boiled out into the haze. Hoke knelt and picked up pitviper after pitviper, two or three to each hand. Standing again, he handled them in the enabling white currents of the drifting pollen grains. His mama, looking on, faded toward invisibility. Hoke lifted a handful of serpents to her in heartfelt farewell. The woods rang with a shout, his own, and the haze pivoting around Hoke's blight elm either drifted or burned away.

Ferlin burst into the clearing.

My God, he said. Way you uz yellin, I figgered somebody'd done kilt you.

No, said Hoke, bagging the snakes in his hands. I'm just out here laudin God.

Alone? said Ferlin, closing the distance between them.

Only takes two or three, said Hoke.

Not countin them divilish snakes there, who's yore second, Pilcher?

Hoke gestured at the tuliptree, realizing as he did that Ferlin was unlikely to have seen his mama stranded amid its blazing pink flowers. He set his crokersack down and dropped a friendly arm over Ferlin's shoulder.

How bout you? he said.

[AUTHOR'S NOTE: I owe a significant debt to Dennis Covington's *Salvation on Sand Mountain: Snake Handling and Redemption in Southern Appalachia* for much of the background of this story. Charles McGlocklin, the End-Time Evangelist, whom I quote three times from Covington's book, is a real person, but all the other characters and situations are imaginary; resemblances to real human beings, living or dead, or to actual situations in the histories of real snakehandling congregations are entirely co-incidental.]

SELECT CRITICAL BIBLIOGRAPHY

Cady, Jack. *The American Writer: Shaping a Nation's Mind,* New York: St. Martin's Press, 1999.

Chase, Richard. *The American Novel and Its Tradition,* Baltimore: Johns Hopkins University Press, 1957.

De Camp, L. Sprague. *Literary Swordsmen and Sorcerers—The Makers of Heroic Fantasy*, Sauk City, WI: Arkham House, 1976.

Delbanco, Andrew. *The Death of Satan—How Americans Have Lost the Sense of Evil*, New York: Farrar, Straus & Giroux, 1995.

Delbanco, Andrew. *Required Reading: Why Our American Classics Matter Now*, New York: Farrar, Straus & Giroux, 1997.

Disch, Thomas M. *The Dreams Our Stuff Is Made Of: How Science Fiction Conquered the World*, New York: The Free Press, 1998.

Fiedler, Leslie A. *Love and Death in the American Novel*, Normal, IL: Dalkey Archive Press, 1997.

Goldthwaite, John. *The Natural History of Make-Believe—A Guide to the Principal Works of Britain, Europe, and America*, New York: Oxford University Press, 1996.

Hardwick, Elizabeth. *American Fictions*, New York: The Modern Library/Random House, 1999.

Howe, Irving. *A Critic's Notebook*, New York: Harcourt Brace Company, 1994.

Kazin, Alfred. *On Native Grounds—An Interpretation of Modern American Prose Literature*, New York: Harcourt Brace Company, 1995.

Kazin, Alfred. *God and the American Writer*, New York: Vintage Books, 1998.

Menand, Louis. *The Metaphysical Club*, New York: Farrar, Straus & Giroux, 2001.

Perkins, David. *Is Literary History Possible?* Baltimore: Johns Hopkins University Press, 1992.

Shattuck, Roger. *Candor & Perversion: Literature, Education, & the Arts*, New York: W. W. Norton & Company, 1999.

Tompkins, Jane. *West of Everything: The Inner Life of Westerns*, New York: Oxford University Press, 1992.